THE
PUSHCART PRIZE, XXII:
BEST OF THE
SMALL PRESSES

THE 1998 PUSHCART PRIZE XXII

BEST OF THE SMALL PRESSES

*Edited by
Bill Henderson
with the
Pushcart Prize
editors.*

PUSHCART PRESS
WAINSCOTT NY 11975

Note: nominations for this series are invited from any small, independent, literary book press or magazine in the world. Up to six nominations—tear sheets or copies, selected from work published, or about to be published, in the calendar year—are accepted by our December 1 deadline each year. Write to Pushcart Press, P.O. Box 380, Wainscott, N.Y. 11975 for more information.

Acknowledgments

Selections for The Pushcart Prize are reprinted from publications with the permission of authors and presses cited. Copyright reverts to authors and presses immediately after publication.

Distributed by W. W. Norton & Co.
500 Fifth Ave., New York, N.Y. 10110

Library of Congress Card Number: 76–58675
ISBN: 1–888889–01–2
        1–888889–07–1 (paperback)
ISSN: 0149–7863

Manufactured in The United States of America
by RAY FREIMAN and COMPANY,
Jamestown, Rhode Island 02835

In Memoriam:

MICHAEL M. REA (1927–1996)

INTRODUCTION

by BILL HENDERSON

Our ELECTRONICALLY DRIVEN times lack a sense of history. The prevailing mood seems to believe if it's not happening now, it's not worth thinking about. The buzz. The Fax. The E-mail. TV and Internet news blather. These are the gods of our contemporary pundits.

But the American small press movement has had a history, and in it are real heroes. Allen Ginsberg was such a hero. When he died in April, 1997, we lost a voice from our past that constantly reminded us of the values of the non-conforming, the genuine and the gentle. Almost all of today's small presses can trace their roots to publication of Ginsberg's *Howl* by Lawrence Ferlinghetti's new small press, City Lights, in the fall of 1956. At this moment, the beat movement was born and by the 1960's the revolution of "the littles" against the commercial monopolies was in full flower and bloom.

I knew Ginsberg only slightly. He and I served quietly as Board members of American P.E.N. in the early 80's. I remember one particular meeting, a sun sparkled afternoon at P.E.N. headquarters in Soho. Norman Mailer had just been elected President and he wanted to change things. I forget what things. E. L. Doctorow thought the changes were a dangerous precedent. The two of them sat at the head table hollering at each other, a school yard brawl. Ginsberg and I sat in the back row of folding chairs, near Harvey Shapiro, who had just retired as editor of the *New York Times Book Review.* While Mailer and Doctorow duked it out, Allen stood up and walked across the room behind Shapiro's chair. Without a word he began to massage

9

Harvey's back. While the dozens of Board members watched, and the thunder from the head table rolled on, Ginsberg administered to the startled Shapiro the best back massage he probably ever had. I am not sure how long Ginsberg massaged and the racket continued. It may have been minutes or a half an hour. But as he massaged and the sun streamed into the room it wasn't Mailer or Doctorow who won the argument. It was Ginsberg's gesture we remembered—his peace, his gentleness.

Over the years I saw Ginsberg from time to time. I recall him and Robert Lowell reading their poetry before a throng at St. Mark's church. Again it was Ginsberg who kept the peace when Gregory Corso interrupted Lowell's reading: "We are not your students!" he screamed again and again every time Lowell started to read. Finally Ginsberg quietly suggested that Lowell be allowed to continue. Corso stomped from the church bearing his infant child with the child's mother right behind him. Lowell continued.

In the early days of the *Pushcart Prize*, Ginsberg volunteered as a contributing editor, as so many good people have done over the years. We accepted one of his nominations for reprint, a poem "Crash" by David Cope, and noted that it was suggested by a fellow named Gins*burg*. He never mentioned it. Burg? Berg? OK by him.

A few words about this edition. I know that every year I proclaim that the book you hold is better than any *Pushcart Prize* before it. That's because it usually is. The stats: PPXXII includes more selections (over 70) by more new presses (19) than ever before in this series. We welcome for the first time: *American Letters and Commentary, Autonomedia, Bakunin, Calyx, Chattahoochee Review, Countermeasures, Counterpoint, Crosstown, Icon, Marlboro Review, Notre Dame Review, Oxford American, Orion Press, Solo, Tamaqua, Third Coast*, University of Iowa Press, White Pine Press and Zeitgeist Press. Altogether 52 presses are represented by reprinted stories, essays and poems (also a record) and many more are listed in the honorable mention section. As usual, most of our writers are new to the series.

Thanks for this astute, eclectic and just plain wonderful selection belongs to our PPXXII editors who sorted through thousands of nominations that arrived directly from small press editors and from our 200-plus Contributing Editors.

Heather McHugh is our guest poetry co-editor. She is a professor and writer in residence at the MFA program at the University of Washington and also at Warren Wilson College. Her books include *Shades* (1988), *Broken English: Poetry & Partiality* (1993) and *Hinge & Sign: Poetry, 1969–1993* (1994), a finalist for the National Book Award, all published by Wesleyan University Press. Her poems have appeared in *Pushcart Prize V, VIII* and *XIII*. She makes her home in Eastport, Maine.

Marvin Bell joins us again as poetry editor. He and Carolyn Kizer selected the poetry for PPXVI, and as any past poetry editor of this series will confess, it is an exhausting and impossible job—so many worthy poems, so little room. It has taken Marvin six years to recover, but I am glad that he is back. Marvin is the author of nine titles and, most recently, *The Book of the Dead Man* (Copper Canyon Press, 1994). He is Flannery O'Connor Professor in the MFA Creative Writing Department at the University of Iowa. He has received the Lamont Award, a Guggenheim Foundation grant and an NEA Fellowship.

I also thank Anthony Brandt who once again read the essays for Pushcart with his usual impatience for cant, verbosity and academic jive. Tony is compiling *The Pushcart Book of Essays*—the best essays from over two decades of PP.

Finally my appreciation to Rick Moody, who has taken on added fiction reading responsibilities with me. Rick has been honored by terrific reviews for his novel, *Purple America* (Little, Brown, 1997), and also for the film version of his novel, *The Ice Storm*, which won top honors for the best screen play at the 1997 Cannes Film Festival. The film was directed by Ang Lee and stars Kevin Kline and Sigourney Weaver. A few year's ago, Rick won Pushcart's Editors' Book Award for his novel, *Garden State* (1992). He previously appeared in *PPXX* with "The Ring of Brightest Angels Around Heaven" (*Paris Review*), from his fiction collection of the same title. His essay "Demonology" follows.

A final word about a good friend who died in 1996. Michael M. Rea devoted a substantial part of his life and his funds to the annual Rea Award for the Short Story. Selected by distinguished panels of judges, the winners of the Rea Award to date are Cynthia Ozick, Robert Coover, Donald Barthelme, Tobias Wolff, Joyce Carol Oates, Paul Bowles, Eudora Welty, Grace Paley, Tillie Olsen, Richard Ford, Andre Dubus and Gina Berriault. I am happy to report that Michael's award will be kept alive and thriving into the future by his widow, Elizabeth.

It is the spirit of people like Michael and Elizabeth Rea, and Allen Ginsberg and thousands of small press writers, editors, readers and supporters that we annually celebrate in these pages.

THE PEOPLE WHO HELPED

FOUNDING EDITORS—*Anaïs Nin (1903–1977), Buckminster Fuller (1895–1983), Charles Newman, Daniel Halpern, Gordon Lish, Harry Smith, Hugh Fox, Ishmael Reed, Joyce Carol Oates, Len Fulton, Leonard Randolph, Leslie Fiedler, Nona Balakian (1918–1991), Paul Bowles, Paul Engle (1908–1991), Ralph Ellison (1914–1994), Reynolds Price, Rhoda Schwartz, Richard Morris, Ted Wilentz, Tom Montag, William Phillips. Poetry editor: H. L. Van Brunt.*

SERIES EDITORS—Rick Moody (fiction); Marvin Bell (poetry); Anthony Brandt (essays)

GUEST POETRY CO-EDITOR—*Heather McHugh*

CONTRIBUTING EDITORS FOR THIS EDITION—*Rita Dove, DeWitt Henry, Andrei Codrescu, Frederick Busch, Carol Muske, Alice Schell, Andre Dubus, Ruth Stone, Tom Paine, Dennis Vannatta, Jewel Mogan, Maxine Kumin, Susan Wheeler, Philip Booth, Bruce Weigl, Jane Cooper, Philip Dacey, Richard Burgin, Daniel Stern, Robert Schirmer, Joseph Maiolo, Siv Cedering, Trudy Dittmar, Cyrus Cassells, Naomi Shihab Nye, Robert McBrearty, Michael Waters, Richard Jackson, Tomaž Šalamun, Arthur Smith, Vern Rutsala, Jane Hirshfield, Tony Quagliano, Kim Addonizio, Christopher Buckley, Eileen Pollack, Caroline Langston, Sigrid Nunez, David Wojahn, Kay Ryan, Maura Stanton, Stuart Dybek, Rick Bass, Sherod Santos, Kent Nelson, Ann Townsend, Mark Irwin, Molly Bendall, Kathy Callaway, Thomas Kennedy, A. Manette Ansay, Pamela Stewart, Steve Barthelme, Jack Marshall, Jim Barnes, Michael Kaniecki,*

C. S. Giscombe, John Allman, Susan Mitchell, David Jauss, Raymond Federman, Wally Lamb, Cleopatra Mathis, Kenneth Gangemi, David Lehman, Edward Hoagland, George Keithley, David Baker, Daniel Orozco, Robert Phillips, Dave Smith, Hope Edelman, Joan Murray, Thom Gunn, Steven Huff, Robert Dana, Karen Bender, M. D. Elevitch, Ted Wilentz, S. L. Wisenberg, Edmund Keeley, Richard Garcia, Josip Novakovich, Leonard Michaels, Norman Lavers, George Williams, Lisel Mueller, Dan Masterson, Ron Tanner, Tom McNeal, H. E. Francis, Robert Wrigley, Michael Bowden, Rosellen Brown, Jay Meek, Mark Halliday, Susan Mates, Adrian C. Louis, Daniel Meltzer, Melissa Malouf, Carol Snow, Stephen Dunn, Donald Revell, Kim Edwards, Richard Tayson, Brenda Miller, Mary Peterson, Susan Bergman, Harold Jaffe, Jim Daniels, Eugene Stein, Rebecca McClanahan, Karla Kuban, Bin Ramke, Philip Levine, Jim Simmerman, Joyce Carol Oates, Reginald Gibbons, Stanley W. Lindberg, Roger Weingarten, Antler, Gary Gildner, J. Allyn Rosser, Christina Zawadiwsky, Lois-Ann Yamanaka, Jean Thompson, D. R. MacDonald, Melissa Pritchard, Laura Kasischke, Timothy Geiger, Marianne Boruch, Lou Mathews, Karen Fish, William Matthews, Susan Moon, Laurie Sheck, Elizabeth Spires, Diann Blakely, James Harms, Aga Shahid Ali, David Romtvedt, Nora O. Keller, Ha Jin, Mark Jarman, Gary Fincke, Linda Bierds, Lloyd Schwartz, Maria Flook, Len Roberts, John Drury, Gibbons Ruark, Mark Cox, Robin Hemley, Kathy Mangan, Michael Stephens, Rachel Hadas, Tony Hoagland, Jane Miller, Pattiann Rogers, Steve Stern, Henry Carlile, Stephen Corey, Barbara Selfridge, James Reiss, Alan Shapiro, Richard Kostelanetz, David Rivard, Edward Hirsch, Stuart Dischell, C. E. Poverman, JoEllen Kwiatek, Michael Martone, Ralph Angel, Fatima Lim-Wilson, Jennifer Atkinson, Tony Ardizzone, Martha Collins, Lynne McFall, Arthur Sze, Michael Collier, Sandra Tsing Loh, Kelly Cherry, Eamon Grennan, Debra Spark, Molly Giles, Elizabeth Inness-Brown, Billy Collins, Henri Cole, Carl Dennis, Marilyn Hacker, Dean Young, Sharon Solwitz, Clarence Major, Thomas Lux, William Olsen, Alberto Ríos, Pinckney Benedict, Ed Ochester, Michael Dennis Browne, Pat Strachan, Sandra McPherson, Brenda Hillman, Campbell McGrath, Walter Pavlich, Eleanor Wilner, David St. John, Sharon Olds, Gerry Locklin, Lee Upton, Gail Mazur, Andrew Hudgins, Joe Ashby Porter, Paul Zimmer, Maureen Seaton, Philip Appleman, Erin McGraw, Robert Pinsky

14

ROVING EDITORS—*Lily Frances Henderson, Genie Chipps*

EUROPEAN EDITORS—*Liz and Kirby Williams*

MANAGING EDITOR—*Hannah Turner*

EDITOR AND PUBLISHER—*Bill Henderson*

CONTENTS

19

THE
PUSHCART PRIZE, XXII:
BEST OF THE
SMALL PRESSES

COURTING A MONK

fiction by KATHERINE MIN

from TRIQUARTERLY

WHEN I FIRST SAW my husband he was sitting cross-legged under a tree on the quad, his hair as short as peach fuzz, large blue eyes staring upward, the smile on his face so wide and undirected as to seem moronic. I went flying by him every minute or two, guarding man-to-man, or chasing down a pass, and out of the corner of my eye I would see him watching and smiling. What I noticed about him most was his tremendous capacity for stillness. His hands were like still-life objects resting on his knees; his posture was impeccable. He looked so rooted there, like some cheerful, exotic mushroom, that I began to feel awkward in my exertion. Sweat funneled into the valley of my back, cooling and sticking when I stopped, hands on knees, to regain my breath. I tried to stop my gape-mouthed panting, refashioned my ponytail, and wiped my hands on the soft front of my sweatpants.

He was still there two plays later when my team was down by one. Sully stole a pass and flipped to Graham. Graham threw me a long bomb that sailed wide and I leapt for it, sailing with the Frisbee for a moment in a parallel line—floating, flying, reaching—before coming down whap! against the ground. I groaned. I'd taken a tree root in the solar plexus. The wind was knocked out of me. I lay there, the taste of dry leaves in my mouth.

"Sorry, Gina. Lousy pass," Graham said, coming over. "You O.K.?"

"Fine," I gasped, fingering my ribs. "Just let me sit out for a while."

I sat down in the leaves, breathing carefully as I watched them play. The day was growing dark and the Frisbee was hard to see.

23

Everyone was tired and played in a sloppy rhythm of errant throws and dropped passes.

Beside me on the grass crept the guy from under the tree. I had forgotten about him. He crouched shyly next to me, leaves cracking under his feet, and, when I looked up, he whispered, "You were magnificent," and walked away smiling.

I spotted him the next day in the vegetarian dining hall. I was passing through with my plate of veal cordon bleu when I saw him sitting by himself next to the window. He took a pair of wooden chopsticks out of the breast pocket of his shirt and poked halfheartedly at his tofu and wilted mung beans. I sat down across from him and demanded his life story.

It turned out he wanted to be a monk. Not the Chaucerian kind, bald-pated and stout, with a hooded robe, ribald humor and penchant for wine. Something even more baffling—a Buddhist. He had just returned from a semester in Nepal, studying in a monastery in the Himalayas. His hair was coming back in in soft spikes across his head and he had a watchful manner—not cautious but receptive, waiting.

He was from King of Prussia, off the Philadelphia Main Line, and this made me mistrust the depth of his beliefs. I have discovered that a fascination for the East is often a prelude to a pass, a romantic overture set in motion by an "I think Oriental girls are so beautiful," and a vise-like grip on the upper thigh. But Micah was different. He understood I was not impressed by his belief, and he did not aim to impress.

"My father was raised Buddhist," I told him. "But he's a scientist now."

"Oh," said Micah. "So, he's not spiritual."

"Spirit's insubstantial," I said. "He doesn't hold with intangibility."

"Well, you can't hold atoms in your hand," Micah pointed out.

"Ah," I said, smiling, "But you can count them."

* * *

I told Micah my father was a man of science, and this was true. He was a man, also, of silence. Unlike Micah, whose reticence seemed calming, so undisturbed, like a pool of light on still water, my father's silence was like the lid on a pot, sealing off some steaming, inner pressure.

Words were not my father's medium. "Language," my father liked to say, "is an imprecise instrument." (For though he said little, when he hit upon a phrase he liked, he said it many times.) He was fond of Greek letters and numerals set together in intricate equations, sym-

24

bolizing a certain physical law or experimental hypothesis. He filled yellow legal pads in a strong, vertical hand, writing these beauties down in black, indelible felt-tip pen. I think it was a source of tremendous irritation to him that he could not communicate with other people in so ordered a fashion, that he could not simply draw an equals sign after something he'd said, have them solve for x or y.

That my father's English was not fluent was only part of it. He was not a garrulous man, even in Korean, among visiting relatives, or alone with my mother. And with me, his only child—who could speak neither of his preferred languages, Korean or science—my father had conspicuously little to say. "Pick up this mess," he would tell me, returning from work in the evening. "Homework finished?" he would inquire, raising an eyebrow over his rice bowl as I excused myself to go watch television.

He limited himself to the imperative mood, the realm of injunction and command; the kinds of statement that required no answer, that left no opening for discussion or rejoinder. These communications were my father's verbal equivalent to his neat numerical equations. They were hermetically sealed.

When I went away to college, my father's parting words constituted one of the longest speeches I'd heard him make. Surrounded by station wagons packed with suitcases, crates of books and study lamps, amid the excited chattering and calling out of students, among the adults with their nervous, parental surveillance of the scene, my father leaned awkwardly forward with his hands in his pockets, looking at me intently. He said, "Study hard. Go to bed early. Do not goof off. And do not let the American boys take advantages."

This was the same campus my father had set foot on twenty years before, when he was a young veteran of the Korean War, with fifty dollars in his pocket and about that many words of English. Stories of his college years constituted family legend and, growing up, I had heard them so often they were as vivid and dream-like as my own memories. My father in the dorm bathroom over Christmas, vainly trying to hardboil an egg in a sock by running it under hot water; his triumph in the physics lab where his ability with the new language did not impede him, and where his maturity and keen scientific mind garnered him highest marks and the top physics prize in his senior year—these were events I felt I'd witnessed, like some obscure, envious ghost.

In the shadow of my father's achievements then, on the same campus where he had first bowed his head to a microscope, lost in a chalk-dust mathematical dream, I pursued words. English words. I committed myself to expertise. I studied Shakespeare and Eliot, Hardy and Conrad, Joyce and Lawrence and Hemingway and Fitzgerald. It was important to get it right, every word, every nuance, to fill in my father's immigrant silences, the gaps he had left for me.

Other gaps he'd left. Staying up late and studying little, I did things my father would have been too shocked to merely disapprove. As for American boys, I heeded my father's advice and did not let them take advantage. Instead I took advantage of them, of their proximity, their good looks, and the amiable way they would fall into bed with you if you gave them the slightest encouragement. I liked the way they moved in proud possession of their bodies, the rough feel of their unshaven cheeks, their shoulders and smooth, hairless chests, the curve of their backs like burnished wood. I liked the way I could look up at them, or down, feeling their shuddering climax like a distant earthquake; I could make it happen, moving in undulant circles from above or below, watching them, holding them, making them happy. I collected boys like baubles, like objects not particularly valued, which you stash away in the back of some drawer. It was the pleasant interchangeability of their bodies I liked. They were all white boys.

Micah refused to have sex with me. It became a matter of intellectual disagreement between us. "Sex saps the will," he said.

"Not necessarily," I argued. "Just reroutes it."

"There are higher forms of union," he said.

"Not with your clothes off," I replied.

"Gina," he said, looking at me with kindness, a concern that made me flush with anger. "What need do you have that sex must fill?"

"Fuck you, Micah," I said. "Be a monk, not a psychologist."

He laughed. His laughter was always a surprise to me, like a small disturbance to the universe. I wanted to seduce him, this was true. I considered Micah the only real challenge among an easy field. But more than seduction, I wanted to rattle him, to get under that sense of peace, that inward contentment. No one my age, I reasoned, had the right to such self-possession.

We went for walks in the bird sanctuary, rustling along the paths slowly, discussing Emily Dickinson or maple syrup-making, but always I brought the subject around.

26

"What a waste of a life," I said once. "Such indulgence. All that monkly devotion and quest for inner peace. Big deal. It's selfish. Not only is it selfish, it's a cop-out. An escape from this world and its messes."

Micah listened, a narrow smile on his lips, shaking his head regretfully. "You're so wonderfully passionate, Gina, so alive and in the world. I can't make you see. Maybe it is a cop-out, as you say, but Buddhism makes no distinction between the world outside or the world within the monastery. And historically, monks have been in the middle of political protest and persecution. Look at Tibet."

"I was thinking about, ahem, something more basic," I said.

Micah laughed. "Of course," he said. "You don't seem to understand, Gina, Buddhism is all about the renunciation of desire."

I sniffed. "What's wrong with desire? Without desire, you might as well not be alive."

The truth was that I was fascinated by this idea, the renunciation of desire. My life was fueled by longing, by vast and clamorous desires; a striving toward things I did not have and, perhaps, had no hope of having. I could vaguely imagine an end, some point past desiring, of satiety, but I could not fathom the laying down of desire, walking away in full appetite.

"The desire to renounce desire," I said now, "is still desire, isn't it?"

Micah sunk his hands into his pockets and smiled. "It's not," he said, walking ahead of me. "It's a conscious choice."

We came to a pond, sun-dappled in a clearing, bordered by white birch and maples with the bright leaves of mid-autumn. A fluttering of leaves blew from the trees, landing on the water as gently as if they'd been placed. The color of the pond was a deep canvas green; glints of light snapped like sparks above the surface. There was the lyric coo of a mourning dove, the chitter-chitter of late-season insects. Micah's capacity for appreciation was vast. Whether this had anything to do with Buddhism, I didn't know, but watching him stand on the edge of the pond, his head thrown back, his eyes eagerly taking in the light, I felt his peace and also his sense of wonder. He stood motionless for a long time.

I pulled at ferns, weaved their narrow leaves in irregular samplers, braided tendrils together, while Micah sat on a large rock and, taking his chopsticks from his breast pocket, began to tap them lightly against one another in a solemn rhythm.

"Every morning in the monastery," he said, "we woke to the prayer drum. Four o'clock and the sky would be dark and you'd hear the hollow wooden sound—plock, plock, plock—summoning you to meditation." He smiled dreamily. The chopsticks made a somewhat less effectual sound, a sort of ta ta ta. I imagined sunrise across a Himalayan valley—the wisps of pink-tinged cloud on a cold spring morning, the austerity of a monk's chamber.

Micah had his eyes closed, face to the sun. He continued to tap the chopsticks together slowly. He looked singular and new, sitting on that rock, like an advance scout for some new tribe, with his crest of hair and calm, and the attentiveness of his body to his surroundings.

I think it was then I fell in love with him, or, it was in that moment that my longing for him became so great that it was no longer a matter of simple gratification. I needed his response. I understood what desire was then, the disturbance of a perfect moment in anticipation of another.

"Wake-up call," I said. I peeled off my turtleneck and sweater in one clever motion and tossed them at Micah's feet. Micah opened his eyes. I pulled my pants off and my underwear and stood naked. "Plock, plock, who's there?"

Micah did not turn away. He looked at me, his chopsticks poised in the air. He raised one toward me and held it, as though he were an artist with a paintbrush raised for a proportion, or a conductor ready to lead an orchestra. He held the chopstick suspended in the space between us, and it was as though I couldn't move for as long as he held it. His eyes were fathomless blue. My nipples constricted with the cold. Around us leaves fell in shimmering lights to the water, making a soft rustling sound like the rub of stiff fabric. He brought his hand down and I was released. I turned and leapt into the water.

A few nights later I bought a bottle of cheap wine and goaded Micah into drinking it with me. We started out on the steps of the library after it had closed for the night, taking sloppy swigs from a brown paper bag. The lights of the Holyoke range blinked in the distance, across the velvet black of the freshman quad. From there we wandered the campus, sprawling on the tennis courts, bracing a stiff wind from the terrace of the science center, sedately rolling down Memorial Hill like a pair of tumbleweeds.

"J'a know what a koan is?" he asked me, when we were perched at the top of the bleachers behind home plate. We unsteadily contemplated the steep drop off the back side.

"You mean like ice cream?" I said.

"No, a ko-an. In Buddhism."

"Nope."

"It's a question that has no answer, sort of like a riddle. You know, like 'What is the sound of one hand clapping?' Or 'What was your face before you were born?'"

"'What was my face before it was born?' That makes no sense."

"Exactly. You're supposed to contemplate the koan until you achieve a greater awareness."

"Of what?"

"Of life, of meaning."

"Oh, O.K.," I said, "I've got it." I was facing backwards, the bag with the bottle in both my hands. "How 'bout, 'What's the sound of one cheek farting?'"

He laughed for a long time, then retched off the side of the bleachers. I got him home and put him to bed; his forehead was feverish, his eyes glassy with sickness.

"Sorry," I said. "I'm a bad influence." I kissed him. His lips were hot and slack.

"Don't mind," he murmured, half-asleep.

The next night we slept in the same bed together for the first time. He kept his underwear on and his hands pressed firmly to his sides, like Gandhi among his young virgins. I was determined to make it difficult for him. I kept brushing my naked body against him, draping a leg across his waist, stroking his narrow chest with my fingertips. He wiggled and pushed away, feigning sleep. When I woke in the morning, he was gone and the *Ode to Joy* was blasting from my stereo.

Graham said he missed me. We'd slept together a few times before I met Micah, enjoying the warm, healthful feeling we got from running or playing Ultimate, taking a quick sauna and falling into bed. He was good-looking, dark and broad, with sinewy arms and a tight chest. He made love to a woman like he was lifting Nautilus, all grim purpose and timing. It was hard to believe that had ever been appealing. I told him I was seeing someone else.

"Not the guy with the crew cut?" he said. "The one who looks like a baby seal?"

I shrugged.

Graham looked at me skeptically. "He doesn't seem like your type," he said.

"No," I agreed. "But at least he's not yours."

29

Meanwhile I stepped up my attack. I asked endless questions about Buddhist teaching. Micah talked about *dukkha;* the four noble truths; the five aggregates of attachment; the noble eightfold path to enlightenment. I listened dutifully, willing to acknowledge that it all sounded nice, that the goal of perfect awareness and peace seemed worth attaining. While he talked, I stretched my feet out until my toes touched his thigh; I slid my hand along his back; or leaned way over so he could see down my loose, barely-buttoned blouse.

"Too bad you aren't Tantric," I said. I'd been doing research.

Micah scoffed. "Hollywood Buddhism," he said. "Heavy breathing and theatrics."

"They believe in physical desire," I said. "They have sex."

"Buddha believes in physical desire," Micah said. "It's impermanent, that's all. Something to get beyond."

"To get beyond it," I said petulantly, "you have to do it."

Micah sighed. "Gina," he said, "you are beautiful, but I can't. There are a lot of guys who will."

"A lot of them do."

He smiled a bit sadly. "Well, then . . . "

I leaned down to undo his shoelaces. I tied them together in double knots. "But I want you," I said.

My parents lived thirty miles from campus and my mother frequently asked me to come home for dinner. I went only once that year, and that was with Micah. My parents were not the kind of people who enjoyed the company of strangers. They were insular people who did not like to socialize much or go out—or anyway, my father was that way, and my mother accommodated herself to his preferences.

My mother had set the table in the dining room with blue linen. There were crystal wine glasses and silver utensils in floral patterns. She had made some dry baked chicken with overcooked peas and carrots—the meal she reserved for when Americans came to dinner. When it came to Korean cooking, my mother was a master. She made fabulous marinated short ribs and sautéed transparent bean noodles with vegetables and beef, pork dumplings and batter-fried shrimp, and cucumber and turnip kimchis which she made herself and fermented in brown earthenware jars. But American cuisine eluded her; it bored her. I think she thought it was meant to be tasteless.

"Just make Korean," I had urged her on the phone. "He'll like that."

My mother was skeptical. "Too spicy," she said. "I know what Americans like."

"Not the chicken dish," I pleaded. "He's a vegetarian."

"We'll see," said my mother, conceding nothing.

Micah stared down at his plate. My mother smiled serenely. Micah nodded. He ate a forkful of vegetables, took a bite of bread. His Adam's apple seemed to be doing a lot of work. My father, too, was busy chewing, his Adam's apple moving up and down his throat like the ratchets of a tire jack. No one had said a thing since my father had uncorked the Chardonnay and read to us the description from his well-creased paperback edition of *The New York Times Guide to Wine*.

The sound of silverware scraping on ceramic plates seemed amplified. I was aware of my own prolonged chewing. My father cleared his throat. My mother looked at him expectantly. He coughed.

"Micah studied Buddhism in Nepal," I offered into the silence.

"Oh!" my mother exclaimed. She giggled.

My father kept eating. He swallowed exaggeratedly and looked up. "That so?" he said, sounding almost interested.

Micah nodded. "I was only there four months," he said. "Gina tells me you were brought up Buddhist."

My father grunted. "Well, of course," he said, "in Korea in those days, our families were all Buddhist. I do not consider myself a Buddhist now."

Micah and I exchanged a look.

"It's become quite fashionable, I understand," my father went on. "With you American college kids. Buddhism has become fad."

I saw Micah wince.

"I think it is wonderful, Hi Joon," my mother interceded, "for Americans to learn about Asian religion and philosophy. I was a philosophy major in college, Micah. I studied Whitehead, American pragmatism."

My father leaned back in his chair and watched, frowning, while my mother and Micah talked. It was like he was trying to analyze Micah, not as a psychiatrist analyzes—my father held a dim view of psychology—but as a chemist would, breaking him down to his basic elements, the simple chemical formula that would define his makeup.

Micah was talking about the aggregates of matter, sensation, perception, mental formations, and consciousness that comprise being in Buddhist teaching. "It's a different sense of self than in Christian religions," he explained, looking at my mother.

"Nonsense," my father interrupted. "There is no self in Buddhist doctrine. . . ."

My mother and I watched helplessly as they launched into discussion. I was surprised that my father seemed to know so much about it, and by how much he was carrying forth. I was surprised also by Micah's deference. He seemed to have lost all his sureness, the walls of his conviction. He kept nodding and conceding to my father certain points that he had rigorously defended to me before. "I guess I don't know as much about it," he said more than once, and "Yes, I see what you mean" several times, with a sickening air of humility.

I turned from my father's glinting, pitiless intelligence, to Micah's respectfulness, his timid manner, and felt a rising irritation I could not place, anger at my father's belligerence, at Micah's backing down, at my own strange motives for having brought them together. Had I really expected them to get along? And yet, my father was concentrating on Micah with such an intensity—almost as though he were a rival—in a way in which he never focused on me.

When the dialogue lapsed, and after we had consumed as much of the food as we deemed polite, my mother took the dishes away and brought in a bowl of rice with kimchi for my father. Micah's eyes lit up. "May I have some of that, too, Mrs. Kim?"

My mother looked doubtful. "Too spicy," she said.

"Oh, I love spicy food," Micah assured her. My mother went to get him a bowl.

"You can use chopsticks?" my mother said, as Micah began eating with them.

"Mom, it's no big deal," I said.

My father looked up from his bowl. Together, my parents watched while Micah ate a large piece of cabbage kimchi.

"Hah!" my father said, suddenly smiling. "Gina doesn't like kimchi," he said. He looked at me. "Gina," he said. "This boy more Korean than you."

"Doesn't take much," I said.

My father ignored me. "Gina always want to be American," he told Micah. "Since she was little girl, she want blue eyes, yellow hair." He stabbed a chopstick toward Micah's face. "Like yours."

"If I had hair," said Micah, grinning, rubbing a hand across his head.

My father stared into his bowl. "She doesn't want to be Korean girl. She thinks she can be 100 percent American, but she cannot. She has Korean blood—100 percent. Doesn't matter where you grow up— blood is most important. What is in the blood." He gave Micah a severe look. "You think you can become Buddhist. Same way. But it is not in your blood. You cannot know real Buddha's teaching. You should study Bible."

"God, Dad!" I said. "You sound like a Nazi!"

"Gina!" my mother warned.

"You're embarrassing me," I said. "Being rude to my guest. Discussing me as if I wasn't here. You can say what you want, Dad, I'm American whether you like it or not. Blood's got nothing to do with it. It's what's up here." I tapped my finger to my temple.

"It's not Nazi," my father said. "Is fact! What you have here," he pointed to his forehead, "is all from blood, from genetics. You got from me!"

"Heaven help me," I said.

"Gina!" my mother implored.

"Mr. Kim—" Micah began.

"You just like American girl in one thing," my father shouted. "You have no respect for father. In Korea, daughters do not talk back to their parents, is big shame!"

"In Korea, girls are supposed to be submissive doormats for fathers to wipe their feet on!" I shouted back.

"What do you know about Korea? You went there only once when you were six years old."

"It's in my blood," I said. I stood up. "I'm not going to stay here for this. Come on, Micah."

Micah looked at me uncertainly, then turned to my father.

My father was eating again, slowly levering rice to his mouth with his chopsticks. He paused. "She was always this way," he said, seeming to address the table. "So angry. Even as a little girl."

"Mr. Kim," Micah said, "Um, thank you very much. We're . . . I think we're heading out now."

My father chewed ruminatively. "I should never have left Korea," he said quietly, with utter conviction.

"Gina," my mother said. "Sit down. Hi Joon, please!"

"Micah," I said. "You coming?"

We left my father alone at the dining-room table.

"I should have sent you to live with Auntie Soo!" he called after me.

My mother followed us out to the driveway with a Tupperware container of chicken Micah hadn't eaten.

On the way home we stopped for ice cream. Koans, I told Micah. "What is the sound of Swiss chocolate almond melting?" I asked him. "What was the vanilla before it was born?"

Inside the ice-cream parlor the light was too strong, a ticking fluorescence bleaching everything bone-white. Micah leaned down to survey the cardboard barrels of ice cream in their plastic cases. He looked shrunken, subdued. He ordered a scoop of mint chocolate chip and one of black cherry on a sugar cone and ate it with the long, regretful licks of a child who'd spent the last nickel of his allowance. There was a ruefulness to his movements, a sense of apology. He had lost his monk-like stillness and seemed suddenly adrift.

The cold of the ice cream gave me a headache, all the blood vessels in my temples seemed strung out and tight. I shivered and the cold was like fury, spreading through me with the chill.

Micah rubbed my back.

"You're hard on your father," he said. "He's not a bad guy."

"Forget it," I said. "Let's go."

We walked from the dorm parking lot in silence. There were lights going on across the quad and music spilling from the windows out into the cool air. What few stars there were seemed too distant to wage a constant light.

Back in my room, I put on the Rolling Stones at full blast. Mick Jagger's voice was taunting and cruel. I turned out the lights and lit a red candle.

"O.K., this is going to stop," I said. I felt myself trembling. I pushed Micah back on the bed. I was furious. He had ruined it for me, the lightness, the skimming quality of my life. It had seemed easy, with the boys, the glib words and feelings, the simple heat and surface pleasures. It was like the sensation of flying, leaping for the Frisbee and sailing through the air. For a moment you lose a feeling for gravity, for the consciousness of your own skin or species. For a moment you are free.

I started to dance, fast, swinging and swaying in front of the bed. I closed my eyes and twirled wildly, bouncing off the walls like a pinball, stumbling on my own stockings. I danced so hard the stereo skipped, Jagger forced to stutter in throaty monosyllables, gulping repetitions.

I whirled and circled, threw my head from side to side until I could feel the baffled blood, brought my hair up off my neck and held it with both hands.

Micah watched me dance. His body made an inverted-S upon my bed, his head propped by the pillar of his own arm. The expression on his face was the same as he'd had talking with my father, that look of deference, of fawn-eyed yielding. But I could see there was something hidden.

With white-knuckled fingers, I undid the buttons of my sweater and ripped my shirt lifting it off my head. I danced out of my skirt and underthings, kicking them into the corner, danced until the song was over, until I was soaked with sweat and burning—and then I jumped him.

It was like the taste of food after a day's starvation—unexpectedly strong and substantial. Micah responded to my fury, met it with his own mysterious passion; it was like a brawl, a fight, with something at stake that neither of us wanted to lose. Afterward we sat up in bed and listened to *Ode to Joy* while Micah, who had a surplus supply of chopsticks lying around the room, did his Leonard Bernstein impersonation. Later, we went out for a late-night snack to All-Star Dairy and Micah admitted to me that he was in love.

*   *   *

My father refused to attend the wedding. He liked Micah, but he did not want me to marry a Caucasian. It became a joke I would tell people. Korean custom, I said, to give the bride away four months before the ceremony.

Micah became a high-school biology teacher. I am an associate dean of students at the local college. We have two children. When Micah tells the story of our courtship, he tells it with great self-deprecation and humor. He makes it sound as though he were crazy to ever consider becoming a monk. "Think of it," he tells our kids. "Your dad."

Lately I've taken to reading books about Buddhism. Siddhartha Gotama was thirty-five years old when he sat under the Bodhi-tree on the bank of the river Neranjara and gained Enlightenment. Sometimes, when I see my husband looking at me across the breakfast table, or walking toward me from the other side of a room, I catch a look of distress on his face, a blinking confusion, as though he cannot remember who I am. I have happened on him a few times, on a Sunday

35

when he has disappeared from the house, sitting on a bench with the newspaper in his lap staring across the town common, so immersed in his thoughts that he is not roused by my calling of his name.

I remember the first time I saw him, that tremendous stillness he carried, the contentment in his face. I remember how he looked on the rocks by that pond, like a pioneer in a new land, and I wonder if he regrets, as I do, the loss of his implausible faith. Does he miss the sound of the prayer drum, the call to an inner life without the configuration of desire? I think of my father, running a sock under heated water thousands of miles from home, as yet unaware of the daughter he will raise with the same hopeful, determined, and ultimately futile, effort. I remember the way I used to play around with koans, and I wonder, "What is the sound of a life not lived?"

Nominated by TriQuarterly

DEMONOLOGY

by RICK MOODY

from CONJUNCTIONS

They came in twos and threes, dressed in the fashionable Disney costumes of the year, Lion King, Pocahontas, Beauty and the Beast or in the costumes of televised superheroes, Protean, shape-shifting, thus arrayed, in twos and threes, complaining it was too hot with the mask on, *Hey, I'm really hot!*, lugging those orange plastic buckets, bartering, haggling with one another, *Gimme your Smarties, please?* as their parents tarried behind, grownups following after, grownups bantering about the schools, or about movies, about local sports, about their marriages, about the difficulties of long marriages, kids sprinting up the next driveway, kids decked out as demons or superheroes or dinosaurs or as advertisements for our multinational entertainment-providers, beating back the restless souls of the dead, in search of sweets.

They came in bursts of fertility, my sister's kids, when the bar drinking, or home-grown dope-smoking, or bed-hopping had lost its luster; they came with shrill cries and demands—little gavels, she said, instead of fists—*Feed me! Change me! Pay attention to me!* Now it was Halloween and the mothers in town, my sister among them, trailed after their kids, warned them away from items not fully wrapped, *Just give me that, you don't even like apples*, laughing at the kids hobbling in their bulky costumes—my nephew dressed as a shark, dragging a mildewed gray tail behind him. But what kind of shark? A great white? A blue? A tiger shark? A hammerhead? A nurse shark?

She took pictures of costumed urchins, my sister, as she always took pictures, e.g., my nephew on his first birthday (six years prior), black-faced with cake and ice cream, a dozen relatives attempting in turn to read to him—about a tugboat—from a brand new rubberized book. *Toot toot!* His desperate, needy expression, in the photo, all out of phase with our excitement. The first nephew! The first grandchild! He was trying to get the cake in his mouth. Or: a later photo of my niece (his younger sister) attempting to push my nephew out of the shot—against a backdrop of autumn foliage; or a photo of my brother wearing my dad's yellow double-knit paisley trousers (with a bit of flair in the cuffs), twenty-five years after the heyday of such stylings; or my father and stepmother on their powerboat, peaceful and happy, the riotous wake behind them; or my sister's virtuosic photos of *dogs*—Mom's irrepressible golden retriever chasing a tennis ball across an overgrown lawn, or my dad's setter on the beach with a perspiring Löwenbräu leaning against his snout. Fifteen or twenty photo albums on the shelves in my sister's living room, a whole range of leathers and faux-leathers, no particular order, and just as many more photos loose, floating around the basement, castoffs, and files of negatives in their plastic wrappers.

She drank *the demon rum,* and she taught me how to do it, too, when we were kids; she taught me how to drink. We stole drinks, or we got people to steal them for us; we got reprobates of age to venture into the pristine suburban liquor stores. Later, I drank bourbon. My brother drank beer. My father drank single malt scotches. My grandmother drank half-gallons and then fell ill. My grandfather drank the finest collectibles. My sister's ex-husband drank more reasonably priced facsimiles. My brother drank until a woman lured him out of my mother's house. I drank until I was afraid to go outside. My uncle drank until the last year of his life. And I carried my sister in a blackout from a bar once—she was mumbling to herself, humming melodies, mostly unconscious. I took her arms; Peter Hunter took her legs. She slept the whole next day. On Halloween, my sister had a single gin and tonic before going out with the kids, before ambling around the condos of Kensington Court, circling from multifamily unit to multifamily unit, until my nephew's shark tail was grass-stained from the freshly mown lawns of the common areas. Then she drove her children across town to her ex-husband's house, released them into his supervision, and there they walked along empty lots, beside a brook, under the stars.

When they arrived home, these monsters, disgorged from their dad's Jeep, there was a fracas between girl and boy about which was

38

superior (in the Aristotelian hierarchies), Milky Way, Whoppers, Slim Jim, Mike 'n Ikes, Sweet Tarts or Pez—this bounty counted, weighed and inventoried (on my niece's bed). Which was the Pez dispenser of greatest value? A Hanna-Barbera Pez dispenser? Or, say, a demonic *totem pole Pez dispenser?* And after this fracas, which my sister refereed wearily (*Look, if he wants to save the Smarties, you can't make him trade!*), they all slept, and this part is routine, my sister was tired as hell; she slept the sleep of the besieged, of the overworked, she fell precipitously into whorls of unconsciousness, of which no snapshot can be taken.

In one photograph, my sister is wearing a Superman outfit. This from a prior Halloween. I think it was a *Supermom* outfit, actually, because she always liked these bad jokes, degraded jokes, things other people would find ridiculous. (She'd take a joke and repeat it until it was leaden, until it was funny only in its awfulness.) Jokes with the fillip of sentimentality. Anyway, in this picture her blond hair—brightened a couple of shades with the current technologies—cascades around her shoulders, disordered and impulsive. *Supermom.* And her expression is skeptical, as if she assumes the mantle of Supermom— raising the kids, accepting wage-slavery, growing old and contented— and thinks it's dopey at the same time.

Never any good without coffee. Never any good in the morning. Never any good until the second cup. Never any good without freshly ground Joe, because of my dad's insistence, despite advantages of class and style, on *instant coffee.* No way. Not for my sister. At my dad's house, where she stayed in summer, she used to grumble derisively, while staring out the kitchen windows, out the expanse of windows that gave onto the meadow there, *Instant coffee!* There would be horses in the meadow and the ocean just over the trees, the sound of the surf and *instant coffee!* Thus the morning after Halloween, with my nephew the shark (who took this opportunity to remind her, in fact, that last year he saved his Halloween candy *all the way till Easter, Mommy*) and my niece, the Little Mermaid, orbiting around her like a fine dream. My sister was making this coffee with the automatic grinder and the automatic drip device, and the dishes were piled in the sink behind her, and the wall calendar was staring her in the face, with its hundred urgent appointments, e.g., *jury duty* (the following Monday) and *R & A to pediatrician;* the kids whirled around the kitchen, demanding to know who got the last of the Lucky Charms, who had to settle for the Kix. My sister's eyes barely open.

Now this portrait of her cat, Pointdexter, twelve years old—he slept on my face when I stayed at her place in 1984—Pointdexter with the brain tumor, Pointdexter with the Phenobarbital habit. That morning—All Saints' Day—he stood entirely motionless before his empty dish. His need was clear. His dignity was immense. Well, except for the seizures. Pointdexter had these seizures. He was possessed. He was a demon. He would bounce off the walls, he would get up *a head of steam,* mouth frothing, and run straight at the wall, smack into it, shake off the ghosts and start again. His screeches were unearthly. Phenobarbital was prescribed. My sister medicated him preemptively, before any other chore, before diplomatic initiatives on matters of cereal allocation. *Hold on, you guys, I'll be with you in a second.* Drugging the cat, slipping him the Mickey Finn in the Science Diet, feeding the kids, then getting out the door, pecking her boyfriend on the cheek (he was stumbling sleepily down the stairs).

She printed snapshots. At this photo lab. She'd sold cameras (mnemonic devices) for years, and then she'd been kicked upstairs to the lab. Once she sold a camera to Pete Townshend, the musician. She told him—in her way both casual and rebellious—that she didn't really like The Who. Later, from her job at the lab, she used to bring home *other people's pictures,* e.g., an envelope of photographs of the Pope. Had she been out to Giants Stadium to use her telephoto lens to photograph John Paul II? No, she'd just printed up an extra batch of, say, Agnes Venditi's or Joey Mueller's photos. *Caveat emptor.* Who knew what else she'd swiped? Those Jerry Garcia pix from the show right before he died? Garcia's eyes squeezed tightly shut, as he sang in that heartbroken, exhausted voice of his? Or: somebody's trip to the Caribbean or to the Liberty Bell in Philly? Or: her neighbor's private documentations of love? Who knew? She'd get on the phone at work and gab, call up her friends, call up my family, printing pictures while gabbing, sheet after sheet of negatives, of memories. Oh, and circa Halloween, she was working in the lab with some new, exotic chemicals. She had a wicked headache.

My sister didn't pay much attention to the church calendar. Too busy. Too busy to concentrate on theologies, too busy to go to the doctor, too busy to deal with her finances, her credit-card debt, etc. Too busy. (And maybe afraid, too.) She was unclear on this day set aside for God's awesome tabernacle, unclear on the feast for the departed faithful, didn't know about the church of the Middle Ages, didn't know about the particulars of the Druidic ritual of Halloween—it was a Hallmark thing, a marketing event—or how All Saints' Day emerged as an alternative to Halloween. She was not much preoccupied with, nor attendant to articulations of loss nor interested in how this feast in the church calendar was hewn into two separate holy days, one for the saints, *that great cloud of witnesses,* one for the dearly departed, the regular old believers. She didn't know of any attachments that bound together these constituencies, didn't know, e.g., that God would *wipe away all tears from our eyes and there would be no more death,* according to the evening's reading from the book of Revelation. All this academic stuff was lost on her, though she sang in the church choir, and though on All Saints' Day, a guy from the church choir happened to come into the camera store, just to say hi, a sort of an angel (let's say), and she said, *Hey Bob, you know, I never asked you what you do.*

To which Bob replied, *I'm a designer.*

My sister: *What do you design?*

Bob: *Steel wool.*

She believed him.

She was really small. She barely held down her clothes. Five feet tall. Tiny hands and feet. Here's a photo from my brother's wedding (two weeks before Halloween); we were dancing on the dance floor, she and I. She liked to *pogo* sometimes. It was the dance we preferred when dancing together. We created mayhem on the dance floor. Scared people off. We were demons for dance, for noise and excitement. So at my brother's wedding reception I hoisted her up onto my shoulder, and she was so light, just as I remembered from years before, twenty years of dances, still tiny, and I wanted to crowd-surf her across the reception, pass her across upraised hands, I wanted to impose her on older couples, gentlemen in their cummerbunds, old guys with tennis elbow or arthritis, with red faces and gin-blossoms; they would smile, passing my sister hither, to the microphone, where the wedding band was playing, where she would suddenly burst into song, into some sort of reconciliatory song, backed by the wedding band, and there would be stills of this moment, flash bulbs popping, a spotlight on her face, a tiny bit of reverb on her microphone, she would smile and concentrate and sing. Unfortunately, the situation around

41

us, on the dance floor, was more complicated than this. Her boyfriend was about to have back surgery. He wasn't going to do any heavy lifting. And my nephew was too little to hold her up. And my brother was preoccupied with his duties as groom. So instead I twirled her once and put her down. We were laughing, out of breath.

On All Saints' Day she had lunch with Bob the angelic designer of steel wool (maybe he had a crush on her) or with the younger guys from the lab (because she was a middle-aged free spirit), and then she printed more photos of Columbus Day parades across Jersey, or photos of other people's kids dressed as Pocahontas or as the Lion King, and then at 5:30 she started home, a commute of forty-five minutes, Morristown to Hackettstown, on two-laners. She knew every turn. Here's the local news photo that never was: my sister slumped over the wheel of her Plymouth Saturn after having run smack into a local deer. All along those roads the deer were upended, disemboweled, set upon by crows and hawks, and my sister on the way back from work, or on the way home from a bar, must have grazed an entire herd of them at one time or another, missed them narrowly, frozen in the headlights of her car, on the shoulders of the meandering back roads, pulverized.

Her boy lives on air. Disdains food. My niece, meanwhile, will eat only candy. By dinnertime, they had probably made a dent in the orange plastic bucket with the Three Musketeers, the Cadbury's, Hot Tamales, Kit Kats, Jujyfruits, Baby Ruths, Bubble Yum—at least my niece had. They had insisted on bring a sampling of this booty to school and from there to their afterschool play group. Neither of them wanted to eat anything; they complained about the whole idea of supper, and thus my sister offered, instead, to take them to the *McDonald-Land play area* on the main drag in Hackettstown, where she would buy them a Happy Meal, or equivalent, a hamburger topped with *American processed cheese food,* and, as an afterthought, she would insist on their each trying a little bit of a salad from the brand new McDonald's salad bar. She had to make a deal to get the kids to accept the salad. She suggested six mouthfuls of lettuce each and drew a hard line there, but then she allowed herself to be talked down to two mouthfuls each. They ate indoors at first, the three of them, and then went out to the playground, where there were slides and jungle gyms in the reds and yellows of Ray Kroc's empire. My sister made the usual conversation, *How did the other kids make out on Halloween? What hap-*

42

pened at school? and she thought of her boyfriend, fresh from spinal surgery, who had limped downstairs in the morning to give her a kiss, and then she thought about *bills, bills, bills,* as she caught my niece at the foot of the slide. It was time to go sing. Home by nine.

My sister as she played the guitar in the late sixties with her hair in braids; she played it before anyone else in my family, wandering around the chords, "House of the Rising Sun" or "Blackbird," on classical guitar, sticking to the open chords of guitar tablature. It never occurred to me to wonder about which instruments were used on those AM songs of the period (the Beatles with their sitars and cornets, Brian Wilson with his theremin), not until my sister started to play the guitar. (All of us sang—we used to sing and dance in the living room when my parents were married, especially to *Abbey Road* and *Bridge Over Troubled Water*.) And when she got divorced she started hanging around this bar where they had live music, this Jersey bar, and then she started hanging around at a local record label, an indy operation, and then she started *managing a band* (on top of everything else), and then she started to sing again. She joined the choir at St. James Church of Hackettstown and she started to sing, and after singing she started to pray—prayer and song being, I guess, styles of the same beseechment.

I don't know what songs they rehearsed at choir rehearsal, but Bob was there, as were others, Donna, Frank, Eileen and Tim (I'm making the names up), and I know that the choir was warm and friendly, though perhaps a little bit out of tune. It was one of those Charles Ives small-town choruses that slips in and out of pitch, that misses exits and entrances. But they had a good time rehearsing, with the kids monkeying around in the pews, the kids climbing sacrilegiously over that furniture, dashing up the aisle to the altar and back, as somebody kept half an eye on them (five of the whelps in all) and after the last notes ricocheted around the choir loft, my sister offered her summation of the proceedings, *Totally cool! Totally cool!*, and now the intolerable part of this story begins—with joy and excitement and a church interior. My sister and her kids drove from St. James to her house, her condo, this picturesque drive home, Hackettstown as if lifted from picture postcards of autumn, the park with its streams and ponds and lighted walkways, leaves in the streetlamps, in the headlights, leaves three or four days past their peak, the sound of leaves in the breeze, the construction crane by her place (they were digging up the road),

43

the crane swaying above a fork in the road, a left turn after the fast-food depots, and then into her parking spot in front of the condo. The porch by the front door with the Halloween pumpkins: a cat's face complete with whiskers, a clown, a jack-o'-lantern. My sister closed the front door of her house behind her. Bolted it. Her daughter reminded her to light the pumpkins. Just inside the front door, Pointdexter, on the top step, waiting.

Her keys on the kitchen table. Her coat in the closet. She sent the kids upstairs to get into their pajamas. She called up to her boyfriend, who was in bed reading a textbook, *What are you doing in bed, you total slug!* and then, after checking the messages on the answering machine, looking at the mail, she trudged up to my niece's room to kiss her good night. Endearments passed between them. My sister loved her kids, above all, and in spite of all the work and the hardships, in spite of my niece's reputation as a firecracker, in spite of my nephew's sometimes diabolical smarts. She loved them. There were endearments, therefore, lengthy and repetitive, as there would have been with my nephew, too. And my sister kissed her daughter multiply, because my niece is a little impish redhead, and it's hard *not* to kiss her. *Look, it's late, so I can't read to you tonight, okay?* My niece protested temporarily, and then my sister arranged the stuffed animals around her daughter (for the sake of arranging), and plumped a feather pillow, and switched off the bedside lamp on the bedside table, and she made sure the night light underneath the table (a plug-in shaped like a ghost) was illumined, and then on the way out of the door she stopped for a second. And looked back. The tableau of domesticity was what she last contemplated. Or maybe she was composing endearments for my nephew. Or maybe she wasn't looking back at my niece at all. Maybe she was lost in this next tempest.

Out of nowhere. All of a sudden. All at once. In an instant. Without warning. In no time. Helter-skelter. *In the twinkling of an eye.* Figurative language isn't up to the task. My sister's legs gave out, and she fell over toward my niece's desk, by the door, dislodging a pile of toys and dolls (a Barbie in evening wear, a poseable Tinkerbell doll), colliding with the desk, sweeping its contents off with her, toppling onto the floor, falling heavily, her head by the door. My niece, startled, rose up from under covers.

44

More photos: my sister, my brother and I, *back in our single digits,* dressed in matching, or nearly matching outfits (there was a naval flavor to our look), playing with my aunt's basset hound—my sister grinning mischievously; or: my sister, my father, my brother and I, in my dad's Karmann-Ghia, just before she totaled it on the straightaway on Fishers Island (she skidded, she said, *on antifreeze or something slippery*); or: my sister, with her newborn daughter in her lap, sitting on the floor of her living room—mother and daughter with the same bemused impatience.

My sister started to seize.
The report of her fall was, of course, loud enough to stir her boyfriend from the next room. He was out of bed fast. (Despite physical pain associated with his recent surgery.) I imagine there was a second in which other possibilities occurred to him—hoax, argument, accident, anything—but quickly the worst of these seemed most likely. You know these things somewhere. You know immediately the content of all middle-of-the-night telephone calls. He was out of bed. And my niece called out to her brother, to my nephew, next door. She called my nephew's name, plaintively, like it was a question.

My sister's hands balled up. Her heels drumming on the carpeting. Her muscles all like nautical lines, pulling tight against cleats. Her jaw clenched. Her heart rattling desperately. Fibrillating. If it was a conventional seizure, she was unconscious for this part—maybe even unconscious throughout—because of reduced blood flow to the brain, because of the fibrillation, because of her heart condition; which is to say that my sister's *mitral valve prolapse*—technical feature of her *broken heart*—was here engendering an arrhythmia, and now, if not already, she began to hemorrhage internally. Her son stood in the doorway, in his pajamas, shifting from one foot to the other (there was a draft in the hall). Her daughter knelt at the foot of the bed, staring, and my sister's boyfriend watched, as my poor sister shook, and he held her head, and then changed his mind and bolted for the phone.

After the seizure, she went slack. (Meredith's heart stopped. And her breathing. She was still.) For a second, she was alone in the room, with her children, silent. After he dialed 911, Jimmy appeared again, to try to restart her breathing. Here's how: he pressed his lips against hers. He didn't think to say, *Come on, breathe dammit,* or to make similar imprecations, although he did manage to shout at the kids, *Get the*

45

hell out of here, please! Go downstairs! (It was advice they followed only for a minute.) At last, my sister took a breath. Took a deep breath, a sigh, and there were two more of these. Deep resigned sighs. Five or ten seconds between each. For a few moments more, instants, she looked at Jimmy, as he pounded on her chest with his fists, thoughtless about anything but results, stopping occasionally to press his ear between her breasts. Her eyes were sad and frightened, even in the company of the people she most loved. So it seemed. More likely she was unconscious. The kids sat cross-legged on the floor in the hall, by the top of the stairs, watching. Lots of stuff was left to be accomplished in these last seconds, even if it wasn't anything unusual, people and relationships and small kindnesses, the best way to fry pumpkin seeds, what to pack for Thanksgiving, whether to make turnips or not, snapshots to be culled and arranged, photos to be taken—these possibilities spun out of my sister's grasp, torrential futures, my beloved sister, solitary with pictures taken and untaken, gone.

EMS technicians arrived and carried her body down to the living room where they tried to start her pulse with expensive engines and devices. Her body jumped while they shocked her—she was a revenant in some corridor of simultaneities—but her heart wouldn't start. Then they put her body on the stretcher. To carry her away. Now the moment arrives when they bear her out the front door of her house and she leaves it to us, leaves to us the house and her things and her friends and her memories and the involuntary assemblage of these into language. Grief. The sound of the ambulance. The road is mostly clear on the way to the hospital; my sister's route is clear.

I should fictionalize it more, I should conceal myself. I should consider the responsibilities of characterization, I should conflate her two children into one, or reverse their genders, or otherwise alter them, I should make her boyfriend a husband, I should explicate all the tributaries of my extended family (its remarriages, its internecine politics), I should novelize the whole thing, I should make it multigenerational, I should work in my forefathers (stonemasons and newspapermen), I should let artifice create an elegant surface, I should make the events orderly, I should wait and write about it later, I should wait until I'm not angry, I shouldn't clutter a narrative with fragments, with mere recollections of good times, or with regrets, I should make Meredith's death shapely and persuasive, not blunt and

46

disjunctive, I shouldn't have to think the unthinkable, I shouldn't have to suffer, I should address her here directly (these are the ways I miss you), I should write only of affection, I should make our travels in this earthly landscape safe and secure, I should have a better ending, I shouldn't say her life was short and often sad, I shouldn't say she had her demons, as I do too.

Nominated by Conjunctions *and Sigrid Nunez*

ELEGY ENDING IN THE SOUND OF A SKIPPING ROPE

by LARRY LEVIS

from QUARTERLY WEST

I.

All I have left of that country is this torn scrap
Of engraved lunacy, worth less now

Than it was then, for then it was worth nothing,
Or nothing more than

The dust a wren bathes in,

The fountain dry in the park off the Zelini Venac,
The needles of pines dry above it,

The green shutters of the fruitsellers' stands closed
For the afternoon so that in the quiet it seemed

The wren was the only thing moving in the whole city
As it beat its wings against the stone

To rid itself of lice as the dust rose around it.

The sound of its wings, I remember, was like the sound
Of cards being shuffled, as repetitive

And as pointless.

The characters met on faint blue paper.
They were thin as paper then.

They must be starving now.

*

I don't feel like explaining it,
And now I have to.

To illustrate its money, the State put lovers on the money,

Peasants or factory workers staring off at something
You couldn't see, something beyond them,

Something that wasn't Titograd.
They kept looking at it with their faces

Averted, as if they were watching it take place.

In the casinos, these two lovebirds would lie there
Absorbed in it, staring beyond the green felt

Counters of roulette & baccarat tables, beyond the action,
Beyond the men & women in formal attire.

*

Then someone told me what the money meant,
What they kept looking at:

They were watching the state wither away.

When I tried to imagine it, all I could see
Was a past

Where the ancient goat paths began reappearing,
Crisscrossing a straighter footpath,

Nothing else there except three pedestals lost in moss,

And a man washing a cart horse with soap & tepid
Water, &, at that moment, placing

A plaster of sticky leaves over the sores on the horse's

Withers, the long muscle in the mare's neck rippling
As he does so, as she goes on grazing without the slightest

Interruption, standing there in the shade of an oak
At the exact spot where the Palace of Justice

Finally turned into the mist it had always resembled.
In the moment before it vanished

Flies still buzzed in lopsided circles in the courtroom

And a witness accidentally inhaled one while testifying,
And then *apologized* to the court, apologized

For inhaling the fly, but no one knew what to say,
The room grew suddenly quiet, & then everything disappeared,

And a crowd strolled out of the matinee into a village
That was waiting for them, strolled casually

Out of history,

And into something else: forgetful, inexact,

A thirst, an arousal, a pairing off with whomever they desired,

Strangers even, trysting against the walls,

Or in a field of dandelions, on wagonbeds, the moment
Scripted in the involuntary,

Lovely convulsion of thighs lathered as a horse's back,
Because, as Marx said,

Sex should be no more important than a glass of water.

*

I can't imagine it back.

I can't get the miles of dust rubbed away from it,
Or the layers of sheetrock.

The fruitseller's stand on Lomina Street with its closed
Green shutters was what

Reminded me of Big Sur in 1967,

Reminded me of the beach at Lucia with the vacant
Concession stand, the two unemployables

Entwined like salt in a wave inside it, asleep,
Naked in each other's arms.

I can't imagine it enough.

I can't imagine how to get back to it, with something
In your eye, something always in your eye,

And everything becoming a scrap of paper:

The sprawl of the surf there & the cries of the lovers
Just pin-ups or illustrations behind the counter now:

"Gimme a Coke. Gimme a hotdog too, then," someone
Says to him, tattoos from the Navy over

His forearms, not liking what he does, not
Imagining doing anything now

Except this. Just this.

What withered away?

I watch the guy working fast & suddenly it's *me* who's

Wrapping the hotdogs in waxed paper, *me* who
Half turns, grabs the lids & straws for the Cokes,

Adds it up without pausing & hands them the change.

I can't imagine it enough, & even if I could, one day

That, too, would be the wave's sprawl on the empty rocks,
The hunger in the cries of the gulls.

He pulls the shutters down & locks it up.

"Gimme This & Gimme That. You O.K., Mr. Sea?"
He says to the sky, to the gulls,

To the slur of water receding
On the rocks, to the empty sprawl of the wave

Showing its hand at last before it folds.

II.

The lovers must have stepped out of their money
A few days after the State stepped out

Of its thousand offices.

At night you could look up, & all the black glass
Of the windows would glint back at you

Once, as if in recognition.

The lovers must have stepped out because I *saw* them

Sitting at one of the tables outside the Moskva & shouting

At each other, shouting so loudly

They did not notice their friends beginning
To gather around them.

I gazed past them at the crowds on Terazije passing by
Amid the smells of exhaust

And grilled meat & the odor the sticky bark of the trees
Gave off in the summer afternoon,

The leaves still exhausted & not turning or
Falling or doing anything yet

Above it all. I liked them. I liked the way the leaves
Had a right to be there & say nothing about it

Hanging there, motionless, without expression,
Without faces, not looking at all

Like passing generations but exactly as leaves look

When they're still, looking as if
They are refusing to enlist, looking as they always did,

If I glanced up from the book I was reading,
And rubbed my eyes,

And tried to trace her shape I had thought
I'd memorized,

But hadn't.

Her shape like the sun on the roads.

*

Too bad, with all the evacuations,
All the troop movements & closed offices,

Each black window shining like a contradiction,

"You'd think the parliament would . . .
You would think out of common *decency*, that. . . ."

But the state did not wither away,
It looked just the same, with the rain

Falling between the treeless, bleached yellow
Of cheap housing projects, the rain

Showing them the way home, showing them the Future:

When they get there they find her uncle living
With them, he's eating dinner

When they arrive, he's sucking on a fish bone
When they walk in.

In a few weeks Failure & Limitation
Shows its hand in the cold bud

Of her body refusing to open itself,
Refusing to wake up in the morning,

And the uncle by the end of the summer walking naked
Through the apartment, pausing one day

Beside her, leaning over her a little, not to
Seduce her but to show her a few things,

To introduce her to

The real head of state grinning through its veil

Of skin as if there was

This joke, something just between

The two of them.

And later the uncle just grins at her,

Grins and says nothing.

*

Love's an immigrant, it shows itself in its work,
It works for almost nothing.

When the State withers away it resembles
The poor sections of Wichita or Denver.

They held hands the first day & walked under the trees,
And so they were warned about the trees,

About straying into the parks.

A fuzzy haze of green in someone's yard comes back,
But then it forgets it's there.

The streets are forgetting they are streets
And they cross other streets

And at the intersections those streets
Begin to forget.

Most of the stores are boarded up, most of what
Is left is braced with 2x4's in X'x

Over the doors like spells with no power in them,
The sun like neglect bathing the walls,

Bathing the beams you can see right through to,

It's always the day after the day after here,
And every rebellion's a riot,

The riot goes on though no one's there, the streets
Looking burned still, looking as inexplicable

To them as it did the first day
They saw it,

The *days* are inexplicable,
Their unvarying routine where children not yet

In school peer through the chain link
Of a storm fence above the boulevard & the traffic

To watch for the cops,

Where their older brothers with their girlfriends
Sprawl on a car seat ripped out

Of a van & placed here to overlook the city, the river,
Its history an insult in which

They were property.

When it was over, history became a withered arm,
And everyone entered history & no one could find them.

The children keep staring through the chain links

Of the storm fence. The older ones on the car seat
Get high from a glass pipe & watch

The planes on the runway taxi & take off,
They get high again & watch the planes

Glide in & land, & do one last hit before
They stand up & one of them pisses into a small ravine

Of trash. The five year old girl keeps peering
Through the storm fence without letting

Her attention stray

Because the price of freedom is eternal vigilance,
Her brother tells her, laughing,

And because the task assigned to her is sacred.
I can't imagine her enough.

I remember standing in broken glass at the foot
Of a stairway, the woman beside me

Frightened & crying, & the way the glass felt
Like a river freezing under my feet.

I remember how expensive it all seemed,

And after we had split up, in the years that followed,
I would feel my body turn

Slowly away from others so that it could live alone,
So that each afternoon it could

Become wholly a body. It swept the floors of the house
Each day until it was a routine,

Until it became the finite, thoughtless beauty
Of habit.

Whenever the body swept, it could forget.

And the habit was neither pleasure nor work but an act
That kept the stars above it

In the night, kept the pattern of the stars
From rattling out of their frames,

Whether you could see them above you or not,
Whether you looked up & noticed them or not,

The body swept the floors & kept the light above it.

This is why

The girl keeps squinting through the storm fence,
This is why the task assigned to her is sacred,

Why her love for her brother
Is unconditional,

And though she suspects that her brother
Will one day turn into mist behind her

A space on the car seat, that he will
Disappear like the others have,

It hasn't happened yet.

I swept the floors to let the worlds blur
Into one another.

But the lovers, the emigrants?
I never see them anymore.

I don't know where they went.

III.

I remember the idiot in the park near Zeleni Venac,
Standing there without a shirt on,

With his fly undone,

The way he'd hold his penis in one hand, & simply howl
And keep howling to anyone passing by

On Lomina street, because, as Ratko explained to me,
He believed that he held one end of a leash

In his hand, & that the other end was held by his Master,
And now that it had been snapped in two

He would never find him, this Master he had waited for,
This owner whose whistle he listened for

In the faint blue stillness of the summer daybreak.

In the mornings he would seem calm & play cards
Without understanding them with the others

Who slept in the park & tolerated him, but by
Late afternoon, he would begin

To stammer & beg beside the dry fountain, the pine needles
So dry by now they seemed

About to ignite above him, & then, at the certain moment,
He would seem to realize

What had happened, he would become completely still
At that moment, & then. . . .

Then the howling would start up again.
It was not the howling of an idea.

It was the flesh being flayed.

*

My friend Ratko used to drink brandy constantly

In little sips throughout the day & could lie
So beautifully about anything

That the government awarded him, each year, a grant

To write stories, but of course he never wrote them
Except on the air as he walked with friends

Through the city.

Continuing his almost endless commentary,
Asking if the idiot did not admit, without knowing it,

The great truth

About us, that a broken string or snipped-off thread
Is all we remember, & that even this is

Less real than the pulpy flesh he held between his fingers.

History has a withered arm.

And the love of these two adhering to paper, delusional,
Vestigial, the daydream of Capitalism,

The last transaction of the State by which it vanishes,

The flies caking the face of the horse standing there
In its innocence again,

I can't imagine them enough to bring them back.
After a while, when any subject is forbidden,

All thought is deviationist.

And the young schoolteacher in Rijeka is . . . *where* by now?
And the young Muslim poet from Sarajevo is . . . *where* by now?

And the harmless, lazy bellman at the Atina Palace is . . .
Where by now?

And the pipe smoking translator with his office overlooking
Princip Street & the river,

Who was last heard on the phone shouting to someone
As the beams & windowglass let go of themselves

In the laughter that shatters all things is . . . *where* by now?

*

Those nights when I couldn't sleep in Belgrade,
When I could no longer read,

When there was no point in going out because everything
Was closed, I'd glance at the two of them

On their worthless currency, as if I might catch them
Doing something else, & once,

I turned from their portrait to the empty street
Beneath the window, the thick trees like a stillness

Itself in the night,
And . . . I *saw* them there. This time they were

Fucking in the rain, their clothes strewn beneath them

On the street like flags

After a war, after some final defeat—fucking each other
While standing up, standing still in the rain & the rain falling

In sheets as if there were no tomorrow left
In it, as if their mouths, each wide open & pressed against

The other's mouth, stilling the other's, & reminding me
Of leaves plastered to the back of a horse

Trotting past after a storm, leaves plastered to the side
Of a house by the wind, to what is left of some face . . .

Had taken the breath out of everything. I thought of
The horse passing easily

Under the exhausted looking mulberry trees, under the leaves
And the haunted scripture—

Some of its characters shaped like blossoms, others
Like a family of crows taking flight, others like farm tools,

Some of them moving in circles like swirls in a current—

All of it written in the cracked, weathered Cyrillic of some

Indecipherable defeat, though once its shapes had been

Perfect for showing one things, clear as a girl's face,

The girl who skipped rope in her communion dress,
        Dry & white as a petal—
    Jeden, Cesto?, Nema, Zar ne?
                    Chaste and thoughtless as the thing she chanted

And then lost interest in, until I could hear only the endless,
Annoying, unvarying flick of the rope each time

It touched the street.

Nominated by Quarterly West, *Jane Cooper and David Wojahn*

THE BEAUTY TREATMENT

fiction by STACEY RICHTER

from MISSISSIPPI REVIEW

SHE SMILED WHEN SHE saw me coming, the Bitch, she smiled and stuck her fingers in her mouth like she was plucking gum out of her dental work. Then, with a little pout, like a kiss, I saw a line of silver slide towards my face. I swear to God, I thought she'd pried off her braces. I thought she'd worked one of those bands free and was holding it up to show me how proud she was to have broken loose of what we referred to, in our charming teenage banter, as oral bondage. The next thing I knew, there's blood all over my J. Crew linen fitted blouse, in edelweiss—a very delicate, almost ecru shade of white, ruined now. There's blood all over the tops of my tits where they pushed out my J. Crew edelweiss linen shirt and a loose feeling around my mouth when I screamed. My first thought was fuck, how embarrassing, then I ran into the girls' room and saw it: a red gash parted my cheek from my left temple to the corner of my lip. A steady stream of blood dripped off my jawline into the sink. One minute later, Cyndy Dashnaw found the razor blade on the concrete floor of the breezeway, right where the Bitch had dropped it.

Elizabeth Beecher and Kirsty Moseley run into the bathroom and go Oh my God, then drag me screaming hysterically, all three of us screaming hysterically, to Ms. B. Meanwhile, the Bitch slides into her Mercedes 450SL, lime green if you can believe that—the A1 primo daddylac of all time—and drives off smoking Kools. I'm in the nurse's office screaming with Ms. B calmly applying pressure and ordering Mr. Pierce, the principal, to get in gear and haul my ass to the emergency room. This is what you get from watching too much TV,

I'm thinking, and believing your workaholic father when he tells you during one of his rare appearances that you're the Princess of the Universe to which none can compare. And then watching teenage girls from Detroit on *Montel,* for God's sake—the inner city—froth and brag about hiding razors under their tongues and cutting up some ho because she glanced sideways at the boyfriend: I mean, help me. This is the twentieth century. My father's a doctor. The Bitch's father is a developer who's covered half of Scottsdale with lifestyle condos. We consume the most expensive drugs, cosmetics and coffee known to man. Tell me: what was she thinking?

I went to the emergency room where the nurse gave me a shot to stop the screaming and eventually my mother came down and the nurse had to give her a pill to stop her from screaming, too. Once Mother had sufficiently calmed, she paged Dr. Wohl, who'd done her tits, and had him run down and stitch me up with some special Indonesian silk that would make me look, he promised, like a slightly rakish movie star. Afterwards, during the healing process, was when my mother really started broadcasting the wonders of Smith College and Mount Holyoke or, if worse came to worst, Mills. Women's colleges were so liberating, she said, waving her tennis elbow around to signify freedom. It was such a blessing, she said, to study without all that nasty competition and distraction from boys. That's when I knew I was in for it. If my mother, who wanted nothing more than for me to marry a Jewish doctor like she had—to duplicate her glorious life and marry a Jewish doctor and live bored and frustrated in the suburbs and flirt with the other bald, wrinkled, fat, ugly doctors at the tennis club on Wednesday afternoons—if *this* mother was trying to usher me away from the prying eyes of young, male, pre-med students, I knew it was all over for me. I knew my looks were shot.

And another thing—as if I would actually relish the thought of living with a bunch of chicks in hormonal flux after one prime example, the Bitch, my best friend, sliced a gill into my cheek for no apparent reason. Why did she do it? they kept asking. What happened between you two? Ask her yourself, I replied. Ask the Bitch. But I knew she would never tell. How could she? It was bad enough that they took her down to the police station and put her in a cell without air conditioning until her daddy showed up with *two* lawyers and escorted her out of there like she was Queen of the May Parade. It was bad enough that she got kicked out of Phoenix Country Day and had to go to Judson—

Judson, where bad kids from California with parents who didn't want them were sent to board. At Judson, even the high school students had to wear uniforms.

Uniforms, ha ha, it served her right. After The Accident, as my mother called it, or The Beauty Treatment, as my father referred to it, I was treated like that guy my verbal teacher at Princeton Review told us about, the prodigal son, but a female version. Did I shop? I shopped 'til I dropped, amen, hallelujah. I had all the latest stuff from the stores *and* the catalogs. I had six pairs of Doc Martens, a set of sterling flatware (for my dowry), and a ravishing Chanel suit. We flew to New York to get the suit. All this accompanied by the message—through word and gesture of Arthur and Lilly, doting parents—that no matter what I had, I could not have enough. Not only did I deserve this, I deserved all this and more. I had suffered, and every available style of Swatch would bring relief.

The Bitch, meanwhile, was slogging through her days in a tartan plaid skirt and kneesocks. She was locked in a world without jewelry, handbags, or, indeed, accessories. White shirt, button-down collar—no patterns, no decorations, no excuses. They couldn't even wear a demure white-on-white check. We got the lowdown from the Judson Cactus Wrens at soccer matches—big, bitter girls who charged the ball with clenched teeth and didn't even talk among themselves at halftime. They told us about the uniform requirements with a weird, stiff pride, like they were army recruits or something. Talk about future sadistic Phys Ed instructors, those Wrens were hard. Every time we had a game against them, half the Country Day girls got convenience periods and skipped out on a nurse's pass.

Even when I really did have my period, I never got a pass. I wasn't afraid of anything anymore, as long as the Bitch wasn't on the Judson soccer team, which she wasn't. I mean, what could happen to me that was worse than what I had already gone through? Getting kicked in the shin? A torn earlobe? Being snubbed by Bobby England? Give me a break. I'd seen pain and passed through it. I was a superhero. I was a goddamn Jewish Joan of Arc riding a Volkswagen convertible in a lemon-yellow Chanel suit. After a few months, so many people had asked me what was wrong with my face that it stopped bothering me and I began to have a little fun with it. I even managed to work in some of my vocabulary words.

"I was on the back of Johnny Depp's motorcycle. He tried to feel me up, like the callow youth he is, and we wiped out."

And, "I was wearing Lee Press-On Nails and had the most vehement itch."

Or my personal favorite, "My father did it by accident, whilst beating me zealously," which got horrified looks, especially from medical personnel.

All in all, things weren't so bad for me. Everyone at school was being really nice, and I was getting extra time to make up my homework. This while the Bitch had to either go straight home from school or go directly to the shrink. Even her stupid, doting mother thought she was crazy for a day or two; I know because her mom and my mom are friends, though I must say the relationship is, oh, a bit *strained*. The Bitch must have put them off with a fake story because if she ever told the truth they'd put her in the nuthouse with her schizophrenic brother where she probably belongs. She must have told them that I had stolen her boyfriend (not) or shafted her on a dope deal (double not). She must have told them something that would have sounded plausible on *Oprah* or *Montel*, something gritty and real—the kind of thing they wanted. When the truth is the Bitch started hating me one day out of the clear blue, after we'd been friends since we were ten years old, because I wanted to go into a store and buy the sheet music for "Brokenhearted," a song made famous by the singer Brandy.

The Bitch hated Brandy. The Bitch was going through what Mr. Nesbit, our school counselor, referred to as a *phase*. The Bitch, natural-born white girl, with a special pair of Mormon panties in her dresser and her own frequent-flyer miles on her own credit card, wanted to be a homegirl. She had her dishwater hair done up in scrawny braids and got paste-on acrylic nails with a charm on the ring finger that said "Nubian." She wore deep-brown lipstick from the Soul Collection at Walgreen's. When her braids got frizzy, which didn't take long, she slicked them back with Afro Sheen.

I, on the other hand, did not wish to be a homegirl. I figured it was my lot to try to survive as a rich, white Jewish girl who could not do the splits and therefore would never be a cheerleader, and it would be fruitless to reach for anything else. I had nothing against black people, though it's true I didn't know any. Was it my fault there weren't any black families clamoring to send their children to Phoenix Country Day? Was it my fault my parents trundled me off to a snooty private school? Hell no! I was a pawn, a child, and the worst sin I was guilty of, according to those tablets Moses obtained, was taking off my bra

66

for Bobby England and ridiculing my loving parents whenever I got a chance. Thus, I had no longings to be a homegirl, and it pissed the Bitch off. She said I was spoiled (and I say: it takes one to know one). She said we should aim to be tough. She said black chicks were the coolest and saw the world for what it really was—a jungle, a merciless, dog-eat-dog world.

Which struck me as strange, especially considering the Bitch had the sweetest dog in the world named, perhaps ironically, Blackie. Blackie was getting pretty old but had some spunk in her still. Right up to the day of the razor incident, the Bitch and I would take her out to the golf course in the evenings and let her bite streams of water shooting from the sprinklers. That dog was great. We both loved Blackie and urged her to go get the sprinklers, to really kill 'em; then she would lie down panting in the wet grass and act like she was never going to get up. The Bitch and I frequently discussed what we would do if tragedy struck and the dog died. Blackie was fourteen and had been the Bitch's companion almost her entire life. The void, the terrible void that would be left behind. We discussed filling it with taxidermy. She would have her stuffed, the Bitch said, in the sprinkler-biting posture, because that was when Blackie was the fucking happiest, and we were the happiest sharing in her joy. She would put it on her credit card.

The loss of Blackie loomed all the more ominous, I suppose, since the Bitch's adoring father basically never came home from work and the Bitch's mother was preoccupied trying to get the schizophrenic brother either into or out of commitment. The brother was smoking a lot of pot and talking to little guys from Canada or Planet Centaur, it just depended. On occasion he'd be struck by the notion that the Bitch was The Bride of Pure Evil, and one day he stuck a fork in her thigh. In return, she bit him, then took off her shirt and showed him her tits, which mortified him so badly he ran around the house for a while, then curled up in the corner. After that, if he was slipping, she'd wear a nursing bra at home so she could flash him if he got out of line.

All the while Blackie padded around after the Bitch, hoping for attention. She was a nuzzler, and even if the Bitch was busy doing something else, she would insinuate her nose underneath one of her hands and just freeze there, pretending to be petted. It was touching. At night she would fall into a twitchy sleep beside the Bitch's bed, and every now and then she would struggle to her feet and go stick her

67

nose under the Bitch's arm or foot for a minute and hold it there. It was like she had to touch the Bitch every so often to make sure she was still okay. That dog was great. In fact, Blackie was probably the one creature she could count on, aside from me, and I could see why her decrepitude made the Bitch nervous.

So, around the time Blackie was fading and her brother was going insane, the Bitch started acting even more homegirl and tough and was irked to high hell that I wouldn't get with the program. She was listening to all this gangsta rap in her Mercedes and never taking off her wraparound shades until the teacher made a specific and pointed request. I mean, even our favorite teacher, Mrs. DeMarzo, who talked like Katherine Hepburn, had to tell her to take them off. She had all these garments from the mall in extra-large sizes which she referred to as "dope." Of course, do I have to mention the Bitch is not one iota interested in actually hanging with the homegirls? I mean, she's not driving down to the South Side and having her Alpine stereo gouged from her dashboard while she rounds up some sistahs to talk jive with, or whatever. She is hanging with me and the other fair students of Phoenix Country Day School as always, but she's acting like she's too cool for us, like she's doing us a favor.

Was she annoying? God yes, but I never considered dumping her. The thing was that with me, in private, she wasn't so bad. I mean, the Bitch lived right down the street and we'd been best friends since fourth grade, when being best friends really meant something. I'd seen only one miracle in my sixteen dull years of life and the Bitch had been its agent. Actually, the miracle wasn't much, but it was enough to make me believe that there was some kind of power floating around in the universe and that the Bitch had a little influence with it. I figured if I stuck close to her, my life would periodically be visited by blessings and magic, like in fairy tales. What happened was this: we're eleven years old, sitting in my room on top of my rainbow Marimekko print comforter, beneath the Olympische Spiele München posters, talking animatedly and intimately about whatever. Suddenly, the Bitch gasps and points to the candy-colored Venetian glass chandelier my mother brought back on the trip to Europe she took without my father. A beat of time passed. And then the chandelier winked out.

Actually, the power had gone out in the whole neighborhood. If there'd been a sound or a pulse in the light, I hadn't noticed it, and when I asked the Bitch why she'd pointed at the chandelier, she said,

"Because I knew something was going to happen." Oh my God, was I a bored little girl. Did I ever want to hitch my star to someone who knew something was going to happen.

So, I overlooked her flaws, her erratic behavior, her insistence I smoke Kools and endure the strains of gangsta rappers calling me a bee-atch because at least around her, things were interesting. I tried to make light of her attitude, figuring it would pass, but I wasn't sacrificing anything of myself, understand? I mean, I wanted that Brandy sheet music. I didn't care that I couldn't play the piano or any other musical instrument. That wasn't the point. I wanted "Brokenhearted" because it had this great picture of Brandy, a beautiful girl, on the cover and I thought it was cool. Me, *I* thought it was cool. Well, the Bitch was just not having any of this. For one thing, Brandy's black, which apparently is her territory, and she's the big fucking expert. For another thing, she says Brandy is "an ugly little crossover wimp" and not a real homegirl and I'm an asshole if I like her. I mean, like: so what? So, I like Brandy. So shoot me. So pitch a fit, which she did, peeling out in her 450SL and leaving me in the parking lot of a C-mall. So slice my face with a fucking razor blade.

Which she did the next time I saw her and I haven't seen her since, except for that one time at her shrink's office. This was after Mother had gotten all high and mighty because I'd only scored 590 on the quantitative part of the SAT, since math was right after lunch and frequently I attended stoned. Of course, Lilly couldn't give a shit if I did math or not; she hires an accountant to balance her checkbook, but since my youthful beauty was trampled, she'd reasoned that I should fall back on my next best asset—the mind. Oh those smart girls! Do men ever love those clever girls! She said it over and over, with a fake, bright smile, when she thought I wasn't paying close attention.

By then I wasn't half as worried about my sullied good looks as she was. Dr. Wohl said we could smooth out the lumps with dermabrasion during summer vacation, plus he wasn't entirely wrong about the rakish charm. I'd begun wearing black Anna Sui numbers and hanging out at The Coffee Plantation in Biltmore Fashion Square, where the neo-beatnik kids considered me sort of a god. I rarely spoke and they were under the impression I had a boyfriend in France. I'd also realized the scar sort of went with the curves of my face, it cupped my cheekbone—I mean, if you're going to have a major facial scar, this was the one to have. One girl with piercings all over her nose came up to me and asked where I had it done.

It wasn't like I looked normal, but I was learning to adjust. I was feeling okay about myself—I rented *The Big Heat,* where the heroine gets coffee flung in her face, and I was beginning to feel like being slightly maimed was kind of romantic. I mean, I got noticed, and I looked just fine from the right side. Still, Lilly was putting all bets on the intellect and had dragged Arthur into her camp. Together they forced me to take a Princeton Review class to get my test scores up. I hated it all except vocabulary. Perfidy: betrayal, the deliberate breaking of trust. Refractory: resisting treatment, unmanageable. My verbal was 780. Seven-eighty—that's almost perfect! I couldn't believe they were making me. It had been years since they'd forced me to do anything. It was cutting into my spare time, and it wasn't only me who suffered: I knew the neo-beatniks would be lost without their tragic center. Finally I went on strike and refused to eat in the dining room. I just took a plate, retired to my room, locked the door, and put on my headphones. A couple days of this, I thought, and they'll go into serious parenting withdrawal.

The second day Mom caved and weaseled her way in. She said I could quit the class if I'd do something for her. She said she'd talked to the Bitch's mother, and she'd said her therapist had recommended I go to one of the Bitch's sessions. She "wasn't happy," Lilly said; she was "having trouble adjusting." This was like one of those moments when my mother gets all doe-eyed and yearns to save the environment, tears well up, etc., but a second later it's *snap!* time for a manicure. On the other hand, she was dead serious, and I knew this was my chance to get out of that fucking class. Even so, I wouldn't have done it. I wasn't scared of anything then except the Bitch. I thought I saw her a million times, in the mall or the Cineplex; I saw her big, smiling head gliding through the crowd, and then a swish of silver. At the last minute it was never her—the big head always morphed into some alternate head—but whether I created it or not, I felt like I was being stalked. Then I had these dreams where the Bitch and I were just hanging out, dancing to Chaka Khan, just hanging out like before when everything was normal—and those really gave me the creeps. I did not want to see her. No Bitch for me.

70

But then I changed my mind. Young and foolish I am. Also, I loved the idea of going to see the Bitch's shrink. I pictured a distinguished man, with gray at his temples, gasping at the sight of my scar when I walked in the room. Then, he would look at me with infinite compassion. I would take a seat on the leather lounger. My outfit is DKNY. My shoes are Kenneth Cole. The Bitch would be sitting in a straight-backed chair, her hair in cornrows. The Doctor would shake his head reproachfully.

"I never dreamed the wound was so dramatic," he says.

The Bitch would blush. I notice her body racked by waves of contrition. In her arms is an album by Brandy. A CD would be more practical, but I like the way an album fills up her arms.

"This is for you," she'd say. "I've learned that it's okay for us to like different things. I celebrate your appreciation of Brandy."

I thank her. The Doctor looks on approvingly. I can tell by his glance he thinks I'm a brave and noble girl. A few minutes later I leave. The Bitch is weeping softly. I feel a light, crisp sense of forgiveness. The Doctor has offered me free therapy, if I should ever want to share my burdens.

Well, I'm here to tell you, buddy, it wasn't like that at all. First, there's no lounger, and the doctor is a streaked blond chick about my mother's age. I arrive late and she shows me to the office where the Bitch is already sitting on a swivel chair. She barely looks up when I enter the room. My dress is DKNY. The Bitch is dressed like white trash in jeans and a T-shirt of normal proportions. She looks like hell. I mean, *I* look better than she does. I was always prettier than her, but she used to seem intriguing. Before, if she was in a room, you felt her presence immediately. The girl knew how to occupy space. Something came out of her—a lot of pesky teen rage, but at times, something nicer. She had that glow, at least to me; she had a sense of excitement and wonder. But in the office, it's missing. She seems dull, not bright, and the truth is, right away I feel sorry for the Bitch.

The Shrink looks like she came straight out of a Smith alumni magazine—Ann Taylor suit, minimal makeup, low-heeled leather shoes. The picture of emotional efficiency. Her office, too, is a symphony in earth tones. She checks me and the Bitch out, then says something like, "Katie's been grappling with the conflict that occurred between the two of you, and now she needs to know how you feel about it."

71

She does not blink twice at my scar. She does not look at me with infinite compassion. I realize whose turf I'm on. She's an employee, and the Bitch's father writes the paychecks.

"I feel okay," I say. I keep trying not to look at the Bitch, but she's unavoidable. After hallucinating her face a million times, it's unnerving how unfamiliar she seems. She's gained weight, but it seems like she's not really there. There's something inert and lumpen about her. No rage, no nail charms. Nothing extreme. She's just examining her shoes—for God's sake—clogs.

"Just okay? Because Katie and I have been discussing the impact of the cutting, and for her it's really been quite profound."

The Bitch does not say anything. The Bitch is not looking at me. The Bitch is sitting with her head down and her mouth closed like the first day she came to school with her braces. Then I realize something. "She's not even looking at it," I say. "She won't even check out my scar!"

I look at the Shrink like she's some kind of referee. She, apparently, is having none of that, and sits quite calmly glancing at me and the Bitch as though we were a light piece of entertainment intended to gaily pass the time. This goes on for a while. The Bitch looks at her clogs and a brown spot on the carpet. I look at the Bitch for as long as I can, then start reading the spines of the Shrink's books. *Personality Disorders*—ha, that should come in handy. I can hear her breathing, which is odd, because in all the years we hung out together I never noticed her breathing. It's like she's alive in some weird, biological way—the way those pithed frogs were alive in Mr. Graham's class. Alive but damaged.

Finally, the Bitch clears her throat. She raises her head until her eyes hit the scar. She starts to wince, then freezes. I can tell she's trying to control her expression but all the color empties out of her face in a smooth, descending line, like she's been pumped full of pink fluid and someone has pulled the plug.

That was when I knew for sure: I looked like shit, absolutely and for certain. I'd been fooling myself until then, believing I looked dashing and rascally, but in the shock on my best friend's face I saw the truth. I was ruined.

The Bitch started to cry. I started to cry. The Shrink tried to calmly glance at us as if we were a light piece of entertainment, but you could sense the strain. I pulled a Kool out of my bag and lit it. The Shrink finally cracked and shot me a dirty look, but I was beyond caring. I realized, after all I'd been through, that I still smoked Kools, just like the Bitch always had, like she'd encouraged me to, and the thought of that made me cry even harder. Something switched then, and I wasn't crying about my face anymore. I was crying because the Bitch was the Bitch and the friend I'd had since I was a kid, the friend who knew for certain something was going to happen to us, something magical and vivid, was lost forever. She was lost to us both. The wonder had been extinguished.

Eventually I got a hold of myself and squashed the Kool out in a piece of damp Kleenex. The Bitch had slumped over in her swivel chair and I didn't even want to look at her. My thoughts: fuck, shit, etc. It was weird. I began to feel practically like she was my friend again, us having had a simultaneous cry. I did not want that. I wanted her to stay the Bitch.

"Jesus Christ," she says, unprompted by the Shrink.

I notice her braces are off. She's not looking at me. It's too much for her.

"Fuck," she says, to the spot on the carpet, "I'm so sorry."

Okay: I'm a girl who's going to Smith College. I'm going to Smith and then I'm going to law school to become a criminal lawyer who champions the rights of the victimized and oppressed. I'm going to have two cars, a Volvo for transportation and a Jag for thrills. I'll cut a feline figure in my Agnes B. clothes and I'll have a drawerful of jewels. Maybe I'll even get married to some average-looking dork, but I will never be pretty and I will never be loved by the handsome men who roam this earth. My dear mother told me long ago that youth and beauty will get you everything. Well, mine's fucked up and now I'll never have Everything. No magic, no wonder, no fairy tales.

The plan was to walk out of there with a light, crisp sense of forgiveness, but help me. I sat in a sea of beige and looked at the Bitch in her clogs, fat, miserable and afraid, and I knew: if I really forgave her, something vast and finite would open up inside me, some place wide and blue, and I couldn't go into such a place. It would be like some kind of health spa—where you go in naked, without any things. God, would I ever be lost in a place like that.

So I said, "Oh Katie, that's okay babe! No problema! I forgive you!" with a hint of fake innocence in my voice—a little dose of manufactured niceness. She turned white again and the Shrink started urging me to get in touch with my feelings, but you know, I had my finger right on them.

73

Later, when I got home, I went into the bathroom and stared at myself in the mirror for a while. It was the same mirror Katie and I used to stare at in the pitch black while chanting "Bloody Mary, Bloody Mary" over and over until we hallucinated the beheaded head of Mary, Queen of Scots, emerging in reflection, dripping like a porterhouse steak. She fought her way up from the land of the dead to punish us for tempting the dark with the sight of her terrible wound. Mary with her disgusting necklace of blood—she was a perfidious one! I didn't look anything like her. In fact, I had a certain glow about me. I was so radiant I looked almost pretty. From the right side, I actually was pretty.

Nominated by Steven Barthelme

ODE TO MEANING

by ROBERT PINSKY

from THREEPENNY REVIEW

Dire one and desired one,
Savior, sentencer—

In an old allegory you would carry
A chained alphabet of tokens:

Ankh Badge Cross.
Dragon,
Engraved figure guarding a hallowed intaglio,
Jasper kinema of legendary Mind,
Naked omphalos pierced
by quills of rhyme or sense, torah-like: unborn
Vein of will, xenophile
Yearning out of Zero.

Untrusting I court you. Wavering
I seek your face, I read
That Crusoe's knife
Reeked of you, that to defile you
The soldier makes the rabbi spit on the torah.
"I'll drown my book," says Shakespeare.

Drowned walker, revenant.
After my mother fell on her head, she became
More than ever your sworn enemy. She spoke
Sometimes like a poet or critic of forty years later.

Or she spoke of the world as Thersites spoke of the heroes,
"I think they have swallowed one another. I
Would laugh at that miracle."

You also in the laughter, warrior angel:
Your helmet the zodiac, rocket-plumed
Your spear the beggar's finger pointing to the mouth
Your heel planted on the serpent Formulation
Your face a vapor, the wreath of cigarette smoke crowning
Bogart as he winces through it.

You not in the words, not even
Between the words, but a torsion,
A cleavage, a stirring.

You stirring even in the arctic ice,
Even at the dark ocean floor, even
In the cellular flesh of a stone.

Gas. Gossamer. My poker friends
Question your presence
In a poem by me, passing the magazine
One to another.

Not the stone and not the words, you
Like a veil over Arthur's headstone,
The passage from the Proverbs he chose
While he was too ill to teach
And still well enough to read, *I was*
Beside the master craftsman
Delighting him day after day, ever
At play in his presence—you

A soothing veil of distraction playing over
Dying Arthur playing in the hospital,
Thumbing the Bible, fuzzy from medication,
Ever courting your presence.
And you the prognosis,
You in the cough.

Gesturer, when is your spur, your cloud?
You in the airport rituals of greeting and parting.
Indicter, who is your claimant?
Bell at the gate. Spiderweb iron bridge.
Cloak, video, aroma, rue, what is your
Elected silence, where was your seed?

What is Imagination
But your lost child born to give birth to you?

Dire one. Desired one.
Savior, sentencer—

Absence,
Or presence ever at play:
Let those scorn you who never
Starved in your dearth. If I
Dare to disparage
Your harp of shadows I taste
Wormwood and motor oil, I pour
Ashes on my head. You are the wound. You
Be the medicine.

Nominated by The Threepenny Review, *Stuart Dischell and Lloyd Schwartz*

GROUNDED

fiction by CLAIRE DAVIS

from THE GETTYSBURG REVIEW

ONLY AN HOUR AGO Wava Haney had grounded her son, Kyle, forever, but there he was, kicking down the gravel driveway as though he had every right. She knelt on the shop floor, the chair braced against her thigh, one hand supporting the dowel while she cranked on the wood clamp with the other. Her fingers were glossed with glue, and the chair, her best work yet, teetered on the edge of completion. Lifting her fingers from the clamp, she eyed the configuration for balance. She knew what it *should* look like, this Shaker style, ladder-back chair, bird's-eye maple, with a plank seat chiseled and sanded by her own hands, those hands calloused until she'd lost the tactile details of every day—the embossed flowers on her favorite teacups, the hairs blushing her arms. The chair lingered in a suspension of glue and faith eminently perishable. On her haunches, she looked out the door. Two precious days off from waitressing at the cafe. Two days in which she'd planned to finish this chair. Start another. She'd as soon pretend she hadn't seen Kyle, wipe her hands and wait in the shade of a tree for his sorry return, then give him a righteous piece of her mind. She rose to her feet, studied the chair. This was a critical stage; it could all go so badly.

She slapped her hands across the butt of her jeans, thinking too late, as she always did, that she should have used a towel. He was on the turn in the drive, and if she didn't hurry he would be gone. She hiked her arms and tried running, but her ankles wobbled. Should it feel this way at thirty-six? Her upper arms jiggled and she felt absurd. She slowed to a jog.

The driveway was a piece of work—a half-mile of pitching turns, hills and dips that in winter meant night shifts pushing through random drifts behind the plow on her four-wheel drive Custom Ford pickup. You wouldn't think it, to see it now, in the dog days of summer, trees wilted, waiting for the final crisp of autumn. Roadside weeds were varnished with dust. The green grasshoppers of June had turned brown and percolated in the shrubs.

She caught up as he turned onto the highway—two lanes and no shoulders, common to Montana. "Where do you *think* you're going?" she asked.

He slowed. She could see her effect in the set of his chin. She touched his arm and he didn't snatch it from her, and even in her anger she was grateful for that.

"Did you hear me?"

"Yes, ma'am," he said, as he always did when angry, as though he needed that distance of courtesy.

"You're grounded."

"Yes, ma'am."

"Then where are you going?"

"Away from you."

He'd stopped and was watching her with all the astuteness of a fifteen-year-old, already gathering his defenses. She stepped to the high side of the road, trying to appear taller. She was no more used to looking up than he was looking down. All that bone didn't fit him yet. He used it like a borrowed body. She supposed he'd gotten his height from his father, though she preferred to think it was some wild-card gene from her own short side of the family. He was dressed in Levis, T-shirt, and high-top sneakers, a jacket tied around his waist. No water, no food, no spare clothes. "You won't last a day," she said.

"You going to give me the chance to find out?"

"Probably not."

She could see them as others might—a logger, or better yet, a couple on a leisurely drive, startled by the scenery, heads ducked to better see the mountains packed in the frame of car windows. They would welcome the sight of a mother and son on the side of the road. "Isn't that nice," they would say.

"Get home," she said. "We'll forget it happened."

He walked ahead. She stood a moment in disbelief. "You're too young to run away," she called, though the fact was, he was too old. At five, ten, even thirteen, he could have been bullied back up the drive,

79

hauled by the arm into the house and sat on the couch for a dressing down. But at fifteen he was becoming a man, too strong to tackle.

He lengthened his stride, one to every two of hers.

"Eighteen is old enough. When you're eighteen, I'll lock the door after you." She tried not to breathe heavily. She was past showing weakness to anyone. It had been her first lesson as a single mother in rural Montana, where a woman alone didn't so much gather disapproval as disinterest. "This is ridiculous," she said.

He cut into a fallow field, sour with leafy spurge. Knapweed broke flower heads down their jeans and bunched in the cuffs. She chugged behind, convinced he would tire even as she did, that he would grow hot and thirsty and bored with his own dogged rebellion. Wava settled into a rhythm of walking, jogging in short bursts when she got too far behind. He was having an easy time of it while she struggled with weeds, hummocks, and prairie dog holes. Three-foot conical hills topped the wild oats, the industry of ants shivering on the surface. She believed he could be worn down. There was nothing beyond this stumbling valley but the Swan Mountains to the left and the Missions hard on the right. When Kyle hit the bog edging the Clearwater River, his high-tops swilled with water. He looked for a shallow wade or a felled tree to cross. He must have known he'd be stopped by the river, she thought, and beyond that by the mountains, all that implacable rock. An innocent in the pitting of wills, he must have thought she would give up. She felt disillusioned. He simply did not believe in her.

He appeared disinterested, turning away, his neck craning back to study the side of the mountains where a red-tailed hawk circled on the thermals. "Sharp-shinned hawk," she said, giving him an excuse to talk, an argument to cover his embarrassment. She had a keen sense of what it felt to be fifteen and daring and foolish. She was less certain as to how it felt to be thirty-six and a mother whose son was running away. He started back toward the highway, his sneakers squeezing water with each step. Good: easier to keep up on blacktop.

Given other circumstances, taken at her own accustomed pace, she'd have enjoyed this walk. In the fourteen years she had lived in Montana, how much of it had been spent doing just this, striking off across fields, bullying her way through cheatgrass or forests with the pine pitch smell she'd come to love better than her own baking. It was something perverse in her that preferred this above everything— putting herself in a place where everything most precious could be lost. Time. Direction.

She suspected Kyle had been incubating this idea for some time now. In this he was her son, predicating each move, imperfectly planned perhaps, but planned. It went beyond their fight. It was a product, she thought, of the hours he spent sitting on the back stoop studying the commotion of wind in grass, or the flight of birds. It came of example.

When her husband Joe had first brought them to Montana, enacting the whim and transporting her and one-year-old Kyle out of the Midwest and into the West, she was still young and able to be swayed. Joe was a woodworker, neither particularly adept nor inspired, but he tried. "All that lumber," he'd said. "We'll buy a small place with lots of trees." He chucked her under the chin with a finger. "Don't you see it's like free wood then. We're dying here. All the costs—you, the baby, the wood." She wondered how she could have been so witless as to believe that. Five years later he ran off with Katie Hitchet, who'd commissioned a set of bookcases. The only redeeming grace was that he'd left his tools. The bookcases Wava burned. She regretted that, in a way—those beautiful birch planks. But it made a hell of a bonfire.

On the highway, Wava kept her pace and temper at twenty feet behind. To the right, a pileated woodpecker knocked its head against a tree, rapping like a determined visitor. They passed the Riding High Ranch, where the signpost listed over an assemblage of derelict Studebakers. A flock of peacocks roosted on roofs, shat on windshields and dismembered fenders. They screamed in a frenzied chorus, their fanned tails trembling in the sunlight. Wava and Kyle passed a lumberyard and then a small herd of cattle stupefied with the first heat of the day. When she looked at Kyle again, he'd stuck his thumb up for a ride. What next, she wondered.

"Have you ever heard a thing I've told you?" she asked. "Hitchhiking is *stupid*. You don't know what's out there."

He was jogging backwards, joyfully wagging his thumb in the air. Wava's heart thickened as she looked over her shoulder and in the distance saw a car, a glint off the windshield like the proverbial light at the end of a tunnel, like the oncoming train. Kyle was running to leave her behind, and the car was coming on, nearing, then passing and slowing to a stop fifty yards ahead. The passenger door swung open. Kyle loped up to the car, leaned down to see who was driving, then glanced back at her and got in. The door slammed. Wava ran. She ran, wishing for better shoes. She thought to get the license number, but all she could see was sunlight, a frieze on the bumper, two blurs in the

81

front seat. She wanted, more than anything, to see Kyle's face while he was still here, still hers to look at. She was within twenty feet when the gears engaged and the car started pulling away. She could see the driver checking for traffic. "Wait," she yelled. The taillights flickered. "I'm coming," she called. The exhaust fumed, but the car waited on the side of the road.

THE MISSION MOUNTAINS VEERED OFF as they drove down the highway, she in the back, swathed in dog hair—golden retriever, she thought—Kyle up front, his head rigidly forward, and Jessup Taylor driving. Sup he called himself, with liver-spotted hands, and a face of indeterminate age. Sup hummed, his bass voice lush and resonant, out of place in the small car with upholstery tufts seeping out of torn seams and dog hair pooling on the floor. Glancing in the rearview mirror, he smiled. "Where you two going?"

"We're not together," Kyle answered. "As far as you'll take me," he added.

"Seeley Lake," Sup said. "Once a week, need it or not, I go to Seeley Lake for a little excitement. Course, given my age and the nature of the place, it's an exercise in futility, but I try. And you, ma'am?"

"Wherever you take my son."

Sup flicked a look into the rearview mirror, then over at Kyle. "Thought you weren't together."

Kyle flinched. His neck looked delicate from behind, white beneath the short-cropped black hair. She'd never seen anything so vulnerable. "He's running away. From me," she said.

"He's not doing a very good job of it," Sup said, downshifting into a turn, five feet from where the bank lolled down into trees brazed with the noon light—ponderosas, fir, scrub larch, and lanky aspen whose leaves had already gone gold above the red dogwood and bunchgrass.

Sup's head bobbed into each turn, his passengers ignored, as if it were normal to find himself transporting both a runaway and the runned-from in his car, as though there were a world of mothers tethered to runaway sons, and perhaps for him this was true because he was old, had seen enough to believe anything possible, and life with all its attendant quirks was no longer a dilemma. Wava envied him.

"Everyone runs away least once in his life, or contemplates the idea," Sup said. "I thought about it, once, maybe two, three times. But it always seemed a coin better saved." They drove in quiet, the road paralleling the forest and link of lakes—Summit, Alva, Inez, bright glimpses of the foliage—unfolding like a drunken stagger, one mile forward, two back on itself in a series of horseshoe curves. They passed a stand of tamarack and a falling magpie. Wava cranked her window open, and the dog hair drifted and fell.

"Your dog still got any hair?" Wava asked.

"Sorry," Sup said. "He's lost more than I ever owned." He rolled his window down, and the hair wheeled in the air and drafted out. Sup hummed a few notes. "But he's a good dog." He looked over at Kyle. "Stays put where I tell him. Where's it you plan to run to? You got somewhere to go?"

"You can let me out anywhere, sir."

"You trying to get rid of me too? This is not your lucky day, boy." He drove on.

Minnesota, Wava thought. That's where they all go eventually, Minnesota or California.

Kyle leaned forward, his hands fidgeting with the seat belt. "Idaho," he said.

"Idaho?" Sup slapped the steering wheel. "Now *that's* a change for the better." He grinned. "How you going to live?"

"I'll get a job."

"You don't look a day over sixteen—minimum wage and a handful of hours." And from the backseat, Wava could see how Kyle blushed with pleasure to be thought older than he was, even if only a year. "You got money?" Sup asked.

"Yes, sir, seventy-three dollars," Kyle said, as if it were all the money in the world—one year's savings, chopping and stacking wood for the elderly Geneva Norwitch, who lived alone with her dogs and spavined horses down the valley.

"Well, you're an accommodating boy. Seventy-three dollars, sir, he says. Why don't you just hand it over and get it done with—save yourself a knock on the head?" He shook his finger at Kyle. "You got to consider who you're going to meet on the road. But you're thrifty. I'll say that for you, if not real smart."

"And he's an *honors* student," Wava said, intending irony but sounding boastful. And why not? How could she not be proud? What he was, she had made him. Kyle was gazing out the side window.

"No offense, ma'am," Sup said. "We'll be coming into Seeley Lake soon, and all the better that I'm out of it." On the outskirts of town, Sup asked, "Can you tell me why you're leaving?"

"She thinks she owns me." The answer was practiced. Believed.

83

"She does. Heart and soul, boy," Sup said.

As if that didn't work both ways.

THEY WALKED HIGHWAY 83 eastbound out of Seeley Lake. As earlier, Wava kept a few steps behind, the road two lanes of long, slow ascents. She thought about the chair in her woodshop, about the glue that might shirk its grip, the laddered rungs slipping, then she looked up and saw her son moving farther from their home with more determination than she could ever account for. He was furious. Embarrassed. His shoulders were slumped under the new backpack he'd bought in the hardware store. He hadn't spoken a word to her since Seeley Lake. And didn't he have every right to feel angry with her? Wava punched her hands into her jeans. No. How was she supposed to know what that old man was going to do?

Sup had dropped them off at the True Value Hardware store, an oversized log cabin like all the other Seeley Lake buildings—a tidy collection of logs gummed with oil, antlers and skulls lofted into every available cornice. In the store, Wava veered off into the wood finishing aisles. She loved the color cards—pecan, cherrywood, mahogany, teak—the stacked cans of stains and oils, lacquers and waxes. She loved the hiss of a newly opened can, the look of grain revealed with stain, how cheesecloth glided over well-sanded wood. She could use some tung oil. She pulled herself away and followed Kyle. He was looking at hatchets. He eyed the top-of-the-line then pulled a mid-priced one from the shelf.

He ran his thumb lightly down the steel while Wava winced. "Good edge," he said.

She took the hatchet from him. The balance was wrong: wrists would pop and ache. It would not cleave cleanly. That's what novices didn't understand. For them the edge was all. She pulled a better one from the rack, placed them both in his hands. "Feel the difference?"

He held them awkwardly. "No," he said.

She moved his hands down the handle. "Yeah," he said. "Oh, yeah." And he handed the new hatchet to her to hold as he moved down the aisle. She swung it as she walked. They could use it at home. A person could always use a good hatchet. It had become an excursion, she thought. There was really nothing desperate about it.

She loved tools—oiling wood handles, cleaning and sizing router bits in the proper felt pockets, alert to the dings, flakes, and splinters that could diminish months of work. Joe'd respected the function of

84

tools but not the tools themselves. The labor and the means always secondary to the product. And wasn't that indicative of something larger in him? "You're too damn critical," he'd say, one foot raised on the table or chair he'd just finished. "I'm just trying to help," she'd offer, and he'd look her over while picking his teeth. "*Yeah*," he'd say. "I *can tell*," or, "*Who asked for it?*" And so, wasn't it a relief when it all came apart? Yes.

At the counter, Kyle bought the backpack, the hatchet, and a pocketknife. He was down to a twenty, some singles, and odd change. He slipped the items into the pack while she looked at postcards. "We could send this one to ourselves," she teased him. "Having a good time, glad you're here." He broke into a smile. Yes, she thought, this could be turned around.

"Anyone here got a runaway?"

A sheriff stood in the door. Kyle ducked his head and started to move. Wava reached out and snatched at his sleeve, hauling herself back to his side.

"Who's got the runaway?" the sheriff repeated, then spotted them. He was a squat man, a lightweight, bearing down with all the authority of Swan County winking from the badge on his front pocket. "You got the runaway?"

Wava nodded while Kyle shook his head.

"How old are you?" he asked Kyle.

They spoke at the same time.

"Eighteen."

"Fifteen."

Kyle pulled away and the sheriff's strangely delicate hand circled Kyle's wrist. There were handcuffs prominent in the sheriff's back trouser pocket. She could see Kyle and herself in the back of the sheriff's car, the siren silent, no blue lights, but cruising at sixty with intent down the highway, back to their home and abandoned on the front stoop. Then what? Wait for Kyle to run again. She blamed herself—what, after all, did she know about raising boys? She was an only child, from the Midwest, where all the boys she knew in childhood were cornfed at proper tables, wore tight jeans, and carried themselves with the arrogance of their fathers.

"You got some ID?"

Kyle shook his head.

"He's got his mother," Wava said. "Is that ID enough?"

"It is *if you are*."

"I am."

"Is she?" He turned to Kyle and the boy kept silent. People were gathering in a clutter, slowing down to see better, leaning in as they walked by.

Wava jabbed Kyle with an elbow and whispered, "This is no time to fool around."

"Maybe we should just go down to the office—"

"She is. She's my mother."

Wava smiled. "Told you so."

The sheriff was breathing through his nose. "This is not a game. I got some old man at the office worrying about a runaway. Now I *got* to investigate."

"I can handle it," Wava said. "I know you're trying to help." She saw herself as he saw her, shirt slipping out of her jeans, sweat stains under her arms and breasts, her hair coarse from the sun. She looked small, foolish, and fierce. The sheriff's eyebrow hitched, and she knew he did not believe her. If she could handle it, they wouldn't be here. "You're just interfering—"

"Where's your father?" he asked Kyle.

Wava settled on her heels. "I'm divorced," she said, not that it was any of his business.

A woman standing at Wava's elbow nodded and whispered, "It's a hard road."

Wava singled out the woman. "You got something to do?" The woman hissed and backed away. And then Wava rounded on the sheriff, because he was the cause of it all—her snapping at the woman who meant only sympathy—because he assumed any father was better than none. She lifted her chin level with the badge on his chest. "Are you done with us? I'm his mother. We're out for a walk." She leaned up into his face. *"This is not your business."*

The sheriff released Kyle's wrist. He was steadying his temper with deep breaths. "Then take your walk somewhere else. Ravalli County maybe." He stepped off and said under his breath, "God damned ungrateful. I'd probably run too."

After that, nothing remained in Seeley but to stand by as Kyle made his purchases at the IGA: a loaf of bread, peanut butter, a six-pack of Coke, and two apples.

They were heading up yet another incline, and it stretched onward for a half a mile. They were entering the real heat of the day. Her underwear, damp with sweat, bunched and crept where it had no business. She twisted her hair up and wiped her neck with her shirt collar.

She was stewing in her own skin. Considering the wealth of crazed conversations that day, the sheriff's parting comment was probably the most remarkable. What had she done to merit it? Lose a husband, take on a job while trying to learn a skill to keep the clothes on their backs, the food in their bellies, the sky from falling. *I'd probably run too.* Well, God damn it, when was the last time she'd had that luxury?

"Slow down," she yelled. The highway edged a lake sheltered in a hollow of hills, the reflected trees more significant than the real. They passed the island where the millionaire built his log-cabin mansion— six kitchens, fifteen fireplaces. A for-sale sign hung roadside. He had one year on the lake before burning his yacht for insurance and firing off his own head. She could not conceive a proper reason for suicide. She could not imagine the necessity of it. The whole prospect of death and dying was deterrent enough. But how much did a person have to lose before the end was worth more than the means? Her mouth went dry. The water looked clean, the hills unmoved. "I'm thirsty," she called.

"You should have bought something to drink," he yelled back.

She jogged to where he waited, pulled her pockets inside out. "No money."

"You should have thought of that before," he said and started walking.

"What? I should have read your mind, grabbed my purse, packed a dinner—"

He stopped.

"I'm thirsty," she repeated. "Pretend I'm a stranger. Pretend I'm some bum on the road who needs a drink and not the mother who gave birth to you, who watched your head crown between her knees."

He opened his pack. "That's gross."

"You don't know the half of it," Wava said as she pulled out two Cokes, handed one to him. "Thanks." She took a long pull. He shrugged the backpack, seated it in the duff of pine needles, then walked down to the lake. Wava folded herself to the ground. Subterranean mushrooms whoofed under her, and a cloud of brown spore patinated her arms. She wiped the sweat under her breasts with the tail of her shirt and leaned back against the tree. Kyle was bending over, picking at the knots in the laces, taking off his shoes. When he was five, she'd bought him a pair with Velcro fasteners. When she showed him how they worked, all he'd said was, *I can tie my shoes.* He put them on, but there was no delight. It was clear he believed she hadn't enough faith in him.

Kyle dove into the water. The afternoon light sliced through the trees. She counted the limbs overhead like a blessing. Pine was good for primitives—plank tables, benches, bookcases. The soft imprint of hammers gave them character, the respect of use and age. After three years of working with the more expensive hardwoods, she retained a fondness for pine. She loved the open-hearted wood with all its knot-holes and failings that relentlessly taught forgiveness. If she had a sin-gle great attribute, it would be her belief in the character of wood, that each wood had its own best use, each plank its order in design or-dained by the symmetry of grain, and that grain preordained by the clemency of weather, by soil or rock face, by the event of seasons.

Belly up to the sun, Kyle floated in the water. Wava's kidneys felt battered from the long walk and the sudden intake of fluids. She re-lieved herself in privacy, then walked down to the lake. She set her shoes next to her son's and stepped into the lake fully clothed. The cold water wicked up her thigh, her buttocks. She slipped deeper until her breasts floated and the sweat washed away. Dog paddling awhile, she kept her head dry above the water. She had always been a coward about full immersion, each time a battle of will between herself and the unknown. And yet she persisted. She held her breath, squeezed her eyes shut, and ducked under. She floated beneath the surface, and when the ringing in her ears faded and her heart calmed, she heard the hum and kick of her son swimming.

HER SHOES SQUEAKED when she walked, the lake water trickling from her jeans into her shoes. But she felt refreshed, ready to do battle. She tried to vary the pitch. "Hey, listen to this," she said, and pumped her foot in her shoe. When she finished he stood there, uncomprehend-ing. "It's *Stars and Stripes Forever,* you know, John Philip Sousa."

He rolled his eyes. "Don't you ever get tired?" he asked.

"You should try an eight-hour shift with the meatloaf special," and she balanced her arms out in front of her. "How about you?" she asked, trying to keep the hope out of her voice.

He turned away and started walking.

"That's my boy," she said. "Never say die." And that was probably her own damn fault too. His stamina—built on long nights at the cafe as a little boy when she couldn't afford a babysitter and he'd play qui-etly at one of the tables, sneaking sips of cold coffee left by customers. When he faded, she carried him out to the parking lot and lay him in the back of the truck bed—the cap windows cranked open or shut, depending on the weather. She'd check on him in the spare moments, between late-night customers—drunks trying to revive with food, or the truckers hunched over tables talking into the tableside phones, hands cupped around the mouthpieces. Hamburgers hissed, fried chicken crackled, and she'd bolt through the back door to lean against the pickup and listen to her son, still safe, still asleep while coyotes choraled in the distance. Hardly an ideal childhood. Not even a reasonable one.

All totaled, including the ride from Sup, they had covered nearly twenty miles. They were still on 83, alongside the Blackfoot-Clearwater Wildlife Management Range, an elk and wildlife preserve. A long, flat pasture, with hills bucked up against its western border. They passed signs with binoculars stenciled on—wildlife viewing areas—though in summer when tourists arrived, the elk ranged miles up and away in the high country of the Bob Marshall Wilderness Preserve. A curious idea, given that, in season, hunting was allowed, the hunters advised to return the radio collars to the department of fish and game. Didn't that make it uncomfortably like shooting a pet? Removing the collar after the dog is hit on the road?

"Could you kill something?" she asked Kyle.

He stopped, shifted the pack on his shoulder. "Why, is there something you want dead?"

"I could carry that pack for a while," she said.

He shook his head. "I can do it. You *never* think I can do it."

"No." She shook a finger at him. "I *know* you can. Why the hell do you think I'm here?"

He stepped back, turning his head so she wouldn't see how pleased he was. Maybe she had done too much. Maybe all these years she worked the extra hours, did the extra chore herself, she hadn't so much given as taken from the boy?

"You never said—could you kill something? Elk? Deer?"

He led off again. "I won't make the county line by dark."

"I could—kill something—but I'd have to be damned hungry first," she said, and thought it couldn't be wearing a collar. He slowed down, and she trotted up alongside him. Her son hadn't answered, and that seemed significant. There were things mothers should have of their sons before handing them over—a sense of their experience. "Did you ever see anything die? Something sizable." Her hands spread apart. "Something that counts?"

"Sure." Then he reconsidered. "Do roadkills count?" he asked.

She nodded and thought about her parents, but that was unfair. They had been *in* the car. She had been fifteen hundred miles away with the excuse of raising her own son. She would spare Kyle that, if she could—leaving too soon, too angry, and too proud to go back. But she couldn't think about that now—the wages of being someone's child. She had her hands full being a parent. "My father used to slaughter hogs—a sledge to the head." Her arm swung down, and she stopped, fixing the spot at her feet as if there were a pig at the end of her reach. "Jesus, he had *arms* on him." She looked at her own. "Then he'd hoist it up by the hind feet to a crossbar and slit its throat." Kyle was staring at the road, his nose wrinkled. "They were big hogs, hung their length from a crossbar, their heads swinging just about the height of my head. I could look in their eyes if I wanted to." She stepped off. The sun was over the western hills. Meadowlarks sang, perched on the tips of lamb's ear, and the shadows of clouds rolled over the fescue like animals grazing. They stood side by side, looking at the shadows, the mountains, the sky around them, everything but each other.

"Did you? Look in their eyes?" he asked.

She nodded her head. "Always."

"Cripes." He walked away. "Why?" he asked over his shoulder.

"Because I was ten years old. Because nothing frightened me then." What kind of child does that? Touches the dead, looks it in the eye? She had been a strange child. So who was she to question Kyle's behavior? Though the only time her father had been upset was when he'd found her, knees crooked over the crossbar and swinging like one of those hogs. She'd wanted to know how they saw the world, inverted, the sky become ground, the grass heaven. Her parents had been horrified. But then what, after all, frightens parents more than their own children's curiosity?

They laid her parents out in oak coffins. Closed caskets. Their neighbor sent her pictures, printed on the back of one, "your father," and on the other, "your mother," as if she wouldn't know them. A car passed, and another, none slowing down for a better look at the odd pair vagrant in the road. Wava slipped a hand into her blouse to ease the stitch in her side.

"I killed a rabbit once," he said.

Wava nodded, as if that were reasonable.

"I lobbed a rock at it, hit it square on the head. It didn't have time to be surprised." His eyebrow lifted, as though he still found that surprising himself. "Never thought I'd hit it. That it would die."

She studied him from the corner of her eye, the sweat beading on his lip, the chin still hairless—skin like the bottom of a baby's foot. He seemed impossibly young, still bewildered by his own actions, a rock and a rabbit, cause and effect. "Why?" she asked.

He blushed, swiped at the hair over his forehead. "I wanted a lucky rabbit's foot."

The day's sun had wilted the weeds. Wava's arms were lacquered with sweat. In the grasses, beetles drowsed on the underside of the blades, and dragonflies fumbled through the air. She was thirsty, but reluctant to ask him for another drink. The meadow was spent with the day's heat, and the first early evening breezes were still moments away, the land pendent with expectation.

"Did you take it?" she asked. "The rabbit's foot?"

"No," he said. "The rabbit was dead. How lucky could it be?"

IT WAS DARK by the time they stopped. Their clothes had dried, though the inseams in Wava's jeans remained damp and chafed her thighs. She took off her shoes, rubbed the weals on her feet. Her hair had hardened in snarls. They camped in an abandoned shed, one of many sagging houses and barns along 200 heading south to Missoula. They were in the Garnet Range that had drifted from Idaho almost ninety million years prior, along with the Sapphire and Bitteroot mountains, escaped to Montana. All this traffic, coming and going, Wava thought.

Her skin itched—no-see-ums, whose bite didn't bother until after they'd fled, and what kind of defense could you have against that? Still she slapped at her arms, disinclined to let them get away with it. It was chilly. They had a hatchet and wood, but no matches. She sat on the dirt floor, under a star-pierced roof. The wall across from her buckled outward, and through the yawning pitch between wall and foundation, sage and knapweed grew rampant.

Coyotes yapped from the fields outside. "There are big cats around here—mountain lions. Wolves. Rats," Wava said.

"Elk, mule deer, skunk," Kyle said.

"The occasional psychopath," Wava added. "He can use your new hatchet on us."

"You're not going to scare me back home."

Wava stretched her feet in front of her, locked her arms over her chest. "Steaks would taste good."

91

"We don't have a fire to cook them, anyway."

"I'd eat them raw. Damn, I'm tired." She took a bite of the peanut butter sandwich he offered her. "So, remind me. Why are we running away?"

"You grounded me. *Forever.*"

She shrugged. "And you can see how long that lasted. If you'd just done what I told you in the first place—"

"I can't do a *damn* thing without you ordering me around."

"Watch your language. I do not."

He pointed a finger at her. "You don't even know when you're doing it."

"I'm a parent. Your only parent. I'm *supposed* to give you order in your life." She wished she still smoked. She'd have matches then, and she could light a fire. Maybe the whole god-damned shed. "I take orders every day of my life." Bucking hot plates to customers until her arms were pinked with the heat, Rod, the owner and cook, shuffling kettles counter top, waiting for the next spurt of customers. He had six daughters, none of whom he thought level-headed enough to work for him. And Wava figured that was his own damned fault.

Kyle had moved off to the far side of the shed, kicking at the sagebrush. She was tempted to list her acts of benevolence like a catalogue of his sins. "Checking for snakes?" she asked, and he returned to sit ten feet from her. "You want to be an adult? Then act like it. Adults don't run away." And that was nonsense, of course. They ran with regularity, off to work, to lovers. Put holes in their heads. They had better timing was all, a greater ingenuity for excuses—financial ruin, change of life, you don't understand me. I never meant to fall in love with her, meaning I never meant to fall out of love with you. But there it is. Take care of the boy.

"Well, you're the adult all right," Kyle said. "*You* don't run from nobody."

"You talking about your dad? Christ. Don't bother. He invented his own excuses when he left. No. This is not his doing. This is yours. You take care of your own reasons." She walked over and squatted in front of him. "But you tell me of one time, just one, when I wasn't there."

She stood, dusted her knees and walked to where her shoes slumped in the dirt.

"Maybe I just want to be alone," Kyle said.

"Funny you should say that. I don't." Wava slipped her shoes on and limped to the door. She leaned on the remains of the jamb. People were selfish. They learned it as children. They were generous only in blame. The moon hung low and huge in the sky. It would ascend and shrink, but still it would be there, night after night after night. As a child, how many times did it have to rise before she'd believed it would always rise to fall? Such things must have come easier back then.

She could have left. Fifteen years ago. Ten years ago. It was done all the time. She had simply chosen not to. It was all so absurd, her son running from the only one who had stayed, her standing there, tired in the doorway, the moon rising yet another time. She could sleep, and Kyle would run. She could stay awake, and Kyle would run.

"You go on," she said. "You meet other people. Someday, you'll find yourself a woman who knows that you save your peas for the last and assumes it's because you like them least. You'll have to tell her otherwise. Then some morning, you'll slip out of your wife's bed, maybe step on your children's toys, and you'll wonder if it's worth it all. You'll think about leaving. I suspect it comes easier with practice."

She shuffled back into the room. She could barely make out his shape against the wall.

"You going somewhere?" he asked.

She shrugged. "Maybe."

"You can hardly walk."

"I'll hitch," she said.

"That's stupid."

She walked out the door. The wind ruffled the grasses and she stepped off into the gratifying silence. She was cut loose and it was terrifying. Wonderful. Wasn't this what she'd been preparing for all along? Marriage and friendship, sons and daughters, were just a respite between you and the knowledge that every choice you make is yours alone. The moon was nearing its zenith, and trust seemed a damned thin thing to rely on. She crossed a small hummock, stumbled on the downside and caught herself short of falling, or turning back to look at the shed a last time. She could not afford to consider what she left behind. The field seemed deeper in the night and the hills kinder—the edges planed clean in silhouette. It was seductive, she thought, this running away. She could just keep going. She watched her feet carefully, stepping clear of the prairie dog holes, through the chewed turf and buckled grasses where elk had rolled out of sleep. Her arms swung at her side, and she waded through the knee-high grass. She heard the clatter of Kyle's possessions banging in his backpack as he raced up from behind.

"You act like it's my fault," he said.

93

"It is. Surprised?" She struck off toward the road.

He caught up to her, his feet catching the grass. "How do *you* like it?" he asked.

"I don't know. I haven't been on this end long. But does it scare you? Now that it's me leaving?"

"You going home?"

She stopped. She could see his face in the moonlight, his eyes bright and frightened. She turned away and kept walking. Kyle hesitated, and then there was the sound of his feet treading behind her own.

SHE STRUCK OFF WITHOUT DIRECTION. They would argue and talk. Perhaps they would walk east, or south to discover what came of the moon's progress. She wondered what they would see, what would become available to them because they'd placed themselves here and now. They'd flush deer whose antlers oriented like a compass against the stars and range behind them to the edges of cities. They'd walk the concrete sidewalks and loiter to hear the streetlamps buzzing. Avenues lined in maples, oaks, and weeping birch. There would be homes with dogs yawning on the stoops, doors clamped tight, and hallways they didn't know by feel. Where men and women clung to each other, their children spent in fretless sleep under the benediction of gabled roofs. They'd pass like shadows, the city falling behind. Past cemeteries, a march of crosses and stone angels anchored in decline. They'd traverse water and mountains, hillocks of cedar—old-growth groves with hoary skin. And on the downslope, where wind sheers toppled trees and lightning forged revelations, they would trace the wood beneath the skin. She would instruct her son—the cambium, the heartwood, the pith, the soul—she would speak as mothers never can, and he would understand as sons never have. And in this world, where all things *are* possible, they will turn the corner to find their house, tied to the land, open as they'd left it with the woodshop still redolent of glue and all the clever tools in their ordered place, safe beneath the crown of cottonwoods, beneath the sky, the night suspended.

Nominated by Robert Wrigley

THE BALLOON

by MARY RUEFLE

from THIRD COAST

Rain scanty, fodder scarce. Or the children's feet
are muddy. There's no bread. A sheep ate the heart
of Thomas Hardy, so that another sheep's heart
had to do in the terrible pinch and be laid to rest
next to the novelist's wife. Have you ever seen
a sock stiffening with real blood, as if it had
a sweet red voice like the hard-to-speak-to toys
we had a heart to heart with when we were ten?
Some persons are picking through the rubble.
Someone's found a colander and is sifting
for his other shoe, some coins, his daughter, her bear,
the bear's undazzled eye—
which he finds and sews on his coat
and only then can the bear see the man for what he is,
an animal that needs to be talked to.
At this time a black balloon rises over the municipal
ruins, and no one knows what it means.

Nominated by Mark Cox, Tony Hoagland, William Olsen, David Rivard, and Dean Young

PREACHER

by STEVE YARBROUGH

from THE GEORGIA REVIEW

IF HE'S ALIVE TODAY, he must be sixty-five. For all I know, he still lives somewhere on the outskirts of Indianola, Mississippi, north of town maybe, out close to Fairview Baptist Church. He may still be driving tractors, working now for somebody I grew up with. He may spend his days in the cotton field, or he may spend them driving along the levees of catfish ponds, pulling a seine or lowering a probe into the water to measure the pond's oxygen level.

If he lives in the town or in the countryside nearby, he can, if he chooses, enter any restaurant he wants to, and he will be served. If he buys his groceries at Piggly Wiggly, he will know that there are no longer two water fountains in the store—one painted white, one painted black. Both water fountains were removed many years back, and with a few exceptions, white people no longer shop at that store at all. Should he fall ill, he can appear at Hull Brothers' Clinic, and if he does so he will find today only one waiting room, with soft chairs and couches on which people of either race may sit.

If he lives in the town or anywhere nearby, chances are he knows several of the black officers on the city police force or at least a few of the black deputies who work for the sheriff's department. Perhaps when he encounters any of these law enforcement officers they exchange pleasantries. For all I know, they may be his relatives or the sons of men he once knew when he was driving a tractor for my grandfather.

It's a safe bet that, if he is alive, he owns a television set and at some point in the last year and a half watched at least a portion of the O.J. Simpson trial. It's also a safe bet that when he heard that former detective Mark Fuhrman had used the word *nigger* at least forty-one times and boasted that he had beaten black suspects and planted evidence to implicate those suspects in crimes they might or might not have committed, he remembered a lonely spot on a gravel road north of Indianola, the way the air smelled at midnight in the fall of 1962, how he could hear the tires of an approaching car crunching gravel even before the headlights exposed his shadow on the ground in a pool of white light.

*

Everybody, black and white alike, called him Preacher. My grandfather said he was called that because of his clothes. Unlike a lot of the black farmhands, he did own a suit, which you might chance to see him wearing on a Sunday as he walked home from whatever church it was that he attended. The suit, as I recall it now, was brown, and he wore it with a matching brown tie, a white shirt, and a brown hat.

On weekdays, when he was out in the field on Grandpa's old red-bellied Ford tractor, he dressed well too. He wore matching khaki pants and work shirts and a beige felt hat. Somehow, he always managed to keep his work boots looking clean, even when the rice and cane tires on that Ford tractor were throwing up huge clods of gumbo.

My father, who farmed with Grandpa, had a different theory about Preacher's nickname. He said Preacher had gotten it because he was so pious. Dad said that back in the fifties, Preacher had worked for another local farmer. One day Preacher was out in the middle of a big field and the western horizon started turning purple, as it does in the Delta when one of those swift violent thunderstorms is on the way. Preacher knew he couldn't make it to headquarters before the storm hit, so he hopped down off his tractor and ran for the nearest road ditch. When he reached it, he lay down.

Dad said the man who owned the farm drove by and saw the tractor standing in the field. Then he saw Preacher. He stopped his truck, got out, and walked over to the side of the road. He asked Preacher (who was not then called Preacher) what in the hell he was doing. Preacher looked up at him and said, "The Bible says *Fear God.*"

The story sounds apocryphal. Like so many stories white Deltans love to tell about blacks, it stresses the black man's fear of natural elements, and it places him where most white Deltans would like him to

97

remain: in a prone position. But it contains, I believe, at least one kernel of truth. Preacher did fear God.

God was all he feared. I once saw him break up a knife fight on the porch of the little country store my grandmother ran. When one of the men who'd been involved in the fight turned on Preacher, Preacher uttered two words. *Try it.* The man with the knife chose not to.

He did not fear dogs, even though many white people in the Delta had trained their dogs to go crazy whenever a black person set foot in their yards, and he did not fear snakes. The dogs he would talk to—*Easy boy, lay down and be still*—and the snakes he would kill. I must have seen him slice in two at least fifteen cottonmouths at one time or another. He didn't come up behind them with the hoe the way Dad had taught me to; he walked right up in front of them, and when he brought the blade down, in one smooth flashing motion, he did not grunt or grit his teeth or exhibit emotion.

He did not fear children. Neither their presence nor their questions caused him any discomfort. Many times I walked up behind him when he was busy, hunkered down behind a cultivator rig out in the middle of a hot dusty field. When I asked him what he was doing, he always responded with plenty of detail, as if the information might actually be of use to a six-year-old boy. "I'm resetting the cultivator sweeps," he'd say, "and changing the depth on them gauge wheels. Soil's sandy here, and your grandpa don't want me to plow too deep."

He displayed the same kind of patience in the fall of 1962, when, on the first of three successive Sunday mornings, my grandfather appeared at the Sunflower County Courthouse to get him out of jail. He had been charged, as he would be on each of the next two weekends, with disorderly conduct and fined fifteen dollars—half a week's pay for a tractor driver in Indianola, Mississippi, in 1962.

That first Sunday morning the jailer told my grandfather Preacher had been staggering along at the edge of town, singing and shouting obscenities. While the jailer delivered this information, Preacher waited quietly in a cell a few feet away. His dress was as immaculate as ever. His pants and shirt were clean, and his shoes showed no trace of mud.

In the truck, on the way home, my grandfather said, "Preacher, what'd you do?"

"I was walking down the road, eating a bag of popcorn. Police pulled up behind me, right close to the city-limit sign, and rolled down the window and told me to get in." As he answered the question, Preacher

98

stared straight ahead, keeping his gaze trained on the ridge of loose gravel in the middle of the road.

Grandpa said, "They generally wouldn't arrest a person for that."

Preacher said, "I'm sure they *generally* wouldn't."

Grandpa probably drummed his fingers on the wheel while he drove. He did that whenever he felt nervous. "Some folks wouldn't agree with what I'm fixing to say," he told Preacher, "but as far as I'm concerned, there's nothing wrong with going into town on Saturday night and getting a little bit rowdy."

"I don't see a problem with that neither, Mr. Yarbrough," Preacher said. "And between the two of us, Sir, if I had wanted to get rowdy, I imagine I would have done it."

"But the fact remains that you didn't."

"No Sir, I didn't."

"You was just eating popcorn."

"Yes Sir."

"They let you finish it?"

"No Sir," Preacher said. "They pitched the sack into the ditch back yonder by the city limit sign."

They were five or six miles from town by that time, almost home. Grandpa said, "You reckon the bag's still back there?"

"Could be."

"But it could not be?"

Preacher said, "Mr. Yarbrough, that bag was near about full. Somebody's liable to have come along and eat it."

"Damp and all?"

Preacher said, "I've seen people eat a lot worse."

*

To understand what happened on the last Saturday night in October of 1962, the fourth Saturday in a row on which Preacher had an encounter with the Indianola police, you have to know certain things about Grandpa and certain things about the Delta.

A century earlier, there had been four slaves for every white person in Sunflower County. If you factored in the value of slaves, Issaquena County, a few miles south of Indianola, was the second richest county in the United States. In fact, four of the river counties were among the thirty-six richest counties in the country. But if you discounted slave value, according to James C. Cobb in his history of the Delta (*The*

99

Most Southern Place on Earth, 1992), the figures dropped dramatically. The antebellum Delta planter was well aware that much of his wealth was in the form of black bodies.

Neither the slaves nor their owners found the land hospitable. Mosquitoes and water moccasins were the only natural inhabitants of the place ever since the Treaty of Doak's Stand, signed in 1820, had removed the Choctaw Indians to areas farther west. Malaria, cholera, and typhoid fever plagued the inhabitants of Delta plantations, and throughout the rest of the South, slaves lived with the constant fear that their owners would sell them to a Delta planter.

The Civil War freed the slaves, but it didn't alter several basic facts. The soil of the Delta was still some of the most fertile in the world, the environment was still harsh and dangerous, and cotton was still a labor-intensive crop. Somebody had to plant it, tend it, and pick it. And more often than not, the somebody was a black person.

The early decades of the twentieth century saw planters placing ads in hill-country papers in an attempt to lure blacks to the Delta. For a time they were successful. But by the end of the First World War, blacks had started to migrate north to places like Chicago and Detroit, where manufacturing offered more attractive opportunities. At the same time, poor whites from the hills moved in.

Grandpa's family had been part of that migration from the hills. They had come to Sunflower County in 1920, and as sharecroppers they worked plantation land for portions. They and others like them did many of the same things blacks did on a plantation, but blacks did some things poor whites weren't allowed to do. Blacks held the domestic positions, just as they had in slave times. They served as cooks, nannies, drivers. They entered the Big House through the back door, true enough, but at least they went inside. The animosity poor whites felt for blacks was often deadly.

My grandfather, however, had never shared this animosity. He used the word *nigger,* but he used it in much the same way he used such words as *Baptist, farmer, school-bus driver* or *Indian*—all words he might have used to describe himself; he was one-quarter Choctaw and happy enough about it, just as he was happy enough to be a farmer.

He was happy enough, I believe, to know that between 1920 and 1962 he had managed to raise his family's standard of living. He didn't own land, but he no longer sharecropped either. He rented sixteenth-section land from the county and grew cotton and rice and soybeans. To supplement his income, he drove the bus.

In 1956, the year I was born, he and my father installed an indoor bathroom, and in 1958 they bought a television set, which other families from sixteenth-section lands would sometimes come and watch on Saturday evenings, while we all sat around the living room eating popcorn. By any standard except one—that of the blacks who worked as field hands—all of us were poor.

The Delta's social structure never quite let us forget it. We didn't belong to the country club, and at high school football games we didn't sit in the reserved section. When the circus came to town, we occupied the general admission seats, halfway between the reserved section and the benches at the end of the ring, which were always allotted to blacks. Like black people, we were treated brusquely in such establishments as pharmacies and the better clothing stores along Front Street. And occasionally we suffered brushes with the law.

One of my uncles, who lived a few miles away in Greenville, was in and out of jail. He worked on a tugboat, and when he got off work he generally made it no farther than the Marina before he bought his first beer. His first beer was never his last. Several times he was arrested for fighting on the docks, though he never hurt anyone and usually ended up being pushed into the water. Various other relatives—blessedly distant—had done time in Parchman. We had one car thief in the family, a couple of check kiters, and a cousin named Everett who was briefly on the FBI's wanted list—he was a truckdriver who had apparently misplaced a load of unmarked gravestones.

Grandpa, like Dad, was a law-abiding man. He drank nothing stronger than Barq's Root Beer, he never engaged in shady dealings of any sort, he never missed a payment on any of his farm equipment. But even he had once—back in 1961—found himself in the clutches of the Indianola police.

He and I had just gotten haircuts at Gayden Smith's barbershop. The barbershop, now in downtown Indianola, was at that time situated out on Highway 82 between L&H Auto Parts and Lott's Appliances. The three businesses stood side by side, their gravel parking lots small and crowded. People parked their pickup trucks wherever the notion struck them, sometimes blocking the view of drivers attempting to back out of the parking lot into 82.

Grandpa couldn't see the westbound lane of 82. So he inched backward, looking over his shoulder, doing his best to see if anything was coming.

101

Something was. An Indianola police department car. Brakes screamed, and the cruiser veered toward the center stripe.

As I have said, Grandpa was one-quarter Choctaw, but that morning his face looked completely white. He rested his forehead against the wheel and whispered, "Shit."

The worst, however, was still on its way. It barreled toward us in the form of Officer Stan Melton—a little over six feet tall, blond, and heavily muscled. Looking at him, you might suspect he'd been a wonderful football player, but the truth was that he'd graduated from high school the previous year without ever starting a game. He was one of those who looked marvelous on the sideline but who, when it came time to deliver a blow, couldn't mash a marshmallow. He had grown up in the country, not far from our house, and he'd ridden Grandpa's school bus. He was the kind, Grandpa said, who liked to make trouble. He threw spitballs at high school girls and stuck straight pins into the rear ends of first- and second-graders. Several times Grandpa had put him off the bus and made him walk.

Stan pulled a pad from his pocket. "Mr. Yarbrough," he said, "I'm fixing to charge you with reckless driving. You like to run me clean off the road."

Grandpa said, "I couldn't see you, Stan. You know how folks park here."

Stan said, "Ignorance ain't no excuse."

"I'm not talking about ignorance," Grandpa said. He ran his tongue over his bottom lip, like he sometimes did when he was trying to make a hard decision. Then he added: "Though seeing you in that uniform does summon the word *ignorance* to mind."

Stan charged Grandpa with reckless driving and using abusive language against an officer of the law.

The following week, Grandpa appeared in court to dispute the charges. Dad and I went with him. It was hard not to notice that all of the other people who were in the courtroom that day, facing charges, were black. They waited quietly in a row at the back of the courtroom. When the presiding magistrate called their names, they went quietly forward. The most common charge against them was loitering.

I was sitting next to Grandpa. "What's loitering?" I asked.

"Just kind of hanging around."

"What's wrong with that?"

"Nothing," he said, "at least as far as I'm concerned."

102

The magistrate did not agree. Every single one of the black people was pronounced guilty as charged. In three cases Stan had been the arresting officer.

Finally Grandpa's turn came. The magistrate, who also owned the gin where Grandpa took his cotton, as well as a large plantation out on the Sunflower River, listened to Stan's account of the event, then to Grandpa's. Then he cleared his throat.

"This is a regrettable event," he said. "Mr. Yarbrough, Patrolman Melton's not the most experienced member of the police force, so maybe this time we can just excuse his youthful zeal."

He banged his gavel. "Dismissed."

Leaving the courtroom that day, Grandpa said, "I guess even a poor man's business is worth something."

*

Did this awareness of Grandpa's—that so much depended on the worth of your business—make him do what he did the last Saturday night in October of 1962? Did it account for his pensiveness that afternoon? He hadn't said much all day. He hadn't said much for two or three days.

It had been dry for almost a week, so he and Dad and Preacher had kept the picker in the field around the clock. We'd had a lot of rain that fall, as I recall, and way too much cotton was still in the field. Before too long, if we didn't get it picked, it would mildew and sell below grade.

I wasn't much help, but I did what I could. After the picker dumped a load of cotton in the trailer, I would tromp it down, packing it as tightly as possible. You wanted to get as much cotton in one trailer as you could, and you wanted to get that trailer to the gin, which was backed up because of the sudden rush, and get it empty and pull it home. We only owned three trailers. If they were all at the gin at the same time, there was nothing we could do except sit around and worry.

Along about four o'clock, it rained. We hauled the trailer, half-full, to the headquarters shed. Grandpa told Preacher to go on home and take off until Monday. Unlike some farmers, Dad and Grandpa never worked on Sunday, no matter how desperately they wanted to get the crop in.

As they left the shed, Grandpa said, "Preacher? You aim to go to town?" By that time Grandpa had learned that Preacher's arresting officers had been the same ones each time: Stan Melton and an older man named Ford Cash.

Preacher turned around. He removed his hands from his pants pockets and crossed his arms over his chest. "I might," he said, "if it quits raining. There's a movie on at the Honey I wouldn't mind watching."

"Be careful."

"Yes Sir, I sure will. I'm always careful when I go to town."

At supper that night, Grandpa said, "I reckon Preacher's in Indianola now, looking at the movie and getting ready to go to jail."

"He's in Indianola," Grandma said, "but I doubt he's watching any movie."

Grandpa's fork paused on the way to his mouth. "What you think he's doing, then?"

Grandma wrinkled her nose. "I imagine he's down on Church Street."

I didn't know what *down on Church Street* meant, but I knew that Grandpa believed in Preacher, just as I did, and Grandma didn't. And though I loved Grandma as much as I loved my own mother, I felt a gap opening between us. It was a gap that would grow larger as I grew older, and it was the kind of gap that would eventually open between me and a lot of other people I loved, including my mother and father. It would eventually make me leave the place where I'd grown up and turn me into the most peculiar species of outsider: the one who can close his eyes and walk around a place without ever stumbling, guided by sound and smell, by the feel of the dirt beneath his feet.

I said, "I bet Preacher's watching the movie," and then I went on and finished my supper. By the time I went to bed I'd forgotten the whole discussion.

But Grandpa hadn't. Maybe his inability to forget it had left him unable to sleep at all. I never asked, and he never said. Late that night, when he appeared beside my bed and asked if I wanted to go to town with him, I wiped the sleep from my eyes, got up, and dressed.

*

Marie Road intersects Highway 82 at what was once the western edge of Indianola. The town stretches beyond that point now, with a Wal-Mart to the west, two or three small businesses, and a used-car lot. But in 1962, when you got to the red light at Marie and 82, you had left town behind and were about a half mile out in the country. One house stood on the corner near the light, and another one stood three-quar-

104

ters of a mile from the highway. In between those two houses, there were no others.

Cotton fields stretched out on both sides of the road. Turnrows, which tractors and pickers used to turn around on, ran along the road ditches. Near the city-limit sign, there was a single grove of trees in between the turnrow and the road ditch. I had ridden by many times with Dad or Grandpa and seen field hands resting there, doing their best to stay out of the sun.

As we bumped and occasionally slid over the muddy turnrow, Grandpa said, "We'll just pull in behind them trees up there and sit a spell and see if anything interesting happens."

"You think they're gonna arrest Preacher?"

"I don't know," he said. "Could be."

"Why are they doing it?"

"I don't know," he said. "I'd kind of like to see."

"Have you got a gun?"

"Lord no."

"What if they start shooting?"

"If they start shooting, we'll start driving."

We parked behind the trees. Grandpa said it was about eleven-thirty, and he wondered if I'd ever been up this late before. He said he'd always liked it late at night—he didn't mind driving a tractor or a picker at night nearly as much as he did in the daytime. At night, he said, it was cool and quiet, and while you drove you had a lot of time to think. Some folks were scared of the dark, but he never had been, and he bet I wouldn't be either.

The sound of his voice must have lulled me. I became aware of something cool and hard against my cheek—the window glass. Though I had wanted badly to stay awake, I couldn't stop myself from snuggling down into my jacket and closing my eyes.

It was Grandpa's hand that woke me. He had laid it on my knee. "Wake up," he whispered. "I think there's fixing to be something to see."

*

I live in California now, and I have two girls, ages six and seven. As I write these words, near midnight on a Tuesday in October of 1995, I do so with the expectation that one day they will read them, and with the hope that they will feel the hand of a man they've never known, that they'll hear his voice telling them to wake up, because there's something he wants them to see.

Through the trees, in the darkness, the face of the man walking along the road was impossible to distinguish. But the erect bearing was familiar. So was the hat. He walked like a man who was bound for a specific destination, a man who aimed to get where he was going in his own good time.

He looked straight ahead, toward that point where Marie Road bent west. He did not look over his shoulder, even though he could not have failed to hear the noise of the approaching car. Within a few seconds he was bathed in the glow of the headlights, but he stopped walking only when the police car pulled up beside him. I saw him turn to look at the driver.

"Stay here," Grandpa said, and for the first time that night, I felt real fear. Sweat popped out on my forehead. Something large and hard had lodged in my throat.

But I did what he told me. I sat there in the cab of his pickup truck, and I watched while the scene played itself out. I saw it the way you see a silent movie: the characters moved their lips, but no words reached my ears. I could have rolled my window down, but I chose not to.

My grandfather walked in front of the police car, right into that glaring white light and around to the driver's side door. He stood beside Preacher, rested one hand on top of the car, and leaned down toward the driver. He talked to him calmly, without making any gestures.

The other policeman must have been Ford Cash, who sat with his face against the passenger-side window glass, much as I had done. He was thinking, I imagine, that my grandfather was a churlish man, to be so bent on spoiling such harmless fun.

*

It would make a better ending if I could say that a few moments later my grandfather and Preacher walked over to the truck, that Grandpa took his place behind the wheel, Preacher took my seat, and I moved over so that I sat between the two of them, one of my thighs touching Grandpa's and the other touching Preacher's. It would make a better ending if I could say that on the way home, Preacher put his arm around my shoulders and Grandpa said, "Did you see the look on that jackass's face?"—to which Preacher said, "I wouldn't take a million dollars for it."

It would make me feel a lot better about the place and the people I came from if I could say that the next day, my grandfather picked up the phone and called the chief of police and the mayor, telling them both that if Stan Melton or Ford Cash or any other member of the Indianola police force ever again without just cause accosted Preacher or anyone else who worked for him, he would hire an attorney and pursue justice to heaven and beyond.

But of course things didn't happen that way.

While Grandpa and Preacher walked over to the truck, Stan turned the cruiser around and burned rubber, heading back toward town.

Grandpa and Preacher got into the truck. Before the truck ever moved, Grandpa said what he must have felt he had to say, knowing as he did that though a poor white man's business was worth something, it wasn't worth much.

"If you aim to stay alive," Grandpa told Preacher, "you better start coming home earlier. And choose a different route."

Nominated by Robin Hemley, Philip Levine and Josip Novakovich

STONEHENGE

by ALBERT GOLDBARTH

from BELLINGHAM REVIEW

Each morning he'd anoint the room's four corners
with an arc of piss, and then—until
he was forcibly halted—beat his forehead open
on the eastern wall, the "sunrise wall,"
incanting a doggerel prayer about God
the Flower, God of the Hot Plucked Heart; and
she, if loose in the halls, would join him,
squatting in the center of the room and masturbating
with a stolen bar of soap. This isn't *why*
they were sent to the madhouse: this is what
they needed to do *once in* the madhouse: this
is the only meaningful ritual they could fashion
there, created from the few, make-do
materials available. It isn't wondrous strange
more than the mega-boozhwah formulaic splendor
of my sister's wedding ten, eleven years ago:
her opulent bouquet of plastic flowers
(for the wilting pour of wattage at the photo session),
nigglingly arranged to match the *real* bouquet
she carried down the aisle, bloom per bloom;
the five-foot Taj Mahal of sculpted pastel sherbet;
endless "Fiddler on the Roof"; I'm sorry
now I cranked my academic sneer hauteur in place
all night. I'm sorry I didn't lose myself
like a drunken bee in a room-sized rose,
in waltzing Auntie Sally to the lush swell

108

of the band. We need this thing. There's not one
mineral in Stonehenge that our blood can't also raise.
One dusk, one vividly contusion-color
dusk, with my fists in my pockets and
a puzzle of fish-rib clouds in the sky, I
stopped at the low-level glow of a basement window
(Hot Good Noodles Shop) and furtively looked in:
a full-grown pig was splayed on the table,
stunned but fitfully twitching, it looked as if
it had grasshoppers under its skin. A man and a woman
slit that body jaw-to-ass with an ornate knife,
and then they both scooped out a tumble
of many dozens of wasps, preserved
by the oils of living pig to a beautiful black and amber
gem-like sheen. I saw it. Did I
see it? From inside this, over their wrists
in the tripes, they carefully removed
the wooden doll of a man and the wooden doll of a woman
maybe two inches tall, a tiny lacquered sun
and matching brass coin of a moon, and then
a child's-third-grade-version of a house
made out of pallid wax: a square of walls,
a pyramid roof, and a real smoking chimney.

Nominated by Mark Cox, Karla Kuban, J. Allyn Rosser, and Jim Simmerman

WOMEN DREAMING OF JERUSALEM

fiction by RACHEL KADISH

from STORY

THERE IS A SAYING among some in Jerusalem that when the messiah comes and our world merges with the next, the entire city will be replaced. This is because there are two Jerusalems. A Jerusalem on earth, and a Jerusalem on high.

At the end of days, Jerusalem on high will descend to earth, and replace the Jerusalem we know. We do not need to worry about getting lost in the new Jerusalem, we do not need to worry about stumbling over an unfamiliar curbstone on our way to the bakery or falling into the mouth of an unexpected well as we leave the office of the dentist. Jerusalem on high is a replica of Jerusalem on earth. Only different, in every way different.

In the kitchen of the Jerusalem Battered Women's Shelter, two women stand facing away from each other. They have no interest in speaking. They have been sent here in the afternoon heat by a sharp-faced Israeli social worker, who has instructed them to make up: They are not to leave this room until they have overcome their differences.

They are not interested in overcoming their differences. Tamar, Irina. Two straight-backed women, ushered into a windowless kitchen, a door shut behind them. They are interested in their anger. It holds their attention like nothing in memory, makes each of them tremble as she understands her own power to stare at the

110

other with undisguised contempt if she chooses, or to ignore the other with the barest shift of the eyes, wrists flickering disdain. The social worker tells them that here at the Shelter they must all get along, but these two women know better. They understand that they have left behind nights of starting with a pounding heart at every shift of their husband's sleep-heavy body; they have come to a place of safety. They do not have to be afraid of rages echoing in furniture-less rooms, a child standing in the bedroom doorway, roused by cries in the night. They are, finally, free. And this is the measure, the grain and weave of their new freedom: No one can stop them from hating each other.

From the Shelter's anteroom the Israeli social worker listens to the silence from the kitchen, rolls her eyes at the American volunteer sitting at the front desk. It is so difficult to get these immigrant women to behave in a reasonable way. You would think it would be the Sabra women, with their geometric jewelry and quick retorts, who would be the troublemakers. You would think it would be the new immigrants, stumbling on the syllables of an unfamiliar language, who would be the most cooperative.

But the Israeli women gossip together about the actors on the television. They trade recipes, exchange clothing from hastily packed suitcases, comb the hair of each other's children. It is the immigrants, the Ethiopians and the Russians, who refuse to speak.

For three days now, there has been nothing but spite and silence. The four Russian women folding laundry on one side of the main bedroom, jerking their children back by the elbows when they seem in danger of touching one of the Ethiopian children. Admonishing them in loud and wailing tones that leave the children inscrutable and moody. On the other side of the steam pipe, three Ethiopian women congregate, glancing over to the Russians from time to time and pronouncing soft phrases in Amharic.

The Shelter's five Israeli women have exhausted themselves trying to reason with the Ethiopians, the Russians, trying to lure Marina into speaking with Kessaye by asking them to cook supper together (the banging of pots under the cold stream of the sink, the slamming of the refrigerator door, and two separate suppers: a cold borscht, a spicy vegetable stew). Now some of the Israeli women amuse themselves with obstacles: They push beds closer together, leave only one pot available when a Russian and an Ethiopian both need to boil water. They fan each other and roll their eyes and wait to see how the

Ethiopians and Russians will maneuver without acknowledging each other's presence.

It started with the metal bowl Natasha put into the microwave, which sent smoke ringing up to the ceiling and left the microwave and part of one wall blackened by the time one of the Israeli women saw the flames.

Tali, the Israeli social worker, set the microwave down on her desk with a thump. The Israeli women looked at their feet and laughed, nudged each other. Tali did not laugh. "What, no one broke it?" she continued. "A microwave oven just breaks on its own, all by itself? Catches fire without anyone having touched it?" Harsh Hebrew syllables falling on still afternoon air. The Russians looked impassively at cracks in the walls, like gloomy children waiting out a teacher's tirade. The Ethiopian women's glances were birdlike, ricocheting off the walls, settling finally like shadows at their own feet. Tali shrugged her irritation. If this was the way they wanted it. All right, then. The microwave would not be replaced until the women raised the money.

One of the Ethiopian women stepped forward like a schoolgirl reciting, "Natasha broke," she said.

The insults came first, the silence after. The Ethiopian women were primitive savages, their children had lice. The Russians sweated even when their flesh was cold and clammy, they smelled and had hairy lips. Their legs were bigger than big trees.

"At least we don't jump out of windows," Natasha said, and smirked into the horror blossoming on Tamar's face. Tamar, whose mother had nearly become the third Ethiopian to step out a window on the absorption center's eighth floor. No one told them the cubicle had carried them so far above the rocky ground.

"At least we don't go crazy when they put us in elevators because we think someone is shutting us in a cage," Natasha continued, watching Tamar's soft brown eyes harden to silvery pebbles. "Flailing at the walls like animals."

"But our husbands," Tamar hissed, "aren't drunkards who can't tell day from night." The other Ethiopian women held their breath. They waited to see how the Russians would respond.

Natasha shrugged. "Our husbands at least aren't still swinging from the trees," she said.

"And all of our husbands beat us. So go to sleep already why don't you," one of the Israeli women called from her cot, her daughter curled sleepily beside her. "No, please Yael," another Israeli clapped her hands, "don't interrupt. This is just getting interesting. I want to hear us insult each other's husbands. Now that would be entertainment."

"My husband is too good for all of you," Natasha muttered.

The Ethiopian women watched the Russian women turn away, then retreat to their own cots at the far corner of the room.

"Ignorant savages," a Russian woman called over her shoulder.

The Israeli social worker had not expected an argument to continue so long. For three days she has observed in silence, only this afternoon announcing her conclusion to the American volunteer: Tamar and Irina are the best hope for making peace between the groups.

Tamar and Irina, standing in the kitchen like two implacable monuments.

The problem between the Ethiopians and the Russians, according to Tali, who works a finger into the corner of her eye beneath her eyeglasses, is not race. Nothing as simple as race, Tali explains to the American volunteer. The problem is this: The Russians are jealous, the Ethiopians are jealous. The Ethiopians are beloved by everyone. It's not that the Russians aren't welcome, didn't the country promise to take in all Jews. It's just that Israelis are getting a little tired. Immigrants are, no one likes to admit, a burden. The Russians are used to Soviet ways, they demand everything from the government. Things even Israelis don't have: jobs, benefits, services. And they come in with black market trailing behind them like a stink. The Ethiopians don't make demands. The Ethiopians, at least, are grateful.

"They don't know anything, you know," Tali says. "The Ethiopians. I hear the villages are dust and sticks. So of course they're jealous of the Russians—Russians, at least, know how to make do." She giggles into one hand, looks over her shoulder to be certain none of the Ethiopian women is listening. "Would you believe some of the Ethiopians have never seen a flush toilet?"

After a moment the social worker removes her eyeglasses and holds them in one hand, resting the other hand lightly on the metal desktop. "They all come to this country with such faith, don't they," she says. "They think this place is going to fix everything." She shrugs, then she pats her hand evenly on the desk: once, twice, three times. "No wonder they can't understand it when their husbands still beat them here."

113

In Jerusalem on high, the night sky is a deep blue that would sing with ripples were you to throw a stone toward the stars. In Jerusalem on high, a woman might lay down on hard earth with a stone for a pillow and sleep without waking. Jerusalem on high has steep hills and winding alleys. The setting sun lights the city the color of the crescent of your fingernail. That pink, that brown, that white.

Jerusalem on earth is the home of this season's most popular rock band. Its religious Jewish neighborhoods are expanding, as is its Chinese restaurant. The new mall on King George Street sells platform shoes and cellular telephones. There is a discount for soldiers. In East Jerusalem, a vendor selling lightbulbs and blue jeans calls out to a man in a white head-dress who stands puzzling over the ruins of a demolished house. "I know a place where your family can stay for a while," he says.

The Jerusalem Battered Women's Shelter occupies a secret location, it has already moved twice and may have to move again. The telephones at the Shelter are not equipped with the city's new callback service. Every now and then someone suggests cutting off telephone communication from the Shelter altogether: These women cannot be trusted, they will call the outside world and reveal their location in a desperate attempt to revisit love. But this policy has not been adopted. It is felt that it is enough to move the Shelter to unmarked locations from time to time, so those outside cannot find it, and those inside do not know precisely where they are located and cannot cause undue trouble.

There has been talk of adopting this policy for the State of Israel.

When Tamar and her family joined the group awaiting airlift in Addis Ababa, they had been walking for days. The evening was a pale orange, the clouds distant and weightless as they passed silently along the final stretch of the road into the city. A message had come to Tolleka and the other Jewish villages: Take what you can carry and walk to the south. The time is near. All those who were fit for the walk would leave at dawn.

Hours later, with the rising sun, the village took flight. Past low quiet hilltops, past sleeping Christian huts with empty doorways, the village was moving silently south, bundles and baskets in hand. Walking in the heat of day, walking into evening and night. Plumes of dust rose between the walkers so that at times Tamar could see only an occasional peering face. Somewhere ahead was Tamar's husband, but he did not

114

turn back to find her. Tamar moved ahead with the feather weight of her mother's hand on her shoulder. In the haze that enveloped her, she saw ghosts. She saw the rain Tolleka had prayed for that winter but which had never come. She saw her husband as he had been the first time he had spoken to her, when his voice bent toward her like a new branch. A skinny and broad-shouldered boy crouched on a narrow platform by the edge of a field of green shoots; his knees rested on the pile of stones he had gathered so that his slingshot might frighten away birds. Raising his head, he looked at Tamar for a pained instant, as if her slight form bore all the answers he might need. Tamar saw her grandmother, lame in one leg, who had stayed behind in Tolleka with the old men and the women in childbirth. When the women have recovered we will come, the old men had said, but Tamar's grandmother had shaken her head. I am old, she had answered Tamar's protests. The others will prepare for their journey. Before they have finished their preparations I will die. Now she repeated to Tamar softly: *Don't worry for us. If the bandits come for Tolleka we will manage. God will show a way, it has happened before.* Tamar walked through pillars of dust. She saw, before her eyes, Israel: a stretch of green, a rocky stream, shady steps of the Temple. A place to lay her head, rest her feet. A place to take her mother's hand from her shoulder, rinse the dirt from its fine creases, lift her face and see her husband's eyes filled with peace.

In Addis Ababa, the village settled into a cluster of gray apartments. Word spread daily from the embassy: not yet. Not today. Tamar rocked the coughing child of one of the families sharing their apartment. On the street below, the men stood squinting at traffic and spoke in low voices. Months passed, the word spread out from the walls of the embassy: not today. Tamar's mother sang to her: In Israel we will have a garden and a well, a beautiful home.

And then the night. The instructions needed no repeating. They were to come, now. They were to bring none of their belongings. A bus would carry them to the place. Everyone at the embassy was being taken, there was no time to wait for those who had not yet arrived in Addis Ababa.

At the airfield, thunderous noises shook the darkness. Tamar found herself amid an endless expanse of people: as thick as stars in the sky, more people than she had ever seen. The Jews of Ethiopia stood on the tarmac, dark liquid eyes searching the faces beside them as if seeing them for the first time, studying the familiar curve of a lip, the puckered scar above a cheekbone, the bright white of a numbered tag pasted on a long-creased forehead. Doing as others showed her, Tamar pasted a tag on her forehead and one on her mother's. The villages of Jews murmured, nestled close to each other. Words passed through them like spreading ripples: It was the Redemption. They were to be carried to Jerusalem. Someone had heard the blast of a ram's horn, it must be true. They would be the ones, out of all the generations they would be the ones, to greet the messiah. The whispers collided, rose and fell against crosscurrents of rumor: It was a trick, someone had heard that at last the rebels were coming to finish off the Jews. Gathering them in Addis Ababa had been a trap after all, not one of them would survive.

But here were pale-skinned men carrying papers, hurrying among them. When these men asked in halting Amharic for quiet, the crowd was silent; when they asked for village leaders, men stepped forward without a word. *It is time,* the whisper passed through Tamar. *They are taking us.* The village became a line, curving in silence toward another village behind it. Even the babies made no sound. A man making marks on a sheaf of papers stopped near Tamar. He was middle-aged and burly, his skin marked by sun and wind. He was gazing at the villages curving across the tarmac, stretching on to the horizon. The people filing one by one: young women carrying babies in slings, old men clutching the shoulders of their grown grandchildren. Lowering his papers slowly to his side, the man lifted a trembling hand in air. Strange words of wonder or benediction escaped his lips. Tamar could have opened her mouth then, she could have told the man in Amharic of visions in plumes of dust, nights of soft footfalls. Instead she held her head high with understanding. This was a man accustomed to speaking of such things every day: a man from the Promised Land.

In the airplane, they sat crowded together on the floor and waited for instructions from the men with the papers. They would be in Israel by sunrise, the men said through an interpreter. When the airplane pushed forward faster and faster and then lifted with terrifying labor into the sky, Tamar's mother breathed prayers of joy. The holy land. Tamar's mother had not believed until now that they were being taken to Jerusalem but now she knew it was true, because they moved up into the clouds until all was white. They were going to the city above, Jerusalem on high: Jerusalem wandering about the heavens like a kid straying peaceably from the flock at dusk.

116

On the airplane Tamar's husband detached himself from the group crowded against the window and made his way to her. "It is our greatest day," he told her. Tamar started at his touch on her shoulder. Uncertain, she looked up at him, into the awe spreading on his face. Her husband, who for not providing him with a child had accused her of not keeping the laws of purity, scheming against him. Outside the window, a sea of white rippled beneath a bright blue sky. Tamar's husband leaned over her, shy like a boy. His voice broke with pride. "I am Israel now," he said.

Later, Tamar joined her mother at the window. "Moshe has changed his name," she said, but her mother only gripped her arm and gestured toward the window. "Look how beautiful," her mother whispered.

Three months later, in their house outside the absorption center in Be'er Sheva, Tamar's mother would set her basket of laundry gently on the floor. "Everywhere, Jews." Tamar's mother laughed aloud, a delicate unfamiliar sound. "Everywhere Jews," she said.

Jews running for buses and standing in lines. Jews farming and marketing. Tamar shook her head in confusion. Who could have dreamed it: so many Jews with white skin.

Tamar's mother walked to the concrete doorstep of the house. She stepped out the door, walked through the weed-tangled dust of the yard, made a slow circle around the house. Tamar, sitting on a stool in the kitchen, watched from the windows as her mother passed behind the telephone pole, around the narrow tree in the alley between their house and the next, along the path separating their house from the sun-beaten road, back to the front door. Tamar's mother stepped gently into the house.

"It is not as I thought it would be," she said after a moment. "But it is enough." She patted her palms together softly, once and then again. "It is good to be here together."

That week Tamar lay awake at night listening to cars passing on the road outside their ground-floor window. She had dreamed again of that first day in the hotel-turned-absorption-center outside Tel Aviv. The hotel manager holding her mother in the corner of the elevator, her mother's arms pinned to her sides, as an interpreter insisted to Tamar. *Tell your mother we're not putting her in a cage.* An exhausted Israeli hotel manager, holding tight to the woman beating at him like a frightened bird so that she would not scratch him bloody. On the eighth floor of the hotel Tamar's mother retreated to a corner of the room, shuddering, her breath ragged, she refused to speak. Tamar, unfolding a blanket at the foot of a high bed, turned to see her mother gripping the sill of the window. Her mother, leaning forward as if to step from the window. Her mother, leaning forward as if to step from this sill toward her dreams. Voices shouting from the street below, wind combing through her hair.

Lying in bed, Tamar listened to the silence of the desert surrounding this Israeli city of Be'er Sheva. There was beauty somewhere in this country, of this Tamar was sure, but she had searched and had not found it. She saw only the still shadows of this plaster-walled house. She saw only that she was a woman from a foreign country lying motionless beside her husband in a bedroom by the side of a road, and the sigh that broke loose from the hollows of her bones frightened her because it was a foreign sound, sung in a foreign language, deserving of no shelter in this rock-strewn landscape.

Beside her Israel cried out in his sleep, sat up in bed. He fumbled for the wall switch and squinted at Tamar in the blinking fluorescent light. He looked at her as a buyer looks at fruit, carefully and with an eye to detail. He brushed his fingers against the dark spot on the thin part of Tamar's upper arm where he had gripped to cast her against the wall, so he would cast away this cursed country with its cursed bureaucracy.

He would cast it away. Days of air shimmying over parking lots with nothing but desert behind them, days of standing in lines with others so eager for approval they nodded at every Israeli they saw. The woman behind the desk said his Hebrew must improve before he would be ready for carpentry training and how many more lessons, how many more speeches about history and Judaism and proper behavior in this shouting shoving country, as if he had no culture and manners of his own, how many more must a man endure before he could leave this cursed city in the middle of nowhere? He was not an infant to be disciplined by a woman. He was not a child in a schoolyard. He was in control of his own destiny. This country with its cursed conjugations. At least in Ethiopia his enemy did not smile at him. He was a man. Not an immigrant. Language flowed from him like water from a rock. Here, social workers wearily repeated: *Come back next week, we'll see what we can do.*

Tamar felt the questioning touch on her arm and she understood why Israel had to strike her. She understood that he was not to blame for the rage that stiffened his gait some evenings so that she taught herself to stand opposite him without flinching, taught herself to en-

118

dure without a sound. Lying in bed beneath the shuddering of the light, Tamar understood that her husband was not to blame. It was not his fault. This country had defeated him.

Sitting cross-legged in bed, Israel rubbed the back of his neck. This is not what I thought we would be, he said.

At the Jerusalem Battered Women's Shelter, twelve women cut loose from their moorings sleep in one room. Their children lie alongside them on their low cots or curl together on blankets on the floor. During the days while volunteers play with the children, the women work in the kitchen or in the laundry room. They iron and fold and chop side by side, but some go about their work in fierce silence. For days it has been like this. The Ethiopian woman named Tamar stepping toward the Russian woman named Irina. Tamar reaching over Irina's shoulder for a frying pan. Drawing it past the Russian woman's face, Tamar pauses. A thought sings in her mind: She does not have to endure pain. She does not have to endure insult. She will not, any longer, endure anything.

Irina can hear her own breathing. The Ethiopian women are never like this, they always look away, their eyes take flight like swallows. Why is it that this one's wordless hatred bores into her, strikes her like steady blows falling in utter silence? Irina cannot help it: She stumbles backward.

Moving slowly, Tamar lowers the frying pan and crosses to the other side of the kitchen. The women standing beside Irina watch Tamar as she walks. When she has reached the other side of the room the murmur begins in Russian: Who does this one think she is, a princess?

Irina, chopping onions, is drained of all thought. She will not listen to the murmurs, she will not try to understand this Ethiopian woman. Why should she try to understand anything. Why should she, in this wearying and numbing country.

When the Russian volunteer at the absorption center had told Irina that she and her husband were the generation of the desert, she had decided that he was an arrogant fool.

"I myself came here from Moscow, so listen closely," the man said. "I don't have to give you advice, this advice I'm giving you for free."

Irina stroked the head of her son Boris, sitting heavy in her lap. She did not listen while the volunteer spoke of the Bible, told her of children of Israel wandering in the desert. Irina looked out the window at the tops of palm trees.

"Forty years they wandered, and they died there," the man's Russian was flecked with Hebrew phrases, his chin lifted in pride. "And do you know why?"

Irina, concentrating on the sound of palm fronds in wind.

The man said, "For their children. The Jews who escaped slavery died in that desert, they never saw the Promised Land. But they gave their own lives over to wandering, so that their children could live free in Israel."

Irina thought of Gorky.

"Being an immigrant won't be easy, you know. You won't know how to mail a letter here. You won't know how to buy food. Even your thoughts will be wrong." The man's voice rose in irritation, but Irina would not turn her head from the window. "When you come here you put yourself into the desert so that your children can someday be at home. What is foreign to you will be everyday to them. You will always be an immigrant, but they will be natives. And they will not understand you."

Irina thought of oranges.

Oranges on a fall afternoon, in honor of her wedding. Buttoning her into the white dress passed along from her grandmother, Irina's mother had cried. Irina was beautiful, so beautiful. She was their treasure, did Irina know that? The most lovely girl in Gorky. Pale brown hair in long smooth curls, such a straight nose, no one would guess she was Jewish. And Irina's light blue eyes, eyelashes long and so dark, eyelashes like soft dark feathers. *You are our joy,* Irina's mother said. Her father's touch on her arm was bashful as he walked her to the chuppah, he reached a hand to Irina's cheek and quickly turned away from her kiss, as if he could not bear for this unaccountably beautiful daughter to witness the depth of his love.

That night, alone in their own apartment, David had told her that her eyes were as clean and fresh as the ocean. He said her face was a perfect jewel. Her face was his pride, he had known he loved her the moment they met.

The first time David hit her it was sunset. The second, a morning gray with the threat of snow. She learned to turn her body so that his fists hit hip not belly, arm not rib. She learned the signs of his anger. It was not hard. In the morning she rose and prepared his breakfast on the gas stove, and they sat opposite each other at the kitchen table until they left for work. When he rose to leave, he kissed her hard on the mouth and reached, yawning, for the door.

She was a teacher of mathematics, the school only a twenty-minute bus ride into town, half an hour when she stopped on the way to leave the new baby with her mother. David worked as an engineer. In the evenings, they sat after dinner with friends and speculated into the night about where they would go when their visas were approved. They compared stories of foreign cities, counted the days until their next appointments with the immigration officials. "Criminals, all of them," David insisted, and there were nods around the table.

Most nights it was Simon who made the toasts, his girlfriend Asya who poured the vodka. "To America, to Israel, to Argentina or Spain. To wherever they'll let a wandering Jew go," Simon pronounced. "To Felix's nose, may it grow ever more mountainous." Felix laughed aloud, turned in profile for their admiration. "May Felix's nose be a monument that will outlive us all, may the KGB someday scale its peaks and plant a flag declaring it new territory for Soviet expansion." Simon dropped his voice to a stage whisper. "And may they fall dead of the shock when they understand here is one territory they can't expel the Jew from."

David rose, steadying himself on the table. An elaborate wave of the hand, begging Simon's pardon. "To my son Boris," David said. "And to my wife Irina, princess of Gorky." Irina hesitated, the others' glasses raised in air around her, but all she could see in David's smile was playfulness.

They tipped back their glasses with murmurs of *l'chaim*. Holding Boris asleep in her lap, Irina looked at David hopefully. David stood at the table, his voice trembling as he whispered, "To all of you, the best friends a man could have."

The evening David returned home with their visas, he danced Irina across the kitchen floor. They hugged Boris between them until the boy struggled to be let go. Then they set him on the floor and wheeled about the room, just the two of them, as if music filled the lamp-lit kitchen and flung their steps wide.

That night when David left the apartment he hugged Irina and Boris hard. "I'm going to buy our ticket," he said. "Our ticket to pave our way in Israel." And when he returned in the morning he carried wood. Slung over his shoulder, strapped to his back, and more to come by car that afternoon. He had all but emptied the bank account, he told Irina with a widening grin. Not a ruble left beyond what they needed to see them through to departure. Old Yakov had said that wood was the most valuable thing a person could bring to Israel, and he knew the way to ship it. "Forget cash, the government will hardly let you take any. And forget any ideas of selling your grandmother's silver when you get there. Israel is overflowing with immigrants looking to sell old junk. As for finding a job the day you arrive, don't think you'll be the first Russian engineer in Israel." Yakov had slapped a hand to the back of David's neck and leaned close. "What Israel needs is top-quality hardwood. Bring enough for someone to build a floor in a fine house, and demand top prices. You'll start up in fine style."

The wood was heavy and smooth, honey-colored with darker lines feathering gently up and down the wide planks. David had plans for a rich brown varnish, he knew how they would ensure that the wood reached Jerusalem without getting scratched. And then, what opportunities they could have. What freedom. Any thought in their heads, they could shout from the rooftops. They would stand atop that stack of wood and see the future, choose their path and begin.

That evening they piled the wood in their kitchen, stacked it the length of the linoleum floor and as high as their elbows, and David stood in the bedroom doorway while Irina hushed Boris to sleep. The unfinished wood drove splinters into Irina's skin when David laid her carefully down and she did not care, she held David's shoulders as if these were the two pillars of the world and they made love on top of the wide boards that could have fallen at any moment but only shifted and sighed, so that Irina thought of cool planks beneath someone's bare feet in Jerusalem, a firmament beneath her own and her husband's and her son's new lives.

In Jerusalem she learned to mop the floor of their new apartment with a rubber strip and let the water stream from drainage holes to splash sidewalks full of Jews. In Jerusalem she watched the trucks jolt up the street and had to remind herself that she must stay out of their paths just as in Gorky. They were driven by Jews, these trucks. Trucks, driven by Jews. Buses. In the supermarket, a Jewish clerk. At the street corner Jews throwing their hands at each other and shouting politics. Independence Day, an airshow, Jews streaming up into the sky, trailing puffs of blue and white. She was blinded with Jews, she stumbled on the street from staring. Their boldness overwhelmed her. She tried to describe it in the letters she wrote back to Felix in Gorky, to Simon and Asya in their new home in America. But she could not. Instead, she wrote of the markets. In Gorky the stores had only a few items, bare brown shelves, lines for butter and eggs. Here in Jerusalem, the open-air markets overflowed, and you could sample from every stall:

honeyed dates from one, pistachios from another, fresh strawberries from a third, and everywhere oranges. She carried Boris through the market twice a day, and each time she made a feast for him from stall to stall. A country overflowing with milk and honey, figs and halva and sweet sesame bread.

It will cost to revarnish the wood, the buyer said. He stepped around the planks carefully, and David followed him in a tight circle around the kitchen of their apartment. The wood occupied nearly all the space in the room; for weeks they had been eating their meals on it, Irina maneuvering around the boards to reach the stove. When David was not in the apartment, Irina had begun changing Boris' diapers on a cloth laid on the wood. This was the first buyer who had agreed even to come to the apartment. "I'll give you one thousand shekels," the man said. David hooted and held out the tray once again. The man took a cookie and ate it in one bite. "Do you think you're the only person in this city with a roomful of planks?" he said through his chewing. "Every Russian in the country thinks he's got the best varnish yet to come to the Middle East. Let me tell you, at that price you'll never sell it." Motioning Irina for his jacket, the buyer muttered, "At least the Ethiopians don't bring floors."

The man in the market chased her down the row of stands. Grabbing her arm, he marched her back to the vendors of pears and cookies. "Memorize this one's face," he told them. Irina stood mute. Four Jews with hair of steely black and gray catalogued her features from beneath wearily lowered lids. "What do you think, you can just eat a meal here for free every day?" The man shook Irina with every phrase. "Don't you have shame?" Irina felt the strength drain out of her body until there was nothing holding her up but the vendor's crushing fingers, no substance to her but Boris' weight on her hip. An old man with a basket of eggs, a woman with a string bag full of vegetables, slowed in the aisle. Irina heard the woman snicker, the man's grunt of agreement and she understood that she was no longer the person she had seen in the mirror that morning.

A thousand figures wove through the aisles of the marketplace, a thousand glimmers of light shot through the green thatch overhead. At the end of the market where bright planes of sunlight cut in from the street, the vendor released her arm. *Russian freeloader,* he called to her back. She tripped into the crowded sidewalk, stumbled toward the street. And then she realized. Dropping to one knee in the hurrying crowd, she held her son at arm's length. He waited, plump cheeks flushed, for her to speak. Kneeling on the sun-struck street with strangers rushing and dodging around her, Irina heard the droning voice of the man at the absorption center: Here in Jerusalem, she was not a proper mother. Here in Jerusalem, she was nothing. She had let them memorize her son's face.

"But that's just what I paid for the wood," David was saying to the Israeli. His mouth soft like a child's, his forehead furrowing. Irina rushed forward, stepped in front of the buyer. "Twice that," she insisted. "Twice." The buyer zipped his jacket, turned for the door. "I've got a family to support too," he said.

She argued with the buyer. She used every trick she knew, she threatened to tell everyone of his miserliness. The man shrugged. "Who told you you could get that kind of money in Israel for a wood floor," he said. She told him of her own serious medical condition, very serious. And of her elderly grandmother, come only this week from the Soviet Union, needing special shoes, a fragile woman. She told him, despairing, the truth: Of the books and clothing they needed, the food and the furniture, and when they settled she knew that the profit would cover hardly a month's expenses. David leaned heavily against the pile of wood. He said nothing. But when Irina shook hands with the buyer and the man closed the apartment door behind him, David looked up at her with a hatred she thought he had left behind in Gorky.

When Irina was brought to the Jerusalem Battered Women's Shelter, she knew that she could never live with David again. She knew that Boris would have to forget his father.

Standing silent in the kitchen of the Shelter, Irina can imagine a city of Jerusalem. It is a place of ringing footsteps, Irina's Jerusalem, where pistachios are piled high in barrels and wooden floors sigh beneath the whisper of a broom. It is a place which will purify all, redeem all. It is a place where there will be no need to think of expenses, of vodka, of voices clenched like fists.

In the main room of the Jerusalem Battered Women's Shelter, the contest is in full swing. One of the Israeli women is laughing, and this time even the Russians and Ethiopians listen attentively.

"That's nothing," the woman is saying. "*My* husband threw a can of athlete's foot spray at me." She spreads her arms wide, dips in a curtsy. "He even tried to set it on fire first."

"Bravo, Yossi," another woman says. Her face is flushed, she claps her hands. "Yossi gets the creativity award."

One of the Ethiopian women sets her infant on a bed. She hesitates. Then she speaks in Hebrew. "Do you think if we leave here we'll be safe?"

A Russian woman busies herself remaking a bed. Quietly she says, "I'll be safe. My husband isn't a degenerate. He's a bank teller."

The first Israeli woman to speak stands suddenly. She walks through the room, between women kneeling beside tubs of water to wash their hair, women lying across cots, the sun stretching toward them from the front room where the social worker sits. She passes the other Israeli women, the Ethiopians on one side of the heating pipe, the Russians on the other. "It's good to be with all of you," she says after a moment.

Some of the women turn away, others smile and reach out a hand to brush her shoulder.

"It's good," she says when she has completed her circle.

She is moving herself and her daughter to a small apartment of their own, in a location arranged by the Shelter. She is not going back to her husband. She says this is the first time she has seen that women can make it on their own. She is afraid, it will not be easy. But she is going to try this new life. She promises to invite them all to her new home as soon as she has it set up for company.

In the kitchen of the Jerusalem Shelter, two women. Irina, Tamar. A fly loops near the ceiling, skitters along the kitchen walls, neither woman makes a motion to swat it.

The Israeli social worker opens the kitchen door, peers in. Behind her, the American strains to see. "You two haven't settled this thing yet?" the social worker demands, tilting her head as the fly escapes past her through the door.

There is no word from the two women.

A shuffling of feet, the sound of Hebrew and English murmurs, the door is closed once again.

Irina does not want to leave the Shelter. The old men strolling outside, the students rushing for the bus, frighten her. Among them she will be anyone and no one. Without David, she will slip into the crowd and be lost.

Tamar stands perfectly still. She is listening to the beating of her heart in a foreign language: She no longer knows whether it is Hebrew or Amharic. Only that it is foreign. How can she summon her mother from Be'er Sheva as the social worker urges her? Her mother, who

125

told her that if Tamar were only patient and good, Israel's violence would disappear.

Irina Rosovsky sighs, a sigh so deep it surprises her as it escapes. Across the room Tamar Dapre laughs. Neither woman moves.

The Israeli social worker at the front desk lays down her nail file. Slowly she presses her fingertips to her temples. Sometimes she thinks she would like to leave this Shelter behind. Surely there are many other places to be, where one does not have to be so continually wary of danger.

But she knows she is needed here. She knows that caution is necessary at the Shelter. If there is anything she learned as a child, it is the necessity of caution. Don't read in such a dark room you'll strain your eyes. Don't cross the street without looking both ways. Don't run barefoot so close to the barbed-wire fence. Don't kick the can lying crushed in the gutter it might be a bomb. Her Hungarian grandfather clutching her hand as they reached the street corner, as if to anchor this precious granddaughter against a swift and unpredictable wind.

Sometimes the Israeli social worker cannot remember what city she lives in. Sometimes, nodding with drowsiness on the bus home from work, she imagines that she is in her grandfather's hiding place in Hungary, she is a child spending a war in a closet with no windows. Outside the windowless closet a village is carried away, floats among the fields, wanders about the Polish countryside in a ribbon of train cars and is gassed.

In the mornings the Israeli social worker buys milk for the Shelter's children, makes certain there are cleaning supplies and bars of soap, white cheese and soft bread. She leaves the grocery bags in the kitchen, purses her lips, settles at the desk with her coffee. And she listens to the immigrant women, who do not know that she understands Russian. Israel is a shithole. Israel has disappointed them. The Ethiopian women stand at the windows with an expression the social worker understands although she does not know a word of their language. All those years of persecution, all those years of suffering, must add up to something. Israel cannot after all be a country like any other, can it?

The social worker imagines the Shelter wandering above her as she passes through the city on her errands. She imagines it hangs etched against the clouds, patient, expectant. In her thoughts she tries to ignore it, outrun it, dodge it in the intricacies of alleyways, and when she turns to find it still drifting there, she shakes a fist to the sky.

126

She would like a house. It is not much to ask, after all. A house by the sea, a house with plants and a balcony, and windows in every room. Jerusalem wearies her; Netanya is where she wants to be. Her boyfriend Yair, back from army reserve, says that when he's through with his studies they can have their wedding at Gan HaPa'amon. He says he's tired of reserve duty, he's tired of patrols in the territories. He'd rather be studying engineering. He says there's no excuse for holding on to other people's fields and orchards anymore. No freedom in a demolished house. Let them give the damn land for peace, who wants land at such a cost?

He wants to live in a house by the sea with her. He wants to paint the walls a fresh white. He wants to buy a floor of imported wood, lay his mattress on it and sleep a dreamless sleep.

In the Jerusalem Battered Women's Shelter, some of the Israeli women are at it again. "What's the worst Ehud ever did to you?" one asks another. "Come on, try to remember, what's the craziest thing he ever did." She adds her own story for encouragement. "Once Yakov picked up the challah board. To go after me with it. And he chased me covered in flour."

"Once I made Ehud so angry he ran me into the yard," a blonde-haired woman with rings under her eyes speaks up hesitantly. "Without his clothes on. He gave the neighbors a show."

"Were they impressed?" Penina asks dryly from her cot.

"Not really. He's not much to look at." As soon as she has spoken the blonde-haired woman claps a hand over her mouth. Laughter bursts out from all around her, and after a few seconds she joins in, her shoulders shaking soundlessly.

In the Shelter's front office, the American volunteer grimaces. She thinks these Israeli women ought to show some deference in light of the seriousness of their own predicament. She has seen these women, after all, as they arrive at the Shelter: lips bloodied, ribs dark with bruises, eyes blackened and swollen.

And now they laugh about it. Isn't it disrespectful, the American wonders, to treat the past so lightly? But she has promised herself that here in this fiercely beautiful Jerusalem she will be open to everything she sees, so she tries not to let her disapproval show.

In the kitchen of the Jerusalem Battered Women's Shelter, two women cut loose from their moorings listen to each other's breathing. It has been this way for a long time. They do not speak. If they turn to look at each other they will have to see from the fading bruises on each other's bodies that they are not in Jerusalem on high but rather in Jerusalem on earth, and they will know that they must now give up on their bitterness and make compromises. It passes through both of their minds that they could after all do this. That they will. That they might just in a moment turn, and greet each other by name.

But to turn is to concede everything. To shed the mantle of their suffering and to acknowledge that no one will ever appreciate what they have endured.

It is an impossible choice. How can anyone ask it of them. How can anyone who does not understand dare to demand they turn their backs on all that has passed and face each other, with stumbling speech and still-grieving hearts.

The thing about Jerusalem on high is this: Is it exactly like Jerusalem on earth. But there are no people. Or when there are people, they appear only for an instant, figures flickering across the horizon and then gone. Cisterns echo faintly the sound of the breeze, stones lie on the hard ground awaiting weary heads. But no one comes. No one can live in Jerusalem on high for very long. One can dream the city forever, but when one arrives one finds that something is not right. One finds something quite unexpected. The weight of one's own bundle of dreams has pulled the city to earth once again.

Jerusalem on high is a city lonely for its people. It longs for them just as they long for their beloved home. It recites their faces by heart just as they recite the names of its streets and corridors. It knows the dreams they dream in Amharic and in Russian. In English and Ladino and Yiddish. In Hebrew. In Arabic.

Jerusalem on high wanders patiently among the clouds. The city says prayers. The city dreams.

Tamar, facing the smoke-stained kitchen wall, imagines that this Russian woman behind her might know how to explain to a mother trembling with confusion. She might perhaps know how to explain to Tamar's mother that Tamar has decided to find an apartment for the two of them. How to explain that Tamar has decided to leave her husband behind.

Irina passes a hand across an overturned soup pot, fingers the knife-marred counter. She wonders whether this straight-backed woman with her marvelous stillness might know what future this city will hold for her son.

They delay turning, each waiting for the other to speak. Tamar waits for Irina, Irina for Tamar. Surely the other will scuffle her feet on the tile floor, will turn suddenly and say *you have suffered, I see now that you have suffered.*

But at this moment in this silent kitchen, their anger is their most priceless, their only, possession. In it, they know who they are. Standing with their backs to each other, they know each other as no one else does. Each of them makes the other real, each of them anchors the other and keeps her from becoming a slip in the wind. Standing with their backs to each other, they are miracles: tears burning in their eyes, water from a rock. In their throats, words trembling unspoken. They are not the people of the desert. They are the people who stand on the brink of the Promised Land, and they will not be disappointed.

Nominated by Story *and Joyce Carol Oates*

ATOMIC BRIDE

by THOMAS SAYERS ELLIS

from PLOUGHSHARES

For Andre Foxxe

A good show
Starts in the
Dressing room

And works its way
To the stage.
Close the door,

Andre's cross-
dressing, what
A drag. All

The world loves
A bride, something
About those gowns.

A good wedding
Starts in the
Department store

And works its way
Into the photo album.
Close the door,

Andre's tying
The knot, what
A drag. Isn't he

Lovely? All
The world loves
A bachelor, some-

thing about glamour
& glitz, white
Shirts, lawsuits.

A good dog
Starts in the yard
And works its way

Into da house.
Close your eyes,
Andre's wide open.

One freak of the week
Per night, what
A drag. Isn't

He lovely? All
The world loves
A nuclear family,

Something about
A suburban home,
Chaos in order.

A good bride starts
In the laboratory
And works his way

To the church.
Close the door,
Andre's thinking

Things over, what
A drag. Isn't
He lovely? All

The world loves
A divorce, something
About broken vows.

A good war starts
In the courtroom
And works its way

To the album cover.
Close the door,
Andre's swearing in,

What a drag.
Isn't he lovely? All
The world loves

A star witness,
Something about
Cross-examination.

A good drug starts
In Washington
And works its way

To the dancefloor.
Close the door,
Andre's strungout,

What a drag,
Isn't he lovely? All
The world loves

Rhythm guitar,
Something about
Those warm chords.

A good skeleton
Starts in the closet
And works its way

To the top of the charts.
Start the organ.
Andre's on his way

Down the aisle,
Alone, what an encore. All
The world loves

An explosive ending.
Go ahead Andre,
Toss the bouquet.

Nominated by Jim Simmerman

GIVE THE MILLIONAIRE A DRINK

fiction by MIKE NEWIRTH

from THE BAFFLER

THEY COME FROM ALL over to the town of East Hampton, this celebrated place at the end of the island. Private jets shoot off hourly from Dallas and L.A., the chilled Porsches and Saabs arrive from Montclair and Rye, matron busloads depart the Park Avenue swelter in a huff of opera and facials, and they come packed five to a Camaro from Woodside and Asbury Park. They crowd the same streets gridded by Dutch burghers of centuries past, fill the landscape like Baptists in a church, and with their tanned arms thrown up and their eyes upon their lord they sing of the coin of the realm, of padded pockets, of the alchemical wish: *I can buy this.* I can pull things near to me, I levitate as you descend, I will pile the stuff of cash so high as to keep me forever out of my grave. . . .

Nobody could guess why the internationally known supermodel decided to piss in the bar sink at the Apex Grill. Two a.m., the hour most socially permissible for decadent stunts, barroom crowded with angular bodies and faces gone shiny with cosmopolitans and blue martinis, called for again and again with the same stubby wave. The bartender, blurred bulk in white shirt and French apron, watched idly as the tall woman with the charred gold mop of hair crawled up on top of the bar, nailed hand rubbing the makeup from her face, her smiling mouth the long slot of a cigarette machine. As she stepped to the chrome rails and rucked up her dress, silk scraping silk, there were shrieks and the

134

sound of a man slapping himself to vulgar effect, and the bartender remembered an afternoon decades past, lying in bed with his first girlfriend, she sashaying above him in his boxer shorts, giggling, this as piss of drink sprays from the center of that trained and shaped and photographed body, and the bar sink fills like a cistern.

After, a distinguished anesthesiologist, lean, leathery, hair varnished like a helmet, holds up a credit card. "Buy the lovely lady whatever she wants to drink." Cheers, applause, the bartender straightens up and, moving so slowly through time, reaches for the cassis and champagne.

His date, a twenty-year-old with an unblemished accusing Andover face: "What is your fucking *problem.*"

"You need to be more celebratory." His gaze locked to the swaying flushed model, all the swelled faces in the long mirror, cell phone before him on the bar like a gray fish. "I already *told* you what you're here for."

Slow late afternoon: stray cats prowl the village dumpsters. All the good people—those drowning in that hearty moral sea of accumulated wealth—are stretched out at the gleaming beach. A famous comic actor known for his films of family entertainment (homespun wisdom interspersed with hilarious belches and pratfalls), and for his witty endorsements of a fine tortilla chip, walks up and down the main street carrying a large bottle of vodka. His fishing vest and floppy hat add a near-tint of gentility. The actor's eyes resemble cathode ray tubes. When his cell phone rings he shifts the bottle and flips it open, and keeps on walking. He speaks with the air that is trapped for years at the bottom of a western mine.

Three teenage girls stand before the window of a crowded shop. Stylish clothes for women, all and entirely in the color of white. Frocks and gowns and underwear, all the same hue of elegance and emptiness, the blankness of a frame, slices of nothing. Beside those white garments, the girls throb in their hiphuggers and tight striped shirts, slurping on pacifiers. Sixteen and already their faces engraved with a Russian century of bored malaise. "There is nothing I wouldn't do to spite my father," one says.

"If only I wasn't *here,*" says another.

Tea is served on the veranda of the American Hotel to a rowdy party of options traders. Oh, they've done all the good drugs, been tapped for entrance at many velvet ropes, they've fucked all the slim blonde women (and then watched, snifters in hand, as all the women melted together in the foamy hot tub on the moonlit deck, every last gawky white boy fantasy fulfilled categorically). But now the intrusion of china cups and pale sandwiches flusters their paid-for vacation hoohrah. Their practiced repose comes apart, up through the mucus of the body's past rise the fumbling second-string ballplayers and zitty homeroom monitors. "This is *bogus*," Troy says.

"Hey. Waitress. Can't you bring us some *port*, or something?" calls out Ken, twisting for assurance his gold-flashing diver's watch.

"The bar will not be open until six, sir," she replies.

"Bitch," says Trevor, knocking a teacup off the rail.

At the Telephone Mama, the choice nightspot of this season, the one the Jersey tourists and Astoria orthodontists are *simply* better off not even knowing about, the line snakes out into the parking lot: bare thighs of celebrant applicants brushed, bruised, by the slow flow of fancy rolling metal. Who are these people? Shaky background zombies from *Night of the Flesh-Eating Corporate Raiders*, the never-made Corman salute to the rapacious 1980s? The men fluff their chest hair through the slits of silk shirts, if they have it; the smooth-skinned blondies, those delicate boys with pursed mouths disparaging, they are either blood-leached and serious old money, or else homosexual. Reaching the door, three black kids from Valley Stream are turned away: "We have a dress code," says the enormous doorman. Through the door thumps a vintage Funkadelic side; inside the young women twitch like wraiths on the dance floor, white shawls slipping from their shoulders and breasts. Cursing, the blacks drive off into the night.

In the narrow aisles of the town supermarket: a wealthy man in his fifties argues with his girlfriend, half his age. She is wearing a thong bikini, and her tanned skin is like fine fudge or mink: a thing sheiks might buy by the yard. When he sweeps his arm, his IWC chronometer and gold bracelet tick, clanking: his voice is low, savaging. She flips her ashy hair precisely, cloyingly. "I won't go," she says. "Not unless André goes." At the cash register a townie—belly, navel, nipples distended, jaw shame-slacked, oily hair—hands over a sheaf of food stamps. The proper patrons line up elsewhere, piling their soda crackers and Pellegrino up on the other conveyor, as if something were catching.

That well-known actor loiters in the Rexall, chatting discretely with the pharmacists. He leaves, buying quantities of cough drops and breath mints. In five years, perforated liver shipping poison to his brain, he'll have taken to passing out candy from his pockets to alarmed children on the streets.

136

An internationally famous woman, even locally a celebrity of some substance, watches the washed-up wetbrain cross the street from within the armored capsule of her Range Rover. She feels towards him a chundering mix of contempt and fear: he's a has-been, for sure, reduced to kiddy pablum and shilling for snacks, but once he was actually a Hollywood player, the realest kind. She's on top now, the ultimate hostess, a lasery visionary of taste and purchases and decor, with magazines and recipe clubs and catalogs, a carpet-bombing of commerce spread across the hick heartland; but, you know, she doesn't really *do* anything which any Miss Baltimore Homemaker of 1961 could not improve upon. Behind the flat flawless heatproof glass of the vehicle, her smile is pulled into place by hydraulics, exposed teeth carved from a single block of titanium. But beyond it she's shaking as though from a palsy. Recently, one of the dowagers she courted had whispered to her the cruel, glittering news—"for your own good, dear," the withered bitch had said—that her daughter, that hard-cheeked rider of deceit and ponies, was sleeping with the contractor on her Sag Harbor cottage, with whom, truthfully (and known to none other), *she* had last slept not two weeks previous. Unlikely, but it *could* get around. Ten thousand dollars had gone towards quieting the tale of baby ducks (briefly needed for a photo shoot) murdered beneath the wheels of her vehicle. This perfect woman, no one guesses at her days of shudder and terror, what she endures to prop up this exemplary life of buying and placing. *Cross me and die,* this famous hostess thinks, waiting for the light to change.

July glides into August, the frictionless summer everlasting. Everybody is from England or into junk bonds or forcing themselves to vomit or working on a novel or bisexual temporarily. More telephones are stolen out of Range Rovers. Most of the dogs receive grooming. Some of the townies get laid.

It is still 2 a.m. at the Apex Grill. The supermodel lurches in, shaky, bad news. Her miniskirt offers up her sintered ass. Nobody is surprised by this, no one notices. Bound to her shoulders is the soft black leather Prada knapsack which every woman here was required on peril of her soul to purchase for this summer. The Prada bags, shapeless, hang from the backs of the women like elegant hide pupae. But the model has replaced the Prada bag's signature gold-plated zipper ornament with a Tiffany keychain, a miniature infant's bottle in platinum. This particular Prada bag was made in Malaysia, in a factory thrown up in an enormous corrugated shed, hand-stitched by women whose arms bear curing burns and knife scars, women with hair coarse as rope and stalled faces, and some weeks later the model purchased it at the East Hampton Saddlery for $570 because her agent and *Country* magazine had touted it as the summer's prime accessory, and of course, they were right.

"I would like a . . . cosmopolitan," she whispers to the bartender. Her mind has been expertly muted to a soft blue Xanax blur. Beneath it, though, is something real: a throbbing kodachrome snapshot of the night, five years before, she sucked a photographer, somewhere in the Montauk dunes. Two months later she had a shoot in *Interview*, so it was undoubtedly worth it, she knows, but still . . . The memory's buzz will outlast her looks and career. The bartender sets a cocktail glass before her and spills out her drink. Her fingers flutter like moths on the hard stem of the glass.

The bartender slips further down his bar, wiping spills with a white dinner napkin. He pauses before a man and two women sagged with drink and exhaustion, but the man waves him away. "We still have our ménage to look forward to," says the black woman with grayed skin and dropping gold jewelry.

"Yes," the man agrees. "If only for its own sake."

"Oh, you think that's the important thing," says the other woman. She looks close to forty, as do they all.

"What I think," he says, "is it is something we are going to do. Any other definition is just somebody being intentionally morbid and obtuse, *Nancy*."

"Pay up," says the first woman.

"Have another drink," says the man, words leaking out through his puffy face. "Let the impatience build a little."

"Is your head up your ass or what," the bartender says, quietly, to the barback, a pocked, stumbling local boy, who has let the ice tub deplete to meltings. "Fill that up and then go home. Get out of my sight."

He's not really a good person, this bartender.

But this is his life, East Hampton to Aspen and back, selling the best legal drug in America to the rich folk, enabling their little scenes and gaudy reckless purchasing, all that passes for history these days. His secret knowledge tends to weigh him down: that the dollar's what it's all about, and this is just a dance of fancy smoke and notions.

Out in the parking lot, watched only by the stars and valet, that sly pretty Andover girl wanders in slow, dazed circles. The anesthesiolo-

138

gist is long gone, back to Scarsdale. Tonight there was a late supper with a stocky, rapacious bond trader, a manic transplant from Kansas for whom all the dollars made and spent were their own nonstop coitus. They went to Apex, where his waved credit card produced champagne. She listened to his mouth, saying things like, "Damn shit, I sure do love this Dom." He followed her into the toilet. "Let's ignite ourselves," holding out the vial of cocaine. Then went right up her *skirt,* $30 panties split down the middle, her forearms bruised where he planted her against the hot air blower. The entrance of three dazed Chanel matrons gave her a chance to run. "*What?*" he said behind her. "Bitch," as she slipped coins into the phone. She cries, wondering only what, specifically, she'd expected—the bastard dropped two hundreds on dinner, to say nothing of the drugs and bar tabs, the cost of it all, she knows at what sum the numbers add up—cries nonetheless, and waits for her taxi to come.

Nominated by The Baffler

WHAT THE WATER KNOWS

by SAM HAMILL

from DESTINATION ZERO: POEMS 1970–1995 (White Pine Press)

What the mouth sings, the soul must learn to forgive.
A rat's as moral as a monk in the eyes of the real world.
Still, the heart is a river
pouring from itself, a river that cannot be crossed.

It opens on a bay
and turns back upon itself as the tide comes in,
it carries the cry of the loon and the salts
of the unutterably human.

A distant eagle enters the mouth of a river
salmon no longer run and his wide wings glide
upstream until he disappears
into the nothing from which he came. Only the thought remains.

Lacking the eagle's cunning or the wisdom of the sparrow,
where shall I turn, drowning in sorrow?
Who will know what the trees know, the spidery patience
of young maple or what the willows confess?

Let me be water. The heart pours out in waves.
Listen to what the water says.
Wind, be a friend.
There's nothing I couldn't forgive.

Nominated by Jane Hirshfield and Arthur Sze

JESSICA, THE HOUND & THE CASKET TRADE

by THOMAS LYNCH

from WITNESS

> *She went to a long-established, "reputable" undertaker. Seeking to save the widow expense, she chose the cheapest redwood casket in the establishment and was quoted a low price. Later, the salesman called her back to say the brother-in-law was too tall to fit into this casket, she would have to take the one that cost $100 more. When my friend objected, the salesman said, "Oh, all right, we'll use the redwood one, but we'll have to cut off his feet."*
> —Jessica Mitford, *The American Way of Death*

T HE SAME MORTICIAN who once said he'd rather give away caskets than take advantage of someone in grief later hung billboards out by the interstate—a bosomy teenager in a white bikini over which it read *Better Bodies by Bixby* (not the real name) and the phone numbers for his several metro locations.

I offer this in support of the claim that there are good days and there are bad days.

No less could be said for many of the greats.

I'm thinking of Hemingway's take on Pound when he said, "Ezra was right half the time, and when he was wrong, he was so wrong you were never in any doubt of it." But ought we be kept from "The River-Merchant's Wife" by his mistaken politics? Should outrage silence the sublime?

The same may be asked of Mr. Bixby's two memorable utterances.

Or, as a priest I've long admired once said, "Prophesy, like poetry, is a part-time job—the rest of the time they were only trying to keep their feet out of their mouths." I suppose he was trying to tell me something.

Indeed, mine is an occupation that requires two feet firmly on the ground, less for balance, I often think, than to keep one or the other from angling toward its true home in my craw.

I sell caskets and embalm bodies and direct funerals.

Pollsters find among the general public a huge ambivalence about funeral directors. "I hope you'll understand it if I never want to see you again," the most satisfied among my customers will say. I understand.

And most of the citizenry, stopped on the street, would agree that funeral directors are mainly crooks, "except for mine . . . " they just as predictably add. "The one who did my (insert primary relation) was really helpful, really cared, treated us like family."

This tendency to abhor the general class while approving of the particular member is among the great human prerogatives—as true of clergy and senators as it is of teachers and physicians. Much the same could be said of time: "Life sucks," we say, "but there was this moment . . . " Or of racial types: "Some of my best friends are (insert minority) . . . " Or of the other "(Insert sex)! You can't live with them and you can't live without them!"

Of course, there are certain members of the subspecies—I'm thinking lawyers, politicians, revenue agents—who are, in general and in particular, beyond redemption and we like it that way. "The devil you know's better than the one you don't . . . " is the best we can say about politicians. And who among us wants a "nice" divorce attorney or has even one fond memory involving a tax man? Really, now.

But back to caskets and bodies and funerals.

When it comes to caskets I'm very careful. I don't tell folks what they should or shouldn't do. It's bad form and worse for business. I tell them I don't have any that will get them into heaven or keep them out. There's none that turns a prince into a frog or, regrettably, vice-versa. There isn't a casket that compensates for neglect nor one that hides true love, honorable conduct or affection.

If worth can be measured by what they do, it might help to figure out what caskets "do" in the inanimate object sense of the verb.

How many here are thinking HANDLES? When someone dies, we try to get a handle on it. This is because dead folks don't move. I'm not making this part up. Next time someone in your house quits breathing, ask him to get up and answer the phone or maybe get you some ice water or let the cat out the back door. He won't budge. It's because he's dead.

There was a time when it was easier to change caves than to drag the dead guy out. Now it's not so easy. There's the post office, the utilities, the closing costs. Now we have to remove the dead. The sooner the better is the rule of thumb, though it's not the thumb that will make this known.

This was a dour and awful chore, moving the dead from place to place. And like most chores, it was left to women to do. Later, it was discovered to be a high honor—to bear the pall as a liturgical role required a special place in the procession, special conduct and often a really special outfit. When hauling the dead hither and yon became less the chore and more an honor, men took it over with enthusiasm.

In this it resembles the history of the universe. Much the same happened with protecting against the marauding hordes, the provision of meaty protein sources, and more recently, in certain highly specialized and intricate evolutions of food preparation and child care.

If you think women were at least participant and perhaps instrumental in the discovery of these honors, you might better keep such suspicions to yourself. These are not good days to think such thoughts.

But I stray again. Back to business.

Another thing you'll see most every casket doing is being horizontal. This is because folks that make them have taken seriously the demonstrated preference of our species to do it on the level. Oh, sure—it can be done standing up or in a car or even upside down. But most everyone goes looking for something flat. Probably this can be attributed to gravity or physics or fatigue.

So horizontal things that can be carried—to these basic properties, we could add a third: it should be sturdy enough for a few hundred pounds. I'm glad that it's not from personal experience that I say that nothing takes the steam out of a good funeral so much as the bottom falling out.

And how many of you haven't heard of this happening?

A word on the words we're most familiar with. *Coffins* are the narrow, octagonal fellows—mostly wooden, nicely corresponding to the shape of the human form before the advent of the junk food era. There are top and bottom, and the screws that fasten the one to the other are often ornamental. Some have handles, some do not, but all can be carried. The lids can be opened and closed at will.

Caskets are more rectangular and the lids are hinged and the body can be both carried and laid out in them. Other than shape, coffins and caskets are pretty much the same. They've been made of wood and metal and glass and ceramics and plastics and cement and the dear knows what else. Both are made in a range of prices.

But *casket* suggests something beyond basic utility, something about the contents of the box. The implication is that it contains something precious: heirlooms, jewels, old love letters, remnants and icons of something dear.

So casket is to coffin as tomb is to cave, grave is to hole in the ground, pyre is to bonfire. You get the drift? Or as, for example, eulogy is to speech, elegy to poem, or home is to house or husband to man. I love this part, I get carried away.

But the point is a *casket* presumes something about what goes in it. It presumes the dead body is important to someone. For some this will seem like stating the obvious. For others, I'm guessing, maybe not.

But when buildings are bombed or planes fall from the sky, or wars are won or lost, the bodies of the dead are really important. We want them back to let them go again—on our terms, at our pace, to say you may not leave without permission, forgiveness, our respects—to say we want our chance to say good-bye.

Both coffins and caskets are boxes for the dead. Both are utterly suitable to the task. Both cost more than most other boxes.

It's because of the bodies we put inside them. The bodies of mothers and fathers and sons, daughters and sisters and brothers and friends, the ones we knew and loved or knew and hated, or hardly knew at all, but know someone who knew them and who is left to grieve.

In 1906, John Hillenbrand, the son of a German immigrant, bought the failing Batesville Coffin Company in the southeastern Indiana town of the same name. Following the form of the transportation industry, he moved from a primarily wooden product to products of metal that would seal against the elements. *Permanence* and *protection* were concepts that Batesville marketed successfully during and after a pair of World Wars in which men were being sent home in government boxes. The same wars taught different lessons to the British for whom the sight of their burial grounds desecrated by bombs at intervals throughout the first half-century suggested permanence and protection were courtesies they could no longer guarantee to the dead. Hence the near total preference for cremation there.

Earth burial is practiced by "safe" societies and by settled ones. It presumes the dead will be left their little acre and that the living will be around to tend the graves. In such climates any fantasies of permanence and protection thrive. And the cremation rate in North America has risen in direct relation to the demographics and geographics of mobility and fear and the ever more efficient technologies of destruction.

The idea that a casket should be sealed against air and moisture is important to many families. To others it means nothing. They are both right. No one need explain why it doesn't matter. No one need explain why it does. But Batesville, thinking that it might, engineered the first "sealed" casket with a gasket in the 1940s and made it available in metal caskets in every price range from the .20 gauge steels to the coppers and bronzes. One of the things they learned is that ninety-six percent of the human race would fit in a casket with interior dimensions of twenty-five inches and exterior dimensions of six-foot, six-inches.

Once they had the size figured out and what it was that people wanted in a casket—protection and permanence—then the rest was more or less the history of how the Hillenbrand brothers managed to make more and sell more than any of their competition. And they have. You see them in the movies, on the evening news being carried in and out of churches, at gravesides, being taken from hearses. If someone's in a casket in North America chances are better than even it's a Batesville.

We show twenty-some caskets to pick from. They're samples only. There are plenty more we can get within a matter of hours. What I carry in blue, my brother Tim, in the next town, carries in pink. What I have tailored, Tim carries shirred. He carries one with *The Last Supper* on it. I've got one with the *Pietá*. One of his has roses on the handles. One of mine has sheaves of wheat.

You name it. We've got it. We aim to please.

We have a cardboard box (of a kind used for larger appliances) for seventy-nine dollars. We also have a mahogany box (of a kind used for Kennedy and Nixon and Onassis) for nearly eight grand. Both can be carried and buried and burned. Both will accommodate all but the tallest or widest citizens, for whom, alas, as in life, the selection narrows. And both are available to any customer who can pay the price.

146

Because a lot of us tend to avoid the extremes, regardless of how we elect to define them, we show a wide range of caskets in between and it would look on a chart like one of those bell curves: with the most in the middle and the least at either end. Thus, we show three oak caskets and only one mahogany, a bronze, a copper, a stainless steel, and six or seven regular steels of various gauges or thicknesses. We show a cherry, a maple, two poplars, an ash, a pine and a particle board and the cardboard box. The linings are velvet or crepe or linen or satin, in all different colors, tufted or ruffled or tailored plain. You get pretty much what you pay for here.

I should probably fess up that we buy these caskets for less than we sell them for—a fact uncovered by one of our local TV news personalities, who called himself the News Hound, and who was, apparently, untutored in the economic intrigues of wholesale and retail. It was this same News Hound who did an exposé on Girl Scout cookie sales—how some of the money doesn't go to the girls at all, but to the national office where it was used to pay the salaries of "staff."

It was a well-worn trail the News Hound was sniffing—a trail blazed most profitably by Jessica Mitford, who came to the best-selling if not exactly original conclusion that the bereaved customer is in a bad bargaining position. When you've got a dead body on your hands it's hard to shop around. It's hard to shop for lawyers when you're on the lam, or doctors when your appendix is inflamed. It's not the kind of thing you let out to bids.

Lately there has been a great push toward "pre-arrangement." Everyone who's anyone seems to approve. The funeral directors figure it's money in the bank. The insurance people love it since most of the funding is done through insurance. The late Jessica, the former News Hound, the anti-extravagance crowd—they all reckon it is all for the best, to make such decisions when heads are cool and hearts are unencumbered by grief and guilt. There's this hopeful fantasy that by pre-arranging the funeral, one might be able to pre-feel the feelings, you know, get a jump on the anger and the fear and the helplessness. It's as modern as planned parenthood and pre-nuptial agreements and as useless, however tidy it may be about the finances, when it comes to the feelings involved.

And we are uniformly advised "not to be a burden to our children." This is the other oft-cited *bonne raison* for making your final arrangements in advance—to spare them the horror and pain of having to do business with someone like me.

147

But if we are not to be a burden to our children, then to whom? The government? The church? The taxpayers? Whom? Were they not a burden to us—our children? And didn't the management of that burden make us feel alive and loved and helpless and capable?

And if the planning of a funeral is so horribly burdensome, so fraught with possible abuses and gloom, why should an arthritic septuagenarian with blurred vision and some hearing loss be sent to the front to do battle with the undertaker instead of the forty-something heirs-apparent with their power suits and web browsers and cellular phones? Are they not far better outfitted to the task? Is it not their inheritance we're spending here? Are these not decisions they will be living with?

Maybe their parents do not trust them to do the job properly.

Maybe they shouldn't.

Maybe they should.

The day I came to Milford, Russ Read started pre-arranging his funeral. I was getting my hair cut when I first met him. He was a massive man still, in his fifties, six-foot-something and four hundred pounds. He'd had, in his youth, a spectacular career playing college and professional football. His reputation had preceded him. He was a "character"—known in these parts for outrageous and libertine behavior. Like the Sunday he sold a Ford coupe off the used-car lot uptown, taking a cash deposit of a thousand dollars and telling the poor customer to "come by in the morning when the office is open" for the keys and paperwork. That Russ was not employed by the car dealer— a devout Methodist who kept holy his Sabbaths—did not come to light before the money had been spent on sirloins and cigars and round after round of drinks for the patrons of Ye Olde Hotel—visiting matrons from the Eastern Star, in town with their husbands for a regional confab. Or the time a neighbor's yelping poodle—a dog disliked by everyone in earshot—was found shot one afternoon during Russ' nap time. The neighbor started screaming at one of Russ' boys over the back fence, " . . . when I get my hands on your father!" Awakened by the fracas, Russ appeared at the upstairs window and calmly promised, "I'll be right down, Ben." He came down in his paisley dressing gown, decked the neighbor with a swift left hook, instructed his son to bury "that dead mutt" and went back upstairs to finish his nap. Halloween was Russ' favorite holiday which he celebrated in more or less pre-Christian fashion, dressing himself up like a Celtic warrior, with an

148

antlered helmet and mighty sword which, along with his ponderous bulk and black beard and booming voice, would scare the bejaysus out of the wee trick-or-treaters who nonetheless were drawn to his porch by stories of full-sized candy bars sometimes wrapped in five-dollar bills. Russ Read was, in all ways, bigger than life so that the hyperbole that attended the gossip about him was like the talk of heroes in the ancient Hibernian epics—Cuchulainn and Deirdre and Queen Maeve, who were given to warp-spasms, wild couplings, and wondrous appetites.

When he first confronted me in the barber's chair, he all but blotted out the sun behind him.

"You're the new Digger O'Dell I take it."

It was the black suit, the wing tips, the gray striped tie.

"Well, you're never getting your mitts on my body!" he challenged.

The barber stepped back to busy himself among the talcums and clippers, uncertain of the direction the conversation might take.

I considered the size of the man before me—the ponderous bulk of him, the breathtaking mass of him—and tried to imagine him horizontal and uncooperative. A sympathetic pain ran down my back. I winced.

"What makes you think I'd want anything to do with your body?" I countered in a tone that emphasized my indignation.

Russ and I were always friends after that.

He told me he intended to have his body donated to "medical science." He wanted to be given to the anatomy department of his alma mater, so that fledgling doctors could practice on him.

"Won't cost my people a penny."

When I told him they probably wouldn't take him, on account of his size, he seemed utterly crestfallen. The supply of cadavers for medical and dental schools in this land of plenty was shamefully but abundantly provided for by the homeless and helpless who were, for the most part, more "fit" than Russ was.

"But I was an All-American there!" Russ pleaded.

"Don't take my word for it," I advised. "Go ask for yourself."

Months later I was watering impatiens around the funeral home when Russ screeched to a halt on Liberty Street.

"OK, listen. Just cremate me and have the ashes scattered over town from one of those hot-air balloons." I could see he had given this careful thought. "How much will it cost me, bottom line?"

I told him the fees for our minimum services—livery and paperwork and a box.

"I don't want a casket," he hollered from the front seat of his Cadillac idling at curbside now.

I explained we wouldn't be using a casket as such, still he would have to be *in* something. The crematory people wouldn't accept his body unless it was *in* something. They didn't *handle* dead bodies without some kind of handles. This made tolerable sense to Russ. In my mind I was thinking of a shipping case, a kind of covered pallet compatible with fork-lifts and freight handlers, that would be sufficient to the task.

"I can only guess at what the balloon ride will cost, Russ. It's likely to be the priciest part. And, of course, you'd have to figure on inflation. Are you planning to do this very soon?"

"Don't get cute with me, Digger," he shouted. "Whadasay? Can I count on you?"

I told him it wasn't me he'd have to count on. He'd have to convince his wife and kids—the nine of them. They were the ones I'd be working for.

"But it's *my* funeral! My money."

Here is where I explained to Russ the subtle but important difference between the "adjectival" and "possessive" applications of the first-person singular pronoun for ownership—a difference measured by one's last breath. I explained that it was really *theirs* to do—his survivors, his family. It was really, listen closely, "the heirs"—the money, the funeral, what was or wasn't done with his body.

"I'll pay you now," he protested. "In cash—I'll pre-arrange it. Put it in my Will. They'll have to do it the way I want it."

I encouraged Russ to ponder the worst-case scenario: his wife and his family take me to court. I come armed with his Last Will and Preneed documents insisting that his body get burned and tossed from a balloon hovering over the heart of town during Sidewalk Sale Days. His wife Mary, glistening with real tears, his seven beautiful daughters with hankies in hand, his two fine sons, bearing up manfully, petition the court for permission to lay him out, have the preacher in, bury him up on the hill where they can visit his grave whenever the spirit moves them to.

"Who do you think wins that one, Russ? Go home and make your case with them."

I don't know if he ever had that conversation with them all. Maybe he just gave up. Maybe it had all been for my consumption. I don't know. That was years ago.

When Russ died last year in his easy chair, a cigar smoldering in the ash tray, one of those evening game-shows flickering on the TV, his son came to my house to summon me. His wife and his daughters were weeping around him. His children's children watched and listened. We brought the hearse and waited while each of the women kissed him and left. We brought the stretcher in and, with his son's help, moved him from the chair, then out the door and to the funeral home where we embalmed him, gave him a clean shave, and laid him out, all of us amazed at how age and infirmity had reduced him so. He actually fit easily into a Batesville Casket—I think it was Cherry, I don't remember.

But I remember how his vast heroics continued to grow over two days of wake. The stories were told and told again. Folks wept and laughed out loud at his wild antics. And after the minister, a woman who'd known Russ all her life and had braved his stoop on Halloween, had had her say about God's mercy and the size of heaven, she invited some of us to share our stories about Russ and after that we followed a brass band to the grave, holding forth with "When the Saints Go Marching In." And after everything had been said that could be said, and done that could be done, Mary and her daughters went home to the embraces of neighbors and the casseroles and condolences and Russ' sons remained to bury him. They took off their jackets, undid their ties, broke out a bottle and dark cigars and buried their father's body in the ground that none of us thought it would ever fit into. I gave the permit to the sexton and left them to it.

And though I know his body is buried there, something of Russ remains among us now. Whenever I see hot-air balloons—fat flaming birds adrift in evening air—I sense his legendary excesses raining down on us, old friends and family—his blessed and elect—who duck our heads or raise our faces to the sky and laugh or catch our breath or cry.

In even the best of caskets, it never all fits—all that we'd like to bury in them: the hurt and forgiveness, the anger and pain, the praise and thanksgiving, the emptiness and exaltations, the untidy feelings when someone dies. So I conduct this business very carefully because in the years since I've been here, when someone dies, they never call Jessica or the News Hound.

They call me.

Nominated by Witness

151

LIVING WITH STRIPES

by KAY RYAN

from THE SOUTHERN REVIEW

In tigers, zebras,
and other striped creatures,
any casual posture
plays one beautiful set of lines
against another:
herringbones and arrows
appear and disappear;
chevrons widen and narrow.
Miniature themes and counterpoints
occur in the flexing and extending
of the smaller joints.
How can they stand to drink,
when lapping further complicates
the way the water duplicates their lines?
Knowing how their heads will zigzag out,
I wonder if they dread to start sometimes.

Nominated by Jane Hirshfield

OXYGEN

fiction by RON CARLSON

from WITNESS

In 1967, THE YEAR BEFORE the year that finally cracked the twenti-eth century once and for all, I had as my summer job delivering med-ical oxygen in Phoenix, Arizona. I was a sophomore at the University of Montana in Missoula, but my parents lived in Phoenix, and my fa-ther, as a welding engineer, used his contacts to get me a job at Ayr Oxygen Company. I started there doing what I called dumbbell main-tenance, the kind of make-work assigned to college kids. I cleared de-bris from the back lot, mainly crushed packing crates that had been discarded. That took a week and on the last day, as I was raking, I put a nail through the bottom of my foot and had to go for a tetanus shot. Next, I whitewashed the front of the supply store and did such a good job that I began a month of painting my way around the ten-acre plant.

These were good days for me. I was nineteen years old and this was the hardest work I had ever done. The days were stunning, starting hot and growing insistently hotter. My first week two of the days had been a hundred and sixteen. The heat was a pure physical thing, magnified by the steel and pavement of the plant, and in that first week, I learned what not to touch, where not to stand, and I found the powerhouse heat simply bracing. I lost some of the winter dormitory fat and could feel myself browning and getting into shape.

Of course, during this time I was living at home, that is arriving home from work sometime after six and then leaving for work some-time before seven the next morning. My parents and I had little use for each other. They were in their mid-forties then, an age that I've since found out can be oddly taxing, and besides they were in the mid-dle of a huge career decision which would make their fortune and

153

allow them to live the way they live now. I was nineteen, as I said, which in this country is not a real age at all.

I was having a hard ride through the one relationship I had begun during the school year. Her name was Linda Enright, a classmate, and we had made the mistake of sleeping together that spring, just once, but it wrecked absolutely everything. We were dreamy beforehand, the kind of couple who walked real close, bumping foreheads. We read each other's papers. I'm not making this up: we read poetry on the library lawn under a tree. I had met her in a huge section of Western Civilization taught by a young firebrand named Whisner, whose credo was "Western civilization is what you personally are doing." Linda and I had taken it seriously, the way we took all things, I guess, and we joined the Democratic Student Alliance and worked on a grape boycott, though it didn't seem that there were that many grapes to begin with in Montana that chilly spring.

And then one night in her dorm room we went ahead with it, squirming out of our clothes on her hard bed and we did something for about a minute that changed everything. After that we weren't even the same people. She wasn't she and I wasn't I; we were two young citizens in the wrong country. I see now that a great deal of it was double- and triple-think, that is I thought she thought it was my fault and I thought that she might be right with that thought and I should be sorry and that I was sure she didn't know how sorry I was already, regret like a big burning house on the hill of my conscience, or something like that, and besides all I could think through all my sorrow and compunction was that I wanted it to happen again, soon. It was confusing. All I could remember from the incident itself was Linda stopping once and undoing my belt and saying, "Here, I'll get it."

The coolness of that practical phrase repeated in my mind after I'd said good-bye to Linda and she'd gone off to Boulder where her summer job was working in her parents' cookie shop. I called her every Sunday from a pay phone at an Exxon station on Indian School Road, and we'd fight and if you asked me what we fought about I couldn't tell you. We both felt misunderstood. I'd slump outside the door as far as the steel cord allowed, my skin running to chills in the heat, and we'd argue until the operator came on and then I'd dump eight dollars of quarters into the blistering mechanism and go home.

The radio that summer played the number one song, "Little Red Riding Hood," by Sam the Sham and the Pharaohs over and over along

154

with songs by the Animals, even "Sky Pilot." This was not great music and I knew it at the time, but it all set me on edge. After work I'd shower and throw myself on the couch in my parents dark and cool living room and read and sleep and watch the late movies.

About the third week of June, I burned myself. I'd graduated to the paint sprayer and was coating the caustic towers in the oxygen plant. I was forty feet up an extension ladder reaching right and left to spray the tops of the tanks. Beneath me was the pump station that ran the operation, a nasty tangle of motors, belts and valving. The mistake I made was to spray where the ladder arms met the curved surface of the tank and as I reached out then to hit the last and furthest spot, I felt the ladder slide in the new paint. Involuntarily I threw my arms straight out in a terrific hug against the superheated steel. Oddly I didn't feel the burn at first nor did I drop the spray gun. It certainly would have killed me to fall. After a moment, long enough to stabilize my heartbeat and sear my cheekbone and the inside of both elbows, I slid one foot down one rung and began to descend.

All the burns were the shapes of little footballs, the one on my face a three-inch oval below my left eye, but after an hour with the doctor that afternoon, I didn't miss a day of work. They've all healed extraordinarily well, though they darken first if I'm not careful with the sun. That summer I was proud of them, the way I was proud not to have dropped the spray gun, and proud of my growing strength, of the way I'd broken in my work shoes, and proud in a strange way of my loneliness.

Where does loneliness live in the body? How many kinds of loneliness are there? Mine was the loneliness of the college student in a summer job at once very far from and very close to the thing he will become. I thought my parents were hopelessly bourgeoisie, my girlfriend a separate race, my body a thing of wonder and terror, and as I went through the days, my loneliness built. Where? In my heart? It didn't feel like my heart. The loneliness in me was a dryness in the back of my mouth that could not be slaked.

And what about lust, that thing that seemed to have defeated me that spring, undermined my sense of the good boy I'd been, and rinsed the sweetness from my relationship with Linda? Lust felt related to the loneliness, part of the dry, bittersweet taste in the lava-hot air. It went with me like an aura as I strode with my burns across the paved yard of Ayr Oxygen Company, and I felt it as a certain tension in the tendons in my legs, behind the knees, a tight, wired feeling that I knew to be sexual.

The loading dock at Ayr Oxygen was a huge rotting concrete slab under an old corrugated metal roof. After I burned my face, I was transferred there. Mr. Mac Bonner ran the dock with two Hispanic guys that I got to know pretty well, Victor and Jesse, and they kept the place clean and well organized in a kind of military way. Industrial and medical trucks were always delivering full or empty cylinders or taking them away and the tanks had to be lodged in neat squadrons which would not be in the way. Victor, who was the older man, taught me how to roll two cylinders at once while I walked, turning my hands on the caps and kick-turning the bottom of the rear one. As soon as I could do that, briskly moving two at a time, I was accepted there and fell into a week of work with them, loading and unloading trucks. They were quiet men who knew the code and didn't have to speak or call instructions when a truck backed in. I followed their lead.

There were dozens of little alcoves amid the gas cylinders standing on the platform and that is where I ate my lunches now. Victor and Jesse had milk crates and they found one for me and we'd sit out of sight up there from 11:30 to noon and eat. There was a certain uneasiness at first, as if they weren't sure if I should be joining them, but then Victor saw it was essentially a necessity. I wasn't going to get my lunch out of the old fridge on the dock and walk across the yard to eat with the supply people. On the dock was where I learned the meaning of *whitebread,* the way it's used now. I'd open my little bag: two tuna sandwiches and a baggie of chips, and then I'd watch the two men open their huge sacks of burritos and tacos and other items I didn't know the names of and which I've never seen since. During these lunches Victor would talk a little, telling me where to keep my gloves so that the drivers didn't pick them up, and where not to sit even on break. One day Jesse handed me a burrito rolled in white paper. I was on the inside now; they'd taken me in.

That afternoon there was a big Linde Oxygen semi backed against the dock and we were rolling the hot cylinders off when I heard a crash. Jesse yelled from back in the dock and I saw his arms flash and Victor, who was in front of me, lay the two tanks he was rolling on the deck of the truck and jumped off the side and ran into the open yard. I saw the first rows of tanks start to tumble wildly, a chain reaction, a murderous thundering domino chase. As the cylinders fell off the

156

dock, they cartwheeled into the air crazily, heavily tearing clods from the cement dock ledge and thudding into the tarry asphalt. A dozen plummeted onto somebody's Dodge rental car parked too close to the action. It was crushed. The noise was ponderous, painful, and the session continued through a minute until there was only one lone bank of brown nitrogen cylinders standing like a little jury on the back corner of the loading dock. The space looked strange that empty.

The yard was full of people standing back in a crescent. Then I saw Victor step forward and walk toward where I stood on the back of the semi. I still had my hands on the tanks.

He looked what? Scared, disgusted, and a little amused. "Mi amigo," he said, climbing back on the truck. "When they go like that, run away." He pointed back to where all of the employees of Ayr Oxygen Company were watching us. "Away, get it?"

"Yes, sir," I told him. "I do."

"Now you can park those," he said, tapping the cylinders in my hand. "And we'll go pick up all these others."

It took the rest of the day and still stands as the afternoon during which I lifted more weight than any other in this life. It felt a little funny setting the hundreds of cylinders back on the old pitted concrete. "They should repour this," I said to Victor as we were finishing.

"They should," he said. "But if accidents are going to follow you, a new floor won't help." I wondered if he meant that I'd been responsible for the catastrophe.

"I'm through with accidents," I told him. "Don't worry. This is my third. I'm finished."

The next day I was drafted to drive one of the two medical oxygen trucks. One of the drivers had quit and our foreman Mac Bonner came out onto the dock in the morning and told me to see Nadine, who ran Medical, in her little office building out front. She was a large woman who had one speed: gruff. I was instructed in a three-minute speech to go get my commercial driver's license that afternoon and then stop by the uniform shop on Bethany Home and get two sets of brown trousers and short-sleeve yellow shirts worn by the delivery people. On my way out I went by and got my lunch and saw Victor. "They want me to drive the truck. Dennis quit, I guess."

"Dennis wouldn't last," Victor said. "We'll have the Ford loaded for you by nine."

The yellow shirt had a name oval over the heart pocket: David. And the brown pants had a crease that will outlast us all. It felt funny

157

going to work in those clothes and when I came up to the loading dock after picking up the truck keys and my delivery list, Jesse and Victor came out of the forest of cylinders grinning. Jesse saluted. I was embarrassed and uneasy. "One of you guys take the truck," I said.

"No way, David." Victor stepped up and pulled my collar straight. "You look too good. Besides, this job needs a white guy." I looked helplessly at Jesse.

"Better you than me," he said. They had the truck loaded: two groups of ten medical blue cylinders chain-hitched into the front of the bed. These tanks were going to be in people's bedrooms. Inside each was the same oxygen as in the dinged-up green cylinders that the welding shops used.

I climbed in the truck and started it up. Victor had already told me about allowing a little more stopping time because of the load. "Here he comes, ladies," Jesse called. I could see his hand raised in the rearview mirror as I pulled onto McDowell and headed for Sun City.

At that time, Sun City was set alone in the desert, a weird theme park for retired white people, and from the beginning it gave me an eerie feeling. The streets were like toy streets, narrow and clean, running in huge circles. No cars, no garage doors open, and, of course, in the heat, no pedestrians. As I made my rounds, wheeling the hot blue tanks up the driveways and through the carpeted houses to the bedroom, uncoupling the old tank, connecting the new one, I felt peculiar. In the houses I was met by the wife or the husband and was escorted along the way. Whoever was sick was in the other room. It was all very proper. These people had come here from the Midwest and the East. They had been doctors and professors and lawyers and wanted to live among their own kind. No one under twenty could reside in Sun City. When I'd made my six calls, I fled that town, heading east on old Bell Road, which in those days was miles and miles of desert and orchards, not two traffic lights all the way to Scottsdale Road.

Mr. Rensdale was the first of my customers I ever saw in bed. He lived in one of the many blocks of townhouses they were building in Scottsdale. These were compact units with two stories and a pool in the small private yard. All of Scottsdale shuddered under bulldozers that year; it was dust and construction delays, as the little town began to see the future. I rang the bell and was met by a young woman in a long silk shirt who saw me and said, "Oh, yeah. Come on in. Where's Dennis?"

I had the hot blue cylinder on the single dolly and pulled it up the step and into the dark, cool space. I had my pocket rag and wiped the wheels as soon as she shut the door. I could see her knees and they seemed to glow in the near dark. "I'm taking his route for a while," I said, standing up. I couldn't see her face, but she had a hand on one hip.

"Right," she said. "He got fired."

"I don't know about that," I said. I pointed down the hall. "Is it this way?"

"No, upstairs, first door on your right. He's awake, David." She said my name just the way you read names off shirts. Then she put her hand on my sleeve and said, "Who hit you?" My burn was still raw across my cheekbone.

"I got burned."

"Cute," she said. "They're going to love that back at . . . where?"

"University of Montana."

"University of what?" she said. "There's a university there?" She cocked her head at me. I couldn't tell what she was wearing under that shirt. She smiled. "I'm kidding. I'm a snob, but I'm kidding. What year are you?"

"I'll be a junior," I said.

"I'm a senior at Penn," she said. I nodded, my mind whipping around for something clever. I didn't even know where Penn was.

"Great," I said. I started up the stairs.

"Yeah," she said, turning. "Great."

I drew the dolly up the carpeted stair carefully, my first second-story, and entered the bedroom. It was dim in there, but I could see the other cylinder beside the bed and a man in the bed, awake. He was wearing pajamas, and immediately upon seeing me, said, "Good. Open the blinds will you?"

"Sure thing," I said, and I went around the bed and turned the mini-blind wand. The Arizona day fell into the room. The young woman I'd spoken to walked out to the pool beneath me. She took her shirt off and hung it on one of the chairs. Her breasts were white in the sunlight. She set out her magazine and drink by one of the lounges and lay face down in a shiny green bikini bottom.

While I was disconnecting the regulator from the old tank and setting up the new one, Mr. Rensdale introduced himself. He was a thin, handsome man with dark hair and mustache and he looked like about three or four of the actors I was seeing those nights in late movies after my parents went to bed. He wore an aspirator with the two small nostril tubes, which he removed while I changed tanks. I liked him immediately. "Yeah," he went on, "it's good you're going back to college. Though there's a future, believe me, in this stuff." He knocked the oxygen tank with his knuckle.

"What field are you in?" I asked him. He seemed so absolutely worldly there, his wry eyes and his East-coast accent, and he seemed old the way people did then, but I realize now he wasn't fifty.

"I, lad, am the owner of Rensdale Foundations, which my father founded," his whisper was rich with humor, "and which supplies me with more money than my fine daughters will ever be able to spend." He turned his head toward me. "We make ladies' undergarments, lots of them."

The dolly was loaded and I was ready to go. "Do you enjoy it? Has it been a good thing to do?"

"Oh, for chrissakes," he wheezed, a kind of laugh, "give me a week on that, will you? I didn't know this was going to be an interview. Come after four and it's worth a martini to you, kid, and we'll do some career counseling."

"You all set?" I said as I moved to the door.

"Set," he whispered now, rearranging his aspirator. "Oh absolutely. Go get them, champ." He gave me a thin smile and I left. Letting myself out of the dark downstairs, I did an odd thing. I stood still in the house. I had talked to her right here. I saw her breasts again in the bright light. No one knew where I was.

From the truck I called Nadine telling her I was finished with Scottsdale and was heading—on schedule—to Mesa. The heat in the early afternoon as I dropped through the river bottom was gigantic, an enormous, unrelenting thing and I took a kind of perverse pleasure from it. I could feel a heartbeat in my healing burns. My truck was not air conditioned, a thing that wouldn't fly now, but then I drove with my arm out the window through the traffic of these desert towns.

Half the streets in Mesa were dirt, freshly bladed into the huge grid which now is paved wall to wall. I made several deliveries and ended up at the torn edge of the known world, the road just a track, a year maybe two at most from the first ripples of the growth which would swallow hundreds of miles of the desert. The house was an old block home gone to seed, the lawn dirt, the shrubs dead, the windows brown with dust and cobwebs. From the front yard I had a clear view of the Santan Mountains to the south. I was fairly sure I had a wrong address

160

and that the property was abandoned. I knocked on the greasy door and after five minutes a stooped, red-haired old man answered. This was Gil, and I have no idea how old he was that summer, but it was as old as you get. Plus he was sick with emphysema and liver disease. His skin, stretched tight and translucent on his gaunt body, was splattered with brown spots. On his hand several had been picked raw.

I pulled my dolly into the house, dark inside against the crushing daylight and was hit by the roiling smell of dog hair and urine. I didn't kneel to wipe the wheels. "Right in here," the old man said, leading me back into the house toward a yellow light in the small kitchen where I could hear a radio chattering. He had his oxygen set up in the corner of the kitchen; it looked like he lived in the one room. There was a fur of fine red dust on everything, the range, the sink, except half the kitchen table where he had his things arranged, some brown vials of prescription medicine, two decks of cards, a pencil or two on a small pad, a warped issue of *Field and Stream,* a little red Bible, and a box of cough drops. In the middle of the table was a fancy painted plate, maybe a seascape, with a line of Oreos on it. I got busy changing out the tanks.

Meanwhile the old man sat down at the kitchen table and started talking. "I'm Gil Benson," his speech began, "and I'm glad to see you, David. My lungs got burned in France in 1919 and it took them twenty years to buckle." He spoke, like so many of my customers, in a hoarse whisper. "I've lived all over the world including the three A's: Africa, Cairo, Australia, Burberry, and Alaska, Point Barrow. My favorite place was Montreal, Canada because I was in love there and married the woman, had children. She's dead. My least favorite place is right here because of this. One of my closest friends was Jack Kramer, the tennis player. That was many years ago. I've flown every plane made between the years 1938 and 1958. I don't fly anymore with all this." He indicated the oxygen equipment. "Sit down. Have a cookie."

I had my dolly ready. "I shouldn't, sir," I said. "I've got a schedule and better keep it."

"Grab that pitcher out of the fridge before you sit down. I made us some Koolaid. It's good."

I opened his refrigerator. Except for the Tupperware pitcher, it was empty. Nothing. I put the pitcher on the table. "I really have to go," I said. "I'll be late."

Gil lifted the container of Koolaid and raised it into a jittery hover above the two plastic glasses. There was going to be an accident. His

161

hands were covered with purple scabs. I took the pitcher from him and filled the glasses.

"Sit down," he said. "I'm glad you're here, young fella." When I didn't move he said, "Really. Nadine said you were a good-looking kid. This is your last stop today. Have a snack."

So began my visits with the old Gil Benson. He was my last delivery every fourth day that summer, and as far as I could tell, I was the only one to visit his wretched house. On one occasion I placed one of the Oreos he gave me on the corner of my chair as I left and it was there next time when I returned. Our visits became little three-part dramas: my arrival and the bustle of intrusion; the snack and his monologue; his hysteria and weeping.

The first time he reached for my wrist across the table as I was standing up to go, it scared me. Things had been going fine. He'd told me stories in an urgent voice, one story spilling into the other without a seam, because he didn't want me to interrupt. I had *I've got to go* all over my face, but he wouldn't read it. He spoke as if placing each word in the record, as if I were going to write it all down when I got home. It always started with a story of long ago, an airplane, a homemade repair, an emergency landing, a special cargo, an odd coincidence, each part told with pride, but his voice would gradually change, slide into a kind of whine as he began an escalating series of complaints about his doctors, the insurance, his children, naming each of the four and relating their indifference, petty greed, or cruelty. I nodded through all of this: *I've got to go.* He leaned forward and picked at the back of his hands. When he tired after forty minutes, I'd slide my chair back and he'd grab my wrist. By then I could understand his children pushing him away and moving out of state. I wanted out. But I'd stand—while he still held me—and say, "That's interesting. Save some of these cookies for next time." And then I'd move to the door, hurrying the dolly, but never fast enough to escape. Crying softly and carrying his little walker bottle of oxygen, he'd see me to the door and then out into the numbing heat to the big white pickup. He'd continue his monologue while I chained the old tank in the back and while I climbed in the cab and started the engine and then while I'd start to pull away. I cannot describe how despicable I felt doing that, gradually moving away from old Gil on that dirt lane, and when I hit the corner and turned west for the shop, I tromped it: forty-five, fifty, fifty-five, raising a thick red dust train along what would some day be Chandler Boulevard.

162

Backing up to the loading dock late on those days with a truck of empties, I was full of animal happiness. The sun was at its worst, blasting the sides of everything and I moved with the measured deliberation the full day had given me. My shirt was crusted with salt, but I wasn't sweating anymore. When I bent to the metal fountain beside the dock, gulping the water, I could feel it bloom on my back and chest and come out along my hairline. Jesse or Victor would help me sort the cylinders and reload for tomorrow. I spent eight dollars every Sunday calling Linda Enright. I became tight and fit, my burns finally scabbed up so that by mid-July I looked like a young boxer, and I tried not to think about anything.

A terrible thing happened in my phone correspondence with Linda. We stopped fighting. We'd talk about her family; the cookie business was taking off, but her father wouldn't let her take the car. He was stingy. I told her about my deliveries, the heat. She was looking forward to getting the fall bulletin. Was I going to major in geology as I'd planned? As I listened to us talk, I stood and wondered: who are these people? The other me wanted to interrupt, to ask: hey, didn't we have sex? I mean, was that sexual intercourse? Isn't the world a little different for you now? But I chatted with her. When the operator came on, I was crazy with Linda's indifference, but unable to say anything but, "Take care, I'll call."

Meanwhile the summer assumed a regularity that was nothing but comfort. I drove my routes: hospitals Mondays, rest homes Tuesdays, residences the rest of the week. Sun City, Scottsdale, Mesa. Nights I'd stay up and watch the old movies, keeping a list of titles and great lines. It was as much of a life of the mind as I wanted. Then it would be six a.m. and I'd have Sun City, Scottsdale, Mesa. I was hard and brown and lost in the routine.

I was used to sitting with Gil Benson and hearing his stories, pocketing the Oreos secretly to throw them from the truck later; I was used to the new carpet smell of all the little homes in Sun City, everything clean, quiet and polite; I was used to Elizabeth Rensdale showing me her white breasts, posturing by the pool whenever she knew I was upstairs with her father. By the end of July I had three or four of her little moves memorized, the way she rolled on her back, the way she kneaded them with oil sitting with her long legs on each side of the lounge chair. Driving the valley those long summer days, each window of the truck a furnace, listening to "Paperback Writer" and "Last Train

163

to Clarksville," I delivered oxygen to the paralyzed and dying, and I felt so alive and on edge at every moment that I could have burst. I liked the truck, hopping up unloading the hot cylinders at each address and then driving to the next stop. I knew what I was doing and wanted no more.

Rain broke the summer. The second week in August I woke to the first clouds in ninety days. They massed and thickened and by the time I left Sun City, it had begun, a crashing downpour. I didn't want to be late at the Rensdales'. I was wiping down the tank in the covered entry when Elizabeth opened the door and disappeared back into the dark house. I was wet from the warm rain and coming into the air conditioned house ran a chill along my sides. The blue light of the television pulsed against the darkness. When my eyes adjusted and I started backing up the stairway with the new cylinder, I saw Elizabeth sitting on the couch in the den, her knees together up under her chin, watching me. She was looking right at me.

"This is the worst summer of my entire life," she said.

"Sorry," I said, coming down a step. "What'd you say?"

"David! Is that you?" Mr. Rensdale called from his room. His voice was a ghost. I liked him very much and it had become clear over the summer that he was not going back to Pennsylvania.

Elizabeth Rensdale whispered across the room to me, "I don't want to be here." She closed her eyes and rocked her head. I stood the cylinder on the dolly and went over to her. I didn't like leaving it there on the carpet. It wasn't what I wanted to do. She was sitting in her underpants on the couch. "He's dying," she said to me.

"Oh," I said, trying to make it simply a place holder, let her know that I'd heard her. She put her face in her hands and lay over on the couch. I dropped to a knee and, putting my hand on her shoulder, I said, "What can I do?"

This was the secret side that I suspected from this summer. Elizabeth Rensdale put her hand on mine and turned her face to mine so slowly that I felt my heart drop a gear, grinding now heavily uphill in my chest. The rain was like a pressure on the roof.

Mr. Rensdale called my name again. Elizabeth's face on mine so close and open made it possible for me to move my hand around her back and pull her to me. It was like I knew what I was doing. I didn't take my eyes from hers when she rolled onto her back and guided me onto her. It was different in every way from what I had imagined. The dark room closed around us. Her mouth came to mine and stayed there. This wasn't education; this was need. And later, when I felt her hand on my bare ass, her heels rolling in the back of my knees, I knew it was the mirror of my cradling her in both my arms. We rocked along the edge of the couch, moving it finally halfway across the den as I pushed into her. I wish I could get this right here, but there is no chance. We stayed together for a moment afterward and my eyes opened and focused. She was still looking at me, holding me, and her look was simply serious. Her father called, "David?" from upstairs again, and I realized he must have been calling steadily. Still, we were slow to move. I stood without embarrassment and dressed, tucking my shirt in. That we were intent, that we were still rapt made me confident in a way I'd never been. I grabbed the dolly and ascended the stairs.

Mr. Rensdale lay white and twisted in the bed. He looked the way the dying look, his face parched and sunken, the mouth a dry orifice, his eyes little spots of water. I saw him acknowledge me with a withering look, more power than you'd think could rise from such a body. I felt it a cruel scolding, and I moved in the room deliberate with shame, avoiding his eyes. The rain drummed against the window in waves. After I had changed out the tanks, I turned to him and said, "There you go."

He rolled his hand in a little flip toward the bed table and his glass of water. His chalky mouth was in the shape of an O, and I could hear him breathing, a thin rasp. Who knows what happened in me then, because I stood in the little bedroom with Mr. Rensdale and then I just rolled the dolly and the expired tank out and down the stairs. I didn't go to him; I didn't hand him the glass of water. I burned: who would ever know what I had done?

When I opened the door downstairs on the world of rain, Elizabeth came out of the dark again, naked, to stand a foot or two away. I took her not speaking as just part of the intensity I felt and the way she stood with her arms easy at her sides was the way I felt when I'd been naked before her. We looked at each other for a moment; the rain was already at my head and the dolly and tank were between us in the narrow entry, and then something happened that sealed the way I feel about myself even today. She came up and we met beside the tank and there was no question the way we went for each other about what was going on. I pushed by the oxygen equipment and followed her onto the entry tile, then a moment later turning in adjustment so that she could climb me, get her bare back off the floor.

165

So the last month of that summer I began seeing Elizabeth Rensdale every day. My weekly visits to the townhouse continued, but then I started driving out to Scottsdale nights. I told my parents I was at the library, because I wanted it to sound like a lie and have them know it was a lie. I came in after midnight; the library closed at nine.

Elizabeth and I were hardy and focused lovers. I relished the way every night she'd meet my knock at the door and pull me into the room and then, having touched, we didn't stop. Knowing we had two hours, we used every minute of it and we became experts at each other. For me these nights were the first nights in my new life, I mean, I could tell then that there was no going back, that I had changed my life forever and I could not stop it. We never went out for a coke, we never took a break for a glass of water, we rarely spoke. There was admiration and curiosity in my touch and affection and gratitude in hers or so I assumed, and I was pleased, even proud at the time that there was so little need to speak.

On the way home with my arm out in the hot night, I drove like the young king of the desert. Looking into my car at a traffic light, other drivers could read it all on my face and the way I held my head cocked back. I was young those nights, but I was getting over it.

Meanwhile Gil Benson had begun clinging to me worse than ever and those prolonged visits were full of agony and desperation. As the Arizona monsoon season continued toward Labor Day, the rains played hell with his old red road, and many times I pulled up in the same tracks I'd left the week before. He now considered me so familiar that cookies weren't necessary. A kind of terror had inhabited him, and it was fed by the weather. Now most days I had to go west to cross the flooded Salt River at the old Mill Avenue Bridge to get to Mesa late and by the time I arrived, Gil would be on the porch, frantic. Not because of oxygen deprivation; he only needed to use the stuff nights. But I was his oxygen now, his only visitor, his only companion. I'd never had such a thing happen before and until it did I thought of myself as a compassionate person. I watched myself arrive at his terrible house and wheel the tank toward the door and I searched myself for compassion, the smallest shred of fellow feeling, kindness, affection, pity, but all I found was repulsion, impatience. I thought, surely I would be kind, but that was a joke, and I saw that compassion was a joke too, along with fidelity and chastity and all the other notions I'd run over this summer. Words, I thought, big words. Give me the truck keys and a job to do, and the words can look out for themselves. I had no compassion for Gil Benson. His scabby hands, the dried spittle in the ruined corners of his mouth, his crummy weeping in his stinking house. He always grabbed my wrist with both hands, and I shuffled back toward the truck. His voice was so nakedly plaintive it embarrassed me. I wanted to push him down in the mud and weeds of his yard and drive away, but I never did that. What I finally did was worse.

The summer already felt nothing but old as Labor Day approached, the shadows in the afternoon gathering reach although the temperature was always a hundred and five. I could see it when I backed into the dock late every day, the banks of cylinders stark in the slanted sunlight, Victor and Jesse emerging from a world which was only black and white, sun and long shadow. The change gave me a feeling that I can only describe as anxiety. Birds flew overhead, three and four at a time, headed somewhere. There were huge banks of clouds in the sky every afternoon and after such a long season of blanched white heat, the shadows beside things seemed ominous. The cars and buildings and the massive tin roof of the loading dock were just things, but their shadows seemed like meanings. Summer, whatever it had meant, was ending.

I sensed this all through a growing curtain of fatigue. The long hot days and the sharp extended nights with Elizabeth began to shave my energy. At first it took all the extra that I had being nineteen, and then I started to cut into the principal. I couldn't feel it mornings which passed in a flurry, but afternoons, my back solid sweat against the seat of my truck, I felt it as a weight, my body going leaden as I drove the streets of Phoenix.

"Oy, amigo," Jesse said one day late in August when I rested against the shipping desk in the back of the dock. "Que pasa?"

"Nothing but good things," I said. "How're you doing?"

He came closer and looked at my face, concerned. "You sick?"

"No, I'm great. Long day."

Victor appeared with the cargo sheet and handed me the clipboard to sign. He and Jesse exchanged glances. I looked up at them. Victor put his hand on my chin and let it drop. "Too much tail." He was speaking to Jesse. "He got the truck and forgot what I told him. Remember?" He turned to me. "Remember? Watch what you're doing." Victor took the clipboard back and tapped it against his leg. "When the tanks start to fall, run the *other* way."

But it was a hot heedless summer and I showered every night like some animal born of it, heedless and hot, and I pulled a cotton T-shirt over my ribs, combed my wet hair back, and without a word to my parents, who were wary of me now it seemed, drove to Scottsdale and buried myself in Elizabeth Rensdale.

The Sunday before Labor Day, I didn't call Linda Enright. I rousted around the house, finally raking the yard, sweeping the garage, and washing all three of the cars, before rolling onto the couch in the den and watching some of the sad, throwaway television of a summer Sunday. In each minute of the day, Linda Enright was in my mind. I saw her there in her green sweater by her father's rolltop. We always talked about what we were wearing and she always said the green sweater, saying it innocently as if wearing the sweater that I'd helped pull over her head that night in her dorm room was of little note, a coincidence, and not the most important thing that she'd say in the whole eight-dollar call, and I'd say just Levi's and a T-shirt, hoping she'd imagine the belt, the buckle, the trouble it could all be in the dark. I saw her sitting still in the afternoon shadow, maybe writing some notes in her calender or reading, and right over there, the telephone. I could get up and hit the phone booth in less than ten minutes and make that phone ring, have her reach for it, but I didn't. It was the most vivid Linda had appeared to me the entire summer. Green sweater in the study through the endless day. I let her sit there until the last sunlight rocked through the den, broke and disappeared.

Elizabeth Rensdale and I kept at it. Over the Labor Day weekend, I stayed with her overnight and we worked and reworked ourselves long past satiation. She was ravenous and my appetite for her was relentless. That was how I felt it all: relentless. Moments after coming hard into her, I would begin to palm her bare hip as if dreaming and then still dreaming begin to mouth her ear and her hand would play over my genitals lightly and then move in dreamily sorting me around in the dark and we would shift to begin again. I woke from a brief nap sometime after four in the morning with Elizabeth across me, a leg between mine, her face in my neck, and I felt a heaviness in my arm as I slid it down her tight back that reminded me of what Victor had said. I was tired in a way I'd never known. My blood stilled and I could feel a pressure running in my head like sand, and still my hand descended in the dark. There was no stopping. Soon I felt her hand, as I had every night for a month, and we labored toward dawn.

In the morning, Sunday, I didn't go home, but drove way down by Ayr Oxygen Company to the Roadrunner, the truckstop there on

McDowell adjacent to the freeway. It was the first day I'd ever been sore and I walked carefully to the coffee shop. I sat alone at the counter, eating eggs and bacon and toast and coffee, feeling the night tick away in every sinew the way a car cools after a long drive. It was an effort to breathe and at times I had to stop and gulp some air, adjusting myself on the counter stool. Around me it was only truck drivers who had driven all night from Los Angeles, Sacramento, Albuquerque, Salt Lake City. There was only one woman in the place, a large woman in a white waitress dress who moved up and down the counter pouring coffee. When she poured mine, I looked up at her and our eyes locked, I mean her head tipped and her face registered something I'd never seen before. If I used such words I'd call it horror, but I don't. My old heart bucked. I thought of my professor Whisner and Western Civ; if it was what I was personally doing, then it was in tough shape. The gravity of the moment between the waitress and myself was such that I was certain to my toenails I'd been seen: she knew all about me.

That week I gave Nadine my notice, reminding her that I would be leaving in ten days, mid-September, to go back to school. "Well, Sonnyboy, I hope we didn't work your wheels off."

"No, ma'am. It's been a good summer."

"We think so, too," she said. "Come by and I'll have your last check cut early, so we don't have to mail it."

"Thanks, Nadine." I moved to the door; I had a full day of deliveries.

"Old Gil Benson is going to miss you, I think."

"I've met a lot of nice people," I said. I wanted to deflect this and get going.

"No," she said. "You've been good to him; it's important. Some of these old guys don't have much to look forward to. He's called several times. I might as well tell you. Mr. Ayr heard about it and is writing you a little bonus."

I stepped back toward her. "What?"

"Congratulations." She smiled. "Drive carefully."

Some of my customers knew I was leaving and made kind remarks or shook my hand or had their wife hand me an envelope with a twenty in it. I smiled and nodded gratefully and then turned businesslike to the dolly and left. These were strange good-byes, because there was no question that we would ever see each other again. It had been a summer and I had been their oxygen guy. But there was more: I was young and they were ill. I stood in the bedroom doors in Sun City and said, "Take care," and I moved to the truck and felt something, but I couldn't even today tell you what it was. The people who didn't know, who said, "See you next week, David," I didn't correct them. I said, "See you," and I left their homes too. It all had me on edge.

The last day of my job in the summer of 1967, I drove to work under a cloud cover as thick as twilight in winter and still massing. It began to rain early and I made the quick decision to beat the Salt River flooding by hitting Mesa first and Scottsdale in the afternoon. I had known for a week that I did not want Gil Benson to be my last call for the summer, and this rain, steady but light, gave the excuse I wanted. The traffic was colossal, and I crept in a huge column of cars east across the river noting it was twice as bad coming back, everyone trying to get to Phoenix for the day. What I am saying is that I had time to think about it all, this summer, myself, and it was a powerful stew. I imagined it raining in the hills of Boulder, Linda Enright selling cookies in her apron in a shop with curtains, a Victorian tearoom, ten years ahead of itself as it turned out, her sturdy face with no expression telling she wasn't a virgin anymore, and that now she had been for thirty days betrayed. I thought, and this is the truth, I thought for the first time of what I was going to say *last* to Elizabeth Rensdale. I tried to imagine it, and my imagination failed. When I climbed from her bed the nights I'd gone to her, it was just that, climbing out, dressing and crossing to the door. She didn't get up. This wasn't "Casablanca" or "High Noon," or "Captain Blood," which I had seen this summer, this was getting fucked in a hot summer desert town by your father's oxygen delivery man. There was no way to make it anything else.

Even driving slowly, I fishtailed through the red clay along Gil's road. The rain moved in for the day, persistent and even, and the temperature stalled and hovered at about a hundred. I thought Gil would be pleased to see me so soon in the day, because he was always glad to see me, welcomed me, but I surprised him this last Friday knocking at the door for five full minutes before he unlocked the door looking scared. Though I had told him I would eventually be going back to college, I hadn't told him this was my last day.

Shaken up like he was, things went differently. There was no chatter right off the bat, no sitting down at the table. He just moved things out of the way as I wheeled the oxygen in and changed tanks. He stood to one side, leaning against the counter. When I finished, he made no move to keep me there, so I just kept going. I wondered for a moment if he knew who I was or if he was just waking up. At the front door, I said, "There you go, good luck, Gil." His name quickened him and he came after me with short steps in his slippers.

"Well, yes," he started as always. "I wouldn't need this stuff at all if I'd stayed out of the war." And he was off and cranking. But when I went outside, he followed me into the rain. "Of course, I was strong as a horse and came back and got right with it. I mean, there wasn't any sue-the-government then. It was late in 1919. We were happy to be home. I was happy." He went on, the rain pelting us both. His slippers were all muddy.

"You gotta go," I told him. "It's wet out here." His wet skin in the flat light looked raw, the spots on his forehead brown and liquid; under his eyes the skin was purple. I'd let him get too close to the truck and he'd grabbed the door handle.

"I wasn't sick a day in my life," he said. "Not as a kid, not in the Navy. Ask my wife. When this came on," he patted his chest, "it came on bang! Just like that and here I am. Somewhere." I put my hand on his on the door handle and I knew that I wasn't going to be able to pry it off without breaking it.

Then there was a hitch in the rain, a gust of wet rain, and hail began to rattle through the yard, bouncing up from the mud, bouncing off the truck and our heads. "Let me take you back inside," I said. "Quick, Gil, let's get out of this weather." Gil Benson pulled the truck door open, and with surprising dexterity he stepped up into the vehicle, sitting on all my paperwork. He wasn't going to budge and I hated pleading with him. I wouldn't do it. Now the hail had tripled, quadrupled in a crashfest off the hood. I looked at Gil, shrunken and purple in the darkness of the cab; he looked like the victim of a fire.

"Well, at least we're dry in here, right?" I said. "We'll give it a minute." And that's what it took, about sixty seconds for the hail to abate, and after a couple of heavy curtains of the rain ripped across the hood as if they'd been thrown from somewhere, the world went silent and we could hear only the patter of the last faint drops. "Gil," I said. "I'm late. Let's go in." I looked at him but he did not look at me. "I've got to go." He sat still, his eyes timid, frightened, smug. It was an expression you use when you want someone to hit you.

I started the truck, hoping that would scare him, but he did not move. His eyes were still floating and it looked like he was grinning, but it wasn't a grin. I crammed the truck into gear and began to fishtail along the road. At the corner we slid in the wet clay across the street and stopped.

I kicked my door open and jumped down into the red mud and went around the front of the truck. When I opened his door, he did not turn or look at me, which was fine with me. I lifted Gil like a bride and he clutched me, his wet face against my face. I carried him to the weedy corner lot. He was light and bony like an old bird and I was strong and I felt strong, but I could tell this was an insult the old man didn't need. When I stood him there he would not let go, his hands clasped around my neck and I peeled his hands apart carefully, easily, and I folded them back toward him so he wouldn't snag me again. "Good-bye, Gil," I said. He was an old wet man alone in the desert. He did not acknowledge me.

I ran to the truck and eased ahead for traction and when I had traction, I floored it, throwing mud behind me like a rocket.

By the time I lined up for the Tempe Bridge, the sky was torn with blue vents. The Salt River was nothing but muscle, a brown torrent four feet over the river bottom roadway. The traffic was thick. A ten-mile rainbow had emerged over the McDowell Mountains.

I radioed Nadine that the rain had slowed me up and I wouldn't make it back before five.

"No problem, Sonnyboy," she said. "I'll leave your checks on my desk. Have you been to Scottsdale yet? Over."

"Just now," I said. "I'll hit the Rensdales' and on in. Over."

"Sonnyboy," she said. "Just pick up there. Mr. Rensdale died yesterday. Remember the portable unit, O.K.? And good luck at school. Stop in if you're down for Christmas break. Over."

I waited a minute to over-and-out to Nadine while the news subsided in me. It was on Scottsdale Road at Camelback where I turned right. That corner will always be that radio call. "Copy. Over," I said.

I just drove. Now the sky was ripped apart the way I've learned only a western sky can be, the glacial cloud cover broken and the shreds gathering against the Superstition Mountains, the blue air a color you don't see twice a summer in the desert, icy and clear, no dust or smoke. All the construction crews in Scottsdale had given it up and the bright lumber on the sites sat dripping in the afternoon sun.

In front of the Rensdales' townhouse I felt odd going to the door with the empty dolly. I rang the bell and after a moment, Elizabeth appeared. She was barefoot in jeans and a T-shirt, and she just looked at me. "I'm sorry about your father," I said. "This is tough." She stared at me and I held the gaze. "I mean it. I'm sorry."

She drifted back into the house. It felt for the first time strange and cumbersome to be in the dark little townhouse. She had the air conditioning cranked way up so that I could feel the edge of a chill on my arms and neck as I pulled the dolly up the stairs to Mr. Rensdale's room. It had been taken apart a little bit, the bed stripped, our gear all standing in the corner. With Mr. Rensdale gone you could see what the room was, just a little box in the desert. Looking out the window over the pool and the two dozen tiled roofs before the edge of the Indian Reservation and the sage and creosote bushes, it seemed clearly someplace to come and die. The mountains now all rinsed by rain were red and purple, a pretty lie.

"I'm going back Friday." Elizabeth had come into the room. "I guess I'll go back to school."

"Good," I said. "Good idea." I didn't know what I was saying. The space in my heart about returning to school was nothing but dread.

"They're going to bury him tomorrow." She sat on the bed. "Out here somewhere."

I started to say something about that, but she pointed at me. "Don't come. Just do what you do, but don't come to the funeral. You don't have to."

"I want to," I said. Her tone had hurt, made me mad.

"My mother and sister will be here tonight," she said.

"I want to," I said. I walked to the bed and put my hands on her shoulders.

"Don't."

I bent and looked into her face.

"Don't."

I went to pull her toward me to kiss and she leaned away sharply. "Don't, David." But I followed her over onto the bed, and though she squirmed, tight as a knot, I held her beside me, adjusting her, drawing her back against me. We'd struggled in every manner, but not this. Her arms were tight cords and it took more strength that I'd ever used to pin them both against her chest while I opened my mouth on her neck and ran my other hand flat inside the front of her pants. I reached deep and she drew a sharp breath and stretched her legs out along mine, bumping at my ankles with her heels. Then she gave way and I knew I could let go of her arms. We lay still that way, nothing moving but my finger. She rocked her head back.

173

About a minute later she said, "What are you doing?"

"It's O.K.," I said.

Then she put her hand on my wrist, stopping it. "Don't," she said. "What are you doing?"

"Elizabeth," I said, kissing at her nape. "This is what we do. Don't you like it?"

She rose to an elbow and looked at me, her face rock hard, unfamiliar. "This is what we do?" Our eyes were locked. "Is this what you came for?" She lay back and thumbed off her pants until she was naked from the waist down. "Is it?"

"Yes," I said. It was the truth and there was pleasure in saying it.

"Then go ahead. Here." She moved to the edge of the bed, a clear display. The moment had fused and I held her look and I felt seen. I felt known. I stood and undid my belt and went at her, the whole time neither of us changing expression, eyes open, though I studied her as I moved looking for a signal of the old ways, the pleasure, a lowered eyelid, the opening mouth, but none came. Her mouth was open but as a challenge to me, and her fists gripped the mattress but simply so she didn't give ground. She didn't move when I pulled away, just lay there looking at me. I remember it was the moment in this life when I was farthest from any of my feelings. I gathered the empty cylinder and the portable gear with the strangest thought: *It's going to take me twenty years to figure out who I am now.*

I could feel Elizabeth Rensdale's hatred, as I would feel it dozens of times a season for many years. It's a kind of dread for me that has become a rudder and kept me out of other troubles. That next year at school, I used it to treat Linda Enright correctly, as a gentleman, and keep my distance, though I came to know I was in love with her and had been all along. I had the chance to win her back and I did not take it. We worked together several times with the Democratic Student Alliance, and it is public record that our organization brought Robert Kennedy to the Houck Center on campus that March. Professor Whisner introduced him that night, and at the reception I shook Robert Kennedy's hand. It felt, for one beat, like Western Civilization.

That bad day at the Rensdales' I descended the stair, carefully, not looking back and I let myself out of the townhouse for the last time. The mud on the truck had dried in brown fans along the sides and rear. The late afternoon in Scottsdale had been scrubbed and hung out to dry, and the elongated shadows of the short new imported palms along

174

the street printed themselves eerily in the wet lawns. Today those trees are as tall as those weird shadows. I just wanted to close this whole show down.

But as I drove through Scottsdale, block by block, west toward Camelback Mountain, I was torn by a nagging thought of Gil Benson. I shouldn't have left him out there. At a dead-end by the Indian School canal I stopped and turned off the truck. The grapefruit grove there was being bladed under. Summer was over; I was supposed to be happy.

Back at Ayr Oxygen, I told Gene, the swingman, to forget it and I unloaded the truck myself. It was the one good hour of that day, one hour of straight work, lifting and rolling my empties into the ranks at the far end of the old structure. Victor and Jesse would find them tomorrow. They would be the last gas cylinders I would ever handle. I locked the truck and walked to the office in my worn-out work shoes. I found two envelopes on Nadine's desk: my check and the bonus check. It was two hundred and fifty dollars. I put them in my pocket and left my keys, pulling the door locked behind me.

I left for my junior year of college at Missoula three days later. The evening before my flight, my parents took me to dinner at a steakhouse on a mesa, a western place where they cut your tie off if you wear one. The barn-plank walls were covered with the clipped ends of ties. It was a good dinner, hearty, the baked potatoes big as melons and the charred edges of the steaks dropping off the plates. My parents were giddy, ebullient because their business plans which had so consumed them were looking good. They were proud of me, they said, working hard like this all summer away from my friends. I was changing, they said, and they could tell it was for the better.

After dinner we went back to the house and had a drink on the back terrace, which was a new thing in our lives. I didn't drink very much and I had never had a drink with my parents. My father made a toast to my success at school and then my mother made a toast to my success at school, and then she stood and threw her glass out back and we heard it shatter against the stucco wall. A moment later she hugged me and she and my father went in to bed.

I cupped my car keys and went outside. I drove the dark streets. The radio played a steady rotation of exactly the same songs heard today on every 50,000-watt station in this country; every fifth song was the Supremes. I knew where I was going. Beyond the bright rough edge of the lights of Mesa I drove until the pavement ended, and then I dropped onto the red clay roads and found Gil Benson's house. It was

175

as dark as some final place, and there was no disturbance in the dust on the front walk or in the network of spider webs inside the broken storm door. I knocked and called for minutes. Out back, I kicked through the debris and weeds until I found one of the back bedroom windows unlocked and I slid it open and climbed inside. In the stale heat, I knew immediately that the house was abandoned. I called Gil's name and picked my way carefully to the hall. The lights did not work, and in the kitchen when I opened the fridge, the light was out and the humid stench hit me and I closed the door. I wasn't scared, but I was something else. Standing in that dark room where I had palmed old Oreos all summer long, I now had proof, hard proof that I had lost Gil Benson. He hadn't made it back and I couldn't wish him back.

Outside, the bright dish of Phoenix glittered to the west. I drove toward it carefully. Nothing had cooled down. In every direction the desert was being torn up, and I let the raw night rip through the open car window, the undiminished heat like a pulse at my neck. At home my suitcases were packed. I eased along the empty roadways trying simply to gather what was left, to think, but it was like trying to fold a big blanket alone. I kept having to start over.

Nominated by Witness *and Melissa Pritchard*

BLACKLEGS

by BRIGIT KELLY

from TAMAQUA

The sheep has nipples, the boy said,
And fur all around. The sheep
Has black legs, his name is Blacklegs,
And a cry like breaking glass.
The glass is broken. The glass
is broken, and the milk falls down.

The bee has a suffering softness,
The boy said, a ring of fur,
Like a ring of fire. He burns
The flowers he enters, the way
The rain burns the grass. The bee
Has six legs, six strong legs,
And when he flies the legs
Whistle like a blade of grass
Brought to the lips and blown.

The boy said, The horse runs hard
As sorrow, or a storm, or a man
With a stolen purse in his shirt.
The horse's legs are a hundred
Or more, too many to count,
And he holds a moon white as fleece
In his mouth, cups it like water
So it will not spill out.

And the boy said this. I am a boy
And a man. My legs are two
And they shine black as the arrows
That drop down on my throat
And my chest to draw out the blood
The bright animals feed on,
Those with wings, those without,
The ghosts of the heart—whose
Hunger is a dress for my song.

Nominated by Tamaqua, *Marianne Boruch and Elizabeth Spires*

NOT THE PLASTER CASTERS

fiction by JANICE EIDUS

from UNBEARABLES (AUTONOMEDIA)

I WAS NOT A MEMBER of the Plaster Casters. I was a free agent. Although—on the surface, at least—I did exactly what the Plaster Casters did. That is, we all made plaster casts of the penises of rock stars. But the Plaster Casters got all the glory, all the publicity. Even though *I* did it first.

The Plaster Casters, you see, did it for the power they thought it gave them—the power that would lead them to the fifteen minutes of fame they wanted so much. Which they got. Big deal. Fifteen minutes.

I wanted no glory, no money. I didn't need fifteen minutes. I had a lifetime, and another, far greater, agenda. I never hired a publicist, never contacted a journalist to write up my exploits, nor to take photos of me looking wacky and sexy, stirring up a vat of my plaster mixture with a come-hither look on my face, or sitting on Jimi's lap, or cuddling up to Rod. I was as different from the Plaster Casters as Picasso from a greeting-card illustrator.

I was an artist, with an eye trained to recognize natural beauty when I saw it. And rock stars were definitely objects of natural beauty, with their lean, hard bodies, their long hair flowing down their backs, their bejeweled ears, necks, and fingers. Rock stars were like Greek statues with attitude.

And so I created homages to them. My sculptures were vehicles through which I rendered both them, and myself, immortal. I iso-

179

lated their most beautiful, most artistic feature, and I re-created it, re-invented it. Like the poet said—art is about making it new, making it *your own*. And I certainly did that: when I was finished, after the rock stars had gone, I gave each plaster cast my signature. I painted my initials—the initials of my real name, my given name, the name everyone but me has long forgotten, since everyone else now knows me as Not the Plaster Casters. I used a shimmery, otherwordly silver, a shade of my own creation, a shade that nobody else can ever copy or match. And each initial looks exactly like the letter it is, and yet simultaneously, like a female body, as well, a sensuous female with full breasts, slim waist, and perfectly balanced, rounded hips. My signature is the symbol for me, of course, for my own erotic beauty; again something those homely Plaster Casters with their chubby bodies and scraggly hair just didn't have, couldn't measure up to.

My ageless, creamy-skinned beauty—which has only been enhanced over time—is such that the rock stars would beg me to sleep with them, would grow keenly aroused as I patted the plaster firmly onto their members. But I never gave in. I never slept with a single one, and, believe me, there were times I desired one or another of them so much I could hardly breathe. But I had no choice: I had to be pure, objective. What if I had fallen in love? My art might have suffered, and that would have been intolerable. Besides, my body never went hungry. I had my ways.

Meanwhile, I was doing them all, all the greats: Jimi, Bobby, the two Keiths, David, Mick, Paul, and so many others, all colors, all sizes. Even Janis wanted in: "Can't you do a boob this time?" she asked.

"For you, okay," I agreed.

Her face lit up with her kooky, lopsided smile.

In fact, I ended up doing both her boobs, which turned out, surprisingly, to be small and delicate.

And Janis, Jimi, the two Keiths, and all the others—all of them—they understood the difference between me and the Plaster Casters. They knew the Plaster Casters were mere publicity-seekers. But after all, they wanted publicity, too. So they let those clumsy girls paw them and poke them this way and that, but they never respected them or found them erotic, never thought of them as anything more than dumb groupies. With me, though, they were respectful, in awe. Together, we sought immortality, not just a write-up in *Rolling Stone*. After all, compared to immortality, an orgasm isn't that big a deal.

Their desire to let me sculpt them came from a place deep inside, a place not sullied by commercialism and greed, the very place where their own art came from: Jimi's wild guitar playing, Janis' raw, untamed voice, David's androgynous personae, Bobby's esoteric lyrics. And to this day, only they—these beautiful, fierce rock icons—are ever allowed to see my work. Dealers are banned from my studio; the public is never invited in. Only the rock stars themselves, so wide-eyed and respectful as they follow me from sculpture to sculpture. And when, at the end of their tour, they ask me what the silver initials stand for, I tell them they're not initials, just abstract, silvery shapes. And sometimes one might add, "Well, you know, those silver shapes also look a lot like a woman's body—like your body, Not the Plaster Casters." But I merely smile enigmatically.

I'm always distancing myself—planning the next one I'll be doing, for instance, even as I'm casting the member of another. After all, my work is never done. Not by a long shot. There are new ones to conquer, new ones all the time, new ones whenever I blink. And believe me, I know how to separate the real ones from the wannabes, the pretenders, the flashes in the pan. Next week, for instance, I'm doing Michael. The week after, Bono. And the week after that, there's Axl on Wednesday, and Slash on Thursday. Madonna—like Janis—also wants to pose. "I'm bigger than Janis," she bragged over the phone. I didn't deign to reply; my art is not about size or competition. And Bruce and Rod and Billy all want to come back, to do it a second time, to "re-live the high," they say.

They all call *me*. They know where to find me. I'm never cruel, but I'm always honest. Sometimes I just have to say: "I'm sorry, but you don't have it, that star quality, that beauty, that thing that I, as an artist, require." I had to tell that to Michael's brothers, for instance. Some accept my refusal with dignity. Others weep and beg. Others hang up abruptly, stunned and ashamed. It saddens me to hurt them, but there's no room in art for pity.

The ones I say "yes" to, though, are euphoric. They grow overeager. "When? Tonight? Tomorrow?"

"Whoa," I tell them. "Slow down."

And then, on the given date—sometimes I make them wait weeks, or even months—they fly in from L.A. or London or Seattle, and they arrive at my private studio, way up here, far away from any big city, high in the mountains, where I can best maintain my distance, my anonymity, my purity.

"You look so young," they always say, when I first greet them at the door.

I smile modestly, and then I show them around, giving them the tour. They grow silent, too much in awe to speak, as I lead them from sculpture to sculpture. Sometimes one might whisper under his breath, "Wow, that Jimi, man," or, "Those Plaster Casters had nothin' on you," or one might even sniffle and shed a tear or two, but other than that, they're as quiet as if in church.

Then, when we've finished the tour, I show them where to stand, where to hang their flannel shirts and baseball caps, their lycra biking shorts and headbands.

They begin to strip—some slowly, some hurriedly, some with bravado, some with a sheepish grin.

Meanwhile, I stir up the plaster, watching them all the while, assessing their size, their shape.

"Really, you look as young as I do," the baby-faced ones from Seattle always say, as I mold the plaster onto their flesh, firmly yet delicately, with my special touch.

"It's the art," I tell them. "It keeps me young."

Then, as I stroke the plaster gently, smoothing it down, I add, "It's *you*. You keep me young."

Of course, they want to sleep with me, just as their rock forefathers did. They grow aroused and needy. "I want you," they all say. "You're so sensuous, so ripe."

I thank them, and then I explain that for art's sake, I can't.

"I understand," they sigh. "Your art is bigger than we are."

Again, I smile enigmatically. And when it's time for them to leave, I allow them one kiss goodbye, but no more than that, even when my body craves much, much more. "Goodbye, Not the Plaster Casters," they wave, when I finally send them on their way.

"Goodbye," I wave back, standing at my doorway, watching them walk down the long, winding mountain path.

"Goodbye," I wave a second time, when they turn around for one final look, hoping to preserve me—Not the Plaster Casters—forever in their memories. And I don't begrudge them that final look. After all,

I already have *them* with me *forever,* here in my studio, hardened and perfectly formed—to do with what I will. And *that*—like my silver initials—is my secret, the part of my artistic process I keep all to myself, the part that really keeps me so beautiful, so eternally young, so eternally ripe.

Nominated by Kim Addonizio

WHAT THE ANIMALS TEACH US

by CHARD DENIORD

from HARVARD REVIEW

that love is dependent on memory,
that life is eternal and therefore criminal,
that thought is an invisible veil that covers our eyes,
that death is only another animal,
that beauty is formed by desperation,
that sex is solely a human problem,
that pets are wild in heaven,
that sounds and smells escape us,
that there are bones in the earth without any marker,
that language refers to too many things,
that music hints at what we heard before we sang,
that the circle is loaded,
that nothing we know by forgetting is sacred,
that humor charges the smallest things,
that the gods *are* animals without their masks,
that stones tell secrets to the wildest creatures,
that nature is an idea and not a place,
that our bodies have diminished in size and strength,
that our faces are terrible,
that our eyes are double when gazed upon,
that snakes do talk, as well as asses,
that we compose our only audience,

that we are geniuses when we wish to kill,
that we are naked despite our clothes,
that our minds are bodies in another world.

Nominated by Tom Lux

NEW YORK DAYS, 1958–1964

by CHARLES SIMIC

from THE GETTYSBURG REVIEW

Even the old Romans knew. To have a poet for a son is bad news. I took precautions. I left home when I was eighteen. For the next couple of years, I lived in a basement apartment next to a furnace that hissed and groaned as if it were about to explode any moment. I kept the windows open in all kinds of weather, figuring that then I'd be able to crawl out to the sidewalk in a hurry. All winter long I wrote bad poems and painted bad pictures wearing a heavy overcoat and gloves in that underground hole.

At the Chicago newspaper where I worked, I proofread obituaries and want ads. At night I dreamed of lost dogs and funerals. Every payday I put a little money aside. One day I had enough to quit my job and take a trip to Paris, but I treated my friends to a smorgasbord in a fancy Swedish restaurant instead. It wasn't what we expected: there was too much smoked fish and pickled herring. After I paid the bill, everybody was still hungry, so we went down the street for pizza.

My friends wanted to know: When are you going to Paris? "I've changed my mind," I announced, ordering another round of beers. "I'm moving to New York, since I no longer have the money for Paris." The women were disappointed, but the fellows applauded. It didn't make sense, me going back to Europe after being in the States for only four years. Plus, to whom in Paris would I show my poems written in English?

"Your poems are just crazy images strung arbitrarily together," my pals complained, and I'd argue back: "Haven't you heard about surrealism and free association?" Bob Burleigh, my best friend, had a degree in English from the University of Chicago and possessed all the critical tools to do a close analysis of any poem. His verdict was: "Your poems don't mean anything."

My official reply to him was: "As long as they sound good, I'll keep them." Still, in private, I worried. I knew my poems were about something, but what was it? I couldn't define that "something" no matter how hard I tried. Bob and I would often quarrel about literature till the sun came up. To show him I was capable of writing differently, I wrote a thirty-page poem about the Spanish Inquisition. In the manner of Pound in his *Cantos*, I generously quoted original descriptions of tortures and public burnings. It wasn't surrealism, everybody agreed, but you still couldn't make heads or tails of what was going on. In one section, I engaged Tomás de Torquemada in a philosophical discussion, just as Dostoyevsky's Ivan did with the Grand Inquisitor. I read the poem to a woman called Linda in a greasy spoon on Clark Street. When we ran to catch a bus, I left the poem behind. The next morning, the short-order cook and I tried to find it buried under the garbage out back. But it was a hot summer day, and the trash in the alley smelled bad and was thickly covered with flies. So we didn't look too closely.

Later, I stood at the corner where we caught the bus the night before. I smoked a lot of cigarettes. I scratched my head. Several buses stopped, but I didn't get on any of them. The drivers would wait for me to make up my mind, then give me a dirty look and drive off with a burst of speed and a parting cough of black smoke.

I LEFT CHICAGO in August 1958 and went to New York, wearing a tan summer suit and a blue Hawaiian shirt. The weather was hot and humid. The movie marquees on 42nd Street were lit up twenty-four hours a day. Sailors were everywhere, and a few mounted policemen. I bought a long cigar and lit it nonchalantly for the benefit of a couple of young girls who stood at the curb afraid to cross the busy avenue.

A wino staggered up to me in Bryant Park and said: "I bark back at the dogs." A male hooker pulled a small statue of Jesus out of his tight pants and showed it to me. In Chinatown I saw a white hen pick a card with my fortune while dancing on a hot grill. In Central Park the early morning grass was matted where unknown lovers lay. In my hotel room I kept the mirror busy by making stranger and stranger faces at myself.

"Sweetheart," a husky woman's voice said to me when I answered the phone at four in the morning. I hung up immediately.

187

It was incredibly hot, so I slept naked. My only window was open, but there was a brick wall a few feet outside of it and no draft. I suspected there were rats on that wall, but I had no choice.

Late mornings, I sat in a little luncheonette on 8th Street reading the sports pages or writing poems:

> In New York on 14th Street
> Where peddlers hawk their wares
> And cops look the other way,
> There you meet the eternal—
> Con-artists selling watches, silk ties, umbrellas,
> After nightfall
> When the crosstown wind blows cold
> And my landlady throws a skinny chicken
> In the pot to boil. Fumes rise.
> I can draw her ugly face on the kitchen window,
> Then take a quick peek at the street below.

It was still summer. On advice from my mother, I went to visit an old friend of hers. She served me tea and cucumber sandwiches and asked about my plans for the future. I replied that I had no idea. I could see that she was surprised. To encourage me, she told me about someone who knew at the age of ten that he wanted to be a doctor and was now studying at a prestigious medical school. I agreed to come to a dinner party where I would meet a number of brilliant young men and women my age and profit by their example. Of course, I failed to show up.

At the Phoenix Book Shop in the Village, I bought a book of French stories. It was on sale and very cheap, but even so I had only enough money left to buy a cup of coffee and a toasted English muffin. I took my time sipping the lukewarm coffee and nibbling my muffin as I read the book. It was a dark and rainy night. I walked the near-empty streets for hours in search of the only two people I knew in the city. Not finding them home, I returned to my room, crawled shivering under the covers, and read in the silence, interrupted only by the occasional wailing of an ambulance:

> Monsieur Lantin had met the girl at a party given one
> evening by his office superior and love had caught him in
> its net.

She was the daughter of a country tax-collector who had died a few years before. She had come to Paris then with her mother, who struck up acquaintance with a few middle-class families in her district in the hope of marrying her off. They were poor and decent, quiet and gentle. The girl seemed the perfect example of a virtuous woman to whom every sensible young man dreams of entrusting his life. Her simple beauty had a modest, angelic charm and the imperceptible smile which always hovered about her lips seemed to be a reflection of her heart.

After midnight my hotel was as quiet as a tomb. I had to play the radio real low with my ear brushing against it in the dark. "Clap your hands, here comes Charlie," some woman sang, a hot Dixieland band backing her up, but just then I didn't think it was very funny.

WHILE THE WEATHER was still good, I sat on benches in Washington Square Park or Central Park, watching people and inventing stories to go along with their faces. If I was wearing my only suit and it rained, I sat in the lobbies of big hotels smoking cigars. I went window-shopping almost every night. An attractive pair of shoes or a shirt would make me pay a return visit even after midnight. The movies consumed an immense amount of my time. I would emerge after seeing the double feature twice, dazed, disoriented, and hungry. I often had toothache and waited for days for it to go away. I typed with two fingers on an ancient Underwood typewriter, which woke my hotel neighbors. They'd knock on my walls until I stopped. On a Monday morning while everyone else was rushing off to work, I took a long subway ride to Far Rockaway. Whenever the subway came out of the ground, I would get a glimpse of people working in offices and factories. I could tell they were hot and perspiring. On the beach there were only a few bathers, seemingly miles apart. When I stretched out on the sand and looked up, the sky was empty and blue.

When I was on the way home late one night, a drunk came out of a dark doorway with a knife in hand. He swayed and couldn't say what he wanted. I ran. Even though I knew there was no chance he would catch up with me, I didn't stop for many blocks. When I finally did, I no longer knew where I was. Around that time, I wrote:

Purse snatchers
Keep away from poor old women
They yell the loudest.
Stick to young girls,
The dreamy newlyweds
Buying heart-shaped pillows for their beds.
Bump into a drunk instead,
Offer a pencil to sell.
When he pulls out a roll of bills,
Snatch all he's got and split.
Duck that nightstick
Or your ears will ring
Even in your coffin.

I AM NOT EXAGGERATING when I say that I couldn't take a piss without a book in my hand. I read to fall asleep and to wake up. I read at my various jobs, hiding the book among the papers on my desk or in the half-open drawer. I read everything from Plato to Mickey Spillane. Even in my open coffin, some day, I should be holding a book. *The Tibetan Book of the Dead* would be most appropriate, but I'd prefer a sex manual or the poems of Emily Dickinson.

The book that made all the difference to my idea of poetry was an anthology of contemporary Latin-American verse that I bought on 8th Street. Published by New Directions in 1942 and long out of print even then, it introduced me to Jorge Luis Borges, Pablo Neruda, Jorge Carrera Andrade, Drumond de Andrade, Nicholas Guillen, Vicente Huidobro, Jorge de Lima, César Vallejo, Octavio Paz, and so many others. After that anthology, the poetry I read in literary magazines struck me as pretty timid. Nowhere in *The Sewanee Review* or *The Hudson Review* could I find poems like "Biography for the use of the birds" or "Liturgy of my Legs" or this one, by the Haitian poet Emile Roumer, "The Peasant Declares His Love":

High-yellow of my heart, with breasts like tangerines,
you taste better to me than eggplant stuffed with crab,
you are the tripe in my pepper-pot,
the dumpling in my peas, my tea of aromatic herbs.
You're the corned beef whose customhouse is my heart,
my mush with syrup that trickles down the throat.
You're a steaming dish, mushroom cooked with rice,

crisp potato fried, and little fish fried brown . . .
My hankering for love follows you wherever you go.
Your bum is a gorgeous basket brimming with fruits and meat.

The folk surrealism, the mysticism, the eroticism, and the wild flights of romance and rhetoric in these poets were much more appealing to me than what I found among the French and German modernists that I already knew. Of course, I started imitating the South Americans immediately:

> I'm the last offspring of the old raven
> Who fed himself on the flesh of the hanged . . .
> A dark nest full of old misfortunes,
> The wind raging above the burning tree-tops,
> A cold north wind looking for its bugle.

I WAS READING Jakob Boehme in the New York Public Library on 42nd Street on a hot, muggy morning when a woman arrived in what must've been last night's party dress. She was not much older than I, but the hour and the lack of sleep gave her a world-weary air. She consulted the catalog, filled out a slip, received her book, and sat down at a table across from mine. I craned my neck, I squinted in my nearsighted way, and I even brushed past her a couple of times, but I could not figure out what she was reading. The book had no pictures, and it wasn't poetry, but she was so absorbed that her hair fell into her eyes. Perhaps she was sleeping.

Then, all of a sudden, when I was absolutely sure she was snoozing away, she turned a page with a long, thin finger. Her fingers were too thin, in my opinion. Was the poor dear eating properly? Was she dying of consumption? Her breasts in her low-cut black dress, on the other hand, looked pretty healthy. I saw no problem there.

Did she notice me spying on her? Absolutely not, unless she was a consummate actress, a budding Gene Tierney.

Of all of the people I watched surreptitiously over the years, how many noticed me and still remember me the way I remember them? I just have to close my eyes, and there she is, still reading her mysterious book. I don't see myself and have no idea what I look like or what clothes I'm wearing. The same goes for everyone else in the large reading room. They have no faces; they do not exist. She's reading slowly and turning the pages carefully. The air is heavy and muggy and the ceiling fan doesn't help. It could be a Monday or a Thursday, July or August. I'm not even certain if it was 1958 or 1959.

I went to hear Allen Tate read his poems at New York University. There were no more than twenty of us all together: a few friends of the poet, a couple of English professors, a scattering of graduate students, and one or two oddballs like me seated way in the back. Tate was thin and dapper, polite, and read in what I suppose could be described as a cultivated Southern voice. I had already read some of his essays and liked them very much, but the poetry, because of its seriousness and literary sophistication, was tedious. You would have to be nuts to want to write like that, I thought, remembering Jorge de Lima's poem in which he describes God tattooing the virgin: "Come, let us read the virgin, let us learn the future . . . /O men of little sight." Not a spot on her skin without tattoos: "that is why the virgin is so beautiful," the Brazilian poet says.

ON A HOT NIGHT in a noisy, crowded, smoke-filled jazz club, whiskey and beer were flowing, everyone was reeling with drink. A fat woman laughed so hard, she fell off her chair. It was hard to hear the music. Someone took a muted trumpet solo I tried to follow with my left ear, while with my right I had to listen to two women talk about a fellow called Mike, who was a scream in his bathing suit.

It was better to go to clubs on weeknights, when the crowd was smaller and there were no tourists. Best of all was walking in after midnight, in time to catch the final set of the night. One night when I arrived, the bass and drums were already playing, but where was Sonny Rollins, whom I came to hear? Finally we heard a muffled saxophone: Sonny was in the men's room, blowing his head off. Everybody quieted down, and soon enough he came through the door, bobbing his shaved head, dark shades propped on a nose fit for an emperor. He was playing "Get Happy," twisting it inside out, reconstituting it completely, discovering its concealed rhythmic and melodic beauties, and we were right there with him, panting with happiness.

It was great. The lesson I learned was: cultivate controlled anarchy. I found Rollins, Charlie Parker, and Thelonious Monk far better models of what an artist could be than most poets. The same was true of the painters. Going to jazz clubs and galleries made me realize that there was a lot more poetry in America than one could find in the quarterlies.

AT ONE OF THE READINGS at NYU given by a now forgotten academic poet of the 1950s, just as the professional lovers of poetry in the audience were already closing their eyes blissfully in anticipation of the poet's familiar, soul-stirring clichés, there was the sound of paper being torn. We all turned around to look. A shabby old man was ripping newspapers into a brown shopping bag. He saw people glare at him and stopped. The moment we turned back to the poet who went on reading, oblivious of everything, in a slow monotone, the man resumed ripping, but now more cautiously, with long pauses between rips.

And so it went: the audience would turn around with angry faces, he'd stop for a while and then continue while the poet read on and on.

MY FIRST JOB in the city was selling dress shirts in Stern's Department Store on 42nd Street. I dressed well and learned how to flash a friendly smile. Even more importantly, I learned how to let myself be humiliated by the customers without putting up the slightest resistance.

My next job was in the Doubleday Bookstore on 5th Avenue. I would read on the sly while the manager was busy elsewhere. Eventually I could guess what most of the customers wanted even before they opened their mouths. There were the bestseller types and the self-help book types, the old ladies in love with mysteries, and the sensitive young women who were sure to ask for Khalil Gibran's *The Prophet*.

But I didn't like standing around all day, so I got a job typing address labels at New York University Press. After a while they hired another fellow to give me help. We sat in the back room playing chess for hours on end. Occasionally, one of the editors would come and ask us to pick up his dry cleaning, pay an electric bill, buy a sandwich or a watermelon.

Sal and I took our time. We sat in the park and watched the girl students go by. Sal was a few years older than I, and a veteran of the Air Force. When he was just a teenager, his parents died suddenly and he inherited the family bakery in Brooklyn. He got married and in two years had ruined the business.

How? I wanted to know. "I took my wife to the Latin Quarter and Copacabana every night," he told me with obvious satisfaction. He joined the Air Force to flee his creditors. Now he was a veteran and a homespun philosopher.

Sal agreed with H. L. Mencken that you are as likely to find an honest politician as you are an honest burglar. Only the church, in his view, was worse: "The priests are all perverts," he confided to me, "and the Pope is the biggest pervert of all."

"What about Billy Graham?" I asked, trying not to drop my watermelon.

"That's all he thinks about," Sal assured me with a wink.

The military was no better. All the officers he had met were itching to commit mass murder. Even Ike, in his opinion, had the mug of a killer.

Only women were good. "If you want to have a happy life," he told me every day, "learn to get along with the ladies."

AFTER SEVERAL FLEABAG HOTELS, I finally found a home at Hotel Albert on 10th Street and University Place. The room was small, and of course the window faced a brick wall, but the location was perfect, and the rent was not too high. From Friday noon to Sunday morning, I had plenty of money. The rest of the week, I scraped by on candy bars for lunch and hamburgers or cheap Chinese food for dinner. Later I would buy a glass of beer for fifteen cents and spend the rest of the night perfecting the art of making it last forever.

My first poems were published in the Winter 1959 issue of *The Chicago Review*, but other publications came slowly after that: the mail brought me rejection slips every day. One, I remember, had a personal note from the editor that said: "Dear Mr. Simic, you're obviously an intelligent young man, so why do you waste your time writing so much about pigs and cockroaches?"

To spit on guys like you, I wanted to write back.

AFTER WORK ON FRIDAYS, my friend Jim Brown and I would tour the bars. We'd start a few beers at the Cedar Tavern, near our rooms, then walk over to the San Remo on MacDougal Street, where Brown would have a martini and I would drink red wine. Afterwards, we would most likely go to the White Horse, where Brown had a tab, to drink whiskey. With some of the regulars, Brown would discuss everything from socialism to old movies; I didn't open my mouth much, for the moment I did and people heard my accent, I would have to explain where I came from, and how, and why. I thought of printing a card, the kind deaf panhandlers pass around, with my life story on it and an abbreviated account of the geography and history of the Balkans.

Around midnight Brown and I would walk back to the Cedar, which was packed by then, and have a nightcap. Over hamburgers, Brown would harangue me for not having read François Rabelais or Sir Thomas Browne yet. Later, lying in my bed, with drink and talk float-

194

ing in my head and the sound of creaking beds, smokers' coughs, and love cries coming from the other rooms, I would not be able to sleep. I would go over the interesting and stupid things I had heard that night.

For instance, there were still true believers around in those days who idealized life in the Soviet Union and disparaged the United States. What upset me the most was when some nice-looking, young woman would nod in agreement. I reproached myself for not telling her how people over there were turned into angels at the point of a gun. My shyness and cowardice annoyed me no end. I couldn't fall asleep for hours and then, just as I was finally drifting off, one of my rotten teeth would begin a little chat with me.

WITH THE ARRIVAL of the Beats, both as a literary movement and as a commercial venture, the scene changed. Coffee shops sprang up everywhere in the Village. In addition to folk singing and comedy acts, they offered poetry readings. *Where the Beat Meet the Elite,* said a banner over a tourist trap. "Oh God, come down and fuck me!" some young woman prayed in her poem, to the horror of out-of-town customers.

But New York was also a great place for poetry: within the same week, one could also hear John Berryman and May Swenson, Allen Ginsberg and Denise Levertov, Frank O'Hara and LeRoi Jones. I went to readings for two reasons: to hear the poets and to meet people. I could always find, sitting grumpily in the corner, someone with whom it was worth striking up a conversation. The readings themselves left me with mixed feelings. One minute I would be dying of envy, and the next with boredom and contempt. It took me a few years to sort it all out. In the meantime, I sought other views. I'd spot someone thumbing an issue of *The Black Mountain Review* in The Eighth Street Bookstore and end up talking to them. Often that would lead to a cup of coffee or a beer. No matter how hip you think you are, someone always knows more. The literary scene had a greater number of true originals then than it has today—autodidacts, booze hounds, and near-derelicts who were walking encyclopedias—for example Tony, an unemployed bricklayer, who went around saying things like: *Even the mutes are unhappy since they've learned to read lips,* and *It took me sixty years to bend down to a flower.*

Then, there was the tall, skinny fellow with graying hair I talked to after hearing Richard Wilbur read at NYU. He told me that the reason contemporary poets were so bad is because they were lazy. I asked what he meant, and he explained: "They write a couple of hours per week, and the rest of the time they have a ball living in the lap of luxury with rich floozies hanging on their arms and paying their bills. You've got to write sixteen hours per day to be a great poet." I asked him what he did, and he muttered that he worked in the post office.

During one of my rare trips back to Chicago to visit my mother, Bob Burleigh told me about a terrific young poet I ought to meet. His name was Bill Knott. He worked nights in a hospital emptying bedpans and was usually at home during the day. He lived in a rooming house not too far away, so we went to see him.

An old woman answered the bell and said Bill was upstairs in his room. But when we knocked there was no answer. Bob shouted, "It's me, Bob." Just as we were about to leave, I heard a sound of hundreds of bottles clinking together, and the door opened slowly. Soon we saw what it was: we had to wade through an ankle-deep layer of empty Pepsi bottles to advance into the room. Bill was a large man in a dirty, white T-shirt; one lens of his glasses was wrapped with masking tape, presumably broken. The furnishings were a bed with a badly stained mattress, a large poster of Monica Vitti, a refrigerator with an old TV set on it, and a couple of chairs and a table with piles of books on them. Bob sat on the bed, and I was given a chair after Bill swept some books onto the floor. Bill, who hadn't sat down, asked us: "How about a Pepsi?" "Sure," we replied. "What the heck!" The fridge, it turned out, contained nothing but rows and rows of Pepsi bottles.

We sipped our sodas and talked poetry. Bill had read everything: we spoke of René Char, and Bill quoted Char from memory. Regarding contemporary American poetry, we were in complete agreement: except for Robert Bly, James Wright, Frank O'Hara, and a few others, the poets we read in the magazines were the most unimaginative, dull, pretentious, know-nothing bunch you were ever likely to encounter. As far as these poets were concerned, Arthur Rimbaud, Hart Crane, and Guillaume Apollinaire might never have existed. They knew nothing of modern art, cinema, jazz. We had total contempt for them. We bought magazines like *Poetry* in those days in order to nourish our rage: Bob and I regularly analyzed its poems so we could grasp the full range of their imbecility. I did not see any of Bill Knott's poems that day, but later he became one of my favorite poets.

BACK IN NEW YORK, I had a long talk with Robert Lowell about nineteenth-century French poetry. We were at a party following a reading at the Y. It was late, and most people had gone home. Lowell was seated in an armchair, two young women were sitting on the floor, one

196

on each side of him, and I was on the floor facing him. Although he spoke interestingly about Charles Baudelaire, Tristan Corbiere, and Jules Laforgue, what had me totally captivated were not his words, but his hands. Early in our conversation, he massaged the women's necks; after a while he slid his hands down inside their dresses and worked their breasts. They didn't seem to mind, hanging on his every word. Why wasn't I a great poet? Instead of joining in, I started disagreeing with him, told him he was full of shit. True, I had flunked out of school in Paris, but when it came to the French vernacular, my ear could not be faulted. Lowell did not seem to notice my increasing nastiness, but his two groupies certainly did. Finally, I said good night and split. I walked from the upper West Side down to my room in the Village, fuming and muttering like an old drunk.

ANOTHER TIME I was drinking red wine, chain-smoking, and writing, long past midnight. Suddenly, the poem took off, the words just flowing, in my head a merry-go-round of the most brilliant similes and metaphors. *This is it!* I was convinced there had never been such a moment of inspiration in the whole history of literature. I reread what I'd written and had to quit my desk and walk around the room, I got so excited. No sooner was I finished with one poem than I started another even more incredible one. Toward daybreak, paying no attention to my neighbor's furious banging on the wall, I typed them out with my two fingers and finally passed out exhausted in the bed. In the morning, I dragged myself to work, dead tired but happy.

When evening came, I sat down to savor what I wrote the night before, a glass of wine in my hand. The poems were terrible! Incoherent babble, surrealist drivel! How could I have written such crap? I was stunned, depressed, and totally confused.

Still, it wasn't the first time this had happened: nights of creative bliss followed by days of gagging. With great clarity I could see every phony move I had made, every borrowing, every awkwardness. Then I found myself in a different kind of rush: I had only seconds left to rip up, burn, and flush down the toilet all these poems before the doctors and nurses rushed in and put me in a straightjacket. Of course, the next night, I was at it again, writing furiously and shaking my head in disbelief at the gorgeous images and metaphors flooding out of my pen.

I have thrown out hundreds of poems in my life, four chapters of a novel, the first act of a play, fifty or so pages of a book on Joseph

197

Cornell. Writing poetry is a supreme pleasure, and so is wiping the slate clean.

TODAY PEOPLE SOMETIMES ASK me when I decided to become a poet. I never did. The truth is, I had no plans: I was content merely to drift along. My immigrant experience protected me from any quick embrace of a literary or political outlook. Being a suspicious outsider was an asset, I realized at some point. Modernism, which is already a collage of various cultures and traditions, suited me well. The impulse of every young artist and writer to stake everything on a single view and develop a recognizable style was, of course, attractive, but at the same time I knew myself to be pulled in different directions. I loved Whitman, and I loved the Surrealists. The more widely I read, the less I wanted to restrict myself to a single aesthetic and literary position. I was already many things, so why shouldn't I be the same way in poetry?

One evening I would be in some Village coffee shop arguing about Charles Olson and Projective Verse, and the next evening I would be eating squid in a Greek restaurant, arguing in Serbian with my father or uncle Boris about Enrico Caruso and Beniamino Gigli, Mario Del Monaco, and Jussi Bjorling.

On one such evening, a nice, old, silver-haired lady, pointing to three other silver-haired ladies smiling at us from the next table, asked Boris and me: "Would you, please, tell us what language you are speaking?"

Boris, who never missed an opportunity to play a joke, made a long face, sighed once or twice, and—with moist eyes and a sob in his voice—informed her that, alas, we were the last two remaining members of a white African tribe speaking a now nearly extinct language.

That surprised the hell out of her! She didn't realize, she told us, now visibly confused, that there were native white African tribes.

"The best kept secret in the world," Boris whispered to her and nodded solemnly while she rushed back to tell her friends.

It was part of being an immigrant and living in many worlds at the same time, some of which were imaginary. After what we had been through, the wildest lies seemed plausible. The poems that I was going to write had to take that into account.

Nominated by David Lehman

KARMA LOLLIPOP

by ALBERT SAIJO

from BAMBOO RIDGE

WHITEMAN CENTRAL BREAKDOWN—THINGS START
TO WOBBLE & FALL APART—GLASS SHATTERS METAL
CORRODES FERROCONCRETE WEATHERS &
CRUMBLES—WHITEMAN CENTRAL BECOMES POOR—
DIRT POOR—MORE POOR THAN A 3RD WORLD
COUNTRY—SO POOR IT CAN'T EVEN SUPPORT A
WEALTHY CLASS—WHITEMAN RETURNS TO HUNTER
FORAGER MODE—WHITEMAN'S LAND BECOMES TERRA
INCOGNITA—THEN ONE DAY INTO THIS NOT NECES-
SARILY UNHAPPY SITUATION IN WHICH HARDLY
ANYTHING IS HAPPENING BUT LIFE THERE COMES
NOVELTY—1ST IT'S THEIR MISSIONARIES—THEY ARE
NOT WHITE—THEY ARE ELFIN & YELLOW—THEY HAVE
HIGH CHEEKBONES SLANT EYES & BLACK HAIR—THEY
SAY THEY ARE FROM AN ADVANCED HYPERTECH
CIVILIZATION ACROSS THE GREAT WATER TO THE
WEST IN THE DIRECTION OF THE SETTING SUN & THEY
POINT IN THAT DIRECTION SO WHITEMAN UNDER-
STAND—THEY TALK LOUD—THEY SAY WHITEMAN OUR
BURDEN—THEY SAY BUDDHA LOVE WHITEMAN EVEN
IF WHITEMAN BACKWARD DIRTY & HEATHENISH—
THEY WANT WHITEMAN TO CLEAN UP & PUT ON
CLOTHES—THEIR TRIP SEEMS TO BE BUDDHA LOVES
YOU SANITATION & DON'T LET NUTHIN HANG OUT—
SO BIG DEAL IF THAT'S ALL THEY WANT—BUT THEY
BROUGHT THE KONG HONG FLU—LESS SAID ABOUT IT

THE BETTER—THEN COME THE SOCIAL SCIENTISTS—
THEY ARE FROM ANOTHER ADVANCED
TECHNOCIVILIZATION OF SMALL BROWN PEOPLE
WHERE ALTERED NEURONAL TISSUE CULTURED ON
SEWER SLUDGE GROW INTO GIANT BRAINS THAT RUN
EVERYTHING—ORGANIC BIOTECH TO THE MAX OR
NOTHING—A MARVEL OF THE NEW GOOK SCIENTIFIC
IMAGINATION—THEY SAY HEY WHITEMAN YOU DON'T
MIND IF WE SET UP OUR CAMP IN YOUR YARD DO
YOU—WE WANT TO STUDY YOU—YOU'RE VERY INTER-
ESTING TO US—HEY WHAT'S THAT TOOL YOU GOT IN
YOUR HAND—LOOK FELLAS IT'S AN ARCHAIC VICE
GRIP—WE WANT THAT—THEY GIVE WHITEMAN A MESS
OF CHEAP BEADS & A TIN MIRROR & THEY TAKE HIS
VICE GRIP—AND THEY LEAVE THE YELLOW YAW
YAWS—ALMOST 100% MORTALITY FOR WHITEMAN ON
THAT ONE—CLOSE—THE YELLOW YAW YAWS ARE LIKE
THE HEARTBREAK OF PSORIASIS ONLY MUCH MUCH
WORSE—AGAIN LESS SAID ABOUT IT THE BETTER—
THEN COME THE POWER & BUCKS PEOPLE—THEY ARE
SHORT WITH BROAD FLAT FACES & PERFECT ALMOND
EYES YOU'D DIE FOR—THEY DON'T GIVE A SHIT FOR
NUTHIN BUT POWER & BUCKS—DERE DA GUYS WHO
GOT THE VAPORIZOR GUNS—YOU GET IN THEIR WAY
THEY POINT THE VAPORIZOR AT YOU & PULL THE
TRIGGER—WHEN THE FORCE HITS IT TURNS YOU INTO
A PUFF OF INNOCUOUS VAPOR—NO GORY CORPSE—
MAYHEM MADE SANITARY—A GIANT STEP FORWARD
FOR CIVILIZATION—A MARVEL OF THE MONGOL SCI-
ENTIFIC IMAGINATION WITH ITS SURREAL
MATHEMATIC TURNS FLESH TO VAPOR—NOW BEFORE
THE VERY EYES OF WHITEMAN THESE ADVANCED
NONWHITE NATIONS ARE DIVIDING UP WHITEMAN'S
LAND INTO WHAT THEY CALL SPHERES OF INFLU-
ENCE—THEY ARE GOING TO PUT A GRID ON
WHITEMAN'S LAND & SELL IT OFF DIRT CHEAP FOR
KIWI PLANTATIONS WITH WHITEMAN DOING THE
GRUNTWORK—THEN ONCE THE PLANTATIONS ARE IN
THEY AUTOMATE PLANTATIONS—NOW WHITE MAN
ON THE DOLE & REALLY BEGINNING TO GET IN THE

WAY OF PROGRESS—SO THESE SUPERTECH NATIONS
ROUND UP WHITEMAN THAT IS THE REMNANT POPU-
LATIONS OF WHITEMAN STILL SCATTERED HERE &
THERE & THEY PUT THEM INTO WHAT THEY CALL
RELOCATION CENTERS THAT CAN MEAN ANYTHING
OR NOTHING LIKE RESERVATIONS—NOW THESE NON-
WHITE ADVANCED MEGATECH NATIONS BEGIN
FIGHTING AMONG THEMSELVES—INEVITABLY—ALL
POLITICS IS BULLSHIT—THEY MAKE WHITEMAN'S
LAND INTO A BATTLEGROUND FOR THEIR WARS—
THESE WARS HAVE NOTHING TO DO WITH WHITEMAN
BUT THEY ARE TRASHING HIS LAND—MEANTIME
AMIDST ALL THE CHAOS OF THIS MOTHER OF ALL
WARS ONLY THE MENEHUNES OF THE WORLD REMAIN
CLEAR CENTERED ON TIME NEUTRAL EACH A VERI-
TABLE SWITZERLAND OF THE UNIVERSAL POETIC
GENIUS

Nominated by Bamboo Ridge

OUT OF THE WOODS

fiction by JOSIP NOVAKOVICH

from DOUBLETAKE

DENA'S VISION WAS blurry. The stucco on a brick house on the corner of Vlaska Street seemed to her to be detached from the walls, as if it were the building's aura. She wondered whether being malnourished during the Balkan wars had damaged her sight. She looked for the offices of an ophthalmologist on Nazorova Street, in the hills, past several embassies and an orphanage. When she saw two men with patches of white gauze on their eyes, strolling with sticks, back and forth in front of one building, she knew the clinic had to be there. She walked inside and sat down in the waiting room among a quiet group of people who stared ahead of them vacantly. A man in front of her seemed to have no irises, only large pupils, even though his eyes were wide open and sunlight filled the room. The light warmed her knees. She stretched her miniskirt and was upset that she had forgotten to put on a longer one. But then, what difference did it make among the nearly blind?

It did seem to make a difference to the doctor, a tall man with a few streaks in his stark black beard. She crossed her legs, but then felt that her thigh was exposed, so she uncrossed them, but the doctor was now sitting straight ahead of her, and from his angle he could probably see up her thighs. Not that that should be such a big deal—on a beach it would be normal. She brought her knees together and put her hands in her lap.

"Do you wear glasses?" His voice was a sonorous baritone. And she was struck by how pink his gums and white his teeth were—probably the result of German dentistry.

"No, I never have."

"And this is the first time that your vision has been blurry?"

"The first time that I noticed, and the first that I had an eye ache and also a headache."

"Do you have any medical conditions?"

"I'm alive, that's a medical condition, isn't it?"

"Are you ill, allergic to any drugs, suffer from a chronic condition, such as asthma?"

"Not that I know of. But now that you mention it, I am breathing kind of hard, aren't I?" Her breath was almost a wheeze, and she looked down at her breasts, which rose and fell, with an effort, almost a pain.

The doctor shone an ophthalmologic light into her eyes, and she could smell soap on his hands. He poked an instrument into her ears, showed her the alphabetical and numerical charts, put her chin on a black plastic rest, and kept giving her different lenses. Through some lenses, the picture blurred even more; through others, it became sharper, but smaller. "Yes, this is better," she said. "Better." Static electricity seemed to glide over her legs, and she wondered whether she was feeling his gaze. But how could a gaze project any photons, or whatever it was, that she could feel?

"All right," Dr. Glavni said, and stood behind her. He touched her temples and forehead. "Close your eyes." His fingers passed over her eyelids and cheeks, and she remembered a priest putting his hands on her head, to dispense forgiveness after she confessed that she'd stolen her father's wine. That was a long time ago, in Glina.

"It's good to relax," Dr. Glavni said, "because a tense eye distorts the image more than a relaxed one."

"Are my eyes very bad?" Dena asked.

"No, they are beautiful. They do need a minor correction, though. Some astigmatism in the left eye, and myopia—minus one diopter— in the right eye. Good-bye."

Dena liked her glasses. They made her look like an intellectual—a professor of linguistics or a lawyer. She enjoyed thinking that the glasses decreased her attractiveness to the outside world and increased the attractiveness of the outside world to her. Her glasses made a statement to everybody around her. It's more important how you look to me than how I look to you. I'm the subject, you're the object. But she knew that the liquid clarity that the glass added to her dark blue eyes could actually make her look more seductive, veiled yet exposed.

While getting used to the sharpness of the world and to the tickle on the bridge of her nose, she walked into a photo shop in Ilica. She had a dozen pictures of young women, part-time prostitutes, all refugees from Bosnia, who needed work. She thought that she had a good business sense. So she could work out of her two-bedroom apartment, two tricks at a time. The rent was high—seven hundred German marks per month, higher than an average salary. She wanted to buy the apartment so she would not have to pay rent, and then she could do something mellow and honest, like run a boutique.

In the shop she looked at pictures of a naked woman, lying sideways on a cement fence. Her thin waist ascended into broad hips in a bright line. Dena pulled several photos out of her deerskin purse. "Could you do these women, like your woman on the wall, in color? I want to make a classy catalogue. How much would you charge?"

"Hum." He bit the pencil eraser, and looked her up and down. "Not much. An hour of your time."

Dena took a swing to slap him. She missed, and a nail on her middle finger bent as it scraped against his nose. As she rushed out of the shop, he shouted, "I only wanted to take pictures of you!"

She was surprised at her reaction. After all, he was good-looking, clean. Now she would have to look for another photographer, and it might cost her. She went home, and after taking a bubble bath, spent an hour looking for her glasses. She realized that she hoped that the lost glasses would warrant another trip to the ophthalmologist.

She called up her mother, a stooped old woman, who had aged terribly after her husband was executed in front of her. Whenever Dena was busy, her mother baby-sat Igor.

Dena took Igor, her five-year-old son, to get a haircut.

"I don't want a haircut," he said.

"But the hair's in your eyes. Doesn't that bother you? You'll go blind."

She did not cut Igor's hair, and she called Dr. Glavni. "I've lost my glasses. Can I come over right away and get another prescription?"

"Sure, but if you can wait a day, I can mail it to you."

"The mail is slow and unreliable."

"After work I've got to go downtown anyhow, so if you are around, let's say, at the Ban Café, I could meet you there, at six."

"Wow, that's like a date!"

"Would you like it to be?"

"To tell the truth, I don't remember how you look because my vision was so screwed up that day. I'd have to take a good look at you before I could tell you."

At six she walked back and forth under the sculpture of Ban Jellacic, the Croatian governor who had helped put down the Hungarian national revolution in the last century and who had partly inspired a Croatian national revolution in this one. The sculpture of the man in a tall hat pointed a saber to the south toward Krajina, where the Serbs had established their ministate. The original one—she remembered seeing pictures in the newspapers—had pointed north toward Hungary. And who knows where the sculpture would point next. East, perhaps. She looked up at the clock on a metal post on the western side of the square. Since she left her glasses, she had to squint to make out the time, and that was not enough, so she pressed her eyelids together a little with her fingers, and that sharpened her vision. Six-fifteen. Meanwhile a man who looked slightly familiar kept walking back and forth, winking at her. To avoid him, she walked into the café, and there was the doctor, winding his pocket watch.

"Fashionably late, am I?" she said.

"No, that's no longer the fashion."

"Are you sure you don't need a pair of glasses yourself, if you couldn't see me from here?"

"Oh, that's fine. I was reading the newspaper. Here's your prescription." He handed her a blank piece of paper.

"Doc, are you kidding me? *You* need a prescription."

"I know I do, but I also know that I am giving you a better one now. Forget these damned crutches. If you keep losing your glasses, it'll cost you a lot and confuse your eyes. Take a trip, let's say a boat ride down the Adriatic, or a hike in the woods, where you'd have to look into the distance, and then if you still need glasses, come back."

"Are you kidding?"

"Seriously. You seem to be a natural kind of person."

"What's that supposed to mean?"

"Nature will heal you."

"Where do you get that, that I am natural?"

"The way you move. You are in touch with your body."

"In touch . . . that's a pretty loose connection to have with your body. I'm not only in touch—I am squeezing it, biting it, in fact, I *am* my body. And are you in touch with yours?"

205

"Yes, I like the way you move."

"You aren't answering my question."

"Yes, I am. The fact that I like how you move, how you breathe, how your lips pout . . . shows I'm in touch with my male self. Can I kiss you?"

"I didn't ask you whether you were in touch with *my* body."

"Well, I am." He leaned over and kissed her lips, softly. She kept her eyes open, and he did, too. Their noses slid against each other. Their nostrils widened. Her lips tingled.

And then she burst out laughing.

"What's so funny?" he said.

"Your eyelashes are tickling me."

"Your place or mine?"

"I've heard that line before."

"Where?"

"Your place," she said.

"I mean where have you heard it?"

"No, you don't, silly hypocrite. But that is how barflies talk. Are you a barfly and a womanizer?"

"No, but it's not too late, is it?"

"Yes, it is." She pulled him by his brush-like beard with both of her hands to her lips.

They made love in the shower, on rugs, in chairs, on the kitchen counter. And they talked, and joked, pretending constantly to be misunderstanding each other. They were not only playful but serious, too. Nenad told her about his childhood, which he'd spent in the same house where he now lived. As a child he had spent entire weeks without anybody to speak to, in silence, without music. His parents did not talk to each other for an entire year and then got divorced, and the father went to Argentina, never to be heard from again, and the mother, who worked too hard as a teacher and tutor after hours, died of breast cancer when he was still in his teens. And there was more he could tell her, he said, but he would tell her once they got to know each other better.

Dena told him about the Serb massacre near her town, Glina. Her husband was impaled on a hot machine-gun barrel, and she was raped in a devious way. "An officer told me, 'I don't like rape. It's too dry, too much work. But I want to sleep with you. If you don't, I'll let the whole brigade rape you. And I want to see that you are excited. So let me first massage you, and we'll be real gentle.' And so the officer massaged me in exotic oils that he claimed came from the Caucasus."

"And you got excited like that?" Nenad paced, grabbed a plate, and shattered it against the wall. "Damn! Damn!"

"If someone had a gun to your head and massaged your ass, you'd feel excited, too. The hairs on my body stood up, I shivered, and . . . "

"Spare me the details."

She paused. She wanted to tell him how the officer had kept her in his barracks for two months, apart from her son, whom he took along on his rounds to the front lines to show him the artillery pieces as though he were his kid. She was not allowed to read, to watch TV, to walk, to see people; the officer put her into a sensory deprivation limbo, in a dark room, for days at a time, and when he visited, he poured honey over her and licked her, with an infinite patience and a determination to excite her senses, while she shivered from hatred mixed with lust.

"He kept his word," she said. "He didn't let anybody else rape me, and he put me on the bus to Bosanski Brod, from where we went to a camp to Opatija. It wasn't really a camp but a tourist hotel. Since tourism was dead, we were allowed to stay there, with aromatic pine breezes from the South Alps and the salty air from the sea." She wanted to tell Nenad that to get out of the refugee camp, she had resorted to prostitution—not exactly to selling her body, but renting it. There was absolutely no other way for her to get money, to get out.

As though Nenad could guess what she had not told him, he continued pacing, swearing. He drank a bottle of red wine without putting it down. She watched his pointed Adam's apple rise into his beard and fall out of it. The tip of his Adam's apple stretched the skin so that the skin turned white, bloodless. When he was done, his face was red, as though he had been choking. The wine made his lower lip glisten, and the wine flowed down his beard into his white shirt, and stained it. He was breathing hard now, and she was about to joke that perhaps he suffered from asthma, but she did not say it.

She had hoped that she could share everything with him. Probably there were things that he could not tell her—and perhaps things that he could not tell himself. She could not understand how someone could be like that, unwilling to hear the truth, no matter how ugly. Not hearing the truth was even uglier, and wishing not to hear it was a betrayal, self-betrayal, the ultimate adultery of diluting the truth with wishful thinking.

But she soon forgot, or nearly forgot, this day of confessions.

Nenad and she took a trip to Korcula, an island in the south of the Adriatic, and stayed in a hotel room overlooking a rocky beach and a round fortification with stone walls.

As Dena watched Igor shrieking with happiness and Nenad laughing with joy, she realized that her sight had improved: far out to sea, she saw distant sailboats and seagulls in a sharp detail. Her ocular crisis might have been caused by a dizzy spell. Since glasses would probably have ruined her sight, she felt grateful to Nenad for giving nature a chance to cure her vision.

Later, as they ate grilled squid with lime and tomatoes and onions, Igor slept in the shade on an air mattress, over crooked roots sticking out of the ground and smoothed over by feet that had stepped and tripped over them during three decades of robust tourism. A warm wind brought out the pine smell, and mixed it with the smell of the sea and olives and other scents that were hard to decipher, but which made you feel alert and curious. Perhaps similar scents had driven Marco Polo, who'd spent his childhood at Korcula, mad with curiosity and on to China. But these scents made Dena exceedingly happy, and started her dreaming of the happinesses that were still remote.

"We are having such a great time," Dena said, "just as if we were on a honeymoon."

"Don't mention honeymoons. We don't know each other that well."

"Well, how come you aren't married? You are thirty-eight—right?—and you've never been married. At this rate, you never will be. You'll let life pass you by."

"Life will pass anyhow. Just relax."

"I'm not proposing anything. OK, I won't bring it up again." She slurped lemonade until a lemon seed got stuck in the straw. She lifted the straw and squeezed the seed out of it, and said, "You think you're something, don't you?"

"You do. Obviously. I don't. I know I'm not stable enough to take care of myself, let alone of others."

"Do you tell that to your patients?"

Igor moved his arms in sleep as though he were swimming, and Dena and Nenad laughed at him.

After the trip, Dena did not answer the phone for a week, exasperating Nenad, who rang her doorbell every evening. On the eighth evening she missed his company, and answered the door. They took a walk, and Nenad told her the new jokes he'd heard at work. They laughed, and soon they made love, like adolescents who have no place of their own and no money for hotels, in a lanternless and narrow street, against a wooden gate, and in a park, leaning against a wind-struck tree that showered them with smooth round chestnuts that bounced on the cobblestones with dull thuds.

Dena conceived, and told him that they were expecting. If he did not want a family, he should pay for the abortion, and they would never see each other again.

Dena and Nenad got married, and she and Igor moved into Nenad's house on Nazorova Street.

Nenad was busy. After hours, he spent time at meetings of the Croatian Social Liberal Party, the second strongest party in Croatia, which held about 30 percent of the parliament seats. He could become a minister of health, or an ambassador to Germany, or mayor of Zagreb.

Dena, who stayed home, cooking, tutoring Igor, and reading, had developed new ambitions. Now, she wanted to become a physician, and so she studied chemistry and physics for the university entrance exams.

They were both overworked. After a month they did not have sex frequently. Dena thought, That's what men are like—once the conquest is certified with a signature, they yawn.

Sometimes, when she was anxious, she went to the attic and smoked. Because of her pregnancy, however, she did eventually manage to kick the habit, for the time being.

During the final month of her pregnancy, Nenad took off from work and stayed home with her. In the hospital, he held her hands when she had powerful contractions. The labor went on for more than a day and a night. Dena sweated, panted, moaned, and said, "You'd better love us after all this."

He delivered the baby and wept. He described the sensation to Dena as a surge of fear and joy, with a unique worry for another life, a little crying, red-faced life, which opened its milky blue eyes at him in blank wonder. They named the child Robert, and soon, Bobo.

Bobo was breast-fed for a year. Dena formed an intimacy with Bobo that demoted Nenad to the periphery of her affections. Bobo slept with them in the same bed, and climbed all over her, sucking and slurping loudly. Dena could see that Nenad felt left out of all this. He often watched them with a frown before he went to his office, or the parliament, or wherever he went, away from home. Dena did not worry.

As soon as Bobo stopped breast-feeding, Dena felt left out, too, and now she wanted to be with Nenad. But he was busy with his politics, and he ignored her, and the little time he had at home he spent playing with Bobo.

In May, Zagreb was cluster-bombed, and Dena had nightmares: she's trying to get out of a burning house. And she's hanging down from ropes above a barrel of hot oil, and as her pelvis sinks in and burns, the officer says, Now you'll be hot and smooth. And, she's running through the woods, and she falls into a pit where a white tiger is puking hundreds of purple fingers with golden wedding rings.

When she shrieked, Nenad turned the lights on, and they drank tea, and she leaned on him, her ear against his beard. Her anxiety attacks kept her fidgety even during the day. Whenever he went out, she smoked in the basement, or in the attic, or in the street.

He discovered that she smoked and kept tabs on her budget to prevent her from buying cigarettes.

One evening when she got back from a brief get-together with her girlfriends, he said, "Where were you?"

"At my mother's."

"Why do you smell like a tavern? Like booze, tobacco, and lousy coffee."

"Because that's what we drank."

"You are lying."

"You are impossible. Why would I?"

"I mean, look at your clothes! You wear miniskirts, high heels. And why do you wear that scarlet lipstick? Who do you need to wiggle your ass at? I've seen how men look at you."

"I need to stay attractive for you, so you won't look at other women. You think I don't see what you look at? Double standards."

"Double standards. For a man it's natural to look at different women."

"So it's natural for men to look at me. Why are you so upset about it!"

"Because you've got a whore hormone floating around," he said.

"You are a brutal asshole."

He slapped her. She kicked him. He pushed her down into an armchair, and said, "Don't ever kick me again."

Once, when Nenad was away at a conference of his political party in Split, Dena ran into a man who used to visit her—a computer programmer, an ex-hippy with long hair, who treated computers as a mind-expanding drug. She went with him to his apartment, and they kissed fleetingly, drank wine, and watched cyberporn. Pretty soon they had sex. He kept staring at the screen behind her during sex, and she felt as though she were a computer accessory, an inflated mouse for him to move his cursor around, or, more likely, a bit of physical to augment his virtual reality. Dena enjoyed the sensation of freedom, of being frivolous despite marriage; and she thought that she was having sex to spite the marriage in which she could not be free enough to do such an innocuous thing as to smoke an occasional cigarette. Her marriage was threatening to become a bondage situation, a little like being a sex slave in the Serb army, except that there was hardly any sex in her marriage. And now, because she felt so free she even accepted the money, the hundred German marks that the programmer offered her—so the programmer would not owe her anything and she would not owe him anything, and moreover, she would have money to do with as she pleased, buy cigarettes and makeup. But she had not enjoyed this casual sex and afterward had a hangover. The memory of the programmer's bad breath disgusted her.

The programmer called her in the morning and wanted to get together again, and she said, "No, never again."

"Unless you get together with me, I'll let your husband know what we did last night."

"That's not a persuasive argument. You mean, if I don't sleep with you, you're going to tell him that I sleep with you. That's silly. Get lost, and don't ever call here again."

Afterward, when Nenad came home from the party conference, Dena felt both guilty and free enough to know that she was not missing anything out there, and certainly not anything from her past. She wanted to make her home life work. She put flowers in vases around the apartment, taught Igor to play chess, and read baby books to Robert.

Nenad also seemed to be trying to make the marriage work. He bought Dena a present, a gold necklace with a large ruby. He cooked now and then so Dena could study. She thought that he probably was a good man.

But mostly he was busy, and when they sat at their dinner table, she looked across and wondered who this man sitting there was, and what they had together, and thought of asking him, "Excuse me, have we met before?" but she didn't.

One evening when he got home from work, Nenad said, "I smell cigarettes, again!"

"Here you go again. I didn't smoke inside."

"But you smoked. It's like a man saying, I didn't come inside, to prove that he did not have sex after visiting a prostitute."

"A beautiful analogy."

"And not inappropriate. Guess who I saw today?"

"I hate guessing," Dena said. She had a feeling of panic in her chest, she was short of breath, but she maintained an exterior calm. "This city has a million people in it. You could have seen anybody."

"And so could you, from what I found out—the photographer told me about your wanting to make an album. You wanted to be a madam!"

"So? You believe him? And what if I did? That doesn't mean that I'd sleep with the clients."

"I've heard rumors before. And I was blind to them. Deaf. I thought I was the only one, but I was the only one who did not have to pay. But I paid, of course."

"So what's the problem? That was all before you. I couldn't talk to you about anything that happened during the war, let alone after it. How do you think one gets out of a refugee camp?"

"You could have stolen, that would have been better."

"You've been spoiled; you've had it too easy. Good degrees, good jobs, politics."

"Well, forget politics now. You've ruined my politics. In the Balkans, a man with a wife like you is disqualified. If I can't run my own house, what can I do?" He sat down, and poured himself a shot of Black Label on ice. "On the other hand, if we were in the States, it would be the same; a wife with a bad reputation, that would ruin me. Can you imagine if Hillary Clinton moonlighted on the side as a whore?"

"But wasn't he a slut, and he was still elected?"

"Here, there's no difference between the past and the present. Once a war, always a war. Once a whore, always a whore."

"I quit before I met you. You were proud to marry me—weren't you?—you thought you were a damned patriot, saving a war victim, a raped woman—you were saving the continent, you were so full of yourself, you did not even look at me as a person but as a war case, probably as a stepping stone in your political ambitions."

Nenad gathered all her lingerie and set fire to it in the furnace. The clothes crackled, and burned blue and orange and hissed.

"What are you doing that for?"

"You have to ask?"

"We have a family together. You have to behave respectfully toward me, if only because of them."

"Oh, yeah? I think we should get a divorce."

"Do as you please. But I'll sue you. I need to take care of the kids."

"I'd take them with me."

"I'm not so sure."

"I have political influence."

"During the trial, you'd lose your political influence. You've said as much yourself."

"Hmm . . . I'll give you three months to prove yourself. You really feel no guilt, do you?"

"For what? For surviving?"

From that day on, Nenad did not speak to his wife. When they drove to town, he sat in the front with Igor, and she in the back with Bobo. The children talked, played, cried, but Nenad did not talk to his wife. He pretended that she did not exist. They did not sleep together, either. They never looked into each other's eyes.

Sometimes she talked to him, without knowing whether he listened. Dena complained: "In the Balkans, apparently, women are nothing. The woman is the last hole on the flue. Except when men get horny." She considered the option of divorcing him, and although she would have liked it, she decided that because of the children she was not free to be impulsive. She would bear it, and maybe the crisis would be over one day.

Nenad stayed at work more than usual, and at home he read children's books to the kids. When she read to them, she could see that he was jealous. They loved their kids, and hated each other, but their love for the children was stronger than their hatred for each other.

One evening, however, Nenad did talk. He pulled out a letter, addressed to her. It was a pornographic letter, starting with "Don't you remember?" and ending with "Let's do it again."

She read it. "I've never known anybody by that name. It must be one of your political competitors trying to screw you."

"But I am not in politics anymore."

"They're making sure that you won't be. How come you're so blind? You're a fucking blind ophthalmologist."

"Don't you know it! Aren't you scared of disease, disgrace, dis—? . . . "

Nenad slapped her hard, several times. She fell into an armchair and cried. The children cried and held on to each other and trembled in the corner of the room.

"Don't hit Mom," Igor said.

"He's right," she said. "You are scaring them."

As he looked at the children, he was startled. Their teeth were chattering.

"My dear children. Everything will be all right." He approached them to hug them, but they ran to her, and she embraced them.

"All right. This must change," he said. "We've grown too selfish. Let's make a happy family, let's pretend, maybe even join a church, sing cheerful songs, for their sake."

He was still too proud and vengeful to sleep with her, or to look into her eyes, and he easily lapsed into days of silence. He clearly suffered and tried to change his stony disposition. He suggested that they take a trip, to the Plitvice lakes, in the recently liberated Krajina.

And so they did take a trip, on the last day of September, when the leaves turned and each tree became a giant wildflower, as though the earth had reverted to an earlier era, where forests were God's garden.

"Boys, let's go fishing," Nenad said.

"And Mummy, too," said little Bobo.

"And Mummy, too," Nenad said.

They drove, and Nenad whistled. When they got to Plitvice early in the morning, the mist hung over the lakes.

They paddled in two boats—Dena with Bobo, and Nenad with Igor.

"Dad, I won't fish," Igor said. Dena could hear them talking on the water, the sound carried. "I don't want to hurt them."

"What shall we do then?" Nenad asked.

"Let's gather mushrooms."

"No, you can't do that," Nenad said. "There are mines in the hills."

Dena put Bobo in his car seat in front of her and paddled gingerly, so as not to wake him. She enjoyed the sight, or rather, the lack of sight, when she reached the middle of the lake. She could not see the shore or any color, just gradations of gray, as though she had sunk into a penciled drawing. She did not know whether it was mist or rain, but mused dreamily that the mist was a rain that had forgotten to fall, or a cloud that had forgotten to rise. Or if the mist was a rain, it was a fine one, one that fell so that you could not see that it did, because it had forgotten to make drops. The particles floated, touched her face, wandered through her hair, soaked her shirt, and drifted away from her, and she drifted away from them. The mist silenced the water, except for a waterfall in the distance, and the water lay still, unwindblown, unruffled. Baby dragonflies flitted and zigzagged on the surface. A seagull, exiled from the sea, glided and landed on a rock that stuck out of the water near the boat's path.

She dipped the varnished paddle into the lake and when she lifted it, the paddle ladled and spilled the water, to be tasted by her knees, ossified tongues.

Several drops fell on Bobo's cheeks but did not wake him up. He lay tranquil, smooth, his little hands clasped in fists. When she neared the shore, she saw many downed trees. Their roots brought up circles of dark earth. Some trees may have fallen the year before and were still sucking at the earth, as at a breast.

One fir tree had fallen over together with the large rock it had grown on. The tree roots clasped the rock and wouldn't let go. Another tree had peeled away from its rock, leaving the rock clean.

After the mist had drifted away, the sky turned intensely blue, evergreen trees grew dark green, and beeches and oaks began to sing in red and orange keys. Among the colors, clouds clashed—black and gray and white, like an old photograph, merging into the new colorful one.

As she landed against the wooden dock, and stood on the canoe unsteadily with Bobo in her arms, she heard Nenad's shout, "Stop, don't go any farther!" And then she heard crackling branches, running feet. She climbed out, and without tying down the canoe, rushed toward the woods. "Where are you, Igor where are . . . ?" She heard Nenad shouting, and his call was cut short by an explosion. It echoed from the hills, so that it sounded like a cascade of explosions. She feared it could be her son, and even that it could be Nenad. She ran toward a scream. Over a hump of soil she saw Nenad kneeling

215

among orange leaves stained with scarlet blood. Bobo woke up and cried. She panicked.

"Oh my God, he's dead, dead!" shouted Nenad.

Dena put the car seat with Bobo on the ground, and fumbled through the leaves, but could not see Igor. She only saw streaks of flesh. Nenad gripped her from behind, and said, "Stay still. There could be other mines!"

"Let me go. I hope there are. Let me go!"

She stumbled and vomited, and the red and orange turned green in her head, and she could see nothing but the green, and wondered whether she'd gone blind. Now it did not matter. What mattered was that Igor was dead, scattered, ungatherable, probably not even a resurrection could piece him together. Nenad held her up, and he picked up Bobo.

Dena kept groaning. Nenad wiped her face with his white handkerchief, and said, "One thing is strange. I haven't seen his shoes, his clothes, not even a scrap of them, as though . . . "

He left her with Bobo in her arms and searched farther, in widening circles. "Don't," she said. "There could be more mines around."

"That would be all right," he said. "It's all my fault. When he was far enough so that I could not catch him, he said he was running away from home."

Dena's larynx rose up toward her mouth as she was about to shout at Nenad in rage, and only a quiet choking sound came out. Nenad shrieked something she could not understand, and he held up a foot with a hoof. "It's a fawn! Maybe he's alive!"

They found the tail of the fawn, as well. And then Nenad moved farther away, and she stood with Bobo in her arms. She looked up at the sky, to pray to God, but she did not know how.

She looked up an oak tree, and there she saw Igor, high up, and grinning.

She shouted with joy, then said angrily, "You saw us down here? Why didn't you say something?"

"What was there to say?" he said. "Dad did not speak, and I did not want to speak to *him* anymore, to show him what *that* was like."

"Come down, you rascal."

And Igor did, chuckling.

There was another explosion, far away, and it echoed against the mountains. Before Dena could decide whether she should worry about Nenad, or whether the explosion was too far for that, Nenad emerged from the woods slowly. When he heard Igor, he lifted his head and squealed, like a delighted child. Now they all huddled together, and talked eagerly, as one joyful family, amidst light-refracting, dank particles that drifted from the nearby waterfalls and shrouded them in the graceful spectrum of vision and sound.

Nominated by Richard Burgin, John Drury, Robin Hemley, Susan Moon

MISSING IT

by DAN BROWN

from MATTER (Crosstown Books)

The thing about the old one about
The tree in the forest and nobody's around
And how it falls maybe with a sound,
Maybe not, is you throw the part out
About what there isn't or there is,
And the part of it that haunts is still there.
Still there in that the happening, the clear
Crashing there, still encompasses
Everyone condemned to missing it
By being out of the immediate
Vicinity. Out of it the way
You're out of all vicinities but one
All the time. Till presently you've gone
Out of all vicinities to stay.

Nominated by Billy Collins

THE TWELVE PLAGUES

fiction by GERALD SHAPIRO

from THE MISSOURI REVIEW

W HEN THE PHONE RANG, Rosenthal was kicking a canvas to shreds in the middle of his studio. He'd already thrown a can of wet brushes against the far wall and had kicked a tray of paint across the room, leaving an attractive boat-shaped smear of burnt sienna sailing along the whitewashed floorboards. The place should have been condemned, and so should Rosenthal: trapped inside another night of failure in a season of failure, locked in a listless, drifting orbit around a failing sun.

"Kenneth Rosenthal?" the woman's voice asked him.

"That's me," he panted into the receiver, still frenzied from his exertions. He wiped a damp hand across his brow.

"Kenneth Rosenthal, the painter?"

"The one and only," he muttered. "Who's this?"

"Naomi Glick is my name. I hope this isn't an awkward moment. I'm calling on behalf of the Rivka Hirschorn Kissner Foundation in New York City. Perhaps you've heard of us? We're devoted to supporting the work of unknown visual artists who are of interest and significance to the American Jew," the woman said. Her voice was portentous, as if she were reciting something etched on tablets of stone. "I am very pleased to inform you, Mr. Rosenthal, that you are this year's winner of the Rivka Hirschorn Kissner Prize. My heartfelt congratulations."

The Who? The What? But she'd said the word "prize." He stood with the phone pressed to his head, chilling his ear like an ice pack.

"I'm one of several judges," Naomi Glick continued. "We comb the length and breadth of this country, Mr. Rosenthal—the Judaic highways and byways, artistically speaking. We receive slides from scores

219

of exhibitions at reputable galleries around the United States. We're tireless in our pursuit of new Jewish visual artists. We take this work seriously. Some years no one is deemed worthy, and in those years we decline to award the Kissner Prize to anyone. Our standards are high. Your series of paintings, *The Twelve Plagues,* recently came to my attention, and it took my breath away."

"*The Twelve Plagues!* How'd you hear about them?"

"The slides arrived in the mail last month. We received them from—let's see, I have it right here—the Umpqua Valley Arts and Crafts Festival, Roseburg, Oregon. Roseburg—is that by any chance a Jewish name?"

"I don't think so, Mrs. Glick."

"Call me Naomi, Kenneth—please. Such insufferable paintings, these *Twelve Plagues* of yours," she purred. "Obnoxious in the very deepest sense of the word, like a set of precocious eight-year-old boys yammering away. I should know. My son Max is eight years old, and someday soon I may kill him."

"Oh. Well." He hesitated. "Does that mean you liked them?"

"Positively haunted. All that slashing, the paint knifed onto the canvas as though it were trying to burrow through to the other side! All those reds and oranges and blacks saying to themselves, what in the name of God are we *doing* in these paintings? How can we get out of here? All that energy flaming up toward heaven, like it couldn't wait to get out of the frame! I adored them, Kenneth. They're what Jewish art is all about."

Rosenthal remembered the exhilarating, frightening experience of painting them, how they'd come to him like a bundle of gifts—no, like a string of anonymous letter-bombs in the mail—all twelve of them done in a week and a half of hysteria, a series of seizures a year ago, his last sustained and successful creative burst before something vital inside him dried up and blew away. Since then he'd wandered around his studio in a daze, an orphan in the wilderness.

"You don't know—you can't *possibly* know—what this means to me," he said into the receiver, and then he paused. He had no idea of what to say next; he'd never won anything before, in twenty years of labor at the easel. He'd entered one competition after another, submitted slides to foundations, shown his work in art festivals and fairs; he'd come close to recognition, so close he could feel it on his fingertips, but it had eluded him year after year. "To be recognized by such a prestigious foundation—to be honored by my own people,"

220

he heard himself say in a choked voice, and then he stopped. Who was he kidding? His people? When had he last stepped foot into a synagogue?

"You'll be interested to know that you're the very first winner of the Rivka Hirschorn Kissner Prize to live west of the Hudson River," Naomi Glick continued. "Oregon, of all places! Fur trappers, Lewis and Clark, Sacajawea—salmon fishing and lumber mills! One wouldn't have thought a Jew could survive in such a place! Are there Jews in Oregon?"

"There are Jews everywhere, Mrs. Glick. There are Jews in Yokohama."

"Our previous winners have all been New Yorkers," Naomi Glick continued, "which is natural, I suppose, given the fact that most serious American visual artists do seem to live in the New York area. Not that you're not serious, of course—I wasn't implying that at all. Believe me, we wouldn't have awarded you the Kissner Prize if you weren't absolutely first rate—and unknown, of course. But then you don't need me to tell you that, do you?"

Rosenthal surveyed the wreckage of his studio, the canvasses strewn here and there, the paints exploded, the brushes in splinters. "No," he said.

"Your paintings will be displayed at the Apawamis Jewish Community Center, the jewel of Westchester County, a monument to what money can buy, you'll love it, you really will," Naomi Glick went on. Her voice began to speed up, as though she were at a pay phone, running low on small change. "We'll arrange for shipment of the paintings. You'll be flown to New York for the awards presentation, there'll be a big dinner hosted by the donors, Sheldon Sperling and his wife Bernice, we'll invite the cream of New York's art critics and gallery owners to the awards ceremony, you'll be the toast of Apawamis, everyone will praise you to the skies, you'll have a lovely time. Believe me, Mr. Rosenthal, are you excited, of course you are, it's time to *shep* some *nakhes*, you lucky man."

A letter on Kissner Foundation stationery arrived three days later setting out the details of Rosenthal's upcoming trip to New York. He would have to give a short speech at the awards ceremony and then answer questions from the audience. The prize money and the airline tickets were on their way. He'd be met at La Guardia. Did he have any food allergies or preferences? All food would be prepared in a kosher

221

kitchen during his visit, and no travel would be scheduled on the Sabbath, out of respect for his religious beliefs.

His religious beliefs! Rosenthal had a mirthless chuckle over that one. Once upon a time he'd believed. As a boy, he'd even toyed with the thought of becoming a rabbi. What had happened to his childlike devotion, his dutiful affection for God! Hebrew school from four to six in the afternoon, two or three days a week; training for his Bar Mitzvah, learning the entire portion of the Torah by heart; Sunday school; services on Friday nights and again on Saturday mornings, fasting, praying, chanting, beating his breast—at the age of thirteen he was a little Yeshiva *bucher, davening* with the best of them, rocking back and forth on his heels, locked in a dialogue with the Almighty. But once he'd finished with his Bar Mitzvah, stuffed all the gifts he'd received, the neckties, the wallets, the pen-and-pencil sets into a drawer, Rosenthal found himself without much left to say to God.

The trouble had been brewing for a while. In his teens he'd become increasingly aware that there was something despicable about his parents' version of Judaism, a kind of self-righteous, self-pitying one-upmanship. No one else had suffered like the Jews, his parents told him—no one else knew what deprivation was. Oh, sure, here and there in the history of the world, from time to time some other group had had their knuckles rapped with a ruler—but not like the Jews, *nothing* like the Jews. Competitive Suffering! It was an arcane athletic event his parents had invented, governed by one very simple rule: the Jews win. No arguing. Blow the whistle, the game's over, Jews win again. No matter what sorrow, what agony you might think had befallen you or your family or your people, you lose, because nothing that ever happened to anybody could compete with What Happened To The Jews.

Rosenthal remembered his Uncle Irwin coming to the house for dinner, a bleak little man so pale and nondescript that he tended to blend into the wallpaper. "When I was a child, we were so poor we ate grass," Uncle Irwin said during momentary conversational lulls at the family's dining room table. "I never tasted sugar until I was thirty-one years old. That's because we were Jewish. Nobody wanted us to have anything. That's why we had to eat grass. Pass the sugar, will you?"

The first time Uncle Irwin had said this—Rosenthal would have been perhaps nine—the pronouncement carried real drama with it (it beat the crap out of his mother's stories about hand-me-down shoes, for instance); but as the years went by and Irwin told the same story again and again, it lost its tragic bulk in Rosenthal's imagination, and floated up airily into the realm of comedy. Occasionally when Uncle Irwin wasn't there, Rosenthal would impersonate him: "We ate dirt. Sometimes when we had water, we made dirt soup. But we didn't have water very often. Once in a while they took away our dirt, and then we had to eat clothing. Shirts tasted pretty good—a little salt, a little pepper. But then they took away our salt and pepper, because we were Jews and they didn't want us to have any."

"You should be ashamed of yourself," Rosenthal's mother told him. "Such a comedian. Your Uncle went through a lot of deprivation. I'm talking about real deprivation, young man—not a joke."

By the time he was in college, Rosenthal's attitude had soured even further. His first semester, his philosophy professor spent the first ten weeks debunking various arguments supporting the existence of God. One after another, St. Anselm, Bishop Berkeley, Aquinas and the rest of them collapsed like so many mobile homes in a hail storm. At the holiday break, Rosenthal went home and called Rabbi Kravitz, the man who'd blessed him the day of his Bar Mitzvah. "I'm having a spiritual crisis," Rosenthal said. "I think I might be turning into an atheist. Can I come in to see you? It's kind of an emergency."

"This is a terrible week for me," Rabbi Kravitz said. He coughed into the phone.

"Look, I appreciate that, but I really need to talk to somebody."

"Listen to me, Kenny," Rabbit Kravitz said in his deep, tomb-like voice. "God exists. Trust me on this. He hears what you're saying and he's appalled. He's saying to himself, what's got into Kenny Rosenthal?"

"If there's a God, Rabbi Kravitz, just tell me this: why is there so much evil in the world? Why is there so much suffering?"

"You think you're the only one in the world who wonders about God's purpose? You think nobody's ever asked why there's suffering in the world?"

"No, I didn't think that."

"Well, you're not, my young friend," Rabbi Kravitz said in an aggrieved voice. "Listen—you're a Jew. You were born a Jew, you were raised a Jew, you're going to die a Jew. When the Nazis come to town, you think they're going to ask you if you're an atheist or not? You're a Jew! Into the ovens! It doesn't matter what kind of nonsense a professor tries to cram into your head, you're a Jew. Does that answer your question?"

Before Rosenthal could answer, the rabbi had hung up.

A month after the phone call from the Kissner Foundation, early on a Sunday afternoon that promised showers, a small, fragile-looking man in a seersucker sports coat met Rosenthal at La Guardia airport. The old man doffed his Yankees cap, revealing an ancient skull the color of aged parchment. "So you're the lucky artist," he muttered, and snatched Rosenthal's overnight bag with gnarled fingers. "I'm Sheldon Sperling," he said as they walked toward the parking lot. "Call me Chub, why don't you—everybody does. My wife and I, we're the donors of the prize you won. Don't worry, we can afford it. I'm in corporate law. Was, I should say—I just retired about two months ago, seventy-nine years old. Corporate law was my life—I still dream about it every few nights. Merger dreams, mostly—they're like flying dreams, tremendous sense of power there."

The car was a Mercedes station wagon, a big yellow tank of a car. Mr. Sperling threw Rosenthal's bag in the back. Slowly they drove through a skyless wasteland of urban blight, then gradually the scenery turned greener and the world opened up again as they left the city behind and entered lush, heavily wooded suburbs. "I'm taking you to your hotel—you can freshen up there for a while, then we'll send somebody to pick you up and bring you to dinner at our house. Our daughter Rachel came home just for this event. Isn't that something? Flew in from Chicago just for the occasion. She's some daughter. Married to a hotshot in marketing out there, the guy makes nothing but money. Heckuva guy. They've got one girl, beautiful, named Elena. Is that some name? Find that one in the Bible. I love that name. Our only grandchild."

"Gee," Rosenthal said. "That's some name."

"Our other daughter, Stephanie—married to a urologist. He has his own clinic, he's written up in medical journals all the time. They're in the south of France now, driving around drinking wine. Then there's our youngest, Randy, lives in the city. He won't be coming up this year. He says he can't get away. You'd like him—he's a designer. Very artistic guy."

"Sorry I won't get to meet him," Rosenthal said in a sadly philosophical tone, as if he'd really been hoping to meet the whole clan. They lapsed into silence. The streets had turned into avenues lined by arching maple trees, their leaves forming a continual canopy over the road, the afternoon light dappling the foliage.

"Before we get to the hotel, I have to ask you something," Sperling said. "Can I call you Dan?"

"Ken—it's Ken," Rosenthal said.

"It's not really my question, it's my wife's question. You ready?"

"Go right ahead."

"What the heck were you doing with those *Twelve Plagues*, anyway? Those paintings—what were you thinking about? What is that, is that your idea of Jewish art?" They stopped for a red light.

"Excuse me?" Rosenthal asked.

"Relax, don't get your hackles up. I mean, personally I don't care. I'm a lawyer, give me a contract I'll tell you what I think of it. Art is not my cup of tea. My wife, on the other hand—well, it's a different story. That's all I'm saying."

Rosenthal sat silently for a moment, mulling this over. You wait twenty years to win a prize, and now that you win one, you have to listen to this? Some aging shyster critiques your oeuvre for you? What had they brought him here for, anyway? "So, you're saying your wife didn't like my work?" he asked at last. "Is that it?"

"It isn't a question of liking or not liking. I'm just saying, you might want to think about what the heck you were doing, because *some* people might ask, that's all." The light changed and they pulled out into traffic again. "It doesn't bother me, understand. But *some* people," Sperling said, and then his voice trailed off. They drove on to the hotel, a nondescript brick building distinguished only by the extravagance of its landscaping. Sperling sat grimly at the wheel while Rosenthal got out of the car. "Just think about it, that's all," he called out. The Mercedes drove off, leaving Rosenthal standing at the curb with his bag.

At the check-in desk, the reservations clerk said, "Oh, so you're the Kissner winner this year." She flashed a lifeless smile at Rosenthal. "Congratulations on your prize. The room is taken care of—courtesy of the Kissner Foundation. Please don't make any long-distance phone calls—the phone is not taken care of. Neither is room service. And don't ask for anything special from Housekeeping. Last year's winner ran up a bill like you wouldn't believe. And whatever you do, don't watch HBO. It's not covered."

The bed was small but firm, and Rosenthal surprised himself by slipping into a light sleep. He awoke at a quarter to six, feeling refreshed and terror-stricken. He showered slowly, rehearsing the acceptance speech that he'd written for the occasion and had been practicing on and off for weeks. He wasn't very experienced at public speaking, but the tone of this speech seemed okay to him—a few jokes to establish the fact that he was an ordinary fellow, then the meat of the thing, short without being abrupt, humble but not groveling.

The shower itself felt wonderful; it was dark in there, and safe; the hot water hit him in the nape of his neck and cascaded down his back like a light massage. There was nobody in there but him, nobody saying, "So what the hell were you doing with those *Twelve Plagues*, anyway?" He got out reluctantly and towelled off, avoiding his gaze in the brightly lit mirror.

Rosenthal slowly got into his good clothes. Then he sat on the bed and looked at the blank television screen. Why had he come here? How could he have thought this prize would change the basic realities of his life, when nothing ever had changed them before? Flying three thousand miles to accept an award and shake hands with strangers—it was just the kind of thing that Lenore, his ex-wife, had warned him against in *The Price of Arrogance*, one of the series of cautionary treatises she'd written for him after their divorce, in an effort to "set him straight on life." Oh, he'd been set straight, all right.

By the time the phone rang, Rosenthal had retreated so far into himself that he thought the ringing sound was coming from the next room. After a few rings he summoned the presence of mind to pick it up.

"This is Chub Sperling. Did you get a nap in?"

"Yes—yes, I did."

"Good. I'm sending my daughter, Rachel, to pick you up. She's the one with the daughter. Her husband's the marketing hotshot. Nothing but money."

The yellow Mercedes drove into the hotel's circular driveway twenty minutes later. The last benevolent sheen of afternoon light had drifted over the world and was gone, and Rosenthal felt a faint chill in the air as he stepped out of the hotel's lobby and walked toward the car. Rachel, a tanned woman Rosenthal's age, smiled at him from the driver's seat and extended a hand for him to shake once he was in the car. "I've seen your paintings at the Jewish Community Center," she said in a faint, neutral voice. "They're interesting, and I had a question I wanted to ask you about them." She pulled out into traffic.

Rosenthal waited for her to go on, but nothing followed. "Well, it certainly is nice that you flew back East like this," he said after a moment, then added, "Your dad told me all about you, your sister, your brother."

"He told you about Randy? Did he mention the Italian boys?"

"Uh, no. I don't remember anything like that."

"Randy's got a lot of friends—they all happen to be good-looking Italian guys. My dad's still puzzled about it; he'll be the last to know. For the rest of his life he'll be sitting around saying, 'So when's Randy going to get married?'"

Neither of them made much of an effort at conversation during the drive to the Sperlings' house, a route which wound through hushed neighborhoods, stately homes set on lawns as lush and manicured as expensive toupees. At last they swung around a corner and pulled into the driveway of a mustard-colored house with a pillared entryway.

The front door of the house swung open and Bernice Sperling appeared, flanked by the massive pillars. She stood frozen between them for a moment like Sampson in Gaza, and though she was petite and silver-haired, Rosenthal immediately noted something oddly massive in her demeanor, a stern, predatory cast to her chin that made it possible for him to imagine her toppling those pillars with two good shoves.

Then the tableau came to life and she approached him, arms extended. "Ken! So good to meet you," she said. "Congratulations on winning the Rivka Hirschorn Kissner Prize. *Mazel tov!* I hope you realize what a great honor the Kissner Foundation has bestowed on you." She fixed him with a shrewd, puckered smile. "I've spent quite some time with your paintings," she said, then she stopped short, as if trying to hide another sentence that was trying to peek mischievously out of her mouth like a second tongue. The smile faded. "Maybe you can explain them to me over dinner. Well, come in, come in." She linked an arm through Rosenthal's and led him inside.

As they walked inside, a timer went off in the kitchen, and Mrs. Sperling clapped a hand to her throat. "Amuse yourself, Ken, for just a minute or two—I've got some last-minute preparations to attend to." She scurried back toward the kitchen, leaving him to roam on his own.

The house was decorated in an amazing array of Judaica. In the large, formal living room, a Chagall lithograph hung over the fireplace, flanked by two large brass menorahs. The Chagall was shamelessly whimsical, lit with all kinds of iridescent splashes and flying cattle, so *shtetl*-sentimental it might as well have come complete with canned Klezmer music blaring from a hidden speaker. Around the room the walls sagged with Jewish art; there were several reproductions of Rembrandt's etchings of Amsterdam's Jews, and most of the wall facing the fireplace was given over to posed group portraits of bearded, black-robed nineteenth century rabbinical students, all of them stern as corpses. Jewish literature crammed built-in bookcases everywhere Rosenthal looked.

A small woman with an aging ballerina's taut face and a wide, expressive mouth approached Rosenthal as he perused the bookshelves; she waved a long, bony hand out to him, palm down, as if she might be expecting him to kiss it. "Naomi Glick," she said. "We spoke on the phone. I simply adore your work."

"Oh, thank you," Rosenthal said. "I'm so glad you're here."

"I'm still amazed that I've never heard of you," she said. "It was thrilling to call you and tell you you'd won. The high point of my year. Oregon. Oregon! What an ironic place to live! You're a darling painter. I love what you've done with the plagues; the judges all got together and met several times and reviewed a number of other possible choices and no one had the slightest difficulty in settling on you, you were our favorite, our absolute unanimous choice, you lucky boy." She leaned into his ear like a conspirator and whispered, "Sit next to me at the table. I've got to have *someone* to talk to. The Sperlings are sweethearts, but they're a bit too . . . *devout,* shall we say, for my taste."

Naomi Glick led Rosenthal into the dining room, where an elderly couple were chatting with Mr. Sperling. "Ken, this is Milton Steinhaus," she said, and Steinhaus, a stooped, balding fellow, impeccably dressed, shook Rosenthal's hand. "Call me Milton," he said in a heavy middle-European accent. "Eighty-three years old last Thursday, and I've still got my sense of humor. That's why Chub and Bernice still like me—I'm a lively, irreverent old guy with an appreciative eye for the ladies." He ran a finger across his pencil line moustache, then delicately jerked at the bottom of his shirt cuffs, extending them a fraction of an inch beyond his sports coat.

Naomi Glick put a hand on Rosenthal's arm. "Isn't he something? Eighty-three years old. A lively old guy." She turned toward the elderly woman standing next to Steinhaus. "And here's his adorable wife, Harriet."

"I'm Bernice's oldest friend," Harriet Steinhaus said. "I love her like a sister. Like a *sister.* We've been in the same artistic appreciation group over forty years. Is that some kind of record, or what?"

At that moment Rachel and Bernice Sperling burst into the dining room, both of them laden with platters. The table groaned with food: roast chicken, potato pancakes with applesauce, carrot tsimmes, and a large spinach salad crowded in among the plates and glasses. "Sit, everyone—sit!" Bernice cried, and Naomi Glick planted Rosenthal firmly in the seat next to her, at the end of the table farthest away from the Sperlings. The process of passing platters began. "I always get a little emotional at the start of a Kissner Prize dinner," Mrs. Sperling began. "I tell you, I don't mind the cooking, the baking, the cleaning that always goes into this dinner. No amount of work is too much to revere the blessed memory of Rivka Hirschorn Kissner—a gifted Jewish artist, a painter of immense promise."

"She finished three paintings, all of them bad," Naomi Glick whispered in Rosenthal's ear. "My dog is more artistic when he's taking a crap."

"She died too young, may she rest in peace," Mrs. Sperling continued, nodding sadly. "In Palestine, fighting with her last breath for the establishment of a Jewish homeland."

"An incompetent terrorist, too," Naomi Glick added, tickling Rosenthal's ear with her whispers. "She blew herself up trying to set the King David Hotel on fire."

"So as you can well imagine, this is all a labor of love," Bernice Sperling said with a sigh, and nodded to Rosenthal with a noticeable quiver in her chin. She raised her glass. "To the memory of Rivka Hirschorn Kissner, *olev ha sholom.*" Everyone drank. "Eat, please. Go ahead," she said. "Enjoy. *Ess, ess gesundheit.* I have to ask Ken a question or two before I get started, just out of curiosity. You don't mind, Ken?"

Here it came. "No, of course not," Rosenthal said, bracing himself.

"First let me explain something to you. Chub and I don't judge the competition, and we don't judge the judges, either. We're not experts. We're just the donors. Am I making myself clear?"

"Of course."

"Good. So humor me," Mrs. Sperling said. "Let me have a minute." She inhaled deeply before beginning to speak. "In the Bible," she said, "there were only ten plagues, not twelve. Ten was enough for God, Ken—you had to add two more. God made the rivers run with blood, he set plagues of frogs and lice and hail upon the Egyptians. But Pharaoh's heart was hardened."

Naomi Glick leaned into Rosenthal's ear again. "He couldn't help it, the poor man, he had hardening of the heart," she whispered, and pounded a fist hysterically on Rosenthal's thigh under the table. He stared at her. Who was it she resembled? And then of course, there it was: Spencer Pelovsky, the clown prince of Rosenthal's Hebrew school class, remembered most vividly for farting into the microphone the day of his Bar Mitzvah. Naomi Glick's flat prankster's face, the wide, idiotic mouth—it was Spencer Pelovsky reborn, thrumming with impish delight. Staring at her, Rosenthal suddenly realized that he'd never really liked Pelovsky worth a nickel.

"So God sent three days of total darkness," Bernice Sperling continued. "He sent locusts, he killed all the livestock of the Egyptians and saved the livestock of the children of Israel." She looked around the table. "How many was that?"

"That's seven, dear," Mr. Sperling said.

"What am I leaving out? Rachel dear, you were Bat Mitzvahed, you can answer this one."

"Flies?" Rachel offered. "Mosquitoes? Gnats? I don't know."

"The money we spent on her religious education," Mr. Sperling grumbled.

"What else? Anybody?" Bernice Sperling called out.

"Boils," Naomi Glick said. "Lovely plague. Heathen though I am, I remember my Bible."

"Okay, so flies and boils, then finally the climatic plague, the killing of the firstborn. That was enough for God, but not for you, Ken—you had to add a couple of your own. Why? What for?"

Rosenthal sat silently, sucking in a chest full of air.

"And the two you added? What was that, some kind of statement? *Call waiting?* That's a plague? That's something God visited upon the Egyptians in order to free his people? We're talking about *our* people here, Ken. The children of Israel. Call waiting—what is that, some kind of joke?"

"Well, no, not really," Rosenthal said in a mild voice.

"And the other one—the other plague, what was that one again?"

He sighed. She *knew* what it was, and he knew that she knew. She was just doing this to prolong the moment. "Lack of available parking, Mrs. Sperling," he said in a tired voice.

"Right! That's it. *Lack of available parking!* What is that, anyway? That's a plague?" Bernice Sperling looked down at her plate and pushed some food around with her fork. Then she put the fork down and raised a hand to her forehead.

"Bernice, don't let it upset you," Harriet Steinhaus said. Under her breath she muttered, "Expert judges. Feh."

Rosenthal leaned back in his chair and turned his head toward Naomi Glick. She'd been sitting primly, her head lifted high, her hands folded in her lap. He waited for her to say something now, something in her own defense as well as in his. But she said nothing.

"I went over to the Center and I looked at those paintings," Mr. Steinhaus said. "I'm a lively old guy, but I don't know much about art. So I said to myself, Milton, this is Jewish art? Because if this is Jewish art, I'll stick with *goyishe* art, thank you very much."

"Well, enough of this," Mrs. Sperling said with a sniff in her voice, and abruptly arose from the table. "Some of us connect with the story of our people's deliverance from slavery into freedom. Some of us feel that connection, some of us share the pain our people have suffered throughout the ages. For others—well, there's no point in belaboring it," she announced, wiping her hands together as if scrubbing away a stain. "Now, you'll forgive me if we don't have dessert. Normally I would have made something fantastic—I'm known for my desserts."

"She makes an angel food cake you'd kill for," Harriet Steinhaus said.

"But there's going to be food at the reception at the Jewish Community Center," Mrs. Sperling continued. "So we'll have our dessert there. I'll just clean up a little and we'll be off," she said, and walked into the kitchen.

Naomi Glick leaned over to Rosenthal and whispered, "I've got to smoke a cigarette or I'm going to do something I'll regret." She slid out of her chair and was nearly out of Rosenthal's reach before he grabbed her wrist and stopped her. "Where were you?" he asked. "Just then, when they were beating me with baseball bats—what are you, deaf?"

"But they're the *donors*, dear boy. The donors! They bought the *right* to beat you up a little. Why do you think people give money for prizes?"

He let her wrist slide through his fingers, and a moment later he heard her sneaking out the front door. Mr. Sperling and Milton Steinhaus made their way around the table removing the dinner plates, and Rosenthal stood up and began to help them—but Harriet Steinhaus leaned across the table and clutched his sleeve.

"Sit a minute," she said. "I want to talk to you." She waited until he was seated, then fixed him with a steady glare. "More than forty years Bernice and I have been together in the art appreciation group. I'd do anything for that woman. She's like the sister I never had. If it wasn't for Bernice Sperling, would I know about Chaim Soutine?" she said. "Would I know about Jacques Lipchitz? Could I tell you the difference between a Modigliani and a plate of linguini? Would I know Jack Levine's work like I know the back of my hand? Would I have an original Saul Steinberg hanging over my piano if it wasn't for her?

231

Whenever there's a show, an exhibition of Jewish art anywhere within a day's drive, our group is there, thanks to Bernice. Did you know that Rembrandt was Jewish, by the way?"

"Well, yeah, there's some theory about that," he said vaguely.

"It's no theory! The man was Jewish! I'm telling you, I know something about art. The Soyer boys, Raphael and Moses—our group met them when they were nothing, when they couldn't sell a painting to buy breakfast. Harold Rosenberg gave a lecture—we were in the front row. Clement Greenberg offered a three-week seminar—all of us were there, taking notes like crazy. We were talking about Barnett Newman and Mark Rothko before *anybody* was talking about Barnett Newman and Mark Rothko. Not that that's my idea of art, mind you. Very disturbed people. All that depression! Did you know that Jackson Pollock was Jewish, since we're talking?"

"He was?"

"A self-hating Jew. The worst kind. A *shanda*. As far from Chagall as you can get. Now Chagall, there was a Jewish artist. Better than Rembrandt, for my money. Chagall—there was a person—a *mensch*. He painted like an angel—it's like *Fiddler on the Roof* on canvas."

So that was it, Rosenthal told himself—artistic value could be measured by the quality of your Zero Mostel impersonation. He understood now; once again he'd failed to pass muster. He'd live with it—he'd been living with failure, artistic and personal, for so many years already—another season of failure wouldn't kill him. Lenore, his ex-wife, should have been here—she could have been taking notes on another treatise for his benefit. *The Value of Ethnic Identity, or Why You Shouldn't Be Such A Smart-Aleck All The Time.*

But another thought crowded Rosenthal's mind, puffing up like a balloon in his imagination and pushing Lenore and her treatises into the shadows. He'd never realized it before, but it was plain to him now, as plain as a sign stencilled on the wall: whatever else happened to him, no matter how miserable his existence, he'd be a painter the rest of his days.

"I know why you did it," Harriet Steinhaus said, leaning toward him with her eyebrows arched imperiously.

"Did what?"

"The extra two plagues. I know why you did it." She cocked her head at him. "You can't fool me. I have you figured out."

Rosenthal was about to protest when he felt Naomi Glick's bony hand on his shoulder. "What did I miss?" she whispered in his ear and

232

she slid back into her chair. "I didn't hear any explosions. Did anything happen?"

He shook his head, determined to ignore her, and smiled at Harriet Steinhaus—a conciliatory smile, he hoped. At least the rest of them, the Sperlings, Harriet and Milton, even Rachel, for that matter, *believed* in something, he told himself. Even he believed in something. He'd forgotten that, or had stuffed it away somewhere in his attic, but now, under attack at the dinner table, he recalled it.

"Okay, everybody, we can't be late for the awards ceremony. We've got the guest of honor!" Mr. Sperling said. He rubbed his hands together in an exaggerated show of enthusiasm. "Rachel, you ride with your mother and me. Naomi, why don't you come with us, too? We can talk about next year's competition. Milton, would you and Harriet mind giving our winner a ride?"

"For you, darling, we'd do anything," Harriet Steinhaus said.

"Milton knows the way to the Center," Bernice Sperling said to Rosenthal. "We'll see you there in fifteen minutes, tops. Practice your speech!"

It would have been a fine plan, except that Milton Steinhaus didn't, in fact, know the way to the Apawamis Jewish Community Center, and Harriet didn't either. It took twenty minutes for this to come to light—twenty minutes of turning and twisting through unlit streets. "Are you sure we're going the right way?" Rosenthal asked at one point, sure that they'd passed the same corner three times already.

"I'm living in New York seventy-eight years," Milton Steinhaus said. "I was just a kid when I come over here. Believe me, I'll get you there." He flipped on the windshield wipers, though it wasn't raining. "All the money in Westchester County, you think they could spring for some streetlights." The car sailed through a four-way stop, and Rosenthal decided it might be better to handle this situation with his eyes closed.

Finally, after they'd cruised up and down every street in Apawamis, plus most of Rye, Port Chester and a portion of Scarsdale, Steinhaus pulled to the side of the road and shut off the engine. He pounded the steering wheel and said, "Son of a bitch. Son of a bitch."

Harriet, in the front passenger seat, blew out a ragged breath and bowed her head. "Bernice is going to be very upset about this," she said softly.

233

"That's okay," Rosenthal said, patting her arm. "Don't worry. We'll find a phone, we'll call, we'll get directions, we'll be there in no time."

"You have to understand, this woman is my dearest friend," Harriet Steinhaus continued. "I'd put my hand in a fire for her."

"It's not that bad," he crooned to her. "We'll find a phone, we'll get directions. It'll be okay—we just have to find a gas station."

"I know why you did it," she said suddenly, lifting her head and wagged a finger at him. "I've thought about it. I know something about Jewish art, let me tell you. Some people, you know, they say 'I don't know much about art, but I know what I like.' Not me. I say I do know something about art, and that's why I know what I like, Kenny. And what I don't like."

"Don't start," her husband advised her. "Your blood pressure."

"I could go look for a phone," Rosenthal suggested.

"Sometimes I think I could write a *book* about Jewish Art. You don't spend over forty years in an artistic appreciation group and come away from it not knowing a thing or two about art. Our group discussed your paintings at length, you'll be glad to know," Harriet Steinhaus said. "When we heard that the judges had given you the Kissner Prize, we all got out slides of your work—we hadn't seen it before, you understand—and we looked. I'll be honest with you, some of us were a little angry. But I figured you out. I know why you did it." She turned to him and smiled; he saw her eyes gleam in the darkness of the car.

"Mrs. Steinhaus, maybe we could talk about it while we're driving. We're going to the Center, right? Because if we are—"

"We're having a conversation," she said. She took the keys out of the ignition and plopped them into her purse.

"Harriet, sweetheart, is this a good idea?" Mr. Steinhaus asked.

"Okay, fine," Rosenthal offered. "We're not going to the Center. We're having a conversation. You figured me out. You got the goods on me. So tell me, why did I do it?"

"You did it," she said, her eyebrows raised, "because you wanted to shock people—you wanted to be a bad boy."

"No, that's not it," Rosenthal said.

"You did it because you hate the culture that produced you. Because you're angry, you're bitter, you're ashamed. Six million of your people died, and you make jokes. Ten plagues were enough to free the children of Israel from their bondage in Egypt, but ten plagues aren't enough for you. Call waiting! Lack of available parking! Joker! Criminal!"

"That's ridiculous."

234

"I know why you did it," Harriet Steinhaus said after the briefest of pauses, the note of triumph still ringing in her voice. "Okay, you ready? Don't tell me why you did it. I *know* why you did it. You did it to get back—to get back at your parents, and at your people. You did it out of spite, you did it to be vicious."

"Mrs. Steinhaus—"

"That's it, isn't it," she said, nodding in victory. "I hit it on the head, didn't I? Of course I did. Milton, didn't I tell you? I *knew* I knew why he did it."

Rosenthal opened the passenger side door and got out. He shut the door and leaned in through the open window. "Look, stay here, keep the doors locked, I'm going to look for a phone," he said. "I'll be back."

"Mr. Spite. Mr. Vicious," Mrs. Steinhaus spat at him. Her head rose higher on her neck and she looked at him haughtily.

Rosenthal stood by the car musing silently for a moment, running a hand carelessly through his hair. Then he took two steps away, and as he'd half expected, the engine suddenly roared to life, and the vehicle sped away into the dark.

The evening air was balmy and benevolent, soft against his cheeks. He put his hands into his pockets and began to walk, first slowly and then with more purpose, towards a vague light he could see at the far end of the street—surely something was there, some kind of store or service station where there might be a phone. After several blocks he stopped at another darkened street corner. Where the hell was he? The lights he'd been headed toward seemed as far away as they had when he'd started. What else was there to do but push on?

Somehow he'd get back to Oregon, that ironic place—back to the splattered gloom of his studio, where his work, his blessed and awful work, awaited him. He'd spend evenings reading Lenore's post-divorce treatises by lamplight, combing their turgid prose for answers to Harriet Steinhaus's embittered questions. Somewhere in one of them—perhaps in *Get Over It: How Ken Rosenthal Needs To Shape Up and Stop Being So Angry*—he might find what he was looking for. Or perhaps—yes, he liked this—perhaps the answer lay in a painting he had yet to begin, a blank canvas standing in a corner, waiting to catch his eye.

Rosenthal looked carefully to the right and to the left, and then, as he stepped off the curb, he began to deliver his acceptance speech. What the hell, he told himself—why waste the only speech he'd ever written? And besides, he'd rehearsed it so carefully that he felt he knew it by heart. He walked briskly through the shimmering darkness, declaiming as he went to an audience of fire hydrants, stray dogs, parked cars; soon he'd left his memorized speech behind, and was thanking everyone he'd ever known in his life.

Nominated by Robin Hemley, Wally Lamb and Josip Novakovich

MATINÉE IDYLLS

by MOLLY BENDALL

from AMERICAN POETRY REVIEW

My window, barely attached by its butterfly hinge,
still reveals the shabby green awnings
across the street. If someone would only
mend the place. What's the latest in traffic?

I'm tucking away a few numbers on scraps and try
not to notice the black complacency of my phone.
Then I imagine his arrival:
He appears like a museum exhibit, hunted and ambushed

and always, graceful.
My face feels taut. I'm turning into brass.
I've kept his stash in my purse since
Wednesday—the litany—black beauties, white crosses.

But I can't live ashamed anymore.
In my letter to the city I say,
        "Dear ornamental pear, Dear old park at my disposal,
I need a new coat with thick cuffs,

I need walls with a real paint job . . ."
While I practice a stance,
my appliances only throw their color to each other
begging for words like bakelite glamour.

* * *

Why don't we sit down at our usual place—
the hat-box-of-a-table, and retrieve

a momentary thing, like a Tuesday.
I am fond of your jacket, but I do think the darkness

should go down the front.
Midsummer has turned a suspicious cheek to me

rather than become the relief I'd counted on.
The turbaned one by your aqua pool?

A business associate?
I heard the snap of her compact

when I swung the gate. I could have been her,
and worn the gold sandals that light up against

the floral tiles. (That's another
reward I give myself when I need some mercy.)

You've carved an almost tropical
space around yourself.

It's all blurry to you. But look, past the verandah,
above the jasmine,

where the horizon is tissue paper thin,
that's where I'll help you one last time.

                    *   *   *

" . . . yes, I left my martini back there on the vanity."
The mirror doubling her, her glass.
"Only a past to conceal . . . "

She crosses herself with her perfume.
He's getting ready, rushing in a belted coat
around a medley of packages and boxes.

238

"I'll send for the rest."
"On your way out, notice the trumpet vine,
it's so skillfully tangled."

Now their predicament, their cigarette smoke—they're so cavalier.
Once they'd rendez-voused to suit themselves
and left the misled behind.

Even their seaside table had risen
into the cloying sky. The diving pelicans
and yachts, aloof in their hemispheres.

The two of them had thrown their last worries
into the ocean of disapproval
leaving a cool, rational sound on the air.

Nominated by Aga Shahid Ali, Carol Muske, Diann Blakely Shoaf

WE HAVE TIME

fiction by PAUL L. ALLMAN

from WITNESS

N ED FELM HAD VOLUNTEERED willingly and with full knowledge to allow the government, in conjunction with the prison he was attending, to douse his testicles with radiation. This was during 1961, when radiation was new and mysterious, and testicles were not.

The prison radiation program was part of an experiment hosted by the military branch of the government. Because the military was involved, there was money for the volunteers. Because testicles were involved, the money was good. And so Ned Felm, who was in this prison as an inmate, volunteered.

Ned signed a great many papers. At first, he tried to read the documents, but the stack was high and the type small and the language dense and warped, so he skimmed instead, while a man wearing a gray single-breasted suit with thin lapels stood behind Ned, muttering softly and kindly about the gift that the prison program was giving to society.

There was a choice to be made at the end of the document: vertical or horizontal, as in, "Would the subject when given a non-binding preference select (given no prior indications and/nor third-party inclinations in reference to preferability) a mode hitherto to be in all future duplicates of said release form to be known and acknowledged as (select one) vertical 'Vertical' or horizontal 'Horizontal'?"

Ned picked 'Horizontal' because he thought he might be able to nap during the experiment. What it really meant was that Ned, standing like all the rest of the volunteers, would have the radiation gun aiming at his testicles horizontally, that is, with the direction of the beam parallel with the floor, as opposed to the vertical method, in which the gun

240

would be perpendicular to the floor, shooting upwards, through and past the testicles into the organs.

When he saw, Ned was glad what he picked.

It is only fair to Ned Felm to describe the incident by which he found himself incarcerated. He was convicted of what is written and shall forever be recorded as 'Assault with Intent to Maim.' Few but Ned's relatives and the victim and of course the jury knew that Ned's conviction translated into 'Biting Off the Ear of a Police Officer while Resisting Arrest in a Drugstore.'

Ned had gone to the drugstore, seeking a remedy for his cold. In his unhealthy state, Ned at first could not find the cold remedies, and had to be directed to the correct aisle, twice. Ned felt a sense of irritation that the remedies were not more clearly displayed. Then, there were too many remedies to choose from. And the garish packaging was hurting Ned's sore eyes.

Ned stood in the aisle, rocking slightly on his heels, comparing the ingredients listed on the boxes in their fine, small, delicate print, with their long, complex, unpronounceable names. The language of the boxed cold remedies was impenetrable to sniffling Ned, who had long ago rejected the Catholic church for its intentional obfuscation. And so naturally he felt as if he was once again being made the victim of a carefully constructed mystery that was designed to make him give up inquiring and wearily open his wallet, while hoping for the miracle that seemed promised by the magical language.

He set the boxes back on the shelf and approached the high counter that hid most of the pharmacist.

"Yes?" said the pharmacist.

"Do you have a cold remedy that won't make you sleep?"

The pharmacist named a name. Ned found the box with that name, but noticed that the remedy contained caffeine. He returned to the high counter, saying, "Do you have one that won't keep you awake?"

The pharmacist named another, which Ned found. But upon reading the instructions on the box, it was clear that it wouldn't keep the sufferer awake because it was bound to put him right to sleep.

Ned returned to the pharmacist's counter, holding two boxes. "Isn't there one," said Ned, "that will not put you to sleep or keep you awake?"

The pharmacist recommended the one remedy that would keep Ned awake, suggesting he take an over-the-counter sleeping aid at night, to counter the effects.

Then Ned flung the boxes in the air. One could argue that the weariness of this particular gesture—a quick flip of the hands—is no different than the weariness that causes others to sigh and pay the cashier and leave. But the pharmacist—a man in a smock, a man with a license to dispense difficult and powerful powders from behind a high counter—diagnosed disrespect in Ned's flung boxes. The proud pharmacist was provoked into calling Ned Felm 'Young Man,' as in, "Young Man, you pick up those boxes right this minute, or I'm calling the police."

Ned was indeed a young man of twenty, much younger than the pharmacist. He had proposed marriage only once and been rejected only once by that time. It had happened recently and would be introduced by Ned's lawyer at the trial as probable cause for Ned's behavior, which was also introduced at the breakfast table by the mother of Ned's near-fiancée as good cause to be glad that her daughter had rebuffed the young hot-head, Ned Felm, who had rebuffed church, did you know, see where that gets you. The daughter had agreed, saying, "One conviction leads to another, Mother." All at the table had laughed at this, especially Dad, who was hiding his disappointment that Ned would not be his son-in-law, not be around for holiday suppers. He liked the Felm boy because he was high-impact; an impulsive, athletic youth; a former high school defensive back who often got kicked out of games for spiking the ball after making an interception. Ned Felm could not help expressing himself in rule-rankling ways, and the near-fiancée's father liked that about him, even though Ned himself would have said it was his greatest fault and the source of his most frequent shames.

Ned had done it again in the pharmacy, in front of the proud pharmacist who had sold condoms to Ned on so many other occasions, who was now phoning the police. Ned had spiked the cold remedies. The pharmacist had commanded Ned to pick them up. Ned picked up the boxes and also many more items on the shelf below the counter: Life-Savers, throat lozenges, antacids, gums. These Ned flung, up again, and they fell softly at Ned's feet, as if loosened from the gut of a piñata.

Ned started to enjoy it. This was always the case with him, when he stepped a little over the line out of frustration. Whatever was bugging Ned was immediately relieved, replaced by the joy of recklessness. Then he would do it again. It was like a cure, in a way, though a childish one.

Ned cured himself a few more times at the pharmacy, bending gracefully at the waist and swooping up with his hands full of nickel items, scattering them in the air. Strangely enough, the repetition of the toe-touching type of movement in which Ned was engaged loosened his sinuses and freed his breathing. Unfortunately, it had also constricted the breathing of the pharmacist, who had stepped out from behind the high counter and was angrily shoving Ned down the aisle.

It was the cold-remedy aisle, and therefore Ned was inspired to more stupidity, on a much more grand scale. Whole shelves were cleared by the sweep of his arms (his sinuses now as clear!) but not a box nor a bottle had been broken; there had been no damage but disorder. (This would be introduced by Ned's lawyer as evidence of mere horseplay on the part of the reckless youth, and then stricken from the record as irrelevant.)

The policeman, a pancake aficionado by the name of Edwin, was waiting near the end of the aisle, hands on his hips. Behind him, crouching to see, was the cashier—Bettina, a young girl who hated the stuck-up pharmacist, who would state from the witness chair that he had once told her that "the customer was always right, but not as right as the pharmacist." Bettina would lose her job because of that testimony, and then ostracize herself by taking the drugstore to court, winning the case and her job back, causing customers to avoid the drugstore. The pharmacist finally begged her to go away, giving her enough money to land her in New York, where she attended college and became, eventually, the first female lawyer in the firm of Bline, Stremper, and Grouse.

(Ned had once kissed Bettina on the neck at a dance while her boyfriend was sneaking a smoke behind the American Legion. This was never entered as evidence anywhere, by anyone.)

Shoved by the pharmacist, Ned found his shoulder submerged in Edwin the cop's large and soft blue belly. Soon Edwin's arms were around him and Ned was lifted in the air.

"Let's all go home now!" crowed Edwin, inexplicably. (The policeman claimed at the trial that he was speaking literally, though other witnesses avowed that Edwin's 'home' was usually a euphemism for jail. Ned's lawyer argued that Ned would have certainly known this, and based his reaction accordingly. It was debated in court whether 'accordingly' included Ned twisting like a strong serpent in Edwin's arms and climbing up, as it were, onto the policeman's head.)

Nobody could have known at the time—not the pharmacist, Bettina the cashier, Edwin the policeman, and maybe not even Ned—that Ned's scramble up the blue mountain that was Edwin was not an attack on the policeman, but a scramble to safety. For Ned was frightened and ashamed, and he was climbing up the first available height to get away from himself. Ned wanted it to be over and it would not be over.

Then Edwin, with the weight of Ned on his shoulders and on his now-hatless head, toppled to the drugstore floor, howling for help. The pharmacist pulled at Ned's legs. Ned responded by burrowing deeper into the warmth of the policeman, burying his face into Edwin's fleshy neck, finding his ear with his now cleared-up nose, and then, as if he had been possessed by the spirit of a disoriented puppy, drunk on too much play, Ned took a firm bite of Edwin's pink ear.

It was a well-fed ear that had been kept clean, and the gristle as it was introduced between Ned's teeth was satisfying to chomp, so he chomped. The screaming of Edwin was something to hear. And Ned, driven as he was always to persevere, persevered by biting harder, and all of his fears and stresses and confusions and angers were released through his jaws. And though it looked and sounded to all witnesses to be an attack, it was an act of love, Ned was telling himself as he bit harder on the ear, an act of love.

Ned, during his time on the witness stand, said nothing about how he felt like a dog at the time, about the bite as an act of love—even though it might have gotten him a lighter sentence through an insanity plea—because he was ashamed. His mother had gone to the stand to recall Ned's many other acts of biting people, claiming that her son, at the age of three, once bit her foot while she was sleeping on the beach, and she had to be carried to the car.

Ned's legal defender introduced as evidence a handful of pencils once belonging to Ned that had been chewed to splintery frazzles, calling each pencil a 'cry for help,' causing Ned's mother to weep. Bettina fidgeted in her seat in the gallery, glancing at Ned, whose hair was badly combed. His cold had worsened in jail.

Edwin, with an enormous bandage wrapped around his head, a bandage that bulged horribly where his ear had been re-sewn, took the stand. He described how he lay sobbing on the drugstore floor while the pharmacist tried to pry Ned's jaws open for the ear, as Bettina begged Ned to give it back. Some of the jurors wondered silently if the bulge in the bandage was because the ear was swollen to gigantic proportions, due to trauma. This intrigued them for a while, picturing Edwin's ear.

Edwin, after each question by the prosecutor, would tilt his head, with his face inclined toward the jury box, cup his hand behind his bandaged ear and ask for the question to be repeated.

Seven years, four with good behavior. Ned got a lecture on good behavior from the judge. Ned heard the lecture, absorbing it all, especially the part about becoming a productive member of society.

It was Ned's contention, after his conviction—in fact it had occurred to him immediately after his crime—that he needed to be cured of his impulse to disrupt. He didn't hate society and its rules, it was just that something inside him was operating outside of those rules, and occasionally it would burst out of its hiding place and consume everything.

He promised the prison psychiatrist that he would go to church when he got out, take whatever cold remedies were available, plus the sleeping aids, if need be. And he meant it. Ned wanted to belong. He was tired of not belonging. To prove it, Ned attended the prison chapel, volunteering for the choir. He accepted a job as a janitor. He volunteered for the medical experiment. Ned wanted to belong.

The radiation gun thumped and knocked thickly as it fired on Ned's testicles. A man with a fading tattoo of a frigate on his arm, who wore a lead smock smeared with what looked like plaster, crouched behind a screen. The man in the gray single-breasted suit, who had produced the soothing murmur while Ned signed the release forms, was now settled behind a desk in a small office with a thick window looking out into the laboratory. Whenever Ned looked at the man behind the window, the man was looking into Ned's eyes. Ned never caught him looking at his genitals. He took it as a sign of the experiment's validity.

After each session, Ned was given a bottle of Coca Cola. It was not made clear whether this was intended as a tonic or a reward, and hadn't been mentioned in the contract. But after five years of good behavior, after he had received his check from the government for volunteering for the experiment and been released from prison, Ned would think of a bottle of Coca Cola as the symbol of his rehabilitation.

Ned took to drinking Coke when he felt the need to reinforce his devotion to society. His taste for the soda was the first and most noticeable side-effect of the radiation treatments.

Ned settled in downtown Milwaukee, not far from his boyhood home in the suburbs, choosing a small apartment situated above a bakery. The bakery reminded Ned of his odd jobs as a teenager, babysitting for his aunt and uncle. The baby's dirty diapers had smelled like bread dough. Ned had forgotten about this association while he was in prison, and now it came sweeping back over him as he lay on his cheap metal bed in the small apartment above the bakery. It kept Ned from getting too hungry from the smells.

He got a job waving an orange flag at road construction sites, which required Ned to awaken early, which he did without fail. One day, when it was cold and bright, Ned was waving along a column of cars when he spotted his old near-fiancée driving a station wagon with three children sitting in the back seat. She appeared to be very unhappy, possibly because of the construction delays, and did not recognize Ned. She squinted her eyes in the daylight as her three children bounced up and down, smacking each other on the head.

Once, a police car had whizzed by during a slow period, braked suddenly, reversed, and rolled to a stop beside Ned. Edwin was there, peeking out. He was very fat; the ear facing Ned was the good ear. Ned leaned his body sideways toward the hood of the police car, to look through the windshield so he could see Edwin's other ear, but Edwin sped away, leaving a cloud of gravel dust in his place. Ned waved his orange flag weakly in the direction of the departing police car.

A doctor with connections to the military or the prison or both would visit Ned periodically, to ask questions. His name was Belnik; he was thin and white-haired and smoked filtered cigarettes. When Doctor Belnik sat in one of Ned's wooden chairs, his slender legs seemed crossed even when they weren't. He would ask about Ned's 'functioning.' It was finally explained to Ned that 'functioning' meant something sexual, and that the doctor's follow-up visits would take on more meaning when Ned was espoused and considering a family.

"How are things in that department?" ventured Doctor Belnik, tapping his ash into a clean tin-foil pot-pie container provided by Ned for the occasion.

"The functioning department?"

"We can call it romance."

"Not so hot," admitted Ned.

"No stimulation whatsoever?"

"Not to speak of."

"We have time," offered Belnik.

Ned was encouraged by the 'we.'

Ned realized that Doctor Belnik was becoming disappointed in his progress, and wondered if he might be forced to go back to prison to finish his sentence. Yet the laconic doctor seemed somehow relieved by his disappointment. After the first few questions of each interview, Belnik would grow quiet, smoking and thinking. The visits, instead of satisfying the needs of medical research, turned into casual sessions in which both men smoked and looked out of the window, occasionally remarking on the off-season trades made by the Milwaukee Braves baseball team, or the consoling presence of Milt Pappas when he was on the mound.

Ned, as a lonely and somewhat confused young man, anticipated these sessions with the doctor by buying seeded buns and fresh milk for the coffee. Doctor Belnik was secretly touched by these gestures. He would sometimes stay on for hours, drinking the coffee, smelling the bakery, watching the sky above this modest pocket of Milwaukee turn gray, darkening the room until the little desk lamp in the corner of Ned's room seemed to be radiating butter.

Doctor Belnik invited Ned to supper at his house one Friday night, when Ned did not have to retire early for work. The doctor had explained in hushed but gentle tones to his wife Brenda about Ned's reckless mistake and his unfortunate incarceration. He mentioned nothing about the experiment; in fact, the experiment was little on his mind these days.

Brenda, healthy and wide, was understanding about Ned's situation, and she was happy to have a young guest in her house who could eat her food. Ned's un-Jewish condition was improved somewhat by his former rejection of the Catholic church. And her daughter, Rachel, who was twenty-three and socially disadvantaged on account of her looks, could benefit from the company.

Rachel was indeed homely, needing thick glasses to see, needing big clothes to wear. Ned noticed at once that her milky white face was a face that would stay young for a long time. Drinking his Coca Cola at the Belniks' dining-room table, Ned thought it might be rewarding to watch Rachel's face for a long time, watching patiently and without judgment for signs of aging, just as he was being watched by Rachel's father for medical signs of whatever he was watching for.

Within two months, with four dinners per month at the Belniks', Ned made public his thoughts about the Belnik girl, and he and Rachel were engaged.

Thin Doctor Belnik was so outweighed by his wide wife and his solid daughter, that his reservations about the match went unvoiced. If Brenda was willing to overlook Ned's un-Jewish heritage, why couldn't the doctor set aside his concerns about the prison radiation experiments? Yet Doctor Belnik found himself preoccupied with the experiments once again, much more than before. At night, in Belnik's dreams, nightmarish grandchildren swarmed over the doctor, chewing his face. And his sessions with Ned in the apartment above the bakery took on a new intensity, now that Belnik's concerns were both medical and familial.

Unable to do anything about the upcoming wedding, Belnik turned his anxiety toward the prison's radiation program. He filed a flurry of false reports based on Ned's condition, claiming irreparable damage to the subject Ned Felm, and recommended that the experiments be stopped until further research could be done.

But the doctor could not stop the wedding, nor, in his heart, did he want to. For he loved his daughter Rachel and had grown to love Ned, the gangly and chastised young man with the orange flag in his hand and the radioactive heat in his loins.

Ned's mother was at the ceremony, in tears, with the scarred teethmarks in her heel turning pink under her stockings. Ned's father, who disliked Jews and was glad they were getting Ned, whom he disliked even more, declined to attend.

Brenda Belnik and Ned's mother became very close friends and extremely compatible grandmothers after little Samuel was born to Ned and Rachel. Doctor Belnik had overseen the birth, delivering his own grandson. He sweated heavily throughout Rachel's labors, afraid of what he would see. But Samuel was perfectly loud and fat, and Doctor Belnik was happier than he had been for a very long time, holding that little bloody boy.

Belnik had stopped filing false reports to the government and the prison about his patient because he was afraid of getting caught, but those organizations had lost interest in the experiment anyway. The side-effects of the experiments, whatever they were expected to be, would have to proceed on their own, without governmental supervision.

But the results did not escape the attention of Doctor Belnik. While playing with his healthy grandson in the yard, Belnik would sometimes remark in the privacy of his thin white head that the side-effects of the experiment with the radiation in prison had netted a warm friendship with Ned, a husband for his daughter, the robust Samuel, two inseparable older women who were presently talking in low tones inside the kitchen, and the death of Ned Felm at the age of thirty-four from cancer, well before Rachel's face had begun to show any traces of her age.

Nominated by Witness

DOOR

by DANA LEVIN

from COUNTERMEASURES

Then the uprush of air—
Then the cellar doors
    banging back,
the strong dusk light falling in
    like a stanchion,
a gold nail hammered through the blackened trees—
    Can you see it? You,
psyche, burden, friend?
    This is the first time I can speak, the first time
I've seen you
    recede from the front in a fission of mist, the doors of this keep
flying open in the auric light—
    And I can smell

the green smell of straw
    puddled in urine, the musk of fur
coming up from the hutches, laid out in a row in the leaning
    light,
the blood smell of rust
    in the hinges of these open doors—Are you
that sound and rush of flapping wings,
    back there behind me where no birds are roosting. I want
to look back

    in the black deep and the golden light, if I had two faces
and could stand, always, at
    the distinction, on the wooden step

between the gold shaft and the cellar
    beneath me,
I could be like the eye in the center of my head—always to see and
  never
    to enter, never to feel
the light pierce and the darkness snuff it,
    the darkness down and the light
pierce it,
    the exhausting round of wounding and healing, I don't want
to feel, but can't bear
    not feeling.

the light swift through the cottonwood leaves, their edges enflamed
    but their bodies
in shadow, black spades oranged
    in the orange-gold light—
I don't know how
    to get out of this beauty, I was shut up so long
in darkness and weeping, but here
    the rabbits are black stones on fire in the grass,
their blackness burning, as if the light is leaving
    thumbs of fire

on my standing body,
    as I stand on this step between the sun
and the cellar,
    can you tell me if this
is the place I must enter, to burn without consumption
    in the ice-fired night?
Will I burn from the inside out like a star, will I burn from the
  outside in
    in wood-fire,
is it blaze,
    is it anguish,
to be the conscious sun that does not die,
    for isn't life fire, living the human burning torch—

    And then a slight wind like a pointing finger,
    lifting toward the flame-struck field.

Nominated by Countermeasurers, *Richard Tayson*

KNOWING YOUR PLACE

by SYLVIA WATANABE

from MICHIGAN QUARTERLY REVIEW

Before settling in Grand Rapids, my husband and I spent life out of graduate school on freeways, in U-Haul trucks, pursuing tenure at 55 mph. We traveled back and forth along I-80 from California, to New York, to California, to Michigan, jettisoning ballast along the way. The boxes of old Christmas cards were the first to go, along with the deep freeze that could hold five hundred pounds of meat. Next went the barbells, king-sized sofa bed, a mutual interest in geology (complete with rock collection), and *The History of Western Civilization* by Will and Ariel Durant. Somewhere in Wyoming I abandoned my fear of driving in the dark. On our second pass through California, I stopped putting rice out for the family ghosts. Bill, my husband, was reassuring. "They'll just go to Honolulu," he said. "They still know the way to your mother's house."

I have come to think of home as where I am not. As a place I've just left, or a place where I have not yet arrived. There are others too—perfect strangers—who have apparently given these matters some thought. I usually meet these people when I am walking down a street somewhere. "Chink!" they yell from their cars, as they speed past, "Why don't you go home!"

I was born and raised in Hawaii, on an island maybe eighty miles around. There was no such thing there as a perfect stranger. If people yelled at you from their cars, they were liable to get the epithets right.

And if you talked to anyone long enough, you would probably discover that their cousin Albert was related to your uncle Mitsuo's brother-in-law's wife.

It would have been impossible not to form those kinds of ties in a landscape where everything—the weather, the fact you were surrounded by water, the distance to anywhere—conspired to make you stay put. But none of what made leaving so difficult prevented the outside—including an enormous variety of exotic plant and animal life, as well as most of the human population—from moving in. My Japanese grandparents, who were Confucian Buddhists on my mother's side and Confucian Presbyterians on my father's, were among the "exotics" who put their roots down in the Islands and never considered anywhere else home again.

Back in Japan, my mother's mother said, everyone occupied a place that was already decided. She said, "I came to Hawaii to make my own place." She was first made to understand, however, that there was *no* respectable place for an unmarried, non-Christian Japanese female without English except employment as a domestic, then marriage. Only after the births of five children, the death of a son, and widowhood—once more single, but forever respectable—could she finally make a place for herself as head of her family and keeper of the rituals binding us to whatever had come before Hawaii. It was she who taught my mother, then me, that the dead are hungry and must be fed, that home was where they could find their way to us.

My father's parents were a different story. "They were missionaries," he says—as if that explains everything about them. They were educated in Japan by American Presbyterians who persuaded them to go to Hawaii and attempt to convert the Japanese workers on the sugar plantations. When my grandparents emigrated it was not so much with the hope of making a place for themselves, but with the confidence that wherever they went, their place in the Lord was already secure. "Thy Kingdom Come," my grandfather wrote in a letter to one of his teachers. "All Christians must realize that it is their responsibility to Christianize the world."

This belief wasn't shaken when he and my grandmother were informed soon after arriving that the church was unwilling to provide long-term support for their "subsidiary efforts." In present-day academic parlance, they were not tenure track. When support ran out, they didn't complain; the Lord would provide. They looked for other ways to secure a living. Grandmother held classes in American cookery and English conversation. Grandfather worked, at various times, as an insurance salesman, bookkeeper, and postman. They moved from one island to another before finally being called by one of the plantation communities on Maui to establish a Japanese language school. My grandparents regarded it as intrinsic to their teaching efforts to "instill" in their students "American ways of thinking, ways of doing, ways of worshipping, as well as the spirit of Democracy." How could they know then that manifest destiny had nothing to do with them?

"We came because they called us," my grandfather said later. "Perhaps they could not get anyone else who knew both English and Japanese—though our English was not the best. Most of the community were from poor farming families back in Japan, and they could hardly read and write in Japanese. So we taught the children. The parents always had something to translate—immigration papers, bank papers, personal letters. One way or another, I guess you could say, we spread the Word."

In some families there are lawyers, or architects, or investment bankers; in my father's there are missionaries. Before his parents there was his mother's mother who labored for years among the Ainu in northern Japan. More recently his youngest sister converted to Mormonism and went off on a mission to Okinawa. My husband believes that we are carrying on the family tradition. "What else would you call what we've been doing since graduate school?" he asks, and then points out that, as adjunct writing instructors, we too spread the word, go where we're called, and labor under the necessary misapprehension that a higher power will provide.

Bill is the first to receive the call to a tenurable position. We are living in Hayward, California, and the English department with tenure is in Allendale, Michigan. It is true that we have always talked of settling on the West Coast, where family is near, but tenure means health insurance, the end to camping out in a chancy job market, and maybe someday a house of our own. While I am apprehensive about my own lack of a position, something is bound to open up. And when Bill sug-

254

gests that I use the breather to write fulltime, who am I to resist, he being the higher power who will provide.

After many bad adventures in moving, we decide that this time we will get it right. We will not hold a garage sale. We will not scour the dumpsters of all the local liquor stores for cardboard boxes. We will not mail our belongings ahead by Greyhound and the USPS to the houses of relatives all over the state. We will not hire a fifty-foot moving van to drive ourselves, even if it is the only truck left at U-Haul. We will not attempt to drive the entire distance in just two days. We will *not* start packing the night before.

Many weeks before we are scheduled to leave, Bill goes from room to room, measuring things. He measures the bookcases, the queen-sized bed, the dining set, the dressers, the computer work stations, and writes all the figures down on a yellow pad. He opens cupboards and drawers and, after looking inside and doing more calculations, scribbles more figures. When he is finished, he makes a sweeping gesture that takes in the entire apartment, and announces, "We can break most of this stuff down and fit it into a five-by-ten trailer."

"What about that?" I ask, indicating the suddenly enormous looking, foam-padded sofa.

"We'll leave it," he says.

"What about the mattress on the bed?" I ask.

"We'll get a new one; you always said that one was lumpy."

"What about all the kitchen stuff? What about our clothes? What about the books?" I am beginning to feel depressed.

"Ah, the books." Bill looks thoughtful. "Well, maybe we'll need a six-by-twelve and a car top carrier. And—" he adds, as gently as possible, "We'll have to cut down on the load—way down."

Out of curiosity and desperation, I begin calling moving companies. The three questions these places always ask are: How big is the load? How much does it weigh? Do you live upstairs?

The last is the only question I can answer with certainty—at least until the third call I make.

"Do you live upstairs?" the man at the other end of the line asks.

"No," I explain, "We live downstairs, on the ground floor."

He says, "How many flights up did you say that was?"

"One," I reply. "Downstairs."

"But you still have to go up those stairs in order to get out of the apartment, don't you?" he points out.

I can't disagree with the logic of that.

"Well then, you live up one flight," the man says.

So, down is up. What can I say to the other two questions? The load is big, it is enormous, it weighs on us.

One night we are sitting in front of the TV, drinking beers and watching the NBA playoffs, when Bill suddenly sits up, stricken. "I forgot to measure the television," he says. We have also forgotten the teak stereo cabinets, the record collection, the cassette tapes, the tape deck, the speakers, and all the rest of the sound equipment—not to mention the box of baseball bats in the storage cage and the bicycle he took apart to ship here by Greyhound and never put back together again.

Whenever we are at the mall we spend a lot of time at the electronics counter in Macy's. There we wistfully handle the two-inch televisions, the portable CD players, the notebook computers, and the micro-cassette recorders you can carry in your pocket. Bill says, "Just think how easy it would be to move if we could miniaturize."

My grandfather liked to describe how he and my grandmother arrived in the Islands with all their belongings in a single trunk. Although he himself had always been fond of a well-made suit, they were embarking on a new life in which it would be necessary to put aside such worldly tastes. And of course, he would add almost as an afterthought, they could not expect the church to pay their moving expenses.

The tenured missionaries sent to the Islands by the American Board of Commissioners for Foreign Missions had all of their expenses covered. Their move from Boston to Honolulu is described by James Michener in the novel, *Hawaii*. For years I worked in the education department of the museum run by their descendants, and my job was nothing more than to research, catalogue, and make up stories about all the items in the many trunks that came over from Boston. It is quite literally true—not to mention metaphorically significant—that among the things these missionaries brought with them were the disassembled pieces of a two-story, woodframe, New England-style house. As they themselves recognized, they were not mere purveyors of a spiritual doctrine, they were instruments in the grand (some might even say Faustian) endeavor of transplanting an entire material culture. Judging from the present state of "develop-

256

ment" in the Islands, the success of this endeavor has surely surpassed even their wildest dreams.

But when it is not possible either to dismantle and move your entire apartment building or to pare five roomsful of possessions down to a single trunk and the clothes on your backs, the questions remain: what do you take with you and what do you leave behind?

This is the time to face up to the fact that you probably don't need a drawer full of harmonicas. That you will not learn Russian, or take tap dancing lessons, or pick up the alto sax. That you will never manage another recreational baseball team, or put together the ten-speed you took apart and whose headgear you can no longer find. This is the time to realize that you will never again wear the size two black bolero jacket that you can't remove from its drycleaning bag without instantly attracting every white cat hair in the apartment. This is the time to part with the collection of ceramic bunnies that your cousin in Germany continues to send you every Christmas, as well as the dusty box, unopened from the time it was stored in your parents' basement, containing every piece of homework from elementary school.

Then there are things that you would like to discard but cannot, the things you never desired to collect but that have accrued nonetheless. These are the memories: the swastika on the carport wall. The dog excrement smeared on the front stoop. The young white men in the pickup pursuing you down the street as you walked home from work. These are the words: Gook. Nip. Dink. Flip. Slope. Slant. Slant eyes. Rice eyes. Dogeater. Yellowskin. Yellow housenigger. Chink. Jap. These are the questions: What's your nationality? What kind of a name is that? Where is it from? I mean, where are *you* from? Well then, where are your parents from? Is *he* your husband? No, I mean where are you *really* from?

I am a Japanese Confucian Buddhist Presbyterian from Hawaii. My mother's mother and father were born in Yamaguchi Prefecture in Japan. My father's father and mother were born in Fukushima and Gifu. They are all dead now. My husband is a Scotch Irish German Christian Scientist Puritan Agnostic. His great great great great great great great great great great great great great grandfather, John Coggeshall, became the first governor of Rhode Island after testifying in the trial of Anne Hutchinson and being forced to leave the Massachusetts Colony. He is dead now too.

Here is a photo of my grandfather, taken when he was still a very young man. He is dressed in a white suit, his arms full of roses. There is something Wildean and un-Presbyterian about his pose, about the way he gazes languidly upon the flowers.

Here he is again with a group of friends on Mt. Haleakala. They have just been to watch the sun rise. Grandfather kneels in the front row, straw Panama in hand, as immaculately dressed as ever.

Here is a formal portrait of him and my grandmother, taken in a photography studio. My grandmother so small and neat. Her beatific smile. Her slim legs crossed at the ankles, her hands folded in her lap. She has on a western-style dress and a little black pillbox, such as she often wore, the net in front half covering her face. Grandfather stands next to her with his perfect posture, his perfect suit, his arms hanging at his sides. His expression is familiar: the gaze off to the distance beyond the frame of the camera. His eyeglasses glint so I can't see his eyes. On the back of the photo someone has written, "27th Anniversary, 11/41."

A couple of weeks later, early on the morning of December eighth, the Military Police came to my grandparents' house. My grandfather, grandmother, and two youngest aunts were the only ones living there. My father was working in Honolulu and the next three oldest children were all away at college.

It was very dark, as my aunt Dorothy remembers. Everyone was roused from sleep by the sound of loud knocking at the front door. When Grandfather went to answer, he was confronted by armed MPs who told him to get dressed, then took him out to a truck parked in the front drive. After posting a guard they went back inside and searched the house.

Grandfather was taken to the Maui County jail where he was incarcerated in an eight-by-ten cell for six months before being shipped to a temporary holding facility outside of Honolulu. Just before his departure he wrote a letter to the Maui Headquarters for Military Intelligence, asking permission for one last visit with his family. The letter says:

> Dear Lieutenant Sir,
>   I, as an internee, hereby respectfully submit this petition for granting me your special permission to visit my home in Waikapu, only one and a half miles from here, just once, before my transference to the place designated by the Military Authority.

It is not from selfishness, but from a natural humanness, that I desire to meet my family before my long departure.

The house I have lived in for many years is where my six children grew up. The furniture, house goods, utensils, plants, orchids, and everything in it are dear to me. I hope to have my last meal with my wife, aged mother-in-law, and two young daughters. It will not take more than three or four hours [This has been crossed out in the draft, and changed to "four or five hours"]. We will use English only in our conversation under the Military Guard to be provided for me. I will not say anything regarding the War or about the Detention Camp and will observe the rules and regulations we are given to follow.

I have been a faithful resident of Hawaii for 35 years, never committed any crime of any nature, even the slightest offense. I have never been disloyal to America, the country of my six children, and the country we, my wife and I, chose for our last resting place. Now I shall be sent from my family for long duration, under the suspicion of which I have no knowledge. I realize truly the present situation of this country, so I am contented with the treatment I am now being dealt, but I fearlessly state here in the presence of our Living God that I am innocent though it is not the purpose of this letter to clarify my innocence.

I earnestly ask you for permission to visit my home, just once, at any hour of any day before my sad departure.

Respectfully submitted by
Yakichi Watanabe

The Military Authority granted him his request.

A few days later when my father went to visit him at the facility outside of Honolulu, Grandfather—always the man of words—asked for a Spanish dictionary. "They are sending us to New Mexico," he said, "And I hear they speak Spanish there."

The day before Bill and I are to begin our drive to Michigan, we go down to the nearest U-Haul to pick up the trailer. We talk to someone named Frank, who confirms, after looking it up in his book. that we'll be more than okay with a six-by-twelve, which is the maximum size that a Ford Fairmont can pull. He asks where we are headed and when

259

we tell him, vaguely (because we are not sure ourselves), somewhere in the vicinity of Grand Rapids, he says, "I'm from Wyoming."

Bill and I look at each other, then he says to Frank, "That's great. There's some beautiful country in Wyoming."

Frank laughs. "If you like Dutchmen." Then he explains that he is talking about Wyoming, Michigan—a township in the greater Grand Rapids area. "Yep, there sure are a lot of Dutchmen there."

I glance again at Bill, who is staring at the blond, blue-eyed Frank. "Are *you* Dutch?" Bill asks.

Frank says, "Hell, no. I considered myself lucky when I got out."

Bill hitches the trailer to our car, and we drive back to our apartment without exchanging a word.

Early the next morning, with the help of Bill's son, who has driven up from Southern California, we begin loading the trailer. When we are done, it is a job of engineering precision from top to bottom, front to back—each object fitting the next, like pieces in a Rubik's Cube. Bill looks at his watch and notes that it isn't even eleven o'clock; we'll be on our way even earlier than we'd planned. But when we walk around to the side, to admire our work from a different perspective, his son says, "It's probably nothing, but is the back end of the Ford always that close to the ground?" Now that he mentions it, the front end also seems a bit higher than usual, with the entire chassis sloping backward at a twenty-five-degree angle. As we stand there debating whether this is a peculiar design feature we have never noticed before, one of the other tenants in our building calls out as he walks by, "Looks like you've got more than you can handle!"

We stare after him in dismay as he strolls, whistling, to his car and drives off. Bill goes over to the manager's office and calls Frank at U-Haul who informs him that we can solve our problem by redistributing the load. Just make sure to put the heaviest things over the axles and the lightest things up front, Frank says. Bill and his son set about unloading the trailer, while I pack the car with what we have been referring to as "odds and ends." When I am done, they take the entire backseat, as well as most of the front. The plan had originally been to put the cat in the back, but since it is now full I will have to carry her on my lap. For the time being, I leave her on the passenger side, looking pathetically out the window.

By now Bill and his son have finished re-loading. It is not as precise a job as the first time, but they have managed to get everything back inside—except for two large boxes, containing old textbooks from college. The slope of the chassis is down about two degrees, which is not that much of an improvement when we consider that the interior of the car is completely jammed as well. There is nothing to do but lighten the load. As Bill's son gets into his truck to head back down to San Diego, we are throwing our college textbooks into the dumpster at the far end of the parking lot.

Hayward is in the San Francisco Bay Area where there are lots of hills. Each time we struggle up one hill, the inertia of the trailer pulls in the opposite direction. Whenever we hit a downhill, the trailer looms in the rearview, threatening to race full-out over the top of the car. With every bump, sparks fly; the hitch, which extends below the bumper, scrapes bottom hard. After we have gone a couple of miles in this fashion, we pull up to a dumpster in a Denny's parking lot where we empty out the backseat. Next follows a stop at the back entrance of the city library where we leave more boxes of books placed neatly beside the overnight book return. After each jettisoning of ballast, we look hopefully at our Ford, which continues to retain its backward tilt. By now it is getting late, so we head for a friend's house in San Francisco—a drive that usually takes thirty minutes during off-traffic, without an overloaded trailer. Of course it's now at the peak of rush hour.

The next morning, Bill takes everything out of the trailer for the third time. Our friend had kindly offered to let us store part of the load in her basement. "Then you'll have to come back and see us again," she says. I burst into tears.

Along with two large bookcases, we also leave the barbecue, more books, our entire record collection, the teak stereo cabinets, and all the sound equipment. Bill says, "There must have been a reason the first time I forgot to measure all this." After reloading the trailer with what remains, we note optimistically that the car is now tilted at an improved fifteen-degree angle, and we again proceed on our way. As we are driving on the beautiful Oakland Bay Bridge, over beautiful San Francisco Bay, I have the cat on my lap and we are gazing out the passenger seat window, thinking mournful thoughts and watching our beautiful city falling away.

Suddenly Bill says, "Oh, oh, trouble."

I say, "Like we haven't had trouble already."

He says, "This is serious. Smoke."

I look out the rear window, and there it is—a black, metallic-smelling cloud billowing out the back. We speculate that maybe if we slow down, it will get better, and it does.

261

I can't resist asking, "Does this mean that we will have to drive at 30 miles an hour all the way to Michigan?"

He doesn't answer.

That night we make another unexpected stop in Applegate, at a little motel with a fire station motif.

Bill rises early and spends the morning under the hood. He closes it back up without attempting surgery; there is nothing he can do to make our Ford pull that trailer any faster. When we figure it out, we have been averaging 33 miles a day, including backtracking, and at this rate, we won't get to Grand Rapids for another three months.

That's when we decide to Make Our Move with Corrigan. After looking up their address in the phone book, we drive over and leave them our load. Next we go to U-Haul and drop off the six-by-twelve. Now the car behaves well, but the cat has meanwhile decided that she has had enough. As we are crossing the Sierras she begins to yowl.

"She's driving me crazy," Bill says. "Why don't you stop her?"

By now I am also weeping uncontrollably. When we don't turn around and go back, or—as the cat would prefer—stop this minute right where we are, I quit weeping and she crawls under the front passenger seat and refuses to emerge.

This is August of 1988; it's been a summer of record heat. There is drought everywhere, and the reports over the radio say that the corn crop is dying all across the Midwest. It is 115 degrees when we get to the Nevada desert. A little less than halfway across, we stop for gas, and I drag the cat out from her hiding place. She is a rag; barely conscious. I plunge her into the ice chest and attempt feline resuscitation. From that point on, we decide to travel at night.

The night is still hot, but it is not as bad as during the day. The darkness and the desert go on forever. I think of my grandfather in that other desert all those years ago. "At night," he writes, "When there is only the sound of the wind, I look out across the sand. I cannot see far, but I can feel the miles and miles of desert out there, big as an ocean. The sound of the wind is the sound of the ocean. And if I close my eyes and breathe in, I can smell the ocean and imagine myself home once again."

As we cross the Great Salt Lake I try to see it with his eyes. After spending his life on small green islands, how alien this landscape would have seemed . . . and yet, perhaps how familiar—as if, in his desolation, he had been traveling it for a very long time.

When the bombs fell on Pearl Harbor, his place in the world, like that of thousands of others, was blown to bits. Over and over, in the letters he wrote after first being taken into custody, he tries to recover that place. Unsure of the charges against him, he protests his innocence. He has learned English, he says, "to assimilate myself to American life, in every respect." And if that is not sufficient evidence of his loyalty, none of his children has "ever visited a foreign country. They were expatriated from Japan in order to confirm their American Citizenship. I have helped hundreds of other Japanese children in their procedure of expatriation from Japan, without taking any fee."

But all of his arguments miss the point. It is precisely the means he uses to assert his innocence that prove his guilt. His knowledge of English and "American ways" had made him a leader in what had now become the enemy community. By encouraging loyal citizenship among the American-born Japanese, he merely helped to create unwanted complications. How much easier things might have been all the way around if the United States government had not been dealing with citizens having constitutional rights.

When he was unsuccessful at recovering his lost place, my grandfather decided, finally, to accept that too. "We can hope, someday, though not in our lives, that all people of the world will truly wake up to the Will of Our God and live, all races, harmoniously. Thy kingdom come." The most difficult journey he ever had to make was not between his home on Maui and the internment camp in New Mexico. It was not a journey measured in geographical distance, but in the space, the entire desert between two nouns: Missionary. Alien.

My husband and I have lived in Grand Rapids for the last eight years. It is a town of clean, well-kept streets and house-proud neighborhoods. People have conservative—most would say "family"—values and strong religious convictions, primarily of a Calvinist bent. They vote Republican. They seem to know their place in the world.

Since our arrival, Bill and I have moved three times. In our first apartment we lived across the hall from a college student with a fondness for heavy metal music at two in the morning. In our second apartment we lived downstairs from a World War II veteran with

Alzheimers. One morning, after I'd gone to the market, the front door was ajar while I set the bags of groceries down in the kitchen. When I went to close the door, the World War II veteran was in our living room, looking dazed. I asked if he needed help, and he turned toward me. He froze for an instant, his eyes as round as saucers, then he ran out of the apartment yelling, "The Japs are here!"

And so I am.

Bill now has tenure at his college. I write and occasionally teach. We own a house in a tree-shaded neighborhood, with woods and a little lake nearby, and where all the men are named Bud, Ted, Bob, Jim, Skip—and Bill adds, "Or Bill." On Saturdays in the summer, these men with one-syllable names can be heard calling to each other when they go outside to mow their lawns.

Bud, our next-door neighbor, is eighty years old. He brings us fresh strawberries, cucumbers, and tomatoes from his garden. I give him macadamia nuts that my parents have sent me. Bud says that he too has spent some time in Hawaii. "Not like the tourists," he is quick to add. For a while, when they were going there every winter, he and his wife considered it a second home.

When Bill and I decided to dig up our backyard and put in flowers, Bud lends us his sod cutter. He comes over to help us dig up the sod and turn over the soil. Another time he brings us an enormous spool, made out of wood and metal, that he has constructed in his basement shop. "Thought you could use something like this for the cord on your electric mower," he says.

One day in early fall the doorbell rings, and it is Bud announcing, "It's time to get your driveway ready for winter." Bill steps outside and sees that Bud has already hauled over a 5-gallon can of resurfacing material and all the necessary equipment.

"But shouldn't we do your driveway first?" Bill asks.

"Already done," Bud replies.

When I am outside working in the garden, he likes to come over and chat. He tells me stories about his travels. He talks about how he went to Egypt one time, about how he's often visited Europe.

"I like England because I can speak the language," he says. "But France . . . France is another story."

"I've been to France; it's a beautiful country," I reply.

Bud shakes his head. "The French—they just don't care for Americans." Then he looks at me, recognition dawning in his eyes. He real-

264

izes whom he is speaking to. "But they wouldn't have given *you* any trouble," he says.

The more things change, the more they stay the same.

A memory comes to me of my grandfather as a very old man in his nineties. He is in a white cotton T-shirt and long white cotton underwear, crouched on the floor of his study over a roll of rice paper, ink brush in hand. He is scribbling over and over in Japanese: Thy kingdom come. Thy kingdom come. A prayer. A hope. An unfinished notion.

Perhaps my mother's mother was right, and home is where the dead can find their way to us. If that is so then perhaps, too, home can be a place on a page, made out of words.

Lately I have been feeling restless, and I find myself thinking of the road at night—of the sound of the tires rushing over the blacktop and the darkness flowing around the car. Though we don't speak of it much, I know Bill feels this too. The other morning I found him sitting at the dining room table with an MLA joblist and an opened road atlas.

"Not that we have any serious intentions. Not in this bad job market," we say.

But occasionally we look around our nice little house and express the longing to "pare things down." And whenever we are at a department store, we cannot resist stopping off at the electronics counter to check out the miniature appliances.

Nominated by Michigan Quarterly Review *and Joyce Carol Oates*

EXECUTIVE SUITE

by MICHAEL HEFFERNAN

from WITNESS

Why should those of us in the working world
allow our time to be impinged upon
by others whose refusal to participate
reflects a lack of resolution on their part
which we quite reasonably despise them for?
It really is easier to stay up all night
than it is to wake up early in the morning.
The unexamined life is well worth living,
if we insist on getting something done
in place of what we might have come to find
on close inspection. Moral imperatives
or programs for the cleansing of the heart
can manifest themselves in a good day's work
just as effectively as in wild dreams,
being brought to bear believably enough
from evidence we develop at first hand
rather than from the spillage of weak minds
left free to rhapsodize in the wee hours.
Most normal people access waking life
with no perceptible detriment to their souls
(such as they are, such as they need to be),
and even perhaps some tangible benefit,
however negligible to those of us
who keep to ourselves the visions we have achieved,
while lunatics tell lies that no one hears
about the unspeakable stars that make no noise.

Nominated by Gibbons Ruark, David St. John

CARP

fiction by JESSICA ROEDER

from THE THREEPENNY REVIEW

MARY JASPER'S father came to visit one month after Mary and her mother moved into their new house. He had not lived with them for two years. When he arrived, Mary's mother was at the grocery store buying a box of coffee rolls because she had woken up with a taste for them. Since the out-of-court settlement that gave Mary's mother enough money to build the house, all of the mornings had been like that. Mary would wake to find her mother waiting in the living room, tapping her knee excitedly with her one good hand. Always Mary's mother had an idea of what they would eat for breakfast—something sweet, perhaps sticky, nothing they had in the house. Mary was ten years old that year, just old enough, she thought, to know that the breakfasts mattered. Faithfully, she ate whatever treat her mother chose.

Mary had not seen her father since well before the out-of-court settlement, though he had left a message on their answering machine the day it hit the newspaper. "Guys," his message said. "Good news for you. Your vengeance on bus drivers everywhere. Later." After the message played, Mary's mother stared at the machine as if she saw his face there and was not pleased with it. Mary said, "That's Dad for you." Her mother turned away, but not quick enough. Mary saw her face change, gather in on itself, and she knew her mother was craving alcohol, running through her old catalogue of who all might be to blame.

Now, Mary watched through the crack in the door's curtains as her father parked on the grass. His blue car sloped down alarmingly in the front, and the engine made a hee-hee sound. After he turned the key, he smiled into the rear-view mirror, baring his teeth, and then he tilted

267

his head back and checked inside his nose. Mary retreated to the wall of glass in the living room.

To Mary, the wall of glass was the house's best feature, though she knew that its French doors would open easily if a burglar ever tried. She liked the wall of glass because it was made of panes, each one slightly smaller than her face, because often a woodpecker would throw himself against it, fighting his own unflappable reflection, and because it opened the whole of the room to the slope of trees and rough grass that ended in the lake. That summer, their first on the lake, a flock of mallards lived there, as well as a lone goose Mary and her mother called Crazy Eddie, who walked once around their house each evening at dusk. Mary spent most of her days in her mother's canoe, floating, lying down so that she would not be visible from the shore, listening to the sounds of tree removal and construction, to the ducks, and to the people talking on the deck of the model home, the only other structure on the lake that already had glass in the windows. Mary wondered what the visitors thought seeing a canoe adrift with no passengers. She thought about the power she held in invisibility. And sometimes, watching clouds pass over the layered depths of the sky, she thought about becoming a pilot and nearly rose right out of being ten years old.

Mary heard her father brushing his boot-soles on their welcome mat. He cleared his throat three times, then rang the bell. Mary tapped her chin and decided to wait until he went away. He rang again, a double ring this time. Mary unlocked the French door and slipped outside.

She crept up on her father. When she saw the neat back of his shirt, its pressed collar standing away from his neck, sweat broke on her forehead and chin. She did not fear her father, but she knew that he hunted and fished. Her best friend at school was a semi-vegetarian— semi because her mother forbade her to give up meat and would not let her leave the table each night until she chewed and swallowed at least one piece of it. Elspeth hated meat because people ate the very animals that did the least harm; chickens never killed for food or anger, nor did steers, pigs, or sheep. Mary had listened to her speeches for months now without expressing an opinion. Most of all, she admired and envied Elspeth for having a code to follow. She kept to herself that she had been on a hunt with her father, had seen him poke his finger through the bullet hole in a duck's wing.

Quiet in her moccasins, she reached her father and plucked at his sleeve. He jumped around with his hands raised karate-style. "My

God, it's you," he said when he saw her. "Don't you ever surprise a man like that again. Do you treat the UPS man that way?"

"It was a joke," she said, and smiled, showing her teeth. She planted her feet squarely. "Mom said you can't come inside."

Her father shrugged his shoulders so that his shirt settled differently on him, closer to his skin. He looked out toward the water. "If that's the way it is. You want to show me that lake while I'm here?"

Mary's mother had also told her never to let him use the canoe; she had set up many rules in case he visited, though he never had. But Mary decided to show him the canoe anyway, then to let him know he was not welcome anywhere on their property. "We have a canoe," she said. She walked off toward the lake, just fast enough through the tall grass that he would have to judge for himself if he was meant to follow her.

But something went wrong when she showed him the canoe. She heard herself rattling on about the new houses going up, how each one was slightly different and none would have a glass wall as their house did. She was counting the houses out for him, telling him about the families that would move into each one, when he swung the canoe onto his head and brought it down to the water's edge. She stopped mid-sentence. "No," she said. "No, you aren't allowed. Mom should be home by now."

"Listen to me," he said. "You've talked enough. I'm taking this canoe out for a quick tour. You can come along or you can go running to your mom like a pig with a burr on its rump."

Mary's father had never talked to her that way, though she had heard him say such things to her mother. Most of the time when he had lived with them, he did not speak to her at all. The house was quiet, and the wall of glass reflected back the trees, the lake, the sky. "Fine," she said, "at least I know how to bail if you're going to sink it."

"Now just don't say anything for a while," her father said. He held out his hand to help Mary into the canoe, but she stepped in on the other side. She sat in front, facing away from him, and took up her paddle correctly, in both hands.

Her father said, "Illinois is just like Florida in the summer. Except no alligators." He shoved off, then shouted directions to her. Mary did what he said, only slow enough that they always turned slightly away from the side she was paddling on. She waited for her father to say something, but he did not. Once, the shadow of an airplane passed over the lake. She looked back to her mother's property and saw her mother standing on the shore, holding close to her chest her small white grocery bag of baked goods.

Mary's father talked. "You think because you live with your mother you know a lot about her. Thing is, I've *thought* about her, not in a wanting way, but seriously. The way you think about a clue in a crossword puzzle. See, she expected that bus door to catch her. Couldn't have wanted anything more. She was trash even before I met her. That woman, she's been asking for some kind of accident all her life. Gives her an excuse to put away cake and Jack Daniels. A woman like your mother doesn't want to work like other people, doesn't want to exercise, lets herself go to fat and then the best she can expect is an accident so someone else has to pick up the tab. At least it's not me anymore. At least there's that."

He kept talking, but Mary did not listen. She had no need for any more words. Her mother had turned and was pressing slowly toward the house. Ever since the accident, Mary's mother kept her head down when she walked. She watched where she was going; she swerved with all her grace, walking around anything in the way rather than stepping over it.

"Carp," he was saying, and her attention caught. "Now carp are a dirty fish. They're fresh-water pigeons. Rats. You know what they are? They're overgrown goldfish. Like all goldfish, they're inbred. They're so stupid they eat whatever people throw in the water. They hit on junk and people's fingers."

Mary turned in her seat and stared at his forehead, hoping to disconcert him. He paused, but only to breathe.

"Now ducks," he said. "See that duck over there, girl?" He jerked his head toward a lone mallard that was standing on one leg in the weeds close to the water's edge. "What do you think that duck is thinking?"

Mary rushed to speak. "He's thinking he's hungry."

"Maybe, for once in his life. To my mind, that duck should be thinking, 'My God, I'm just a carp. I'm a carp with feathers. I'm a carp with goddamn wings.'"

"I like ducks."

"Little girls like ducks. It's one of those things you'll grow out of. Soon enough."

"I'm ten, and I still like them. Take me back."

"Tell you what I'm going to do for you. I'm going to drop you off at the deck over here," he gestured to the model home as it came up on their right. "I'm going to let you run on back to your mom. You can be just like her if you want to. Fine with me." Mary turned to him again. Would she recognize him in a group of fathers if all were dressed the same? His face was red, and he was paddling hard now, alternating sides, to deliver her through the reeds to the model home's deck. Mary checked—no prospectives out there, leaning over the railing to judge the lake water's depth and purity. She needed to see about her mother, and she decided she would walk the quickest way home, through the weeds, though her mother had warned her that deer ticks might well live there.

"I'll keep the boat out awhile," her father said. "*Boat* is a better word than canoe. Keep it as long as I want. I'll watch for carp. I'll put my fingers in the water, then pop their mouths with the oar."

The canoe bumped against the model deck's moorings. Mary began to climb the small ladder. When her feet hit the second wood slat, her breath caught. For an instant, she thought he would grab at her ankles or calves, or insult their thickness. But he did not. He started whistling, not a tune, just three repeated notes. Mary walked quickly. She would not run, but held her hands in fists. His notes grew louder as she moved away from the sandy edge of the shore, into the weeds. She had to swing her arms as she imagined a trail-blazer would swing a machete, just to make it through.

AFTER THE ACCIDENT and before the settlement, Mary's mother had gone through a period of drinking too much. She sat in their one-bedroom apartment and drank gin, not Jack Daniels, from a crystal glass that her mother-in-law had given her long ago. Mary knew that her mother did not particularly like her grandmother, but at the time she would drink from no other glass. "This very glass, can you believe it?" she said sometimes. "This glass is drinking me into the grave. Wouldn't he get a kick out of that?"

When Mary got ready for school each morning, her mother was asleep. Mary washed out the glass that her mother left courteously overturned in the sink, and when she came home from school, her mother was drinking from the glass again, sitting on the couch where Mary slept each night. She stared at the television's blank screen as if she had turned it on.

Except for the glass-washing, Mary knew she did not treat her mother with much kindness. She had no code of ethics, nothing relevant; she could only try to rush herself and her mother through those difficult and embarrassing times. Every day after school, she brought a chair from the kitchen table, sat in front of the television facing her mother, and told her mother everything that had happened to her that day. Her mother said, "Please, honey, let me have some peace and quiet," but Mary kept talking until she had nothing more to report. Sometimes her mother raised her good arm and covered her right ear. The bad arm stayed at her side, the hand pink and curled. With her arm raised that way, she could not drink, and so she would not cover even the one ear for long.

At first, after the accident, Mary had feared that her mother would need her help in dressing. She did not want to handle the limp arm. But her mother got along fine without her, even when she was in a deep drunk. Mary did not know how she dressed, and she did not want to know. At first, the doctors had said that with nerve damage, one never knew; the nerves might heal on their own within the next two months or so. Mary thought her mother was still waiting to heal, all those months later, boring herself on purpose to encourage her nerves. Sometimes when Mary talked to her mother, she did not even look at her, but instead watched the picture that hung on the wall behind her, a grease-damaged needlepoint of the Great Wall that her mother had bought at a Chinese restaurant's going-out-of-business sale.

Then one night, Mary woke to find her mother bent over her on the couch, shaving Mary's legs. She had folded a wet, soapy face cloth on Mary's stomach, right on her sleep shirt, and she was working carefully, making small, concentrated strokes. The face cloth was cold, and Mary did not like to have cold things on her stomach. Mary wanted to ask her mother to stop, but she was afraid that if she startled her, she might slip and make a cut. So she closed her eyes and let her mother finish. The razor made shushing sounds on her legs. Even if the drinking stopped, she thought, she would not be her mother's true child again.

The next morning, Mary's mother was in the kitchen, poaching eggs to put on toast for Mary's breakfast. Mary took the plate without speaking. Neither one mentioned Mary's legs. Mostly, Mary worried about gym class, when the other fifth graders would see.

That evening, Mary's mother went to her first Alcoholics Anonymous meeting. Mary stayed home and worked three weeks ahead in her math book. Afterward, her mother told her that most of the people there had slipped up once or twice after they first stopped drinking, and so Mary should not expect any miracles. She would try going cold turkey. It seemed to be the only way. If she used the crystal glass, Mary should not wash it. Her plan was that eventually, living with such squalor, she would remember to stop drinking again. She had not lost her cleverness, she told Mary. She had used a false name, and had talked about the difficulty of raising a daughter all alone. At the end of the meeting, she helped put away the folding chairs. A few women congratulated her for speaking up her very first time.

WHEN MARY arrived home from canoeing with her father, her mother was in the living room with one of her friends from A.A. This woman was her mother's sponsor, the person responsible for guiding her through the Twelve Steps. Mary was not certain she was supposed to know that the woman was her mother's sponsor—her mother, she thought, was not yet practiced at confidentiality—and so she tried when around her not to let on to anything. The woman was named K.C. She had short hair that changed colors every few weeks. This week her hair was orange-soda orange, and her face stood out in great detail under it as if she carried around her own fluorescent light.

Mary stood outside the wall of glass, watching her mother and K.C. as they talked together. Grass seeds stuck to Mary's socks and the ends of her hair. Mary shook her head, and a few seeds fell into the already-thick grass. Mary's mother read aloud from a spiral notebook. Her mouth moved only enough to form words.

Every once in a while, K.C. would stop her with a question or a comment. Mary's mother shook the notebook as if to smooth the pages, then answered K.C.

Mary heard almost nothing, but she knew her mother was reading what she had written this far for the step she was on now. She had progressed quickly through the early steps—at a pace that clearly alarmed K.C.—but this one, in which she had to write down everything she had done wrong in her life, was beginning, she had told Mary, to stick in her throat. Mary had read through the steps, and she knew that if her mother progressed far enough she would attempt to make amends for all that she had done. Mary feared this step. She did not want her mother to think of something to make up for having shaved her daughter's legs. Her mother, she thought, would be embarrassed then, worst of all in front of K.C., this woman with the kind sayings about forgiveness, the changing face and changing hair. She hoped, in fact, that her mother had forgotten all about the shaving, that they could go on living simply without her father, with ducks and empty houses for neighbors, in their own house with the glass wall.

Mary knew the women had not seen her, and so she went around to the side porch and sat down on the steps. She watched her father's car, which made occasional clicking noises in the late morning heat. Early last week, Mary's grandmother, her mother's mother, had come to visit. She came from out of town, but she only stayed for a small part of the three hours between her flight from Atlanta to Chicago and her next flight from Chicago to Los Angeles. Mary's grandmother had made a success of writing books about the education of young children, and she talked to both Mary and Mary's mother as if they were young children, slowly and with a turned-up brightness in her voice.

Watching her father's car, Mary thought about the conversation between her mother and her grandmother. They had been sitting too closely together on the couch where Mary's mother now sat with K.C. Mary stretched out on the cold hearth.

"So, to illustrate that children should always share, cooperate, I told them the story of the ant and the jar."

"Is this a sad story?" Mary's mother asked. "If it is, Mom, don't tell me. You know I can't take sad stories any more."

"Well, yes, it is sad, Laura."

"Stop."

"The ant dies in a jar full of seeds."

"I asked you not to tell me that."

"You see, it was the ant's own fault."

All of their conversations were similar. Mary hated and understood her grandmother. She knew that she, too, spoke to her mother that way. It was not only her mother's drinking that brought out in those who spoke to her such a desire, a craving to tell her what she did not wish to hear. Maybe her dead hand had something to do with it, Mary thought, or the way she sometimes closed her eyes and her entire face against a voice as if it were a bright light. *Strike me deaf and dumb,* Mary prayed to no one in particular. Sound sprang up: leaves slapping against each other, another plane overhead, Crazy Eddie honking on the shore. She would like to be a goose, the kind that migrated. She picked the seeds from her socks and dropped them inside one of the large green urn-like planters her mother had bought.

When at length she knew that K.C. would not be leaving soon unaided, she went inside. K.C. said, "Hello, Mary," and reached out her hand for shaking.

274

Mary shook K.C.'s hand vigorously, so that K.C.'s knuckles hit against each other. Then she turned to her mother and shook her hand as well. "Dad took the canoe," she said.

"Of course," said her mother. "Well, sit down and talk to K.C." Mary did. She talked about school being out and about the weeds she had tramped through and about the many ways ducks had of outwitting predators. K.C. threw glances toward Mary's mother. Then at last she stood up to leave.

Just as Mary's mother opened the door to let K.C. out, Mary's father came up from the lake to the grassy parking area at the side of the house. K.C. exhaled sharply and took one step toward her car. Mary ran to her father, hoping to let him know the rules again, more clearly this time, for her mother's sake. But she said nothing. Her father walked around her, chin lifted, and started whistling the three notes he seemed to favor. He paused before the third note, the lowest, as if for drama. Mary bet he had noticed K.C., who stood at the base of the side steps now, balanced on one leg as if she were a wading bird.

Mary's father whistled the third note. He drew it out. Then he brushed a dead moth from the hood of his car. It fluttered down and came to an awkward slantwise rest on the grass.

Mary's mother stood stock-still in the doorway. There might be something graceful in her embarrassment, Mary thought. She held her good arm across her chest, her hand squeezing the opposite shoulder. Mary's father was opening his car door when her mother smiled, stuck her hand out, and said, "Wait there, Danny. There are some things I need to say to you."

Mary's father's shoulder blades pinched. Then he relaxed and gestured as if he were throwing something away. Mary wanted to tell him he could not litter there, but he had let nothing go. K.C. planted the hovering foot and bent her head as if in prayer. Mary's mother said, "Danny, it's not all bad, I have a list. I want to say what I need to say."

K.C. scuttled to her car, scooping her keys from her handbag. Mary could have laughed at the two of them, her father and this orange-haired woman, ready to flee from her mother's words when Mary would stay right there. Then K.C. said, "I support you, Janie."

"Janie?" her father said. "What's this about Janie, Laura? You haven't changed that much, you know."

Her mother plucked a bit of lint from her sleeve and released it. K.C. said, "Call me. I'd better go." Just as soon, she was gone. Mary watched K.C.'s Janie disappear from her mother's eyes.

Mary's father said, "Well, I'm leaving, too. Your boat is fine. You've got no complaints in my book. But this place is overrated and overgrown. Overgrown lake, overgrown shoreline, overgrown kid."

Then he slid into his car, slammed the door, and opened and slammed it again. When he had driven away, Mary's mother's face closed down. Her arm dropped. After a moment, with great facial effort, her mother reconstructed a smile. "I almost forgot," her mother said. "I've been waiting all morning to get to those rolls. Come inside. It's too hot out here."

Soon the rolls were gone, and Mary's mother began her worst day yet of not drinking. She phoned K.C. and each of the nine other women on her emergency call-list. Whenever she got an answering machine, she cursed into the phone and, as soon as the beep stopped, left a brittle, worried message. She ate half a package of processed cheese slices, three containers of chocolate pudding, a can of mixed nuts she'd been saving for company, and a bag of frozen vegetables. They had little other food in the house. She chewed to the quick the fingernails on her good hand. After that, her teeth glistened whenever she opened her mouth. Through it all, Mary played solitaire and talked toward her mother about everything that struck her mind. Her words, she feared, could not be trusted to float them through the day. Only, she could not stop long enough to try something new.

At dusk, some of the light drained out of the trees around the house. Mary understood that night would not change anything. From the inside of her speeches and her waiting, she felt a sudden inspiration. She decided to take her mother out in the canoe.

Mary's mother rarely agreed to a canoe ride. Although she had been enthusiastic about buying the canoe and had even read up on the features desirable in one, she feared capsizing and complained about the mosquitoes that bred along the shore. But the day had worn her down, and Mary guessed that her fears, too, had eroded. Before she asked her to come along, she brought the insect repellent in from the garage. She stood close to her mother and held the repellent to her side as if she were in a television ad. "I'll even spray you myself."

Mary led her mother to the lake shore, handed her in, and pushed the boat off, stepping after it. She said, "Now don't worry about paddling. I'll take care of it." Her mother faced forward, away from Mary, and slouched in her seat. Taking her place, Mary tried to think of a song to sing. Nothing came to mind. She sang anyway.

When she saw her father's car parked in the gravel lot beside the model home, she turned back the canoe. Her mother sighed. Mary was not certain her mother had seen the car. All afternoon she had been sighing. Quite possibly, she had not seen the car, and Mary was not about to ask. Her fourth grade teacher had told her that sometimes people sighed only because they breathed improperly. Their bodies could not get enough air any other way.

She looked back. Her father was moving among the weeds on the shore, leaning forward, holding a dog by the scruff. A blue baseball cap sat low on his forehead; she had never seen him in head-covering before. The dog was no one she recognized, but then her father's hunting friends always had dogs to lend him, hounds of various descriptions, all ugly and efficient. The ones she had seen before had sores that flies got into. The best dogs, her father said, paid no mind to flies. To him, the dogs were objects of respect. "You have to treat your dog just right," he liked to say. "You have to treat him well enough he'll do for you, keep him wanting enough he'll have reason to hunt."

Mary did not want to continue the tour of the lake, but her mother sat up straight in her seat now, and her voice was childlike and clear. "You're so good to keep up on what's happening with these houses," she said. "Bring me around and tell me about them."

When Mary looked back again, her father was no longer in sight. She watched the grass for movement, but saw none. His car rested on the gravel. The front tires might have settled an inch or more. "Two visits in one day," she said under her breath.

"Well, talk to me," her mother said. Crazy Eddie was just coming down to the shore. Mary had never discovered where he spent the night. She gave her mother a quick but informative tour.

MARY AND HER mother went to sleep early. The gunshots woke them. "He stuck around," Mary said into the new-wood scent of her room. But she did not like the idea of her father waiting all those hours in his car with the hungry and thoughtless dog. Mary's mother came in and crouched next to her bed. Just then Mary noticed the yapping sounds the ducks were making, less and less.

"Don't be afraid," her mother said from the floor. "Get out of line of the windows."

"It's down by the lake. He's hunting."

"No, it's not the season," Mary's mother said.

"He has something against ducks."

"You think that's your father?"

Mary lifted the curtain away from the window. The shots continued, evenly spaced. "I can't see him. Who else could it be?"

The shooting kept up for several minutes. After almost every shot, there was a large splash. Her father was whistling again, sounds coded for the dog's ears. Mary wondered why the dog did not bark, and she imagined him moving through the water with his mouth closed, paddling up on the wounded ducks. She had always thought her father was an unaccomplished hunter; he seemed to curse far more than other men, and he never tried for anything larger than a duck or a squirrel. But now she understood his strategy of vengeance. He hunted ducks and squirrels because, in his mind, they deserved to be hunted. He bore a private grudge toward small animals, particularly when they massed where they could be seen.

Mary said, "Stay down." Then she turned on the overhead light. She waited for her father to look up toward the house, to see the solid shape she made in the window. But the shots and the splashing continued.

"What are you doing?" her mother said finally.

"Don't worry. He's not even paying attention."

"Should we call the police?"

"Not yet." Mary turned off the light. She hoped they could keep the police out of it. Nothing would embarrass her more than men in neat uniforms seeing all this. Between the trees, the sky was light gray, spotted with clouds. Something moved close to the water, a figure she thought taller than her father, not him at all. "I hope Crazy Eddie is all right," she said.

"That's it," her mother said. "I'm not waiting around for him, we're going to a hotel."

Her mother crawled into the hallway, and Mary followed. "Get my keys if you're going to stand," her mother said. "They're on the TV." Feeling tall on her legs, high above the furniture tops, Mary walked through the living room. She looked out at the trees and the tall silent grass and knew they would not stay another night there. She had moved before. This time, though, she believed she would use an assumed name as her mother did at meetings. She would call herself Grace Claire, but even the name could not make up for much.

When she returned, her mother was kneeling by the door, undoing the multiple locks. Her purse was slung open across her back. She fumbled as if she were drunk, but it was only the day they had passed.

No smell of alcohol. Mary turned the locks, pulled her mother to her feet, and led her by the hand outside.

The night was innocent. Mary smelled the weeds growing and transpiring even in the dark. He mother's hand did not sweat. When they reached the car, her mother laughed.

"That's right," Mary said, "He just wants to ruin it for us, that's all."

They sat in the car, in the two cherry-red bucket seats. Mary's mother put the key in the ignition but did not turn it. "Do you want to talk for a minute?" her mother said.

"Let's go to the hotel," Mary said.

"Well, you see, I forgot my wallet. Let's just crouch down. If he wanted to hurt us, he wouldn't look here."

From the car at the side of the house, Mary watched her father walk up from the lake, up toward the glass wall. He carried four ducks by the bright orange legs. He was not whistling now. His face was closed, concentrated, the face of someone who would not think to whistle. The dog followed close at his heels, carrying nothing, luminous as a peach. They stopped five paces short of the glass wall. Mary's father stacked the ducks on the ground in a neat pile, like firewood.

Mary did not want to hide from her father. If he found her, he would know she had hid. But she slid down in the bucket seat. Her mother whispered, "Do you think he's far enough now? We should talk."

When the shooting started again, Mary answered. "Yes." Then suddenly the shots stopped. "I'll hear you out if you let me sit up far enough to keep an eye on him."

Mary's mother stared. She squinted as if she were about to cry. "All right," she said, dabbing at her nose with the back of her hand. "But please don't go out to him, okay?"

Mary's father made four more trips up the slope of grass, holding ducks each time. Sometimes, he raised his hand, ducks and all, to rub at a spot on his forehead. He stacked the ducks so that all of their beaks pointed toward the house.

"I have to let you know what I've done wrong to you," Mary's mother said. "There's no better time than the present."

The hunting dog splashed into the water again. "Please, Mom, don't," Mary said.

"No, listen to me. When you were born I wouldn't nurse you. Flat out refused. You were half a day old before I called you by name. A name your father chose. I left you with a ten-year-old who fed you popcorn before you were ready. I never put the emergency numbers by the phone."

279

"Please stop," Mary said. But she know it would continue. And it did, all the while her father was bringing the ducks up from the lake, arranging and rearranging them on the grass. She spoke of slights Mary did not remember, though each one hit her like a small pebble and did not fall away. She was sinking with the built-up weight of it, but she told herself she was a girl of good spirits, not one to go under so easily. Her father had worked out a new duck arrangement. Now each duck held the foot of another duck incompletely in its bill.

"I never meant any harm," Mary's mother said, "but that doesn't seem to help us."

Mary wanted to hit the horn, to make a noise loud enough to stop them both, but the night had at last struck her silent. She understood that if her mother called the police later, they would both tell the officer they had no idea who had done the shooting or why he had arranged the ducks so carefully in front of their glass wall. Only by knowing nothing could they stand apart from all that had gone wrong.

On the ground, the ducks were a straight line, a short wall. Mary's father stood back to judge his work. The dog, too, stood in judgment. Eddie the goose walked around the lake. In time, he would reach the other side and keep on walking. He would lose the name that had never been his, really, and he would not return.

When no one was looking, in that one new moment, the sky would become a mirror. In the mirror, all ducks would form a perfect and silent circle. And Mary would go on living, not hoping to know even in adulthood the true source of talk or cruelty.

Nominated by The Threepenny Review *and Sherod Santos*

NO TURN ON RED

by RICHARD JACKSON

from MARLBORO REVIEW

It's enough to make the moon turn its face
the way these poets take a kind of bubble bath
in other people's pain. I mean, sure, the dumpsters
of our lives are filling with more mistakes
than we could ever measure. Whenever we reach into
the pockets of hope we pull out the lint of despair.
I mean, all I have to do is lift the eyelids
of the stars to see how distant you could become.
But that doesn't mean my idea of form is a kind of
twelve step approach to vision. I mean, I don't want
to contribute to the body count which, in our major journals,
averages 13.7 deaths/poem, counting major catastrophes and wars.
I'm not going to blame those bodies floating down some
river in Rwanda or Bosnia on Love's failures. But really,
it's not the deaths in those poems, it's the way Death arrives in a tux
and driving a Lamborghini then says a few rhymed words
over his martini. It's a question of taste, really,
which means, a question for truth. I mean, if someone
says some beastly person enters her room the way Hitler
entered Poland I'd say she'd shut her eyes like a Kurdish
tent collapsing under a gas attack, it makes about
as much sense. Truth is too often a last line of defense,
like the way every hospital in America keeps a bag
of maggots on ice to eat away infection when the usual
antibiotics fail. The maggots do a better job
but aren't as elegant. Truth is just bad taste, then?

Not really. Listen to this: "Legless Boy Somersaults
Two Miles to Save Dad," reads the headline from Italy
in *Weekly World News*, a story that includes pictures
of the heroic but bloody torso of the boy. "Twisted
like a pretzel," the story goes on. Bad taste or
world class gymnastics? Which reminds me. One afternoon
I was sitting in a bar watching the Olympics—the singles
of synchronized swimming—how can that be true?
If that's so, why not full contact javelin? Uneven
table tennis? The 1500 meter dive? Even the relay dive?
Someone's going to say I digress? Look, this is a satire
which means, if you look up the original Latin, "mixed dish,"
—you have to take a bite of everything. True, some would
argue it's the word we get Satyr from, but I don't like
to think of myself as some cloven hoofed, horny little
creature sniffing around trees. Well, it's taste, remember.
Besides my satire is set while waiting at Love's traffic
light, which makes it unique. So, I was saying you have
to follow truth's little detours—no, no, it was taste,
the heroic kid twisted like a pretzel. Pretzels are
metaphysical. Did you know a medieval Italian monk
invented them in the year 610 in the shape of crossed,
praying arms to reward his parish children?
"I like children," said W.C. Fields—"if they're properly
cooked." Taste, and its fellow inmate, truth—how do we
measure anything anymore? Everyone wants me to stick
to a few simple points, or maybe no point at all,
like the tepid broth those new formalists ladle into their
demitasse. How can we write about anything—truth,
love, hope, taste, when someone says the moment, the basis
of all lyric poetry, of all measure and meter, is just
the equivalent of 10 billion atomic vibrations of the cesium
atom when it's been excited by microwaves. Twilight chills
in the puddles left by evening's rain. The tiny spider
curled on the bulb begins to cast a huge shadow. No wonder
time is against us. In 1953, Dirty Harry, a "nuclear device,"
as the phrase goes, blossomed in Nevada's desert leaving
more than twice the fallout anyone predicted.
After thirty years no one admits the measurements.
Truth becomes a matter of "duck and cover." Even Love

refuses to come out of its shelter. In Sarajevo,
Dedran Smailovic plays Albinoni's *Adagio* outside
the bakery for 22 days where mortars killed 22
and the papers are counting the days till the sniper
aims. You can already see the poets lined up on
poetry's dragstrip revving up their 22 line elegies
in time for the *New Yorker* deadline, so to speak.
Vision means, I guess, how far down the road of your
career you can see. And numbers not what Pope meant
by rhythm, but $5 per line. Pythagoras (b. 570 BC)
thought the world was made entirely of numbers. Truth,
he said, is the formula, and we are just the variables.
But this is from a guy who thought Homer's soul was
reborn in his. Later, that he had the soul of a peacock.
Who could trust him? How do we measure anything?
Each time they clean the standard kilogram bar in Sevres,
France, it loses a few atoms making everything else appear
a little heavier. That's why everything is suddenly
more somber. Love is sitting alone in a rented room
with its hangman's rope waiting for an answer
that's not going to come. All right, so I exaggerate, and
in bad taste. Let's say Love has put away its balance,
tape measure and nails and is poking around in its tin
lunch pail. So how can I measure how much I love you?
Except the way the willow measures the universe.
Except the way your hair is tangled among the stars.
The way the turtle's shell reflects the night's sky.
I'm not counting on anything anymore. Even the foot—
originally defined as the shoe length of whatever king
held your life, which made the poets scramble around
to define their own poetic feet. And truth is all this?
That's why it's good to have all these details as
a kind of yardstick to rap across the fingers
of bad taste. "I always keep a supply of stimulants
handy," said Fields, "in case I see a snake;
which I also keep handy." In the end, you still need
something to measure, and maybe that's the problem
that makes living without love or truth so much pain.
I'd have to be crazy. Truth leaves its fingerprints
on everything we do. It's nearly 10 PM. Crazy.

Here comes another poet embroidering his tragic
childhood with a few loosely lined mirrors.
I'm afraid for what comes next. The birds' warning
song runs up and down the spine of the storm. Who says
any love makes sense? The only thing left is
this little satire and its faceless clock for a soul.
You can't measure anything you want. The basis of all
cleverness is paranoia. 61% of readers never finish
the poem they start. 31% of Americans are afraid to speak
while making love. 57% of Americans have dreamt
of dying in a plane crash. One out of four
Americans is crazy. Look around at your three
best friends. If they're okay, you're in trouble.

Nominated by Marlboro Review, *Gary Fincke and William Matthews*

THE KISS

fiction by PAMELA PAINTER

from THE NORTH AMERICAN REVIEW

No ONE CAN GUESS so she finally tells us. Actually Mona doesn't tell, she shows us by sticking her tongue out and there it is—a gold ball the size of a small pea, sitting in the creased rose lap of her extended tongue.

We all lean forward from our pillows on the floor, seven of us, the wrung-out remnants of a grad party in the low-candle stage. Inge asks Mona where she got it done (Cambridge as an undergrad), Raphi our host asks her why (she likes something in her mouth), my boyfriend wants to know what it tastes like (no taste). We're still peering into her mouth so she lifts her tongue slowly, the rosy tip pointing up toward her nose, and there on the glistening downward slope is another gold ball.

"A bah-bell," she says, her tongue still showing off.

And it is. A tiny gold barbell piercing her tongue.

We settle back into our pillows and she closes her mouth.

My boyfriend, a chef at Valentino's, is probably wondering which tastebuds sit in the middle of the tongue and if they are affected and how. Inge, the etymologist, is mouthing the word tongue, no doubt marveling at how the tongue loves to say that word. I can tell we're all wondering something. Our tongues feel heavy in our mouths, empty except for the privileged gold fillings and ivory bondings of the middle class.

It occurs to me that Mona's not able to enjoy her barbell. Enjoy the way the tip of my tongue visits a rough molar, soothes a canker sore moistly healing on its own, or wetly licks the hairy friction of chapped lips.

I say, I wonder what it's like to kiss her?

Everyone shifts and nods as if they were wondering the exact same thing. We turn to the man Mona came with who shrugs and says he doesn't know. They just met three hours ago at Huddle's Pub.

Well, who's going to kiss her? Inge says.

We all look first to the man she came with and then at the other eligible male. No one counts mine, which disappoints him and he lets it show. The man she came with weighs thirteenth-century Inca bones after reducing them to ashes in an autoclave the size of a toaster. Raphi, our host, is a religion major—the Hellenistic culture—who thinks the world is fast approaching a non-religious end. "I'll kiss her," he offers, then defers to the man she came with.

"Wait a minute. Maybe not," Jorie says, holding up her hand. She's in gender studies with me. "Don't you think we should run it by Mona first?"

We all turn belatedly to Mona.

"Oh," she says, "it's all right with me." The gold ball doesn't show when she talks. I wonder if it makes a dent in the roof of her mouth.

The man she came with says, "I'll kiss her." Neither man is looking at Mona.

"You choose," Inge says to Mona.

Mona shrugs and points to Raphi. "You offered first."

He grins.

Oddly, in perfect synch, they both stand up.

"No, do it here," we all say, "here in front of us." But we needn't have worried: they had no intention of leaving.

Mona and Raphi face each other above us. They are the same height. Mona's hands rest on the hips of her black jeans, her elbows jut out claiming space to equal Raphi's greater weight. He has his hands deep in his pockets. We are all aware of his hands in his pockets.

They stand inches apart—two inches apart. She tilts toward him first, just her shoulders and head, and then he catches her tilt, catches her mouth with his mouth. They kiss. They kiss tenderly and well for two people who have just met. Their heads glide with their mouths and their shoulders move ever so slightly. I imagine his tongue filling her mouth, sliding toward the ball, searching, pressing, perhaps turning it, rolling it; her tongue letting him. I imagine their hands aching to touch the other person but refraining as if to abide by some set of rules.

286

No one looks away.

Minutes, but probably seconds, later they stop. "It's pretty far back," Raphi says and we all swallow with him.

Mona turns and sticks out her tongue to show us she thinks not, and we see it's not so far, really. Perhaps an inch and a half.

She turns back to Raphi and they kiss again and we all watch them kiss, even better the second time: harder, deeper, her tongue and his tongue, her generously letting him, that slight tilt, their scrupulous hands.

They pull away. We have all been holding our breath.

Well?

They settle themselves cross-legged and facing each other. I imagine another night such as this for them, moving away from the kiss toward the questions and answers of getting to know someone, and that moment when they invite their hands to join their kiss.

We listen as Raphi describes to Mona the amazingly hard muscle of her tongue, the cool surprise of the tiny gold ball, the flick past the ball underneath. They tilt toward each other.

Raphi's hands talk.

Mona is smiling that smile. She's got what she wanted.

The man she came with leaves first.

My boyfriend leaves with me, but we go home separately. We all go home with something missing on our tongue.

Nominated by Melissa Pritchard

TROUBADOUR

by DAVID ST. JOHN

from COLORADO REVIEW

I remember how my lover wept
That day I left the Academy of Troubadours
   & set out to prove myself & seek my fortune
Along the plains of Acquitaine, taking with me

   Only the rough clothing of my songs.
The rosewood face of my lute had been inlaid
   With carved ivory roses & exquisitely twined
Vines climbing the lute's sloping shoulders

   & up the long length of its polished neck.
My cloak was lined with a violet satin & even
   The wild Tartar angle of my cheekbones
Was something already gossiped about in the courts

   Of Pisa, Rome and Florence—
& as the valet brought my ancient Triumph TR3
   Up before the beach-front restaurant
Where we'd been sharing our somber final meal

   My lover slowly stroked my parted lips
With the hard, varnished backs of her fingernails—
   As if she were strumming her own ebony lap harp—
Saying to me as her glistening Mercedes appeared

So suddenly at the curb like some black
Stallion rising from the nearby waves, O sing well my child
   & remember every heart's a bit like mine, my dear,
Just a simple door thrown open by the lyre's prick. . . .

Nominated by Ralph Angel, Jane Hirshfield

FOR THE RELIEF OF UNBEARABLE URGES

fiction by NATHAN ENGLANDER

from STORY

THE BEDS WERE TO BE separated on nights forbidden to physical intimacy, but Chava Bayla hadn't pushed them together for many months. She flatly refused to sleep anywhere except on her menstrual bed and was, from the start, impervious to her husband's pleading.

"You are pure," Dov Binyamin said to the back of his wife, who—heightening his frustration—slept facing the wall.

"I am impure."

"This is not true, Chava Bayla. It's an impossibility. And I know myself the last time you went to the ritual bath. A woman does not have her thing—"

"Her thing?" Chava said. She laughed, as if she had caught him in a lie, and turned to face the room.

"A woman doesn't menstruate for so long without even a single week of clean days. And a wife does not for so long ignore her husband. It is Shabbos, a double mitzvah tonight—an obligation to make love."

Chava Bayla turned back again to face her wall. She tightened her arms around herself as if in an embrace.

"You are my wife!" Dov Binyamin said.

"That was God's choice, not mine. I might also have been put on this earth as a bar of soap or a kugel. Better," she said, "better it should have been one of those."

That night Dov Binyamin slept curled up on the edge of his bed—as close as he could get to his wife.

290

After Shabbos, Chava avoided coming into the bedroom for as long as possible. When she finally did enter and found Dov dozing in a chair by the balcony, she went to sleep fully clothed, her sheitel still on the top of her head.

As he nodded forward in the chair, Dov's hat fell to the floor. He woke up, saw his wife, picked up his hat, and, brushing away the dust with his elbow, placed it on the night stand. How beautiful she looked all curled up in her dress. Like a princess enchanted, he thought. Dov pulled the sheet off the top of his bed. He wanted to cover her, to tuck Chava in. Instead he flung the sheet into a corner. He shut off the light, untied his shoes—but did not remove them—and went to sleep on the tile floor beside his wife. Using his arm for a pillow, Dov Binyamin dreamed of a lemon ice his uncle had bought him as a child and of the sound of the airplanes flying overhead at the start of the Yom Kippur War.

Dov Binyamin didn't go to work on Sunday. Folding up his tallis after prayers and fingering the embroidery of the tallis bag, he recalled the day Chava had presented it to him as a wedding gift—the same gift his father had received from his mother, and his father's father before. Dov had marveled at the workmanship, wondered how many hours she had spent with a needle in hand. Now he wondered if she would ever find him worthy of such attentions again. Zipping the prayer shawl inside, Dov Binyamin put the bag under his arm. He carried it with him out of the shul, though he had his own cubby in which to store it inside.

The morning was oppressively hot; a hamsin was settling over Jerusalem. Dov Binyamin was wearing his lightest caftan but in the heat wave it felt as if it were made of the heaviest wool.

Passing a bank of phones, he considered calling work, making some excuse, or even telling the truth. "Shai," he would say, "I am a ghost in my home and wonder who will mend my tallis bag when it is worn." His phone card was in his wallet, which he had forgotten on the dresser, and what did he want to explain to Shai for, who had just come from a Shabbos with his spicy wife and a house full of children.

Dov followed Jaffa Street down to the Old City. Roaming the alleyways always helped calm him. There was comfort in the Jerusalem stone and the walls within walls and the permanence of everything around him. He felt a kinship with history's Jerusalemites, in whose struggles he searched for answers to his own. Lately he felt closer to

291

his biblical heroes than the people with whom he spent his days. King David's desires were far more alive to Dov than the empty problems of Shai and the other men at the furniture store.

Weaving through the Jewish Quarter, he had intended to end up at the Wall, to say Tehillim, and, in his desperate state, scribble a note and stuff it into a crack just like the tourists in the cardboard yarmulkes. Instead, he found himself caught up in the rush inside the Damascus Gate. An old Arab woman was crouched behind a wooden box of cactus fruit. She peeled a sabra with a kitchen knife, allowing a small boy a sample of her product. The child ran off with his mouth open, a stray thorn stuck in his tongue.

Dov Binyamin tightened his hold on the tallis bag and pushed his way through the crowd. He walked back to Mea Shearim along the streets of East Jerusalem. Let them throw stones, he thought. Though no one did. No one even took notice of him except to step out of his way as he rushed to his rebbe's house for some advice.

Meir the Beadle was in the front room, sitting on a plastic chair at a plastic table.

"Don't you have work today?" Meir said, without looking up from the papers that he was shifting from pile to pile. Dov Binyamin ignored the question.

"Is the Rebbe in?"

"He's very busy." Dov Binyamin went over to the kettle, poured himself a mug full of hot water, and stirred in a spoonful of Nescafé.

"How about you don't give me a hard time today?"

"Who's giving a hard time?" Meir said, putting down the papers and getting up from the chair. "I'm just telling you Sunday is busy after a day and a half without work." He knocked at the Rebbe's door and went in. Dov Binyamin made a blessing over his coffee, took a sip, and, being careful not to spill, lowered himself into one of the plastic chairs. The coffee cut the edge off the heat that, like Dov, sat heavy in the room.

The Rebbe leaned forward on his shtender and rocked back and forth as if he were about to topple.

"No, this is no good. Very bad. Not good at all." He pulled back on the lectern and held it in that position. The motion reminded Dov of his dream, of the rumbling of engines and a vase—there had been a blue glass vase—sent to rocking on a shelf. "And you don't want a divorce?"

"I love her, Rebbe. She is my wife."

"And Chava Bayla?"

"She, thank God, has not even raised the subject of separation. She asks nothing of me but to be left alone. And this is where the serpent begins to swallow its tail. The more she rejects me, the more I want to be with her. And the more I want to be with her, the more intent she becomes that I stay away."

"She is testing you."

"Yes. In some way, Rebbe, Chava Bayla is giving me a test."

Pulling at his beard, the Rebbe again put his full weight on the lectern so that the wood creaked. He spoke in a Talmudic sing-song:

"Then you must find the strength to ignore Chava Bayla, until Chava Bayla should come to find you—and you must be strict with yourself. For she will not consider your virtues until she is calm in the knowledge that her choices are her own."

"But I don't have the strength. She is my wife. I miss her. And I am human, too. With human habits. It will be impossible for me not to try and touch her, to try and convince her. Rebbe, forgive me, but God created the world with a certain order to it. I suffer greatly under the urges with which I have been blessed."

"I see," said the Rebbe. "The urges have become great."

"Unbearable. And to be around someone I feel so strongly for, to look and be unable to touch—it is like floating through Heaven in a bubble of Hell."

The Rebbe pulled a chair over to the bookcases that lined his walls. Climbing onto the chair, he steadied himself, then removed a volume from the top shelf. "We must relieve the pressure."

"It is a fine notion. But I fear it's impossible."

"I'm giving you a heter," the Rebbe said. "A special dispensation." He went over to his desk and flipped through the book. He began to scribble on a pad of onionskin paper.

"For what?"

"To see a prostitute."

"Excuse me, Rebbe?"

"Your marriage is at stake, is it not?"

Dov bit at his thumbnail and then rushed the hand, as if it were something shameful, into the pocket of his caftan.

"Yes," he said, a shake entering his voice. "My marriage is a withered limb at my side."

The Rebbe aimed his pencil at Dov.

"One may go to great lengths in the name of achieving peace in the home."

"But a prostitute?" Dov Binyamin asked.

"For the relief of unbearable urges," the Rebbe said. And he tore, like a doctor, a sheet of paper from the pad.

Dov Binyamin drove to Tel-Aviv, the city of sin. There he was convinced he would find plenty of prostitutes. He parked his Fiat on a side street off Dizengoff and walked around town.

Though he was familiar with the city, its social aspects were foreign to him. It was the first leisurely walk he had taken in Tel-Aviv and, fancying himself an anthropologist in a foreign land, he found it all quite interesting. It was usually he who was under scrutiny. Busloads of American tourists scamper through Mea Shearim daily. They buy up the stores and pull tiny cameras from their hip-packs, snapping pictures of real live Hassidim, like the ones from the stories their grandparents told. Next time he would say "Boo!" He laughed at the thought of it. Already he was feeling lighter. Passing a kiosk, he stopped and bought a bag of pizza-flavored Bissli. When he reached the fountain, he sat down on a bench among the aged new-immigrants. They clustered together as if huddled against a biting cold wind that had followed them from their native lands. He stayed there until dark, until the crowd of new-immigrants, like the bud of a flower, began to spread out, to open up, as the old folks filed down the fountain's ramps onto the city streets. They were replaced by young couples and groups of boys and girls who talked to each other from a distance but did not mix. So much like religious children, he thought. In a way we are all the same. Dov Binyamin suddenly felt overwhelmed. He was startled to find himself in Tel-Aviv, already involved in the act of searching out a harlot, instead of home in his chair by the balcony, worrying over whether to take the Rebbe's advice at all.

He walked back toward his car. A lone cab driver leaned up against the front door of his Mercedes, smoking. Dov Binyamin approached him, the heat of his feet inside his shoes becoming more oppressive with every step.

"Forgive me," Dov Binyamin said.

The cab driver, his chest hair sticking out of the collar of his T-shirt in tufts, ground out the cigarette and opened the passenger door. "Need a ride, Rabbi?"

"I'm not a rabbi."

"And you don't need a ride?"

Dov Binyamin adjusted his hat. "No. Actually no."

The cab driver lit another cigarette, flourishing his Zippo impressively. Dov took notice, though he was not especially impressed.

"I'm looking for a prostitute."

The cab driver coughed and clasped a hand to his chest.

"Do I look like a prostitute?"

"No, you misunderstand." Dov Binyamin wondered if he should turn and run away. "A female prostitute."

"What's her name?"

"No name. Any name. You are a taxi driver. You must know where are such women." The taxi driver slapped at the hood of his car and said, "Ha," which Dov took to be laughter. Another cab pulled up on Dov's other side.

"What's happening?" the second driver called.

"Nothing. The rabbi here wants to know where to find a friend. Thinks it's a cab driver's responsibility to direct him."

"Do we work for the Ministry of Tourism?" the second driver asked.

"I just thought," Dov Binyamin said. His voice was high and cracking. It seemed to elicit pity in the second driver.

"There's a cash machine back on Dizengoff."

"Prostitutes at the bank?" Dov Binyamin said.

"No, not at the bank. But the service isn't free." Dov blushed under his beard. "Up by the train station in Ramat Gan—at the row of bus stops."

"All those pretty ladies aren't waiting for the bus to Haifa." This from the first driver who again slapped the hood of his car and said, "Ha!"

The first time past, he did not stop, driving by the women at high speed and taking the curves around the cement island so that his wheels screeched and he could smell the burning rubber. Dov Binyamin slowed down, trying to maintain control of himself and the car, afraid that he had already drawn too much attention his way. The steering wheel began to vibrate in Dov's shaking hands. The Rebbe had given him permission, had instructed him. Was not the Rebbe's heter valid? This is what Dov Binyamin told his hands but they continued to tremble in protest.

On his second time past, a woman approached the passenger door. She wore a matching shirt and pants. The outfit clung tightly, and Dov could see the full form of her body. Such immodesty! She tapped at

295

the window. Dov Binyamin reached over to roll it down. Flustered, he knocked the gear shift and the car lurched forward. Applying the parking brake, he opened the window the rest of the way.

"Close your lights," she instructed him. "We don't need to be on stage out here."

"Sorry," he said, shutting off the lights. He was comforted by the error, not wanting the woman to think he was the kind of man who employed prostitutes on a regular basis.

"You interested in some action?"

"Me?"

"A shy one," she said. She leaned through the window and Dov Binyamin looked away from her large breasts. "Is this your first time? Don't worry, I'll be gentle. I know how to treat a black hat."

Dov Binyamin felt the full weight of what he was doing. He was giving a bad name to all Hassidim. It was a sin against God's name. The urge to drive off, to race back to Jerusalem and the silence of his wife, came over Dov Binyamin. He concentrated on his dispensation.

"What would you know from black hats?" he said.

"Plenty," she said. And then, leaning in further, "Actually, you look familiar." Dov Binyamin seized up, only to begin shaking twice as hard. He shifted into first and gave the car some gas. The prostitute barely got clear of the window.

When it seemed as if he wouldn't find a suitable match, a strong-looking young woman stepped out of the darkness.

"Good evening," he said.

She did not answer or ask any questions or smile. She opened the passenger door and sat down.

"What do you think you're doing?"

"Saving you the trouble of driving around like a schoolboy until the sun comes up." She was American. He could hear it. But she spoke beautiful Hebrew, sweet and strong as her step. Dov Binyamin turned on his headlights and again bumped the gear shift so that the car jumped.

"Settle down there, Tiger," she said. "The hard part's over. All the rest of the work is mine."

The room was in an unlicensed hostel. It had its own entrance. There was no furniture other than a double bed, and three singles. The only lamp stood next to the door.

The prostitute sat on the big bed with her legs curled underneath her. She said her name was Devorah.

"Like the prophetess," Dov Binyamin said.

"Exactly," Devorah said. "But I can only see into the immediate future."

"Still, it is a rare gift with which to have been endowed." Dov shifted his weight from foot to foot. He stood next to the large bed unable to bring himself to bend his knees.

"Not really," she said. "All my clients already know what's in store."

She was fiery, this one. And their conversation served to warm up the parts of Dov the heat wave had not touched. The desire that had been building in Dov over the many months filled his body so he was surprised his skin did not burst from the pressure. He tossed his hat onto the opposite single, hoping to appear at ease, as sure of himself as the hairy-chested cab driver with his cigarettes. The hat landed brim side down. Dov's muscles twitched reflexively, though he did not flip it onto its crown.

"Wouldn't you rather make your living as a prophetess?" he asked.

"Of course. Prophesizing's a piece of cake. You don't have to primp all day for it. And it's much easier on the back, no wear and tear. Better for *you*, too. At least you'd leave with something in the morning." She took out one of her earrings, then, as an afterthought, put it back in. "Doesn't matter anyway. No money in it. They pay me to do everything *except* look into the future."

"I'll be the first then," he said, starting to feel almost comfortable. "Tell me what you see."

She closed her eyes and tilted her head so that her lips began to part, this in the style of those who peer into other realms. "I predict that this is the first time you've done such a thing."

"That is not a prophecy. It's a guess." Dov Binyamin cleared his throat and wiggled his toes against the tops of his shoes. "What else do you predict?"

She massaged her temples and held back a naughty grin.

"That you will, for once, get properly laid."

But this was too much for Dov Binyamin. Boiling in the heat and his shame, he fetched his hat.

Devorah took his hand.

"Forgive me," she said, "I didn't mean to be crude."

Her fingers were tan and thin, more delicate than Chava's. How strange it was to see strange fingers against the whiteness of his own.

"Excluding the affections of my mother, blessed be her memory, this is the first time I have been touched by a woman that is not my wife."

She released her grasp and, before he had time to step away, reached out for him again, this time more firmly as if shaking on a deal. Devorah raised herself up and straightened a leg, displayed it for a moment, and then let it dangle over the side of the bed. Dov admired the leg, and the fingers resting against his palm.

"Why are we here together?" she asked—she was not mocking him. Devorah pulled at the hand and he sat at her side.

"To relieve my unbearable urges. So that my wife will be able to love me again."

Devorah raised her eyebrows and pursed her lips.

"You come to me for your wife's sake?"

"Yes."

"You are a very dedicated husband."

She gave him a smile that said, you won't go through with it. The smile lingered, and then he saw that it said something completely different, something irresistible. And he wondered, as a shiver ran from the trunk of his body out to the hand she held, if what they say about American women is true.

Dov walked toward the door, not to leave, but to shut off the lamp.

"One minute," Devorah said, reaching back and removing a condom from a tiny pocket—no more than a slit in the smooth black fabric of her pants. Dov Binyamin knew what it was and waved it away.

"Am I really your second?" she asked.

Dov heard more in the question than was intended. He heard a flirtation; he heard a woman who treated the act of being second as if it were special. He was sad for her—wondering if she had ever been anyone's first. He did not answer out loud, but instead, nodded, affirming.

Devorah pouted as she decided, the prophylactic held between two fingers like a quarter poised at the mouth of a jukebox. Dov switched off the light and took a half step toward the bed. He stroked at the darkness, moving forward until he found her hair, soft, alive, without any of the worked-over stiffness of Chava's wigs.

"My God," he said snatching back his hand as if he had been stung. It was too late though. That he already knew. The hunger had flooded his whole self. His heart was swollen with it, pumping so loudly and with such strength it overpowered whatever sense he might have had. For whom then, he wondered, was he putting on, in darkness, such a bashful show? He reached out again and stroked her hair, shaking but sure of his intent. With his other arm, the weaker arm to which he bound every morning his tefillin, the arm closer to the violent force of his heart, he searched for her hand.

Dov found it and took hold of it, first roughly, as if desperate. Then he held it lightly, delicately, as if it was made of blown glass—a goblet from which, with ceremony, he wished to drink. Bringing it toward his mouth, he began to speak.

"It is a sin to spill seed in vain," he said, and Devorah let the condom fall at the sound of his words.

Dov Binyamin was at work on Monday and he was home as usual on Monday night. There was no desire to slip out of the apartment during the long hours when he could not sleep, no temptation, when making a delivery in Ramot, to turn the car in the direction of Tel-Aviv. Dov Binyamin felt, along with a guilt he could not shake, a sense of relief. He knew he could never be with another woman again. And if it were possible to heap on himself all the sexual urges of the past months, if he could undo the single night with the prostitute to restore his unadulterated fidelity, he would have it tenfold. From that night of indulgence he found the strength to wait a lifetime for Chava's attentions—if that need be.

When Chava Bayla entered the dining room, Dov Binyamin would move into the kitchen. When she entered the bedroom, he would close his eyes and feign sleep. He would lie in the dark and silently love his wife. And, never coming to a conclusion, he would rethink the wisdom of the Rebbe's advice. He would picture the hairy arm of the cab driver as he slapped the hood of his taxi. And he would chide himself. Never, never would he accuse his wife of faking impurity, for was it not the greater sin for him to pretend to be pure?

It was only a number of days from that Sunday night that Chava Bayla began to talk to her husband with affection. Soon after, she touched him on the shoulder while handing him a platter of kasha varneshkes. He placed it on the table and ate in silence. As she served dessert, levelesh, his favorite, Dov's guilt took on a physical form. What else could it be? What else but guilt would strike a man so obviously?

It began as a concentrated smoldering that flushed the whole of his body. Quickly intensifying, it left him almost feverish. He would exclude himself from meals and sneak out of bed. At work, frightened and in ever increasing pain, he ran from customers to examine himself in the bathroom. Dov Binyamin knew he was suffering from something more than shame.

But maybe it was a trial, a test of which the Rebbe had not warned him. For as his discomfort increased so did Chava's attentions. On her way out of the shower, she let her towel drop in front of him, stepping away from it as if she hadn't noticed, like some Victorian woman waiting for a gentleman to return her hankie with a bow. She dressed slowly, self-consciously, omitting her undergarments and looking to Dov to remind her. He ignored it all, feeling the weight of his heart—no longer pumping as if to burst, but just as large—the blood stagnant and heavy. Chava began to linger in doorways so that he would be forced to brush against her as he passed. Her passion was torturous to Dov, forced to keep his own hidden inside. Once, without any protocol with which they tempered their lives, she came at the subject head-on. "Are you such a small man," she said, "that you must for eternity exact revenge?" He made no answer. It was she who walked away, only to return sweeter and bolder. She became so daring, so desperate, that he wondered if he had ever known the true nature of his wife at all. But he refused, even after repeated advances, to respond to Chava Bayla in bed.

She called to him from the darkness.

"Dovey, please, come out of there. Come lie by me and we'll talk. Just talk. Come Doveleh, join me in bed."

Dov Binyamin stood in the dark in the bathroom. There was some light from the street, enough to make out the toilet and the sink. He heard every word his wife said, and each one tore at him.

He stood before the toilet, holding his penis lightly, mindful of halacha and the laws concerning proper conduct in the lavatory. Trying to relieve himself, to pass water, he suffered to no end.

When he began to urinate, the burning worsened. He looked down in the half-darkness and imagined he saw flames flickering from his penis.

He recalled the words of the prostitute. For his wife's sake, he thought, as the tears welled up in his eyes. This couldn't possibly be the solution the Rebbe intended. Dov was supposed to be in his wife's embrace, enjoying her caresses, and instead he would get an examination table and a doctor's probing hands.

Dov Binyamin dropped to his knees and rested his head against the coolness of the bowl. Whatever the trial, he couldn't bear it much longer. He had by now earned, he was sure, Chava Bayla's love.

There was a noise, it startled him, it was Chava at the door trying to open it. Dov had locked himself in. The handle turned again, and then Chava spoke to him through the door's frosted glass window.

"Tell me," she said. "Tell me: When did I lose my husband for good?"

Every word a plague.

Dov pressed the lever of the toilet, drowning out Chava Bayla's voice. He let the tears run down his face and took his penis full in his hand.

For Dov Binyamin was on fire inside.

And yet he would not be consumed.

Nominated by Story

DAVY CRICKET

by DAVID HAYWARD

from ZYZZYVA

I did what I did for Lubbock and the Crickets
and me. The headline they gave this,
Minor League Mascot Ejected in Brawl,
is funny, I know—over-ardent loyalty,
ha ha, the furious blue insect impervious
in his padded suit and by the same cushion
disabled. Still, it hurts. They boo joy
when they boo me, and the players who held me back
might think harder about whose adamant image
they wear on their caps. For as long as I'm in him,
Davy Cricket won't be among the buccaneers
or bears or Indians who have at their center
something alien, some actor. I am what I look like
and want the things I shout for. Foam lips
are lips. The costume makes me nakeder.

Nominated by ZYZZYVA

UMBILICUS

by JAMES ALAN MCPHERSON

from DOUBLETAKE

IN THE LATE FALL of that first year, when I was growing secure in
my solitude, a friend, an Englishman, came to this house and offered
what he believed was an act of compassion: "Now look here," he told
me, "you are becoming a recluse. Why don't you go out once in a
while? At least go out into your own backyard and see how delightful
the fall is. I'm told that way north of here, along the Minnesota bor-
der, it is even more beautiful. Why don't you at least take a drive up
there before winter comes?" His was a call back to the more complex
rituals of life. After some serious reflection, I accepted it as such. I had
always wanted to see the northeastern part of the state, the sources of
the Mississippi. And so, on a Saturday morning, a golden and blue fall
day, I pulled away from the security of this house. I drove northeast-
erly on county roads. I drove very slowly and very carefully from one
rural town to the next. I saw the light brown beauty of harvested fields,
when soybeans and corn and wheat had given up their energy to en-
tropy, to the enigma of renewal, for the risk of winter and the promise
of spring. I saw that life, my own life, too, *all life*, lay under the promise
of an agreement with something outside, and far, far beyond, the lit-
tle roles we play on the surface of things. I am saying that the slow
drive along the backroads reawakened my spirits. I began to recon-
sider the essential importance of risk to the enterprise of life. I mus-
tered sufficient courage to stop several times along the road, once for
lunch, and again for gasoline and oil. I drove as far north as I thought
was necessary, and then I turned around and drove back toward home.
But in the late afternoon, on the far side of Cedar Rapids, the engine

303

of my car began to smoke and burn. By the time I had parked on the narrow road bank, the engine was on fire. It was here that the old sickness began to reclaim its place in my emotions. I began to feel that the burning engine was God's punishment for my abandoning the simple rituals that had become my life. I felt that, because I had left the refuge of my house, I had *earned* this fate. I abandoned the car. I steeled myself to walk back home, or at least to walk as far as the outskirts of Cedar Rapids, many miles down that county road, as a form of self-punishment. I focused my mind on my house, my bed, my table, and I began walking toward these three things, and *only* these three things.

But several miles along that road, approaching dusk, a truck with two men in it stopped just ahead of me. The two men, both white, sat in the truck and waited for me to approach it. "We saw your car smoking back there, brother," the man in the passenger seat said to me. "Can we give you a ride?" The two of them seemed to be laborers, or at least farmers. The gun rack stretched across the rear window took my memories back to the terror of that long road I had traveled to this place. There was the truck, the gun rack, the white faces, the road. But they did not have the oily Southern accent. I accepted their offer, and the passenger moved over and allowed me to take his seat. Now the three of us were squeezed together on the high seat. They gave me a beer, from the remains of a case of beer on the floor, and we drove toward Cedar Rapids. "A lot of our friends don't like the colored," the driver, who seemed the older of the two, announced to me. "But, hell, me and my brother here, we got colored neighbors. We go over to their houses sometimes for parties. They ain't exactly like us, but we like them all the same." We toasted with our beer and talked of the need for more brotherhood in the world, and of the house parties given by their black neighbors in Cedar Rapids. But at the first service station we reached, just on the outskirts of Cedar Rapids, we were informed that no tow truck was available. The attendant advised us to continue on into Cedar Rapids, toward a station where a tow truck could be available.

Now the older of the two men, in the proximity of safety and social gradation seeming to look more and more "poor white," used this opportunity to offer a radical plan. "Now look," he told me. "I already told you that we *like* the colored. We go over to their house parties in Cedar. You know that some colored are our neighbors. Now here's what I'm gonna do. There's a rope on the back of this truck. We can drive on back and tie that rope to the front bumper of your car. Then we'll just tow her on in to Cedar. You can pay us what you were gonna pay the tow truck, plus we'll do it for less money."

The cool fall evening was closing in. I hesitated, but the desperation of the situation caused me to risk some trust. I accepted their offer. With the bargain struck, with the night closing around us, we drove back to the dead car. We drank more beer in celebration of brotherhood, and we even made some jokes. At the car, after the ropes had been tied to link my own wreck to the back end of their truck, the connection, the *umbilicus,* was tightened until my car could be raised so that only its back wheels were grounded. The two brothers cautioned me to take my former place behind the wheel and manage my car as best I could while they drove the truck. I was handed another beer, for toasting our newly struck brotherhood, while we steered in unison toward the distant lights of Cedar Rapids. And so we started out, slowly and jerkily at first, but then with more and more speed.

Legend has it that all the "I" states are flat. This is not so. There are reasons why the Mississippi River begins in Minnesota, and why its tributaries contribute every drop of water in its meandering and then rapid flow down to the Gulf of Mexico. There are hills in this landscape, and hillocks and dales and rills. The expression *from here to there,* with its promise of fixed purpose, is found in the engineering of straight roadways. But, in contradiction to this illusion of purposeful will, nature itself still has something else to say. Nature will not cede an inch, without struggle, to *any* expression of fixed purpose. Something mysterious in nature, or in the restless growing edge of life itself, imposes a counterintention on all illusion of control. The Great River overflows its banks, flows and ebbs, crests and slackens, rushes and lingers, dies, and then is mighty and waterful again, according to its *own* instincts. So also the straightest of roads are forced to acknowledge the rhythms of the lands that lap under them. Such rhythms are gentle under the four wheels of a tractioned car. But under only two wheels, these same rhythms are foreboding. They speak waywardly of the tenuous nature of life. And in the fall, after harvest time, the uniform brownness of the field, or perhaps it is the withdrawal of the subtle shades of green, keeps one close to the recognition that *death* is the very next season *after* life. You must also add to this the horror of the peculiar angle of a windshield looking *up* into the dark, evening sky, closing down on the emptiness all around the roadbed, and over the top of a truck ahead that you cannot really see. And add also the swaying of the elevated car, first leftward, toward possibly oncoming traffic you cannot see, then rightward, toward sharp and narrow embankments, black-dirted and brown-coated and deathly deep. Imagine also the unsteady stretching of the ropes, the *umbilicus*, connecting the two vehicles. It stretches close to breaking when the truck moves uphill; it relaxes, and the weight of the towed car pushes forward freely and crazily, when the towing truck goes down a dale. Such a haphazardly improvised *umbilical cord* cares nothing for *verbal* affirmations of brotherhood. It encourages very bad manners. It permits the front of the towed car to bump the back of the towing truck, and when the towed car brakes—because its driver tries to steady it when it bumps the rear of the truck ahead, and releases the brake when the rope becomes too tight—both car and towing truck begin to sway dangerously. And add more to it. Add to it the fading illusion of rescue, and the more sharply focused recognition that these are two *white men*, blood brothers, both drunk on beer, who are pulling off the rescue. Add also to it the fact that you have had two beers yourself, and that there is a third beer, open but untouched, on the seat beside you. An additional inducement for fear is that, while these two white men say that they like the colored, and while the three of you raised two toasts to *abstract* brotherhood, the world you live in, especially now, does not perceive things in this same idealized light.

Now, in the entire history of this country there has developed absolutely no substantial body of evidence to support either the authenticity, the genuineness, or the practicality of such a web of self-extension, such an *umbilicus*, extending from either extreme of this great psychological divide. There has been no *real* trust between black and white, especially in such life-risking circumstances. With each sway of the car, within every pull and slack of the rope, the improvised *umbilical* cord—up dale and down dale, inching and then swaying toward the evening lights of Cedar Rapids, the old life lessons came back. *There has never been a life-affirming umbilicus between black and white.* And if this is true, then something else must follow. If the rope should break and the car should crash, no one will really care or even attempt to understand just how this failed and sloppily improvised community of purpose had first come into existence. On the evening news, if even there, it will be dismissed as just another roadkill. *I will never be able to reclaim my bed, my table, or the simple, lit-*

tle, self-protective rituals—sleeping and eating and reading and being reclusive—that I had created to protect what remained of my life.

I braked my car and both vehicles, my car and their truck, went off the road.

But the rope, the *umbilicus, held,* while the car and truck swerved into the ditch at the edge of the roadside.

The two vehicles, the three of us, went into the ditch together. There was no moon over the brown harvested fields that evening. There was no magnetic field, no spiritual center. There was only the spilled can of beer, and its acrid scent mingled with the smell of burning oil, inside my car. Death was announcing itself all around.

I had no trust left in me.

But the three of us were unhurt. The two brothers, after inspecting their truck, dismissed the incident as no more than a joke played on the three of us by the rhythm of the road. "Now we told you we like the colored," the older brother announced. "See, the rope is still tight. We can just push our truck out of the ditch and then hook you up again to it. We'll still drive you on in to Cedar."

I paid the brothers much more than I had promised them, and I began walking down the road toward the lights of Cedar Rapids, toward my bed, my window looking out on my backyard, my table, and toward the simple rituals I had worked out for my life. These things still resided on the far side of Cedar Rapids. I walked away from the urgings of my brothers that we could very easily rescue both truck and car from the ditch, that we had only a few more miles to go before hitting Cedar, that they had always been good neighbors to the colored who lived next door. I kept walking away from them. In my own reduced frame of reference, my two rescuers, my brothers, had become two drunk white men, who, through uncaring, had put my life at risk. I walked away, while behind me they pleaded for the unimportance of money and for the practicality of their plan.

I left it to them to cut the rope, the *umbilicus,* connecting my dead car to their truck.

Nominated by Eileen Pollack

THAT HALF IS ALMOST GONE

by MARILYN CHIN

from SOLO

That half is almost gone,
                    the Chinese half,
the fair side of a peach,
                    darkened by the knife of time,
fades like a cruel sun.

In my thirtieth year
                    I wrote a letter to my mother.

I had forgotten the character
                    for "love." I remembered vaguely
the radical "heart."
                    The ancestors won't fail to remind you

the vital and vestigial organs
                    where the emotions come from

    But the rest is fading.
                    A slash dissects in mid air,
ai, ai, ai, ai,
            more of cry than a sigh

(and no help from the phoneticist).

You are a Chinese!
My mother was adamant.

You *are* a Chinese?
My mother less convinced.

Are you *not* Chinese?
My mother now accepting.

As a cataract clouds her vision,
and her third daughter marries
a Protestant West Virginian

who is "very handsome and very kind."

The mystery is still unsolved—
the landscape looms

over man. And the gafferhatted fishmonger—
sings to his cormorant.

And the maiden behind the curtain,

is somebody's courtesan.

Or, merely Rose Wong's aging daughter

pondering the blue void.

You are a Chinese—said my mother
who once walked the fields of her dead—

Today, on the 36th anniversary of my birth,

I have problems now
even with the salutation.

Nominated by Rita Dove and Jane Hirshfield

THE FOREST

fiction by ANDREA BARRETT

from PLOUGHSHARES

LATER THE SQUAT white cylinders with their delicate indentations would be revealed as a species of lantern. But when Krzysztof Wojciechowicz first glimpsed them, dotted among the azaleas and rhododendrons and magnolias surrounding Constance Humboldt's kidney-shaped swimming pool, he saw them as dolls. The indentations cut the frosted tubes like waists, a third of the way down; the swellings above and below reminded him of bodices and rounded skirts. Perhaps he viewed the lanterns this way because the girls guiding him down the flagstone steps and across the patio were themselves so doll-like. Amazingly young, amazingly smooth-skinned. They were sisters, they'd said. The tiny dark-haired one who'd appeared in the hotel lobby was Rose; the round-cheeked one driving the battered van, with her blond hair frizzing in all directions, was Bianca. Already he'd been clumsy with them.

"You are . . . are you Dr. Humboldt's daughters?" he'd asked. The sun was so bright, his eyes were so tired, the jumble of buildings and traffic so confusing. The step up to the van's back seat was too high for him, but neither girl noticed him struggling.

The small one, Rose, had laughed at his question. "We're not related to Constance," she'd said. "I'm a postdoctoral fellow at the institute." The blond one, who called to mind his own mother sixty years earlier, pulled out of the hotel driveway too fast and said nothing during the short drive to the Humboldts' house. He feared he'd hurt her feelings. For the last decade or so, he'd been subject to these embarrassing misidentifications, taking young scientists for children or servants when he met them out of context. They all dressed so casually, espe-

310

cially in this country; their faces were so unmarked—how could anyone tell them from the young people who chauffeured him about or offered trays of canapés at parties? But of course, he should have known these girls, he'd probably met them earlier. And now, as he stepped down into the enormous back garden and moved toward the long table spread with food and drink, the girl called after a flower veered toward a crowd gathered by the pool and left him with the girl he'd affronted.

"Dr. Wojciechowicz?" she said, mangling his name as she steered him closer to the table. "Would you like a drink, or something?"

Reflexively he corrected her pronunciation; then he shook his head and said, "Please. Call me Krzysztof. And you are Bianca, yes?" He could not help noticing that she had lovely breasts.

"That's me," she agreed dryly. "Bianca the chauffeur; Bianca, Rose's sister; *not* related to the famous Dr. Constance Humboldt. No one you need to pay attention to at all."

"It's not . . . ," he said. Of course he had insulted her. "It's just that I'm so tired, and I'm still jet-lagged, and . . . "

Could he ask her where he was, without sounding senile? Somewhere north of Philadelphia, he thought; but he knew this generally, not specifically. When he'd arrived two days ago, his body still on London time, he had fallen asleep during the long, noisy drive from the airport. Since then he'd had no clear sense of his location. He woke in a room that looked like any other; each morning a different stranger appeared and drove him to the institute. Other strangers shuttled him from laboratory to laboratory, talking at great length about their research projects; then from laboratory to cafeteria to auditorium to laboratory; from lobby to restaurant and back to his hotel. He had given a talk, but it was the same talk he'd been giving for years. He had met perhaps thirty fellow scientists and could remember only a handful of their names. All of them seemed to be gathered here, baring too much skin to the early July sun. It was Saturday, he thought. Also some holiday seemed to be looming.

"Do forgive me," he said. "The foibles of the elderly."

"How *old* are you?"

Her smile was charming, and he forgave her rude question. "I am seventy-nine years of age," he said. "Easy to remember—I was born in 1900, I am always as old as the century."

"Foibles forgiven." She—*Bianca,* he thought, *Bianca*—held out her hand in that strange boyish way of American women. Meanwhile

311

she was looking over his shoulders, as if hoping to find someone to rescue her. "Bianca Marburg, not quite twenty-two, but I'm very old for my age."

"You would be in college, then?"

She tossed her hair impatiently. "Not *hardly*. My sister and I were dreadful little prodigies—in college at sixteen, out at nineteen, right into graduate school. Rose already has her Ph.D.—how else do you think she'd have a postdoc here?"

Would he never say the right thing to this bristly girl? "So, then, you . . . what is the project you are working on?" Americans, he'd been reminded these last two days, were always eager to talk about themselves.

"So, then, *I*—*I* should be in graduate school, and I was until two months ago, but I just dropped out, it was seeming stupid to me. Unlike my so-successful sister, Rose, *I* am at loose ends."

She moved a bowl of salad closer to a platter of sliced bread draped with a cloth, then moved it back again. "Which is why I'm driving you around. Why I'm here. I'm sort of between places, you know? Between lives? I got a temp job typing for this Iraqi biophysicist here— see that short guy over by the volleyball net? He hired me because I can spell 'vacuum' and he can't spell anything in English. Eight weeks, typing some grant applications. I'm staying with my sister until I get enough money together to move. I might go to Alaska."

"That's nice," Krzysztof said helplessly.

"Oh, please," she said. "You don't have to pretend to be interested, I'm low on the conversational totem pole here, and you're this big famous scientist, and I know you've got better things to do than talk to me. Go talk to the other famous people. Constance collects them, they're everywhere."

She huffed off—furious, he saw. At him? In the battered leather bag that hung from his shoulder, he felt the bottle he'd carried across the ocean as a special gift for his hostess. But his hostess was nowhere to be seen, and no one moved toward him from the pool or the round tables with their mushroom-like umbrellas. Already the top of his head was burning; and he was all alone and wished he had a hat. Was it possible that these people meant to stay in the sun all afternoon?

Bianca made a brisk circuit through the backyard, looking for some place to settle down. There was Rose, leaning attentively toward Constance's husband, Roger, and listening to him talk about

312

Norway as if she were actually interested. Entirely typical, Bianca thought; Rose submitted herself to Roger's boring monologues as a way of pleasing Constance, who was her advisor. But Rose had forbidden Bianca to go anywhere near Roger, since he'd overheard her in the cafeteria comparing his droopy, fleshy face to that of a camel. Constance herself was holding court from an elegant lawn chair beneath an umbrella, surrounded by graduate students and postdocs and talking about the session she'd chaired at a Gordon Conference two weeks earlier—but Bianca could not bear the way Constance patronized her, and she steered wide of this group. Almost she joined the two girls Constance employed from the small women's college down the road, who were trotting up and down the steps bearing pitchers of iced tea and lemonade; she would have felt at home with them, but Constance had rebuked her, at last week's reception, for distracting the help. The knot of protein chemists at the volleyball net beckoned, Rick and Wen-li and Diego stripped of their shirts and gleaming in the sun, but she had slept with Diego after that reception, and things were still awkward between them. Vivek and Anisha, easing themselves into the shallow end of the pool just as Jocelyn, already cannonball-shaped, curled her arms around her legs and launched herself into the deep end with a splash? No, no, no. Vivek was charming, but Jocelyn was impossible, and she was already whaling down on her young squire. Everywhere Bianca looked there was laughter, chatter, the display of flesh—much of it, Bianca thought, better left hidden—flirtation and bragging and boredom. A standard holiday weekend party, except that all of these people were scientists and many of them were famous; and she was neither. And had, as Rose reminded her constantly, no one to blame for this but herself.

Off by the fragrant mock-orange tree, she spotted the institute's two resident Nobel laureates side by side, in dark pants and long-sleeved shirts, overseeing the scene like trolls. She drifted their way, curious to see if they were clashing yet. Arnold puffed and plucked at his waistband; Herb snorted and rolled his eyes. But the serious drinking had not yet begun, and these were only false charges, still made in fun. Last week she had sat next to Arnold during Winifred's seminar on the isozymes of alpha-amylase, and watched him and Herb shred Winifred in the boastful cross-fire. Arnold had smiled at her.

"Nice to see you gentlemen again," Bianca said, when she reached their circle of shade.

The men stared at her blankly. On the smooth green grass, Arnold's left foot tapped.

"Bianca Marburg," she reminded them. He *had* smiled at her, hadn't he? When she asked that question about the electrophoretic bands?

"You're—in Jocelyn's lab?" Arnold said now.

"Rose Marburg's sister," she said, grinning stupidly.

Herb frowned, still unable to place her. "Don't you—didn't I see you . . . were you *typing*? For Fu'ad?"

She held her hands up like claws and typed the air. *"C'est moi,"* she said. What was she doing here?

"Ah," Arnold said, with his most condescending smile. "You must be helping Constance out. It's a lovely party, isn't it? So well-organized. Constance really amazes me, the way she can do this sort of thing and still keep that big lab churning out those papers."

"Well," Herb said. "But that last pair of papers, really . . . "

Bianca fled. From the corner of her eye, she saw the man she'd driven here, that Polish émigré, physical chemist turned theoretical structural biologist, Cambridge-based multiple-medaled old guy, standing all alone by the bamboo fountain, watching the water arc from the stem to the pool. Pleasing Constance inadvertently, she thought; Constance fancied her home as a place conducive to contemplation and great ideas. Krzysztof raised his right hand and held it over his head, either feeling for hair that was no longer present or attempting to shade his gruesome array of freckles and liver spots from the burning sun.

Quickly Bianca traversed the yard and the patio, slipped through the glass doors and across the kitchen, and ran upstairs to the third and smallest bathroom. The door closed behind her with expensive precision: a Mercedes door, a jewel box door. On the vanity was a vase with a Zen-like twist of grapevine and a single yellow orchid. She opened the window and lit up a joint. Entirely typical, she thought, gazing down at Krzysztof's sweaty pate. That Constance and Arnold and Herb and the others should fly this man across the ocean to hear about his work, then get so caught up in institute politics that they'd forget to talk to him at their party. Had it not been for the lizard-like graze of his eyes across her chest, she might have felt sorry for him.

Of course Constance did not let Krzysztof languish long by the fountain; that would have been rude, she was never rude. After a few minutes he crouched down by the rock-rimmed basin and began touching a blade of grass to the water, dimpling the surface and thinking about van der Waals forces. Perhaps Constance caught the movement and thought he was feeling ill. She rushed to his side, she burbled and babbled. She asked him about common acquaintances at Cambridge. Did he want to swim?—but of course not, he should come sit here; he knew everyone, didn't he? She helped him into a long, low elaborately curved chair, webbed with canvas that trapped him as securely as a fishnet. She seemed unaware that he could not rise from it unaided. And how could he say, as the faces bent toward him politely for one brief moment, then turned back to each other and their animated conversations about meetings he hadn't attended, squabbles among colleagues he didn't know, that in fact he'd forgotten almost all their names and was incapable of attaching those he did remember to the appropriate faces and research problems?

The sun had moved, was moving, so that first his knees then his thighs and crotch were uncomfortably roasted. Constance had brought him to the throne room, he saw. This cluster of chairs, perched where an adrenal gland would be if the pool were really a kidney, held her and him, Arnold and Herb, Jocelyn and Sundralingam. All the senior scientists. Directly across the pool the junior researchers stood in tight circles, occasionally glancing his way; the postdocs and students gathered at the farthest end of the pool, where a group of bare-torsoed, highly muscled young men had set fire to a long grill. The smoke rose in disturbing columns. He made columns in his mind: faces, names, research projects. Then he tried and failed to match up the lists. The girl named Rose walked by and smiled at him, and he smiled back eagerly but she continued to walk, past him and between a pair of those low white cylinders standing among glossy mounds of hosta like dolls in a dark wood. He knew he'd fallen asleep only when his own sudden, deep-throated snore woke him.

It was not dark yet, not nearly, but the sun had dropped and the sky was the most remarkable violet-blue. Perhaps it was six o'clock. A few people still swam in the pool, but most were out, and mostly dressed, and the smell of roasting fowl filled the air. Across the water, on the patio, people milled around the grill and the table with paper plates in their hands. Bottles of wine, bottles of beer, dripping glasses, ice; he was, he realized, very thirsty. And past embarrassment, although the chairs near him were empty now, as if he'd driven everyone away. Somehow he was not surprised, when he rolled sideways in an unsuccessful attempt to pull himself from his lounge chair, to see

Bianca, cross-legged on the grass, smiling ironically as she watched over him.

"Have a nice nap?" she asked.

"Lovely," he said. She seemed happy now; what had he missed? "But you know I *cannot* get up from this thing."

She held out a hand, but it was not enough. "If you would," he said, "just put your hands under my arms and lift . . . "

Effortlessly she hauled him to his feet. "You want to go over toward the tables?"

"Not just yet. Perhaps I'll just sit here for a minute." This time he chose a straight metal chair with a scallop-shell back. He sat gingerly, then more firmly. A fine chair, he'd be able to get up himself.

"How about I go get you some food?"

He sniffed the air. He had no appetite yet, and the smell of singeing flesh was strangely revolting. "Get something for yourself," he said. "Maybe I'll eat later. But I'm terribly thirsty—do you suppose you could bring me a glass of something cold? Just some water?" He remembered, then, the bottle in his bag. "And if you could find two small empty glasses as well," he said. "I have a treat to share with you."

When she returned he gulped gratefully at his glass of cold water. "Do you like vodka?" he asked.

"Me? I'll drink anything."

He reached into his leather satchel and took out the bottle he'd meant to give Constance. "You brought glasses?"

She held out two little paper cups, printed with blue and green daisies. "The best I could do."

"Good enough." He held up the heavy bottle, so that she could see the blade of grass floating blissfully inside. *"Zubrowka,"* he said. "Bison vodka, very special. It is flavored with the grass upon which the bison feed in the Bialowieza forest, where my family is from. A friend brings it to me from Poland when he visits, and I brought it here from Cambridge."

"Cool," she said. "Should I get some ice?"

"Never," he said, shuddering. "We drink this neat, always." He poured two shots and handed one to her. "You must drink it all in one gulp—*do dna*. To the bottom."

"Bottoms up," Bianca said. Together they tossed the shots down. Almost immediately he felt better. Bianca choked and shook her head, her pale hair flying in all directions. He forbade himself to look at her smooth neck or the legs emerging, like horses from the gate, from her white shorts. He focused on her nose and reminded himself that women her age saw men like him as trolls. Even ten years ago, the occasional women with whom he'd forgotten himself had let him know this, and cruelly. How was it he still felt these impulses, then? That the picture of himself he carried inside had not caught up to his crumpled body?

"Take a sip of water," he said.

"It *burns!*"

"Of course. But isn't it delicious?" He refilled the ridiculous cups, and they drank again. She had spirit, he thought. This time she hardly choked at all. He tried to imagine her as the granddaughter of one of his oldest friends, himself as an elderly uncle.

"Delicious," she agreed. "It's like drinking a meadow. Again?"

"Why not?"

Around the left lobe of the kidney came Rose, a platter of charred chicken in her hand. Simultaneously, Krzysztof thought, she seemed to smile at him and glare at her sister, who was caught with the paper cup still at her lips. Was that a glare? He could not figure out what was going on between these sisters.

"Welcome," he said. And then, reluctantly—he could not help basking in Bianca's undivided attention—"Will you join us?"

"I can't just now," Rose said. "But Constance wants to know if you'd like to come over to the patio and have something to eat." She thrust the platter toward his face. "The chicken's great."

"Maybe later."

"Bianca? You want to come eat?"

"No," Bianca said firmly; she seemed to be rejecting more than just the food. For a minute the sisters glared at each other—*Children,* Krzysztof thought; then remembered Bianca's earlier word. *No, prodigies. All grown up*—then Rose made a clicking sound with her tongue and walked away.

Her mouth tasted of meadows and trees, Bianca thought. As if she had been turned into a creature with hooves, suavely grazing in a dappled glade. The joint she'd smoked earlier was still with her, but barely, palely; this warmth in her veins, this taste in her mouth, were from the splendid bison vodka. And this man, whom at first she'd felt saddled with, and longed to escape, was some sort of magician. Now it was beginning to seem like good fortune that everyone else had abandoned him to her care. The two of them rose from their chairs, on their way

317

to join the crowd and examine the platters of food. But the voices on the patio seemed terribly loud, and someone over by the table was shrieking with laughter, a sound like metal beating metal. They drifted toward the Japanese fountain tucked in the shrubbery; the same place she'd seen Krzysztof standing earlier, all alone. He was smiling now, he had a wonderful smile. It distracted her from the odd way his lower lids sagged, exposing their pale pink inner membranes.

"Isn't this a pretty thing?" he asked, and she agreed. There were ferns surrounding one side of the fountain, lacy and strongly scented. She peered down into the stony basin and said, "We could just sit here for a bit."

"We could," he agreed. "If you would not mind lowering me down on this rock."

This time she knew just how to fit her hands into his armpits, and she got him seated with no fuss at all. "So what is it you do, exactly?" she asked. When he hesitated, she said, "You know, I did do a couple of years of graduate work in biochemistry. Remember? It's not like I can't understand."

"I know that," he said. "I know. It's just that no one this whole visit has actually *asked* me anything. And I'm more or less retired now."

"So what did you used to do?"

His whole long life as a scientist stretched behind him, and he could hardly imagine how to tell it quickly. "In Krakow," he said, "where I went to university, I was trained as a physical chemist specializing in polymers. I went to England, just before the Second World War"—he looked at her open, earnest face, and skipped over all that painful history, all those desperate choices—"and after I'd been there a little while, I was recruited to work on a secret project to develop artificial rubber. Then I studied alpha helices and similar structures in polymers, and then did some fiber-diffraction work on proteins. Once I gave up running a lab, I started doing more theoretical things. Thought-experiments. Do you know much thermodynamics?"

"Enough to get by," she said. "But that kind of heavy math was never my strong point."

"I like to think about the thermodynamics of surfaces, and its relationship to the folding of globular proteins. You know, the buried residues inside the assembly and all that. There is a set of equations . . ."

But Bianca shook her head. "Your bad luck," she said. "I'm probably the only person here who can't follow your math."

318

"I can show you something," he said. "Something that will make you understand at once."

"Yes?" she said. She was, she realized, wonderfully, happily drunk. Her companion, who was at least elated, reached into his magic bag once more.

"More vodka?" she said. "I could do another shot."

"Absolutely." The paper cups were soft-edged now, and partly crumpled, but he straightened their edges and filled them one more time. "There's something else in here, though," he said.

He delved around in the capacious bag, searching for the toys he always carried. Sometimes, when he traveled to foreign countries, his audiences were so diverse that he had to bring the level of his standard lecture down a notch, use visual aids so the biologists could grasp what he was saying as well as the biochemists and biophysicists. He had not had to use those aids here at the institute, where the staff prided themselves on their mathematical sophistication. But now his hand found the coil of copper wire, and the little plastic bottle.

"Perhaps," he said, "if there was a way we could get a bowl of water?"

Bianca pointed at the basin just below them. "Water's right here."

Had he not had so much *zubrowka* he might have considered more closely the relationship between the limpid water in the basin and the tiny stream trickling from the hollow bamboo. But he looked at the small pool and the eager, beautiful girl beside him, and without further thought he opened the bottle and poured several ounces of solution into the basin. From the wire he quickly fashioned several simple polygons. "Watch," he said.

She watched. The voices from the patio faded, the ferns waved gently, her vision narrowed until she saw only his hands, the basin, the rocks where they sat. He dipped a wire shape in the basin and blew a large bubble; then another, which he fastened to the first. More wire forms, more bubbles, more joinings—and before her, trembling gently in the air, rose a complicated structure supported by almost nothing.

"See where the faces join?" he said. "Those shapes the film makes as the faces join other faces?" He launched into an explanation of molecular interactions that seemed simplistic to him, incomprehensible to her. "You see," he said, "what a clear visual demonstration this is of the nature of surface tension. I stumbled on this some years ago, blowing regular old soap bubbles for the grandchildren of some friends of mine."

"That wasn't soap?" she said. "What you put in the water?"

"Not exactly—the film it makes isn't sturdy enough. There's glycerine in here, some other things . . . " He added two more bubbles to his airy construction.

There was a theory behind all this, Bianca knew. An idea that this growing structure of soap film and wire exemplified; and she was the only person at this rarefied gathering incapable of grasping what he was trying to explain. Yet as she sat there in the blue air, that bubble-structure elongating while he expounded on his ideas, she felt almost purely happy. Soon she would have to leave this place. Although she was closer to Rose than to anyone else in the world, so close they sometimes seemed to share a soul, she and Rose could not seem to get along now. At night, lying on the couch in Rose's tiny apartment, she could feel the fierceness of Rose's desire that she go back to school and continue the work they'd shared since their father gave them their first chemistry set. Or, if she refused to do that, that she would go away and leave Rose to her own life. It had been a mistake, she knew, to follow Rose here to Philadelphia, graft herself even temporarily into Rose's new world. But her job had only a few weeks to go, and she felt the pull of other places and lives, the same pull that had, in part, made her drop out of graduate school so suddenly.

Soon her whole life would change. But at that moment, sitting on the rocks with Krzysztof, she felt as if he'd led her to a castle from which she'd been barred, opened the front door with a flourish, and then gaily flung open other doors one by one. The rooms were filled with sunlight and treasure. And although they were rooms she'd given up, rooms that from now on would belong to Rose and not her, this moment of remembering that they existed comforted her like balm.

She said, "I had a grandfather who did wonderful tricks. Maybe not as good as this, but still, you would have liked him. He was from your part of the world, I think. I mean the part where you came from originally."

"He was Polish?" Krzysztof said eagerly. That she equated him with her grandfather was something he wouldn't think about now. "You have Polish blood?"

"Sort of," she said. "Not exactly. I'm not sure. Our grandfather's name was Leo Marburg, and the story in our family goes that he had a German name but was born and raised in Poland, near some big forest somewhere. Or maybe it was Lithuania. But somehow he ended up in the Soviet Union, trying to establish vineyards in the Ukraine for the Communists, not long after the revolution. And then—this is all confused, my mother told me these stories when I was little—he came to America, and he worked as a janitor for a while, but then he found a job with one of the big wineries on the Finger Lakes."

"Finger Lakes? What are those?"

She held up her right hand with the fingers outstretched. "Some long skinny lakes all next to each other, out in western New York, where I grew up. The glaciers made them. It's a good place to grow grapes. When he'd saved enough money, he bought some land of his own, and established the winery that my father still runs. I know a lot about making wine. Grandpa Leo was still alive when Rose and I were tiny, and he used to bring us down into the corner of the cellar where he had his lab and show us all sorts of apparatus. The smells—it was like an alchemist's cave. No bubbles, though."

It was astounding, Krzysztof thought. What she left out, what she didn't seem to know. That Leo might have been hardly older than him, if he were still alive; what did it mean, that he'd worked once for the Soviets? That he'd escaped, made his way here, worked as a laborer, but then reestablished himself and his real life? "So was he German, really?" he asked. "Or Russian, or Polish?"

"I don't know," she admitted. "He died when I was five or so, before I could ask him anything. Most of what I know about him my mother told me, and she died when Rose and I were still girls. I don't know much history, I guess. My own or anyone else's."

How could she tell him about her mother, whom she still missed every day? And talked with, sometimes, although this was another point over which she and Rose quarreled bitterly. She felt a sudden sharp longing for her sister and craned her head toward the crowd behind her, but Rose had her back to them, she was talking with Vivek. She belonged with these people, as Bianca herself never would. "It's because of Grandpa Leo," she said, "that I studied biochemistry in the first place. Because of him and my father and the winery . . . "

"But you stopped," Krzysztof said. "Why was that?"

She could not explain this to Rose, or even to herself: how could she explain it to him? The argument she and Rose had had, when they were working together on one of the papers that grew out of Rose's thesis—how bitter that had been. At its root had been one small kinetics experiment that Rose interpreted one way, she herself another.

"It's so . . . *pushy*," she said. The easy excuse, and at least partially true. "Science, I mean. At least at this level. When I started I thought it was something people did communally. Everyone digging their own small corner of the field, so that in the end the field would flower—I didn't know it got so vicious. So competitive. I hate all this hustling for money and priority and space and equipment. Actually," she said, "I hate these *people*. A lot of them. I really do."

"We're not very inspiring in groups," Krzysztof said. "That's true." He pulled his hands apart and dropped his wire forms, disrupting the bubbles so that suddenly he held nothing, only air. Science was a business now, and sometimes he could hardly bear it himself. Yet he could remember the excitement of his youth, that sense of clarity and vision; it was this, in part, that had pulled him from Krakow to Cambridge. But not only this.

"Your grandfather," he said. "If what you remember about his youth was true, our families might have come from the same place. In northeastern Poland is this huge forest—the forest where the bison live, where this vodka comes from. That might have been the forest your mother meant in her stories."

"Do you think?"

"It's possible," he said, and he repeated the name he'd told her earlier: Bialowieza. Bianca tried to say it herself. "It's a beautiful place," he said.

"And there are still bison there? Real ones, I mean. Now?"

"There are," he said. "It is partly because of my own mother that they still exist." The whole story swirled before him, beautiful and shapely and sad, but just as it came together in his mind, Bianca leapt up from her seat and held out her hands.

"I could show you something," she said. "Something really beautiful, that you'll never see if we stay here. You probably think this country is ugly, all you ever see are airports and highways and scientists. Do you want to get out of here for a while? We'd only be gone less than an hour, and you could tell me about the bison on the way."

"I don't want to be rude," he said.

"I promise you, no one will notice. I'll have you back so soon they'll never know you're gone."

No one had approached them this last half hour; the other guests had taken root, on the grass and the steps and the chairs, and were eating and drinking busily, arguing and laughing and thrusting their chins at each other. But a threat loomed, in the person of the woman—the wife of Arnold?—standing closest to them. Although she was chattering with a postdoc about her work with adhesives, she was sending glances Krzysztof's way, and these made him shudder. At dinner, the previous night, he'd been stuck with her for an hour while she explained the chemistry of what made things sticky, but not too sticky. As if he didn't know. She worked for some huge corporation; the net result of her work, if he remembered it right, had something to do with those small yellow slips of paper that now littered all other sheets of paper, and on which his colleagues scribbled curt notes. How vulgar she was. If he and Bianca continued to sit by this fountain, the woman would eventually sidle over to them. The possibility was unbearable.

He held out his arms to Bianca. "If you would?" Just then the low cylinders in the shrubberies lit up all at once, casting a warm light on the paths and the pool and the patio—yes, of course they were lanterns, not dolls. Expensive, tasteful lanterns, meant to look faintly Oriental.

"My pleasure," she said. She raised him and held her finger to her lips in a gesture of silence. Then, to his delight, she led him through the ferns and azaleas until they disappeared around the side of the house, unseen by anyone. Krzysztof was too pleased by their cunning escape to tell Bianca how badly he needed to urinate.

They drove toward the glorious red horizon, as if chasing the vanished sun. Although the road was narrow and twisted and sunken, almost like an English road, Bianca drove very fast. Krzysztof clutched the dash at first, but then relaxed; what was left of his hair lifted and fanned in the wind, tugging at his scalp like a lover's hands and distracting him from the pressure in his bladder.

"Is there any of that vodka left?" Bianca asked.

He handed her the bottle and watched as she held it to her lips. "So," she said. "Tell me about those bison."

He stuck one hand through the open window, letting it cut into the rushing breeze like a knife; then tilted it slightly and let the air push his arm up. "I was born and raised in Krakow," he said. Had he told her that already? "But my mother grew up in the country, in this forest where perhaps your grandfather was from. It is so beautiful, you can't imagine—it is the last bit of primeval forest in Europe, the trees have never been cut. There are owls there, and roe deer and storks and bears. And it was the last place where the wild bison, the *zubre*, lived. When my mother was young the Russians controlled that part of Poland and the forest was the tsar's private hunting preserve."

323

"Your mother was Russian?"

"No—*Polish*. Defiantly, absolutely Polish." He almost stopped here, overwhelmed by the complexities of Polish history. But it wasn't important, he skipped it all; it was not her fault that she knew nothing and that, if he were to hand her a map, she could not place Poland more than vaguely. "After she married my father they moved to Krakow—he was an organic chemist, he taught at the university there. During the First World War he was conscripted into the Austrian Army and disappeared. We don't even know where he died. So it was just my mother and me after that. When the war was over and I started university myself, we heard stories about how the German armies trapped in the forest during the war's last winter started eating the *zubre* after they'd finished off the lynx and wild boars and weasels. There were only a thousand or so of them left in the world. The forests had been cleared everywhere else in Europe, and rich people had been hunting them for centuries. Then those German soldiers ate all the rest. What could they do? They were freezing, and starving, and they butchered the *zubre* with their artillery. This made my mother very bitter. Her father had been a forester, and she'd grown up watching the bison grazing on buttercups under the oaks."

Bianca interrupted him—suddenly he seemed old again, he was wandering. And crossing and uncrossing his legs like a little boy who had to pee. Was a bison the same as a buffalo? In graduate school she had once met a man, a philosopher, who raised buffalo with his wife not far from Ithaca and peddled the meat. Lean, dark, a little tough.

"This is Meadowbrook," she said, gesturing at the gigantic houses and formal gardens tucked back from the road they whizzed along; hoping to pull him back to the present. "Isn't that a ridiculous name? All the rich people live here. And so do Rose and I, sort of—she has a little apartment above the garage of one of these estates. It used to be the gardener's quarters—over there, see that big stone house?"

She gestured vaguely, and he ducked his head to see over her shoulder. Whatever house she'd pointed out had vanished. Suddenly she slowed and turned the van down a narrow lane between two stone pillars. "Almost here," she said.

He hurried on with his story, sensing that time was short. He skipped everything personal, all his struggles between the two great wars. He skipped the strange evolution of his mother's heart, the way she had left him alone in Krakow and returned to the forest of her youth, burning with a desire to rebuild what had been destroyed. The

324

way she had turned in disgust from his work, from every kind of science but forestry.

"The bison were gone by the end of the war," he said. "Almost extinct. But near the end of the twenties, a Polish forester started trying to reestablish a breeding stock—and my mother moved back to the Bialowieza, to help him. There were a few in a zoo in Stockholm, and some in zoos in Hamburg and Berlin. A few more had survived the war in the south of Poland. And my mother and this man, they brought some females from that little group to the forest, and borrowed bulls from the zoos, and they started a breeding program. From them come all the European bison left in the world. There are several thousand of them now—because of my mother, you see? My own mother."

They were in a forest of sorts right now—the lane grew narrower and turned into a dirt track, and trees brushed the side of the van. When they emerged into a small clearing, Bianca stopped the van without saying a word in response to his tale.

"I run here," she said. "Almost every night. It's a park, this place. But no one comes here, I never see any people. I like to run just before dark." For a second he pictured her, pounding down the dirt paths; perhaps this explained her extraordinary legs. She came around to his side of the van and helped him down the awkward step.

"It's beautiful," he said. Why had he been telling her that story? The forest, his mother, the starving soldiers; the bison, so huge and wild, just barely rescued from oblivion. That part ended happily. The rest, which he would never tell Bianca, did not: during the Blitzkrieg the German army had overrun the forest in a matter of weeks. Then it had passed to the Russians, then back to the Germans; swastikas had flown from the roofs. The resident Jews had been slaughtered under those ancient oaks, and the farmers and foresters had been deported. His mother had disappeared. And all the while he had been safe in England, unable to persuade her to join him. Unable to save her, or anyone. In test tubes he had grown chains of molecules, searching for something that might be turned into tires for planes and jeeps.

"It's a national park now, that forest," he said, unable to let the story go. Then the pressure in his bladder grew unbearable, and he said, "Would you excuse me for a minute?" He stepped behind an oak and into a thorny tangle, disappearing in the brambles. Behind him, Bianca was puzzled and then amused as she heard the long splatter of liquid on leaves, a pause, more splatter, a sigh. The sigh was one of pleasure; even this simple act was no longer reliable, and Krzysztof felt

325

such relief as his urine flowed over the greenery that he was hardly embarrassed when he emerged and Bianca gently pointed out the bit of shirttail emerging from his fly like a tongue.

After he tidied himself, Bianca led him across a muddy field and into the trees at the far edge of the clearing. The sky had turned a smoky violet gray, truly dusk, all traces of red disappeared and with them the color of the leaves and Bianca's hair.

"No bison here," she said cheerfully. "But I think we made it just in time. This whole area—I hate this area, it's one giant suburb. This is the only bit of real woods left for miles. But something kept eating everything Rose planted in her garden, and when I started jogging here I found what it was. Be quiet now."

He was. He was exhausted, remarkably drained, the vodka swirling through his veins. The marzipan-like taste of the bison grass; was it that flavor the secretive, lumbering creatures had craved as they grazed? The only time he had visited his mother in the forest, just before he left for England, she had fed him a dish of wild mushrooms, wild garlic, and reindeer, washed down with this vodka. He had tried to persuade her that war was inevitable. Her hair was gray by then, she no longer looked anything like Bianca. She lived in a low dark hut by herself and said she would rather die than leave her home again.

A deer appeared in the clearing. He blinked his eyes; it had not been there, and then it was. Bianca inhaled sharply. "Oh," she whispered. "We made it just in time." He blinked again: four deer, then eleven, then seventeen. They came out of the trees and stood in the gathering darkness, looking calmly at each other and at the sky. How beautiful they were. He squeezed Bianca's hand, which was unaccountably folded within his own.

She stood very still. Night after night, during these long strange weeks, she had left Rose's cramped apartment and their difficult quarrels, slipped on her running shoes, and sped down the long driveway, past the houses of the wealthy, across the busy suburban road, and into this park. And almost every night she was rewarded with this vision. She could hear her mother's voice then, as if the deer were transmitting it; they seemed unafraid of her and often stayed for half an hour. Tonight they were edgy, though. Their tails twitched and their ears rotated like tiny radar dishes; their heads came up suddenly and pointed toward the place where Bianca and Krzysztof were hidden. They were nothing like bison. They were dainty and delicate-footed, completely at home here and yet so out of place beyond the confines of this small haven. Still she could not figure out either how or when they crossed the bustling road between the park and Rose's apartment to browse on the lettuce and peas.

She did not have to tell Krzysztof not to speak; he stood like a tree, wonderfully still and silent. But his face gleamed, she saw. As if he'd been sprayed with water; was he crying? Suddenly one doe leapt straight up, turned in the air, and then bounded away. The others quickly followed. It was dark, the show was over.

"You okay?" she whispered.

"Fine," he said. "That was *lovely*. Thank you."

"My pleasure."

She slipped an arm beneath his elbow to guide him back through the muddy part of the field, but he shook her off. He was restored, he was himself. He strode firmly over the ruts and ridges. "It's hard to believe there's a place like this so close to the congestion," he said.

She was behind him, unable to make out his words. "What?" she said.

He turned his head over his shoulder to repeat his comment. As he did so, his right foot plunged into a deep hole. For a moment he tottered between safety and harm, almost in balance, almost all right. Then he tipped and tilted and was down in the mud, looking up at the first stars.

In the emergency room, the nurses and residents were very impatient with them. No one seemed able to sort out Krzysztof's health insurance situation: what were these British papers and cards, this little folder marked *Traveler's Insurance*? Then there was the vodka on his breath, and Bianca's storm of hysterical tears; for some minutes the possibility of calling the police was raised. X-rays, blood tests, embarrassing questions: "Are you his girlfriend?" one nurse said. From Bianca's shocked rebuttal, Krzysztof understood that, just as he'd feared, she had never seen him, not for one moment, as an actual man. Almost he was tempted to tell her how clearly, and in what detail, he'd imagined her naked. She sat in an orange plastic chair and sobbed while he was wheeled in and out of rooms, his veiny white legs exposed in the most humiliating fashion. And this exposure was what distressed him most, although more friends than he could count had met their deaths through just such casual falls. Somehow the possibility of actual bodily harm had not occurred to him as he lay calmly regarding the stars from the muddy field.

"The ankle's not broken," a young doctor finally said. "But it's badly sprained."

"So he's all right?" Bianca kept saying. "He's all *right?*" She could not seem to calm herself and sat, as if paralyzed, while the doctors drew a curtain around Krzysztof and went to work.

An hour later Krzysztof emerged with his lower leg encased in two rigid plastic forms, each lined with a green plastic air-filled pod. Velcro straps clamped the shells around him, as if his ankle were an oyster. A boy young enough to be his grandson had given him two large white pills in a white pleated cup, which resembled in miniature the nurse's cap worn by a woman he'd loved during the war; the woman's name had vanished, as had the pain, and his entire body felt blissful. Bianca carried the crutches, and a sheaf of instructions and bills. She opened the van's side door and tried to help as two men lifted Krzysztof from the wheelchair and draped him along the back seat.

All the way back to Constance's house, Bianca drove slowly, avoiding potholes and sudden swerves. "Are you all right?" she asked every few minutes. "Is this hurting you?"

Drowsily he said, "I have not felt so good in years." Actually this long narrow seat was more comfortable than the vast bed in his hotel. The jacket Bianca had folded into a pillow beneath his head smelled of her; the whole van was scented with her presence. On the floor, just below his face, he saw nylon shoes with flared lumpy soles and socks and shirts and reeds and a bird's nest, a canvas sack and a withered orange. Behind his seat was a mat and a sleeping bag. "Do you sleep in here?" he asked.

"I have—but not these last weeks. I'm so sorry, I never meant—I can't *believe* this happened."

"My fault," he said. "Entirely. You mustn't blame yourself."

"Everyone else will," she said bitterly. "Everyone."

Should she bring him straight back to his hotel? But she had to stop at Constance's house, let Constance and the others decide what was best for him. Perhaps Constance would want to have him stay with her. It was past eleven, they'd been gone for hours; and although Bianca had had plenty of time to call from the hospital, the phone booth had seemed impossibly far away, and malignant. Now the only honest thing to do was to show up, with her guilty burden, and admit to everyone what had happened. Behind her, Krzysztof was humming. Stoned out of his gourd, she thought; she would have given anything for their positions to be reversed.

328

"Talk to me," he said. "It's lonely back here. All I can see is the back of your head."

"Those bison," she said. "Are they anything like our buffalo?"

"Similar," he said. "But bigger. Shaggy in the same way, though."

"I heard this thing once," she said. "From a friend of my mother's, who used to visit the winery when Rose and I were little girls. He was some kind of naturalist, I think he studied beetles. Once he said, I think he said, that the buffalo out west had almost gone extinct, but then some guy made a buffalo refuge in Montana, and stocked it with animals from the Bronx Zoo. Like your mother did, you see?" For a minute her own mother's face hovered in the air lit by her headlights.

The van slowed and made a broad gentle curve—Constance's circular driveway, Krzysztof guessed. "In Polish," he said dreamily, "the word for beetle is *chrzaszcz*." Bianca tried to repeat the word, mashing together the string of consonants in a way he found very sweet. How pleasing that after all she'd paid attention to his stories. Their slow progress through the afternoon and evening had culminated properly among the deer, not here, and all of it had been worthwhile.

"We're here," she said. "Boy, this is going to be *awful*—just wait for a minute. I'll tell everyone what's going on, and we'll see what to do."

She turned and touched his head, preparing to face her sister.

"Don't worry," he said gently. "I'll tell everyone I asked you to take me for a drive. I had a lovely evening, you know. I'm very glad to have met you."

Neither of them knew that out back, beyond the rubble of the party, large sturdy bubbles had been forming for hours at the lip of the bamboo fountain, to the mystification of everyone. They did not see the bubbles, nor the inside of the house, because Rose and Constance came flying out the front door to greet the van. Terrified, Bianca saw. And then, as she prepared the first of many explanations, the first clumsy attempt at the story she'd tell for years, with increasing humor and a kind of self-deprecation actually meant to charm in the most shameful way, she saw their faces change: that was rage she saw, they were enraged.

In an instant she had thrown the van into gear again and stomped on the gas. Krzysztof said, "Where . . . ?" and as they lurched back onto the road, leaving behind Constance and Rose and the fountain and the lanterns, the squabbling scientists, the whole world of science, she said, "Back to your hotel, you need to be in your own bed."

Back, Krzysztof thought. Back to the airport, back to England, back across the ocean and Europe toward home; back to the groves of Bialowieza, where his mother might once have crossed paths with Bianca's grandfather. Might have escaped, like him; might have survived and adopted another name and life during all the years when, in the absence of family or friends, her only son shuttled between his laboratory and his little flat and the rooms of women who one by one had tried and failed to comfort him. Back and back and back and back. Where had his life gone?

He thought, *Back*, but Bianca—her foot heavy on the accelerator— thought, *Away*. She had her wallet and her sleeping bag and her running shoes and her van; and she drove as if this were the point from which the rest of her life might begin.

Nominated by Philip Levine

FRAGMENTS FROM THE BURNT NOTEBOOKS OF O. FLEMING

by FRANK POLITE

from ICON

1a
. . . (jokes) i.e. the one about the real estate agent in
Mingo, Fla . . .

3
I have since corrected this view as quoted in Mayfield's
monograph (1985) on flamingo dream studies, from
"cocks rampant" to "cocks heraldic." Today that observ-
ation would read, "Incredibly, all adult male flamingos
have the same recurrent dream; that of being designated
Cocks Heraldic on the weathervanes of Mars."

3c
In Flamingo, *storyteller* and *philosopher* are synonymous
terms, but in degree. Both tell tales, but the philosopher
tells the tallest tales.

3d
Flamingo feathers are compressed thoughts
about themselves as a species. The sum of flamingo
culture (i.e. history and literature) is recorded

in the spina, barbules, and vanes of each
flamingo's feathery mass.

7
. . . a joke to us with significant details missing
and no punchline, i.e. "Hidden and alert like the pit
of an exotic fruit."

18b
Klerb is correct in stating that all flamingo jokes
are self-referential (i.e. the one about the real estate
agent in Mingo, Fla.), but he then goes on to
cite the Bird Club Story as an example—which,
texturally, cannot be flamingo in origin.

18c
. . . vulnerability of flamingo studies—the naivete,
errors, inconsistencies, bias, and outright conscious
falsehood. See O. Fleming in FS, Fall, 1987, "The
Flamingos of Hialeah."

18d
. . . from migratory Chants—the Beloved
as the *Far-fetched,* and the Seeker as the *Far-fetcher.*
Farfetcher is often used as a variant of Flamingo in
the *Meta Sudans,* Beak-cusp Barbule IX.

19
Flamingos refer to themselves, to their species, as
Flamingo. The odds against humans actually hitting on
the term are astronomical, but it did happen. Flamingo
culture celebrates this as a Splendid Event, since it
gives them special status in the bird world. The robin
name, we are told, is *Cree,* and eagle, *Sonshiker.*

20d
. . . i.e. to a philosopher no tale is too tall to tell.
Klerb confuses this with "telltale" which is not
a flamingo concept.

22

Flamingo sensibility is particularly ∇◁♣◁☼⌐ (wounded?)
by the Britannica's description of their dwellings as
"truncated cones of marl and mud piled a few inches up
in a shallow lagoon."

22a

εε∇⊠꙰εϕϕ<△϶ . . . Randall again misunderstands flamingo
humor, a fault embedded in the 'storyteller' exegesis. In
the joke, "the one about the real estate agent in Mingo,
Fla." it is, and is not, mere word play (which includes
the self-referential) that tickles the flamingo funny bone,
but the humor implicit in the phrase, "the one about."
One, or any unit of measure, to a flamingo equals
lunacy. And Mingo, Fla., existing only in self-referential
wordplay, could not support the concept of real estate
agents laying claim to or selling plots of themselves.
Thus, the joke is entire unto itself as "The one about the
real estate agent in Mingo, Fla," with no preface,
punchline, or explication. To a flamingo, the line is a
complex treatise on the essential absurdity of any
symbolic representation of Reality, other than the joke
itself, or the tallest tale.

38

. . . as for instance, "for what it's worth." Flamingos
preface every utterance with "For what it's worth," and
then, over eons compressed that to a hiss which became
increasingly inaudible. Now it is visually experienced as a
barbule that never again need be "said." Flamingos, in
effect, read each other like books. Flocks of Britannicas
swarming together. Whole libraries in flight.

38a

. . . and (flamingos) have no conception of measure-
ment, hence they have no science. It is useless to tell
a flamingo that it migrates thousands of miles since
distance is realized in feathers read or metaphors
appreciated. Something like, but not nearly, the way

Cheyenne measured distance by how many moons
it took to travel from place to place.

39
Flamingos tell the tallest tales. They are the philosophers
of the bird world. "But," a wing-tip vane reads, "it takes an
artist to make a tale believable, which is why Plato is
more compelling, say, than Aristotle."

39a
. . . the passage cited from Holy Scripture, *In the
Beginning was the Word and the Word was made Flesh,*
to explain their species as Illuminated Manuscripts.

62c
FLAMENCO—"so you know it's from our mating dance
and not from the ritual movements of Andalusian
gypsies."—Accordia Spina XX

75
ɖ✝▽◁♡◇γ ϯ≠°° . . . fragment of a flamingo hymn to the
Sun (rendered into English by Wardle, Vane Accordia IV)
which is also (in Spina XX) a lover's lament:

FLAMING O
Flamingo
Flamingo
Flaming O
Flaming   O

Where O, where are you going,
leaving me alone
on fire
without the power
of flight.

Nominated by Icon

CIVILIZATION

fiction by TOMÁS FILER

from CHICAGO REVIEW

PERFECTO IS BACK. Ostentatious, on his own bench now a hundred feet down the sea-walk. I suppose he thinks that's a public statement. Peace again, with the old borders? Fine with me, I won't have to suffer his stinking cigars. But is it possible? I stood with this man on Thomas Ince's staircase; we faced the lion together. We rode with Carlos. Impossible.

I was a fool expecting a primitive like him to manage such a leap of the imagination. He didn't even understand what Ince's movie was about. Greek tragedy? Huh? And differences of vision aside, I should have known he'd never be able to see Carlos as I did. They were brothers, after all. A prophet in his own land, et cetera. Impossible.

We shouldn't have been friends. When I'm not talking or writing, I doubt my life. Perfecto is a warrior, a gardener who's content to let his muscles speak for him. Did you catch the Bulls game last night, *compadre?* What? Eh?

We have to be friends. I knew that when I turned my back on him in 1919. I knew it seventy-five years later when I began hearing the voices of our canyon. I knew it in 1985 when, failed at the business of making a living, my children grown and my wife dead, I decided to make a life and sat down beside Perfecto Padilla on this very bench. We just started talking. We hadn't talked since 1919! Imagine that.

For the next ten years we sat here every afternoon, at four o'clock when the weather was warm, breathing as best we could, resigned by now to the stew of poison rolling back from the cliffs over traffic gridlocked on the Coast Highway. Behind us the afternoon parade of spandexed cyclists, roller-bladers and joggers, the teen-age surfers

335

whizzing by on skateboards to catch their evening wave. We sat here, both of us waiting for something we were afraid to speak of. Until Monday, June 6th, 1994.

Our bench (ours till June 6th, ours because we carry walking sticks) faces Santa Monica Bay. It's situated on the edge of the sea-walk that runs from Venice to Temescal Canyon. That's a half mile south of where Thomas Ince built his city above the staircase in 1916. Cement bunkers housing condos flank Sunset Boulevard there now as it dumps more commuters onto the Coast Highway, a Jack-in-the Box urban slum.

Never mind, I can see it all just as it was the day we rode to Inceville. Ice plants galloping down the dunes spewing yellow and pink flowers sticky with crystal come. The air scrubbed by a spring rain and on every patch of bare earth the new grass tender as hair sprung up for the mountain's newborn. *Green.* The exact shade old Corot envisioned for the skies of heaven. I've never seen grass so green in all the years since.

"Look up there, boys," Carlos said, reining in his stallion beside the Colossus of Rhodes, his hand lifting mine (his sleeve shining from Doña Florentina's charcoal iron).

And there it was, on the highest ridge of the seven hills, crowning Mr. Ince's staircase, a dome of gold gleaming under a sun just risen like a pearl behind the scarf of night fog still wrapped around the cliffs of High Topanga. You catch the morning's mood, the emotions that overwhelm me remembering that day.

"Are you out of your mind, *compadre?*"

Perfecto said that first in 1919, three years after we did the staircase scene. Tormented by memories of recent events in France, I'd mentioned to him dreams I was having about his brother Carlos at Inceville. Then he added, unforgivably, given my poetic and philosophical intent:

"You were out cold when they shot that scene, Webb."

I just walked away then, for sixty-six years. Things got messier when he said it again on June 6th, 1994. The day started out like any other since we'd declared peace in 1985 (as a result of my overtures). Perfecto and I live a block apart, five minutes' walk from the beach (but we take forty). I walked over as usual to the cottage off Canyon Drive where he lives with his daughter Elena. Coffee and doughnuts, a pee. We spent out usual quarter hour patrolling the crosswalk at Mesa Drive, using our walking sticks to discipline speeding commuters. We chatted for five minutes with the Sweeper, a seven-foot Hercules of color who resides in the pedestrian tunnel under Pacific Coast Highway.

336

We often saw the Sweeper disappearing down the sea-walk, on his knees, broom and pan in hand. His mind gone, his work known, he greets the glassy stares of beachgoers with the smile of a saint. Perfecto says he's trying to sweep the world. At home in his tunnel, our Sweeper seems oblivious to the stink of dog shit that drives us on.

We were sitting on this very bench last June 6th when Santa Monica staged a D-Day tribute to some local heroes. News to us. It began with three warships anchored offshore shooting blanks from cannons. Perfecto was diving for the pavement when a jogger explained. Next we had to witness four old fools fake a landing in a Harbor Patrol boat done up as an LCT. They weren't actors—these were the sole survivors of an entire battalion long since relieved of duty under the stones of Normandy.

"The survivors are the heroes?" I hadn't been waiting here ten years to watch the celebration of another war.

"Not my war," Perfecto mumbled.

I should have realized he was upset. Remembering our history, I should have shut up then. I should have known better, talking to a veteran the way I did. But Perfecto just got a little pale and rigid, so I risked another shot at those dreams I'd had about Carlos, trying in a quiet and reasonable manner to explain my point of view.

Perfecto sat there like a rock till I was done, then he said it again, "You were out cold when they shot that scene, Webb."

He angered me, of course, but given our history, I would have dropped the matter if he hadn't said, "It was Wild Bill Hart and Pinto Ben on the staircase, *compadre*. My brother Carlos wasn't riding any horse that afternoon." Tonally, this remark was more offensive than the words might suggest. Then he brought up that damned old man in his white robes again, and he laughed. I am not a violent man by nature, but we both carry walking sticks.

So, here we are. I mean here I am, and there he is a quarter of a mile down the sea-walk. Peace. As in *Requiescat in pace*. Odd, but I suspect he's waiting too. What else does he have to do anymore?

"Webster, don't you dare get out of Carlos's sight!" My mother said that on April 11, 1916, as good a place as any to begin looking at how all this started. Mother was worried because 25,000 extras would be on the staircase with us.

"And you behave, Perfecto Padilla," she said, hoisting me up into Carlos's arms. Perfecto was already aboard, bitching because his big brother made him sit on Rojo's rump (where he'd get the shaking up he usually deserved).

337

"Hang on to the saddlehorn, dear!"

"What, Mom?" I had lain awake until 4 A.M. listening for Rojo. You couldn't mistake his hoof-beats, especially in a canyon where every sound reverberates. Carlos's horse, a roan stallion, weighed nearly half a ton. People in Santa Rosalia spoke his name with awe in crisis situations, knowing Carlos was close.

It's dawn, I'm nine years old and Perfecto is thirteen, already a hulk (though you wouldn't notice it next to his brother). "Hang on, son!" Huh? I can't wake up. Carlos holds me tight against his chest with one arm. I feel the play of muscle in his rein arm, hardly a twitch even when he jumps Rojo over a fallen sycamore in the creek bed. What a horse. I'm awake now.

At the mouth of our canyon, we headed north. There was no seawalk then. Mostly sand ribboning the coastline all the way to San Francisco, a dirt road as far as you dared drive. Twenty miles north at the Rindge Ranch—become Malibu today—range riders took pot shots at you.

Carlos was dressed in his Sunday finest. I suppose he was hoping Mary Ellen Sundance would smile at him on the set. He smelled of mothballs and the sweet red onions his father grew on the Padillas' little mesa. Perfecto complained about the stink of Bay Rum he'd slathered on too, but I didn't mind. The air tasted of iodine and salt.

Rojo trotted neatly around starfish and the snaky nests of brown kelp beached by an ebbing tide. It was a blue light still, almost dark under the Huntington Cliffs, which were furrowed then, collapsed in deluges and earthquakes since. Dunes rolling eastward (gone now too) were studded with yellow coreopsis trees and white spears of yucca in full flower.

Passing the ruins of Long Wharf south of the Japanese Village, Carlos waved to one of Mr. Ince's stars, Señor Sessue Hayakawa, doing his morning t'ai chi chuan in a circle of gulls. Then he said, "Hold on to your socks, boys," and gave Rojo his head. The white water in front of us was all frilled in silver by the fins of big Corbina fish rooting for sand crabs. Rojo didn't exactly shy at them, just waltzed it up a bit, with a couple of swerves and bounces which inspired some profanity from Perfecto in his rear seat. Well, it was a pleasure being aboard that big horse dancing north all the way to Inceville!

Inceville (the actual studio, that is, not to be confused with the set Mr. Ince built) was the prototype for MGM and the mammoth movie factories to follow. To get to its central complex of offices and editing

338

rooms, you turned right at Santa Ynez Canyon, just past the set for the Palace of Versailles. The creek running by the dirt road was gorged from last night's rain and Rojo didn't like it much when the banks kept collapsing inches from his hooves. Spooked by a rented elephant staked in front of the Taj Mahal set, he nearly shook me off. You could still hear the surf behind us and the cañon wrens were making a sweet racket wishing us good morning.

We were the first extras to arrive, though a goodly portion of the local population was already at breakfast inside the commissary. This population, for the interest of movie buffs not read up on Inceville, included (in addition to the usual laborers, carpenters, and technicians) the 110 performers of the 101 Wild West Show, several Keystone Kops, ninety-seven horses in a stable that could house 200 animals, and a herd of cattle.

The commissary, which could feed 300 extras at a clip, was a wood frame building like all the rest. I clearly recall a wren's nest in the porch rafters, a cup of moss and spiders' webs holding five white eggs dotted red on a lining of feathers. Inside, men laughing and shouting, the banging of silver and dishware. It didn't seem to bother the wrens.

Hitching up Rojo in front of the commissary, Carlos said, "Listen, Webster, you too *hermanito tonto*, my stupid little brother . . . " (no one else in Santa Rosalia dared speak like that to Perfecto, even at thirteen, but Carlos was a giant), "they'll pay you one silver dollar and the lunch is free, so behave, get me? I'll set you up at the foot of the stairs, and you just sit tight until you hear ACTION. I'll be busy, see?" (It seems odd now to realize that Carlos's speech patterns in everyday life—unlike crisis situations—remind me of a later star, James Cagney).

Of course Perfecto and I suspected Carlos has come up here just to see Chief Sundance's daughter, Mary Ellen. (Should heroes risk love? This question lingers too). Mary Ellen lived with her father in the Sioux encampment and I'm pretty sure Carlos was over there during the shooting, but I've never admitted that to Perfecto. It was close enough, especially for a man on a horse. Just past the dressing rooms that bordered the five main stages, next door to the sets for the English village and the Sphinx, below the stables and the Mesopotamian Temple, right under the brow of the hill where Mr. Ince built his staircase.

Carlos had no sooner finished his speech than there was a rumble, a backfire that made us jump, and Mr. Ince pulled up in his black Hupmobile convertible (the one they used in the Mack Sennett movies).

Who did we face? What is left of this great man besides his almost forgotten movies? A black homburg on his head, a cigar in a brown blunt face. A broad-chested stump of a man straining at the seams of a single-breasted, pinstriped suit.

Being human, of course, Mr. Ince saw nothing but Carlos, and I could tell the great man was thinking what we all knew: *star material.* Until, as if exhausted by so much splendor, his gaze dropped and he saw me, the runt beside the hero.

"Good," he said, and his lips pulled back from his tobacco-stained teeth in a smile of great sweetness. "Good boy, you'll remember this."

Then he turned again to Carlos, who was grooming Rojo (his mind on Mary Ellen Sundance, not stardom). "Son," Mr. Ince said, "that's a smashing horse you've got there. I'd like you to ride him in the stair-case scene today. See Kit Carson over at casting." He meant Kit Carson Junior, you understand.

Mr. Ince flicked a wooden match with his thumbnail to re-light his cigar, one of those black Italian twists as I recall. "And son, come by tomorrow, will you? I can always use a good man on a horse."

"At your service, sir," Carlos replied.

Sad to tell, Carlos Padilla would soon be in the service of an employer with intentions more subtle than Mr. Ince's. To see this in proper context, to help you understand what service in the United States Military must have meant to him, I have to tell another story. Fade Out, if you will, Fade In.

* * *

It's one month earlier, a March morning in 1916, and I ask you to imagine a snarl of tawny hide and nerves trembling in a dappled shade, an arroyo surrounded by trees bowed overhead to the memory of water. Two fierce golden eyes spiked by sunlight glaring down at you from the limb of a sycamore; baying dogs already bloody making fools of themselves, two dead, the rest trying to climb the tree—tumbling down, snapping at each other—as Lico Pena and Leo Carrillo show up with rifles.

"Webster Hanford Hayden, Perfecto Padilla!" Mother cries, "Oh damn fool boys get away from there!"

Wounded, the lion will make a run for it, possibly killing more than dogs this time (to read in a mother's mind what's unthinkable to two immortal boys). Standing in a creek bed, rocks underfoot haired in

340

weeds still slippery from winter floods, we're as likely as the sycamores to pull out of here quick.

After a swat at Perfecto (she always blamed him when I got in trouble, everyone did), Mother holds me so close I can feel her heart pounding. I look up into a rain of bobby pins, a mass of dark blonde hair shaken loose from its bun. Overhead a clerestory of sycamore leaves shaped like green hands reaches down. Then Lico Pena fires the first shot and misses.

"Oh," Mother cries as the big cat poises to spring, "Where in heaven's name is *Carlos*?"

It was like that, you see. Every good woman in Santa Rosalia Canyon, Anglo or Mexican (known equally as housewives in those days), turned to Carlos in crisis situations. There was something about him that said to the world: Here I am, use me.

Mother's words are no sooner out of her mouth than I feel the rocks jump under my boots and somewhere downstream there's a thrashing in the water willows and bracken fern. Mother turns toward the west, knowing before we do that Carlos will be riding up from the Padillas' barn. The first thing I see galloping straight at me is the white blaze on Rojo's muzzle, his great anvil of a brow thrust out from 1000 pounds of horse. A humming sound, a mother's cries of relief (and remember, mountain lions have been mistaken for a woman screaming, they do not roar like MGM's Leo). All this cut by a steaming volley of Spanish that sends Leo Carrillo and Lico into retreat with their rifles.

Then Carlos speaks to us in English, using the deep round tones (think of a bronze bell) he saves for crises. "Tie up those dogs, you crazy kids," all the while circling the tree, reins in one hand, the loop of his *reata* whirling in the other. Bareback! He took no time for a saddle when he got Mother's message.

I should add, for otherwise this scene might seem incredible, that Carlos had recently been training Rojo to rope cattle for a round-up north of Topanga Canyon. Even we, his witnesses, couldn't believe our eyes, imagine his intentions. Except perhaps for Mother whose faith in Carlos was boundless. "Oh, dear," she said (quite calmly, though she did pinch my ear), "he's dressed for church."

Carlos wore a low-crowned black hat tilted to one side (by fashion, not budged by his gallop), with the *baraquejo*—chin strap—just below his lower lip. Twenty-dollar gold pieces were set onto his silver spurs as rosettes. Leo Carrillo, who wrote a book when he became famous, remembered Carlos as wearing a blue broadcloth jacket over a white shirt,

341

and snug pantaloons with a bell at the bottom to accommodate his small boots. Leo always insisted that Carlos, though a giant, had small feet. That boy was so seldom off his horse, Leo said, why would he need big feet?

Still, all this splendor might be forgotten if Carlos Padilla had been dealing with just one treed lion. Our canyon suffered that year from a plague of lions. Its sponsor was Gandolph Smith, a squatter on the Padillas' land grant currently suing them for ownership rights (Perfecto's father, Don Guillermo, confessed during this episode that his family were flawed Americans, careless with their land and generous with their neighbors).

Gandolph Smith had a single source of income: two slaughter houses up in Santa Monica had contracted to dump their offal in an arroyo behind his ranch—this after beach riots were set off in 1915 by a stew of rotten skulls and guts contaminating local waters (pollution was less subtle in those days). It was to Gandolph's arroyo that the lions came to feed. Many soon grew too lazy to hunt for living prey, though a few dogs disappeared, and coyotes following the lions bit the tails off three calves.

When Don Guillermo and my father led a deputation to voice a protest, Gandolph's response was lofty. "This," he pronounced, "is how I make my living." (This a half century before developers and real-estate salesmen swarmed into Santa Rosalia Canyon).

However, except for the stink that sometimes wafted up the canyon on sea breezes, many of our neighbors were able to ignore this embarrassment. Some even celebrated it and held barbecue-watches for the condors that began commuting down from Ventura to gorge on the mess in Gandolph's arroyo, an awesome sight: black wings nine feet across, talons the size of gaffing hooks.

Then, one Sunday when my father was out of town on location with D. W. Griffith, our neighbor Mr. Machado heard a bawling from his barn that was not a milking call. He found two of his finest Herefords gutted (whether this was the work of a rogue lion yearning for something warmer than carrion, a bear, or marauding coyotes, no one ever knew).

Simultaneously, my own mother, sitting on our kitchen porch while editing one of Dad's screenplays, found herself facing a lion. He was crouched on our backyard fence, licking his paws, and he stank from his last meal in Gandolph's arroyo. He must have looked magnificent wreathed in the flowers of Mother's favorite cup-of-gold vine. At least my little brother thought so.

342

Clarence Eugene, playing in his sandbox under the fence, had just reached up to stroke this beauty when Mother, using language never heard before by him—she was Viennese—ran without hesitation (as Clarence remembers it) straight at the beast, a broomstick her lance.

It was no contest. The slatboard fence toppled over. The lion fled. Mother, foolishly, set our three dogs loose (two were dead minutes later) and with Clarence in her arms ran for the Padillas' barn where Carlos would be grooming Rojo to ride in the Sunday parade at Saint Monica's church. On the way she spotted me (out of earshot, or pretending to be) following Perfecto who was, classically, following the dogs. Sighting Incensia, Carlos's sister, Mother handed her Clarence and a message for Carlos, then hurried on to deliver the *Oh fool boys* aria with which I introduced her.

Now, most of us, boys or not, would have simply shot that lion if we'd had a gun like Leo Carrillo and Lico Pena. Even Mother, I suspect, if brooms came equipped with triggers. Carlos Padilla, however, while he owned a rifle, only wielded a lasso on that Sunday morning. Had his sister misunderstood Mother's message? Could it have had something to do with his falling in love with Mary Ellen Sundance at Mass the week before? Or did he already have a plan to rid us of Gandolph? I wish I'd been prescient enough to ask. These questions linger three-quarters of a century later.

I didn't count, but again credibility demands that Carlos must have missed the lion at least three times. Shadows were beginning to deepen in the glade when his *reata* looped past batting paws and snapping fangs to close on the beast's throat. How did it get to be night in the morning? Night, I can see it. Now, landing a lion in the dark on a short rope might be compared to hooking a shark with your feet in water. The thought still makes me shudder.

Coolness prevailed, Eluding clawed swipes which could have gutted him, and guided by Carlos in some language private to heroes, Rojo towed that lion screaming and spitting down the creek bed. Where? Where else?

Dusk, screams, and caterwauling, beastly and human, thumps and the bang of slammed doors splintering. No witnesses except to sounds, but the voices of our canyon speak to me: Rojo's hooves make quick work of the front door and the lion, guided by Carlos, is delivered to Gandolph Smith. I doubt that Carlos said. "Here is your lion. Señor Smith, now make a living," but I savor the notion.

No one was killed. Carlos always exerted absolute control in crisis situations. Carrion deliveries from the slaughter houses ceased the next week, and not long afterward Gandolph was seen heading east in his buckboard.

Asked how he'd used the lion to rid us of a plague, then finished off the lion without a gun, Carlos just smiled. Never mind, I can see eighty years ago far clearer than the print in this morning's *Times*. Carlos leads that roped lion tame as a chastened hound up Rustic Canyon where the springs run fresh year round, up the mountain where the old people used to worship, to a wilderness he knows. I see a lion freed from Gandolph's carrion. I see a tall boy on a red horse, saddleless, his Sunday clothes immaculate, riding home.

* * *

A month later, surrounded by 25,000 extras, Perfecto and I stood at the base of Mr. Ince's staircase. Carlos had pointed out two cameras set up in mobile wooden towers; a third was somewhere under the steps focused on our feet. Perfecto swears Mr. Ince was taking long shots with a Bell and Howell from the gondola of a hot air balloon, but I doubt that. With electrically-run cameras not yet in common use, most were either hand-cranked or run by some sort of wind-up mechanism. All were large and heavy by modern standards, not something you'd casually tuck into a balloon.

Primitive toys? Hardly. Mr. Ince—and David Griffith not far away over in Hollywood—were using the lenses of these behemoths to catch the leaps of time, the ironies and tragedies of history. Without sound. In *silence*. Imagine that if you can in 1996. The silence. The relief of that, the possibilities.

Carlos had told us to start running when someone shouted ACTION through a bullhorn—megaphones, they were called then. "Run where?" I was scared to death. I'd never been in a mob scene before. "Where's Carlos?" I said.

"Guess," Perfecto said.

"Run where?" I said.

"*Up* the stairs, dummy," Perfecto said, "To the city."

Even I, a nine-year-old boy, could see the capital dome through all those extras—a blaze of gold limning thousands of butts and backs. I remember that much clearly.

Then someone shouted ACTION.

The images flicker. No sound but the breathing of the actors until that shout, a sort of voice-over effect, nothing the audience in a darkened theater would experience, not in the movie—anyway, this was long before talkies. Maybe it was one of the directors (four of them, Perfecto says), but my best guess is Mr. Ince or God because I could swear that shout came from above our heads.

*   *   *

I never told my parents what happened to me on Mr. Ince's staircase. To begin with it would have been disloyal to Mother. As much as Dad admired Carlos, he understood the vicissitudes of the business, and would never have allowed his son to become involved in a mob scene. Mother had granted me permission, exhausted by my whining on the day Carlos rebuilt our backyard fence (the one the lion knocked down). She never dreamed Carlos might fail her. Well, no one knew yet that Carlos was in love.

A few lapses follow. Seventy-eight years have passed since our day at Inceville, and circumstances then make it necessary to rely for some details on the questionable memory of Perfecto Padilla. For example, while declaring me *non compos* when I mention a winged horse. Perfecto insists he saw a bearded old man in white robes standing at the top of Mr. Ince's staircase.

Later, my own mother actually saw Mr. Ince's movie and she never sighted any old man. So, if we accept Perfecto's version, this character must have ended up on the cutting room floor, as they say. I wish I knew, I wish I could talk to Mr. Ince again, because if that old man was really *in Mr. Ince's script,* it changes the whole story.

Long ago I read something by a Frenchman named de Goncourt whose conceit it was to view our earth as a museum; I seem to recall he declared a sort of Armageddon would befall us if we ever achieved the perfection envisioned by Mr. Ince in his movie. De Goncourt's museum had a caretaker, a bearded patriarch, who on the earth's final day stood by the exit doors declaring to one and all:

"It's closing time."

Absurd, except when I imagine de Goncourt's caretaker as a dead ringer for the old man Perfecto saw. Never mind, these French always take the dark view, and of this much I'm certain: Mr. Ince was American to the core.

As you may recall, Perfecto also claimed William S. Hart took Carlos's part on the staircase (for young readers not up on film history, William Hart and his horse Pinto Ben were the first big cowboy stars). Doubting Perfecto or not, I have to confess Perfecto's reporting must have had an effect, because even before his big brother left for France, I couldn't see Carlos on that staircase anymore (my dreams about the winged horse came later).

Instead, there was this weathered, whip-thin type, different but not much different from the heroes of all the Western ballets to follow— Gary Cooper, John Wayne, Henry Fonda, Clint Eastwood (white as snow under their leather chaps, of course, unlike Leo Carrillo who got all the comedy parts). Try as I might, all I could see was William Hart thundering up our staircase; and always the mob (or the Masses as I suspect Mr. Ince named us in his script) parting before him.

Carlos lost to me for almost eighty years! It hurts to be reminded of things like that. And so my small war started again on June 6th. Perfecto just wouldn't let up, insisting his damned old man was at the top of our staircase. But the situation didn't really escalate until he laughed again at my dreams about Carlos on a winged horse, and that's when I whacked Perfecto Padilla with my walking stick.

* * *

Back in 1916 some people said Mr. Ince's set was as big as the one going up for D. W. Griffith's epic film, *Intolerance.* My father laughed at that. "The only thing Ince's got as big as David Llewelyn Wark Griffith, Sonny, is an ego." Ego? A new word to me. It seems Dad, some dreams still intact, had been reading Sigmund Freud on the recommendation of an old pal from the Provincetown Players, the great American playwright, Eugene O'Neill.

Dad, a starving playwright himself once, had come west to be a writer for D. W. Griffith and the studios that buried him. He became a good father and provider, unlike his friend O'Neill who lived a messy life—one son a suicide, I believe—before receiving the Nobel Prize for literature in 1936. In any case, big cannot be argued—the set for Mr. Griffith's *Intolerance,* the walls of ancient Babylon, currently towered over cottages along Sunset Boulevard in Hollywood.

However, this is history too: the set that William Ince built above the staircase took sixty carpenters three months to build, and materials alone cost $80,000, far from peanuts in those days. All for a sequence that lasted one minute and three-quarters, 100 feet of film.

But if for no other reason than the number of bodies Mr. Ince put into motion, I'm convinced he couldn't have failed to capture an enormity of energy, chutzpah, and hope on the staircase he built. Guesswork again—I've never been able to watch the movie, and I've grown to hate its title.

When he got past big, Dad (employed by Mr. Griffith in 1916) insisted Mr. Ince's movie was sure to be a flop. "Sonny," he said, "You're too young to understand such things yet, but for the record, Ince's montage techniques—his cross-cutting, the close-ups, everything—is monkey-see-monkey-do stolen from Griffith. Even so, most of his pictures are filmed like stage plays. No action, sonny."

"Doesn't Mack Sennett work for Mr. Ince, Dad?" Just the week before Perfecto and I had watched a black Hupmobile convertible rocking on the cliff edge above Bundy Bath House. "A blonde lady in a white dress and four Keystone Kops were hanging on for dear life, Dad, while a gang of crooks took potshots at them, and *then* . . ."

"Exceptions don't make the rule, son."

*   *   *

It's my pleasure to report that even Dad's imagination was finally struck by what Mr. Ince built. One day, scouting locations for Mr. Griffith, he took me with him to the top of Griffith Park (not, sadly, named for the great director, but a homicidal millionaire, Colonel Griffiths Jenkins Griffiths, who after shooting his wife almost dead, gave the land to the city).

From there, from Griffith Park—eighteen miles away—even Dad could see William Ince's set on the bluff above the seven hills (where it lasted, endured awhile—alas, did not prevail—before being destroyed by fire, by looting, by the times). "Why," Dad said, "that's not a set, sonny, it's architecture."

And so we looked at it together, my father and I, from that great distance—the gold dome of the capitol building and towers of the city Mr. Ince built to celebrate his theme—a splendor set against the sea which rose like a shining dam on that spring day to hold back the sky. Mr. Ince's movie was in release by then and he'd been invited to the White House by President Wilson, another advocate for peace.

347

"Well," my father said, "well, well." His boss, Mr. Griffith, was still shooting *Intolerance* over in Hollywood and running out of money. Dad wasn't worried. Peace was all the rage that year. In a little village south and east of Mr. Ince's set, they would even name a street for peace, Via de La Paz. You can drive down it to this day, but be careful at its dead end—the cliffs are sliding.

* * *

It's hard to go on, to confess my naivete, as I sit here alone on my concrete bench. But I want to remind you that no one else arrived on horseback that day at Inceville, and no one else arrived so very early, excepting Mr. Ince. Minor actors, the common run of extras, if they weren't locals, all took the red trolley line to the ruins of the Long Wharf just north of Santa Monica Canyon, where buckboards awaited them.

"Good." Mr. Ince said to me that morning, "Good boy, you'll remember this." Could it be that he sensed I'd try some day to write this story about his set? Of course, Perfecto swears Mr. Ince was looking at him, not me, as a possible recruit for stardom.

No question that Carlos was too busy thinking about Mary Ellen Sundance to pay much attention to Mr. Ince's offer; he never showed up for work the next day. I take that, however, to be evidence of character, not slackness—stardom of the sort Mr. Ince offered just wasn't Carlos's style.

As for Carlos's absence during the staircase scene, a disappointment to me, what can I say, finally? Perfection is elusive. Maybe heroes should be flawed, should fall in love and fumble on occasion, so we can know them as human, like us, so we can bear some responsibility too. Who of us would want to be as perfect, as lonely as God? I don't know, though I suspect some of us need our dreams of heroes, to live by.

The truth is, as Perfecto reminded me on June 6th, I can't claim to be a witness anyway. Just after somebody shouted ACTION to 25,000 extras, I fell down. Luckily the staircase was made of wood painted to *look* like marble, a relatively soft landing. Still, I'm lucky to be alive to tell what I do know. Perfecto didn't see my fall, and the cameras kept rolling.

The next thing I remember is the beach whizzing by, Carlos arms around me, and Perfecto complaining as usual on Rojo's rump. We had to make up a story for Mother on the way—I had a black eye.

Thomas Ince's movie was very popular for awhile. In 1916 it helped get President Wilson reelected on the peace platform.

In 1917, as you know, President Wilson declared war on Germany. The effect on Mr. Ince's box office receipts was disastrous, and Mr. Griffith's *Intolerance* fared even worse. From what I've read, this marked the beginning of the end for these great filmmakers, though like Perfecto in his final years of boxing, they stayed in the ring. Bravo.

William Hart, the cowboy star, left with Mr. Ince's luck, along with Mack Sennett and his Keystone Kops, the 101 Ranch Wild West Show, and the Sioux Indian tribe—some to Paramount, others to the Army. Perfecto, lying about his age, followed his big brother to "the France" (as he calls it), but suffered no ill effects from his first war except grief and a lifelong passion for boxing.

Carlos? As you'd expect, he was among the first to enlist (he always is), but only after President Wilson made it clear to him that this was the Great War to End Wars. A War for Peace, as they say. In the cavalry, of course, though Rojo was declared too skittish for military duty. And Carlos was not among the chosen who rode. For a time he polished the boots of white men in fashionable Squadron A of New York City, until the Army declared horses obsolete and Carlos was issued a machine gun.

What happened to him overseas? I don't know, the voices of our canyon fail me here. May I guess that by now his unstained heart was broken, as they say? May I guess that without a horse, his finger on the trigger, Carlos lost it, as they say? That crawling across treeless plains plowed deep in the blood of his brothers, dreams of Rojo winged for battle exhausted Carlos Padilla and made him stupid, a careless warrior whose feet were too small. But no bullet could touch him. The rest is history, not a guess. In 1918, during a mustard gas attack at Chateau-Thierry, Private Carlos Padilla removed his mask. The Army diagnosed it as an act of panic. In 1919 Carlos died in his sleep. Mary Ellen did not wait for him.

*   *   *

To this day I remain troubled by that old man Perfecto claims was standing at the top of Mr. Ince's staircase. Was he really in the great man's script? Our local historian, Betty Lou Young, reassures me. In her perception, the Masses in Mr. Ince's movie would not have stood still for exit lines pronounced by some "Caretaker."

She declares Mr. Ince's plot and theme to be Grecian, that its final scene followed a battle for a new world, led by a secret society of "crazed women" (you understand I'm quoting Betty Lou) who have pledged themselves to bear no more "cannon fodder"—that's how people talked in those days. Where we all came in, Betty Lou says, eternal peace had been proclaimed and was being celebrated by the Masses—our scene, our moment, *us*—rushing up Mr. Ince's staircase to the capital of Civilization. That's what Mr. Ince called his movie.

* * *

I regret nothing! Admittedly, I was the one who declared war. Maybe if someone with the talents of our current Secretary of State, Mr. Christopher, were in charge of public affairs locally, he'd advise me to make another overture. But what's the use? I know what Perfecto would say. I know what I'd do. And this time he might kill me. Look at those hands, *hams!* Eighty men decked in Ocean Park Arena, the fifty years since spent hauling the roots of Padilla Grass out of rich men's gardens.

Sometimes, sitting here looking out over Santa Monica Bay, my thoughts wander as they often do lately, and I see that cowboy star, what's-his-name, on our staircase, and I edit him as Mr. Ince might, as I edit Perfecto's damned old man. Sometimes, I hear a humming overhead where Mr. Ince or God shouted ACTION long ago, and looking up to the top of our staircase, I see a dark prince armed only with a *reata,* astride a Pegasus trained to rope lions in air untainted by carrion.

I think thoughts like that, while Perfecto sits on his bench a quarter of a mile away, watching the roller-bladers in their tights and discussing the World Cup soccer scores with some other old fool. I think of last June 6th, watching the celebration of another war, trying to talk to that man about Mr. Ince's staircase and his brother Carlos and a horse with wings, but what's the use?

Where was I? Did I say Mr. Ince alone braved the drive from Culver City each morning in his Hupmobile convertible, early, bright and early, rain or shine? He was an up-and-at-'em sort of fellow with an eye for the open road and an eye for the story. Not much to slow the great man down in April but arroyos and canyons (though in winter rains even he might have chosen a horse, faced by flooded roads of gumbo

350

mud). He passes truck farms on some flat stretches, but it's mostly desert still before we steal the Owens Valley water. Each March, rolling seas of green and gold and purple stretch as far as the eye can see around the little islands of Culver City, Santa Monica, and Beverly Hills—lupine, poppies, the lavender spires of wild turnips tangled in spinning fields of yellow mustard seeded by Father Serra in 1779.

And as Mr. Ince drives on into autumn, his nostrils sprung wide by the bite of roadside sage crushed beneath his tires, this gorgeous sea becomes a plain all gray and umber, torch dry before he reaches winter and . . . Where was I?

Oh yes, the fires. Fires on the plain, fires on the mountain, until at night it seems as if the sun has risen. The fires continue to plague us, as you know, in the city too now, while Perfecto and I sit here waiting for the messengers of God.

"Carlos." The word catches in his throat. Old men grow wary of speaking aloud the names of their ghosts. "It was Carlos on the staircase, Webb."

I feel something the size of a small ham patting my knee, not lightly—clenched, it once decked seventy-eight contenders in the Ocean Park Arena. The gesture is swift, the diplomacy heavy. We're an old couple, shy in tenderness. But I think we'll be able to talk again, two old men who sometimes hear each other. We'll talk, glad to be here for another sunset in peace or war. Friendship, the last romance.

Nominated by Molly Giles

OYSTERS AND OTHER WORKERS

by TURNER CASSITY

from THE CHATTAHOOCHEE REVIEW

The only jewel that is biological,
Except as greed is biological, a pearl
Is not described in cut or carat. As with flesh,
Its luster, shape, and color, not its kilos, count.
It is its raw inclusion that creates the pearl;
Is it to irritation that the body owes?
Creative as the serpent's question in the mind
A serpent's tooth infecting the Edenic clay.
And do the divers whose existence is the nacre,
Like the miners whose is carbon, when the gem
Is in its mounting have their bitterness for Eve
Or for the Mammon who she is at one remove?
The irritant is value-added for the shellfish,
The diamond grace-under-pressure of the coal.
Ghost of the Slaver, Captain of the Dhow, Mine Captain,
Admit what well you know: the VAT begins
At nil; the pearl of great price may have been a black.

Nominated by The Chattahoochee Review

THE WINGS

fiction by KRISTIN KING

from CALYX

WHEN THEY WERE married in the Salt Lake Temple, she saw how it would be after she died, in the resurrection. Marriage was a dry run for immortality, a message from God telling them what it would be like. Wing-back chairs, crystal-and-gold chandeliers, oak, marble, stained glass letting in the daylight, beige walls with paintings of Christ beckoning his rag-clad followers, ceilings so high she could hardly see them. She thought of God in the spaces between the walls, airy, just beyond what she could see, so big He filled the entire place, or standing just behind her, vanishing when she turned. When she and her husband were married, they were covered in white up to their necks, and all their guests were covered in white. The temple was even covered in white. Her husband stood in the inmost room, the holiest, loveliest, right there next to God's heart, she thought, separated from her by a curtain, and then he pulled her in. This is how it would be.

On Sunday morning, oh, it was always so hard to get everyone in order. The boys wouldn't be dressed, or they would dress in nice shirts and pajama bottoms, or they would not have remembered to brush their teeth until they were almost out the door. She had to find the right dress, remember what she'd worn all those last Sundays, find some pantyhose that matched. Her husband, though, was always there, right on time, perfect. Once they got to church, they sat in the fifth row. There were always the same number of songs before the Sacrament, two. The bishop told them what was going on in the ward, like a holy news reporter. Then they took the Sacrament, then different people (it didn't matter who) talked about the Lord.

353

There at church everyone knew what to do. The little one was even old enough not to bang his legs against the seat.

On Sunday night, this particular Sunday night, she was satisfied. Things went as planned. The chicken dinner—chicken baked in mushroom sauce and potatoes whipped in her blue mixing bowl—went as planned. The children behaved. On nights like this, she didn't go up on the rooftop. She offered herself up to her husband just like she offered up her sins to God, and then she slept the whole night long. She never woke up once, not even to go to the bathroom.

On Monday morning after everyone had left, she sat on the living room couch with a cup of honey tea. Everyone was where they were supposed to be: at school, at work. The boys would come home for lunch and she would make them split pea soup and tuna fish sandwiches. For dinner it would be lasagna; she'd have to start that early.

In between the lunch and dinner, though, she wasn't sure what would happen. That was bad, three hours where anything might happen. But it would be fine; she'd read her scriptures, the Book of Mormon, the part where Alma says to his people that Christ can never vary from what's right, that Christ's course is one eternal round. Yes, everything would be all right.

That night she turned on the electric heater and waited for her soft husband to come to bed. She hoped he wouldn't want anything and when he kissed her she turned away. When he lay back down, she put her arm around his body and kissed his shoulder. Good night, she said.

Sometimes, like tonight, when she couldn't sleep, she would open the window and go out to the roof. Part of the roof, just for decoration, slanted just past her window; she would climb up that part like a cat, with her bare feet and her hands. She would go up partway to the top, where the roof narrowed to a point, staying on just by using the friction between her body and the red roof tile. Or she might climb toward the back of the house, where the roof flattened out. There, it was covered with sticky black tar. Afterward, when she came back, her hands and feet would be gritty with bits of red roof tile and sometimes sticky with black tar, and she'd get bits of tar or red tile on her white sheets. But before that happened she could feel the cool air and look at the darkness; she could feel how nighttime felt without her husband.

In the morning she had things to do. After breakfast there were spots of blackberry jam on the table that she had to wipe off, hope they wouldn't stain. A drawer that could be organized. In a few days she would have to make cookies for the ward party because it was her turn.

354

She could go to the grocery store today, especially since her husband was out of shaving cream and they were a little low on catsup.

At night he asked her, Why don't you want to do it, and she said, I won't mind, really. It was just not important for her. Not interesting. She would rather feel the wisps of his chest hair with her fingers, have his arm protecting her back. She was willing enough, though, and when they finished she reached for a roll of toilet paper to clean it all up, then she went into the bathroom and sat on the toilet, letting it drip away from her. This had to be better than douches, because douches just push it up farther. Not that she didn't want any more babies, oh no, because she did. Really she did.

When she came back to bed she watched him sleep, because he was beautiful. She smelled the sweet smell of Drakkar on his neck. She wondered what she would smell like wearing Rose Petal, and would it clash with his cologne? She put her head down on the pillow and tried to relax, breathing in and out with her chest, then her abdomen, then her sides. She stared at the wall. Then she saw a puff of white out the window.

Who are you? she called, and when nothing answered she got up and opened the window, and the puff flew away to a tree in the neighbor's yard. She climbed out onto the roof for a better look, and the puff of white flew behind her house, so she had to climb all the way to the top of the roof, standing up and holding onto the pointed edge with her hands. She saw long red hair, softly clawed feet, wings that folded perfectly into the body. Come back, she said, and she almost lost her balance trying to see the angel's face. But the angel didn't pay any attention, just lifted its clawed foot to its mouth and nibbled on it. Then it unfurled its wings, each of them six feet long, and flew off toward the south.

In the morning she didn't want a bubble bath but she wanted her honey tea. She wanted to call Sister Mortensen but she didn't. She thought she might want to make the cookies that day instead of the day after, so she got out the butter and nutmeg and milk and eggs and sugar and flour and put it all in a mixing bowl, but then she looked closely and noticed there were bugs crawling around in the flour, and she had to take everything outside and dump it in the garbage. She hosed the bowl down before she brought it back in the house, but even so she was a little worried that the bugs might have crawled someplace, so she got out the bleach and disinfected the floors and then the cabinet. By the time that was done the boys were home, so she didn't have any time to go to the store and get more flour. Butter too, she'd used up most of the butter.

At dinner she made up for not baking cookies like she should have by getting a pound cake out of the freezer and serving it after the spaghetti casserole. Really, they didn't go together, but no one seemed to mind. In bed her husband seemed happier than ever, so she lay there and thought about the scriptures. Her body was a temple, not to be defiled by passionate thoughts or actions or anything else—dirty words, coffee, wine. In real life you had to have a slip of paper, signed by your bishop, in order to go into the temple. Everyone protected the temple. But your body had nobody to protect it but you.

After he was asleep she had an idea, and she went downstairs to get a bit of leftover pound cake. She went back upstairs to the bedroom window, opened it, held the pound cake out at arm's reach. The angel had been hovering in the next yard, and it circled close, closer, and looked at the pound cake with its small black eyes, but would not take it. She put the pound cake on the roof and shut the window and watched. The angel flew closer and closer until she could see its body, saw that it had tattoos on its legs, pink flowers circling green dragons the way the tattoos circled the angel's legs. Then the angel grabbed the pound cake with its clawed foot and flew away.

Night after night it was like that. The angel would fly closer and closer, until the woman could sit on top of the roof and hold the food (a bit of apple, a piece of bread, who knows what angels like best?) away from her body, and the angel would come. She could see parts of the naked angel, enough to know it was a woman, but she would look away from those parts, ashamed, down to the tattooed legs or up at the dirty white wings. She grabbed at the wings once, not knowing why, but the angel backed off the edge of the roof and rose high above her. The angel did not come back that night.

Days the woman could not seem to do anything after everyone had left, so she went back to bed and watched the red digits on her alarm clock shift. Things went undone: crumbs of toast sat on the carpet and were taken away by ants, lunches didn't get ready in time, the toy Count from Sesame Street lay on the kitchen floor for two days before she noticed him and put him back in his Sesame Street house. Her husband pretended not to notice, figuring, she thought, it was that time of the month. But all that time, she was planning. She would catch the angel by its tattooed legs and *make* her carry her to where the angels go. Yes, and she would carry a bag of rice, dyed green, and drop it on the way so she could find the angel's home again in the morning, after everyone had left.

One night she stood on the tarred part of the roof and offered the angel, who was crouching in a tree, some raisins. The angel moved toward the woman and opened her wings, looking as if she would take hold of the woman with them and pull her toward her chest. Then the woman saw the tattoos weren't just on the angel's legs, but climbed up the sides of her body and spread out toward her wings. The woman touched the angel on her soft stomach, in the safe place between the pubic hair and the breasts, and the angel folded in on herself like a little piece of origami. Then the woman stroked the soft wings, smoothing the feathers that were sticking out awkwardly, flicking away the white dandruffy bits of dead skin. The angel opened her wings a little and made a soft bird cry. The woman offered her raisins again, but the angel didn't take them. She just watched the woman for a while, smelling sweaty and creamy and nicely sour, then moved her head back and forth the way birds do when they are about to fly, and beat her wide wings at the air until she lifted up.

The woman wanted to do that, too. She spread her arms but they were not wings, and they did not lift her up. She walked to the side of her roof and wondered for a minute what would happen if she walked right off the edge. Then she thought, in the morning they would find me and what would they think? Possessed by demons. Yes, that was it. There was once a bishop who wanted to know more about the occult, who studied Church books and then academic books and finally the books written by people who loved the devil, until one day he lifted three feet off the floor of the dining room and started banging his head on the ceiling. His wife called a man in the Stake Presidency who called a man in the Quorum of the Twelve, who came over and prayed softly to the Lord for an hour until the man fell to the floor, having learned his lesson. Who sells eternity to get a toy?

She scooted down the roof and climbed back in the window. The grains of roof tile fell off her feet onto the floor, and she left them there when she got back into bed. She rolled her husband's body over onto hers, and he said, Huh? She tried to pray but how could she, there was nothing to say if she wasn't going to say she was sorry. Then she went to sleep. She dreamed of dark holes that make you disappear if you touch them. She dreamed she was disappearing.

In the morning the can opener didn't work; every time she tried to use it the detachable attachment came off, and she couldn't make any tuna fish. The boys had to have peanut butter for lunch instead. When she walked by the broom closet, the little whoosh of wind she made caught the broom and it fell down, clackety-clack-bang. A candle fell out of her hand and rolled into the fireplace, got covered with ashes. The dishwasher leaked and when she pulled out the lower rack to take a look she found a lump of seaweed in it: how did seaweed get in her house? It was the house, yes, it had to be the house against her. It didn't like her on its roof? She didn't know. Or maybe it was what she knew in the back of her head, that she couldn't have both things, the angel and the perfect house. She could only have one or the other.

Saturday night she lay in bed and tried to sleep. When she shut her eyes, a voice like the man on television earlier that night told her about the New World snowy egret, its long neck and long legs, the way male and female together cared for the young, how millinery had nearly wiped it out. She could feel her husband pawing at her with fuzzy bear hands and she turned toward him, but in her half-sleep she was still there, with the snowy egret. Afterward she got up and sat on the toilet while the semen leaked out, and then she went back to bed and tried to sleep, tried to sleep, until she couldn't stand it and she *had* to go out onto the roof with the peeled orange she had by the bedside (so yes, she had planned it, she had to say that, she was guilty of meaning to do it) and wait for the angel. When the angel finally came, she fed her the way she would feed a lover, the way her husband fed her cream puffs once until she laughed and turned her head away. She fed her slice by slice, not pulling her hand away until the angel's wet lips touched her fingers. Then she stroked the feathers on the angel's wings, and she touched the inky tattoo on her thigh to feel whether the skin was smooth or rough. She could feel (oh so lightly) the outline of leaves on the angel's legs, and she could smell (only just barely) flowers, like lilies.

When she went back to bed she stroked her husband's leg to see if it felt like the angel's, but it was just hairy. She rubbed the hairs on his thigh and felt them with her finger pads. Then she had to feel his penis; that would be softer, smoother, and it was. When she cupped it in her hand, she felt it start to grow, and she started rubbing and squeezing it the way she saw him do when he thought she was asleep. She felt tremendous, ticklish, as if she were as big as an airplane or rolling through dandelions. Her whole body itched. By the time he woke up she was already on top of him, and by the time they were done she had licked, bitten just as much as he.

358

On Sunday morning she panicked when she woke up, as if someone were dying. Her heart beat fast, it must have been 140 beats a minute, until she checked to see that her husband and boys were all there. Then she opened her closet door and the bar that held all the clothes hangers fell, everything crashing to the ground. She shut the door, quick, but nobody came to yell at her and she opened it again and picked out a dress. Her husband could fix the bar on Monday but until then all her clothes would have to be on the floor. Dust would settle on them, bugs crawl over them.

Later, when she cracked open an egg to make breakfast, a chick popped out, said Cheep, and fell onto the counter, dead. She wanted to sit down then, quit, cry, but she couldn't let the boys see the chick. She took it outside to give it a proper burial, and when she got back in the house her dress had somehow gotten dirt on it.

But the husband and the boys, they were spotless. After breakfast they all got in the car and drove to church. They sat down and then Sister Mortensen sat down with her five little girls, all of them wearing the dresses Sister Mortensen had sewn, lavender floral prints with puffy sleeves. She'd have sewn dresses for her girls, too, only she didn't have girls, she had boys. She brushed another bit of dirt off her own dress, bought at a store in the mall. And then the other thing was, how would she have found the time for all that sewing? She noticed a bit of slime near the hem of her dress, probably from the chick. She didn't know why she hadn't changed into another dress.

When they passed the Sacrament around, she didn't take it, even though Sister Mortensen was watching. Next week she would take it; she'd shut the blind and not go near the angel, not once.

After church she asked the bishop if they could talk, and they went into his office. She didn't know how she could say to him, I have been, night after night, going up to my roof for love of an angel. In the end she said, I desire a woman. He wanted to know, Who, does she reciprocate, and she couldn't say. Have you acted on it, he said, and she said, No. Keep your scriptures nearby, he said, hold them close to your heart. This is grave but with the help of the Lord we will prevail. The bishop's forehead wrinkled and she left the room, embarrassed.

That evening her husband came back from going to the temple (or so he said), and something wasn't right; he had a funny glow like he'd had his face near a fire. He grinned with all his teeth and held the oldest boy upside down by his legs, to shake out all the yellow, he said laughing, and the oldest boy laughed, too. The boy struggled and then

359

fell on the ground with a bang, but then he sat up again and untied her husband's shoelaces. I have a present, her husband said, and he took saltwater taffy out of his pockets to give to them.

I have a present for you, too, he said to her later, when they were in the bedroom, and he gave it to her: a purple nylon leotard with a hole between the legs, black panties, and a black dress that looked as though it had been shrunk. Oh, she said. Put them on, he said. Oh, she said. Do I take off the garments? she said. Is that against the rules? and he rubbed his hand all though her hair and down her neck, so it tingled and she had to pull away. She could put the leotard on, and the panties, but the dress was so tight he had to help her pull it over her shoulders, and he had to zip up the zipper. It was long and sleek and dark.

Turn around for me, he said, smiling. Should I ? she said. Sure, he said. She spun around in her stocking feet. She didn't feel holy enough. When he pulled her toward the bed she said, Let's sleep with the blind shut, I can't sleep with it open. She pulled the covers up over her body like a turtle and shut her eyes. She thought holy thoughts, and half fell asleep. After he had finished and put her black panties back on she woke up a little and watched the ceiling, which spinned. Spun. She was not going to open the blinds, she was not going to go out there, that was that. Final. She'd wake him up first, tell him she wanted it, before she would go out there again. If she went out, would it all spin, the stars, the moon, or would it be the house spinning under her? She was not going to go out. In the morning, at six-fifty, she would wake up, make lunches, make orange juice from concentrate. Little glasses for her and the children, a big glass for her husband. By seven-thirty they would all be gone. Not going out. Then she would sit around reading her scriptures. She was not going out. Or maybe there wouldn't be time for that; she'd have to take a shower and clean the house before ten, when she had to meet with Sister Jensen to plan out the songs for the next Sunday. Then she remembered what she was wearing, and she meant to take it all off and put her garments back on, but instead, feeling the way the black panties pushed into her skin, she moved her legs a little to make the panties push even better. She fell asleep and woke up once, when she thought she heard the sad sound of claws at the window.

In the morning the alarm didn't go off. Her husband had to go to work without shaving, dirty-chinned, and then the younger boy hit the older boy on the cheek, hard, and how could she send him to school with a bruise? What would they think? Then she went back to bed, forgot all about Sister Jensen and when Sister Jensen came all she could find to wear was a cotton dress with a rip down the side, held closed by a safety pin. Tattered. The day was tattered. Wouldn't it be getting better, though? Wouldn't the house calm down, now that she was done with the angel?

That night she had no mushroom sauce, so she tried to use tomato sauce instead. The chicken came out looking bloody, with loose clumps of tomato looking like raw bits of skin. Poor carcass, her son said. Her husband ate, maybe to be kind, maybe thinking he would be rewarded later, ha! As soon as she thought that, she thought, I should not be thinking that about him, poor thing.

All the men in her life fidgeted after dinner. The younger boy ran his train around the living room carpet, saying vrr-r-rr, and the older boy switched the television set on and off. Her husband unbuttoned his pants and walked from room to room, Looking for something, he said every time she asked. She went upstairs and took off everything for him, even the garments, and put on a T-shirt nightgown, but by the time he finally sent the boys to bed and came upstairs she was asleep, the blankets wrapped tightly against her body. In her dreams, giant headless chickens flew at her, enraged. Then she thought she felt her husband reaching for her in the dark, and after that, when she thought perhaps he was still working at it, she thought she heard the pitter-patter of her son's footsteps. Laughing in whispers, just outside the door, listening to them. She started awake; she rolled over to touch her husband and he was not there. Where was he? In the bathroom? She waited but she didn't hear anything. She got up and then she thought, the roof.

She opened the window and climbed up the grainy red tile, but no one was there. Then she heard sounds, like soft breathing and touching. She climbed toward the back of the house, where the black tar was, and no one was there. It was cold, and she tried to cover herself better with her T-shirt nightgown, but a bit of wind came and exposed her pubic hair. Suddenly she thought—and why hadn't she ever thought this before?—that someone could see her, out there on the roof! She hurried back toward the tile, nearly falling off the roof, and clambered up it, then down again toward the bedroom window. But in her way, blocking the window, there was the angel, half-sitting, half-lying, and facing her husband, who was touching her between her legs with his hand. He couldn't! They couldn't! Oh, but didn't she deserve it, such a bad wife, not staying in the house like an ordinary woman but having to come out to the roof every night and, she had to admit, she wanted to do what her husband was doing. It was her fault. She sat down on the roof and the angel looked up at her (probably seeing, like all the neighbors might have seen, those vile pubic hairs), but the woman had to look away so she wouldn't see the places her husband was touching. She would just wait until they were done; that was all.

But she couldn't. The wind snuck in through the holes in the fabric of the tee shirt nightgown, licking her nipples, no matter how tightly she crossed her arms in front of them, and she knew the Lord was looking down on her, shaking his head. And something was coming inside of her, slow like a steamroller, but coming steadily, until she knew what it was. It was what Jesus did when he saw the money-changers. She stood up and ran toward the angel, shouting, Shoo! so that the angel lost her balance and toppled off the roof. She opened her wings just before she reached the ground, and then made a lonely wail and flew away. She flew south without looking back, until she was just a dot in the sky.

Then the woman climbed back in through the window, put on her garments, and went straight to bed, lying stiff and still when her husband followed. In the morning it would be all right again; yes, it had to be. She'd have sheets to wash, breakfasts and lunches to make. In the morning she'd get up, she'd have her honey tea, she'd take her bubble bath, she'd go to the store and buy some more light bulbs to replace the ones that had burned out in the kitchen.

Nominated by Daniel Orozco

FOR THE YOUNG MEN
WHO DIED OF AIDS

by JULIA VINOGRAD

from ZEITGEIST PRESS

The dead lovers are almost as beautiful
as razor-edged spaces in the air where they used to walk.
Do you remember his hand lazily playing
with the rim of a glass, making the ghost of a bell sound
for his own ghost, and the talk didn't even pause?
That glass is whole. Break it; break it now.
Break everything.
How can people go on buying toothpaste
and planning their summer vacations?
Vegetables would care more.
The potato has a thousand eyes all mourning for the lovers
who lived in their deaths like a country
foreign to everywhere for a long time before dying.
A long time watching people look away.
The potato only met them under the earth
after their deaths and still it wept. And we do not.
The ghost bell makes barely a sound forever.
The dead lovers are still in love, but no one else is.
He took his hand with him, a grave is as good
as a briefcase to keep the essentials in:
a smile, bones, a way of biting his lip
just before looking into your eyes.
Shoulder blades cutting into summer like butter.
All the commuters in a rush hour traffic jam

are cursing because the lovers are dying
faster than their cars.
The child sent to bed without dinner cries
for the lovers, also sent to bed early and without.
Unfair. Throw the dishes against the wall. Break them.
The dead lovers are almost as beautiful
as when they were alive.
You can hear the rim of a glass
tolling for the ghosts to come home.
Break the glass, break the ghosts. Pull down the sky.
Break everything.
Dance on the fragments. Scream their names.
Get splinters of ghosts under your skin
torn and bleeding because it hurts,
                because it hurts so bad.

Nominated by Antler

RHYMING ACTION

by CHARLES BAXTER

from MICHIGAN QUARTERLY REVIEW and (*Burning Down The House*
GRAYWOLF PRESS)

after Virgil Thomson°

FOR THE LAST THREE hundred years or so, prose writers have, from
time to time, glanced over in the direction of the poets for some guid-
ance in certain matters of life and writing. Contemplating the lives of
poets, however, is a sobering activity. It often seems as if the poets have
extracted pity and terror from their work so that they could have a
closer first-hand experience of these emotions in their own lives. A
poet's life is rarely one that you would wish upon your children. It's not
so much that poets are unable to meet various payrolls; it's more often
the case that they've never heard of a payroll. Many of them are
pleased to think that the word "salary" is yet another example of eso-
teric jargon.

I myself am an ex-poet. My friends the poets like me better now that
I no longer write poetry. It always got in the way of our friendships, my
being a poet, and writing poems. The one thing that can get a poet ir-
ritated and upset is the thought of another poet's poems. Now that I
do not write poetry, I am better able to watch the spontaneous com-
bustion of poets at a distance. The poets even invite our contempla-
tion of their stormy lives, and perhaps this accounts for their recent

°See chapter 3, "Survivors of an Earlier Civilization," in Thomson's *The State of Music* (1939;
rev. ed., New York: Vintage, 1962).

production of memoirs. If you didn't read about this stuff in a book, you wouldn't believe it.

Prose writers, however, are no better. Their souls are usually heavy and managerial. Prose writers of fiction are by nature a sullen bunch. The strain of inventing one plausible event after another in a coherent chain of narrative tends to show in their faces. As Nietzsche says about Christians, you can tell from their faces that they don't enjoy doing what they do. Fiction writers cluster in the unlit corners of the room, silently observing everybody, including the poets, who are usually having a fine time in the center spotlight, making a spectacle of themselves as they eat the popcorn and drink the beer and gossip about other poets. Usually it's the poets who leave the mess just as it was, the empty bottles and the stains on the carpet and the scrawled phrases they have written down on the backs of pizza delivery boxes—phrases to be used for future poems, no doubt, and it's the prose writers who in the morning usually have to clean all of this up. Poets think that a household mess is picturesque—for them it's the contemporary equivalent of a field of daffodils. The poets start the party and dance the longest, but they don't know how to plug in the audio system, and they have to wait for the prose writers to show them where the on/off switch is. In general, poets do not know where the on/off switch is, anywhere in life. They are usually *off* unless they are forcibly turned *on*, and they stay *on* until they are taken to the emergency room, where they are medicated and turned *off* again.

Prose writers, by contrast, are unreliable friends: they are always studying you to see if there's anything in your personality or appearance that they can steal for their next narrative. They notice everything about you, and sooner or later they start to editorialize on you, like a color commentator at a sports event. You have a much better chance at friendship with a poet, unless you are a poet yourself. In your bad moments, a poet is always likely to sympathize with your misery and in your good moments to imagine you as a companion for a night on the town. Most poets don't study character enough to be able to steal it; they have enough trouble understanding what character *is*.

Of all human occupations, the writing of poetry leaves the most time for concentrated leisure activities. Poets have considerable quantities of time and a low boredom threshold, which makes them fun and scary to be around. With poets, you are likely to find yourself, as I once did, driving around town at two a.m. looking for a restaurant that sells roast beef sandwiches; the sandwiches, in this case, were not for the poet but for his hunting dogs, who had become accustomed to this diet. Loyalty is a religion for poets, and in any case they need the requirements of friendship to fill the other twenty-three and a half hours of the day. They are distractible, however, since they are usually thinking about an image or a favorite phrase or a new approach to the sacred. Prose writers have to spend hours and hours in chairs, facing paper, adding one brick to another brick, piling on the great heap of their endless observations, going through the addled inventory of all the items they've laboriously paid attention to, and it makes them surly, all this dawn until dusk sitting for the sake of substantial books that you could prop open a door with, big novels with sentences that have to go to the far right-hand margin of the page. Fiction writers get resentful, watching poets calling it quits at 9:30 a.m. Writing prose is steady work, but it tends to make prose writers grumpy and money grubbing and longfaced. They feel that they should be rewarded for what they do: observing everything and everybody with that wide-eyed staring look, like a starving cat painted on a velvet canvas.

Poets are the nobility of the writing world. Their nobility has to do with their spiritual intelligence and mind-haunted love for language and their subtle perfectionism. Poets can trace their lineage back to Orpheus, but prose writers can't get back much further than that money grubber, Samuel Richardson, or that jailbird, Cervantes. Like it or not, prose fiction writers have always been part of the middle class; like other members of the middle class, they perk up when the subject turns to money. You can be a prose writer without having any kind of primary relation to the gods, but poets are often god-touched, when they are not being butchered by the gods, and this fate affects them in curious ways. They think about fate often if not obsessively. Like other nobles who spend their days scouting the heavens, however, poets have little understanding of most worldly occupations, except for writing poems and falling in love and having great sex, which is why half of their poems are about writing poems or falling in love and having great sex.

It's a good thing for prose writers that poets generally gave up telling stories in poems around the turn of the century. Each one of the English romantic poets, with the possible exception of Shelley, was a great storyteller, and even Shelley wanted to write, with *The Cenci*, a play that could be produced on the stage; Coleridge's Ancient Mariner has a great story to tell and Keats's story of Lamia has a startlingly nightmarish quality. The story of Don Juan will keep you stimulated and alert, and even Tennyson could tell a story, though there is a softening in Tennyson that gives his narratives a gauzy mix of the medieval and the romantic that we now associate with the paintings of Maxfield Parrish. Despite their great achievements, Pound, Eliot, and Stevens and many other modernists and postmodernists did not care to get themselves involved with extended narratives of any kind. They saw, or thought that they saw, that progressive narrative was itself a fiction, and that it led to a progressivist view of history in which they did not believe. All of their stories have turned into little shards of broken glass, each shard an enclosed historical moment, and part of the experience of reading their poems involves spending hours gluing these pieces of glass together. It is interesting to me that poets have mostly renounced telling stories in their poems, but as an ex-poet I am pleased that they have done so, because it gives me a mission in life.

The stories that poets have always liked to tell tend to be somewhat hypnotic and mesmerizing. One of the reasons for that is that poets have often attended to what I would call narrative echo-effects. The narrative echo-effect is itself an almost subvocal denial of historical progression. You see this in medieval romances and in the ballad tradition.

All ballads love repetitive actions, or cycles of doubled events. You can easily imagine stories like this. Anyone can make them up. In this summarized form, they're not particularly interesting, but I'll give a thumb-nail example. A boy goes to a city park in the spring to fly a kite. The scene is infused with a kind of lyric innocence and bravery. The kite is yellow, and in the wind it rises so that it can hardly be seen. The narrative knows that the child is missing something, but the child does not know what this element is and could not articulate it even if he felt it directly. This is a characteristic of adolescence, having feelings without words to identify them. Conrad Aiken's stories are usually structured in this manner. Years later, when the boy has grown to be a man, he happens to walk into the same park and sees a young woman who is flying a kite. She's with another man, but her blouse is the same yellow as the boy's kite once was . . . and the man who sees her is suddenly struck with what we sometimes call déjà vu, which is only an eerie sense of some repetition, of a time spiral, of things having come around back to themselves. Now that he has words for his feelings, he's able to take some action. It's as if something about these events has started to rhyme. The effect is a bit like prophecy, except prophecy run in reverse, so that it cannot be used for purposes of worldly advancement.

Prophecy run forward gives the prophet the power of forecasting and a habit of denunciation. Prophecy run backward, into rhyming action or déjà vu, gives the participant a power of understanding. A forward prophetic power is worldly and has something to do with magic and foresight; a reverse prophecy, a sense of rhymed events, is unworldly and has something to do with insight. It moves us back into ourselves.

Robert Creeley once said about his stories, "I begin where I can, and I end when I see the whole thing returning." This is an interesting idea about certain kinds of narratives, particularly those that deal with discovery or growth. But the unsatisfactory nature of thinking about fictional form as a circle becomes apparent after a moment or two. The mechanical nature of Creeley's formulation is bothersome. Particularly in short stories, this automatic homing-device would return the reader to a starting point before any initial materials in the story had been really lost from view. The immediate return of a story to its beginning would be like a rhyme that insists too quickly and bluntly on itself. Dramatically, this idea of the story as a circle would turn every journey into a trip around the block. If *every* story is a circle, ultimately returning to a source, then the sense of discovery along the way is slightly fraudulent. It has to be imaginable that any story may want to end up in a different locale from the one where it started. The return to a starting-point is only a discovery if you've forgotten where you started out from in the first place. And you won't forget your starting-point if you know ahead of time that you're bound to end up back there.

It's customary to talk about effective language or effective dramatic structure in fiction, but almost no one ever talks about beautiful action. At first glance, it's a dubious category. For years I have wondered about how to define beautiful action in fiction, and whether it's even possible. I don't mean actions that are beautiful because a character is doing something noble or good. I mean actions that feel aesthetically correct and just—actions or dramatic images that cause the hair on the back of our necks to stand up, as if we were reading a poem. My conclusion is that it often has to do with dramatic repetition, or echo effects. I think of this as rhyming action.

Almost every narrative struggles with two features of action in time. The first, and more common feature involves the change of a situation, its mutation into a new condition. It's what we mean when we say that in a story, something has to happen. One event follows another

369

through a chain of causal events. The dramatic occurrences of a story push us forward toward a new state, a new condition, into the future of manifest possibilities. Any narrative that leads us toward this future also invites us to wonder or to worry how things will turn out. We turn pages, we are in suspense, we wonder whether Dr. Aziz will be convicted of doing harm to Miss Quested.

The other feature of action in narrative time, however, occurs when narratives move in reverse—when they come dramatically or imagistically to a point that is similar to one they have already seemingly passed. We see an image that we half-remember. We hear a voice that we think we have heard before. We watch as someone performs an action that someone else did very much that way years ago. Something about the onward flow of time has been tricked. Poetry is interfering with the onward course of events. We *are* stepping into the same river twice. We discover that there is in fact an illusory quality about the whole concept of progression. These are the stories that poets often like to tell, but most stories have some elements of time-reversal, of what I'd call stutter-memories, or rhyming action. Huck Finn finds himself reliving, under Tom Sawyer's supervision, the flight and liberation of Jim, only this time in the last chapters of his book, in travesty form. In John Hawkes's *Travesty*, a trauma is being re-enacted, re-staged, for the second time. In Alice Munro's "Five Points" Brenda finds herself in present time accidentally playing the role of the exploited fat girl that her boyfriend Neil has told her about in a story.

Any fiction writer who begins to use the techniques of dramatic repetition can imagine the dangers it presents. A flat rhyme is more regrettable than no rhyme at all. An awkward repetition lends to any story a taste of the overdetermined and stagy. Worse, it presents all symmetries as meaningful and interesting. Not every symmetry is beautiful. The bars on a jail are symmetrical but hardly beautiful. The symmetry of jail bars is different from the symmetry of a leaf. Compulsions are often symmetrical. Neurosis often has a terrible symmetry built into it.

For this reason, I recognize that in talking about rhyming action I may be giving what amounts to bad advice to writers. Using echo-effects or rhyming action can feel contrived and corny—mostly, I think, because in life we are seldom conscious of the way things come back to themselves. With that in mind, what I would argue for is the employment of rhyming action with so subtle a touch that the reader scarcely notices it. The image or action or sound has to be forgotten before it

370

can effectively be used again. Rhymes are often most telling when they are barely heard, when they are registered but not exactly noticed.

When we see two similar events separated by time, it's as if we are watching an intriguing pattern unfolding before we know what the pattern is. I don't think that the pattern has to explain itself to be beautiful. It doesn't even have to announce itself. In fact, I think it's often more effective if the echo-effects, the rhyming of action, are allowed to happen without the reader being quite aware of them. If the subconscious or the unconscious gets us into these time-tricks, these repetitions, then it's in the subconscious or the unconscious where they should be felt.

A pattern can also be understood as fate. Americans don't like to talk about fate, and as a culture we are anti-tragic. We live in a country that believes in progress. Our historical luck has made this belief possible. If we lived in Poland or Bosnia, overrun for centuries by invading armies or warring factions, we might very well believe, as Polish writers have tended to believe, in the semi-tragic non-progression of large historical events. Eastern European writing has a somber and sometimes lyric concern with the invisible force of the repeated act or the echoing rhyming image. Think of Kundera, of *The Unbearable Lightness of Being,* a novel that is in part a meditation on Nietzsche's concept of the eternal return, and which is filled with images concerning the impossibility of any singularity. *Once,* it turns out, is *always,* is *forever.*

African writers, with their warring factions and their history of colonialism, have produced in the twentieth century a literature much closer to Central and Eastern European literature than to ours. Bessie Head and Chinua Achebe and Wole Soyinka are, in their different ways, writers obsessed with patterns and rhyming action. Living in a new nation-state does not mean that one lives in a new state of mind. Quite the opposite.

I can imagine someone—probably an American—objecting to all this by saying that the true beauty of a story often has to do with freedom, with choice, and with the feeling of a unique action, a one-time-only occurrence happening in front of our eyes. Americans love singularity. Ah, we say, the unexpected. How beautiful the unexpected is. (No: the unexpected is seldom beautiful.) The more we talk about patterning, the more we reduce the feeling of flowering of event, and the more we increase the impression of heavy-handedness, a kind of artistic overcontrol. All right, yes, perhaps. But I think I'm not just talking about narrative technique here anymore. I think I'm talking about the way some writers may view the world. Technique must follow a vision, a view of experience. No technique can ever take precedence over vision. It must be its servant. It is not the unexpected that is beautiful, but the inevitability of certain literary choices that surprise us with their sudden correctness.

In *Lolita,* the narrator, Humbert Humbert, whose name is already a double, makes a great point, in the early sections of the novel devoted to his American child-love, about her habit of chewing gum, particularly bubble gum. Much of the time when we see her, she's moving the gum around in her mouth, between words—words like "gosh"—and her half-formed sentences.

Late in the novel, long after she's been violated successively by Humbert and Clare Quilty, Humbert goes to Pavor Manor to kill Quilty, who, along with Humbert, has taken most of what it is possible to take from Lolita, including her innocence, which has been visually identified throughout the novel with her bubble gum. Humbert has violated that innocence too; they're both guilty, though Humbert is the one who feels both anger and remorse. Quilty feels nothing but contented satisfied corruption. In any case, in a scene that is both horrible and comic and terrifying, Humbert finds Quilty in Pavor Manor, and after several pages of verbal confrontation, begins to shoot him. The wounding bullets seem to energize Quilty, and he trudges in a magnificent bloody progress up the stairs and down the hall until at last he arrives at his bedroom.

> "Get out, get out of here," he said coughing and spitting; and in a nightmare of wonder, I saw this blood-spattered but still buoyant person get into his bed and wrap himself up in the chaotic bedclothes. I hit him at very close range through the blankets, and then he lay back, and a big pink bubble with juvenile connotations formed on his lips, grew to the size of a toy balloon, and vanished.

In the act of dying, Quilty visually brings forth Lolita. There she is, her visual traceries coming out of his mouth. He has taken her innocence, and it's inside him. The gum is still echoing there, but now it's grown up, gone through adolescence, and become bloody. This is a small example of a visual rhyming effect, the transformation of an im-

372

age from one person to another. What better proxy than Quilty, who is both a gummy and bloody boor, to bring this image back to us?

The first sentence of the last paragraph of James Joyce's "The Dead" is a simple declarative statement. "A few light taps upon the pane made him turn to the window." It's a seemingly innocent pronouncement, and it does not force itself—or anything else—upon us. But in the previous paragraph, Gabriel Conroy has imagined Michael Furey, a "young man standing under a dripping tree," as a part of the "vast hosts of the dead" whose region he is approaching. The next paragraph begins with those few light taps upon the pane.

The narration does not say that the taps are those of falling snow until the next sentence. If we stop at the end of the sentence, and if we bother to remember what Gretta Conroy has just told Gabriel, we will remember that Michael Furey used to announce himself to Gretta by flinging pebbles and stones against her windowpane. That sound has returned. We are hearing its echo. But this time it is brought to us by the snow, which Gabriel has introduced into the story from the moment he walked into his aunts' house, scraping snow from his galoshes.

We're just far enough away from Gretta's story so that we probably have forgotten those taps on the window. But here they are again. Although Michael Furey is dead, the same sound he created is present again at the window. All right: it's just the snow. By this time, however, the entire landscape has been transformed, so that we have entered the region of the past made manifest—the return, not of the repressed, but of the missing and the lost.

In Sylvia Townsend Warner's story "Oxenhope," published in 1971, the protagonist, a man named William, returns by car to a place in the Midlands he visited on a walking tour when he was seventeen. He had taken the walking tour at that age because he felt his mind collapsing before the pressure of adulthood and the prospect of going to a university on a scholarship. The narration describes this condition as "brain-mauling." His mind had gone empty: "all the facts he had grouped so tidily had dissolved into a broth stirred by an idiot." In his walking tour, the boy chanced upon Oxenhope and was taken in by the woman of the house, who gave him milk and scones his first night there.

The first part of Sylvia Townsend Warner's story gives us his activities and his tasks during the month that the seventeen-year-old William stayed on with his hosts at Oxenhope while his mind recovered, but it also filters these memories with William's travels now, as a retired widower of sixty-four, with a grown daughter. One of his tasks, forty-seven years ago, was to clean up the family gravestones, picking the lichen out of the inscriptions with a knife. In present narrative time, he does the job again. But what he really wants to do is return to the streams and the ponds and the lakes he remembers. His memories are narrated as self-enclosed and seemingly unrecoverable:

> The past was in the present—the narrowed valley, the steeper hills crowding into it, the river running with a childish voice. . . . Hauling himself up from waterfall to waterfall, here by a rowan, there by a handful of heather, he had come to a pool, wide enough to swim a few strokes across, deep enough—though it was so clear that its pebbles seemed within hand's reach—to take him up to the neck. He had stripped and bathed in the ice-cold water, threshing about like a kelpie, and then clambered out on a slab of rock to dry in the sun. He had lain so still in his happiness that after a while an adder elongated itself from the heather roots, lowered its poised head with its delicate, tranquil features, and basked on the rock beside him. There they had lain till a hawk's shadow crossed them, and with a flick the adder was gone.

The point is made here, quietly but insistently, that happiness sometimes has a quality of invisibility to it—transparency is possibly a better word. The story is invested in the clearness of the water and the transparency of the boy. William was, in his youth, empty, harmless and unharmed, filled with bad nerves and a sense of wonder. He left no mark upon anything, he cleared and cleaned things instead, even when, as the story subsequently tells us, he went out on Cat Loch with Oliphant, the keeper of the boathouse, and caught a fish. You catch a fish and then you clean it.

Now he is an older man, having been in the foreign service, and walking around these same locales. Without putting too fine a point on it, this is not a promising situation for a short story. The baffling loss of innocence, an older man gazing at his younger self—we've certainly seen this situation before. So far, William's memories are just that: memories, and there are few situations less edifying than those in which an aging person contemplates the past. Nostalgia, after all, usually is memory raised to a level of kitsch.

Many writers would end the story right here disastrously, with the dying fall of memory. Regret and immobility are pretty obviously inadequate dramatic responses to the challenges of recollection and aging. The story needs something else, a counter-movement. A good story is often like a good conversation: just as a conversation carries with it a statement and an answer, good dramatic structuring often involves a call-and-response. This action—William's return to Oxenhope—calls for a return, the action flung back on itself.

So we should not be too surprised at this point, late in the story, when William, staring off in the middle distance of the field, sees an almost invisible boy watching him from a hiding place. William was once almost invisible himself. Now this boy is. "Sliding his glance in the direction of the watcher, he saw two brilliant pink flowers lighting a clump of heather: two outstanding ears with the sun shining through them. The boy had concealed himself very well, but his ears betrayed him." Like William next to the adder, the boy is next to the flower, but not actually concealed by it. We don't have to remember William and the adder, however, for the purposes of this scene, and it's not an exact rhyme anyway.

William returns to his car, the boy following him. "When William was down and approaching his car along the grassed road, he saw the boy approaching it from the opposite direction. Though his ears were no longer translucent, they were certainly the same ears." Translucency, transparency. Sylvia Townsend Warner's story is at this point inflected with an exact intelligence about the tactful relations between an older man and a young boy who are strangers but are filled with a civilized interest in each other. "The air was full of chill and poetry, and it was the moment to put on an overcoat. Ignoring the boy, who was now standing by the car without appearing to have stopped there, William leaned in and released the lid of the bonnet." The boy makes a cry of surprise (the engine is at the back), and they begin to talk.

The boy takes the man to be a stranger to the area and begins to identify the valleys and the hills. Then, in a subtle shift, the boy rouses himself to tell legendary stories about the place. "'Youn's Scraggie Law,'" the boy explains. "'There was a man once, put goats on it. They were Spanish goats. They didna do.'" He then tells a story about a pool where sheep fell in and kicked each other to death. "William had heard that story from Jimmie Laidlaw," the narrator informs us. In other words, the story is at least fifty years old.

Sylvia Townsend Warner has laid down an intricate pattern here, and part of the pleasure of the story involves watching the characters work their way out of it. Observing the movement of the story, we expect the boy to give an account, a little piece of folk-memory, that might have involved William when *he* was a boy in Oxenhope. This the boy does. But as it turns out, it's a visionary, apocalyptic story about Cat Loch, where William once went fishing. Here is what the boy says: "'There was a man once, set fire to it. He was in a boat, and he set fire to the water. There was flames coming up all round the boat. Like a gas ring.'" When William asks the boy what color the flames were, the boy says, " 'They was blue.' "

In the pause that follows, William remembers what actually happened forty-seven years ago. "Oliphant, interminably rowing about the loch for likely places, had thrust down his oar to check the boat's movement. Bubbles of marsh gas rose to the surface. William saw himself leaning out of the boat and touching off their tiny incandescence with a lighted match."

This is what I mean by a beautiful action. It's like a couplet. The loud apocalyptic story the boy tells, and the quiet exact memory of William setting fire to the little bubbles of marsh gas—these two go together perfectly, and they are perfectly right without anyone worrying over their symbolic applications. Apart from the quiet precision of the language, we have been brought around in this episode to earth, air, water, and fire and their capacity to reintegrate someone after a brain-mauling. Furthermore, in a last feeling for stutter-memory, William is no longer transparent. Children want to be transparent, but old people want to be permanent and visible. Through this legend, William has acquired permanent heroic visibility. He is a song, a hero, a successful Orpheus. Here is the story's last paragraph.

> 'Jump in,' William said briskly, and turned the car. When the surface allowed, he drove fast, to please the boy. He put him down at Crosscleugh (there was still a white marble dog in the garden) and drove on. There was no call for a backward glance, for an exile's farewell. He had his tenancy in legend. He was secure.

I have gone on about "Oxenhope" not because it's on the scale of *Lolita* or "The Dead," but because in its modest way, the story creates a beautiful set of dramatic scenes that make intuitive sense.

These scenes feel right when set next to each other. And they feel radiant before the story has been analyzed for its themes. These images—the boy cleaning the gravestones, lying next to the adder by a rock pool, or leaning out of the rowboat to set fire to the bubbles of marsh gas—have a quality of sensible tactile life. I don't think the pastoral and rural setting accounts for their beauty. It's not the countryside but the boy's wonder that transforms these scenes, and wonder is partially created out of the rhyming action. The boy setting fire to the bubbles of marsh gas has a place in the story because the story has already laid before us another dramatic scene, that of a lake of fire, which, if we bother to think about it, is hell, but is, otherwise, just a visionary place. Place another image next to that one of a boy in a rowboat igniting the marsh gas with matches, and you have, if not heaven, at least its close earthly locale. Lazy little explosions, an afternoon of pleasing pointlessness.

"Oxenhope" doesn't force the reader into a jail of symmetrical images. It doesn't sit you up and ask if you've been paying attention. It won't, with nagging small reminders, find you inadequate as a reader. Nabokov, by contrast, with his aristocratic intelligence and fierce game-playing, is capable of giving his readers a failing grade if they forget where they saw that image or that phrase before. *Pale Fire* and *Ada* can sometimes seem more like final exams than novels. They are gorgeous, in their various ways, but their symmetries gently close out much of the world. They have, at times, a suffocating overdetermined beauty.

The feeling of memory in "Oxenhope" is very light. It does not press hard on William as an adult, and its reverberations sound softly, almost inaudibly, in the reader's ear. Memory has not trapped its protagonist, because, if I understand the story properly, it has been communal. *A memory doesn't have to be accurate to be liberating,* the story claims, *it only has to be shared.*

Rhyming action exists in that curious area of writing between conscious intent and unconscious or semi-conscious impulse. The writer who becomes too conscious of what she's doing, using this technique, would create labored and implacable symmetries. We like to think that the craft of writing is conscious and learned. That's why certain features about it can be taught. So how can I argue that the best forms of rhyming action are probably half-conscious? If this technique is used too consciously, it probably won't work. How can I argue for a half-conscious relaxing of the grip, for half-thinking?

377

It feels to me as if I have worked myself into a false position. But in practice I believe it is probably not false at all. When we write, we reread what we have already written. Then, if we are not too anxious, we allow associations to mingle with those elements we have already laid down. We do so in a state of alert attentiveness that welcomes memory and progression and puts them on the same stage and then lets them go. But if we dwell on our intentions too hard, we kill the spirit. Here, in a letter, is Sylvia Townsend Warner on Benjamin Britten's opera *The Turn of the Screw:*

> The boy sang magnificently, and somehow gave the impression of singing with a hallucinated attention to what he had learned in fear and trembling and now was defiantly sure of. And it was so delicately done by the composer, with such bleak avoidance of appearing to dwell on it or turn blue that it was as matter of fact as a snake, an interval of terror and gone in a flash. Lovely!

Wonderful phrase, "bleak avoidance of appearing to dwell on it or turn blue. . . ."

I also love the way that quick terror, its sudden appearance and disappearance, is experienced as lovely. An event becomes beautiful without reference to its ethical character. What can be beautiful about terror? Terror is not lovely when it weighs eight hundred pounds. But when, in art, it is as light as a wingfeather, and as quick, it takes on the rapid half-lost half-found aura of the glimpse, or a dream that has lost all content but its coloration.

The act of writing anything can be as much consent as creation. One agrees to let certain passages come into the work. As a result, the story takes on a quicksilver quality, as memory drifts and glides through it.

Postscript: Sylvia Townsend Warner, for much of her adult life, intended to revise the Scott Moncrieff translation of Proust's *À la Recherche.* . . . She never got the rights from the Proust estate.

Our friends the poets are falling asleep. All this talk of memory probably annoys them. But in ceding progressive narrative to the prose writers in the twentieth century, they have also, in large part, given over to them the poetry of memory. The poetry of memory in this century belongs to Proust and Faulkner and Woolf and Achebe and the others. It is more difficult to say that the Modernist poets wrote the poetry of memory. *The Cantos* is an act of cultural memory but not in equal part personal memory. True also of *The Waste Land*. American poets, in this alarming century, have more often insisted on memory-as-trauma. Anyone can see why. When one thinks of the poetry of memory in this century, one thinks of the shocks that those memories have sustained. An insistence on memory-as-trauma, however, demonizes the entire realm of remembrance—it demonizes, I would say, one's entire foundation of experience in the past. This demonization is one that many poets have bravely explored. But trauma is not a progressive narrative. It is a loop. It begins where it can, and ends when it sees the whole thing returning.

But when it is not traumatized, the action of memory on our present life may be closest to the feeling that rhyme creates, not full rhyme, but half-rhyme, assonance, slant rhyme. One of the features I love about Wordsworth's *The Prelude* is that, although it is written in blank verse, the events within the poem contain a rhyming logic. Memory does not have to attach itself to its replica in our present moments. It can be oblique, sidling, scary and luminous in its distant relatedness to us. The tree branch, the one without bark outside my window now, does not remind me of another tree branch, nor even a bare arm. That would be too easy. It reminds me of something else. And those broken strings hanging from the basketball hoop are like nothing so much as dangling spider webs I remember from . . . another time. What are these trace memories, these images, but visitors or visitations from our pasts? The best visitors are the shy ones. They hardly want to come in. They stand at the doorway. If you look at them too closely, they'll probably run away and disappear.

We have to save them. We have to save them by turning away a little, pretending to do something else, like lifting the hood of the car and tinkering with the engine, before they'll befriend us. These memories, our children, are not all demons. To claim that *all* memory is demonized and traumatic is to count oneself among the permanently damned.

Paradise is less plausible than Hell, but it is surely no less real.

Nominated by Marianne Boruch, Jim Daniels, Gary Fincke, Dave Smith, Lee Upton

THE LIPSTICK TREE

fiction by KIANA DAVENPORT

from STORY

T HEY RAN SILENTLY in single file, the bush so thick they moved by intuition. By morning they would be missed in their village, and by noon they would dwell in the mouths of elders as curses. Darkness hid a wall of matted spiderwebs that flung them backward to the ground, and Kona wept because she was young and terrified. Eva comforted her, and they lay still watching flying foxes like rags in brief ellipses through the trees.

"We're going to die," Kona said.

Eva shook her gently. "No, we're going to be famous." What she meant was that they were going to be remembered, and hated.

Smelling the stench from a nearby village—rotting vegetation, rancid pig fat, the smoke of old fires mixed with human and animal waste—reminded her of home. For a moment something buckled inside her, but Eva was strong, knowing whatever she would become, she was becoming now in flight.

Through fog, lights flickered on the river.

"They're hunting *puk-puks*," she whispered, guiding her cousin toward the banks of the Sepik, where torches danced.

Exhausted, missing her bed of banana leaves, Kona slid down to earth and dozed. Eva sat beside her, watching men in dugouts, poised with spears. Near mudflats, red, glowing discs—crocodile eyes—blinked up at blazing *pitpit* cane. In the dark a man knew the size of a crocodile by the distance between the eyes. Once her father had killed a seven-foot *puk-puk* with only a bamboo spike. Its tail tasted like fish meat and the hide brought a very good price.

Now she lay back thinking of Agnes, whose clan belonged to her father's, so the girls had grown up like sisters. Two years older than Eva, at sixteen Agnes had married and borne her first son. Clan-women had helped her build a small grass hut for birthing, staying nearby in the bush, shouting advice but keeping a distance when she went into labor. Touching her during childbirth would pollute their minds and hands, preventing them from looking at, or cooking for, their husbands.

Observing the taboo of female blood, no man witnessed childbirth for fear of dying or going insane. Only Eva crept close that day, watching Agnes moan, squatting with her head in her hands. After several hours, she screamed. Seeing the baby's head pop out between her legs, Eva fainted.

After the birth of her son, Agnes' head was shaved and dyed with scarlet seeds from the lipstick tree. When her boy was four years old, he was taken away, raised in the men's house so spells would not be cast on him by his mother. Agnes lived with the women in low pig houses made of *pitpit* cane with thatched roofs. There the women slept in semicircles at the end of each hut, with pig stalls along one wall down the middle. When husbands felt the urge to mate, they called their wives into the bush, then returned to sleep in the men's house. Out of sorrow and terrible frustration, sometimes women fell asleep coddling piglets, even nursing them.

Eva watched Agnes grow swayback from load-bearing and child-carrying and digging in the yam fields, while clan-men lay around discussing bride prices, paybacks, and politics. Eva wondered if this was her future—a life of squatting in the bush, of hookworm and tattooed cheeks, and flesh caked with animal fat to ward off night chill and malarial mosquitoes.

This was the legacy of the women of the Sepik, the seven-hundred-mile-long river coiling from northern slope mountain ranges in central New Guinea down through lowlands of the interior and out to the Pacific Ocean on the country's northeast coast. Just north of Australia, it was a country whites called "Stone Age," "The Last Unknown," where they were still addressed as "Masta" and "Missus."

Eva had been a bright child, crawling too early, walking and talking too soon. In primary mission-school, she had taken each English word on her tongue like a sacrament. By secondary school she saw that the white man's language was her passport to the outside world. But before she could even envision that world, one day she woke bleeding.

381

She was washed and oiled, adorned with shells and plumes of bird of paradise, and led into the center of the village. Though not beautiful, Eva was known to be clever and would graduate from secondary school. Her father proudly paraded her in front of village men, dark skin gleaming like wet bark, her kinky hair like luminous coils.

"My daughter is now a woman ready for betrothal. Intelligent, hard-working, and virtuous. Prepare your bride price, fatten your pigs, collect your salt wheels and gold-lip pearl shells. Bring your offerings to our home."

When Eva told Agnes she would soon marry, Agnes wept for her. "Pray for a girl, so you have something to love."

On the night of Eva's first mating with her husband, and ever after, he whispered chants to protect him from the potency of the female who bled without being wounded, who gave birth to other humans, whose power could shrivel his unprotected soul.

One day Eva watched Agnes with her second son, now two years old, walking toward the river, a slow serenity in her stride. She turned back once, waved to Eva through the trees, and plunged into the Sepik. Eva dropped her digging stick and ran toward the river. Crocodiles sunning in the shallows lifted their heads and in slow sighs stretched out chubby, childlike legs ending in claws. Pushing off from mudflats, they drifted, heads submerged. Agnes surfaced, holding her son up like an offering, and a large croc shot forward.

Her head bobbed as the current swept her along. A shiver ran down the tail of the reptile as it lunged into the depths, then shot up with Agnes in its jaws. The son floated momentarily then was pulled under, water around them boiling red. Eva screamed, and could not stop.

Police arrived, shooting *puk-puks* from their launch, then slit their bellies wide. They found eels, herons, a brass trumpet, a camera, a Bible, a dog. They did not find Agnes or her child. The funeral feast continued for weeks taking on the air of a celebration. Agnes' family, ghostly gray in mourning ash, received six slain pigs from her husband's family, plus yams and taros, bananas and sweet potatoes, the last installment of her bride price.

After that, Eva wept each time her husband called her to the bush. Three times she stole from her village and hid in the Lutheran Mission Church.

"I don't want a child," she told the reverend's wife. "I don't want my head painted red like a slave."

Three times her husband, Ernest, dragged her home. The reverend's wife suggested Eva go away from her village to the large coastal town of Wewak, north of where the Sepik met the Pacific Ocean. There she could study to become a nurse's aide, or one day even a nursing sister at the Lutheran Mission Hospital.

"My husband will write you a letter of recommendation," she said. "You're very bright, Eva. There's nothing here for you."

It was such a large idea, she needed time to think, to gather her nerve. By then she had graduated from secondary school and worked as cleaning girl at the hotel in Si-Siara, an old river station two swamps over from her village that drew tourists and foreign traders looking for totemic masks and *kunda* drums made by local tribes. The hotel was clean but decrepit, twenty rooms with exploding wallpaper and rusted light switches.

The owner was a burly Australian with the lashless eyes of a squid, reeking of insect repellent and cigars. Eva suspected, like all whites who settled in her country, he was full of unwholesome secrets. Yet he was married to a New Guinea woman as black as slate, whom he did not beat or scold, and when he talked to Eva he was kind. She had been working there several weeks when he took her aside.

"You're a good worker and a smart girl, you savvy? But guests are goin' on about you."

Eva stepped back, frightened. "Why, Masta? I do not steal."

He sniffed, fluttering his nostrils. "Use a bit of scent now and again. Or I shall have to let you go."

Other cleaning girls showed her their bottles of deodorant. At the pharmacy where jars were labeled "For Heartworm," "For Tapeworm," "For Malaria," she purchased a bottle with a pink, roll-on top. That night she pulled it from her string bag, stroking it in the dark. She had never owned perfume. Next day she bathed in a stream, and dreamily slid on the sticky wax that smelled like stale gardenias.

Scouring a toilet bowl at the hotel, Eva ran her hands over the graceful curve of its belly, flushing it repeatedly. One day she stopped relieving herself in the bush. The toilet, like her new perfume, became a habit. Sometimes, changing barely wrinkled sheets, she thought of the plaited grass sleeping-mats in her village, shared by humans and animals month after month until they shredded.

She watched elders of her clan who bathed only when it rained, who wore white man's hand-me-downs until they turned to rags. She studied her mother, head bowed from a life of carrying her *bilum*—the string bag of burden—hanging down her back from a braided strap across her head. Through the decades she had carried infants in her *bilum*, firewood, arrows and spears during tribal wars. Her mother had even fought in wars. She had never seen her bathe.

Sometimes Eva buried her face in hotel bath towels, inhaling the wonderful odors, and thought affectionately of her grandmother in her short grass skirt, and her grandfather in his "arse grass" and banana leaf penis-wrapper, and how they loosed in the air around them a rich, forlorn rottenness. Yet, her grandfather could split the skull of a wild boar at forty feet with a simple wooden arrow. And her grandmother had once hypnotized a python, dragging it home like a thick garden hose. What white woman could do that?

One day Eva stood watching a cousin serve Australian expatriates in the dining room. The white men sat over lunch observing two educated natives discussing upcoming elections of a new prime minister of Papua New Guinea. The natives were eating pork ribs, loudly crunching the bones. On the walls overhead, photos of earlier days showed tribes of cannibals holding up shrunken heads.

Nervously, the Aussies lit up cigarettes, exhaling profoundly, turning the pictures on the walls into dreams. Eva's tribe was descended from the people on the walls; she had once discussed it with her grandfather.

"Do you remember eating human flesh when you were young, grandfather?"

He answered slowly in Pidgin, *"Time ee got man belong kaikai small no more by and by man ee full up."* When there was man to eat, only a little bit would fill you up.

"But *yu laik em kaikai* white man?" Eva asked. But you liked eating the flesh of the white man?

He shook his head, making a face. *"Meat belong im stink too muss."*

She reflected sadly on how her people were now paid as waiters to serve the white men they once ate.

She was nineteen then, and one day she watched her grandmother, tiny as a pygmy, running down the road. Having borne ten children, old age had come to her as a luxury. Never still, feet calloused and hard as horns, she was always scurrying off to market with yams or freshly caught bats and eels.

"Grandmother," Eva asked, "are you happy?"

The woman cocked her head like a bird, as if considering the question, patted Eva's cheek, spat out a jet of betel-nut juice, and went cackling and spinning down the road. Sometimes Eva found her squatting with other ancient women—teeth rotten, lips and gums like open wounds from chewing betel-nut—weaving their *bilums*, or pounding sago. Work was their life, what they took pride in. It was their only voice.

She grew up listening to these women gossip in the fields, watching them help each other in childbirth and child burial. In the heads of each woman of each clan were libraries of encyclopedic lore, local legends, knowledge of plants and animals, and the twenty kinds of soil along the Sepik. These were the daughters of memory, the true prophets and seers who protected the fertility of the land.

"They have power," the reverend's wife said. "Their secret is, they share. If you go into the white man's world, Eva, this is what you will miss. White women don't share." She had said it wistfully, and there was alcohol on her breath.

The woman was Canadian, married to an Australian of Scottish descent, and they had lived on different missionary posts along the Sepik for over ten years. Eva became her part-time mother's helper while she was in mission-school, and she insisted Eva call her Margaret, rather than "Missus."

Only fifteen years older than Eva, her face had already surrendered. Direly thin, she seemed to be wearing away. When there was news on the wireless of tribal wars in the highlands and pack-rapes by roving "rascals," Margaret's face turned bloodless. This was when Eva noticed the smell of alcohol and suspected she had been too long away from her own kind.

One night, half-asleep in the pig house, Eva heard her husband call her name, and followed him outside. Though he had gone to mission-school like Eva, he had no curiosity about the world. Mostly he and his clan-men lounged in the *haus tambaran,* the spirit house, smoking and storytelling, or stalking the jungle for small game. The smell of beer was heavy on his breath as Ernest knelt over her. Undoing his shorts, he suddenly froze; she had not washed the deodorant from her underarms. His slap was like fire across her cheek.

"You smell of white man," he cried. "How many you been sleeping with, whore!"

He pummeled her stomach and chest with his fists, slapped her face repeatedly until she bled. Women carried her back to the pig house, rubbing her wounds with heated plant stems that numbed the pain.

"You're taking on white man's ways," her mother said in the language of their tribe. "Making your husband look like he 'have no bones.'" It was an old expression that meant a man was not a man. "Stay home in the fields, where you belong."

"Why is it wrong to want to learn?" Eva cried. "My wages go to my husband and father, and still I am beaten!"

For two weeks she washed off the deodorant before she reached home. One day she forgot and men sniffed as she passed them in her village. That night Ernest beat her again, leaving her bleeding in the bush. Slowly, painfully, she turned her head toward the Sepik, just visible through the trees.

Margaret told her that downriver ninety miles, where the Sepik met the Pacific, was where the world began. Great coastal towns where ships the size of villages docked. Towns peopled with Anglos and Malaysians and Chinese, clanless places with no rules where a woman could become anything she wanted to be. Eva pictured herself in a place where no one would watch her, where she could slowly and carefully grow. But she was only nineteen, she had never even crossed the river. She rolled over in the dark.

The hotel owner warned her twice, but she would not use deodorant again. Guests complained that she smelled like wildlife, and the day she was fired, she sat weeping in Margaret's kitchen.

"Resign yourself," Margaret said softly. "Or go away from here."

"How?" Eva cried. "And why must I leave my people? Why can't things just change? I am not the only unhappy one. Why do you think Agnes gave herself to the *puk-puks*?"

Margaret shuddered, looking longingly toward the cupboard where she kept a bottle.

"My dear, don't you think I know? I watch your women giving up. Poison. The rivers. Or they throw themselves over gorges, taking their infants with them. Ten years of this, look at me. People think I'm fifty." Her gaze drifted, then returned. "Stay here, Eva. Help me with the children. Then one day we'll take you to the mission-hospital at Wewak. You can begin medical training." She took her hand. "I could use the company."

Eva was afraid. Moving into the mission-house with Margaret and Reverend Burns would be desertion of her husband. Ernest would

386

be shamed. Bad feelings would grow between the clans. He had borrowed pigs to pay Eva's bride price and had not yet paid it back. There would be tension between the reverend and the villagers. Ernest might kidnap her, take her home, but not divorce her. He might take another wife, he could take many wives, and keep her as valuable labor.

When she told him she had been fired, he beat her again.

"You are my shame. A joke on me. You do not work in fields with the women. Cannot hold a job with white men. Cannot give me a child!"

She closed her eyes with each blow, hoping she was dying. Near dawn, someone gently lifted her head.

"Be still," her cousin, Kona, whispered. "Elders forbid us to come for you. Your mother cried all night."

She poured something bitter between Eva's lips, wiping insects from her wounds.

Eva moaned, trying to stand. "I thought I died."

"We'll both die here," Kona whispered. "Eva, you must help me run away. You're more clever than I. They're marrying me to a man who worked his last two wives to death."

Kona was fifteen. Her beauty had drawn the attention of many suitors, pressing her father to name how many pigs and gold-lip shells he required for her hand.

For five days Eva lay feverish, infected wounds covered with medicinal leaves and plant stems. On the sixth day she went back to work in the fields, thinking constantly of Wewak, wondering how she would be strong enough to leave her village.

One day she stood by the river gathering kindling. Crocodiles were sunbathing on mudflats, and a large one turned, gazing at her, eyelids opening and closing voluptuously. Eva moved closer, and three *puk-puks* slid almost lazily into the water, floating invisibly but for their snouts. Only the large one remained, contemplating her. Suddenly it trembled from snout to tail, a terrible prolonged shudder.

She had often spied on *puk-puks*, the graceful, swirling water-dance of their courtship. Her father said they fetched back millions of years, that they were as old as earth itself. Revered by her people as patron saints of war and hunting, their heads were carved on weapons and prows of dugout canoes. In initiation rites, men's bodies were scarred to resemble crocodile scales.

Slowly, she approached the huge reptile, moving into the water to her knees. Reaching her hand out, she felt an obsessive need to touch it, to stroke its head. It shuddered again, opened its jaws and, hugely, audibly, sighed.

Eva splashed forward. "Agnes, is it you!"

Recognizing the other, she was wrenched out of herself, and for a moment wondered if she were insane. Then slowly, thoughtfully, she rested her hand on its head, its scales like cold, wet stones.

"Are you finally at peace?" she whispered. "Oh, I am so much like you."

The crocodile sighed again, its eyes fixed dreamily on Eva.

"I will live for both of us," she whispered. "I will break away."

Two days later, elections were held for the new prime minister of Papua New Guinea. The man favored by the people lost. Suspecting rigged elections, natives rioted across the country. Stores were looted and burned, women raped by roving packs of "rascals." Nine people were speared to death, one of them Margaret's husband, Reverend Burns, leaving a supply store upriver from Si-Siara. By the time the news reached Eva, a police launch had already docked in town, but no one could penetrate the reverend's house.

Eva was there when they finally broke down the door; inside it was like a tomb. Then Margaret's baby cried and they found her and her three children, hiding in a closet under clothes. She pointed a cocked revolver at the district chief of police, a big, muscular native, and they saw she was gone, just gone. Hearing the news of her husband on the wireless, she had finally snapped.

Eva moved through the crowd and knelt before her, talking softly about dinner, and bathing the children, and maybe a nice, cool drink, until Margaret handed over the revolver like a child. Days later, a mile outside town where a coral airstrip had been left from World War II, a bush-plane lifted her and her children out of the jungle, circling once over tribes wailing with grief. With Margaret gone, Eva felt her chance at another life was over.

Resigned now, she watched clan-women with bellies huge as if from deep, long inhalations. Each year, as rhythmically as the seasons, women swelled, then expelled their babies, had their heads shaved, and their skulls dyed red. Sometimes infants, in turn, swelled—first feet, then legs and stomach—vomiting worms, the mother pulling them from the infant's throat as it suffocated and died. If not worms, then malaria, pneumonia. In one year, twenty-three infants had died. In a second inhalation, it seemed, the women's bellies swelled again, and the cycle repeated itself, death and birth made routine by repetition.

At night, in the fertile smell of the pig house, Eva felt larvae dropping from the thatched rood, insects gnawing, pigs snuffling. She held her head and wept.

"You look at us with shame," her grandmother whispered.

"No," she cried. "I only wanted to learn a better life."

"It is all the same," the old woman said. "Your learn new ways, this becomes that. But it is all the same."

An older, childless couple settled into the mission, big, doughy Brits, at first too stunned to talk. Reverend Hart had florid skin punished by the sun; during services a girdle of sweat grew steadily down his trousers. Sometimes his wife stood near Eva, wheezing, smelling of white shoe polish, and Eva knew they would not become friends.

But one day the woman gave her an envelope with her name on it. "We found this in the desk with things they left behind. I know you helped Margaret with the children. Perhaps she left you something."

Eva walked slowly along the river, stroking the white square in her pocket, her senses so alerted the jungle came at her in twos—a snake choking down another snake, tails slamming in duet, a pig gnawing the skull of another pig, trees suckling each other, fighting for oxygen. She sat down in a broth of orange mist.

It was a letter addressed to the director of the Lutheran Mission Hospital at Wewak, a friend of Margaret's husband, recommending Eva for internship there as medical aide. The letter was signed, but words were crossed out, as if Reverend Burns had planned to draft another version.

"But it is signed!" she cried, hugging the letter, and it seemed the jungle around her loosened its grip. Fog retreated, snow egrets rose in a column, and a dying sun on huge lotus lilies made the river a floating tapestry.

Desperate, Eva sought out the hotel owner's wife, Suliana. She was from a village near the capital city of Port Moresby where native women went to university and wore lip rouge, and even lived alone.

Eva showed her the letter. "Please help me. I want to be . . . a modern woman."

Suliana smoked a cheroot and rubbed her wedding band. "I have watched you, Eva. You're a bright girl. If you leave, you can never come back."

"Why?" she cried. "I don't want to give up my family forever."

"You would return educated, wearing shoes. Your clan would still be wearing mud. What would you say to them? What would you talk about?" She shook her head. "The river flows one way. This I have learned."

Finally, when she felt Eva was sure, she sent a runner downriver to a hamlet called Pondi. "That is where you will cross the Sepik."

All of that week the people of her village prepared for a *Sing-Sing*, officially welcoming the new reverend and his wife. That night would come back to Eva in memory and dreams, the rhythmical stamping and chanting of men drenched in pig fat, steaming like panthers, faces caked in reds and blues and yellows from plant dye and ash.

Legs tasseled in cassowary feathers, crescents of gold-lip pearl shell blazing on their chests, in feathered headdresses and bone nose-plugs, they moved in waves to great thunking heartbeats of slit-gong drums, while women stood aside, swaying with their infants. For hours, bodies whirled, voices chanted, finally climaxing in the sacrifice of the pigs, a prolonged, baffling shower of blood and squeals. In the light of cane-grass torches, Reverend Hart and his wife lifted their heads and closed their eyes, as if waiting to be impaled.

The night before, Eva had squatted beside her mother and grandmother, watching them sleep. Her mother had slowly sat up, handing her a rag wrapped around a handsome, gold-lip pearl shell carved in the shape of a crescent. This was precious currency. No words were exchanged, but she knew her daughter was going.

Now Eva sat with her tribe in firelight, people glowing with the drippings of slaughter. She moved to her father, touching his arm ringed with boar tusks, his kinky hair exploding with trapped fireflies. He would be the angriest, the most unforgiving. She looked at Ernest, he would find better wives. Then she sat beside her grandfather picking lice from his arse grass, snapping them between his nails.

She asked him how the pig was, and he proudly held up a large hunk of pork, as if he had given birth to it. "*Em bilong mi!*" All of this is mine!

She wrapped her arms around his thin shoulders, hugging him, then turned toward her grandmother squatting in a circle with her cronies, little sun-dried birds thoughtfully smoking their pipes. When she was very young her grandmother had dragged her through the bush at night, to stare through the windows of a white man's house lit electrically by generator. They had stood there for hours until he tapped a switch—a miracle—dousing the mysterious light within. Her grandmother had clapped her hands to her mouth, gasping with fear and wonder. Now Eva looked at her, and could not speak.

390

The old woman shook her head, knowing. "You will see. This becomes that. It is all the same."

She held her hands before her navel as if she'd caught a frog, then reached inside her waistband, drawing forth an object wrapped in cobwebs, pressing it on Eva. An ancient watch face, hands long gone, where rust and lice hung captive. She had carried it for years.

"Time!" she whispered, stroking the watch as if it contained Eva's future. Then she patted Eva's face, and cried.

She and Kona ran hard, in fog so thick the villages they passed were soft and blurred like velvet. Stopping for breath, they could still hear the chanting of their village. By now the drums had reached an otherworldly density, clans dancing with ancestral spirits.

Kona suddenly fell to her knees, sobbing. "My family will be shamed. They'll slaughter my piglets, Apinum and Pawpaw. There are no trees in the city, no mango and dragon plums. Who'll give us plant herbs when we're sick? Who'll give payback when we're insulted?"

Eva shook her viciously. "You fool. Wewak's a town, not a big city. There are trees, and a marketplace. We're not going to Sydney across the bloody ocean!"

"*You* will one day," Kona cried. "What then will become of me?"

Eva dragged her forward, continuing downriver, avoiding swamps like aspic quivering in their path. They walked all night and slept all day in rain that resurrected sewage, and woke beneath a dozing python, like giant bracelets hanging from a branch. Since noon, news of their runaway had echoed on slit-gong drums through the jungle. They walked again the next night, paralleling the river, but avoiding the shore and possible search parties in dugouts from their tribe.

Through the hours Eva sustained herself on what Margaret had said. "Feed your mind. Live up to your capacity."

Then she remembered Suliana's words. "You leave the Sepik. It never leaves you."

On the third night they reached the village of Pondi, where a dugout would come to take them across the river. Hiding in the cleft of a banyan tree, they slept fitfully, finally so welted with mosquito bites, they dived into the Sepik. The village was quiet, fast asleep, and in the darkness Eva saw the outline of a boy paddling a canoe. He drifted closer, calling her name.

"Yes," she cried. "We are ready!"

She swam to shore, gathering her things, then waded to the dugout, pulling Kona behind her. But Kona was no longer there, her voice already drifting, calling back from shore.

"Forgive me! I am not brave enough." In the dark they heard her sobs.

The boy stopped paddling, but Eva urged him from behind. "Go! We must go on."

If they were not across the river by first light, they would be intercepted. Eva's husband would take her back to her village as forced labor. Standing carefully, she took an oar, helping point the dugout toward deep waters. Stars shifted, the night deepened, and Kona's cries grew dim. The current fought them, pulling them downriver, so the trip across took almost all night.

In that time Eva fought against the ineffable softness of river fog, like second skin to her, knowing she would never again sleep beside the steamy breath of these waters, or hear the haunting, eerie insistence of bamboo flutes, or feel orphaned piglets draw tenderness from her like fluid. But no man would ever beat her again, of this she was sure.

They paddled silently until contours grew out of the boy's black silhouette, and Eva saw it was a young woman near her age. Night eased, the shore stepped forward, and bats like huge, brown pods hung quivering in trees of a village called Wara.

The girl turned to her. "You're safe. In another district."

By running away to another district, she had officially divorced her husband. By divorcing him, she had renounced her clan.

Stepping ashore, the girl pointed toward the jungle.

"Follow the dirt path up the mountain. One day's walk, you reach a rusting bunker. Downhill, another day, the coast. Climb the bunker, you'll see Wewak, the Pacific Ocean!"

Between Wara and Wewak lay forty miles of swamp, flat bush country, jungle-covered mountain. Eva looked back at the Sepik, shaking, then flung herself against the girl. They held each other, then the girl stepped back. "Hurry. My village wakes."

"Why did you do this?" Eva whispered. "For me, a stranger?"

"It's too late for me. I have children." She handed her some local currency. "*Kina,* from Suliana." Then she pushed her forward. "Go. Become something."

For two hours, Eva moved swiftly, looking neither left or right. She was bright and ambitious, she told herself. Wewak would be easy. The only hard thing would be talking to people. Then she crawled under a bush and sobbed. At day's end she reached the bunker. In the dark, she pulled an old sweater from her *bilum,* falling asleep wrapped in the smell of her childhood.

At dawn she woke and climbed the bunker, a lookout point left from World War II. Fog slowly lifted and, looking down, she shuddered. In the distance was Wewak, tall, hard-edged buildings jangled with sunlight, a harbor suckled by giant ships. Beyond it, the Pacific, melting into the world. She thought of all the things ahead, shoes aching to be worn, shelves of books waiting to be read, and she was breathless.

Beside a stream, she washed her face, smoothed her hair, and inventoried her *bilum.* The reverend's letter of recommendation, a few *Kina,* a gold-lip pearl shell. Deodorant, a rusty watch. She had never owned so much.

She climbed to the top of the bunker again, and studied the horizon, seeing herself decanted into the future, going even further than Wewak. One day she would shave her legs and cross the sea, and walk boulevards of great cities. Asleep alone in the white man's world, she would dream of deep river and remembered soil, and *puk-puks* dancing in the shallows. She would hear the *kunda* drums, and smell the odor of her tribe. And she would wake in birdless dawns, knowing she lived only in the tears of the daughters of memory.

Breaking a seed from a lipstick tree, she touched it to her mouth, delicately rouging her lips, then started down the mountain.

Nominated by Kim Edwards

SOULS

by DANNIE ABSE

from TRIQUARTERLY

"After the last breath, eyelids must be closed
quickly. For eyes are windows of the soul
—that shy thing which is immortal. And none
should see its exit vulnerably exposed,"

proclaimed the bearded man on Yom Kippur.
Grownups believed in the soul. Otherwise
why did grandfather murmur the morning prayer,
"Lord, the soul Thou hast given me is pure"?

Near the kitchen door where they notched my height
a mirror hung. There I saw the big eyes
of a boy. I could not picture the soul
immaterial and immortal. A cone of light?

Those two black zeros the soul's windows? Daft!
Later, at medical school, I learnt of
the pineal gland, its size a cherrystone,
vestige of the third eye, and laughed.

But seven colors hide in light's disguise
and the blue sky's black. No wonder Egyptians
once believed, in their metamorphosis,
souls soared, became visible: butterflies.

Now old, I'm credulous. Superstition clings.
After the melting eyes and devastation
of Hiroshima, they say butterflies, crazed,
flew about, fluttering soundless things.

Nominated by Joan Murray

DENTAPHILIA

fiction by JULIA SLAVIN

from THE CRESCENT REVIEW

I ONCE LOVED A WOMAN who grew teeth all over her body. The first
one came in as a hard spot in her navel. It grew quickly into a tooth, a
real tooth with a jagged edge and a crown, enameled like a pearl. I
thought it was sexy, a little jewel in her belly button. Helen would
bunch up her shirt, undulate like a harem dancer and I'd be ready to
go. Then one day I came home from the mill and Helen called for me
to come upstairs. She sat at the foot of our bed wrapped in a towel,
still wet and shiny from the shower. She lifted her arm. I felt around.
With her arm raised I could see the outline of a row of upper incisors
pressing out just under her skin. My God, I thought, the soft under-
side of her arm looked like a crocodile jaw. She said it'd been itching
and painful there for some time. I told her not to worry. It was noth-
ing. It would go away. I even managed to make her believe me long
enough for her to go to sleep and for me to lay awake all night won-
dering what the hell to do. But in the morning when she scratched my
thigh with a molar that had sprouted in the crease behind her knee, I
called Dr. Manfred.

"Yes, well . . . yes, well. . . . " Dr. Manfred murmured as he exam-
ined Helen's body with a small magnifying glass that looked like the
kind jewelers use to appraise diamonds. With each "yes, well" my
chest expanded, tightening my shirt at the buttons. I thought my ribs
would burst out of my shirt and pile up on the floor like sticks.

"Well what?" I asked.

He drew the glass away from his eye and smiled a phony smile. "I can
see how you thought they were teeth." Then he produced a little scalpel

from his white coat and began to scrape away at one of the teeth on the inside of Helen's elbow. It came off in thin translucent strips like the layers of an onion. Helen squeezed her lips together but didn't complain. She was brave when it came to pain. In a metal bowl, he ground the tooth with a marble pestle into a fine white powder like sand.

"You have calcinosis, my dear," Dr. Manfred said. "It's a calcification condition." He pushed up on a turquoise soap dispenser and rubbed his hands into a fat lather cloud. "Sometimes there's a build up of calcium deposits in the body," he said over running tap water. "We don't normally see the calcification externally, perhaps a plaque in the dermis, a deposit in the nodule. Not a worry, though." He shook his hands dry in the air. "We'll run some blood, check the thyroid. These things usually just go away. Poof."

Helen pinched the sand in the metal bowl between her thumb and index finger, rubbed some into her palm, let it run through her fingers back into the bowl. Dr. Manfred wrote a prescription for a calcium substitute and told her to lay off salt.

In the morning, Helen rolled over and I saw a long series of evenly-spaced holes in the sheet, like boll weevils had been eating the bed. By scraping off the tooth on her elbow, Dr. Manfred had just made room for more. Helen had teeth sticking out all the way up her arm. Her shoulder looked like the back of a stegosaurus. A fool could have told me Dr. Manfred was the wrong kind of doctor.

Dr. Freedman's waiting room had little chairs and little tables with crayons and coloring books. Some kid had already rifled through and scribbled everything green. Green duck, green cow, green Bo-Peep, green sheep. "The dentist sees grown-ups too?" I asked the receptionist.

"Yes, grown-ups too," she assured me in a little voice.

I gave Helen the last grown-up chair and sat in one of the little ones. My knees came to my head. The kid at my table was really upset about all the coloring books being colored in and his mother was telling him to try drawing his own pictures from his imagination. He looked at her like she was stupid. Then he noticed Helen. All the kids were looking at her with their mouths open even when their mothers told them it wasn't polite. Even when Helen smiled at them and said hello they couldn't stop gaping. The row of lowers across her cheekbone was too much.

She was in his office for an hour. I started pacing. Then two hours. The other patients were agitated and the receptionist was making apologies on the dentist's behalf. "I'm sure it's an urgent matter," she said. "You'll want him to give you the time you need when it's your turn."

"What took so long?" I asked driving home.

"I have hyper-stimulated dentin," she said looking out her window at the shadows from the trees. "He wants me to stop taking the calcium substitute. And he wants to see me in a week."

"What for?"

"He says I have twelve cavities." She flipped down the cosmetic mirror on the visor and freshened her lipstick.

"Leave this to me, Hel," I said. "You concentrate on getting well, and leave the rest to me." I reached over and touched her knee.

She turned towards me. "Can you pull over?" She asked. "I need to walk."

"Whatever you want," I said, stopping the truck on the shoulder.

"I'll see you at home," she said, climbing down.

"I'll come too," I said.

"I need to be alone for a while," she said, and closed the door.

The teeth started coming in pretty regularly. Every morning there'd be something new to report, something pressing against the skin, a toughening between her toes, a hard place on her ear. Then a few days would go by with nothing, and I'd think maybe the whole business was going to go away like Dr. Manfred said. But then the cramp Helen had been rubbing on her hip would explain itself with a freshly cut tooth or a red spot above her eyebrow would open up to a molar. "Just how ugly am I, Mike?" She asked one morning, staring out the front at some squirrels who were draining the seeds out of her bird feeders.

I moved her hair away and looked at her face which was blotched and speckled with incisors. "You could never be ugly, Hel," I said. And I meant it.

I spent a lot of spare time chopping and stacking wood in the back, trying to figure out how to keep Helen from being scared, thinking about how much I loved her and how going through this experience together *confirmed* to me how much I loved her. One afternoon I heard her singing in the downstairs bathroom. "Delta Dawn," to be precise. I leaned my ax against the stump and moved over to where I could see her, in front of the medicine chest mirror, rubbing the teeth on her body with peroxide and a chamois cloth like they were little pieces of carved crystal. Her hair was twisted into a new do with a big sunflower barrette and shimmery pink gloss on her lips. She'd bought a new dress. A yellow gabardine that pinched in under her breasts, fit tightly at her waist and buttoned all the way down. I watched her put on earrings—little zircons that picked up the light—and hook a matching necklace behind her neck. Then she looked over and saw me standing there with my hands against the window, my breath fogging up the glass, and screamed bloody murder.

* * *

Helen was at Dr. Freedman's office every other day for this or that. "He says I need another cleaning," she'd say, or, "He wants more x-rays." I'd sit in that kids' waiting room for hours, listening to Helen giggle and squeal in the office. Once, when things got too quiet I went in. I found her giddy and stupid on nitrous.

"You can't expect her to get treatment with no anesthesia," Dr. Freedman said snapping off latex gloves. Helen pulled one out of his hand, blew it up into a five fingered balloon and let it zip across the room. I pulled her out of the office by her wrist.

In the car, Helen was furious. She said I was way out of line. I tried arguing with her but she told me not to bother her, she was cutting a tooth on her neck.

I came home from the mill one night and Helen had left a note saying she had her group. I made a sandwich with a couple of slices of cheese which had hardened around the edges and about a half cup of mayonnaise to mask the taste of some old turkey. Then I watched men's volleyball on ESPN. Helen was undressing when I woke up. Naked, she was a vision in gold, a treasure from King Tut's tomb, a gilded statue covered in jewels. For one sleepy moment, I thought she was the most beautiful thing I'd ever seen. Then I realized what I was looking at.

"Are you insane?" I asked about her rows upon rows of gold fillings. "We can't afford those. What were you thinking?"

"They were a gift from Dr. Freedman."

That put me over the top. I wasn't going to lose the woman I loved to a dentist. I pulled on my pants, threw on a shirt and shoes and grabbed Helen by the wrist. "I thought you'd like them," she cried as I yanked her bathrobe off a nail on the door and dragged her from the house. "I did them for you." I forced her in the truck and peeled out of the driveway. With Helen screaming and grabbing onto the strap above the window, I swerved and cut corners, thirty miles over the speed limit.

Dr. Freedman lived in a new brick split-level connected to his office. He opened his huge front door with a gaudy lion-head knocker. He was in pajamas. Blue silk. Helen was trying to wiggle out of my grip and kicking me in the shins with her sharp little feet.

"Why don't you come in, Mike, and we'll talk it over," Freedman said, trying to sound like he was the one in control and I was the crack brain.

"We don't want any of your handouts," I yelled.

"They were a gift, Mike," he said. "Professional courtesy. For all the business Helen's brought."

"Take 'em out."

"That's not reasonable, Mike. You're not being reasonable." Freedman held his skinny little hands up, his only defense as I moved towards him to bust his mouth in. Helen was screaming. I was hurting her wrist. I let her go and she ran across the lawn. The dentist and I just stood there, like a couple of lazy dogs and watched her run, her feet cutting divots into the dentist's lawn, her teeth opalescent in the moonlight.

I didn't go to work the next day. I couldn't get out of bed. I called the mill and said I had the flu. I called all of Helen's girlfriends to see if they'd seen her. Around noon I drove around to places Helen liked to go—Hatcher's Boutique, Sweet Nothings, Flower Emporium— knowing full well she wouldn't be seen in any of those places now. I bought some roses at the Emporium, came home and watched TV. Five o'clock that afternoon Helen came in. She'd had the gold replaced with porcelain. She thanked me for the flowers and went upstairs for a bath. I stood outside the bathroom door and asked her if she wanted a glass of wine, cocoa, warm towels from the dryer, a sandwich, some music, an inflatable pillow for her neck, anything. No thank you, no thank you, nothing.

"If you want to do something," she called when I ran out of offers and started to move away from the door. "You can wash my back."

I pushed open the door. She sat with her arms resting on the sides of the lion-claw tub like a queen. I lowered myself to my knees. She opened her mouth a little and I kissed her. She didn't kiss me back but she didn't push me away either. I dragged my tongue down her neck and around a circle of pointed teeth that surrounded her nipple like a fortress. She raised her chest. Then I scooped the soap out of the dish and rubbed up a lather. She bent forward causing little murky waves

400

to lap at the sides of the tub. The water was filled with lumps of chalky powder. I looked up at the ceiling to see if the plaster had come loose. Then I looked at her back. The skin was peeling like she'd had a bad sunburn, rolling up and coming off in shavings.

"I know what it looks like," Helen said before I could say anything. "Wash along the edges. It'll help it along."

"Help it along to what?" I managed to ask. Underneath the old skin she was tender, wrinkled and pink like a newborn. I was afraid to touch, worried I'd hurt her. She said it didn't hurt, that it just itched and stung a bit. Then I saw a couple of teeth bob to the surface of the bath water like a row of miniature buoys on a dark and rocky bay.

For a little while it seemed like everything was getting back to normal. Every morning we'd find a couple more teeth somewhere in the bed or swirling around in the shower drain. Throw them out, get rid of them, I said, but Helen saved them in a little Zulu basket. "For jewelry," she said, holding them in her hands like precious stones. "Maybe a necklace." I was so happy and giddy during that time, she could have worn the basket on her head and I wouldn't have objected. I bought her things. I took her dancing even though I'm no dancer.

Freedman cautioned otherwise. "Helen needs very special care during this period," he said. "She's completely defenseless." He'd called me into his office to talk about her recent blood test. There was an excess of calcium carbonate in her blood. He was concerned about the shedding.

"You're looking at me like you think I can't take care of my wife," I said.

Freedman shrugged. I knew he was in love with her. I mean, everybody was in love with Helen. I used to sit on a stool at *The Mug*, where she bartended, drinking diluted whiskey just waiting for a chance to talk to her. Two other guys did the same. But it was my car she slid into after work one snowy night. My lap she swung her leg over. And my hand that slid the ponytail holder out of her long brown hair. Now, she was getting better. She wasn't going to need him anymore. He was losing her and couldn't bear it.

More of the teeth dropped out and the skin on her back healed and in time the calcium in her blood dropped way down.

But then things started to get bad again.

One beautiful Spring morning I came out of the mill and Helen was sitting on the hood of our truck kicking her heels against the tire like a little girl. "My wisdom teeth are coming in," she smiled proudly.

I froze. "Where?" I finally asked.

She lowered her eyes bashfully and raised them. "Down there," she said.

"Oh," I said. What are you supposed to say when your wife tells you something like that? "Oh." She put her arms around my neck and slipped her butt off the hood. She felt like a wisp of grass. Then my brain bucked into action and I realized she was falling. And I was dropping her. I caught her under her arms before she broke on the asphalt.

"I'm fine, Mike. Really fine. Just a little wobbly." She moved away from me and did little herky jerky pirouettes around the parking lot like a glass ballerina on top of a busted music box.

To say the teeth started coming back in would be an understatement. They knocked down doors and busted back in. Bing! Bang! Bing! They grew in mounds on top of one another, in notched clumps like fallen stones from a temple ruin, in clusters like tiled mosaics. They grew straight and crooked and upside down and ingrown. You could sit and watch them grow, see them force their way out. Helen said it didn't hurt. She even got excited when she felt one coming. "Look at that one," she'd squeal. "Oh! Here comes another." And she'd brush and rub them with baking soda and peroxide, spend all day in front of the mirror singing and polishing.

Helen wasn't in Freedman's office fifteen minutes when I lost patience and barged in. He looked at me like he was really tired of my intrusions. Well, too bad for you, I thought. When I came around the chair I saw he had her legs in stirrups. "They're impacted," he said.

The whole business with Dr. Freedman had made me crazy. They were always talking on the phone and laughing and having appointments every day. In my mind, I saw them together, passing the rubber tube of the nitrous tank back and forth. I saw her legs hung over the arms of the chair with Freedman crouched down. "Hope you don't mind the drill," he'd say and think he was so funny as she'd laugh and wrap her arms around his neck, pulling him up into her. I started following her, listening in to her phone calls on the other line. But I was

402

a bad spy. I kept getting caught. "I know you're there, Mike," she'd say on the phone, talking to one of her girlfriends about a beauty makeover in a magazine. "I hear you breathing." And I'd hang up, sit on my hands on the bed. Once she tapped on my car window in the parking lot of the Price Chopper where I'd fallen asleep watching her shop. "Relationships have to be based on trust, Mike," she yelled through the glass. "Or there's *no* relationship." She was getting nasty. She snapped at me all the time. I couldn't do anything right. One night she stormed out of the house on the crutches she had to use now that her legs had gone so stiff. She said she and Dr. Freedman were going to the symphony. "The symphony?" I said from the front stoop.

"Yes," she hissed back. "The symphony."

"What for?" I said.

"For culture," she growled, right up in my face, three little canines on the end of her pointed chin. "You and me, Mike, we have no culture."

That was the night I tried to be with another woman. Robin was a waitress at The Mug who always wanted to get together with me when I only wanted Helen. We went back to her apartment but I didn't like touching her. She felt too soft, squishy. I missed Helen's rough spots, her premolars and molars, her pointy canines and wisdoms, the soft areas next to the hard areas. I missed being inside Helen and the challenge of going around the sharp places. Robin felt like Silly Putty, like I could stretch and bend her and tie her up with herself. I apologized to Robin and got up to go. When we were putting our clothes back on she said there were doctors that could help me with my problem. She said this in a mean way, not in a helpful way.

Helen was in bed when I got home, the sheet pushed down to her waist. In the cool streetlight that shined through the window, I could see the phosphorescent glow of the thick clumps of teeth that stuck all over her back like barnacles. I shucked off my clothes and slid in next to her. We slept on satin sheets, not because they're sexy but satin was the only material that didn't catch on the teeth that covered most of her body now. She perched herself up on her elbows and waited for me to talk. "I want things back the way they were," I said. "I miss us."

In the morning we went to Dr. Freedman's and Helen told him to pull the teeth. All of them. I expected him to tell me I was a hateful son-of-a-bitch but he nodded professionally and spread out his tools. He offered gas, Novocain, a sedative. Helen waved him off. He started with the molars on her rib cage. He used tweezers to pluck out the little teeth on her face and pliers for the bigger molars across her collar bone. He yanked, twisted and pulled and went on to the next. But something bad oozed out of those holes where the teeth had been, not the red blood that inevitably flows after a pulled tooth. This blood was black-red, the kind of blood that comes from deep inside you and doesn't want to be disturbed. Helen let out a low sorrowful moan. "Stop," I said finally. "No more."

I took her to the beach. She wanted to smell the salt and feel the air rush through her teeth, let the sounds of gulls and waves lull her to sleep. By now her beautiful face was covered in teeth. But she was still beautiful. I wrapped her in a satin quilt and put oven mitts on her hands which had become rough and bent. I laid her brittle body against a dune and we stayed there together like that for three days.

She said she was sorry time ran out on us and she wished we'd had kids. She apologized for going to the symphony with Dr. Freedman. "He made me feel pretty," she said. "I know it was wrong."

"I always thought you were beautiful," I said. "I still do."

After the second day she couldn't talk anymore because her tongue had calcified. I told her stories. I made them up out of nowhere. There was the giant turnip that crushed a big city; the eyeballs that took over the world. Her favorite was the talking stadium who fell in love with a cheerleader, got his heart broken, then realized, too late, because he'd already caved in and killed everybody, that his real love was the hot-dog lady in one of his concession stands who had been there all along inside him.

On the third day I woke up at sunrise and saw her looking up at pelicans flying in formation over the dunes. I'd seen pelicans in the Outer Banks of North Carolina, but never this far north. They flew southeast and faded into the horizon. Helen was still looking up. "Whatcha lookin' at, Hel?" I asked and looked where she was looking. But there was nothing up there. Not even a cloud.

Now and then, I stumble on an oasis, palm trees, blue water, and there's Helen leaning on a tree in the yellow dress she was buried in and yellow shoes, holding a banana daiquiri she made for me. I take a drink of the daiquiri but the cold hits my brain and gives me a headache. She says, "Poor baby, let me rub it," and holds out smooth ivory hands. Then she slips through my arms. Dissolves into sand. I grab at her but the more I grab the more sand caves in around me and it's not until I'm buried to the waist that I realize she's gone.

Nominated by The Crescent Review

L.A. DREAM #2

by MAUREEN SEATON

from PRAIRIE SCHOONER

I WAS ON THE LEFT side of the dream which was three-dimensional as all dreams I was watching myself on the left side of the dream I could not see my head but it was me as it is in all dreams and so my eyes were not visible yet the body was mine stretched out on a kind of bed or a bench this is always confusing this detail but it seemed wooden I don't know the period of the dream but I think it was a bench or a pew and I was naked. In the middle of the dream that is in the middle of the screen of the dream I could see a child who Freud (Jung?) said is also me and she could have been her bangs familiar her pixie face she was so little perhaps three or four the phallic stage though truly without a phallus in fact there was no phallus visible in the dream which did not detract the least from the fear. I'm sorry I told you the faint of heart must exit here or the very pure of spirit you may want to close your eyes because what happens next is so devastating and I myself the creator of the dream could not believe it upon waking but also could not deny the sequence of events how the little girl who was me climbed on top of the woman who was me and there was a flash of sex. How terrifying to me the woman both in the dream and in the moment I woke beside the electric fireplace grounded on a street that dead-ends on a river in Chicago. I put the child down on the floor at once and that's crucial but listen I don't know if this is important but listen I can understand now why some people hurt children I can understand the child wanting love so much she will open everything I understand how a woman con-

406

fuses desire and forgets this is a child I understand now I don't want to but I do the universe gave me the body and the child and the camera and told me go ahead and shoot.

Nominated by Prairie Schooner *and S. L. Wisenberg*

NATIVE DAUGHTER

fiction by LEE SMITH

from THE OXFORD AMERICAN

MAMA ALWAYS SAID, "Talk real sweet and you can have whatever you want." This is true, though it does not hurt to have a nice bust either. Since I was blessed early on in both the voice and bosom departments, I got the hell out of Eastern Kentucky at the first opportunity and never looked back. That's the way Mama raised us, not to get stuck like she did. Mama grew up hard and married young and worked her fingers to the bone and wanted us to have a better life. "Be nice," she always said. "Please people. Marry rich."

After several tries, I am finally on the verge of this. But it has been a lot of work, believe me. I'm a very high-maintenance woman. It is *not easy* to look the way I do. Some surgery has been involved. But I'll tell you, what with the miracles of modern medicine available to our fingertips, I do not know why more women don't go for it. *Just go for it!* This is my motto.

Out of Mama's three daughters, I am the only one that has gotten ahead in the world. The only one that really listened to her, the only one that has gone places and done things. And everywhere I go, I always remember to send Mama a postcard. She saves them in a big old green pocketbook which she keeps right by her bed for this very purpose. She's got postcards from Las Vegas and Disney World and Los Angeles and the Indianapolis 500 in there. From the Super Bowl and New York City and Puerto Vallarte. Just this morning, I mailed her one from Miami. I've been everywhere.

As opposed to Mama herself, who still cooks in the elementary school cafeteria in Paradise, Kentucky, where she has cooked for thirty years, mostly soup beans. Soup beans! I wouldn't eat another soup bean if my life depended on it, if it was the last thing to eat on the earth. I grew up on soup beans. Give me caviar. Which I admit I did not take to at first as it is so salty, but now have acquired a taste for, like Scotch. There are some things you just have to like if you want to rise up in the world.

I myself am upwardly mobile and proud of it, and Mama is proud of me, too. No matter what kind of lies Brenda tries to tell her about me. Brenda is my oldest sister who goes to church in a mall where she plays tambourines and dances all around. This is just as bad as being one of those old Holiness people up in the hollers handling snakes, in my opinion. Brenda tells everybody I am going to Hell. One time she chased me down in a car to lay hands on me and pray out loud. I happened to have a new boyfriend with me at the time and I got so embarrassed I almost died.

My other sister, Luanne, is just as bad as Brenda but in a different way. Luanne runs a little day care center at home, which has allowed her to let herself go to a truly awful degree, despite the fact that she used be the prettiest one of us all, with smooth, creamy skin, a natural widow's peak, and Elizabeth Taylor eyes. Now she weighs over two hundred pounds and those eyes are just little slits in her face. Furthermore she is living with a younger man who does not appear to work and does not look American at all. Luanne claims he has Cherokee blood. His name is Roscoe Ridley and he seems nice enough, otherwise I never would let Tiffany stay with them. Of course this arrangement is just temporary until I can get Billy nailed down. I feel that Billy is finally making a real commitment by bringing me along this weekend, and I have cleared the decks for action so to speak.

But speaking of decks, this yacht is not exactly like *The Love Boat* or the one on *Fantasy Island,* which is more what I had in mind. Of course I am not old enough to remember those shows, but I have seen the reruns. I never liked that weird little dwarf guy. I believe he has died now of some unusual disease. I hope so. Anyway, thank goodness there is nobody like that on *this* boat, we have three Negroes who are nice as you please. They smile and say yes ma'am and will sing calypso songs upon request, although they have not done this yet. I am looking forward to it, having been an entertainer myself. These island Negroes do not seem to have a chip on their shoulder like so many in the U.S., especially in Atlanta, where we live. My own relationship with black people has always been very good. I know how to talk to them, I know where to draw the line, and they respect me for it.

409

"Well, baby, whaddya think? Paradise, huh?" This is my fiancé and employer Billy Marcum who certainly deserves a little trip to paradise if anybody does. I have never known anybody to work so hard. Billy started off as a paving contractor and still thinks you can never have too much concrete. This is also true of gold, in my opinion, as well as shoes.

Now Billy is doing real well in commercial real estate and property management. In fact we are here on this yacht for the weekend thanks to his business associate Bruce Ware, one of the biggest developers in Atlanta, though you'd never know it by looking at him. When he met us at the dock in Barbados wearing those one hundred-year-old blue jeans, I was so surprised. I believe that in general, people should look as good as they can. Billy and I had an interesting discussion about this in which he said that from his own observation, *really* rich people like Bruce Ware will often dress down, and even drive junk cars. Billy says Bruce Ware drives an old jeep! I cannot imagine.

And I can't wait to see what his wife will have on, though I *can* imagine this, as I know plenty of women just like her—"bowheads" is what I call them, all those Susans and Ashleys and Elizabeths, though I would never say this aloud, not even to Billy. I have made a study of these women's lives which I aspire to, not that I will ever be able to wear all those dumb little bows without embarrassment.

"Honey, this is fabulous!" I tell Billy, and it is. Turquoise blue water so clear you can see right down to the bottom where weird fish are swimming around. Strange jagged picturesque mountains popping up behind the beaches on several of the little islands we're passing.

"What's the name of these islands again?" I ask, and Billy tells me, "The Grenadines." "There is a drink called that," I say, and Billy says, "Is there?" and kisses me. He is such a hard worker that he has missed out on everything cultural.

Kissing Billy is not really great but okay.

"Honey, you need some sunscreen," I tell him when he's through. He has got that kind of redheaded complexion that will burn like crazy in spite of his stupid hat. "You need to put it everywhere, all over you, on your feet and all. Here, put your foot up on the chair," I tell him, and he does, and I rub sunscreen all over his fat white feet one after the other and his ankles and his calves right up to those baggy plaid shorts. This is something I will not do after we're married.

"Hey Billy, how'd you rate that kind of service?" It's Bruce Ware, now in cut-offs, and followed not by his wife but by some younger heavier country club-type guy. I can feel their eyes on my cleavage.

"I'm Chanel Keen, Billy's fiancée." I straighten up and shake their hands. One of the things Billy does not know about me is that my name used to be Mayruth, back in the Dark Ages. Mayruth! Can you imagine?

Bruce introduces his associate, Mack Durant, and then they both stand there grinning at me. I can tell they are surprised that Billy would have such a classy fiancée as myself.

"I thought your wife was coming," I say to Bruce Ware, looking at Billy.

"She certainly intended to, Chanel," Bruce says, "but something came up at the very last minute. I know she would have enjoyed being here with you and Billy." One thing I have noticed about very successful people is that they say your name all the time and look right at you. Bruce Ware does this.

He and Mack sit down in the deck chairs. I imagine their little bow-head wives back in Atlanta shopping or getting their legs waxed or screwing the kids' soccer coach.

Actually I am relieved that the wives stayed home. It is less competition for me, and I have never liked women much anyway. I never know what to say to them, though I am very good at drawing a man out conversationally, any man. And actually a fiancée such as myself can be a big asset to Billy on a business trip which is what this is anyway, face it, involving a huge mall and a sports complex. It's a big deal. So I make myself useful, and by the time I get Bruce and Mack all settled down with rum and Cokes and sunscreen, they're showing Billy more respect.

Bruce Ware points out interesting sights to us, such as a real volcano, as we cruise toward St. Felipe, the little island where we'll be anchoring. It takes three rum and Cokes to get there. We go into a half-moon bay which looks exactly like a postcard, with palm trees like Gilligan's Island. The Negroes anchor the yacht and then take off for the island in the dinghy, singing a calypso song. It is *really foreign* here! Birds of the sort you find in pet stores, yachts, and sailboats of every kind flying flags of every nationality, many I have never seen before. "This is just *not American* at all, is it?" I remark, and Bruce Ware says, "No, Chanel, that's the point." Then he identifies all the flags for Billy and me. Billy acts real interested in everything but I can tell he's out of his league. I bet he wishes he'd stayed in Atlanta to make this deal. Not me! I have always envisioned myself on a yacht, and am capable of learning from every experience.

For example, I am interested to hear Bruce Ware use a term I have not heard before, "Euro-trash," to describe some of the girls on the

411

other yachts. Nobody mentions that about half the women on the beach are topless, though the men keep looking that way with the binoculars. I myself can see enough from here—and most of those women would do a lot better to keep their tops on, in my opinion. I could show them a thing or two. But going topless is not something which any self-respective fiancée such as myself would ever do.

The Negroes come back with shrimp and limes and crackers, etc. I'm so relieved to learn that there's a store someplace on this island, as I foresee running out of sunscreen before this is all over. While the Negroes are serving hors d'oeuvres, I go down to put on my suit which is a little white bikini with gold trim that shows off my tan to advantage. I can't even remember what we did before tanning salons! (But then I remember, all of a sudden, laying out in the sun on a towel with Brenda and Luanne, we had painted our boyfriends' initials in fingernail polish on our stomachs so we could get a tan all around them. CB, I had painted on my stomach for Clive Baldwin who was the cutest thing, the quarterback at the high school, he gave me a pearl ring that Christmas before the wreck but then I ran off to Nashville with Randy Rash.)

"You feel okay, honey?" Billy says when I get to the top of the little stairs where at first I can't see a thing, the sun is so bright, it's like coming out of a movie.

"Sure I do." I give Billy a little wifely peck on the cheek.

"*Damn,*" Mack Durant says. "You sure *look* okay." Mack himself looks like Burt Reynolds but fatter. I choose to ignore that remark.

"Can I get one of the Negroes to run me in to the beach?" I ask. "I need to make a few purchases."

"Why not swim in?" Bruce suggests. "That's what everybody else is doing." He motions to the other boats, and this is true. "Or you can paddle in on the kickboard."

"I can't swim," I say, which is not technically true, but I have no intention of messing up my makeup or getting my hair wet, plus also I have a basic theory that you should never do anything in front of people unless you are really good at it, this goes not just for swimming but *everything*.

Bruce claps his hands and a Negro gets the dinghy and I ride to the beach in style, then tell him to wait for me. I could get used to this! Also, I figure that my departure will give the men a chance to talk business.

There's not actually much on the island that I can see, just a little shack of a store featuring very inferior products and a bunch of pathetic-looking Negroes begging, which I ignore, and selling their tacky native crafts along the beach. These natives look very unhealthy to me, with their nappy hair all matted up and their dark skin kind of dusty looking, like they've got powder on. The ones back in Atlanta are much healthier in my opinion, though they all carry guns.

I pay for my stuff with some big green bills that I don't have a clue as to their value. I'm sure these natives are cheating me blind. Several Italian guys try to pick me up on the beach, wearing nasty little stretch briefs. I don't even bother to speak to them. I just wade out into the warm clear water to the dinghy and ride back and then Billy helps me up the ladder to the yacht where I land flat on my butt on the deck, to my total embarrassment. "It certainly is hard to keep up your image in the tropics!" I make a little joke as Billy picks me up.

"Easier to let it go," Bruce Ware says. "Go native. Let it all hang out."

In my absence, the men have been swimming. Bruce Ware's chest hair is gray and matted, like a bathmat. He stands with his feet wide apart as our boat rocks in the wake of a monster sailboat, looking perfectly comfortable, as if he grew up on a yacht. Maybe he did. Billy and I didn't, that's for sure! We are basically two of a kind, I just wish I'd run into him earlier in life. This constant rocking is making me nauseous, something I didn't notice before when we were moving. I am not about to mention it, but Bruce Ware must have noticed because he gives me some Dramamine.

Billy and I go down below to dress up a little bit for dinner but I won't let Billy fool around at all as I am sure they could hear us. Billy puts on Khaki pants and a nice shirt and I put on my new white linen slacks and a blue silk blouse with a scoop neck. I am disappointed to see that Bruce and Mack do not even bother to change for dinner, simply throwing shirts on over their bathing trunks, and I am further disappointed by the restaurant which we have to walk up a long steep path through the actual real jungle to get to. It's at least a half a mile. I'm so glad I wore some flats.

"This better be worth it!" I joke, but then I am embarrassed when it's not. This restaurant is nothing but a big old house with Christmas lights strung all around the porch and three mangy yellow dogs in the yard, why I might just as well have stayed in Eastern Kentucky!

We climb up these steep steps onto the porch and sit at a table covered with oilcloth and it is a pretty view, I must admit, overlooking the little harbor. There's a nice breeze too. So I am just relaxing a little bit when a chicken runs over my foot which causes me to jump a mile. "Good Lord!" I say to Billy, who says, "Shhh." He won't look at me.

Bruce Ware slaps his hand on the table. "This is the real thing!" He goes on to say that there are two other places to eat, on the other side of the island, but this is the most authentic. He says it is run by two native women, sisters, who are famous island cooks, and most of the waitresses are their daughters. "So what do you think, Chanel?"

"Oh, I like it just fine," I say. "It's very interesting," and Billy looks relieved, but frankly I am amazed that Bruce Ware would want to come to a place like this, much less bring a lady such as myself along.

"Put it right here, honey," Bruce says to a native girl who brings a whole bottle of Mount Gay rum to our table and sets it down in front of him, along with several bottles of bitter lemon and ice and drinking glasses which I inspect carefully to choose the cleanest one. None of them look very clean, of course they can't possibly have a dishwasher back in that kitchen which we can see into, actually, every time the girls come back and forth through the bead curtain. There's two big fat women back there cooking and laughing and talking a mile a minute in that language which Bruce Ware swears is English though you can't believe it.

"It's the rhythm and the accent that makes it sound so different," Bruce claims. "Listen for a minute." Two native men are having a loud back-slapping kind of conversation at the bar right behind us. I can't understand a word of it. As soon as they walk away together, laughing, Bruce says, "Well? Did you get any of that?"

Billy and I shake our heads no, but Mack is not even paying attention to this, he's drinking rum at a terrifying rate and staring at one of the waitresses.

Bruce smiles at us like he's some guy on the Discovery Channel. "For example," he lectures, "One of those men just said, 'Me go she by,' which is really a much more efficient way of saying 'I'm going by to see her.' This is how they talk among themselves. But they are perfectly capable of using the King's English when they talk to us."

I make a little note of this phrase, the King's English. I am always trying to improve my vocabulary. "Then that gives them some privacy from the tourists, doesn't it?" I remark. "From people like us."

"Exactly, Chanel." Bruce looks pleased and I realize how much I could learn from a man like him.

"Well, this is all just so interesting, and thanks for pointing it out to me," I say, meaning every word and kicking Billy under the table, who mumbles something. Billy seems determined to match Mack drink for drink, which is not a good idea. Billy is not a good drunk.

414

Unfortunately I have to go to the bathroom (I can't imagine what *this* experience will be like!) so I excuse myself and make my way through the other tables which are filling up fast, I can feel all those dark native eyes burning into my skin. When I ask for the ladies' room, the bartender simply points into the jungle. I ask again and he points again. I am too desperate to argue, I stumble out there and find a portable toilet such as you would see at a construction site. Luckily, I have some Kleenex in my purse.

It is all a fairly horrifying experience made even worse by a man who's squatting on his haunches right outside the door when I exit, I almost fall over him. "Oh!" I scream and leap back, and he says something. Naturally, I can't understand a word of it. But for some reason I am rooted to the spot. He stands up slow and limber as a leopard and then we are face to face and he's looking at me like he knows me. He is much lighter-skinned and more refined-looking than the rest of them. "Pretty missy," he says. He touches my hair.

I'm proud to say I do not make an international incident out of this, I maintain my dignity while getting out of there as fast as possible, and don't even mention it to the men when I get back, as they are finally talking business, but of course I will tell Billy later.

So I just pour myself a big drink to calm down, and Billy reaches over to squeeze my hand, and there we all sit while the sun sets in the most spectacular fiery sunset I have ever seen in real life and the breeze comes up and the chickens run all over the place, which I have ceased to mind, oddly enough, maybe the rum is getting to me, it must be some really high proof. So I switch to beer though the only kind they've got is something called Hairoun which does not even taste like beer in my opinion. The men are deep in conversation though Mack gets up occasionally and tries to sweet-talk the pretty waitress who laughs and brushes him off like he is a big fat fly. I admire her technique as well as her skin which is beautiful, rich milk chocolate. I laugh to think what Mack's little bowhead wife back in Atlanta would think if she could see him now! The strings of Christmas lights swing in the breeze and lights glow on all the boats in the harbor. Billy scoots closer and nuzzles my ear and puts his arm around me and squeezes me right under the bust which is something I wish he would not do in public. "Having fun?" he whispers in my ear, and I say "yes" which is true.

I am expanding my horizons as they say.

This restaurant does not even have a menu. The women just serve us whatever they choose, rice and beans and seafood mostly, it's hard to say. I actually prefer to eat my food separately rather than all mixed up on a plate which I'm sure is not clean anyway. The men discuss getting an 85-percent loan at 9 percent and padding the specs, while I drink another Hairoun.

The man who touched my hair starts playing guitar, some kind of island stuff, he's really good. Also, he keeps looking at me and I find myself glancing over at him from time to time just to see if he is still looking, this is just like seventh grade. Still, it gives me something to do since the men are basically ignoring me, which begins to piss me off after a while since Mack is *not* ignoring the pretty waitress. The Negro with the guitar catches me looking at him, and grins. I am completely horrified to see that his two front teeth are gold. People start dancing. "I don't know," Billy keeps saying to Bruce Ware. "I just don't know."

I have to go to the bathroom again and when I come back there's a big argument going on involving Mack who has apparently been slapped by the pretty waitress. Now she's crying and her mother is yelling at Mack who is pretty damn mad, and who can blame him? Of course he didn't mean anything by whatever he did, he certainly wasn't going to sleep with her and get some disease. "Goddamn bitch," he says, and Bruce tells Billy and me to get him out of there, which we do, while Bruce gets into some kind of fight himself over the bill. These Negroes have overcharged us. Bruce's behavior at this point is interesting to me. He has gone from his nice Marlin Perkins voice to a real J.R. Ewing obey-me voice. *Thank God there is somebody here to take charge* I'm thinking as I stand at the edge of the jungle with a drunk on each arm and watch the whole thing happening inside the house like it's on television. The ocean breeze lifts my hair up off my shoulders and blows it around and I don't even care that it's getting messed up, though of course I am somewhat mad at Billy for getting so drunk.

"You okay, honey?" Bruce Ware says to me when he gets everything taken care of to his satisfaction, and I say, "Yes." Then Bruce takes Mack by the arm and I take Billy and we walk back down to the harbor two-by-two, which seems to take forever in the loud rustling dark. I wouldn't be a bit surprised if a gorilla jumped out and grabbed me, after everything that's happened so far! Bruce goes first, with the flashlight. I love a capable man.

When we finally make it down to the beach, I am so glad to see our Negroes waiting, but even with their help it's kind of a problem getting Mack into the dinghy, in fact it's like a slapstick comedy, and I fi-

416

nally get tickled in spite of myself. At this point Mack turns on me. "What are you laughing at, bitch?" he says, and I say, "Billy?" but all Billy says is "Shhh."

"Never mind, Chanel," Bruce tells me. "Mack's just drunk, he won't even remember this tomorrow. Look at the stars."

By now the Negroes are rowing us out across the harbor.

"What?" I ask him.

"Look at the stars," Bruce says, "you see a lot of constellations down here that you never get to see at home, for instance that's the Southern Cross right over there to your left."

"Oh yes," I say, though actually I have never seen *any* constellations in my life, or if I did I didn't know it, and certainly did not know the names of them.

"There's Orion," Bruce says. "See those three bright stars in a row? That's his belt."

Of course I am acting as interested as possible, but by then we've reached the yacht and the Negro on board is helping us all up (they have quite a job with Mack and Billy) and then two of them put Mack to bed. "Scuse me," Billy mutters, and goes to the back of the boat to hang his head over and vomit. Some fiancé! I stand in the bow with Bruce Ware, observing the southern sky, while the Negroes say good night and go off with a guy who has come by for them in an outboard. Its motor gets louder and louder the farther they get from us, and I am privately sure that they are going around to the other side of the island to raise hell until dawn.

Bruce steps up close behind me. "Listen here, whatever your real name is," he says, "Billy's not going to marry you, you know that, don't you?"

Of course this is none of Bruce Ware's business, so it makes me furious. "He most certainly is!" I say. "Just as soon as. . . ."

"He'll never leave Jean," Bruce says into my ear. "Never."

Then he sticks his tongue in my ear which sends world-class shivers down my whole body.

"Baby—" It's Billy, stumbling up beside us.

"Billy, I'm just, we're just—" now I'm trying to get away from Bruce Ware but he doesn't give an inch, pinning me against the rail. "Billy," I start again.

"Hey, baby, it's okay. Go for it. I know you like to have a good time." Billy is actually saying this, and there was a time when I would have actually had that good time, but all of a sudden I just can't do it.

417

Before either my ex-fiancé or his associate can stop me, I make a break for it and jump right down into the dinghy and pull the rope up over the thing and push off and grab the oars and row like crazy toward the shore. I use the rowing machine all the time at the health club, but this is the first time I have had a chance at the real thing. It's easy.

"Come back here," yells Bruce Ware. "Where the hell do you think you're going?"

"Native," I call back to them across the widening water. "I'm going native."

"Shit," one of them says, but by now I can barely hear them. What I hear is the slapping sound of my oars and the occasional bit of music or conversation from the other boats, and once somebody says, "Hey, honey," but I just keep on going straight for the beach which lies like a silver ribbon around the harbor. I look back long enough to make sure that nobody's coming after me. At least those natives can speak the King's English when they want to, and I am perfectly capable of helping out in the kitchen if need be. I'm sure I can pay one of them to take me back to Barbados in the morning. Won't that surprise my companions? Since I am never without some "mad money" and Billy's gold card, this is possible, although I do leave some brand new perfectly gorgeous shoes and several of my favorite outfits on the yacht.

A part of me can't believe I'm acting this crazy, while another part of me is saying, "Go, girl!" A little breeze comes up and ruffles my hair. I practice deep breathing from aerobics, and look all around. The water is smooth as glass. The whole damn sky is full of stars. It is just beautiful. All the stars are reflected in the water. Right overhead I see Orion and then I see his belt, as clear as can be. I'm headed for the island, sliding through stars.

Nominated by The Oxford American

BREATHING LESSONS

by RANE ARROYO

from PLOUGHSHARES

Yet another Puerto Rican
Buddhist. He wants to breathe in
peace, while keeping his rice-
and-beans cooking skills, his accent,

his blue jeans from the Santana
years, his wine and rum collections
housed inside his head. Today's lesson:
fireflies know they're grasshoppers'

illusory stars. And that
Puerto Rico is only
a comma in Time's poem some
have called the Great Antilles.

The word "greater" is too much ego,
an egg which only revolution
can hatch. Fireflies in San Juan
around El Morro are gardens

with feet and wings. He breathes in. In.
It's the breathing out that is
difficult, for it's a loss. Loss
has, in the past, been his source of

knowledge. If he gives that up, then
loss will no longer be a gain, gains.
Meditation is like a game
of monopoly with his

Latino friends. It always ends
with a coup: the upturned board,
hotels thrown into the air,
useless *Get out of jail* cards,

a shower of dollars suddenly
worthless because of the players'
disbeliefs. He feels Puerto Rican
in New York, American

in San Juan, and Catholic
in Buddhist temples. He has blamed
karma for his bad Protestant
lovers. Joy is joy, even if

fleeting, or found when one is
being tortured. Buddha said that.
So did Genet. And Oliver Stone.
So does a fisherman friend who

sleeps with soldiers just to steal their
guns ("In case of an emergency
war!"). He isn't the reincarnation
of Che. He must find other

excuses to breathe below his waist.
His teacher warns him: *Forget yourself,
you are wind.* Does he want to let go
of memories, that Spanish entrée?

No more codfish, pork feet, chicken
breast stuffed with chickpeas and carrots,
steak with baby onions so it is
Venus wearing a pearl necklace.

He sits and waits not to be waiting.
He sits on toilets, sits on buses,
sits at his desk, sits at lunch
counters, sits in a lobby for

the latest physician who
will comfort him ("No, you're not dead").
He sits in the bathtub filled with tears for
an ancient water god long

evaporated into the air.
Baptists once told him to trust that
they would pull him out of the deep
end of the baptismal pool by

his Samson-like pubic hair.
He watches MTV's *The Grind* and
sees men and women reject their
childhood by running away with

their hips. His wet dreams drown him.
He wakes up gasping for air. But
Buddha teaches that most beaches
in Puerto Rico are illusions,

that the naked and the dead are
not obscene but opaque. He longs
for *home.* Longing is thinking so
he takes bigger breaths. In, in, in,

out. He is tired of being
the serpent of the Caribbean
in the tequila bottle. He
is no message floating in

the sea. He has nothing to say. He
is nothing. Nothing hurts his lungs. He
lunges into the Void. But he grows
afraid as he has been so many

countless times when his airplanes
began their descents into San Juan,
urban ghost that embraces
him until he too is breathless.

Nominated by Jim Simmerman

TWO ACCIDENTS: REFLECTIONS ON CHANCE AND CREATIVITY

by LEWIS HYDE

from THE KENYON REVIEW

> Chance and chance alone has a message for us. Everything that occurs out of necessity, everything expected, repeated day in and day out, is mute. Only chance can speak to us. We read its messages much as gypsies read the images made by coffee grounds at the bottom of a cup.
>
> MILAN KUNDERA (48)

I.   The Lucky Find

OUTSIDE my study door a bird has built its nest with the usual twigs and moss but also, in this case, with two strips of paper torn from the sides of my computer printout. The bird did not set out in search of those white strands, of course, but when it happened to find them it knew how to weave a habitable home. "I do not seek, I find": this is Picasso's famous dictum, underlining the wandering portion of his artistic practice. In both cases, an intelligence makes itself at home in the happening world, one not so attached to design or purpose as to blinker out the daily wealth of accidents. "Chance itself pours in at every avenue of sense: it is of all things most obtrusive" (Hacking 200). I happened on that sentence from the philosopher C. S. Pierce late in the day I was writing these paragraphs, as I happened on that bird early in the morning. A friend was stuck writing her thesis when, wandering aimlessly through the library, she happened on a carrel where someone had spread out just the article she needed. Antonio Stradivari, wandering in Venice one day, came upon a pile of broken, waterlogged oars, out of which he made some of his most beautiful violins. A lucky find gave Picasso one of his famous sculptural creations:

> Guess how I made that head of a bull. One day, in a rubbish heap, I found an old bicycle seat, lying beside a rusted handlebar . . . and my mind instantly linked them together. The idea for this *Tête de Taureau* came to me before I had even realized it. I just soldered them together. . . . (Picasso 157)

In classical Greece the accidental find was called a *hermaion,* which means a "gift-of-Hermes," though it should be said that because Hermes was such a duplicitous god his "gifts" can entail both finding and loss. He is generous, but also a thief. In a journal entry Carl Kerényi records how a book of his disappeared on a boat trip: "Does Hermes wish to play . . . with me again? . . . I am left with the feeling of being stolen from, something uncanny, a vague sense of change of circumstances—truly something hermetic" (Kerényi, *Hermes* iv-v). Accidental loss, accidental gain—both flow from Hermes, the single constant being accident.

And yet that formulation doesn't quite catch the tone of things, for with the right kind of attention it is the *happy* accident, the creative accident, that Hermes engenders. Perhaps Kerényi's use of the word "uncanny" bears attention: In hermetic territory, who is to say what is loss and what is gain? It's hard to get your bearings. There's a "change of circumstance," that's all you know, for in uncanny space the terms themselves collapse, and a sudden loss (my computer crashes, my car keys disappear) can flip and become a sudden gain (I slow down, I go walking in the woods).

The idea of "finding" itself bespeaks this indeterminate space. There are many ways in this world to acquire things: you can make something with your labor, you can buy it, you can receive it as a gift, you can steal it, and so on. "Finding" occupies an odd position in any such list. If I pocket a five-dollar bill found in the trash at the edge of a deserted parking lot, am I a thief? How should we describe a farmer who bumps into buried treasure with his plow (this being Aristotle's old example of a chance event)? He gets the gold not by working for it, not as a present from friend or relation, not by stealing it, not by purchase. . . . We are in a shady area here, and shady language is in order. "It fell off the truck" is the American version of what the ancient Greeks meant by a *hermaion*.

To speak of happy accident is not to deny the negative side of chance; we all know that accident can bring great loss and grief, contingency can breed great tragedy. But for the tone that accompanies a "gift of Hermes" we might look at an example that features the god himself. In the *Homeric Hymn to Hermes* we hear how Hermes, newly born, stepped from his mother's cave and bumped into something unexpected—a wood turtle waddling past.

> Hermes picked up the turtle with both hands
> and carried his lovely toy into the house.
> He turned her over and with a scoop of grey iron
> scraped the marrow from her mountain shell.
> And, just as a swift thought can fly through the
> heart of a person haunted with care,
> just as bright glances spin from the eyes,
> so, in one instant, Hermes knew what to do and did it.
> He cuts stalks of reed to measure, fitted them through
> the shell and fastened their ends across the back.
> Skillfully, he tightened a piece of cowhide,
> set the arms in place, fixed a yoke across them,
> and stretched seven sheep-gut strings to sound in
>   harmony[1]

In this way and in this slightly manic mood the young god made the first lyre. He is a little like Picasso with the bicycle parts in the rubbish heap; not everyone would have made something of that encounter ("What's out there?" "Just an old turtle."), but when Hermes is around, coincidence turns fertile.

The ingredients of such prolific moments—surprise, quick thinking, sudden gain, and so forth—suffuse them with humor, not tragedy. Hermes laughs when he happens upon the turtle. Picasso once described his amusement coming upon some sea urchins in a tidal pool: "The sense of sight enjoys being surprised. . . . It's the same law which governs humor. Only the unexpected sally makes you laugh" (Picasso 90). The agile mind is pleased to find what it was not looking for. Someone once said that Picasso painted to do a kind of "research"; the remark annoyed him, and prompted him to formulate his sense of "finding":

> In my opinion to search means nothing in painting. To
> find, is the thing. Nobody is interested in following a man
> who, with his eyes fixed on the ground, spends his life look-
> ing for the pocketbook that fortune should put in his path.
> The one who finds something . . . , even if his intention
> were not to search for it, at least arouses our curiosity, if
> not our admiration. . . .
>
> When I paint, my object is to show what I have found and
> not what I am looking for. (Picasso 71–72)

Whoever the gods of fortune are, they will drop things in your path,
but if you search for those things you will not find them. Wandering is
the trick, and giving up on "loss" or "gain," and then agility of mind.

*

What, if anything, does an accident, lucky find, or chance event re-
veal? For most ancient or believing peoples the answer is simple: ac-
cidents are no accident; they reveal the will of the gods. What happens
on earth follows the designs of heaven, and if it appears to be random
chance that is only because our sight is not capacious enough to see
that apparent chance always follows grand design. An expert on Greek
oracles tells us that in ancient Greece, ". . . the drawing of lots was gov-
erned, not by chance, but by the will of the gods" (Flaceliere 17). Such
has also been the Christian understanding for centuries. In his
Anatomy of Melancholy, Robert Burton writes that "Columbus did not
find out America by chance, but God directed him. . . . It was contin-
gent to him, but necessary to God" (OED *sv contingent*). Even today
in the United States, Amish communities elect their bishops by a lot-
tery, which they understand to reveal God's will in the matter.

In cases where a character like Hermes is taken to be the agent of
chance it now becomes apparent why he is also thought of as a herald
or messenger. With Hermes, contingency is prophecy, at least to those
who have the ears to hear. Hermes gives his followers acute hearing;
they call him "the god of the third ear," the one that can hear an
essence buried in an accident. There is a form of divination associated
with Hermes called *cledonomancy,* derived from *cledon,* which means
an accidental but portentous remark, the language version of a lucky
find. Long ago Pausanias described this oracle of "Hermes-of-the-

426

Marketplace": At dusk as the lamps are being lit the petitioner leaves a "coin of local money" at the image of Hermes, whispers the questions he hopes to have answered, puts his hands over his ears, and walks away. When he takes his hands from his ears, the first words he hears contain the oracle's reply. All the better if the words are uttered by a child or a fool, someone clearly incapable of calculating an effect (Flaceliere 9–10).

Hermes, then, is not only an agent of luck, he helps to draw heaven's hidden meanings out of luck's apparent nonsense. In the modern world we find a similar conjunction of accident and insight, only the discovered meanings now lie in the head rather than the heavens, for we have translated the ancient art of inquiring into the will of the gods into psychological terms. "Divination techniques . . . are techniques to catalyze one's own unconscious knowledge," says Marie Louise von Franz in a typical modern formulation (38). Von Franz was a student of Carl Jung's, and it was Jung in his preface to the *I Ching* who famously announced that when we find meaning in synchronous events (the uncanny encounter in a distant city, say, or the three of spades turned up on the third of May) we are getting insight into "the subjective . . . states of the observer or observers" (xxiv). Freud was less directly concerned with divination, but his understanding of chance was similar. All his lectures on "the psychology of errors" are addressed to an imagined doubter who would say that slips of the tongue "are not worth my explanation; they are little accidents" (27). On the contrary, Freud argues, what hides in the unconscious only "masquerades as a lucky chance," and we must learn to remove the mask (69). Slips of the tongue and other errors "are serious mental acts; they have their meanings"; they "are not accidents" (41). Seeming mistakes will appear "as omens" to all those who have hermeneutic "courage and resolution" (53).

I suppose we will have to say it is no accident how many artists in the twentieth century had a similar understanding at the same time. Picasso believed that no painting can be plotted out beforehand and yet nothing is an accident, a seeming contradiction unless we understand that Picasso believed in the deep self, a personality of which the artist is not necessarily aware. "I consider a work of art as the product of calculations," he once said, "calculations that are frequently unknown to the author himself. It is exactly like the carrier pigeon, calculating his return to the loft. The calculation that precedes intelligence" (Picasso 30). What leads this pigeon-like artist are his

427

desires, his impulses. In a work of art, "what counts is what is spontaneous, impulsive" (21). "Art is not the application of a canon of beauty but what the instinct and the brain can conceive beyond any canon. When we love a woman we don't start measuring her limbs. We love with our desires . . ." (11).

One of Picasso's favorite assignments for a young artist was to have him or her try to draw a perfect circle. It can't be done; everyone draws a circle with some particular distortion, and that distorted circle is *your* circle, an insight into *your* style. "Try to make the circle as best you can. And since nobody before you has made a perfect circle, you can be sure that your circle will be completely your own. Only then will you have a chance to be original" (45). The deviations from the ideal give an insight into the style, and thus Picasso says, "from errors one gets to know the personality" (45).

This, then, is the sense in which an artist works with accidents, yet when he or she is done "there are no accidents. Accidents, try to change them—it's impossible. The accident reveals man" (91). With Picasso, as with Jung and Freud, accidents point to the concealed portion of the man or woman to whom they happened.

Ancient or modern, then, one continuing line of thought holds that accidents break the surface of our lives to reveal hidden purpose or design. The carefully interwoven structures of thought and social practice provide stability and structure, but they bring a kind of blindness and stupidity, too. Gifts of Hermes tear little holes in those fabrics to offer us brief intelligence of other realms.

*

That, at least, is one answer to the question of what a lucky find reveals. But here Hermes himself might come forward to complicate things. When he bumps into the tortoise, he seems to be giving a *hermaion* to himself, and what, we might ask, does *it* reveal? Who is sending a message to whom? In another story Hermes divides some sacrificial meat by lottery: in the Greek tradition a lottery is supposed to reveal the will of the gods, but when a god holds one, whose will is being revealed? The implication seems to be that heaven itself is not immune from chance. When a character like Hermes is around, the gods themselves suffer from uncertainty, and if that is the case an accidental find must sometimes reveal something other than heavenly will or hidden purpose. A remark by Carl Kerényi suggests what this

428

might be: "Chance and accident," he says, "are an intrinsic part of primeval chaos [and] Hermes carries over this peculiarity of primeval chaos—accident—into the Olympian order" (Kerényi, "Primordial Child" 57).

In this conceit the cosmos is an orderly thing surrounded by chaos, confusion, muddle. "Opportunities are not plain, clean gifts," writes the psychoanalyst James Hillman; "they trail dark and chaotic attachments to their unknown backgrounds . . ." (154). It must be that sometimes our assertions about higher order and hidden design are fables we have made up to help us ignore our own contingency. Accidents tear little holes in the fabric of life to reveal, well, little holes. In one of the books he published under the general title *Hermès,* Michael Serres, a French philosopher of science, writes skeptically about our assumptions of underlying unity in things. "The real," Serres suggests, may be "sporadic," made of "fluctuating tatters." Perhaps "the state of things consists of islands sown in archipelagoes on the noisy, poorly-understood disorder of the sea . . ." (xiii). Perhaps accidents reveal, not hidden realms of greater order, but a world of shifting fragments, noise, and imperfection. Accident is the revelation of accident.

In all fairness to the nature of hermetic accidents, however, I must here double back on myself one last time and add that in the case of the tortoise-shell lyre and the lottery I mentioned, when Hermes works with chance he does more than upset the order of things. If Hermes is involved, after a touch of chaos comes another cosmos. Hermes is a god of luck, but more than that, he stands for what might be called "smart luck" rather than "dumb luck." These two kinds of luck figure in Latin mythology, where Mercurius stands for the smart and Hercules for the dumb. "Should a *stupid* fellow have good luck, he owes it to the witless Hercules . . . ," Kerényi writes, referring us to a story in Horace in which "Mercurius once let Hercules talk him into enriching a stupid man. Mercurius showed him a treasure which he could use to buy the piece of land he was working. He did so, but then proved himself unworthy of the Hermetic windfall by continuing to work the same piece of land!" (Kerényi, *Hermes* 24–25).

That is "dumb luck," the luck of all gamblers whose winnings never enrich them, the luck of the grocery store clerk who hits the lottery, quickly spends himself into bankruptcy, and returns to being a clerk. It is sterile luck, luck without change. "Smart luck," on the other hand, adds craft to accident—in both senses, technical skill and cunning. Hermes is a skillful maker of the lyre, and he is canny as well, leveraging the wealth his *hermaion* brings. Hermes "trades up" with his lyre; he doesn't become just a turtle farmer or a lyre maker with an unpaid small business loan. Late in the *Hymn* he sings a song with his new instrument, and the tune seduces his brother Apollo, from whom he has recently stolen a herd of cattle. After Hermes stops singing, the *Hymn* says, "Apollo was seized with a longing he could do nothing about; he opened his mouth and the words flew out: 'Butcher of cattle, trickster, busy boy, friend of merry-makers, the things you're interested in are worth fifty cows. Soon I believe we shall settle our quarrel in peace.' "

Hermes, at this point in the *Hymn,* is actually involved in negotiating for certain divine powers; Apollo not only knows that, he accepts the music of the lyre as a part of the exchange. Under the manic spell of this *hermaion,* Apollo cancels the debt that Hermes incurred by his theft. The point is simply that this lucky find does more than add chaos to Apollo's world. The lyre *is* disruptive, of course—with it Hermes gets the spellbound Apollo to abandon his sense of what should properly happen to a thief. So, on the one hand, a touch of chaos comes into the Olympian order; but, on the other hand, it doesn't endure because Hermes soon weaves his lucky find into the scene he has disturbed (forever after Apollo plays the lyre as part of his own repertoire). Thus does Hermes show us how "smart luck" responds to hermetic windfalls.

*

Perhaps, then, what a lucky find reveals first is neither cosmos nor chaos but the mind of the finder. It might even be better to drop "cosmos" and "chaos," and simply say that a chance event is a little bit of the world as it is—a world always larger and more complicated than our cosmologies—and that smart luck is a kind of responsive intelligence invoked by whatever happens.

A story of scientific discovery makes a good illustration. "Chance favors the prepared mind" is Louis Pasteur's famous aphorism, and his own career abundantly illustrates its meaning. The neurologist James Austin has described one famous case:

> Pasteur was studying chicken cholera when his work was interrupted for several weeks. During the delay, the infectious organisms in one of his cultures weakened. When

injected, these organisms no longer caused the disease. However, this same group of fowls survived when he later reinoculated them with a new batch of virulent organisms. Pasteur made a crucial distinction when he recognized that the first inoculation was not a "bad experiment" but that the weakened organisms had exerted a protective effect. (202)

For chance to "favor the prepared mind" means, first of all, that chance events need a context before they can amount to anything. In evolution, a chance mutation disappears immediately if there is no hospitable environment to receive it; more to the point here, in this example Pasteur had a set of ideas about disease and inoculation and was thereby more able to recuperate his botched experiment. But notice that in addition to having a ready structure of ideas, the prepared mind is ready for what happens. It has its theories, but it attends as well to the anomaly that does not fit them. We therefore get this paradox: with smart luck, the mind is prepared for what it isn't prepared for. It has a kind of openness, holding its ideas lightly and willing to have them exposed to impurity and the unintended.

In a 1920 letter to a friend, James Joyce made a wonderful, quick remark on Hermes that links the god to this receptive mind. Joyce is musing on the mysterious plant, the *moly,* that Hermes gives Odysseus on the road to Circe's house. Classicists aren't sure what the *moly* is in fact (the wild garlic?), but Joyce has a hunch as to what it is in spirit:

> Moly is a nut to crack. My latest is this. Moly is the gift of Hermes, god of public ways, and is the invisible influence (prayer, chance, agility, *presence of mind,* power of recuperation) which saves in case of accident. . . . Hermes is the god of signposts: i.e. he is, specially for a traveller like Ulysses, the point at which roads parallel merge and roads contrary also. He is an accident of providence. (272)

What I like best here is the phrase Joyce underlines: when Hermes is around, his gifts reveal the *presence of mind.* Not some hidden structure of mind, necessarily (not the Oedipus complex or an instinct for beauty), but more simply some wit that responds and shapes, the mind on-the-road, agile, shifty in a shifting world, capable of recuperation, and located especially at the spot where roads "parallel . . . and contrary" converge. Paul Valéry's enigmatic assertion, "the

431

bottom of the mind is paved with crossroads," speaks to me here, for the mind that has smart luck makes meaning from unlikely coincidence and juxtaposition.

How do we come by this wandering, crossroad mind? We already have it, I suppose, but those who take it seriously keep it awake through ritual attention to its gods, something as simple as touching the statute of Hermes as one leaves the town gate or enters the marketplace. At the thresholds where one crosses into territories of increased contingency, such small ritual action brings to mind the mind contingency demands. To go on a journey (or enter the painting studio) without consulting the god of the roads is to invite dumb luck; to take the god into account is to summon the presence of mind that can work with whatever happens. The first lucky find (or unlucky loss!) will reveal whether or not anything has responded to the summons.

II. A Net to Catch Contingency

In the late 1940s D. T. Suzuki, the Japanese Buddhist scholar, lectured at Columbia University, and one of these lectures gave the composer John Cage a key insight into what was already a part of his method. Suzuki drew a circle on the blackboard and sectioned off a bit of it with two parallel lines. The full circle stood for the possible range of mind, while the small part between the lines stood for the ego. Cage remembers Suzuki saying that "the ego can cut itself off from this big Mind, which passes through it, or it can open itself up" (52).[2]

It is especially by our "likes and dislikes," Cage says, that we cut ourselves off from the wider mind (and the wider world). Likes and dislikes are the lap dogs and guard dogs of the ego, busy all the time, panting and barking at the gates of attachment and aversion and thereby narrowing perception and experience. Furthermore, the ego itself cannot intentionally escape what the ego does—intention always operates in terms of desire or aversion—and we therefore need a practice or discipline of *non*intention, a way to make an end run around the ego's habitual operations. The Zen tradition, Cage says, suggests the practice of cross-legged meditation: "You go *in* through discipline, then you get free of the ego." Cage thought his own artistic practice moved in the other direction to the same end: "I decided to go *out*. That's why I decided to use the chance operations. I used them to free myself from the ego" (229).

What do you want for lunch, a hamburger or a hot dog? Flip a coin, and the decision will have nothing to do with your habitual tastes. Would you like silence here, a sustained flute tone, the noise of traffic, or the car alarm? You might hate car alarms, as I do, but with Cage's method "you" and "I" do not get to choose. Cage says:

> I have used chance operations . . . in a way involving a multiplicity of questions which I ask rather than choices that I make. . . . If I have the opportunity to continue working, I think the work will resemble more and more, not the work of a person, but something that might have happened, even if the person weren't there. (52–53)

"Something that might have happened," by haps, per chance. Cage's faith was that this method would, as meditation promises, "open the doors of the ego" so as to turn it "from a concentration on itself to a flow with all of creation" (20). Cage was fond of repeating Meister Eckehart's assertion that "we are made perfect by what happens to us rather than by what we do" (Cage, *Silence* 64); therefore Cage not only allowed things to happen, he developed a practice that encouraged them to do so.

Popular perceptions of Cage tend not to see that for Cage chance operations were a spiritual practice, a discipline. One kind of courting of chance is exactly the opposite of discipline, of course—the young person putting herself at risk, the gambler on a spree, the speculator playing with a relative's money. Cage was a playful man, but these are not his uses of chance, as he himself often struggled to make clear. In recommending nonintention he once explained, "I'm not saying, 'Do whatever you like,' and yet that's precisely what some people now think I'm saying. . . . The freedoms I've given [in a musical score] have not been given to permit just anything that one wants to do, but have been invitations for people to free themselves from their likes and dislikes, and to discipline themselves" (102).

In many ways the discipline Cage recommended was as stringent as that of any monk on a month-long meditation retreat. He asked that intention be thwarted rigorously, not occasionally or whimsically. He *worked hard* at chance. He would literally spend months tossing coins and working with the *I Ching* to construct a score. It took so much time he would toss coins as he rode the New York subway to see friends. One famous piece less than five minutes long took him four

433

years to write. And when a piece was finished it was not meant to be an occasion for improvisation; it was meant to be played *within the constraints* chance had determined. "The highest discipline is the discipline of chance operations. . . . The person is being disciplined, not the work" (219). The person is being disciplined away from his or her "likes and dislikes," away from the ego's habitual attitudes and toward a fundamental change of consciousness.

An even fuller sense of the intentions of Cage's nonintention can be gleaned from the several places where he contrasts his own practice with the work of other artists who might seem, at first glance, to be engaged in a similar enterprise. Cage distanced himself from improvisation, from automatic art, and from methods of spontaneous composition, even though such things might initially seem related to his project. The score for Cage's *Concert for Piano and Orchestra,* for example, "frees" the orchestra at one point, and if you listen to the Town Hall recording of this piece you will hear one of the woodwinds improvise a bit of Stravinsky at that point. "You could look at the part I had given him," Cage later commented, "and you'd never find anything like that in it. He was just going wild—not playing what was in front of him, but rather whatever came into his head. I have tried in my work to free myself from my own head. I would hope that people would take that opportunity to do likewise" (68–69).

For the same reasons, Cage was not drawn to an art like that of Jackson Pollock. Pollock's working assumption was that the wildness of his paintings expressed his deep, primitive, and feeling self, and Cage would argue, I think, that no matter how "deep" the self is, it is still the self. "Automatic art . . . has never interested me, because it is a way of falling back, resting on one's memories and feelings subconsciously, is it not? And I have done my utmost to free people from that" (173). Cage much preferred the incidental drawings that are scattered throughout Thoreau's *Journals:* "The thing that is beautiful about the Thoreau drawings is that they're completely lacking in self-expression" (126).

*

The point of Cage's art, then, is not to entertain nor to enchant but to open its maker (and, perchance, its audience) to the world, to what is the case. In one of his oft-repeated stories, Cage tells of a time when he had just left an exhibit of paintings by his friend Mark Tobey: "I was standing at a corner of Madison Avenue waiting for a bus and I happened to look at the pavement, and I noticed the experience of looking at the pavement was the same as the experience of looking at the Tobey. Exactly the same. The aesthetic enjoyment was just as high" (175). Cage is praising Tobey here, not criticizing him, for Tobey's work had opened its viewer's eyes; he could *see* and enjoy what previously might have been the city's dull and unregarded asphalt skin. Such is one function of twentieth-century painting, says Cage, "to open our eyes," as its music should open our ears (174). As one of Cage's colleagues, the painter Jasper Johns, says: "Already it's a great deal to see anything clearly . . ." (Copeland 48).

I should add here that Cage's ideas have some authority for me because I have had the experience they describe. I first heard Cage himself in 1989 when he gave Harvard's Norton lectures, in his case, a collage of text fragments—drawn from Thoreau, Emerson, the *Wall Street Journal*, older Cage lectures—assembled and ordered through a series of chance operations. I found the lectures sometimes amusing but mostly boring; I walked out of the first one before it was over. But then a funny thing happened. I couldn't get the experience out of my head; the readings had cocked my ear, as it were, so that situation after situation recalled them to me. Nowadays in any city in the world one constantly hears a complicated sound collage—fragments of the radio, phrases coming out of shop doorways, the passing traffic, the honk of horns, the click of a door latch. From all around us, noises join coincidentally at the ear and, like it or not, this is the world we are given to hear. Having heard Cage I hear it more clearly.

Then I spent a summer some years later in Berkeley, California, writing an early draft of this essay and reading Cage's prose pieces and interviews. At the same time I was sitting zazen at the Berkeley Zen Center and often, as I sat, I was suddenly conscious of the sounds around me—of bird song punctuating the drone of a jet plane, for example, with a conversation from a nearby house as a sort of middle theme. These moments of hearing were *amusing*, and I have to wonder if my amusement wasn't the happiness of letting the world happen. I found I could briefly drop my unconscious, reflexive filtering, and when I did, it was as if I'd had water in one ear for years and suddenly it disappeared. In an interview Cage once described his own struggle with his *dislike* of the background drones of machines like refrigerator motors. "I spent my life thinking we should try to get rid of them. . . . What has happened is that I'm beginning to enjoy those sounds, I mean that I now actually listen to them with the kind of enjoyment with which I listen to the traffic. Now, the traffic is easy to recognize as beautiful, but those drones are more difficult and I didn't really set out to find them beautiful. . . . They are, so to speak, coming to me" (97). There is a state of mind that finds the sound of the refrigerator motor interesting, even at 3:00 A.M.

Cage readily admits that the change of mind that leads to this sort of interest is one of the purposes of his purposelessness. "I think that music has to do with self-alteration; it begins with the alteration of the composer and conceivably extends to the alteration of the listeners. It by no means secures that, but it does secure the alteration in the mind of the composer, changing the mind so that it is changed not just in the presence of music, but in other situations too" (99).

Chance operations can change the mind because they circumvent intention. "Everyday life is more interesting than forms of celebration," Cage once said, adding the proviso: "*when* we become aware of it. That *when*," he explained, "is when our intentions go down to zero. Then suddenly you notice that the world is magical" (208). The Tibetan Buddhist teacher, Chogyam Trungpa, once said that "magic is the total appreciation of chance." We are more likely to appreciate chance if we stop trying to control what happens, and one way to do that is to cultivate nonintention. To do it totally is to realize how fully the world is already happening inside us and around us, as if by magic.

In one sense, "art" itself disappears as a result of such a practice. In later years Cage felt that his own technique of composition had changed him, "and the change that has taken place is that . . . I find my greatest acoustic, esthetic pleasure in simply the sounds of the environment. So that I no longer have any need not only for other people's music but I have no need really for my own music" (99–100). An art produced in this spirit is hardly an art at all, at least not in the sense of leaving any durable object behind, any recognizable trace of the ego's intentions. In his book *For the Birds*, Cage tells of a party he once attended: "As I was coming into the house, I noticed that some very interesting music was being played. After one or two drinks, I asked my hostess what music it was. She said, 'You can't be serious?' " (22). It was a piece of his own, as it happens.

Such a piece differs markedly, I think, from the creations that an artist like Picasso makes when a lucky find surprises his eye, or at least the artists differ markedly. To articulate how they differ I want to borrow an idea from the theory of evolution. In his book *Chance and Ne-*

436

cessity, the French biologist Jacques Monod distinguishes between a creation and a revelation, between "absolute newness" and a newness that arises predictably from conditions already present. For example, Monod calls the sugar crystal formed in a cooling sugar solution a "revelation" because its appearance merely reveals a potential already present in the warm solution. It is a foreseeable event and not, therefore, a pure creation. On the other hand, a genetic mutation that survives to become the seed of a new species is a pure creation; nothing in the context out of which it came could have let us foresee what in fact appeared (Monod 87, 116).

In these terms, Picasso's *Tête de Taureau* is a revelation, not a creation. I am actually following Picasso himself when I say this: "The accident *reveals* man," he says (91). In the case of the *Tête de Taureau*, what we see, in case we had not seen it before, is that Picasso's "deep personality" is in love with the bulls and bullfighting. Some of his earliest images are of bullfights (John Richardson's biography reproduces two that Picasso drew when he was nine years old) (30). The bull's head is a part of his mental landscape so it is no surprise when his eye catches a familiar pattern in the handlebars and bicycle seat. It is an accidental find, to be sure, but it is a symptomatic accident. If there were bottle racks or a face of Christ in that rubbish heap, Picasso did not see them. Were Matisse to look over the same rubbish heap he might have found something much more colorful. If the mathematician Benoit Mandelbrot had cast his eye over that rubbish he might have seen a feathery rill of mud or a paisley oil slick. And John Cage? We could not predict what Cage would find, at least not if he came to the rubbish heap carrying the *I Ching* under his arm.

In Cage's terms, then, Picasso's attention to accident is a way of exploring the self, but not of leaving it, and it therefore runs the risk of indulgence and repetition. I am reminded of the theater director Peter Brook's critique of actors who try to get in touch with their "deep" selves: "The method actor . . . is reaching inside himself for an alphabet that is . . . fossilized, for the language of signs from life that he knows is the language not of invention but of his conditioning. . . . What he thinks to be spontaneous is filtered and monitored many times over. Were Pavlov's dog improvising, he would still salivate when the bell rang, but he would feel sure it was all his own doing: 'I'm dribbling,' he would say, proud of his daring" (Copeland 47).

The materials in Picasso's accidental find (the bicycle seat, for instance) are new, but the art he shapes from them returns us to a

437

Picasso we know very well. Picasso, of course, was quite happy to work with accident as a tool of revelation ("From errors one gets to know the personality!"), but Cage was not ("Personality is a flimsy thing on which to build an art."), for Cage was after what Monod would call the "absolute newness" of pure chance (Picasso 45; Cage, *Silence* 90). He was not out to discover any hidden self, nor did he think chance operations would reveal any hidden, already existing divine reality, as ancient diviners thought. "Composition is like writing a letter to a stranger," he once said. "I don't hear things in my head, nor do I have inspiration. Nor is it right, as some people have said, that because I use chance operations my music is written not by me, but by God. I doubt whether God, say he existed, would take the trouble to write my music" (74).

*

If the products of Cage's chance operations are not revelations, either of the self or of the divine, then what exactly are they? As I have said, in one sense they are "nothings," experiences whose lack of purpose has as their purpose the creation of a kind of awareness or attention ("Not things, but minds," was one of Cage's aphorisms [Cage, *Themes* 11]). Nonetheless, while Cage is clearly more interested in consciousness than in art objects, he does sometimes speak as if he were an object maker, describing his works as inventions or discoveries, and his process as a labor to "bring . . . new things into being" (207). This minor theme in his self-descriptions interests me because in it I hear echoes of Monod's idea that pure chance might lead to absolute newness, to creations that could not have been foreseen even if one knew the unrevealed contents of self or cosmos. Almost as a matter of definition, such absolute newness (in either evolution or art) can only arise if the process itself has no purpose, for where there is purpose, creations reveal it and are not, therefore, absolutely new.

Cage once said, for example, that a "happening" should create a thing wholly unforeseeable. In 1952 Cage and a group of friends at Black Mountain College produced one of the first happenings, a mixed theatrical performance whose shape was devised by chance operations (it included Cage reading one of his lectures from the top of a stepladder and the painter Robert Rauschenberg playing records on an old Victrola [Revill 161]). Much later Cage would say: "A Happening should be like a net to catch a fish the nature of which one does

438

not know" (113), a remark that resonates nicely with Monod's sense of "absolute" creation, for in evolution, too, the addition of chance to necessity means that creation always "catches fish" the nature of which can never be predicted. Cases of convergent evolution (in which similar species evolve in similar but distant ecosystems) demonstrate the point nicely. In both Africa and South America, for example, fish that must navigate in muddy water have evolved a method of sensing what is around them that involves broadcasting a weak electric field. For such electrolocation to work, the body of the fish becomes a sort of receiving antenna and must therefore be held stiff, which means the fish cannot undulate to swim the way most fish do. Electric fish, therefore, propel themselves by means of a single large fin that runs the length of the body. In the African species, the fin runs along the fish's back, but in South America it runs along the belly (Dawkins 97–99). Such beings arise from the play of chance and necessity; the nature of electricity necessarily stiffens the body, but the propelling fin is located by haps. Because pure chance is involved, in the evolution of species and in a John Cage happening, "fish" appear, the nature of which no one could have predicted from the original circumstances.

To say this another way, in both cases whatever emerges—no matter how beautiful or useful—is not the fruit of any hidden purpose. Cage, like Picasso, might have been able to say "I do not seek, I find," but in Cage's case his lucky finds never reveal unconscious motives. One of Cage's early innovations was to stick all sorts of objects into the strings of a piano (screws, bolts, pieces of paper), producing unpredictable and novel noises. "I placed objects on the strings, deciding their position according to the sounds that resulted. So, it was as though I was walking along the beach finding shells. . . . I found melodies and combinations of sounds that worked with the given structure" (62–63). If Cage was looking for "what works," it might seem at first that he did have purposes here, and that he was allowing his taste to guide him. But if that is the case it is hard to explain why he never made use of his lucky finds. That is to say, when Cage happened upon a melody he liked he didn't then go on to build with it, repeat it, weave it into a climax, and so forth. To do so would be to promulgate his "likes and dislikes," and by that begin again to shape and solidify the ego. Just as the play of chance in evolution is not directed toward any end, even when durable beauty arises from it, so when chance handed Cage an interesting melody he never took it as a sign of his purposes (as Picasso might), nor did he allow it to

439

arouse his intention. He moved on to let chance decide what happens next.[3]

Thus, and despite the fact that Cage sometimes spoke as if his art produced objects, this line of thought takes us back to his aphorism, "Not things, but minds." Cage was above all dedicated to creating a kind of awareness, believing that if we rigorously allow chance to indicate what happens next we will be led into a fuller apprehension of what the world happens to be. Take what is probably Cage's best known composition, a piece called 4' 33", four minutes and thirty-three seconds of silence broken into three movements (each indicated by the piano player lowering and raising the lid of the piano). The same year this piece was written, in 1952, Cage had a chance to visit an anechoic chamber at Harvard University, a room so fully padded that it was said to be absolutely silent. Alone in the room, Cage was surprised to hear two sounds, one high, one low; the technicians told him these were the sounds of his nervous system and his circulating blood. At that point he realized that there is no such thing as silence; there is only sound we intend and sound we do not intend (228–29; Revill 162–64). Thus 4' 33" is not so much a "silence" piece as a structured opportunity to listen to unintended sound, to hear the plenitude of what happens. The audience at the premiere of 4' 33" "missed the point," Cage once remarked. "What they thought was silence . . . was full of accidental sounds. You could hear the wind stirring outside during the first movement. During the second, raindrops began patterning the roof, and during the third the people themselves made all kinds of interesting sounds as they talked or walked out" (65).

Theories of evolution have shown us that, even though it is difficult at first to imagine how a process that depends on chance can be creative, nonetheless it is by such a process that creation itself has come to be. I have been interested in Jacques Monod's picture of the role of chance in the creation of the biosphere partly because his language resonates with Cage's in so many respects. On the one hand, Monod recognizes that there is a kind of self-protective egotism to all living things, which is to say, all living things perpetuate themselves through invariance (DNA is remarkably stable), and guard themselves against the "imperfections" that chance might visit upon them. On the other hand, invariance means that living things, by themselves, cannot adapt when the world around them changes, nor change to occupy empty niches of the biosphere. In nature, true change requires happy accidents. "The same source of fortuitous perturbations, of 'noise,' which in a nonliving . . . system would lead little by little to the disintegration of all structure, is the progenitor of evolution in the biosphere and accounts for its unrestricted liberty of creation," Monod writes, calling DNA "[a] registry of chance, [a] tone-deaf conservatory where the noise is preserved along with the music" (116–17).

This echoes Cage's aesthetic quite precisely. He was not blind to the fact that cultures and selves guard and replicate their ideals, their beauties, their masterpieces, but he did not cast his lot with durable structures, he cast it with perturbation. He turned toward chance to relieve the mind of its protective garment of received ideas so that it might better attend to the quietly stirring wind or the rain patterning the roof. He made an art that was a sort of net to catch contingency. He cocked his ear for noise, not the old harmonies, sensing that noise can lead to something as remarkable as this world, and believing that, in a civilization as complex and shifting as ours has become, a readiness to let the mind change as contingency demands may be one prerequisite of a happy life.

Notes

[1]All citations to the *Homeric Hymn to Hermes* are from my own unpublished translation. For a good English version with the Greek original, see *Hesiod, the Homeric Hymns and Homerica,* translated by Hugh G. Evelyn-White (Cambridge: Harvard UP, 1914).

[2]Unless otherwise indicated, all of John Cage's remarks are taken from Richard Kostelanetz's wonderfully well-composed book of interviews, *Conversing with Cage.*

[3]Cage was rigorous in his devotion to chance, to the consternation even of his friends. The composer Earle Brown once argued for the mixture of chance and choice: "I feel you should be able to toss coins, and then decide to use a beautiful F sharp if you want to—be willing to chuck the system in other words. John won't do that" (Tomkins 74).

Mark Twain's witticism about Wagner—"His music is better than it sounds"—nicely catches the complexity of my own reaction to Cage (walking out on him and then being haunted). Like Earle Brown, I prefer the play of chance and intention to the purity of Cage's method. But I also realize that he cleared a field no one had entered, and set a marker there. Even those who do not follow him into his field benefit from the sight of that marker.

Works Cited

Austin, James H. *Chase, Chance, and Creativity.* New York: Columbia UP, 1978.
Cage, John. *For the Birds.* In conversation with Daniel Charles. Boston: Marion Boyars, 1981.

————. *Silence*. Middletown: Wesleyan UP, 1961.

————. *Themes & Variations*. Barrytown: Station Hill, 1982.

Copeland, Roger. "Against Instinct: The Denatured Dances of Merce Cunningham." *Working Papers* (Fall 1990): 41–57.

Dawkins, Richard. *The Blind Watchmaker*. New York: W. W. Norton, 1987.

Flaceliere, Robert. *Greek Oracles*. Trans. Douglas Garman. New York: W. W. Norton, 1965.

Freud, Sigmund. *A General Introduction to Psychoanalysis*. Garden City: Garden City Publishing, 1943.

Hacking, Ian. *The Taming of Chance*. Cambridge: Cambridge UP, 1990.

Hillman, James. *Puer Papers*. Dallas: Spring Publications, 1979.

Joyce, James. *Selected Letters of James Joyce*. Ed. Richard Ellmann. New York: Viking, 1975.

Jung, Carl G. Foreword. *The I Ching*. 3rd ed., Bollingen Series XIX. Princeton: Princeton UP, 1967. xxi-xxxix.

Kerényi, Carl. "The Primordial Child in Primordial Times." In C. G. Jung and C. Kerényi, *Essays on a Science of Mythology*. Princeton: Princeton UP, 1969. 25–69.

————. *Hermes, Guide of Souls*. Dallas: Spring Publications, 1986.

Kostelanetz, Richard. *Conversing with Cage*. New York: Limelight Editions, 1991.

Kundera, Milan. *The Unbearable Lightness of Being*. New York: Harper, 1984.

Monod, Jacques. *Chance and Necessity*. New York: Vintage, 1972.

The Oxford English Dictionary. 20 vols. Oxford: Clarendon Press, 1989.

Picasso, Pablo. *Picasso on Art*. Ed. Dore Ashton. New York: Da Capo, 1972.

Revill, David. *The Roaring Silence. John Cage: A Life*. New York: Arcade, 1992.

Richardson, John. *A Life of Picasso. Vol. I: 1881–1906*. New York: Random House, 1991.

Serres, Michel. *Hermes: Literature, Science, Philosophy*. Baltimore: Johns Hopkins UP, 1983.

Tomkins, Calvin. *The Bride & The Bachelors*. New York: Viking, 1965.

Von Franz, Marie-Louise. *On Divination and Synchronicity, the Psychology of Meaningful Chance*. Toronto: Inner City Books, 1980.

Nominated by The Kenyon Review *and Rebecca McClanahan*

ON THE FAILURE NAMED BOSNIA

by P. H. LIOTTA

from CHELSEA

Love no country: countries soon disappear.
—Czeslaw Milosz

Somewhere in Hegel there is a line
    that masks the Janus truth, of how *the owl*
    of Minerva flies only at dusk. Which means,

I say, we see most wisely rearward, and so
    remain dumbfounded by all that confronts us
    in the present tense. And if you read this,

Mr. President, indeed if you read
    anything any mild-spoken citizen
    has ever sent to that great house

where it seems so often no one has ever
    finished composing a thought, let
    alone a sentence, it might be worth

your time to ponder Hegel, in the dark hours
    where I understand you are given over
    to your most buried thoughts, there,

in the stillness of those corridors, where
    the ghosts of the Republic walk
    beside you. Consider how what they

have to tell you is the truth, though it may
    not be your version of it, or mine,
    or ours; but truth, nonetheless.

Some will rise as geysers of earnest passion;
    some who have sinned against the office,
    as you well know, have never repented.

A man's fate, according to Heraklitos,
    is in his character. But what character
    is yours, or ours? We have all

been changed. Think of Aurelius, someone
    I know you read, when he speaks of how
    it is not death that a man should fear;

rather, it is never beginning to live.
    I respect the office, and you, if truth
    be known. But the world has gone before

our eyes. And no one, if not you, will cross
    the river of ash. The owl will fly
    into the shadow's dark soul and we will hear

only the swift whipping of a feathered wing
    crossing the moon's path. So, listen.
    Ask your guards to let you pass, alone.

Listen, tonight, when you pace the cavernous
    absence and the voices of the *Geist*
    of this Republic walk beside you.

They will tell you things you will not want
    to hear, in the carpeted silence beneath
    the dull, flickering sconce. They will call

you by name and when you hear them, do not
        turn away. Remember the clown of
        Kierkegaard, who stood at the proscenium

and announced the stage had broken into flame.
        Remember how the claque exploded
        in laughter? But what if god's clown

were real? And, absorbed through their eyes,
        we became that audience? What would we
        say when the clown's voice crackles,

fists tremble and feet smash through
        the stage? What if it were true? The theater
        is burning now. The best of us on fire.

Nominated by Jay Meek

THE FAMOUS TORN AND RESTORED LIT CIGARETTE TRICK

fiction by ELIZABETH GILBERT

from THE PARIS REVIEW

for Kate

IN HUNGARY, Richard Hoffman's family had been the manufac-
turers of Hoffman's Rose Water, a product which was used at that time
for both cosmetic and medicinal purposes. Hoffman's mother drank
the rose water for her indigestion, and his father used it to scent and
cool his groin after exercise. The servants rinsed the Hoffman's table
linens in a cold bath infused with rose water, such that even the kitchen
would be perfumed. The cook mixed a dash of it into her sweetbread
batter. For evening events, Budapest ladies wore expensive imported
colognes but Hoffman's Rose Water was a staple product of daytime
hygiene for all women, as requisite as soap. Hungarian men could be
married for decades without ever realizing that the natural smell of
their wives' skin was not, in fact, a refined scent of blooming roses.

Richard Hoffman's father was a perfect gentleman, but his mother
slapped the servants. His paternal grandfather had been a drunk and
a brawler, and his maternal grandfather had been a Bavarian boar-
hunter, trampled to death at the age of ninety by his own horses. Af-
ter her husband died of consumption, Hoffman's mother transferred

the entirety of the family's fortune into the hands of a handsome Russian charlatan named Katanovsky, a common conjurer and a necromancer, who promised Madame Hoffman audiences with the dead. As for Richard Hoffman himself, he moved to America, where he murdered two people.

•

Hoffman immigrated to Pittsburgh during World War II and worked as a busboy for over a decade. He had a terrible, humiliating way of speaking with customers.

"I am from Hungary!" he would bark. "Are you Hungary, too? If you Hungary, you in the right place!"

For years he spoke such garbage, even after he had learned excellent English, and could be mistaken for a native-born steelworker. With this ritual degradation he was tipped generously, and saved enough money to buy a popular supper club called The Pharaoh's Palace, featuring a nightly magic act, a comic and some showgirls. It was a favorite with gamblers and the newly rich.

When Hoffman was in his late forties, he permitted a young man named Ace Douglas to audition for a role as supporting magician. Ace had no nightclub experience, no professional photos or references, but he had a beautiful voice over the telephone, and Hoffman permitted him an audience.

On the afternoon of the audition, Ace arrived in a tuxedo. His shoes had a wealthy gleam, and he took his cigarettes from a silver case, etched with his clean initials. He was a slim, attractive man with fair brown hair. When he was not smiling, he looked like a matinee idol, and when he was smiling he looked like a friendly lifeguard. Either way, he seemed altogether too affable to perform good magic (Hoffman's other magicians cultivated an intentional menace) but his act was wonderful and entertaining, and he was unsullied by the often stupid fashions of magic at the time. Ace didn't claim to be descended from a vampire, for instance, or empowered with secrets from the tomb of Ramses, or kidnapped by gypsies as a child, or raised by missionaries in the mysterious Orient. He didn't even have a female assistant, unlike Hoffman's other magicians who knew that some bounce in fishnets could save any sloppy act. What's more, Ace had the good sense and class not to call himself the Great anything, or the Magnificent anybody.

447

On stage, with his smooth hair and white gloves, Ace Douglas had the sexual ease of Sinatra.

An older waitress named Sandra was setting up the cocktail bar at the Pharaoh's Palace on the afternoon of Ace Douglas's audition. She watched the act for a few minutes, then approached Hoffman and whispered in his ear, "At night, when I'm all alone in my bed, I sometimes think about men."

"I bet you do, Sandra," said Hoffman.

She was always talking like this. She was a fantastic, dirty woman, and he had actually had sex with her a few times.

She whispered, "And when I get to thinking about men, Hoffman, I think about a man exactly like that."

"You like him?" Hoffman asked.

"Oh my."

"You think the ladies will like him?"

"Oh my," said Sandra, fanning herself daintily. "Heavens, yes."

Hoffman fired his other two magicians within the hour.

After that, Ace Douglas worked every night that The Pharaoh's Palace was open. He was the highest paid performer in Pittsburgh. This was not a decade when nice young women generally came to bars unescorted, but The Pharaoh's Palace became a place where nice women—extremely attractive young single nice women—would arrive without dates, with their best girlfriends and with their best dresses to watch the Ace Douglas magic show. And men would come to The Pharaoh's Palace to watch the nice young women and to buy them expensive cocktails.

Hoffman had his own table at the back of the restaurant, and, after the magic show was over, he and Ace Douglas would entertain young ladies there. The girls would blindfold Ace, and then Hoffman would choose an object on the table for identification.

"It's a fork," Ace would say. "It's a gold cigarette lighter."

The more suspicious girls would open their purses and seek unusual objects—family photographs, prescription medicine, a traffic ticket—all of which Ace would describe easily. The girls would laugh, and doubt his blindfold, and cover his eyes with their damp hands. They had names like Lettie and Pearl and Siggie and Donna. They all loved dancing, and they all liked to keep their nice fur wraps with them at the table, out of pride. Hoffman would introduce them to eligible or otherwise interested businessmen. Ace Douglas would escort the nice young ladies to the parking lot at night, listening politely as they spoke up to him, resting his hand reassuringly on the smalls of their backs if they wavered.

And at the end of every evening Hoffman would say sadly, "Me and Ace, we see so many girls come and go . . ."

Ace Douglas could turn a pearl necklace into a white glove, and a cigarette lighter into a candle. He could produce a silk scarf from a lady's hairpin. But his finest trick was in 1959, when he produced his little sister from a convent school and offered her to Richard Hoffman in marriage.

Her name was Angela. She had been a volleyball champion in the convent school, and she had legs like a movie star's legs, and a very pretty laugh. She was ten days pregnant on her wedding day, although she and Hoffman had only known each other for two weeks. Shortly thereafter, Angela had a daughter, and they named her Esther. Throughout the early 1960s, they all prospered happily.

●

Esther turned eight years old, and the Hoffmans celebrated her birthday with a special party at The Pharaoh's Palace. That night, there was a thief sitting in the cocktail lounge.

He didn't look like a thief. He was dressed well enough, and he was served without any trouble. The thief drank a few martinis. Then, in the middle of the magic show, he leapt over the bar, kicked the bartender away, punched the cash register open and ran out of The Pharaoh's Palace with his hands full of tens and twenties.

The customers were screaming, and Hoffman heard it from the kitchen. He chased the thief into the parking lot and caught him by the hair.

"You steal from me?" he yelled. "You fucking steal from me?"

"Back off, pal," the thief said. The thief's name was George Purcell, and he was drunk.

"You fucking steal from me?" Hoffman yelled.

He shoved George Purcell into the side of a yellow Buick. Some of the customers had come outdoors, and they were watching from the atrium of the restaurant. Ace Douglas came out, too. He walked past the customers, into the parking lot, and he lit a cigarette. Ace Douglas watched as Hoffman lifted the thief by his shirt and threw him against the hood of a Cadillac.

"Back off me!" Purcell said.

449

"You fucking steal from me?"

"You ripped my shirt!" Purcell cried, aghast. He was looking down at his ripped shirt when Hoffman shoved him into the side of the yellow Buick again.

Ace Douglas said, "Richard? Could you take it easy?" (The Buick was his, and it was new. Hoffman was steadily pounding George Purcell's head into the door.) "Richard? Excuse me? Excuse me, Richard. Please don't damage my car, Richard."

Hoffman dropped the thief to the ground, and sat on his chest. He caught his breath and then smiled.

"Don't ever," he explained. "Ever. Don't ever steal from me. Ever."

Still sitting on Purcell's chest, he picked up the tens and twenties that had fallen on the asphalt, and handed them to Ace Douglas. Then he slid his hand into Purcell's back pocket and pulled out a wallet, which he opened. He took nine dollars from the wallet, because that was exactly all the money he found there. Purcell was indignant.

"That's my money!" he shouted. "You can't take my money!"

"*Your* money?" Hoffman slapped Purcell's head. "*Your* money? *Your* fucking money?"

Ace Douglas tapped Hoffman's shoulder lightly and said, "Richard, excuse me? Let's just wait for the police, okay? How about it, Richard?"

"*Your* money?" Hoffman was slapping Purcell in the face now with the wallet. "You fucking steal from me, you have no money! You fucking steal from me, I own all your money!"

"Aw Jesus," Purcell said. "Quit it, will ya? Leave me alone, will ya?"

"Let him be," Ace Douglas said.

"*Your* money? I own all your money!" Hoffman bellowed. "I own you! You fucking steal from me, I own your fucking *shoes!*"

Hoffman lifted Purcell's leg and pulled off one of his shoes. It was a nice brown leather wing tip. He hit Purcell with it once in the face, then tore off the other shoe. He beat on Purcell a few times with that shoe, until he lost his appetite for it. Then he just sat on Purcell's chest for a while, catching his breath, hugging the shoes and rocking in a very sad way.

"Aw Jesus," Purcell groaned. His lip was bleeding.

"Let's get up now, Richard," Ace suggested.

After some time, Hoffman jumped up off Purcell and walked back into The Pharaoh's Palace, carrying the thief's shoes. His tuxedo was torn on one knee, and his shirt was hanging loose. The customers backed against the walls of the restaurant and let him pass. He went into the kitchen and threw Purcell's shoes into one of the big garbage cans next to the pot-washing sinks. Then he went into his office and shut the door.

The pot washer was a young Cuban fellow named Manuel. He picked George Purcell's brown wing tips out of the garbage and held one of them up against the bottom of his own foot. It seemed to be a good match, so he took off his own shoes and put on Purcell's. Manuel's shoes had been plastic sandals, and these he threw away, into the big garbage can. A little later, Manuel watched with satisfaction as the chef dumped a vat of cold gravy on top of the sandals, and then he went back to washing pots. He whistled a little song to himself of good luck.

A policeman arrived. He handcuffed George Purcell and brought him into Hoffman's office. Ace Douglas followed them in.

"You want to press charges?" the cop asked.

"No," Hoffman said. "Forget about it."

"You don't press charges, I have to let him go."

"Let him go."

"This man says you took his shoes."

"He's a criminal. He came in my restaurant with no shoes."

"He took my shoes," Purcell said. His shirt collar was soaked with blood.

"He never had no shoes on. Look at him. No shoes on his feet."

"You took my money and my goddamn shoes, you animal. Twenty dollar shoes!"

"Get this stealing man out of my restaurant, please," Hoffman said.

"Officer?" Ace Douglas said. "Excuse me, but I was here the whole time, and this man never did ever have any shoes on. He's a derelict, sir."

"But, I'm wearing dress socks!" Purcell shouted. "Look at me! Look at me!"

Hoffman stood up and walked out of his office. The cop followed Hoffman, leading George Purcell. Ace Douglas trailed behind. On his way through the restaurant, Hoffman stopped to pick up his daughter, Esther, from her birthday party-table. He carried her out to the parking lot.

"Listen to me now," he told Purcell. "You ever steal from me again, I'll kill you."

"Take it easy," the cop said.

"If I even see you on the street, I'll fucking kill you."

The cop said, "You want to press charges, pal, you press charges. Otherwise you take it easy."

451

"He doesn't like to be robbed," Ace Douglas explained.

"Animal," Purcell muttered.

"You see this little girl?" Hoffman asked. "My little girl is eight years old today. If I'm walking on the street with my little girl and I see you, then I will leave her on one side of the street, and I will cross the street and I will kill you in front of my little girl."

"That's enough," the cop said. He led George Purcell out of the parking lot and took off his handcuffs.

The cop and the thief walked away together. Hoffman stood on the steps of The Pharaoh's Palace, holding Esther and shouting.

"Right in front of my little girl, you make me kill you? What kind of man are you? Crazy man! You ruin a little girl's life! Terrible man!"

Esther was crying. Ace Douglas took her from Hoffman's arms.

The next week, the thief George Purcell came back to The Pharaoh's Palace. It was noon, and very quiet. The prep cook was making chicken stock, and Manuel the pot-washer was cleaning out the dry goods storage area. Hoffman was in his office ordering vegetables from his wholesaler. Purcell came straight back into the kitchen, sober.

"I want my goddamn shoes!" he yelled, pounding on the office door. "Twenty dollar shoes!"

Then Richard Hoffman came out of his office and beat George Purcell to death with a meat mallet. Manuel the pot washer tried to hold him back, and Hoffman beat him to death with the meat mallet, too.

•

Esther Hoffman did not grow up to be a natural magician. Her hands were dull. It was no fault of her own, just an unfortunate birth flaw. Otherwise, she was a bright girl.

Her uncle, Ace Douglas, had been the American National Champion Close-Up Magician for three years running. He'd won his titles using no props or tools at all, except a single silver dollar coin. During one competition, he'd vanished and produced the coin for fifteen dizzying minutes without the expert panel of judges ever noticing that the coin spent a lot of time resting openly on Ace Douglas's own knee. He would put it there where it lay gleaming to be seen if one of the judges had only glanced away for a moment from Ace's hands. But they would never glance away, convinced that he still held a coin before them in his fingers. They were not fools, but they were dupes for his fake takes, his fake drops, his mock passes and a larger cast of impossible moves so deceptive they went entirely unnoticed. Ace Douglas had motions which he himself had never even named. He was a scholar of misdirection. He proscribed skepticism. His fingers were as loose and quick as thoughts.

But Esther Hoffman's magic was sadly pedestrian. She did the Famous Dancing Cane Trick, the Famous Vanishing Milk Trick, and the famous Chinese Linking Rings Trick. She produced parakeets from light bulbs, and pulled a dove from a burning pan. She performed at birthday parties, and could float a child. She performed at grammar schools, and could cut and restore the neckties of principals. If the principal was a lady, Esther would borrow a ring from the principal's finger, lose it, and then find it in a child's pocket. If the lady principal wore no jewelry, Esther would simply run a sword through the woman's neck while the children in the audience screamed in spasms of rapture.

Simple, artless tricks.

"You're young," Ace told her. "You'll improve."

But she did not. Esther made more money teaching flute lessons to little girls than performing magic. She was a fine flutist, and this was maddening to her. Why all this worthless musical skill?

"Your fingers are very quick," Ace told her. "There's nothing wrong with your fingers. But it's not about quickness, Esther. You don't have to speed through coins."

"I hate coins."

"You should handle coins as if they amuse you, Esther. Not as if they frighten you."

"With coins, it's like I'm wearing oven mitts."

"Coins are not always easy."

"I never fool anybody. I can't misdirect."

"It's not about misdirection, Esther. It's about *direction*."

"I don't have hands," Esther complained. "I have paws."

It was true that Esther could only fumble coins and cards, and she would never be a deft magician. She had no gift. Also, she hadn't the poise. Esther had seen photographs of her uncle when he was young at The Pharaoh's Palace, leaning against patrician pillars of marble in his tuxedo and cuff links. No form of magic existed which was close-up enough for him. He could sit on a chair surrounded on all sides by the biggest goons of spectators—people who challenged him or grabbed his arm in mid-pass—and he would borrow some common object and absolutely vanish it. Some goon's car keys in Ace's hand would turn into absolutely nothing. Absolutely gone.

Ace's nightclub act at the The Pharaoh's Palace had been a tribute to the most elegant vices. He used coins, cards, dice, champagne flutes, cigarettes—any item which would suggest and encourage drinking, sin, gamesmanship and money. The fluidity of fortune. He could do a whole act of cigarette effects alone, starting with a single cigarette borrowed from a lady in the audience. He would pass it through a coin, and then give the coin—intact—back to the lady. He would tear the cigarette in half and then restore it, swallow it, cough it back up along with six more, duplicate them and duplicate them again until he ended up with lit cigarettes smoking hot between all his fingers and in his mouth, behind his ears, emerging from every pocket—surprised? he was terrified!—and then, with a nod, all the lit cigarettes would vanish except the original. That one cigarette he would transform into a stately pipe, which he would smoke luxuriously during the applause.

Also, Esther had pictures of her father during the same period, when he owned The Pharaoh's Palace. He was handsome in his tuxedo, but with a heavy posture. She had inherited his thick wrists.

When Richard Hoffman got out of prison, he moved in with Ace and Esther. Ace had a tremendous home in the country by then, a tall, yellow Victorian house with a mile of woods behind it and a lawn like a baron's. He had only one neighbor, an elderly woman with a similarly huge Victorian home, just next door. Ace Douglas had made a tidy fortune from magic. He had operated The Pharaoh's Palace from the time that Hoffman was arrested, and with Hoffman's permission had eventually sold it at great profit to a gourmet restaurateur. Esther had been living with Ace since she'd finished high school, and she had a whole floor to herself. Ace's leggy little sister Angela had divorced Hoffman, also with his permission, and had moved to Florida to live with her new husband.

What Hoffman had never permitted was for Esther to visit him in prison, and so it had been fourteen years since they'd seen each other. In prison he had grown even sturdier. He seemed shorter then Ace and Esther remembered, and some weight gained had made him more broad. He had also grown a thick beard with elegant red tones. He was easily moved to tears, or at least seemed to be always on the verge of being moved to tears. The first few weeks of living together

454

again were not altogether comfortable for Esther and Hoffman. They had only the briefest conversations, such as this one:

Hoffman asked Esther, "How old are you now?"

"Twenty-two."

"I've got undershirts older than you."

Or, in another conversation, Hoffman said, "The fellows I met in prison are the nicest fellows in the world."

And Esther said, "Actually, Dad, they probably aren't."

And so on.

In December of that year, Hoffman attended a magic show of Esther's, performed at a local elementary school.

"She's really not very good," he reported later to Ace.

"I really think she's fine," Ace said. "She's fine for the kids, and she enjoys herself."

"She's pretty terrible. Too dramatic."

"Perhaps."

"She says, *Behold!* It's terrible *Behold* this! *Behold* that!"

"But they're children," Ace said. "With children, you need to explain when you're about to do a trick and when you just did one, because they're so excited they don't realize what's going on. They don't even know what a magician is, Richard. They can't tell the difference between when you're doing magic and when you're just standing there."

"I think she was very nervous."

"Could be."

"She says, *Behold* the *Parakeet!*"

"Her parakeet tricks are not bad."

"It's not dignified," Hoffman said. "She convinces nobody."

"It's not meant to be dignified, Richard. It's for the children."

The next week, Hoffman bought Esther a large white rabbit.

"If you do the tricks for the children, you should have a rabbit," he told her.

Esther hugged him. She said, "I never had a rabbit."

Hoffman lifted the rabbit from the cage. It was an unnaturally enormous rabbit.

"Is it pregnant?" Esther asked.

"No, she is not. She is only large."

"That's an extremely large rabbit for any magic trick," Ace observed.

Esther said, "They haven't invented the hat big enough to pull that rabbit out of."

"She actually folds up to a small size," Hoffman said. He held the rabbit between his hands like it was an accordion and squeezed it into a great white ball.

"She seems to like that," Ace said, and Esther laughed.

"She doesn't mind it. Her name is Bonnie." Hoffman held the rabbit forward by the nape of her neck, as though she were a massive kitten. Dangling fully stretched like that, she was bigger than a big raccoon.

"Where'd you get her?" Esther asked.

"From the newspaper!" Hoffman announced, beaming.

Esther liked Bonnie the rabbit more than she liked her trick doves and parakeets, which were attractive enough, but who were essentially only pigeons that had been lucky with their looks. Ace liked Bonnie, too. He allowed Bonnie to enjoy the entirety of his large Victorian home, with little regard for Bonnie's pellets, which were small, rocky and inoffensive. She particularly enjoyed sitting in the center of the kitchen table and from that spot would regard Ace, Esther and Hoffman gravely. Bonnie had a feline manner.

"Will she always be this judgmental?" Esther wanted to know.

Bonnie became more canine when she was allowed outdoors. She would sleep on the porch, lying on her side in a patch of sun, and if anyone approached the porch she would look up at that person lazily, in the manner of a bored and trustful dog. At night, she slept with Hoffman. He tended to sleep on his side, curled like a child, and Bonnie would sleep upon him, perched on his highest point, which was generally his hip.

As a performer, however, Bonnie was useless. She was far too large to be handled gracefully on stage, and on the one occasion that Esther did try to produce her from a hat, she hung in the air so sluggishly that the children in the back rows were sure that she was fake. She appeared to be a huge toy, typical and store-bought as their own stuffed animals.

"Bonnie will never be a star," Hoffman said.

Ace said, "You spoiled her, Richard, the way the magicians have been spoiling their lovely assistants for decades. You spoiled Bonnie by sleeping with her."

•

That spring, a young lawyer and his wife (who was also a young lawyer) moved into the large Victorian house next door to Ace Douglas's large Victorian house. It all happened very swiftly. The widow who had lived there for decades died in her sleep, and the place was sold within a few weeks. The new neighbors had great ambitions. The husband, whose name was Ronald Wilson, telephoned Ace, and asked if there were any problems he should know about in the area, regarding water-drainage patterns or frost heaves. Ronald had plans for a great garden and was interested in building an arbor to extend from the back of the house. His wife, whose name was Ruth-Ann, was running for probate judge of the county. Ronald and Ruth-Ann were tall and had perfect manners. They had no children.

Three days after the Wilsons moved in next door, Bonnie the rabbit disappeared. She was on the porch, and then she was not.

Hoffman searched all afternoon for Bonnie. On Esther's recommendation, he spent the evening walking up and down the road with a flashlight, looking to see if Bonnie had been hit by a car. The next day, he walked through the woods behind the house, calling the rabbit for hours. He left a bowl of cut vegetables outside on the porch, with some fresh water. Several times during the night, Hoffman got up to see if Bonnie was on the porch, eating the food. Eventually, he just wrapped himself in blankets, and laid down on the porch swing, keeping a vigil beside the vegetables. He slept out there for a week, changing the food every morning and evening, to keep the scent fresh.

Esther made a poster with a drawing of Bonnie (who looked very much like a spaniel in her rendering) and a caption reading LARGE RABBIT MISSING. She stapled copies of the poster on telephone poles throughout town and placed a notice in the newspaper. Ace Douglas called the local ASPCA for daily updates. Hoffman wrote a letter to the neighbors, Ronald and Ruth-Ann Wilson, and slid it under their door. The letter described Bonnie's color and weight, gave the date and time of her disappearance and requested any information on the subject at all. The Wilsons did not call with news, so the next day Hoffman went over to their house and rang the doorbell. Ronald Wilson answered.

"Did you get my letter?" Hoffman asked.

"About the rabbit?" Ronald said. "Have you found him?"

"The rabbit is a girl. And the rabbit belongs to my daughter. She was a gift. Have you seen her?"

"She didn't get in the road, did she?"

"Is Bonnie in your house, Mr. Wilson?"

"Is Bonnie the rabbit's name?"

"Yes."

"How would Bonnie get in our house?"

"Perhaps you have some broken window in the basement?"

"You think she's in our basement?"

"Have you looked for her in your basement?"

"No."

"Can I look for her?"

"You want to look for a rabbit in our basement?"

The two men stared at each other for some time. Ronald Wilson was wearing a baseball cap, and he took it off and rubbed the top of his head, which was balding. He put the baseball cap back on.

"Your rabbit is not in our house, Mr. Hoffman," Wilson said.

"Okay," Hoffman said. "Okay. Sure."

Hoffman walked back home. He sat at the kitchen table and waited until Ace and Esther were both in the room to make his announcement.

"They took her," he said. "The Wilsons took Bonnie."

●

Hoffman started to build the tower in July. There was a row of oak trees between Ace Douglas's house and the Wilson's house, and the leaves from these trees blocked Hoffman's view into their home. For several months, he'd been spending his nights watching the Wilson house from the attic window with binoculars, looking for Bonnie inside, but he could not see into the lower-floor rooms for the trees and was frustrated. Ace reassured him that the leaves would be gone by autumn, but Hoffman was afraid that Bonnie would be dead by autumn. This was difficult for him to take. He was no longer allowed to go over to the Wilson's property and look into the basement windows, since Ruth-Ann Wilson had called the police. He was no longer allowed to write threatening letters. He was no longer allowed to call the Wilsons up on the telephone. He had promised Ace and Esther all of these things.

"He's really harmless," Esther told tall Ruth-Ann Wilson, although she herself was not sure this was the case.

Ronald Wilson found out somehow that Hoffman had been in prison, and he'd contacted the parole officer, who had, in turn, contacted Hoffman, suggesting that he leave the Wilsons alone.

"If you would only let him search your home for the rabbit," Ace Douglas had suggested gently to the Wilsons, "this would be over very quickly. Just give him a half hour to look around. It's just that he's concerned that Bonnie is trapped in your basement."

"Why would we keep his rabbit? Why would we do that?"

Hoffman said to Ace, "Because of the vegetable garden. Think about this. Vegetables, Ace. Naturally, they are against the rabbit."

"If you would just let him look inside once . . ." Ace repeated.

"We did not move here to let murderers into our home," Ronald Wilson said.

"He's not a murderer," Esther protested, somewhat lamely.

"He scares my wife."

"I don't want to scare your wife," Hoffman said.

"He's really harmless," Esther insisted. "Maybe you could buy him a new rabbit."

"I don't want any new rabbit," Hoffman said.

"You scare my wife," Ronald repeated. "We don't owe you any rabbit at all."

In late spring, Hoffman cut down the smallest oak tree between the two houses. He did it on a Monday afternoon, when the Wilsons were at work, and Esther was performing magic for a Girl Scouts party, and Ace was shopping. He'd purchased a chain saw weeks earlier and had been hiding it. The tree wasn't very big, but it fell at a sharp diagonal across the Wilson's back yard, narrowly missing their arbor, and destroying a substantial corner of the garden.

The police came. After a great deal of negotiating, Ace Douglas was able to prove that the oak tree, while between the two houses, was actually on his property, and it was his right to have it cut down. He offered to pay generously for the damages to the Wilsons. Ronald Wilson came over to the house again that night, but he would not speak until Ace sent Hoffman from the room.

"Do you understand our situation?" he asked.

"I do," Ace said. "I honestly do."

The two men sat at the kitchen table across from one another for some time. Ace offered to get Ronald some coffee, which he refused.

"How can you live with him?" Ronald asked.

Ace did not answer this, but got himself some coffee. He opened the refrigerator and pulled out a carton of milk, which he smelled and then poured down the sink. After this, he smelled his cup of coffee, which he poured down the sink as well.

"Is he your boyfriend?" Ronald asked.

459

"Is Richard my boyfriend? No. He's my very good friend. And he's my brother-in-law."

"Really," Ronald said. He was working his wedding band around his finger as though he were screwing it on tight.

"You thought it was a dream come true to buy that nice old house, didn't you?" Ace Douglas asked. He managed to say this in a friendly, sympathetic way.

"Yes, we did."

"But it's a nightmare, isn't it? Living next to us?"

"Yes, it is."

Ace Douglas laughed. Ronald Wilson laughed, too, and said, "It's a complete fucking nightmare, actually."

"I'm very sorry that your wife is afraid of us, Ronald."

"Well."

"I truly am."

"Thank you. It's difficult. She's a bit paranoid sometimes."

"Well," Ace said, again in a friendly and sympathetic way. "Imagine that. Paranoid! In this neighborhood?"

The two men laughed again. Meanwhile, in the other room, Esther was talking to her father.

"Why'd you do it, Dad?" she asked. "Such a pretty tree."

He had been weeping.

"Because I am so sad," he said, finally. "I wanted them to feel it."

"To feel how sad you were?" she said.

"To feel how sad I am," he told her. "How sad I am."

Anyway, in July he started to build the tower.

Ace had an old pickup truck, and Hoffman used this to drive to the municipal dump every afternoon, so that he could look for wood and scrap materials. He built the base of the tower out of pine, reinforced with parts of an old steel bed frame. By the end of July the tower was over ten feet high. He wasn't planning on building a staircase inside, so it was a solid cube.

The Wilsons called the zoning board, who fined Ace Douglas for erecting an unauthorized structure on his property and insisted that the work stop immediately.

"It's only a tree house," Esther lied to the zoning officer.

"It's a watchtower," Hoffman corrected. "So that I can see into the neighbor's house."

The zoning officer gave Hoffman a long, empty look.

"Yes," Hoffman said. "This truly is a watchtower."

"Take it down," said the zoning officer to Esther. "Take it down immediately."

•

Ace Douglas owned a significant library of antique magic books, including several volumes which Hoffman himself had brought over from Hungary during the Second World War, and which had been old and valuable even then. Hoffman had purchased these rare books from gypsies and dealers across Eastern Europe with the last of his family's money. In the 1950s, he'd given them over to Ace. Some volumes were written in German, some in Russian, some in English.

The collection revealed the secrets of Parlor Magic, or Drawing Room Magic, a popular pursuit of educated gentlemen at the turn of the century. The books spoke not of tricks, but of "diversions," which were sometimes magical maneuvers but were just as often simple scientific experiments. Often, these diversions involved hypnosis or the appearance of hypnosis. Many tricks required complicated acts of memorization and practice with a trained conspirator hidden among the otherwise susceptible guests. A gentleman might literally use smoke and a mirror to evoke a ghost within the parlor. A gentleman might read a palm or levitate a tea tray. Or, a gentleman might simply demonstrate that an egg could stand on its end, or that magnets could react against one another, or that an electric current could turn a small motorized contrivance.

The books were exquisitely illustrated. Hoffman had given them to Ace Douglas back in the 1950s, because he had hoped for some time to recreate this lost conjury in Pittsburgh. He had hoped to decorate a small area within The Pharaoh's Palace in the manner of a formal upper middle-class European drawing room, and to dress Ace in spats and kid gloves. Ace did study the books, but he found that there was no way to accurately replicate most of the diversions. The old tricks called for common household items which were simply not common anymore: a box of paraffin, a pinch of snuff, a dab of beeswax, a spittoon, a watch fob, a ball of cork, a sliver of saddle soap, et cetera. Even if such ingredients could be gathered, they would have no meaning to modern spectators. It would be museum magic, resonating to nobody. It would move nobody.

To Hoffman, this was a considerable disappointment. As a very young man he had watched the Russian charlatan and swindling

461

necromancer Katanovsky perform such diversions in his mother's own drawing room. His mother, recently widowed, wore dark gowns dressed with china blue silk ribbons precisely the same shade as the famous blue vials of Hoffman's Rose Water. Her face was that of a determined regent. His sisters, in childish pinafores, regard Katanovsky in a pretty stupor of wonder.

Gathered in the drawing room as a family, they had all heard it. Hoffman himself—his eyes stinging from the phosphorus smoke—had heard it: the unmistakable voice of his recently dead father, speaking through Katanovksy's own dark mouth. They heard father's message (in perfectly accentless Hungarian!) of reassurement. A thrilling, intimate call to faith.

And so it was unfortunate for Hoffman that Ace Douglas could not replicate this very diversion. He would've liked to have seen it tried again. It must have been a very simple swindle, although an antique one. Hoffman would've liked to have witnessed the hoax voice of his dead father repeated and explained to him fully and, if necessary, repeated again.

·

On the first day of September, Hoffman woke at dawn and began preparing his truck. Months later, during the court proceedings, the Wilson's attorney would attempt to show that Hoffman had stockpiled weapons in the bed of the truck, an allegation that Esther and Ace would contest heatedly. Certainly there were tools in the truck—a few shovels, a sledgehammer and an ax—but if these were threatening they were not so intentionally.

Hoffman had recently purchased several dozen rolls of wide, silvery electrical duct tape, and at dawn he began winding the tape around the body of the truck. He wound long lengths of the tape, and then more tape over the existing tape, and he did this again and again, as armor.

Esther had an early morning flute class to teach, and she got up to eat her cereal. From the kitchen window, she saw her father taping his pickup. The headlights and taillights were already covered and the doors were sealed shut. She went outside.

"Dad?" she said.

And Hoffman said, almost apologetically, "I'm going over there."

"Not to the Wilsons?"

"I'm going in after Bonnie," he said.

Esther walked back to the house, feeling shaky. She woke Ace Douglas, who looked from his bedroom window down at Hoffman in the driveway, and he called the police.

"Oh, not the police," Esther said. "Not the police . . ."

Ace held her in a hug for some time.

"Are you crying?" he asked.

"No," she lied.

"You're not crying?"

"No, I'm just sad."

When the duct tape ran out, Hoffman circled the truck a few times and noticed that he had no way to enter it now. He took the sledgehammer from the flatbed and lightly tapped the passenger-side window with it, until the glass was evenly spiderwebbed. Then he gently pushed the window in. The glass crystals landed silently on the seat. He climbed inside, then noticed that he had no keys, so he climbed out of the broken window again and walked into the house where he found his keys on the kitchen table. Esther wanted to go downstairs to talk with him, but Ace Douglas would not let her go. He went down himself, and Esther slid her head under Ace's pillow and cried in a hard, down-low way.

Downstairs, Ace said, "I'm sorry, Richard. But I've called the police."

"The police?" Hoffman repeated, wounded. "Not the police, Ace."

"I'm sorry."

Hoffman was silent for a long time, staring at Ace.

"But I'm going in there after Bonnie," he said, finally.

"I wish you wouldn't do that."

"But they have her," Hoffman said, and he was now crying, as well.

"I don't believe that they do have her, Richard."

"But they *stole* her!"

Hoffman took up his keys and climbed back into his taped-up truck, still weeping. He drove over to the Wilson's home, and circled their house several times. He drove through the corn in the garden. Forward over the corn, then backwards, then forward over the corn again. Ruth-Ann Wilson came running out, and she pulled up some bricks that were lining her footpath and chased after Hoffman, throwing the bricks at his truck and screaming.

Hoffman pulled the truck up to the metal basement doors of the Wilson's house. He tried to drive right up on them, but his truck didn't have the power, and the wheels sunk into the wet lawn. He honked in long, forlorn foghorn blasts.

463

When the police arrived, Hoffman would not come out. He would, however, put his hands on the steering wheel to show that he was not armed.

"He doesn't have a gun," Esther shouted from the porch of Ace Douglas's house.

Two officers circled the truck and examined it. The younger officer tapped on Hoffman's window and asked him to roll it down, but he refused.

"Tell them to bring her outside!" he shouted. "Bring the rabbit and I will come out of the truck! Bring Bonnie! Terrible people!"

The older officer cut through the duct tape on the passenger-side door with a utility knife. He was able, finally, to open the door, and when he did that, he was able to reach in and drag Hoffman out, both of them cutting their arms over the spilled, sparkling glass of the broken window. Once outside the truck, Hoffman lay on the grass in a limp sprawl, face down. He was handcuffed and taken away in a squad car.

Ace and Esther followed the police to the station, where the officers took Hoffman's belt and his fingerprints. Hoffman was wearing only an undershirt and work pants, and his cell was small, empty and chilly.

Esther asked the older police officer, "May I go home and bring my father back a jacket? Or a blanket? May I please just do that?"

"You may," said the older police officer, and he patted her arm with a sort of authoritative sympathy. "You may, indeed."

•

Back home, Esther washed her face and took some aspirin. She called the mother of her flute student and canceled that morning's class. The mother wanted to reschedule, but Esther could only promise to call later. She noticed the milk on the kitchen counter and returned it to the refrigerator. She brushed her teeth. She changed into warmer autumn boots, and she went to the living room closet and found a light wool blanket for her father. She heard a noise.

Esther followed the noise, which was that of a running automobile engine. She went to the window of the living room and parted the curtains. In the Wilson's driveway was a sturdy white van with grills on the windows. The side of this van was marked with the emblem of the ASPCA. Esther said aloud, "Oh my."

464

A man in white coveralls came out of the Wilson's front door, carrying a large wire cage. Inside the cage was Bonnie.

●

Esther had never been inside the local ASPCA building, and she did not go inside it that day. She parked near the van, which she had followed, and watched as the man in the coveralls opened the back doors and pulled out a cage. This cage held three gray kittens, which he carried into the building, leaving the van doors open.

When the man was safely inside, Esther got out of her car and walked to the back of the van. She found the cage with Bonnie, opened it easily and pulled out the rabbit. Bonnie was much thinner than the last time Esther had seen her, and the rabbit eyed her with an absolutely expressionless gaze of nonrecognition. Esther carried Bonnie to her car and drove back to the police station.

She parked the car and got out, tucking the rabbit under her left arm. She wrapped the light wool blanket she'd brought for her father completely around herself, like a cape. Esther walked briskly into the police station. She passed the older police officer, who was talking to Ace Douglas and Ronald Wilson. She raised her right hand as she walked near the men and said solemnly, "How, Pale-faces."

Ace smiled at her, and the older police officer waved her by.

Hoffman's jail cell was at the end of a hallway, and it was poorly lit. Hoffman had not been sleeping well for several weeks, and he was cold and cut. One lens of his glasses had been cracked, and he had been weeping since that morning. He saw Esther approaching, wrapped in that light gray wool blanket, and he saw in her the figure of his mother, who had worn cloaks against the Budapest winters and who had also walked with a particular dignity.

Esther approached the cell, and she reached her hand between the bars toward her father, who rose with a limp to meet that hand. In a half-mad moment, he half-imagined her to be a warm apparition of his mother and, as he reached for her, she smiled.

Her smile directed his gaze from her hand to her face, and in that instant, Esther pulled her arm back out of the cell, reached into the folds of the blanket around her, and gracefully produced the rabbit. She slid Bonnie—slimmer now, of course—through the iron bars and held the rabbit aloft in the cell, exactly where her empty hand had been only a moment before. Such that Hoffman, when he glanced down from Esther's smile, saw a rabbit where before there had simply been no rabbit at all. Like a true enchantment, something appeared from the common air.

"Behold," said Esther.

Richard Hoffman beheld the silken rabbit and recognized her as Bonnie. He collected her into his square hands. And then, he did also behold his own daughter Esther.

A most gifted young woman.

Nominated by The Paris Review

INVIERNO

fiction by JUNOT DÍAZ

from GLIMMER TRAIN

FROM THE TOP OF Westminister, our main strip, you could see the thinnest sliver of ocean cresting the horizon to the east. My father had been shown that sight—the management showed everyone—but as he drove us in from JFK he didn't stop to point it out. The ocean might have made us feel better, considering what else there was to see. London Terrace itself was a mess; half the buildings still needed their wiring and in the evening light these structures sprawled about the landscape like ships of brick that had run aground. Mud followed gravel everywhere and the grass, planted late in fall, poked out of the snow in dead tufts.

Each building has its own laundry room, Papi said. Mami looked vaguely out of the snout of her parka and nodded. That's wonderful, she said. I was watching the snow sift over itself and my brother was cracking his knuckles. This was our first day in the States. The world was frozen solid.

Our apartment seemed huge to us. Rafa and I had a room to ourselves and the kitchen, with its refrigerator and stove, was about the size of our house on Sumner Welles. We didn't stop shivering until Papi set the apartment temperature to about eighty. Beads of water gathered on the windows like bees and we had to wipe the glass to see outside. Rafa and I were stylish in our new clothes and we wanted out, but Papi told us to take off our boots and our parkas. He sat us down in front of the television, his arms lean and surprisingly hairy right up to the short-cut sleeves. He had just shown us how to flush the toilets, run the sinks, and start the shower.

467

This isn't a slum, Papi began. I want you to treat everything around you with respect. I don't want you throwing any of your garbage on the floor or on the street. I don't want you going to the bathroom in the bushes.

Rafa nudged me. In Santo Domingo I'd pissed everywhere, and the first time Papi had seen me in action, whizzing on a street corner, on the night of his triumphant return, he had said, What are you doing?

Decent people live around here and that's how we're going to live. You're Americans now. He had his Chivas Regal bottle on his knee.

After waiting a few seconds to show that yes, I'd digested everything he'd said, I asked, Can we go out now?

Why don't you help me unpack? Mami suggested. Her hands were very still; usually they were fussing with a piece of paper, a sleeve, or each other.

We'll just be out for a little while, I said. I got up and pulled on my boots. Had I known my father even a little I might not have turned my back on him. But I didn't know him; he'd spent the last five years in the States working, and we'd spent the last five years in Santo Domingo waiting. He grabbed my ear and wrenched me back onto the couch. He did not look happy.

You'll go out when I tell you you're ready. I don't want either of you getting lost or getting hurt out there. You don't know this place.

I looked over at Rafa, who sat quietly in front of the TV. Back on the island, the two of us had taken guaguas clear across the Capital by ourselves. I looked up at Papi, his narrow face still unfamiliar. Don't you eye me, he said.

Mami stood up. You kids might as well give me a hand.

I didn't move. On the TV the newscasters were making small, flat noises at each other.

Since we weren't allowed out of the house—it's too cold, Papi said—we mostly sat in front of the TV or stared out at the snow those first days. Mami cleaned everything about ten times and made us some damn elaborate lunches.

Pretty early on Mami decided that watching TV was beneficial; you could learn English from it. She saw our young minds as bright, spiky sunflowers in need of light, and arranged us as close to the TV as possible to maximize our exposure. We watched the news, sitcoms, cartoons, *Tarzan, Flash Gordon, Jonny Quest, Herculoids, Sesame*

Street—eight, nine hours of TV a day, but it was *Sesame Street* that gave us our best lessons. Each word my brother and I learned we passed between ourselves, repeating over and over, and when Mami asked us to show her how to say it, we shook our heads and said, Don't worry about it.

Just tell me, she said, and when we pronounced the words slowly, forming huge, lazy soap-bubbles of sound, she never could duplicate them. Her lips seemed to tug apart even the simplest constructions. That sounds horrible, I said.

What do you know about English? she asked.

At dinner she'd try her English out on Papi, but he just poked at his pernil, which was not my mother's best dish.

I can't understand a word you're saying, he said one night. Mami had cooked rice with squid. It's best if I take care of the English.

How do you expect me to learn?

You don't have to learn, he said. Besides, the average woman can't learn English.

Oh?

It's a difficult language to master, he said, first in Spanish and then in English.

Mami didn't say another word. In the morning, as soon as Papi was out of the apartment, Mami turned on the TV and put us in front of it. The apartment was always cold in the morning and leaving our beds was a serious torment.

It's too early, we said.

It's like school, she suggested.

No, it's not, we said. We were used to going to school at noon.

You two complain too much. She would stand behind us and when I turned around she would be mouthing the words we were learning, trying to make sense of them.

Even Papi's early-morning noises were strange to me. I lay in bed, listening to him stumbling around in the bathroom, like he was drunk or something. I didn't know what he did for Reynolds Aluminum, but he had a lot of uniforms in his closet, all filthy with machine oil.

I had expected a different father, one about seven feet tall with enough money to buy our entire barrio, but this one was average height, with an average face. He'd come to our house in Santo Domingo in a busted-up taxi and the gifts he had brought us were small things—toy guns and tops—that we were too old for, that we broke right away. Even though he hugged us and took us out to dinner on the Malecón—our first meat in years—I didn't know what to make of him. A father is a hard thing to get to know.

Those first weeks in the States, Papi spent a great deal of his hometime downstairs with his books or in front of the TV. He said little to us that wasn't disciplinary, which didn't surprise us. We'd seen other dads in action, understood that part of the drill.

What he got on me about the most was my shoelaces. Papi had a thing with shoelaces. I didn't know how to tie them properly, and when I put together a rather formidable knot, Papi would bend down and pull it apart with one tug. At least you have a future as a magician, Rafa said, but this was serious. Rafa showed me how, and I said, Fine, and had no problems in front of him, but when Papi was breathing down my neck, his hand on a belt, I couldn't perform; I looked at my father like my laces were live wires he wanted me to touch together.

I met some dumb men in the Guardia, Papi said, but every single one of them could tie his motherfucking shoes. He looked over at Mami. Why can't he?

These were not the sort of questions that had answers. She looked down, studied the veins that threaded the backs of her hands. For a second Papi's watery turtle-eyes met mine. Don't you look at me, he said.

Even on days I managed a halfway decent retard knot, as Rafa called them, Papi still had my hair to go on about. While Rafa's hair was straight and dark and glided through a comb like a Caribbean grandparent's dream, my hair still had enough of the African to condemn me to endless combings and out-of-this-world haircuts. My mother cut our hair every month, but this time when she put me in the chair my father told her not to bother.

Only one thing will take care of that, he said. Yunior, go get dressed.

Rafa followed me into my bedroom and watched while I buttoned my shirt. His mouth was tight. I started to feel anxious. What's your problem? I said.

Nothing.

Then stop watching me. When I got to my shoes, he tied them for me. At the door my father looked down and said, You're getting better.

I knew where the van was parked but I went the other way just to catch a glimpse of the neighborhood. Papi didn't notice my defection until I had rounded the corner, and when he growled my name I hurried back, but I had already seen the fields and the children on the snow.

470

I sat in the front seat. He popped a tape of Jonny Ventura into the player and took us out smoothly to Route 9. The snow lay in dirty piles on the side of the road. There can't be anything worse than old snow, he said. It's nice while it falls but once it gets to the ground it just causes trouble.

Are there accidents?

Not with me driving.

The cattails on the banks of the Raritan were stiff and the color of sand, and when we crossed the river, Papi said, I work in the next town.

We were in Perth Amboy for the services of a real talent, a Puerto Rican barber named Rubio who knew just what to do with the pelo malo. He put two or three creams on my head and had me sit with the foam awhile; after his wife rinsed me off he studied my head in the mirror, tugged at my hair, rubbed an oil into it, and finally sighed.

It's better to shave it all off, Papi said.

I have some other things that might work.

Papi looked at his watch. Shave it.

All right, Rubio said. I watched the clippers plow through my hair, watched my scalp appear, tender and defenseless. One of the old men in the waiting area snorted and held his paper higher. When he was finished Rubio massaged talcum powder on my neck. Now you look guapo, he said. He handed me a stick of gum, which would go right to my brother.

Well? Papi asked. I nodded. As soon as we were outside the cold clamped down on my head like a slab of wet dirt.

We drove back in silence. An oil tanker was pulling into port on the Raritan and I wondered how easy it would be for me to slip aboard and disappear.

Do you like negras? my father asked.

I turned my head to look at the women we had just passed. I turned back and realized that he was waiting for an answer, that he wanted to know, and while I wanted to blurt that I didn't like girls in any denomination, I said instead, Oh yes, and he smiled.

They're beautiful, he said, and lit a cigarette. They'll take care of you better than anyone.

Rafa laughed when he saw me. You look like a big thumb.

Dios mío, Mami said, turning me around.

It looks good, Papi said.

And the cold's going to make him sick.

Papi put his cold palm on my head. He likes it fine, he said.

471

Papi worked a long fifty-hour week and on his days off he expected quiet, but my brother and I had too much energy to be quiet; we didn't think anything of using our sofas for trampolines at nine in the morning, while Papi was asleep. In our old barrio we were accustomed to folks shocking the streets with merengue twenty-four hours a day. Our upstairs neighbors, who themselves fought like trolls over everything, would stomp down on us. Will you two please shut up? and then Papi would come out of his room, his shorts unbuttoned and say, What did I tell you? How many times have I told you to keep it quiet? He was free with his smacks and we spent whole afternoons on Punishment Row—our bedroom—where we had to lie on our beds and not get off, because if he burst in and caught us at the window, staring out at the beautiful snow, he would pull our ears and smack us, and then we would have to kneel in the corner for a few hours. If we messed that up, joking around or cheating, he would force us to kneel down on the cutting side of a coconut grater, and only when we were bleeding and whimpering would he let us up.

Now you'll be quiet, he'd say, satisfied, and we'd lay in bed, our knees burning with iodine, and wait for him to go to work so we could put our hands against the cold glass.

We watched the neighborhood children building snowmen and igloos, having snowball fights. I told my brother about the field I'd seen, vast in my memory, but he just shrugged. A brother and sister lived across in apartment four, and when they were out we would wave to them. They waved to us and motioned for us to come out but we shook our heads, We can't.

The brother shrugged, and tugged his sister out to where the other children were, with their shovels and their long, snow-encrusted scarves. She seemed to like Rafa, and waved to him as she walked off. He didn't wave back.

North American girls are supposed to be beautiful, he said.

Have you seen any?

What do you call her? He reached down for a tissue and sneezed out a double-barrel of snot. All of us had headaches and colds and coughs; even with the heat cranked up, winter was kicking our asses. I had to wear a Christmas hat around the apartment to keep my shaven head warm; I looked like an unhappy tropical elf.

I wiped my nose. If this is the United States, mail me home.

Don't worry, Mami says. We're probably going home.

How does she know?

Her and Papi have been talking about it. She thinks it would be better if we went back. Rafa ran a finger glumly over our window; he didn't want to go; he liked the TV and the toilet and already saw himself with the girl in apartment four.

I don't know about that, I said. Papi doesn't look like he's going anywhere.

What do you know? You're just a little mojón.

I know more than you, I said. Papi had never once mentioned going back to the Island. I waited to get him in a good mood, after he had watched *Abbott and Costello,* and asked him if he thought we would be going back soon.

For what?

A visit.

Maybe, he grunted. Maybe not. Don't plan on it.

By the third week I was worried we weren't going to make it. Mami, who had been our authority on the Island, was dwindling. She cooked our food and then sat there, waiting to wash the dishes. She had no friends, no neighbors to visit. You should talk to me, she said, but we told her to wait for Papi to get home. He'll talk to you, I guaranteed. Rafa's temper, which was sometimes a problem, got worse. I would tug at his hair, an old game of ours, and he would explode. We fought and fought and fought and after my mother pried us apart, instead of making up like the old days, we sat scowling on opposite sides of our room and planned each other's demise. I'm going to burn you alive, he promised. You should number your limbs, cabrón, I told him, so they'll know how to put you back together for the funeral. We squirted acid at each other with our eyes, like reptiles. Our boredom made everything worse.

One day I saw the brother and sister from apartment four gearing up to go play, and instead of waving I pulled on my parka. Rafa was sitting on the couch, flipping between a Chinese cooking show and an all-star Little League game. I'm going out, I told him.

Sure you are, he said, but when I pushed open the front door, he said, Hey!

The air outside was very cold and I nearly fell down our steps. No one in the neighborhood was the shoveling type. Throwing my scarf over my mouth, I stumbled across the uneven crust of snow. I caught up to the brother and sister on the side of our building.

Wait up! I yelled. I want to play with you.

The brother watched me with a half grin, not understanding a word I'd said, his arms scrunched nervously at his side. His hair was a frightening no-color. His sister had the greenest eyes and her freckled face was cowled in a hood of pink fur. We had on the same brand of mittens, bought cheap from Two Guys. I stopped and we faced each other, our white breath nearly reaching across the distance between us. The world was ice and the ice burned with sunlight. This was my first real encounter with North Americans and I felt loose and capable on that plain of ice. I motioned with my mittens and smiled. The sister turned to her brother and laughed. He said something to her and then she ran to where the other children were, the peals of her laughter trailing over her shoulder like the spumes of her hot breath.

I've been meaning to come out, I said. But my father won't let us right now. He thinks we're too young, but look, I'm older than your sister, and my brother looks older than you.

The brother pointed at himself. Eric, he said.

My name's Joaquín, I said.

Juan, he said.

No, Joaquín, I repeated. Don't they teach you guys how to speak?

His grin never faded. Turning, he walked over to the approaching group of children. I knew that Rafa was watching me from the window and fought the urge to turn around and wave. The gringo children watched me from a distance and then walked away. Wait, I said, but then an Oldsmobile pulled into the next lot, its tires muddy and thick with snow. I couldn't follow them. The sister looked back once, a lick of her hair peeking out of her hood. After they had gone, I stood in the snow until my feet were cold. I was too afraid of getting my ass beat to go any farther.

Was it fun? Rafa was sprawled in front of the TV.

Hijo de la gran puta, I said, sitting down.

You look frozen.

I didn't answer him. We watched TV until a snowball struck the glass patio door and both of us jumped.

What was that? Mami wanted to know from her room.

Two more snowballs exploded on the glass. I peeked behind the curtain and saw the brother and sister hiding behind a snow-buried Dodge.

Nothing, Señora, Rafa said. It's just the snow.

What, is it learning how to dance out there?

It's just falling, Rafa said.

We both stood behind the curtain, and watched the brother throw fast and hard, like a pitcher.

Each day the trucks would roll into our neighborhood with the garbage. The landfill stood two miles out, but the mechanics of the winter air conducted its sound and smells to us undiluted. When we opened a window we could hear the bulldozers spreading the garbage out in thick, putrid layers across the top of the landfill. We could see the gulls attending the mound, thousands of them, wheeling.

Do you think kids play out there? I asked Rafa. We were standing on the porch, brave; at any moment Papi could pull into the parking lot and see us.

Of course they do. Wouldn't you?

I licked my lips. They must find a lot of crap out there.

Plenty, Rafa said.

That night I dreamed of home, that we'd never left. I woke up, my throat aching, hot with fever. I washed my face in the sink, then sat next to our window, my brother snoring, and watched the pebbles of ice falling and freezing into a shell over the cars and the snow and the pavement. Learning to sleep in new places was an ability you were supposed to lose as you grew older, but I never had it. The building was only now settling into itself; the tight magic of the just-hammered-in nail was finally relaxing. I heard someone walking around in the living room and when I went out I found my mother standing in front of the patio door.

You can't sleep? she asked, her face smooth and perfect in the glare of the halogens.

I shook my head.

We've always been alike that way, she said. That won't make your life any easier.

I put my arms around her waist. That morning alone we'd seen three moving trucks from our patio door. I'm going to pray for Dominicans, she had said, her face against the glass, but what we would end up getting were Puerto Ricans.

She must have put me to bed because the next day I woke up next to Rafa. He was snoring. Papi was in the next room snoring as well, and something inside of me told me that I wasn't a quiet sleeper.

At the end of the month the bulldozers capped the landfill with a head of soft, blond dirt, and the evicted gulls flocked over the

475

development, shitting and fussing, until the first of the new garbage was brought in.

My brother was bucking to be Number One Son; in all other things he was generally unchanged, but when it came to my father he listened with a scrupulousness he had never afforded our mother. Papi said he wanted us inside, Rafa stayed inside. I was less attentive; I played in the snow for short stretches, though never out of sight of the apartment. You're going to get caught, Rafa forecasted. I could tell that my boldness made him miserable; from our windows he watched me packing snow and throwing myself into drifts. I stayed away from the gringos. When I saw the brother and sister from apartment four, I stopped farting around and watched for a sneak attack. Eric waved and his sister waved; I didn't wave back. Once he came over and showed me the baseball he must have just gotten. Roberto Clemente, he said, but I went on with building my fort. His sister grew flushed and said something loud and rude and then Eric sighed. Neither of them were handsome children.

One day the sister was out by herself and I followed her to the field. Huge concrete pipes sprawled here and there on the snow. She ducked into one of these and I followed her, crawling on my knees.

She sat in the pipe, crosslegged and grinning. She took her hands out of her mittens and rubbed them together. We were out of the wind and I followed her example. She poked a finger at me.

Joaquín, I said. All my friends call me Yunior.

Joaquín Yunior, she said. Elaine. Elaine Pitt.

Elaine.

Joaquín.

It's really cold, I said, my teeth chattering.

She said something and then felt the ends of my fingers. Cold she said.

I knew that word already. I nodded. Frío. She showed me how to put my fingers in my armpits.

Warm, she said.

Yes, I said. Very warm.

At night, Mami and Papi talked. He sat on his side of the table and she leaned close, asking him, Do you ever plan on taking these children out? You can't keep them sealed up like this; they aren't dead yet.

They'll be going to school soon, he said, sucking on his pipe. And as soon as winter lets up I want to show you the ocean. You can see it around here, you know, but it's better to see it up close.

476

How much longer does winter last?

Not long, he promised. You'll see. In a few months none of you will remember this and by then I won't have to work too much. We'll be able to travel in spring and see everything.

I hope so, Mami said.

My mother was not a woman easily cowed, but in the States she let my father roll over her. If he said he had to be at work for two days straight, she said okay and cooked enough moro to last him. She was depressed and sad and missed her father and her friends. Everyone had warned her that the U.S. was a difficult place where even the devil got his ass beat, but no one had told her that she would have to spend the rest of her natural life snowbound with her children. She wrote letter after letter home, begging her sisters to come as soon as possible. I need the company, she explained. This neighborhood is empty and friendless. And she begged Papi to bring his friends over. She wanted to talk about unimportant matters, and see a brown face who didn't call her mother or wife.

None of you are ready for guests, Papi said. Look at this house. Look at your children. Me dan vergüenza to see them slouching around like that.

You can't complain about this apartment. All I do is clean it.

What about your sons?

My mother looked over at me and then at Rafa. I put one shoe over the other. After that, she had Rafa keep after me about my shoelaces. When we heard the van arriving in the parking lot, Mami called us over for a quick inspection. Hair, teeth, hands, feet. If anything was wrong she'd hide us in the bathroom until it was fixed. Her dinners grew elaborate. She even changed the TV for Papi without calling him a zángano.

Okay, he said finally. Maybe it can work.

It doesn't have to be that big a production, Mami said.

Two Fridays in a row he brought a friend over for dinner and Mami put on her best polyester jumpsuit and got us spiffy in our red pants, thick white belts, and amaranth-blue Chams shirts. Seeing her asthmatic with excitement made us hopeful that our world was about to be transformed, but these were awkward dinners. The men were bachelors and divided their time between talking to Papi and eyeing Mami's ass. Papi seemed to enjoy their company but Mami spent her time on her feet, hustling food to the table, opening beers, and changing the channel. She started out each night natural and unreserved, with a face that scowled as easily as it grinned, but as the men loosened their

477

belts and aired out their toes and talked their talk, she withdrew; her expressions narrowed until all that remained was a tight, guarded smile that seemed to drift across the room the way a splash of sunlight glides across a wall. We kids were ignored for the most part, except once, when the first man, Miguel, asked, Can you two box as well as your father?

They're fine fighters, Papi said.

Your father is very fast. Has good hand speed. Miguel shook his head, laughing. I saw him finish this one tipo. He put fulano on his ass.

That *was* funny, Papi agreed. Miguel had brought a bottle of Bermúdez rum; he and Papi were drunk.

It's time you go to your room, Mami said, touching my shoulder.

Why? I asked. All we do is sit there.

That's how I feel about my home, Miguel said.

Mami's glare cut me in half. Such a fresh mouth, she said, shoving us toward our room. We sat, as predicted, and listened. On both visits, the men ate their fill, congratulated Mami on her cooking, Papi on his sons, and then stayed about an hour for propriety's sake. Cigarettes, dominos, gossip, and then the inevitable, Well, I have to get going. We have work tomorrow. You know how that is.

Of course I do. What else do we Dominicans know?

Afterward, Mami cleaned the pans quietly in the kitchen, scraping at the roasted pig flesh, while Papi sat out on our front porch in his short sleeves; he seemed to have grown impervious to the cold these last five years. When he came inside, he showered and pulled on his overalls. I have to work tonight, he said.

Mami stopped scratching at the pans with a spoon. You should find yourself a more regular job.

Papi smiled. Maybe I will.

As soon as he left, Mami ripped the needle from the album and interrupted Felix de Rosario. We heard her in the closet, pulling on her coat and her boots.

Do you think she's leaving us? I asked.

Rafa wrinkled his brow. It's a possibility, he said. What would you do if you were her?

I'd already be in Santo Domingo.

When we heard the front door open, we let ourselves out of our room and found the apartment empty.

We better go after her, I said.

Rafa stopped at the door. Let's give her a minute, he said.

478

What's wrong with you? She's probably face down in the snow.

We'll wait two minutes, he said.

Shall I count?

Don't be a wiseguy.

One, I said loudly. He pressed his face against the glass patio door. We were about to hit the door when she returned, panting, an envelope of cold around her.

Where did you get to? I asked.

I went for a walk. She dropped her coat at the door; her face was red from the cold and she was breathing deeply, as if she'd sprinted the last thirty steps.

Where?

Just around the corner.

Why the hell did you do that?

She started to cry, and when Rafa put his hand on her waist, she slapped it away. We went back to our room.

I think she's losing it, I said.

She's just lonely, Rafa said.

The night before the snowstorm I heard the wind at our window. I woke up the next morning, freezing. Mami was fiddling with the thermostat; we could hear the gurgle of water in the pipes but the apartment didn't get much warmer.

Just go play, Mami said. That will keep your mind off it.

Is it broken?

I don't know. She looked at the knob dubiously. Maybe it's slow this morning.

None of the gringos were outside playing. We sat by the window and waited for them. In the afternoon my father called from work; I could hear the forklifts when I answered.

Rafa?

No, it's me.

Get your mother.

How are you doing?

Get your mother.

We got a big storm on the way, he explained to her—even from where I was standing I could hear his voice. There's no way I can get out to see you. It's gonna be bad. Maybe I'll get there tomorrow.

What should I do?

Just keep indoors. And fill the tub with water.

479

Where are you sleeping? Mami asked.

At a friend's.

She turned her face from us. Okay, she said. When she got off the phone she sat in front of the TV. She could see I was going to pester her about Papi; she told me, Just watch the TV.

Radio WADO recommended spare blankets, water, flashlights, and food. We had none of these things. What happens if we get buried? I asked. Will we die? Will they have to save us in boats?

I don't know, Rafa said. I don't know anything about snow. I was spooking him. He went over to the window and peeked out.

We'll be fine, Mami said. As long as we're warm. She went over and raised the heat again.

But what if we get buried?

You can't have that much snow.

How do you know?

Because twelve inches isn't going to bury anybody, even a pain-in-the-ass like you.

I went out on the porch and watched the first snow begin to fall like finely-sifted ash. If we die, Papi's going to feel bad, I said.

Don't talk about it like that, Rafa said.

Mami turned away and laughed.

Four inches fell in an hour and the snow kept falling.

Mami waited until we were in bed, but I heard the door and woke Rafa. She's at it again, I said.

Outside?

You know it.

He put on his boots grimly. He paused at the door and then looked back at the empty apartment. Let's go, he said.

She was standing on the edge of the parking lot, ready to cross West-minister. The apartment lamps glared on the frozen ground and our breath was white in the night air. The snow was gusting.

Go home, she said.

We didn't move.

Did you at least lock the front door? she asked.

Rafa shook his head.

It's too cold for thieves anyway, I said.

Mami smiled and nearly slipped on the sidewalk. I'm not good at walking on this vaina.

I'm real good, I said. Just hold onto me.

480

We crossed Westminister. The cars were moving very slowly and the wind was loud and full of snow.

This isn't too bad, I said. These people should see a hurricane.

Where should we go? Rafa asked. He was blinking a lot to keep the snow out of his eyes.

Go straight, Mami said. That way we don't get lost.

We should mark the ice.

She put her hands around us both. It's easier if we go straight.

We went down to the edge of the apartments and looked out over the landfill, a misshapen, shadowy mound that abutted the Raritan. Rubbish fires burned all over it like sores and the dump trucks and bulldozers slept quietly and reverently at its base. It smelled like something the river had tossed out from its floor, something moist and heaving. We found the basketball courts next and the pool, empty of water, and Parkridge, the next neighborhood over, which was full and had many, many children. We even saw the ocean, up there at the top of Westminister, like the blade of a long, curved knife. Mami was crying but we pretended not to notice. We threw snowballs at the sliding cars and once I removed my cap just to feel the snowflakes scatter across my cold, hard scalp.

Nominated by Glimmer Train, *Robert Schirmer*

SPARROW

by REGINALD GIBBONS

from NOTRE DAME REVIEW

In the town streets
pieces of the perishing world
Pieces of the world coming into being

The peculiar angle at which a failing gutter descends
from a house-eave; a squirrel's surviving tattered nest of leaves
woven into a high bare crook of an elm tree (the last one alive on this
    street);

the small bright green leafing out of that elm;
a man shaking coins in a dry Coke-cup and saying
Small change, brother? Small change?;
                                 a woman
in scuffed white running shoes and a fine suit hurrying
down the street with a baggy briefcase that must have
papers and her purse and her good shoes in it
Perhaps a small pistol

Gusts rattle the half-closed upstairs window in the old office
    building that's going to be torn down

Skittering across the sidewalk, a scrap of paper with someone's
    handwriting on it, in pencil
A message that will arrive

Things in themselves

A few minutes of seeing
An exalting

Or a few minutes of complete shelter
A protectedness, a brief rest from the changes

Sparrow moments

*

But this emblem I take from the world—
able, fussing, competing
at the feeder, waiting on a branch,
sudden in flight, looping and rushing, to another branch,
quick to fight over mating and quick at mating,
surviving winter on dry dead seed-heads of weeds
and around stables and garbage and park benches,
near farms and in deep woods,
brooding in summer-hidden nests—house sparrow,

song sparrow, fox sparrow, swamp sparrow,
field sparrow, lark sparrow, tree sparrow, sage sparrow,
white-throated sparrow of the falling whistled song
that I hear as a small reassurance—

Would my happiness be that the sparrow not be emblem—
that it be in my mind only as it is outside of my mind, itself,
that my mind not remove it from itself
into realms of forms and symbolic thinking?

My happiness, that is, my best being

Words like branches and leaves,
or words like the birds among
the branches and leaves?

483

They take wing all at once
The way they flee makes flight look like exuberance not fear
They veer away around a house-corner

Nominated by Stuart Dybek, Rachel Hadas, Joyce Carol Oates

RETURN OF THE BOYCEVILLE FLASH

fiction by GORDON WEAVER

from QUARTERLY WEST

> *What becomes of all the little boys*
> *Who never say their prayers?*
> *They're sleeping like a baby*
> *On the Nickel over there.*
> —Tom Waits

PAFKO, SOBER LONG ENOUGH he'd stopped counting the days, wasn't sure what it was he was looking for when he checked out of his Chicago flop and thumbed up to Milwaukee. It was like he was in one of his dreams, doing and feeling like it was him in the dream, watching himself, but knowing it wasn't real because he knew he'd never really do what he was doing.

He just woke up when the flop rousted the residents, shaved standing under the spray in the gang shower like always, dressed in the Goodwill suit and shoes he must have bought to be ready for this, packed his personals in the airline bag he found in trash the day he worked day labor out at O'Hare, ate the flop breakfast, headed out on the el and the CTA bus to thumb the freeway north—as if something not him knew all the time where he was going even if he didn't have clue one why.

If it was like one of his dreams, then he woke up standing on the corner at Farwell and North, checking out what looked the same, what was changed, as confused as waking up from a bout on the skid, entirely blacked out. Like the times he came to on Greyhounds going places he'd never been, sleeping on tables in joints he could have swore he never entered, curled up cold and wet in a park once, still holding the jug put him to sleep, thinking at once about where the jug to start the day could be had.

He knew where he was, suddenly thought of Marino, who had the hook for a hand and intimidated people to come across in the days when Pafko and Marino buddied, worked the two sides of any downtown street, scoring a dollar a block average each hustling the panhandle on shoppers—what in God's name, Pafko wondered, would have become of Marino after they split that time on the row in Minneapolis arguing over the one jug just enough to wake up one of them, not both?

Pafko shook his head, blinked his watery eyes. He knew where he was. There was Hooligan's, like always, where he'd cashed G.I. Bill checks, college days, where it was kicks to see the regulars start off on port wine with beer chasers at six in the A.M., world's largest bar and workingman's friend, supposed to be—except now there was neon advertising the east side's best pub food, and the brick was sandblasted clean. What the hell happened to Hooligan's?

And there was the Oriental, where he worked part-time, high school, set pins in the alley downstairs, and there was the eastside branch library where he read his eyes out under the fluorescents when he was a kid. And there was Oriental Drugs where they hung out those high school days he ran with the Red Arrow Park boys—what must have become of the Red Arrow guys? Pafko wondered.

But there was a lot of new places, a travel agency, a Greek restaurant, *Olympia* and *Gyros* signs, employment agency—check it out for day labor, Pafko thought, maybe something clean with the Goodwill suit and shoes—Honda dealer where Heiser Ford used to be, office supply, a big restaurant, new, German, across from the Oriental, a lot of big glass windows bouncing the mid-morning sun like needles into Pafko's eyes.

He pivoted away from the intersection to look up Farwell, check for Bette and Dad's, Champ's, the Murray Elbow Room where they'd give you the first shot in a water glass so your morning shakes didn't spill it. And there was Champ's but Bette and Dad's and the Elbow Room gone, and Champ's bigger than he remembered, with a big sign, *Champ's*, all lighted up in the bright sunlight, and he knew he was going in, but like a dream Pafko he dreamed, without knowing what he was doing or why.

486

And there *he* was, Pafko, checking himself in one of the big glass windows on North Avenue, seeing if he looked okay. He thought he looked okay. *I look okay. Pretty much,* he figured. Naturally he needed a haircut, and the Goodwill suit was loose, which hid his sprung gut, and out of style, like the suits he wore when he sold all-risk auto insurance to beat the band, fast and fat days, the Goodwill shoes needed shined.

But it was his face, Pafko and he looked pretty okay if he stood straight, took his hand out of his pocket, squared his shoulders. *Sober,* Pafko thought. With change and a few small bills in his pants he felt against his leg, and a hundred inside the sock inside each of his scuffed shoes. He should have popped for a topcoat—even if he wasn't cold, it would have looked better. If anybody should ask, he'd come up with a story for the airline bag carrying his personals.

So he walked up to Champ's heavy glass and brushed metal doors, went in as if that's where he was headed from the minute he left the Chicago flop.

Pafko was blind for a second, Champ's cave-dark after the sharp daylight.

It was like waking up on the skid again. His pupils eased open to show him Champ's. It wasn't at all like it was. It was *big!* The bar was as long as he remembered Hooligan's, tables with tablecloths with glass candleholders, candles burning, winking like stars in night sky, or streetlights when you squinted, half-gone, to clear your vision, and big booths, leather upholstery, brass nail-heads, some Muzak music or maybe FM sounding like it came out of the walls with the faint recessed lighting. Tiffany lamps over the tables and booths, big green plants in planters, and everywhere Packers and Brewers and Bucks pennants, and framed photographs and what looked like cartoon drawings and newspaper headlines, all framed and hung on the long wall in this huge Champ's he didn't recognize. Monster TV screens turned on showing sports shows with no sound on.

A waitress in a get-up showing leg and cleavage, good smelling perfume like a cloud around her, came up to him with an oversize menu in her hands, frozen smile on her face, too-red lips pulled back over too-white teeth, a certified stunner. She said, "Can I get you a table?

"Bar," Pafko said. His croak of a voice always surprised him. He stepped around her and walked to the long bar of the enormous Champ's that wasn't what it was anymore.

If he'd ever sat at a posher bar, it was so long ago—a dozen, fifteen years?—Pafko couldn't remember it. He set the airline bag of personals down beside a stool.

It was such a long bar, the stool he took a padded captain's chair that swiveled without making any noise, a carpeted shelf for his feet in the Goodwill shoes, a padded leatherette rail for his forearms and elbows, the bartop like black slate reflecting no light, and the backbar. Bottles with chrome spouts rising on tinted glass tiers, like organ pipes, filled with every color. The booze glowed softly, seemed to pulse—red, blue, green, orange, gold, yellow, vodkas and gins pure clear as spring water, every shade of brown and tan—labels Pafko couldn't quite read in the dimness, like languages he couldn't read, never heard. Over his head, glassware in all possible shapes hung by their stems from dark wooden racks. To his right, the handles of half a dozen beertaps rose like ceramic statues.

He wanted to say something, knew his dry mouth wouldn't speak, tried to swallow, but there was nothing in his cracked, hot throat to go down. He found his reflection in a space of mirror over the register that looked like a computer rig, knew it was his face looking back at him, as strange to him as if it was someone he dreamed or met somewhere on the skid.

He forced himself to look away, find the waitress with all the leg and cleavage, find customers to check out—there was a man, business suit, head down over a drink, so far down the bar he was almost a shadow in shadows. Swiveling his stool-chair, he found a couple in a booth beyond the tables, man and woman, dressed up looking, leaning toward each other so far their heads nearly touched, whispering or silent, or if they spoke their voices lost in the Muzak music oozing out of the long wall.

Pafko swung himself back around, and in that moment the bartender—gleaming white shirt, black colonel's tie, red vest silver-buttoned, frilly garters on his sleeves to keep his cuffs dry, was there facing him, like he'd popped up out of a secret trapdoor. "Pick your poison," the bartender said, laying a napkin that said *Champ's* in big letters on the bar.

Pafko thought it was Old Man Champion, but bigger, fatter than he remembered him, which was impossible—Old Man Champion had to be dead, long ago . . . if this was Old Man Champion he had to be maybe ninety years old now. But it was Old Man Champion, the big head of meringuewhite hair, bushy eyebrows, walrus mustache, waiting for him to order up, tapping the bartop with his sausage fingers, a heavy gold ring with a big stone on one pinkie.

"Mr. Champion?" Pafko said to what could be a ghost or the real, impossible Old Man Champion. He was surprised he could speak through his dry, hard lips.

"Make it Champ. We're just folks, unless you're here with a summons for me," the possible ghost said, smiled, cocked his head like a big fat old owl. Then Pafko knew it was Jimmy Champion grown old as Pafko, fatter than his old man had been, almost the carbon of his old man.

"Jimmy," Pafko said, and, "I'm guessing you don't recognize me. It's been some years," he said. He took a deep breath, pulled himself up straight in his stool-chair, squared his shoulders, shot a look at the space of backbar mirror to see if he looked okay. *Mostly okay.* Jimmy Champion! Jimmy Champion squinted at him.

"Pafko," Pafko said. "Thaddeus. Teddy." When Jimmy Champion said nothing, he said, "Pafko." There was just a second that felt longer to him, while he waited and hoped and prayed all at once that Jimmy Champion would remember him from way back then.

"You scared me," Pafko said, and, "I thought you were your old man, you're the exact carbon almost exactly," he said. And then Jimmy Champion recognized him, remembered.

"Pafko!" he said, smiled big, put out his big fat hand with the pinkie ring, took Pafko's, squeezed hard, laughed a big laugh the carbon of his old man's. He said, "Pafko for the Christ's sakes!" And he said, "How in the holy hell long's it been? Am I hallucinating or you're actually sitting there after how many goddamn years, a coon's age!"

"A whole lot. I can't exactly recall, time flies so fast," Pafko said.

Jimmy Champion slapped the bar, the smack sound so loud the business suit far down the bar startled, looked up from his drink at them like somebody goosed him. "I will be dipped in shit, this calls for libations!" he said. "I am pleased to have the first of the day in your honor," he said. "Name it, I got it or can get it, auld lang syne," he said.

For just a second, Pafko, grinning like his face would split, for just the smallest second, like a window slid open to light up a dark, empty room, only that long, Pafko thought to ask for a double-on-a-double with a chaser maybe. But the window slid shut—he wasn't positive why—he knew who he was, so said, "Maybe a diet soda, or even a coffee black. It's early in the day for me at my age now."

"Oh, never too early, Teddy," Jimmy Champion said. He poured himself a stiff Wild Turkey over an ice cube in a rock glass, called the waitress with leg and cleavage who smelled so good to bring a black coffee. "I know this character since who laid the Chunk," he said to her when she brought the coffee. "You believe this character took me for my old man, God rest his soul, left us, what, sixteen years ago if it's a day?" he asked her. And he laughed the carbon big laugh of his deceased old man, said, "Bumps!" as he raised his glass, tossed off a good half his Wild Turkey.

Pafko raised the steaming cup to him. "Back at you," he said, sipped, tried to find some taste, flavor in it that would do, and then they talked.

"So what brings you to our fair city after all this time?" Jimmy Champion said.

"Sort of business or pleasure, some of both," Pafko said. He didn't know where the words came from, didn't have a clue to the answer to the question. He said, "I flew in on kind of a whim's what it was," and suddenly thought of the guy who picked him up in a Toyota on the interstate—the guy was about Pafko's age, a talker, the smell of peppermint, some kind of cologne, or maybe a lozenge he sucked to cover his breath. Pafko figured he was maybe half in the bag, a talker, was tempted to ask him if he kept a pint in the glove compartment or under the driver's seat. But didn't for fear it was true, the guy'd offer him a pull.

"And you're still the big insurance mogul I suppose," Jimmy Champion said. When he poured himself another Wild Turkey, held the bottle out to Pafko, Pafko shook his head.

"It fed the bulldog and then some," Pafko said. Jimmy Champion had to go down the bar, serve two more suits who bellied up, talking loud. Pafko swiveled his stool-chair, saw Champ's was steadily filling with suits, a few women, all dressed for offices, talkers and laughers, some carrying briefcases, styled hair, a lot of rings and big gold wristwatches, some gold chains. They ordered up from the bar, and now there were two more waitresses with the leg and cleavage gal, and they came and went from the rail with trays of drinks—martinis and wine coolers and wine, foaming beers in tall pilsner glasses. And Jimmy Champion was joined by another bartender, kid with a matching red vest, sleeve garters, and now the Muzak music stopped or was covered by the voice babble, and there was sound from the monster TV screens' show now. Pafko's coffee was tepid on his tongue, tasted metallic.

He was in Champ's, but it wasn't Champ's. Where was Champ's from back then. Two decades? He closed his eyes, concentrated, brought up Champ's—no tables, just booths and the bar, scarred with cigarette burns, an electric shuffleboard, bumper pool, cigarette machine that worked with a plunger you pulled, Old Man Champion ready to shake the dice cup for a round anytime. The regulars.

The regulars. The old Greek coot, Tsoris, smoking a pipe smelled so bad Pafko kidded he'd take it away, throw it in the commode in the men's. Knees Gazapian, always off on how his bad knees kept him from a career in pro football, which everyone knew was bullshit, and Wheezy O'Brien with *Let Me Tickle You* stitched on the back of his windbreaker, big metal taps on his heels so you heard him a block away. The Neery brothers, all five in their construction job work-clothes. Old timers and young bucks like Pafko, living it up, the good times after they outgrew running with their gangs—Red Arrow Park, the Dago Regiment, Polack Eagles, Fighting Irish, all that behind them because they were *men* then, living it up in Champ's together, charged up on all the energy was going to explode them into futures they couldn't see but knew were waiting, all of them!

"You about ready there?" Jimmy Champion said, pointed at his coffee cup, nodded toward the tiers of bottles on the backbar. Pafko wondered if he saw him sitting with his eyes closed—did he look okay? Now he stared back at Jimmy Champion, Champ's full of people, suits and dressy women, talking, drinking, eating, laughing, silverware clanking on plates, the long bar's stool-chairs almost all occupied. Were people keeping their distance from him at the bar? Maybe he didn't look okay?

"Not just yet," Pafko said, and, "Maybe a diet soda?" And he said, "You do a land office lunch trade, Jimmy," when Jimmy Champion looked funny at him before he filled a glass with Diet Coke from a hissing nozzle on the end of a thin hose.

"Can't complain," Jimmy Champion said. Pafko checked his eyes— oh yes, Jimmy Champion had *his* buzz. Pafko knew the look in the eyes, the sure sound of it in a voice.

"It's all changed," Pafko said. "So big."

"Years ago," Jimmy Champion said. "I bought out the whole building after my old man passed."

"Bette and Dad's?" Pafko asked. "The Elbow Room?"

"They went when the leases ran out. We tore out the walls, did it all over. We're three times the size," he said.

"I don't recognize anybody," Pafko said.

"You wouldn't hardly. You been gone too long, Teddy. The whole east side's changed. We're Yuppieville. Strictly upscale high-rent."

"Really," Pafko said.

"I shit you not," Jimmy Champion said. "You got to go with the flows. The jigs crowded out west and north from the ghetto, so people moved east if they didn't go to the burbs to hell and gone. A lot of refurbishment construction and all since your time, Teddy."

"That's sort of sad," Pafko said.

"You don't catch me complaining," Jimmy said. He said, "Far be it from me to brag on myself, but I'd be embarrassed to tell you my gross." And he said, "So you won't join me in a libation now?" Pafko looked straight at him, into his slightly buzzed eyes, shook his head, picked up his soda, and Jimmy Champion went off down the bar to help his assistant with the drink orders coming and going from the rail with the waitresses. Instead of closing his eyes, Pafko looked at his reflection in the mirror space.

Champ's lunch trade thinned out. He heard the clatter of glassware dumped in the bar sinks, sunlight coming on, shutting off as suits and their dressy women left for their offices or wherever, costumed waitresses passing money and credit cards over the bar to Jimmy Champion, the digital register flashing red numbers in the corner of Pafko's eye. Old Man Champion had a big bronze register that rang loud when the drawer shot open, raised numbers behind a window, made a steely grating noise when the drawer snapped shut.

What became of everybody? Knees Gazapian, Wheezy O'Brien, the Neery boys, the codger Tsoris, the Polacks, Chinski and Kenny Lewandowski, who legally changed his name to Lane so he wouldn't be Polack to anybody didn't know him from when. The Dago Regiment, Frank and Angelo Valenti, Tony Vitucci, and the tough little wop Pafko fought in his only real fight ever for Red Arrow Park, Tommy Cincotta. *Where? What?*

"Got one with your name on it," Jimmy Champion said, there in front of him with the Wild Turkey bottle in his big fat fist.

"Give me a pass on that for a little yet," Pafko said, and "I need to visit your men's, coffee and soda on an empty stomach." He got down out of his stool-chair, moved in the direction Jimmy Champion pointed with the Wild Turkey bottle. Was Jimmy Champion giving him a fish-eye?

Champ's men's room was back in the far darkest end of the room, around a corner where the long wall broke into the kitchen doors. He passed the leg and cleavage waitress, who gave him a funny look too. I probably don't look so good, Pafko thought.

492

He couldn't remember the last time he'd used a men's as nice, clean, as Champ's. It glistened, smelled sweetly of air freshener, white handtowels on rollers, fake marble sinks, a big mirror with a bluish cast in it. He checked himself out—he didn't look so good. Washing and drying his hands—pink liquid soap smelling like flowers—he had a little spell of the shakes, almost ducked into one of the commode stalls to wait it out, but the shakes went away for some reason, so he splashed his face, dried, combed his hair with his fingers because if he had a comb it was back at the bar in his airline bag of personals.

Jimmy Champion was waiting for him. "So," he said when Pafko was seated in his stool-chair.

"So," Pafko said. When Jimmy didn't speak, he said, "This is your down time now, I figure." Champ's was empty, the TV sound off, Muzak music back up.

"Until Attitude Adjustment Hour," Jimmy said, "which comes pretty early for us here. We offer a Double Bubble from three o'clock right on to seven brings them, and then it's dinner shift and late-nighters to who laid the Chunk."

"So," Pafko said.

"So," is all Jimmy said. Pafko searched for something to talk about.

"I meant to ask, Jimmy," he said at last, "if you're married and all. I didn't recall you marrying before I left town."

"Thrice," Jimmy Champion said, holding up three fingers, half-smiling under his walrus mustache. "Four if you'd count my current arrangement, but we didn't formalize it. You'll meet her if you hang around, she comes in during the dinner hours, we always eat supper together," he said.

"You got kids? Children?" Pafko said.

"Also three, by two separate mothers," he said. "You?" Jimmy Champion asked. Pafko had a second afraid the shakes were coming back, but they didn't. "I remember it you were married pretty young, the big tall looker we called Legs, some of us," Jimmy said.

"Just the once," he said, trying to remember any of it. "And only two kids, they're grown. I have to tell you I'm very out of touch for some time in that department, Jimmy."

"Happens in the best of families," Jimmy said, and he said, "Speaking of which, you still have people in Milwaukee?"

"Again very out of touch," Pafko said. Then he asked for another diet soda to keep from having to talk or think about his former wife

493

and two children, about his sister who for all he knew still lived in the neighborhood, her family, any living or dead relatives.

"So where you been in your life, Pafko?" Jimmy Champion said. "I mean, I recall your going to the college for awhile, and then the story was you made big bucks hustling high-risk insurance to jigs or whoever?"

"I had my own company, actually incorporated," Pafko said, but could not remember its name.

"Then you took off somewhere?"

"I sold out for a good position in Kansas City." Pafko remembered Kansas City for just an instant. "That soured, pretty much everything soured, so I went a lot of places after that." He remembered Chicago, Oklahoma City, Chicago again, Minneapolis. He remembered on the skid with Marino. Chicago again—then he went blank until he was in Chicago, a fourth time at least, day labor and drying out for no reason he could figure, the flop he left that morning without knowing why, thumbing north.

"If you don't mind me inquiring," Jimmy Champion said, "are you all right? I mean, you're trembling there." Pafko put both hands on his soda glass.

"I don't know," he said. "I was probably feeling nostalgia or something for the old days before—"

"Before what?" Jimmy said, but Pafko talked through it.

"—I was just living my life without thinking about it, if you get me. For instance I'm trying to remember people from when we were all young bucks, you and me and everybody, Jimmy."

"To be frank, you're sounding on the strange side, Pafko," Jimmy said.

"For instance," he said, "what became of all the guys from the gangs we ran with those days?"

"*Gangs?*" Jimmy Champion said. "If you think you guys were *gangs*, you got another think coming! Read a newspaper. See the TV. Now we got *gangs*, jigs, they sell dope and shoot the shit out of each other over the business."

"Red Arrow Park," Pafko said. "The Dago Regiment, Polack Eagles." Jimmy laughed.

"And maybe you forget I didn't have time for that horsing around, my old man had me at work here all the time."

"I do just now remember that," he said. "But can you tell me what became of those guys? Knees Gazapian, the Valenti brothers, Polack Kenny Lane?"

494

"Sweet jumping Jesus!" Jimmy Champion said. He said, "Gazapian was the big jock, last I ever knew he was coaching football at some high school or junior high in the burbs. I think he was the only one besides you went off to the college to get higher educated. Valenti—Angelo, not Vince," he said, "got a bar over on Brady, has rock and roll bands in to play weekends."

"Chinski?"

Him I remember, the horny sucker, anything hot and hollow, from the cat's ass to a stovepipe! Search me on where in hell's half-acre that one got to," Jimmy said.

"Can you remember them? Can you remember us?" Pafko said.

"You need something to steady yourself there, Pafko," he said. And, "Why would I have occasion to think about ancient history, for the Christ's sakes?"

He waited for an answer while Pafko tried to come up with one, until Pafko said, "I don't know." Jimmy laughed a laugh that was more a snort, turned and walked away down the bar, leaving him alone gripping his soda glass with both hands. It could have been a spell of shakes coming on, but wasn't.

Pafko sat alone at Champ's bar for what seemed like a long time, but he couldn't be sure. He had no sense of time, what a minute or an hour felt like, no sense of how many years, exactly, he'd been gone from this city, not counting the times he and Marino passed through on the skid. He closed his eyes, concentrated. *Why? What?* he asked himself.

No clue about how long he sat alone at Champ's bar, Pafko flinched when Jimmy Champion spoke, standing in front of him. He said, "You talking to yourself there, are you, Pafko?"

"Jimmy," Pafko said. He said, "I think my thoughts wander sometimes."

"Get you something to drink?" Jimmy said.

"For the moment no," he said. And he said, "Something just came to mind here. Jimmy, you remember how we all had nicknames back then? It just came to me, everybody I can remember had a name we gave them, right?"

"So?" Jimmy Champion said.

"Like," Pafko said, "Knees was Knees Gazapian because he hurt his knees playing football, Wheezy O'Brien because of the asthma, Kenny Lane Polack for changing his name, even my wife I married, you referred to her as Legs for how tall she was," he said.

"Why are you talking so loud?" Jimmy said.

Pafko said, "We all had personal names, you remember?"

"I remember," Jimmy said, "for what it's worth," and, "You guys, you and your pals, called me Widesides because of overweight I couldn't help."

"*Widesides!*" Pafko said. "I remember that! We called you Jimmy Widesides!"

"I came by my bulk by hereditary from the old man. That was hurtful to me when I was a kid, Pafko. I thought I'd forgot all that crap until just this minute," he said.

"We didn't mean hurt by it," Pafko said. "Everybody had a name for something personal is what it was, see? Remember mine, Jimmy? I can remember my nickname clear as anything, but see, that's almost all I can remember!"

"You're shouting, Patko. Simmer down," Jimmy Champion said. Pafko swiveled, saw the leg and cleavage gal, the assistant bartender, an old guy wearing cook's whites had all come out of the kitchen, staring at him.

"What was my nickname, Jimmy? Can you remember it?" he said quickly, trying to lower his voice. But he wasn't sure how loud he was. He felt like a shaking spell was coming, wanted whatever he needed to be said before shakes hit him. He looked to Jimmy for an answer, but Jimmy said nothing, shook his head like there was a mess he had to clean up, made a clucking sound with his tongue. "The Boyceville Flash," Pafko said.

"The which?" Jimmy said.

"The Boyceville Flash. After *Andy* Pafko, played outfield for the Braves when they won the Series? Because he was originally from Boyceville, Upstate, remember? Andy Pafko. He was with the Cubs before they traded him here. Remember?" He heard the waitress laugh.

"I suggest you take yourself out of here, Pafko," Jimmy Champion said. He said, "You don't fit quite so good here, Happy Hour's soon, my lot out back's going to fill with Broncos and Beemers, so you better take a hike, okay? I'm sorry, Pafko." Pafko very carefully got down out of his stool-chair, careful not to slip, fall.

"Tell me, Jimmy," he said, groping at his feet for his airline bag of personals, "can you remember *me?* Could you sort of possibly tell me anything about who I was, what sort of person I was, Jimmy?"

"I begin to think you're pure stone cracked," Jimmy Champion said. Pafko heard the waitress and the assistant bartender and the cook laughing back somewhere by the kitchen doors.

"It's possible," Pafko said, "or even possibly my brain's wet for all I know, I sometimes don't remember the least thing, don't know the time of day, but I could be satisfied with anything you might tell me about anything, Jimmy."

"Don't," Jimmy Champion said, "make me to come out from behind this bar and escort you physically, Pafko."

Pafko tried to stand straight, held his personals bag with both hands to keep off shakes. He looked at Jimmy Champion who folded his big arms across his fat chest, at the tiers of bottles rising behind him, glowing, like an organ in a church.

He knew if he just concentrated, ordered up, put money on the bar, he'd be okay. Everything would come easy and clear as always if he just ordered up, asked for Champ's Double Bubble. "You hearing me?" Jimmy Champion said.

Pafko nodded. Before he turned and walked out the door of Champ's, he said, "You were Jimmy Widesides. I was The Boyceville Flash. I'm certain." Going out the door, he heard some words: *bizarre, fucking seedy nutso.*

Outside, eyes squinted and tearing in the hard sunlight, he stood still until he was sure of his balance. He hefted the airline bag, breathed deep, concentrated, remembered the change and small bills in his pants pocket, the hundred pressed against the sole of each foot inside his Goodwill shoes.

Then Pafko started walking. He lacked a clue as to where, any clue as to any point in being where he was. If nothing else, Jimmy Champion—*Widesides Jimmy!*—would make a bar story out of him, tell it to his eastside Yuppie trade, make a joke out of Pafko who was The Boyceville Flash, however long ago that was.

Nominated by Mark Cox and Thomas Kennedy

OLD WOODRAT'S STINKY HOUSE

by GARY SNYDER

from THE YALE REVIEW

The whole universe is an ocean of dazzling light
On it dance the waves of life and death.
—service for the spirits of the dead

Coyote and Earthmaker whirling about in the world winds
found a meadowlark nest floating and drifting; stretched it to cover
   the
waters and make us an earth—

     Us critters hanging out together
     something like two billion years

     Ice ages come one hundred fifty million years apart
     last about ten million
     then warmer days return—

     all the free water in the world flies up and falls again
     within two million years—

     A venerable desert woodrat nest of twigs and shreds
     plastered down with amber'd urine

a family house in use eight thousand years,
            & four thousand years of using writing equals
the life of a bristlecone pine—
A spoken language works
for about five centuries,
lifespan of a douglas fir;
big floods, big fires, every couple hundred years,
a human life lasts eighty,
a generation twenty.

Hot summers every eight or ten,
four seasons every year

twenty-eight days for the moon
day / night   the twenty-four hours

& a song might last four minutes,

a breath is a breath.

Pocket gopher, elk, elk-calf, deer, field mouse,
snowshoe hare, ground squirrel, jackrabbit, deer mouse,
pine squirrel, beaver.
Jumping mouse, chipmunk, woodrat, pika.
House-cat, flying squirrel. Duck, jay, owl, grebe,
fish, snake, grasshopper, cricket, grass.
Pine nuts, rose seeds, mushrooms, paper, rag, twine, orange peel,
    matches,
rubber, tinfoil, shoestring, paint rag, two pieces of a shirt—
                   from 5,086 coyote droppings—
—And around the Great Basin
    human people living eating cattail pollen,
    bullrush seeds, raw baby birds,
    cooked ducks and geese,
    antelope, squirrel, beetles, chub, and suckers—
    ten thousand years of living
             from the
Lovelock Cave—

Great tall woodrat nests. Shale-flakes, sheep-scats, thorns,
heaped up for centuries
placed under overhangs—caves in cliffs—
at the bottom, antique fecal pellets;
orange-yellow urine-amber.
Shred of a bush that grew eight thousand years ago,
                another rain, another name.

    Cottontail boy said "Woodrat makes me puke!
    Shitting on his grandmother's blankets—
    stinking everything up—pissing on everything—
    yucky old woodrat!
    Makes his whole house stink!"

—Coyote says "You people should stay put here,
        learn your place,
                do good things, Me, I'm traveling on."

Nominated by Philip Booth and Sherod Santos

JAMMING TRAFFIC

fiction by RITA ARIYOSHI

from WITNESS

THE HELICOPTER WAS FILLED with new guys, their burger-fed faces still warm from their mothers' good-byes. The hugs of sisters and sweethearts were almost tangible in the folds of their clothes. They had that typical American vacuity in their eyes, a blankness of soul that might be mistaken for innocence but was the result of having led, until this moment, a second-hand life. They had experienced lust and mayhem once removed, in their living rooms, on their screens, since first awareness.

The pilot and the door gunner, old Nam hands of seven and eight months respectively, exchanged conspiratorial glances. "Watch this," gunner Bobby Johnson said over the roar of the engine as the chopper slowed and circled. He looked at new guy Pete Pacheco as if he were about to feast on him. Six-foot-six, a brown giant, and every square inch was mush. A perfect case—medic—the guys whose testosterone tank ran on low. They were missing what Johnson called the K.I. chromosome, the killer instinct. They were hole pluggers, plumbers. With acute pleasure, Johnson sized up the tensile hulk of a man looking out on Vietnam with gee-whiz written all over his face.

Pacheco was from Hawaii, so he was accustomed to a world glowing in a hundred hues of green, but he had never seen, in all his twenty-two years, a green quite like the orderly squares of luminosity stretched out in the Mekong Delta below. He was seeing, for the first time, a rice crop in its full fecundity, an incredible sea of emerald, just before the tips start to go to gold for harvest.

A family—husband, wife, three small children—walked along the walls of the paddies, single file, accompanied by a platoon of ducks.

501

From the air he couldn't see their faces, only the conical coolie hats. The wife had a baby in a sling on her back, a round lump curled in the shadow of her hat. It was a beautiful scene, could be the cover of a tour brochure. Visit sunny Vietnam. Pacheco had already heard about the surf at China Beach.

From the wide edge of its circle, the chopper suddenly aimed for the center, picking up speed, dipping as it neared target. Bobby Johnson shot the children first, one, two, three, "Pazooie," he yelled, then shot the wife in the very moment she raised her face to the swirling heavens and opened her mouth to scream. The chopper pulled up and Pete could see the face of the man, brown as his own, contorted in an anguish he didn't know until that moment was part of the range of human emotions. The man was looking up, shouting something at the chopper while his family lay like crumpled rags around him, staining the green. The chopper swept in again, so close the man's shirt blew in the wind. His hands were up, not in surrender, Pacheco knew instinctively, but in supplication —*take me, don't leave me*. Bobby Johnson obliged.

Radiant, blue eyes burning like a butane flame, the gunner turned to the men in the chopper, pulled his hat down snug on his head and said, "Gentlemen motherfuckers, welcome to fucking Hell." The hugs, the kisses, mothers, sweethearts, tenderness, naiveté, the whole nine yards were blown away in less than five minutes. Television and life merged. You had to do it. You couldn't take babies into battle, couldn't count on them not to break down and get someone killed. There were no thirty-second Pepsi breaks in Vietnam.

It wasn't Pacheco's worst moment in Vietnam, gore for gore, horror for horror, counting by bodies. The first time he killed a man, it was almost an accident. He didn't have time for the luxury of a moral decision. Danny Carew was down, both legs bloody pulps. Pacheco crawled toward him with his arsenal of Q-tips and tourniquets, which is how he sneeringly came to regard his army-issue medic's kit. As he knelt beside the black, twitching grunt, working quickly in the red slime just to dam the flows, he felt, rather than saw, a presence. He grabbed Carew's gun and whirled around shooting. The enemy fired aimlessly as he fell. The enemy couldn't have been more than fourteen, couldn't have weighed more than a skinny girl. He looked like one of the kids who hung around the Ching Lee store on Liliha Street, sucking on *li hing mui* and wet mango, trading milk caps.

Pacheco took some small moral satisfaction in the fact that he vomited after killing the kid. Carew, who would never walk again, tried to comfort him while they waited for the duster, "He would have killed us both. He might have been a kid, but he was the enemy. You did what you had to do, man."

Pacheco looked at the dead boy with his slim torso almost severed across the chest, and was ashamed. When the duster took Carew, they also took the boy's AK-47 and left the flesh behind to rot in the elephant grass.

In the evening Pacheco sat apart looking at the muted mountains bathed in moonlight, dangerously bright. He thought of the time he had crept quietly about his back yard, slingshot in hand, past the car port, stepping gingerly over the coiled hose, so close to the hibiscus bushes he got gold pollen dusted on his bare shoulders. There was a mynah bird owning the lychee tree, clear shot. Slowly he raised up the slingshot, sighted and sent the sharp rock flying. Got it in mid-squawk. The dark wings fluttered as it fell, the white undertips showing in the sunlight, like underwear. He rushed over. There was a hole in its head, something throbbing inside, pulsing. Life, mysterious force. Please die quickly. The bird was gasping air into its little orange beak. Suddenly another mynah came swooping out of the tree, diving at Pete, screaming, followed by a third bird. They pulled up and attacked again, taking turns diving at him, screaming. They drove him back to the hibiscus, then they went and stood beside the wounded bird, cooing softly until it died. Pete didn't go into the back yard for a week. He supposed a cat ate the body. When he was drafted into the army, he asked to be a medic, said he didn't want to kill.

Nobody screamed at you when you killed something in Vietnam. Most times nobody talked to you while you died and the last sounds you heard were not the cooing of kin, but the ear-splitting static of fire power. The delicate boy he shot was probably not missed yet by the mother who carried him. Pete wanted to remember the boy's details so a callus wouldn't form on his own conscience, as thick and protective as the ones his feet earned in a life spent barefoot. He knew it was entirely possible he would get used to killing, that he would take a kind of pride in the outer limits of his actions, as he did in his ability to walk across fields of sharp, hardened lava, and to ride the monster storm waves that rolled into Waimea—the suicide surf. He also knew that Bobby Johnson was not unique, not an alien monster perverted from birth. Someday Johnson would go back to his real life and get married and have kids and maybe be a Little League coach and go to the mall with his wife.

That moonlit night when nothing moved, not even the bamboo, Pacheco thought that his first kill was some kind of a milestone in his life, the point from which nothing would ever be the same. But he was mistaken. There was no one turning point. Vietnam was cumulative. The overflow came the day his platoon burned some miserable thatched village and killed every man, woman, child and chicken. He did a post-carnage check—there were none to save. "Not a goddamn gook left," said one man, who then emptied a round into the dirt road, stirring up dust ghosts. The dead bodies looked like the Pachecos' neighbors. He took some Darvon from his medicine kit.

He didn't prescribe for himself often. There were men who might need the pills more than he did, men with visible, gaping wounds. He thought of his mother, her soft, too-sure voice saying, as she had hundreds of times in childhood when sibling quarrels erupted, "Little birds in their nest agree, why then, oh why can't we?" He swallowed his medicine and dozed in his Darvon nest.

Pacheco did two tours in Nam. They needed medics. The VC had a price on the heads of American medics. For every medic down, twenty soldiers would bleed to death in the field. It was an efficient, clever strategy. There were no Red Cross armbands in Fucking Hell. When the Americans went into battle, they had to have a code word for medic, because the VC would lie in the bushes and yell "Medic," and the poor guy crawling forward with his regulation Q-tips and cotton balls would buy the farm. The other, more compelling reason Pacheco had signed up for the extra tour was he had ceased to believe in a life outside Vietnam. He could not imagine reentering a two-sex world where you could be reasonably sure you would make it through the day, barring a traffic accident, and make it through the night without the sweet detachment of Darvon dreams. Then one day his sister Pua sent him a tape of Gabby Pahinui and his slack key guitar. The man sang "Hii lawe" as if he were weeping for joy and was so happy he almost couldn't stand it, and Pacheco remembered the beauty and peace of home, remembered those exact feelings. Hell had an exit that wasn't chemical. He was honorably discharged.

The whole family came to meet him at the airport, so eager, the tears, the hugs, up to his ears in leis. He had forgotten how sweet the air smelled, how soft upon the skin it was. How could this place exist in the same time, on the same planet? Pua, his mother, his older sister Kaui, his aunties, they had no idea. He had nothing to say to them. They remarked on how quiet he had become.

Whenever he checked the newspaper, Vietnam was page five, after the jellyfish sightings on the south shore, after the budget battle in the legislature, after the shipping news, after the Liberty House white sale. People are bleeding and dying. Young people. They are missing legs, arms, eyes. Mothers who nurtured little boys and packed lunches and poked thermometers and cleaned baseball uniforms got their sons back in anti-fungal body bags. A medic is the garbage man of war. Nobody wanted to hear that. They no longer cared about it. They said: *You are back. You are safe. I can relax. I can skip page five from now on. My boy is back. Praise the Lord.* If they could detect in his duffel bag the smell of burning hay from the roofs of small villages, as he could, they never said a word. He wanted to shake them. He swallowed his uppers.

Pete, because of his size, always slept Japanese-style on a futon on the floor. No bed was big enough, unless it was special order and too much money. He awoke the first morning at home and knew right where he was because birds were singing in the plumeria trees, in the lychee and mango trees dripping with fruit—greedy bulbuls with their beautiful song, doves incessantly cooing, little finches twittering, mynahs quarreling. Nam had no birds left.

Thanks to an uncle in the union, Pete got a job with Matson, unloading containers. He moved his futon to a place of his own so his mother wouldn't shame him into church on Sunday and so he wouldn't shame his mother with his sins. She had a way of pushing at the sides of her upswept hair before saying that Reverend Tamsing missed him and that his life would be wonderful if he would only come back to church.

He was grateful he was sleeping alone the night he dreamed he was in Nam. The dead boy had him by the throat, those slim wrists were hard as wing nuts. They rolled over, Pete was on top. He punched the grinning boy as hard as he could and woke himself with his own scream, his right hand shattered from impact with the concrete floor of his bedroom. He'd never work at Matson again. He couldn't even surf for a while.

He met Cindy, a waitress who could swallow a tray of drinks like they were guava juice. They had a baby girl. The infant's dark hair peeked over the top of the flannel blanket, her shape round as—as the baby that first day in Nam. He wouldn't hold his child. He was terrified of the baby. Every time he looked at her he thought of that other baby sleeping so peacefully on its mother's back, in the shade of her hat. He saw small bodies all askew in a miserable village obscured by smoke. He knew that if he touched little Leilani he would break apart. Neither uppers nor downers helped. Not whiskey, either. Nam owned him forever.

Cindy pleaded with him, begged him to get help. They should go to AA together. They should go to his mother's church.

He'd walk out when she got like that, full of self-pity, giving him guilt. She had no idea what she might unleash, and the leash was fraying. Pete was relieved when she took her little round baby and went back to the Mainland. She had looked at him desperately, one last time before slamming the door.

At times, he missed her. But not the baby. He was afraid of the baby even in his dreams. He was afraid he might hurt her, and equally afraid something might happen to her, that she would die and he wouldn't be able to protect her.

His mother left letters from Cindy out on the kitchen counter. He'd walk out when he saw the familiar writing on the envelope.

When he was broke and couldn't buy dope, he'd go to the VA for medicine, for counseling, for job referral. He saw the slag of war, sitting in wheelchairs, missing limbs, parts of brain, and he wondered why he had tied those tourniquets.

Of the six medics who had gone through training with him and who were his friends, he was the only one to come home. He tried expressing his feeling in music. He wanted to communicate—what? He wanted to shake his head and clear it, but couldn't. Besides, he'd never sound like Gabby. It was too late for him to sing like that and play like that, the music piercing the heart with joy, when he had been to Nam and back.

Pete was arrested making his first heroin buy. He was brought into court in handcuffs and leg irons, like an animal, a pig from the mauka forest. His mother was there, along with Kaui and her husband. He had never seen his mother look so small, like a little girl. When she saw him, her honey-colored face aged eons in moments. Pete vowed he would never put her through this again.

First offense, vet. He got probation.

His mother revved up the church campaign. He wanted to please her, went once, liked the choir in their white nurse dresses singing

"Rock of Ages," but he would have walked out if it wouldn't have embarrassed her. It wasn't that he didn't believe—quite the opposite. He believed every word of Scripture. When he tried to pray, he saw those little children in coolie hats, the Holy Innocents and their parents, up in heaven at God's right hand, whispering bad things about him in God's ear. He could never show his face in heaven.

He stopped in at his mother's when he needed a few bucks, and when he needed to be with someone who didn't really know him and so could continue to love him. Sometimes when he was kicked out of whatever shelter he had for not paying rent, he'd come and sleep on her floor.

Most times he slept under a tree in Aala Park. His sisters couldn't stand the sight of him, said he was taking advantage of their mother. They didn't know that he once in a while stopped in at the offices of their husbands and borrowed money. The husbands never told. Men are usually pretty decent about those things.

Pete's next arrest happened on the Lunalilo Freeway where he happened to be walking stark naked. He had been seized with a compulsion to be free, as if by shedding his clothes he could shed his memories. For a few glorious moments he was utterly free, walking in traffic in nothing but his pelt, the air touching every part of him gently. It made him giddy—or maybe it was the dope. He wanted to stop traffic, snarl up the whole highway, do something monumental for once in his life, but nobody stopped. They veered around him, looked back at the naked giant through rear-view mirrors, sneaky-like. When the police came, he raised his hands like the Vietnamese father, hoping to be shot. They spoke nicely. The ambulance came.

From that time on, he was in and out of Kaneohe State Hospital, the psychiatric ward. With the drugs he took on the outside and the drugs they gave him on the inside, he lost track of time.

Occasionally, over the years, he thought of his daughter. It amazed him that a parent could have a child and that the child would wander so casually in and out of his mind. There was some kind of heresy going on here. He was little better than a stud dog who wouldn't recognize his own pup if it was eating out of the same bowl. He decided to call Leilani, to be a better father, even at a distance. The first time he called, he was surprised she could speak. He had been picturing her still round and curled. She was five. When she was eight he promised her a doll house. It was summer. There were no doll houses. Christmas shipments hadn't come in yet. By Christmas, he was back in Kaneohe. One more thing he didn't finish. He never

507

finished his rehab programs because the truth was, he didn't want to be clean. It wasn't safe.

Years went by before he overcame his embarrassment and called Leilani again. She was thirteen. She didn't mention the doll house, but he heard it in her tone of voice, implying why call if you don't have the doll house like you promised. He asked for a photograph. Cindy wrote back, "You are not entitled to a photograph. You have never spent one thin dime to support your daughter. You just want to satisfy your sick-o curiosity as to what she might look like. You're not a father, you're just a sperm donor. Go screw yourself, Bastard, and leave us *A-lone*." Calling all uppers.

Pete begged money for dope on the Fort Street Mall. He hit up his brothers-in-law. When he was flat, he had his street friends and the surf rats—the haoles always had something. He'd like to say he didn't remember calling his mother in the middle of the night and taunting her, singsong, "Birds in their nest agree . . . " But he did remember, and it didn't matter. The phone call to his mother just wasn't up there with his first day in Nam.

He was forty-three and he wanted to be free of Vietnam. The place was a lover who got into your blood, tantalizing, taunting, putting you through hell, leading you by the hand to the fires. He would strip himself of it once and for all.

He felt again those first glorious moments of utter naked freedom as he stepped into traffic. It felt so good he was sure he would succeed in stopping cars this time. He would explain to people about the little children in the coolie hats, the army-issue body bags. They had no right to their ignorance, to their nice day. He pictured the lines of cars obediently coming to a stop as he stretched his arms out and confessed. They would all look at him and admire him for his courage, waiting for his words. He would speak for all the fallen, the ones taken away in dusters, and the ones left to rot in the elephant grass.

He hardly heard the shouts, "Hey, Lolo," as the cars veered around him. One old Dodge pulled to the shoulder, another Hawaiian blalah. Peter staggered toward him, aware that he might topple over, that his head was an enormous mango without a pit. The man got out of the car, put his arms around him, "I know, brother. I know." Pete sobbed uncontrollably, and bent way over to rest his head on the man's shoulder. "'Not a gook left,'" the guy said.

Gently the stranger eased him into the passenger seat and said, "I'm going to get you some help, brother. Nobody knows who wasn't there."

He drove him to Tripler, the big pink hospital on the hill, built for the invasion of Japan, before the atomic bomb made it unnecessary, promised to make all invasions unthinkable.

The man got him checked in. He came back to see him every day after work, made sure he got in the right programs.

The family was relieved. He was safe and clean, and they were very tired of dealing with him. They sent greeting cards.

Pete was released into yet another rehab program. No contact with anyone outside for thirty days. Inside, nobody presumed to have answers. They just listened. People like himself sat in a circle and took turns speaking their unspeakable private hells, the childhood rapes, the lovelessness, the self-inflicted humiliations, and the failures.

His road friend came to see him when he "graduated," helped him get a job in the produce department of Star Market. He had his own room in a boarding house, his own closet with hangers, an extra pair of pants, three clean shirts. He was happy for the first time since childhood when he'd surf all day off Diamond Head and come ashore with his board, and tourists would shoot him with their little cameras. Then the Veteran's Administration said that if he put in those kinds of hours working at Star, he'd lose his benefits. He couldn't afford that. He quit, went surfing, had a few beers when the sun went down and the sharks cruised. His benefits and welfare always ran out before the end of the month. He worked the Fort Street Mall, developed a routine. He'd go up to a neatly dressed businessman and say, "Hi, am I glad to see you. How's it goin? Hey we gotta have lunch soon. Boy, I'm lucky I ran into you today. I forgot my wallet." While the man was trying to figure out how he knew him, Pete would talk him out of a five. "Thanks, Buddy, I'll call you next week." Pete hated himself for doing it. It had never bothered him before. Now he felt like a loser.

He kept going to rehab meetings, spilling his guts out. When he left the circle of pain and loss, he felt increasingly isolated, as if he had little in common with anyone outside rehab. They all lived in a plastic world, which by its very nature could not bleed. He escaped into his safe haven of uppers and downers, then confessed at the meetings.

You have to try, he was told. You have to make amends to break down walls. It's the ninth step to recovery. He called Leilani, apologized for being a bad dad. All she said was, "That's okay." Sobbing, he hung up the phone, his cries bouncing off some satellite in space, carried thousands of miles in darkness. Later he realized it had been three in the morning, her time.

He began to visit his mother more often, always being careful not to show up when he was stoned. She seemed so pleased with him, in her ignorance, but he could see her disappointment, her sorrow at the sight of him.

One night, a friend asked if he had ever tried free-basing crack. He said there was nothing on this earth like it. They sat down on the sidewalk on King Street in the arches of the old post office. A little flame flickered, rose then fell to a small spark as he sucked in. It was the most intensely pleasurable moment of his life, sexual, his entire being vibrated with pleasure, glowed like Bobby Johnson after a kill. He was walking on burning lava, hissing and crackling. No calluses. He became one with the pain, lost in its fiery magnificence, and entered the flame.

The police found him, alone and dead at five in the morning, when they made their sweep of the streets, before the secretaries in muumuus with paper cups of coffee came along, before the tourists off-loaded from their vans to gape at Iolani Palace.

His funeral was a curious mixture of family, his mother's friends from church dressed in white salvation nurse outfits, his own friends immediately recognizable in their ill-fitting hope as being from the rehab center, and some surfers dressed solemnly, thoughtfully in black tank tops. A young woman with long auburn hair sat beside his mother. It was Leilani, who didn't know what she should be feeling. When he had called her a month ago she had not been warm. She heard him eulogized as "a gentle giant."

He was to be buried with honors in the veterans' cemetery in Kaneohe. The extra-large casket, draped in an American flag, was eased into the hearse. The police escort revved their motorcycles, swung out into the street and stopped traffic on the Pali Highway for the funeral procession of Pete Pacheco. This was the only truth he could show them, and he was finally free.

His daughter was impressed by the escort. She didn't know that in Hawaii the police stop traffic for every funeral, not just for Peter Kaulana Pacheco, fallen hero, wounded 1968, died 1993.

Nominated by Witness

VAN LEEUWENHOEK: 1675

by LINDA BIERDS

from THE THREEPENNY REVIEW

All day, the cooper's hoops squeal and nibble.
Through the single eyepiece of his hand-ground lens,
he watches a spider's spinnerets, then the tail-strokes
of spermatozoa. Now and then, his bald eye unsquints,
skates blindly across his wrist and sleeve—
and makes from his worlds their reversals:
that of the visible and that of the seen . . .

Visible? he is asked, at the market, or the stone tables
by the river. The lip of the cochineal? Starch
on the membranes of rice? But of course—
though a fashioned glass must press and circle,
tap down, tap down, until that which is, is.

Until that which is, breaks to the eye.
It is much like the purslane, he tells them,
that burst from the hoofbeats of horse soldiers:
black seeds long trapped in their casings, until
the galloping cracked them. In the steppes, he says,

or veldt, where nothing in decades had travelled.
Then flowers burst forth from the trauma
of hooftaps, and left in the wake of the soldiers
a ribbon of roadway as wide as their riding.

Smoke now. The screech of a shrinking hoop.
His thoughts are floral with hearth flames and soldiers,
the cords in his bent neck rigid as willow.
Then slowly, below, something yellow begins. Some flutter of
yellow on the glass plate, in the chamber of a tubal heart . . .

By winter, the snows crossed over the flanks
of the horses, felling them slowly. And the soldiers,
retreating, so close to survival, crept
into the flaccid bellies. Two nights,
or three, hillocks of entrails steaming like
breath. Now and then they called out
to each other, their spines at the spines
of the long horses, and the flaps of muscle
thick shawls around them. Then they rose, as a thaw
cut a path to the living.

    . . . A flutter, yellow, where an insect heart ripples
in reflex. But no, it is only light and shadow, light
turning shadow. As the perfect doors, in their terrible
finitude, open and open.

He straightens, feels his body swell
to the known room. Such vertical journeys, he thinks,
down, then back through the magnifications
of light. And the soldiers, their cloaks
like blossoms on a backdrop of snow:
surely, having taken through those hours
both the cradle and the grave,
they could enter any arms and sleep.

Nominated by Henry Carlile

THE APPROPRIATION OF CULTURES

fiction by PERCIVAL EVERETT

from CALLALOO

D ANIEL BARKLEY HAD MONEY left to him by his mother. He had a house which had been left to him by his mother. He had a degree in American Studies from Brown University which he had in some way earned but had not yet earned anything for him. He played a nineteen-forty Martin guitar with a Barkus-Berry pickup and drove a nineteen-seventy-six Jensen Interceptor which he had purchased after his mother's sister had died and left him her money, she having had no children of her own. Daniel Barkley didn't work and didn't pretend to need to, spending most of his time reading. Some nights he went to a joint near the campus of the University of South Carolina and played jazz with some old guys who all worked very hard during the day, but didn't hold Daniel's condition against him.

Daniel played standards with the old guys, but what he loved to play was old-time slide tunes. One night, some white boys from a fraternity yelled forward to the stage at the black man holding the acoustic guitar and began to shout, "Play *Dixie* for us! Play *Dixie* for us!"

Daniel gave them a long look, studied their big-toothed grins and the beer-shiny eyes stuck into puffy, pale faces, hovering over golf shirts and chinos. He looked from them to the uncomfortable expressions on the faces of the old guys with whom he was playing and then to the embarrassed faces of the other college kids in the club.

And then he started to play. He felt his way slowly through the chords of the song once and listened to the deadened hush as it fell over

513

the room. He used the slide to squeeze out the melody of the song he had grown up hating, the song the whites had always pulled out to remind themselves and those other people just where they were. Daniel sang the song. He sang it slowly. He sang it, feeling the lyrics, deciding that the lyrics were his, deciding that the song was his. *Old times there are not forgotten* . . . He sang the song and listened to the silence around him. He resisted the urge to let satire ring through his voice. He meant what he sang. *Look away, look away, look away, Dixieland.*

When he was finished, he looked up to see the roomful of eyes on him. One person clapped. Then another. And soon the tavern was filled with applause and hoots. He found the frat boys in the back and watched as they stormed out, a couple of people near the door chuckling at them as they passed.

Roger, the old guy who played tenor sax, slapped Daniel on the back and said something like "Right on" or "Cool." Roger then played the first few notes of *Take the A Train* and they were off. When the set was done, all the college kids slapped Daniel on the back as he walked toward the bar where he found a beer waiting.

Daniel didn't much care for the slaps on the back, but he didn't focus too much energy on that. He was busy trying to sort out his feelings about what he had just played. The irony of his playing the song straight and from the heart was made more ironic by the fact that as he played it, it came straight and from his heart, as he was claiming southern soil, or at least recognizing his blood in it. His was the land of cotton and hell no, it was not forgotten. At twenty-three his anger was fresh and typical, and so was his ease with it, the way it could be forgotten for chunks of time, until something like that night with the white frat boys or simply a flashing blue light in the rearview mirror brought it all back. He liked the song, wanted to play it again, knew that he would.

He drove home from the bar on Green Street and back to his house where he made tea and read about Pickett's charge at Gettysburg while he sat in the big leather chair which had been his father's. He fell asleep and had a dream in which he stopped Pickett's men on the Emmitsburg Road on their way to the field and said, "Give me back my flag."

* * *

Daniel's friend Sarah was a very large woman with a very large afro hairdo. They were sitting on the porch of Daniel's house having tea. The late fall afternoon was mild and slightly overcast. Daniel sat in the wicker rocker while Sarah curled her feet under her on the glider.

514

"I wish I could have heard it," Sarah said.

"Yeah, me too."

"Personally, I can't even stand to go in that place. All that drinking. Those white kids love to drink." Sarah studied her fingernails.

"I guess. The place is harmless. They seem to like the music."

"Do you think I should paint my nails?"

Daniel frowned at her. "If you want to."

"I mean really paint them. You know, black or with red, white and blue stripes. Something like that." She held her hand, appearing to imagine the colors. "I'd have to grow them long."

"What are you talking about?"

"Just bullshitting."

Daniel and Sarah went to a grocery market to buy food for lunch and Daniel's dinner. Daniel pushed the cart through the Piggly Wiggly while Sarah walked ahead of him. He watched her large movements and her confident stride. At the checkout, he added a bulletin full of pictures of local cars and trucks for sale to his items on the conveyer.

"What's that for?" Sarah asked.

"I think I want to buy a truck."

"Buy a truck?"

"So I can drive you around when you paint your nails."

* * *

Later, after lunch and after Sarah had left him alone, Daniel sat in his living room and picked up the car-sale magazine. As he suspected, there were several trucks he liked and one in particular, a nineteen-sixty-eight Ford three-quarter ton with the one thing it shared with the other possibilities, a full rear cab window decal of the Confederate flag. He called the number the following morning and arranged with Barb, Travis's wife, to stop by and see the truck.

* * *

Travis and Barb lived across the river in the town of Irmo, a name which Daniel had always thought suited a disease for cattle. He drove around the maze of tract homes until he found the right street and number. A woman in a housecoat across the street watched from her porch, safe inside the chain-link fence around her yard. From down the street a man and a teenager who were covered with grease and apparently engaged in work on a torn-apart Dodge Charger mindlessly wiped their hands and studied him.

515

Daniel walked across the front yard, through a maze of plastic toys and knocked on the front door. Travis opened the door and asked in a surly voice, "What is it?"

"I called about the truck," Daniel said.

"Oh, you're Dan?"

Daniel nodded.

"The truck's in the back yard. Let me get the keys." He pushed the door to, but it didn't catch. Daniel heard the quality of the exchange between Travis and Barb, but not the words. He did hear Barb say, as Travis pulled open the door, "I couldn't tell over the phone."

"Got 'em," Travis said. "Come on with me." He looked at Daniel's Jensen as they walked through the yard. "What kind of car is that?"

"It's a Jensen."

"Nice looking. Is it fast?"

"I guess."

The truck looked a little rough, a pale blue with a bleached out hood and a crack across the top of the windshield. Travis opened the driver's side door and pushed the key into the ignition. "It's a strong runner," he said. Daniel put his hand on the faded hood and felt the warmth, knew that Travis had already warmed up the motor. Travis turned the key and the engine kicked over. He nodded to Daniel. Daniel nodded back. He looked up to see a blonde woman looking on from behind the screen door of the back porch.

"The clutch and the alternator are new this year." Travis stepped backward to the wall of the bed and looked in. "There's some rust back here, but the bottom's pretty solid."

Daniel attended to the sound of the engine. "Misses just a little," he said.

"A tune-up will fix that."

Daniel regarded the rebel flag decal covering the rear window of the cab, touched it with his finger.

"That thing will peel right off," Travis said.

"No, I like it." Daniel sat down in the truck behind the steering wheel. "Mind if I take it for a spin?"

"Sure thing." Travis looked toward the house, then back to Daniel. "The brakes are good, but you got to press hard."

Daniel nodded.

Travis shut the door, his long fingers wrapped over the edge of the half-lowered glass. Daniel noticed that one of the man's fingernails was blackened.

516

"I'll just take it around a block or two."

The blonde woman was now standing outside the door on the concrete steps. Daniel put the truck in gear and drove out of the yard, past his car and down the street by the man and teenager who were still at work on the Charger. They stared at him, were still watching him as he turned right at the corner. The truck handled decently, but that really wasn't important.

Back at Travis' house Daniel left the keys in the truck and got out to observe the bald tires while Travis looked on. "The ad in the magazine said two-thousand."

"Yeah, but I'm willing to work with you."

"Tell you what, I'll give you twenty-two hundred if you deliver it to my house."

Travis was lost, scratching his head and looking back at the house for his wife who was no longer standing there. "Where abouts do you live?"

"I live over near the university. Near Five Points."

"Twenty-two hundred?" Travis said more to himself than to Daniel. "Sure I can get it to your house."

"Here's two-hundred." Daniel counted out the money and handed it to the man. "I'll have the rest for you in cash when you deliver the truck." He watched Travis feel the bills with his skinny fingers. "Can you have it there at about four?"

"I can do that."

*   *   *

"What in the world do you need a truck for?" Sarah asked. She stepped over to the counter and poured herself another cup of coffee, then sat back down at the table with Daniel.

"I'm not buying the truck. Well, I am buying a truck, but only because I need the truck for the decal. I'm buying the decal."

"Decal?"

"Yes. This truck has a Confederate flag in the back window."

"What?"

"I've decided that the rebel flag is my flag. My blood is southern blood, right? Well, it's my flag."

Sarah put down her cup and saucer and picked up a cookie from the plate in the middle of the table. "You've flipped. I knew this would happen to you if you didn't work. A person needs to work."

"I don't need money."

"That's not the point. You don't have to work for money." She stood and walked to the edge of the porch and looked up and down the street.

517

"I've got my books and my music."

"You need a job so you can be around people you don't care about, doing stuff you don't care about. You need a job to occupy that part of your brain. I suppose it's too late now, though."

"Nonetheless," Daniel said. "You should have seen those redneck boys when I took *Dixie* from them. They didn't know what to do. So, the goddamn flag is flying over the State Capitol. Don't take it down, just take it. That's what I say."

"That's all you have to do. That's all there is to it."

"Yep." Daniel leaned back in his rocker, "You watch ol' Travis when he gets here."

* * *

Travis arrived with the pickup a little before four, his wife pulling up behind him in a yellow TransAm. Barb got out of the car and walked up to the porch with Travis. She gave the house a careful look. "Hey, Travis," Daniel said. "This is my friend, Sarah." Travis nodded hello. "You must be Barb," Daniel said. Barb smiled weakly. Travis looked at Sarah, then back at the truck and then to Daniel. "You sure you don't want me to peel that thing off the window?"

"I'm positive."

"Okay."

Daniel gave Sarah a glance, to be sure she was watching Travis' face. "Here's the balance," he said, handing over the money. He took the truck keys from the skinny fingers.

Barb sighed and asked as if the question was burning right through her. "Why do you want that flag on the truck?"

"Why shouldn't I want it?" Daniel asked.

Barb didn't know what to say. She studied her feet for a second, then regarded the house again. "I mean, you live in a nice house and drive that sports car. What do you need a truck like that for?"

"You don't want the money?"

"Yes, we want the money," Travis said, trying to silence Barb with a look.

"I need the truck for hauling stuff," Daniel said. "You know like groceries and—" He looked to Sarah for help.

"Books," Sarah said.

"Books. Things like that." Daniel held Barb's eyes until she looked away. He watched Travis sign his name to the back of the title and hand it to him and as he took it, he said, "I was just lucky enough to find a truck with the black power flag already on it."

"What?" Travis screwed up his face, trying to understand.

518

"The black power flag on the window. You mean, you didn't know?" Travis and Barb looked at each other.

"Well, anyway," Daniel said. "I'm glad we could do business." He turned to Sarah. "Let me take you for a ride in my new truck." He and Sarah walked across the yard, got into the pickup and waved to Travis and Barb who were still standing in Daniel's yard as they drove away.

Sarah was on the verge of hysterics by the time they were out of sight. "That was beautiful," she said.

"No," Daniel said, softly. "That was true."

* * *

Over the next weeks, sightings of Daniel and his truck proved problematic for some. He was accosted by two big white men in a '72 Monte Carlo in the parking lot of a 7-11 on Two Notch Road.

"What are you doing with that on your truck, boy?" the bigger of the two asked.

"Flying it proudly," Daniel said, noticing the rebel front plate on the Chevrolet. "Just like you, brothers."

The confused second man took a step toward Daniel. "What did you call us?"

"Brothers."

The second man pushed Daniel in the chest with two extended fists, but not terribly hard.

"I don't want any trouble," Daniel told them.

Then a Volkswagen with four black teenagers parked in the slot beside Daniel's truck and they jumped out, staring and looking serious. "What's going on?" the driver and largest of the teenagers asked.

"They were admiring our flag," Daniel said, pointing to his truck.

The teenagers were confused.

"We fly the flag proudly, don't we, young brothers?" Daniel gave a bent arm, black power, closed-fist salute. "Don't we?" he repeated. "Don't we?"

"Yeah," the young men said.

The white men had backed away to their car. They slipped into it and drove away.

Daniel looked at the teenagers and with as serious a face as he could manage, he said, "Get a flag and fly it proudly."

* * *

At a gas station, a lawyer named Ahmad Wilson stood filling the tank of his BMW and staring at the back window of Daniel's truck. He then looked at Daniel. "Your truck?" he asked.

519

Daniel stopped cleaning the windshield and nodded.

Wilson didn't ask a question, just pointed at the rear window of Daniel's pickup.

"Power to the people," Daniel said and laughed.

* * *

Daniel played *Dixie* in another bar in town, this time with an R&B dance band at a banquet of the black medical association. The strange looks and expressions of outrage changed to bemused laughter and finally to open joking and acceptance as the song was played fast enough for dancing. Then the song was sung, slowly to the profound surprise of those singing the song. *I wish I was in the land of cotton, old times there are not forgotten . . . Look away, look away, look away . . .*

* * *

Soon, there were several, then many cars and trucks in Columbia, South Carolina, sporting Confederate flags and being driven by black people. Black businessmen and ministers wore rebel flag buttons on their lapels and clips on their ties. The marching band of South Carolina State College, a predominantly black land grant institution in Orangeburg, paraded with the flag during homecoming. Black people all over the state flew the Confederate flag. The symbol began to disappear from the fronts of big rigs and back windows of jacked-up four-wheelers. And after the emblem was used to dress the yards and mark picnic sites of black family reunions the following Fourth of July, the piece of cloth was quietly dismissed from its station with the U.S. and state flags atop the State Capitol. There was no ceremony, no notice. One day, it was not there.

Look away, look away, look away . . .

Nominated by Clarence Major

SOME INFORMATION ABOUT 23 YEARS OF EXISTENCE

by JEFF CLARK

from ZYZZYVA

after Michaux

1970

In the shrift, she says, "It is *always* moving, even in slumber, never
    still. It is *always* quivering. Too much swill, Father, and I fear the
    womb will get murky, and the little one, when it emerges, will
    already be a sot."

Pressed, at the coast (the breakers), by the crapulous mass, its
    talking like a boat turning over. Tepid sac that night, powdery
    floes. Taxied through rumble-chambers.

1971

Terror in the birthing room: the little door slides back—

First mews were of pissulence, not want.

In the depot Deliriope.

1972

Antler-nubs cropped, tail docked.

Taken, in the morning, out of my box and into their fetid room. His key-sore hands would then be rubbed.

Thrown into the sea.

Begin inward composition of *Aphorisms of Legless*.

Considering: what will be my first utterance?

1973

First utterance: "Horse horse whose horse?"

Second utterance: *Mal dedans*.

First compositions for musical saw.

1974

Wondering: *Pre-dawn? Preyed on? Prie-Dieu?*

Mother says, "*Please* come—I have Bushmills."

1975–1978

Oil.

Beginning to understand pine trees.

1979

Meditations on Melody and Transparency.

Plug, untree, mourn my first beast.

1980

Tended by Francis in rear of Yeoman's Lounge, Anaheim Sheraton.

Fathoming his pomatum.

Who was Francis?

1981

Homemade birthday card from Auntie, in which is calligraphed:

*The fiend knows the wear of his soles can be traced to two or three
boulevards in particular . . .*

. . . and can't stop walking them!

Her gift: an antediluvian grammar book. Discover that, in "Subjects
for Themes," she has marked, "Of What Use are Flowers?,"
"Street Arabs," "Sailors," "Pluck," "An Old Fashioned Corn-
husking," "Affectation and Naturalness," "Was the Execution of
Jay Unjust?"

Twirling.

1982

First hymns.

Autodialogues begin.

1983

First ejaculation—accidental—: into a jar of bath salts.

Entranced and mortified by crepuscular bird-clatter.

Parable of the Hangared Satellite.

April: receiving, as if in earphones, someone else's thinking.

1984

My impressions are dim impressions. I console myself thus: "My
impressions are merely *not of this dimension.*"

Alas, they are of this dimension, and are like corduroy in the palace
cloak room.

Ruptures.

Church of Evangelical Freedom: Sunday mornings, Wednesday
evenings. Hilarious faux-tongues to the left and to the right.
Inward guffaws.

Sometimes a small wind on the back of the neck.

1985–1987

All notions occur to me beginning, "If I were . . . "

Swaying outside make-out closets.

1988

First Skoal fiasco.

Introduced to a breast: daunted.

Another black August: far away, cannot move anyone with my body.

Yellow paw.

Speech at Elks Lodge: "Thank you, friends, for the generous
    scholarship. Now there will be a cleft in the linoleum, and
    between sash-openings and -closings of flame, you'll see me
    descend."

1989

Defending the goal line Friday night—middle linebacker, with
    150 mg Ephedrine migraine and swollen forearms and an F in
    Humanities, here and there the heart not beating—, saying to the
    boys, in the huddle, "Boys—aren't we beginning to loathe line
    breaks like

"What a fine thing it was to walk that Autumn out of one's
Body and in-
To a death fil-
Led
With ether-booms and no more
Am-
Ber horse-dust-
Ed vials'?"

1990

Blame the Church for my being an emulator.

Writes Auntie, *All I ask is that you show me pictures, that you play
    your records when I have been delivered from the night to your
    stoop mangled, my pant legs torn.*

Excommunicated by Nature.

Waving good-bye to a billow of smoke from a mortuary chimney.

Drawn from my sidewalk into a fashionable party. Standing among
six or seven who discuss film. Am a kind of would-be participant,
eating cheese, occasionally nodding. Someone turning to me,
asking, "What do *you* think of Pasolini?"

"I don't know about that, but I've read *Mrs. Dallow.*"

1991

Parable of the Hangared Satellite. The choice was given it to depart
its hangar and enter the firmament, or to rest immobile inside it,
alone with the wicked technician.

Identical dreams: muzzled dog, queer chandelier.

O good-bye Mother.
O good-bye wombwater.

1992

In depot P, prying open lockers, looking into duffels.

Imitations of Immortality

Wondering: *Remorse? re: Mors?*

Around the neck a noose? Collapsed halo?

1993

Sounds like altos in the deep end.

Encounter first of several scenarios of or including images of
trapped birds.

1994

Quixotism.

Novantiquities.

Sidling to the organ: threnodies.

Remembering how one faded into a last Polaroid, and took a last kiss—before an aurora he and I heard horns in the harbor—he whose pleas now leave me.

1995

Passed out, fell forward into the Royal. Struck some letters with my face: h, m.

Why have I developed no personal logorhythms?

Terror now in the shrift: the little—

Terror now in the Hangar: the little door slides back:

Nominated by ZYZZYVA

THE SECRET NAMES OF WHORES

fiction by DONALD RAWLEY

from PRESS

DELILAH IS A GOOD Christian woman who likes the radio on twenty-four hours a day. First salsa in the morning, horns and maracas and painted guitars, then prayer radio as she cleans houses on slow afternoons. Delilah makes fifty dollars a day and she works six days a week. She's learned her English from sermons. Then in her own bedroom of lavender carpet and silk flowers, she lets Tony Bennett and Frank Sinatra hold her in the yellow-tinged dark. Somnolent and exhausted, the night blooms in silence and shadowed citrus, and the music stays in her dreams.

Her face is healthy brown, innocent, and fat. She is most proud of her ears, tiny things that are her one delicate feature. She keeps her hair rubine, done once a month by her cousin Maria and swept up with black plastic combs to show off her ears. She has thirty pairs of dangling, oversized costume earrings, one for each day of the month, and a filigree gold pair for special occasions.

Delilah saves everything, from glass jars and paper bags to postcards and restaurant honey. She knows this is the way to become rich. Delilah takes everything that is free. It is a protection, and she hoards all of it in a turquoise bungalow built in the twenties—one of hundreds with the perfume of failed women who stayed trapped, the starlets and mistresses who flow through the studios like irrigation water. Now her street is a jungle where weeds become trees and pit bulls in cages snap at flies.

It is here, in this flat waste of drives and lanes with Saint's names, behind Paramount Pictures and below the old Goldwyn Studios, that Delilah has made her home. The immigrant apartments and battered Mexican-style cottages have always been poor, resonating a subliminal decay. They are not lived in long—cheap to rent and never remembered. Here, Armenian women and Mexican women stare from behind rusted screens and poinsettias bought in drugstores, that took in the ground and now cover windows. Their loins are damp with hysteria. They have been taken like a catalogue and will not give their names or speak to strangers, praying for any man who can see the questions they leave taped on walls. On mirrors and cars. The directions out.

Except for Delilah. Her lawn is neatly trimmed with patches of wildflowers, and the bars on her windows have been painted glossy white. She is friendly with other women nearby, women who work at Kodak and film-editing offices, in cocktail lounges and hair salons. They meet for drinks and at church; watch over each other's children and disregard the haunted faces of those women who are just passing through. They have forgotten men, and wearing lipstick every night, and tasting the sweat of a man's thighs. They paint their front doors pink and green and have names for each other, secret names of whores that they say with a wink and another beer.

Delilah is her nickname but now she uses it every day. Her friends are Jane and Iris and Dot, but their whispered names are Dixie, Coco, and Princess, or Thelma who became Jinx, and Sally who is Frosty. Together they save their money in silver-red Valentine's boxes hidden in garages, tend their lemon trees on Sundays, and know they will never move.

Delilah understands Jesus and his pain, how angels walk in morning sun, and the heart in music. There is a wedding dress still crisp in her mother's cedar closet in Santo Domingo. She is saving it for her daughter, Angelica. There are certain things Delilah insists be perfect. One is her living room. Then, her daughter. And most important to the flow of all things is how they celebrate life. Christmas and Easter take months of planning. There are balloons and freshly baked cakes in the sun. There must always be sun.

Angelica is now five and plump as her mother, in lace dresses and tiny white buckled shoes with ribbons pinching her scalp. She likes to squeal and chase field rats that come into their backyard through a hole made by a tractor that backed up. Delilah hates this hole, which leads to Hollywood Memorial Cemetery, and has planted honeysuckle and pink and white ferns that won't take. The only thing covering it is a century plant, grotesque and sharp and covered with webs, and with a single long stem of blossoms that has lasted most of the year.

She'd first seen the flower in January and now it is Easter and not a blossom had gone brown. Waxy and pompous, its giant stem has thrust six feet up and even the wind can't shake it. Delilah can see the brown grass of the cemetery, short and parched as the man who repairs her shoes, but chooses not to look through the hole and becomes cross with Angelica when she tries.

Delilah explains some fields of the dead have good spirits but this place doesn't, that you must hold your breath when you pass by, or they will enter. She knows men and women go there at night to make love, and homosexuals, who frighten her. She leaves the radio on a little louder and crosses herself.

Her daughter is undamaged, and it must stay that way, as virgins always fly straight to heaven if taken too soon. She has not yet explained to Angelica that her father is a criminal, that he sits in a prison in the Dominican Republic, that they have the same face, that all bruises are mistakes and healing is a gift of time women allow, or that all men are a danger of incongruous flesh and their shine only darkens a woman's skin.

She was pregnant with Angelica when she wound up with relatives in Hollywood, looking at signs in English that were stained by auto exhaust and graffiti. She missed rain and shallow tidal pools and walking with a paper thin parasol in the mornings. Delilah missed her church and the smell of its clay walls and spilled wine, but learned her English and walked to the buses that would take her to clean houses that all looked alike.

Now, Delilah has grown accustomed to working for women with high heels who never look her in the eye. Her feet itch from bleach and the sidewalk heat makes her wear pads under her arms. At the end of her day, walking down Santa Monica Boulevard, she prays for the black man to be playing his bongos in front of the dry cleaners and always gives him a full dollar before her marketing. She knows he is from the island, too. When she hears his drums in the stale, confused air, she thinks of mamees who carried fruit in their aprons under Caribbean clouds that hung like a lace fan, Spanish moss, and the threat of Saturday nights.

And today Delilah survives well. There will be balloons for Angelica's Easter, chocolate cake and candy rabbits, and a hunt for eggs with faces painted to resemble blue-eyed, blonde-haired women with long, pasted lashes. She is throwing a little party for Angelica's friends. There will be the laughter of Coco, Dixie, Princess, and Jinx—their children running through the yard, all girls and one little boy who could be a girl—white lilies and pink carnations, and votives lit to the wax eyes of female Saints who say this is right. It is the only way.

Coco is the first to arrive, at eleven, tugging Little Howie, whose father was shot and killed in New York. Little Howie is very pretty. His mulatto skin and curly blonde hair are soft as powder. His green eyes assess everything and he likes to be around the women and their daughters, where he can play with the girls' toys without being teased. The women seem to know what is in store for Little Howie, but love him as they love Coco, an Irish girl who got a bad deal but makes a good living at the cocktail lounge where they meet each Monday for Happy Hour.

The sky is clear over baby blankets on clotheslines, pink as a movie star's lips. Coco and Delilah let the children run off into the back yard as they settle into the kitchen, listening to a gospel Easter show and giggling, pouring a little Scotch in their coffee. Soon Dixie, Frosty, and Princess are there too and the bottle is empty, the children are playing and the air is smoky with cigarettes and baking lasagna. Later, when the women leave, Delilah will start the Easter egg hunt, but for now it is a time for gossip and the steam of ice in coffee cups.

The radio's gospel moves over Delilah's kitchen like the shadow of leaves from the avocado tree, which they surmise is older and sweeter than they are. Cigarettes are stubbed out in glass ashtrays with names like Sunset Casa and the Impromptu Inn on them, places where Delilah has worked and taken linens and towels, and enough ashtrays for all the girls. Delilah has beautiful sheets and guest towels stacked in her linen closet, and the girls have always admired Delilah's way of sifting out things no one will miss.

"It's a gift, if you ask me," Frosty announces, as she has announced every time at Delilah's. "Delilah will wind up with a house in Beverly Hills, because someone won't want it. You know what I mean?"

The girls nod their heads, signaling each other it's time to go, to allow themselves a free Sunday with hidden men and simple passions they won't discuss with anyone. It is Easter. A holiday. As the girls sigh and stub their cigarettes out, listening to their children screaming outside, they are all caught in the same dream. A thought passes through their scrubbed wrists like fire; that somewhere there are women dancing for the first time, rubbing their legs with cream so they shine. Women of reds and glistening pinks that no one sees, and French floral dresses hung indifferently in huge closets. Women with arms full of flowers. Women who have easy births and lucky daughters, seasons nodding to the light like sugar on their tongues.

Today, they leave laughing and a little high on an Easter noon. They will go their secret ways, ready for words only men use, the numb rub when they straddle and pump, undoing the monotonies. As the girls say goodbye, Delilah notices they are looking in different directions, their eyes transfixed on something before them that only they see, their lips curling into smiles. They will be back at six, and no one will say they have been anywhere or done anything worth talking about. Delilah knows, because she has been there too.

*

Delilah is wearing a purple lace dress with white satin bows and an Easter apron. She checks herself in the mirror, then goes out into the backyard with a tray of cake and jelly beans and Coca Cola with paper cups. The children fidget in their folding chairs and a light wind blows the paper tablecloth inches above an old redwood table that she found in the trash. As the children begin to eat, she looks at them and sits down.

"Momma's going to tell a story!" Angelica knows, and bites her paper cup.

"That's right, I am." Delilah is proud of her English. The sun is warm and she is happy at this moment. Later she will have a vodka with the fresh orange juice she will squeeze for *los niños*. And the whole afternoon will stay warm, petted by a light wind and the soul of Jesus.

"Do you believe in ghosts?" Delilah crosses her legs wishing at this moment they were a little thinner. Angelica and Mary Francis and Little Howie begin to squeal.

"Easter celebrates the ghost of Christ who walked this earth and was our savior. They say the only animals who know where Christ is, because his ghost still walks the earth, are the bunnies, and because they can't talk, his secret is safe. But the bunnies like to hide the hens eggs in the bushes to tell us where he is—like a clue—and he gets very, very angry because he doesn't want us to know."

Angelica gets up and stands on her chair, facing the other children like an actress.

"Momma says that movie-star ghosts are next door and Christ won't talk to them."

"That's enough, Angelica."

"Momma says I can't be a movie star, but that's what I want to be." Angelica turns around on her chair, holding her dress with both hands.

"Let me finish my story. Sit down." Delilah is annoyed.

Little Howie whispers, "fatty fatty," and Mary Francis' cola shoots out of her nose as she laughs. Delilah continues.

"So this morning I found one of these bunnies, and I realized that all his eggs are hidden, right here, and that there is a golden egg, and if you find it you get a real prize; but I can't tell you what it is till you find it. Now everyone eat their cake, because when I say so, it'll be time to look for the eggs." Delilah pretends to look at her watch as the children finish their sweets.

The wind has begun to get a little stronger and she can hear it in the palms and the tops of the magnolias in the cemetery. She can hear gospel singers in the kitchen and smell ham and sweet potatoes down the street and finds herself looking at her hands to see if they are still young, then turns to the children, who have been waiting silently.

"Go."

They scream and scatter.

"Wait. Here, I forgot. Take these baskets for your eggs. Now go." Delilah smiles.

As she walks into her kitchen she thinks of the wind on her island, where shells and ferns spoke, where every night was summer and every day a white sheet, how she moved her hips to tin drums and high tides, how her nipples would harden when fog swallowed air at dusk and her husband would close the shutters of their room. She remembers their garden and the squirrel monkey who slept on the roof and bit her hand. She remembers police—boys she had gone to school with—in pressed khaki uniforms and sunglasses, taking her husband away and the radio, always on, with the President's voice and a cheering crowd.

Delilah reasons that is why her radio is still always on; perhaps she will hear the President's voice again, this time speaking the language of Jesus, and tin drums will be heard down the drive. But her island is not important here. Nothing is important here, except blonde women and money and fast cars. She accepts it, except for movies, the ones on Santa Monica with naked women and men, and the smell of urine on the sidewalk; those are the devil's movie stars. Delilah does not believe in movie stars of any kind.

She is glad they built a shopping center on the land in front of the graveyard. Now she does not have to cross herself and hold her breath when she walks by, or see the tourist buses going in and out.

*

"I now quote from the Sermon on the Mount." Delilah is squeezing oranges and she listens to the dramatic pause on the radio, broadcast from a church she has never been to, with a congregation coughing lightly and squirming in the pews. She imagines the church's stained glass is vermilion and ash, bottle blue and orchid, its light focused on the altar like a rainbow.

"Ye are the salt of the earth, but if the salt has lost his savior, where-with shall it be salted? It is thenceforth good for nothing but to be cast out, and to be trodden under the foot of men." She hears amens and several chords of organ music with a tambourine. The wind seems to be building, and her avocado tree is shaking. A full pitcher of orange juice is ready and she pours some into her own glass, which is half full of vodka from the cupboard. She hears the children play-ing, laughing, shouting. The juice is sticking and thickening in pulp between her fingers. She wipes her hands, puts three cubes in her glass, and begins to sip.

"We are the light of the world. A city that is set on a hill cannot be hid. Neither do men light a candle and put it under a bushel, but on a candlestick; and it giveth light to all that are in the house. Let your light so shine before men that they may see your good works and glorify your Father who is in heaven." The preacher's voice vibrates.

"Amen," Delilah whispers under her breath, seeing her husband erect in purple smoke and walking towards her through the shuttered light of their upstairs bedroom, the squirrel monkey scratching on the shutters.

"And think that today of all holy days is for the children to hear God's words as they are spoken here, to give as only a child can give: in in-nocence, not ignorance, running to find the light. Like all of God's lit-tle children, we will run to find the light!"

Delilah echoes the amens of the congregation, who seem to be with her as she closes her eyes, the vodka running down to her toes, think-ing of Coco and Jinx and where they are in Los Angeles—some place

533

secret and held to their hearts like the men who are inside of them for an afternoon, like the husband she will never see again. Delilah remembers his hair smelled of wet ocean roads and salt, and he danced naked in a yellowed field just for her, his mouth open for prayer, his heartbeat the music of dawn.

*

Outside Angelica has found the most eggs but she won't admit she saw her mother hiding them. Still, she doesn't know where the golden egg is, and turns to Little Howie and the pack of girls and puts her basket down in a patch of crabgrass.

"Do you want to see the movie stars?" A hush falls on the girls and they turn their heads slowly, peering at the house. Gospel music is blaring—black voices and clapping hands and high-pitched shouts.

"Sure." Little Howie is the first to step up and take her hand.

Angelica, poised like a ringleader, lowers her voice, something she's heard her mother do. This means she's important.

"I bet the golden egg is through that hole. Where the movie stars are," Angelica says, conspiratorially.

"Your momma will be really mad." Mary Francis twists the bottom of her skirt with her left hand and rubs her nose with her right, trying not to look at the house.

"Momma never comes outside until the music is over. We can be secret agents. And we're all famous and pretty."

The children begin to crawl through past the century plant, then through the hole; following Angelica's lead they pretend it has doors. As each child pops through they squeal. Mary Francis is the last to go, keeping her eye on the house until the very last second, because she knows if her momma did come out she would be O.K. if she was still in the backyard.

On the other side of the wall the music from Delilah's kitchen is faint. Everything is very still, except for an elderly woman getting in her car. The children hide behind a palm tree. Angelica darts to another palm and whispers, "Be careful, she's got a gun. Look for the egg!"

Angelica is floating, knowing this is part of being a movie star, and begins to run, screaming and singing, through graves and unkept flowers and weeds that have been placed at stone markers. She smells things she has never smelled before, like magnolias that have fallen to the ground in great open husks of scent. She can smell mounds of earth sitting next to freshly dug holes. The other children are following her and to all of them it seems like a place in Saturday morning cartoons, with Scooby Doo and Alvin and the Chipmunks and any friend they want, invisible, running beside them. High clouds have bleached the sun, and the children love the feeling of wind on their legs and hair, and shouting across space with no one to hear them. They do not know what mausoleums and crypts are, thinking them little houses with columns and gates and statues. Everyone has their favorite, Angelica's being the biggest and grandest.

"See? I'm a rich movie star. Howie, you are my sister and also a secret agent who's gonna rescue me, but we gotta find the mountain."

Little Howie nods his head and runs with Angelica. The other girls are worried; they are trailing far behind them. Mary Francis looks around and bites her lip.

"We're supposed to hold our breath, remember? If we don't, bad things will happen." The other girls agree, and they begin to walk slowly together, their cheeks fat with air, eyes determined.

Little Howie and Angelica are out of breath and they have stopped at Tyrone Power's tomb, covered with tiny graffiti and overlooking a lagoon of water the color of malachite, full of water lilies and garbage that has collected in the reeds at the edges. Angelica decides to speak.

"This is the mountain, see? And there's the ocean. Now the golden egg is ours, but we're both naked." Little Howie nods his head and takes off his clothes as the other girls come up to the tomb, still holding their breath and woozy. Angelica takes off her clothes and the girls start laughing, letting the air escape, as she and Howie—who's always wanted to be a naked girl on top of a mountain—begin to pose like they are afraid, looking for the villain, from on top of Tyrone Power's tomb.

"We're naked and they're gonna get the egg. Help!" Angelica jumps off the tomb as her clothes begin to blow away. She runs naked to the lagoon, her baby fat shaking and her hair ribbons unraveling on her shoulders. Little Howie is lost in his dreams, still pretending to be a naked girl who's a secret agent and a movie star on top of a mountain with a golden egg.

The other girls have seen Little Howie's weenie before, so they follow Angelica to the lagoon.

"I need to hide. They're looking for me!"

One of the girls finds a fallen palm frond and puts it in front of Angelica, but she is not sure who Angelica is hiding from. Angelica splashes some water from the lagoon on her and looks around, smiling and naked.

"This will make me a movie star for sure."

"And God said, the children of the earth know no wrong; they see with the eyes we have lost, their innocence is our sal-va-tion!" Delilah opens her eyes.

"Amen," she whispers. Delilah realizes she is drunk, that she has been asleep. And suddenly she remembers the children. What time is it? Two o'clock.

"Fear not death, little children, he is but a comfort when thou art tired. He is the future friend to us all."

Delilah wipes her eyes and sets the orange juice in paper cups on a tray and walks unsteadily outside. She realizes it must be the combination of Scotch with coffee, and vodka with her orange juice that did it to her. It doesn't seem possible. She's only had five drinks. Jinx and Frosty could drink her under the table. Princess liked champagne and bought cases of the cheap stuff, Jacques Bonet, which she drank in tall iced tea glasses on the rocks. They were all putting on weight.

She hears the black man with his bongos, realizes he must be with his girlfriend at the triplex down the block, and thinks we all have homes today, on Easter, and none of us is lost. It is God's will.

Delilah drops the tray of fresh orange juice when she sees the backyard. The children aren't there. The paper tablecloth has blown away and is caught on the clothesline. Pieces of chocolate cake, jelly beans, and crumpled napkins are scattered on the lawn. When she begins to shout Angelica's name, she is not sure it is her own voice. She sounds like an angry, drunk man, her voice is so guttural. She sounds like her husband yelling to her on his way to prison, when he stared at her, repeating something she couldn't understand, as the doors closed on the police truck.

"Children, come back! I have to give you your prizes!" She sees the baskets half full of eggs, some tipped over, by the century plant, and her heart begins to palpitate. She can hear her own breath in the sunny wind. It is small and ineffectual.

It is Angelica's fault. She was born mean, a breech birth, and now she is a child filled with godless ideas and too old for her age. They will have to move now, somewhere else. San Diego or Bakersfield. Somewhere where there are no movie stars, no graves, no whores.

Delilah knows they have gone through the hole, and bends down ungracefully to see if she can get through it. The hem of her dress catches on the century plant, and the tip of one of the juicy, sharp

536

leaves scratches her leg, causing a long line of blood to trickle down to her ankles. She barely fits, and as she pulls herself through, she is covered with garden dirt and bits of crushed fern and mint.

"Children!" As she walks into the Hollywood Memorial Cemetery, the sound of her gospel program becomes dimmer.

"Children!" Delilah staggers across the in-ground markers, looking as though she were pulled out of the earth. One of her favorite earrings has fallen off and she touches her ear as she walks, promising not to cry, not to be frightened. She knows she has only a few more hours until the girls get back, and that the children must nap, be fed, and be ready to go home. They will have one more drink for the road, even though they all live on the same two blocks of shade and chain-link fence.

As she walks through the silent land of mausoleums and monuments to studio heads, she crosses herself, thinking there is nothing more horrifying than a graveyard in a high wind, when flower arrangements tip over and spirits dance. She looks for cars on the twisting, narrow lanes that cut through grubby orchards of palms and stone but everyone is home today. Home.

Delilah sees statues of women who died too young and they are made to look like angels, but Delilah knows they weren't—their eyes white stone balls eaten away by car fumes and rain full of sand. She walks past chipped stone doves and marble roses, long sleek sarcophagi of famous men that hold the heat of the sun and rot the bodies inside. And everywhere the wind carries voices, beating against her ears.

She sees the children in the distance and walks rapidly towards them, furious, one purple leather shoe now wet with blood. Again she crosses herself, her lips tightening. As she nears them, she realizes they are playing on top of a movie star's tomb. She reads "Tyrone Power," repeats his name over and over and stops walking. I shall remember you in my prayers, Tyrone Power. She remembers seeing Tyrone Power in *Captain From Castille* in the Dominican Republic, the film already ten years old by the time it played there, scratchy with age and dubbed into Spanish. She remembers a boy put his finger in her, and she let him, grinding down on it because it felt good, and how it came back to her with whispers behind the aloof face of her mother. She remembers her living room of red and gold and its lizards swept out daily. She remembers the shame—that movies made boys do this. She remembers being beaten and how it didn't hurt.

She watches the children, transfixed, and does not comprehend. She sees that Angelica and Little Howie are naked, and the other girls are laughing and watching them as they continue a charade. Delilah begins to cry, large moaning, shaking sobs that force her to her knees and blind her. She will pray for their souls. She will pray for her own soul.

The children suddenly become quiet when they hear the sobbing, turning around to find where it is coming from and see Delilah on her bloody knees, her hair covered in cobwebs. Mary Francis screams, but one of the other girls nudges her in the ribs, telling her to shut up. Slowly Angelica and Little Howie hop down from the top of the tomb and find their wind-scattered clothes, putting them on, embarrassed and flushed.

Delilah can feel the Scotch coming up on her breath and she can't stop crying. She can't see the children, but she can feel her nose running down to her lip. Everything in her mind moves rapidly, drunkenly to a finish, and she is crying because she does not know what it is. Angelica circles her mother, terrified. The children run back to the wall, to the hole, and climb through it. Delilah stays alone on her knees for quite some time, crying because there is nothing left for her to do on this day, because Jesus does not walk through Hollywood Memorial, and Delilah must have him with her at all times.

When the girls return they wink and sip another drink with Delilah, who has put on a fresh dress and cleaned her leg. In May, Coco will have her turn with the children, and Delilah will go to an upholstered bar on Venice Boulevard where the men speak Spanish and palm trees are painted on the walls. Coco will take the children to the beach and Delilah will close her eyes on another man's bed.

Coco wants to make sure Little Howie has behaved himself, and Delilah says he was an angel, a little angel, and that the children have had a grand time. She shakes her head and lisps that Angelica was punished, that she is in her room without cookies and cake.

Delilah is humming to herself as the women and their children leave, words galloping over her starched tongue, a song her mother taught her. How you don't give bread to wolves, because they will spirit your children away, to a place where even the strongest men don't go. Angelica is screaming behind her locked door, and Delilah takes out her crucifix and a piece of lace from the linen drawer, touching it to her face, running it over her eyes so the light around her becomes flowers of ivory and white.

Nominated by Sandra Tsing Loh

BODY PARTS (1968)

by BIN RAMKE

from AMERICAN LETTERS AND COMMENTARY

HISTORY

Divided and divided again against
itself, the body the body. Meiosis and other
forces in the tiny universe, so
solemn and satisfied. Here is a war for you.
In school they would wear fatigues
and say *I was there.* And they were, and are. We trembled
in their wake, wondering. We studied *here.* No *there*
was worth the work and still we suffered.
Where was I? To see is just to see.

THEOLOGY

And then there was God, and the newest theory
and the finest film of desire began to appear
in their eyes, mistaken for tears. A prayer
that would suffice.

There was a time the women
dressed in desire and the men
in meaning, when no one listened
to anything
willowy lingering
wails announced the foreign about to fall
at their feet. Some nice
new accents might arrive
with marble and Italians to carve it, white

blasted from big holes
in the native soil. Full of history is
hard country. There's work across the sea.

ART

Smooth as stone and turn upon turn
surrounds the glister of flesh
monumentally other the only
the library's Psyche the memory
of marble though carved
anything can last
forever, given time enough. Obstacles
strung between us from the start
like wasps flung across the path at a pretty
party, like flagstone. The views, you would say,
some limb severed you still care about
because gone and long missed so nothing else
matters. They were married that way, or we
were at someone's wedding, marbled
and cool in the afternoon under tribal tents
rented metal cool to the touch to sit on.
Champagne, a color, something like that.

Nominated by American Letters & Commentary *and Lee Upton*

KILLER WHALES

fiction by SUSAN DAITCH

from STORYTOWN (Dalkey Archive Press)

I WOKE UP to find Gregor Samsa in my sink. He was enormous, at
least two inches long, blue-black, and very fast. I grabbed a china
teacup, something the last tenant had left in the house, placed it over
him, and slid the covered bug to a position over the drain. I hoped he
would figure that crawling down the hole was his only alternative, al-
though his scutcheoned shell was far too broad to allow him to do so
easily. He was a real monster, and I expected the teacup itself might
move across the stainless steel any minute, its rim scraping the left-
over grit of cleanser and coffee grounds. It was raining into the bay,
rain streaked the kitchen window and ran into pots of baby cacti and
pansies that a catalogue had promised would grow to sequoia dimen-
sions. I opened the window and let it rain in. The spigots and faucets
were soon dotted with tiny convex reflections. My beetle under china
roses slumbered.

The wind dropped, and the rain fell straight down so that a haze of
water bounced from shingles. Gutters turned riverlike and drainpipes
led to miniature versions of Niagara Falls. I walked out into the rain,
stood beside a laurel tree, and looked into my neighbor's window. He
had changed the arrangement of figures set out behind small panes of
glass, and I was glad because I hadn't seen him for a while. A statue of
Saint Francis faced outward from the sill, arms outstretched, one hand
chipped off, white plaster showing through the scratched brown paint
of his robe. He was surrounded by toy sheep, soldiers, a couple of
windup Godzillas, a toy bed with two syringes tucked in it, and a can-
dlestick which had a flame-shaped light bulb where a wick would have

been. I hadn't seen these objects before. I was afraid my neighbor would catch me staring at the sleeping needles as water dripped down my back, but his ground-floor apartment looked empty. Behind a louvered glass door the rooms were dim, tables dusty.

SOME THINGS aren't as different as people like to claim. When I was a child I used to think about language as an odd job lot of words, random and haphazard, you find a string to do the work, to effect meaning. Then the metaphor evolved again. Words were like a school of jellyfish with thousands of tentacles streaming below the surface, and some of those tentacles were attached or stuck together below the waves: the seemingly unconnected jellyfish were really Siamese twins if you looked closely. The connections might be syllables or synonyms. I was a rubberized underwater diver looking for those strands which tied words together. How might *Aztec* be like *Creole* or *Yayoi* like *Ikan?* I don't think I was innocently looking for natural linguistic connections—I deliberately tied tentacles together, ignoring my own stung fingers. Abandoning articulate speech, I turned to origins: I listened to babies, trying to determine when a child begins to drop the nonsense from his or her speech and link the production of sounds to the expression of desire, gratification, or frustration. Crawling, staring, drooling onto tape recorders, they slowly begin to identify clusters of sounds, priming the language pump, it's called. For several years I watched them play and cry, then shifted my attention to unlocking the meaning of monkey chatter and bird songs. I monitored whale calls, seismographic blurps on a blue screen, interpreting each wave as if it were a kind of dangling clause or tense shift, yet often felt lost in the protolanguages of animals and children.

Now I look at words as isolated catatonic patients in a state hospital whose funds have been cut off. It is a scene of bankruptcy where there is no longer any relationship between sound and meaning. The orderlies smoke joints in the unswept halls and take all kinds of pills right out in the chaotic open. They speak of morphine in morphemes, if possible, and I'm even more convinced of the futility of this project, looking for sources.

I WORK AT the university lab annotating the speech of sea animals, particularly the killer whales on loan from Sea World in San Diego. The lab, crescent-shaped, a fingernail clipping in the sand, is underground, equipment separated by plates of glass from huge tanks which contain the animals, and I watch them swim in very blue water. If the animals can see me, through windows on the inner curve, they give no sign. There are manatees, members of the Siren family, and a tank of rare pygmy sperm whales. Black-and-white killer whales are really giant porpoises; they're fast swimmers, able to swallow dolphins and smaller porpoises alive. According to Eskimo legends, killer whales began as hungry wolves who transformed themselves into aquatic creatures, overwhelmed by the seduction of hunting in the Pacific, and once transformed, none of them returned to land. Ferocious in packs, they are known to eat the weak and wounded members of their own families, but in Sea World or here in the lab, there's hardly a chance for cannibalism. In Sea World they performed with swimmers on school vacation; girls held up rings for them to catch at the end of their noses. In enclosed pools the porpoises were fed small live fish, easily caught, no pursuit involved; they consumed meals with matter-of-fact languor of someone on a couch tossing popcorn into his mouth.

The young imitated and learned their mothers' calls, but the question was posed: If one of the mothers died, would the calf remember her call or would it learn the adopted call of some other killer whale? I threw them fish and listened closely, but all our mothers lived, and mimesis continued without interruption. I would pat the whales when they surfaced, and felt something had been added to my identity when they recognized me. Sea World knew our lab was waiting for the possibility of observing the effect of a parent's death on learning calls, but it wasn't an experiment we could perform. In Sea World when a mother died on its own of more or less natural causes, the calf was transferred up north to our lab.

I watched them swim and dive in bluish light and listened to their calls. The patterns of their swimming followed similar curves traced by the device that records their speech, but I wondered if the orphan calf, as she mimicked the chain of sounds produced by some other member of the herd, was able to forget her mother in the middle of an untroubled swim. Did she hear echoes of her mother's call mixed up in another whale's bark? These were questions for electrodes and heart monitors. Her face is smooth, teeth glinted. I was clueless.

Once my neighbor put a fishbowl in his window. Goldfish and guppies swam through a miniature pink castle surrounded by artificial ferns. A naked Barbie doll, or something like one, sat on the sill watching the fish. The doll's knees weren't jointed, so its legs shot straight out, aggressively. On the other side of the broad window ledge another doll was submerged head down in a glass tank, surrounded by rubber fish placed in inquisitive attitudes as if they were watching her, although later it occurred to me the rubber fish setup might have been an ambush. The doll's legs stuck out above the rim and its blonde hair floated in the water. I'm not sure if this was a gesture in my direction, a way of beckoning, teasing, or mimicking, and I never asked. Perhaps the tableau had nothing to do with me at all. Up until then the sill had contained a collection of cigarette lighters shaped like pistols, and a lamp whose base was an Elvis Presley head. I'd thought my neighbor had an interest in things which model themselves after something else, which hide behind another identity or another history, but now I'm not so sure. The last time I saw him he had become very thin and walked slowly, stopping to buy a newspaper at our corner. My neighbor who constructs stories out of ephemera—toys, needles, and nicked-up saints—is dying, and I don't know if there's been anyone in to learn his speech, anyone who could decode those window displays, and say with certainty, *this is what he meant by . . . and I will repeat to you. . . .* I called him before I left, but no one picked up. The light changed slightly over the water, although I couldn't see the sky, but without looking at a clock I knew it was late, locked up the lab, and began to drive away from the coast.

FOUR ALL-NIGHTERS huddled together, a lit island in a dark street: 24-hour Bus Stop Fruit and Vegetables with a marquee constructed of lemons, peaches, and eggplant stacked outside; That's Rentertainment, a video store whose windows displayed life-size cardboard cutouts of muscled actors and animated caricatures that too seemed to glow in the dark; a gas station defended by looping elephantine hoses; and a Greek restaurant. I thought I might see the same people at each, buying eggplant, renting a movie, sitting in the restaurant drinking coffee to stay awake, then driving home.

Electric lights shaped like candles had been placed in each of Demeter's windows, romantic in the rain if you've just driven up for gas and aren't anxious to get home. I parked, seduced by the electric candles, but also because Demeter's aluminum-sided diner reminded me of Sam's, torn down long ago in another city. I used to take a bus from school to Sam's downtown, sitting with friends at a curving formica counter with boomerang shapes embedded in it; we'd order Cokes. The man who fried everything under the sun had a thin, pissed-off face. We watched him. However much we tried to wrinkle our gray skirts and green blazers, we felt trapped and ordinary, while his tattoo of a woman with a whip and dangling cigarette spoke of foreignness. I was sure he hated us because we ordered little more than french fries and showed no visible signs of responsibility. Sam's had an electric sign over the grill. Above the name of the restaurant was a blackboard-colored field split by a hyperbolic curve with a dot of light tracing its trajectory. The spellbinding illusion was that the color of the dot of light changed as it traveled along the curve. Blue hill, green valley, yellow hill, red valley, purple hill, then back to the beginning, a visual metronome. It was mesmerizing when you had nothing to talk about, or even when you did.

The bathroom in Sam's reflected someone's idea of what signified feminine: smudged gray and pink tile, cracked formica threatening to spill its gold glitter. But the feminine was covered by names and numbers scratched into yellow metal, written on walls and mirrors, even the paper towel dispenser: pleadings and demands, secrets made public, ridiculous limericks. The Aztecs and Mayans had chalk talk, pictogramic calendars or talking pictures, and I wondered if the names in Sam's bathroom weren't some kind of message system too. I didn't imagine the rude poems and crooked hearts had anything to do with loneliness. They were just dirty and funny. I saw men and women meet each other at Sam's. They slid into booths, or sat down heavily, somehow they found each other. I tried to listen to their conversations, but from the counter I couldn't really hear anything. Once I heard the phrase *dirty laundry*, several times the word *telephone*, then *letter from Plei-ku*.

We were warned not to go there. The nail in the coffin of our trips to Sam's came when a man was arrested in one of the booths. I don't remember what he was charged with or if he was convicted, but I continued to go there, usually alone. I would have given anything for a weekend job at Sea World swimming with the porpoises, but we lived in a landlocked state. In a small town near two state lines Sam's served as amusement park and laboratory. I saw packages left in the phone booth whose wooden door, an accordion of two panels, easily offered a screen. Women came and went quickly in the late afternoon, not stopping to talk to each other in booths or over the counter. The long-haired men who picked up the packages used the word *babe*, like nothing I'd ever heard before.

My mother's warnings hadn't described them. Her language was so full of omissions that I didn't learn it. I've read of tribes where one language is spoken by men and a quite different one by women, but consider a tribe in which daughters speak a separate language, unrelated to that of their mothers—an impractical invention, ridiculous and fantastic. Let's say they do speak the same language, but in this tribe the language is constructed so that mothers and daughters who take pleasure in contradicting each other are able to do so at every possible opportunity. Every time a spear is hammered, every time a bowl is cast, or fish are fried, they disagree. One says something is blue, the other says no, it's green, one says offense is taken, the other says no, you misinterpret, you always do, and I'm sick of it. The tanks I watch appear serene in comparison; one learns the calls of the other, and that's it. I have no one to repeat my mother's warnings to in any case, except possibly baby killer whales who ignore me, just as a child who is too often told what to do might finally ignore an adult, or try to, so perhaps the result is the same.

AT DEMETER'S the news on the hour is broadcast from a radio kept by the cash register. Mr. Demeter turns it on only late at night when a few drivers or midnight video renters straggle in, and the diner is sporadically empty anyway. The announcer snaps out the words *Persian Gulf*. It's difficult to pronounce these soft syllables with such brittleness. *Pershun. Per-son.*

Sand as fine as powdered sugar, Mr. Demeter echoed something he had once heard.

The radio again: *Tariq, Kerkuk, Baghdad, Mesopotamia,* and *Al Basra* slam into *typhus, typhoid, microorganisms.* Here the tongue lingers. I try to imitate the announcer but am unable to mimic his speech. *Forty thousand body bags have just been ordered, although no shot has been fired.* Demeter hits the cash register so ringing interrupts the newscast. He's not really successful in blocking out the sound, and I imagine if Bartleby suffered paralysis as a result of working in a dead letter office, those who sew and measure zippers and nylon on a body bag assembly line may also linger in future cells saying only *I prefer not to.* No one will guess their histories. I line up the salt and pepper shakers, the sugar dispenser, and the ketchup bottle as if each object represents a sewing machine operator, a packer, a filer of invoices. Windows are streaked with rain, and within That's Rentertainment a clerk is counting orange Video Bucks, another moves a

546

cardboard Julia Roberts out of the window, putting his hands between her legs to lift her and laughing at a man who stares at him, laughing too. Plastic coverings are lowered over fruit and vegetables next door. Under blinking fluorescent lights, daffodils, hyacinths, and paper whites glow like supernatural parodies of themselves.

SOMEONE HAD wiped dust from the jalousied door. Objects had been removed from his window, and it remained empty the next day as well. Just a week before the monster had risen from my drain. Perhaps Gregor Samsa fled with the instinctive knowledge that everything he was used to had been slated to be swept away. I turned on the television, but these kinds of deaths aren't reported, there are so many of them. Even after the news I left it on, providing a blur of sound in the house for a few minutes. I didn't pay attention really, but as something like *America's Most Wanted* or *Unsolved Mysteries* followed the news broadcast it occurred to me that the man behind the grill at Sam's might turn up on one of these programs, computer aged, because it's years later. All kinds of people do, followed by the warning: *If you should see this man or woman, please call. . . .* If this should happen, my mother will say, I told you so, you were lucky to get away unharmed. Perhaps I know her language better than I realize or am ever willing to admit.

THE KILLER whales swim in confined pools. Curves of whale speech snaking across a laboratory monitor resemble the curve of the electric sign in Sam's that held you spellbound, *Drink Coke, Drink Coke, Drink Coke.* I recognize patterns of sound, but the meanings they bark remain elusive. Whether they are arguing or talking about dinner, expressing boredom or depression, the screen doesn't tell me, but I sit and watch. It's late. At Demeter's Mr. D has refused to listen to the radio for the time being, he doesn't want to hear about refugees or nerve gas, so I get a coffee to go and return to work for a few more hours. The microphones are set in the whale pool. I am listening.

Nominated by Dalkey Archive Press

547

EL PERIFÉRICO, OR SLEEP

by JOSHUA CLOVER

from AMERICAN POETRY REVIEW

A man throws ten thousand shovels of gravel at a window screen
propped upside a wheelbarrow so only the powder
passes into the wheelbarrow and the gray rocks fall to the ground.
You musta died once to live like this.
Yeah he says I died once and I had lost my ear
so I was looking for it in a field and the stars were like a seiner's net
and then they were like a system of nerves
and then they were like a sieve I came through
that right back into this country and got a job and married
the woman the first two things
she said to me in that fiery field holding in her hands
my ear were how this country now is full
only of pilgrims and residue and her name is Beatriz ending
like light ends with a *z*.

Nominated by John Allman and Brenda Hillman

ZENOBIA

fiction by GINA BERRIAULT

from THE THREEPENNY REVIEW and WOMEN IN THEIR BEDS
(Counterpoint Press)

". . . and in the innermost room, the holy of the holies, the soul sits alone."
—*Edith Wharton*

SO HIGH AND MIGHTY, like God who gave life to Adam and Eve and set their names down in the Bible, you gave life to me and set my name down in a book. One can't outlive God but I have outlived you, and I say this to you where you lie in your tomb, far across the ocean in a foreign land: Edith, you shall never forgive yourself for wronging me.

Silence, the wind's gone on. No whistlings, no growlings, no loose boards banging. My heart's flapping against my ribs where I could not always hear it before. Pitiful bird, it wants out from where you caged it for me. When the wind sweeps down again, I pray it breaks this house into a thousand pieces and throws onto the snow the mildewed beds nobody's slept in for years and years, where mice make their nests, and the black-crusted pots and the cracked dishes and this splintery rocker where I sit in my gray wrapper that's ages-thin, ages-old like a dead bird's feathers, and this greasy table where you sat us down together, the three of us, your beloved Ethan and your darling Mattie and your dread Zenobia.

Such a kind name you gave to him, a name like his heart beating, muffled deep in chest . . . Eee . . . Thun . . . Eee . . . thun, and such a sweet name you gave to her, a name like a crisp of maple sugar melting in his mouth, like the whirr of a dove's wings . . . Matteee . . . Matteee . . . and such a twisted stick of a name you gave to me. Z is the

549

letter at the end of the alphabet, there's no place after Z. It's a criss-cross gate that nobody can get past if they want to see what's there. Once I saw a dried-up skin from a big lizard that was brought from the underside of this earth. Zenobia ought to be the name of that creature.

Milliner's hats laden with flowers, gowns of silk and velvet, the stitches invisibly tiny, shoes of Spanish leather with fancy heels and jeweled buckles, everything upon you handmade by other persons always bent over their tasks, and pearls, endless strands of pearls, and furs, and ribbons, and billowy lace over your bosom. So proud you were of your bosom, any woman with less than yours you mocked, you pointed out as a failure of a woman, as you did me. Oh, and the many mansions where you dwelled, your Persian carpets, and marble fireplaces, and your pure white bed with tasseled canopy, and high windows that opened onto fragrant gardens. And how many times did you cross the ocean as if it were a lake and belonged to you? How could you be expected to know what my deprivations were, so immensely more than all your possessions, which I did not covet in the least.

Where I'll begin is where you began, though now the truth will be told. Winter, yes, it was winter, ice hard under the snow and the trees encased in ice, when I was brought into his house to tend his mother. And I did tend her, hand and foot, as I had done for so many others, and when she was buried out there under the snow, why then he asked me to marry him and stay on. Yes, it was winter and you were right, a young man of twenty-one would not have asked me if it were spring, seven years older than him, and come into his life in that winter of his mother dying. I did not belong in the spring, I was condemned to remain in that winter of his memory, and the aches of winter got into me. Oh hear me! all parts of me cried. How they begged for love and tending like little children weakly crying, and often I had to lie down, and take my spoon of medicine, and wrap myself warm.

Oh Lord, why did you bring her into my life? Oh Lord, is she my fate? That's how he looked at me. Night after night he turned his back on me. Year after year we lay side by side, untouching. I was not born mean, meanness set in, took its time like a disease. Meanness came and filled up the spaces where his love was not. But how shamelessly, Edith, you made the most of my meanness! You made my hair sparse and tangled and gray, and my body thin as a rake, and my eyes lashless, and my neck scraggy, and you took away my teeth, every one, so poor Ethan had to see his wife's false teeth in a glass every day, and asthma, you gave me asthma, and that was further proof of my bad nature, like God's punishment of me.

But, Edith, I was only around thirty-five when you described me so and not like I am now in my old, old age. Recollect, Edith, how I was in the time when I was still a very young woman, before I ever met him, how my own eyes saw myself. Tall, and how gracefully erect I stood, and how I looked directly at everyone and at children, too, so they'd feel grown-up. My face some thought austere but kindly so, and my hair was black and shone in lamplight and firelight, and my hands were long and gentle. I was the young woman who tended the sick and whose presence was welcomed by them when they opened their eyes and found her sitting at their bedside, knitting or reading.

You likened this house to a gray gravestone and that's how it was for me, still in my youth. I did my chores as he did his, every season of the year, and at night we lay down together in that room at the top of the steep, narrow stairs that I've not climbed in years and years, not since he died. And after awhile, as we lay apart, with his back to me always, I became as empty of love for him as he was empty of love for me. But my heart was hurting over its emptiness, and even in the day I'd slip up to that bed and lie alone to soothe it. Once, when he was out at the mill, I wept, but very quietly so he wouldn't hear if he came into the house. I wept over who I had become, dislikable as he saw me, someone I was not before. It was a grievous thing that had come about.

Before I ever knew Ethan Frome, before I ever knew he was on this earth, there was good in me. A nurse in that doctor's office over in Bettsbridge, that's who I wanted to be, back when I was twenty. A white smock and a white cap on my smooth black hair, and both of us, the doctor and myself, doing good, and there might come a time when he would want me to never part from his side. So I heard he was wanting a nurse and I went, but there was the chosen girl already, her eyes bright for being the chosen one. They knew already she was to be at his side forever. He said to me he'd heard about my gift for caring for the sick and I knew he said gift because that word was to make up for not choosing me. Never would I go back to him, that's what I vowed, but when I was ailing I went to him. I put myself through the humiliation of her dark, bright eyes so sympathetic because she knew why I'd come back.

My feeling for that good doctor helped me to get through the years. That secret feeling, all to myself, helped me to look up into his face and wait for his hands to be placed upon me. It got me up into the train and up the stairs to his office, and he grew older along with me, and that helped. And though he had not chosen me he must have come to cherish me for all the longing in my body. A kind man, he was kind to me, his hands were kind upon my body when my body was young and when it was old, and one day when I was surely old he took my hands in his—we were sitting and facing—and bowed his head, and when he lifted his head his eyes held tears. He'd known all along what my ailment was but he couldn't tell me, he had no words. It wasn't a name in his Disease and Medicine Manual.

The way Ethan complained about my trips to the doctor, about his errands to the post office to pick up the medicines I'd ordered, that way of his was like the way squirrels pack their acorns inside their cheeks. He'd be silent, but the complaints dragged down his face, and, if the tonic made me feel kind of light in the head, I'd want to laugh at how he looked. I had to go up to bed and hide the laughing in my pillow, where it changed itself into grief. Edith, you who had every reason to laugh aloud, how could you know how a laugh that's hid turns itself into grief.

When I asked Mattie Silver to come into this house and help me with the chores, it was not just for my sake, it was for her sake, too. She had no mother or father and was in poor health. Recollect, Edith, that she blossomed while she was here, and recollect I urged her to go down to the dancing in the church basement where she could meet a young man who'd fall in love with her and make her his wife, and recollect I urged her to go to picnics in the summer with other young people round about. I knew it was Ethan who scrubbed the kitchen floor and churned the butter when he thought I slept, doing those chores to spare her, though I pretended not to know this.

Was there a hidden intention in my heart when I asked her to come into this house? Was I wanting a girl who'd be like a ray of sun, who'd stir up some life in that pillar of stone, that Ethan, who'd got old while he was young, while both of us were young? If that was my intention it was not a shameful one. But when I saw that what I longed for from him was given to her, was given to Mattie, why then I banished her. I could not bear how she joined with him to render me so hateful. Tell me, Edith, if you know, what Sarah felt when she banished Hagar, when she sent her out into the wilderness. Mattie carried no child with her as Hagar did. She carried Ethan's love, and I thought his love was as much a treasure as a child. I do not think so now.

Yes, it was cruel of me to banish Mattie. But when they rode that sled down the hill and into the elm and were split asunder forever, that was not my deed, that was not my doing. It was Mattie who was Death's handmaiden, not I, and the night I banished her and Ethan took her down to the train, that was the night she did Death's bidding. Death left that sled waiting there for them, and together they rode down that hill and into the elm, and Ethan sat in front to protect her, wanting to be the one to die if one was to go on living, and she sat behind him, clasping him, and Death sat behind her, clasping them both. Old trickster Death, Life tricked him back.

It hurts my shrunken heart to call him a coward, but he was that. Ethan was a coward. He could have run away with her, he could have borrowed a small sum from a friend in town, enough for train tickets to get them to some place where work was to be had for the asking. He would have paid it back, he was an honest man and everybody knew that. But wasn't there a nettle of dishonesty in his heart? You said his conscience told him not to forsake me, not to leave me with nothing but a poor farm and mill beyond my health to manage. But didn't he forsake me when he chose to die? A forsaking most awful!

Edith, I tell you what I would have done if they had died that night. I would have taken the blame on myself. What else could I do but live out my wretched life, guilty of their deaths? But when they returned into this house, broken in body and spirit, Mattie to spend the rest of her years wracked by pain, whining for me to tend her, which I did, and Ethan grown stonier, a stone man lamely striving to attend to his tasks, why then I saw that I was not to blame. I saw it was their fate and I saw it was my fate to care for them.

Often I mused on what I would have done if they had run away together. Often I used to remember one day in the spring of the year, one day when Ethan was away in town and Mattie had not come to us yet. I saw a young man out by the mill, his easel set up, painting a picture. It was in that time when I began to see how Ethan never cared to look into my face and, whenever he did look, a puzzlement came into his eyes as though he felt a pain somewhere. So I got my courage up and walked out to where the young man sat on a rock, and I stood behind him to see how a painting appears in the very making of it. I stood behind him to keep him from taking notice of me, afraid he would look up into my face the way Ethan looked at me, like I ought not to be there. He turned his head, he looked up at me, and what did he do? He smiled, he said, "Can I take the liberty and make a

553

painting of your mill?" Oh take the liberty and ask afterwards! I liked that, it amused me. He was a stranger, someone I'd never seen in town or passing by on the road. He said he'd come down from the state of Maine and was bound West. He said he wished to be an artist. High mountains and dense tall forests and rushing rivers, that's what he'd paint, and he looked into my face while he told me, and I saw that my face gave him pleasure.

Oh take the liberty! That's what I would have done if Ethan and Mattie had run off together and left me on this forsaken farm. I would have packed my satchel and my portmanteau and climbed aboard a train bound West, and gazed out the window at what there was to see across this vast country. City spires in the midst of wheatfields, and miles of orchards with fruit on the bough, and high bridges over broad rivers, and mountains of clouds the likes of which I'd never seen, and birds of a kind I'd never seen before. And there'd be a city where I'd stay, and there'd be an old couple in a fine house of many rooms, and I'd tend them and see they kept neat, and on my days off I'd wind my black hair in a fashionable way with tortoise-shell combs, and hold my head high, and go out to see what that city had to offer.

Edith, you never looked into my face the way that young painter did. You saw Ethan, you saw the twist of his body and his suffering face, and your heart was moved by what had befallen him. But your heart was unmoved by what befell me that day I came to tend his mother, that winter day I stepped down from the train, and he took my satchel from my hand and said my name, Zenobia, and my own heart was moved by him for the rest of my days.

Nominated by The Threepenny Review *and Andre Dubus*

THE MAN WHO WOULDN'T PLANT WILLOW TREES

by A. E. STALLINGS

from THE BELOIT POETRY JOURNAL

Willows are messy trees. Hair in their eyes,
They weep like women after too much wine
And not enough love. They litter a lawn with leaves
Like the butts of regrets smoked down to the filter.

They are always out of kilter. Thirsty as drunks,
They'll sink into a sewer with their roots.
They have no pride. There's never enough sorrow.
A breeze threatens and they shake with sobs.

Willows are slobs, and must be cleaned up after.
They'll bust up pipes just looking for a drink.
Their fingers tremble, but make wicked switches.
They claim they are sorry, but they whisper it.

Nominated by Ha Jin and Diann Blakely Shoaf

AT LEAST THIRTEEN WAYS OF LOOKING AT LOOK

by GORDON LISH

from PRESS

Listen, you are looking at somebody who just can't wait to look derived. It scares the spunk out of me for me to think they'll come along and look at my writing and say, "Hey, who sent this clown? Where'd he come from? Uh-oh, this bozo's not some kind of vagrant Johnny-come-lately, is he?"

Please, I know all about Bloom and that stuff—and, believe me, I'm not saying it's not terrific stuff, Bloom's stuff. But I'm telling you, the one thing you're looking at when you look at me is somebody who does not want to look like somebody who's exclusively responsible for himself.

Talk about anxiety—as far as I'm concerned, Bloom didn't know what he was talking about when he was talking about anxiety.

Didn't the man ever hear of the Anxiety of the Appearance of Being the Sole Responsible Party in Sight?

Which is why I always knock myself out looking for epigraphs as alibis.

I figure if I can stand my writing in back of the right writer by citing the right epigraph right up front in front of my writing before anybody has had himself a chance to look at my writing, I can maybe sort of look as if I am sort of maybe guilty, all right—

conceded, conceded!—but not without virtue of a certain glamorous association.

You know—the forgivably bastard son of, a traceably impoverished relation to.

All honor to Bloom, you bet—but, honest, I'm always looking to look as if I'm as influenced as anybody can get.

Which is what led me to looking very closely at Wallace Stevens a little bit ago—epigraph-hunting.

Well, I had the notion it would look pretty wonderful on me for me to look as if I'd spent some deep time looking at Wallace Stevens.

(Which can have the effect of getting you to believe Wallace Stevens spent some deep time looking at you, you know?)

So when the poems had me stumped (except for a couple or three that probably had me no less stumped but that, anyhow, knocked me flat), I started looking all around inside of Stevens' daughter's selection of Stevens' letters—and, boy, did I find wild provocation for wild postures of derivation and so forth.

Get this.

The man's wife was named Elsie.

Okay, the fifth-most of the most romantic sensations of my childhood (the first-most I felt in the vicinity of myself, the second-most in the ditto of my mother, the third-most in that of one of my grammar-school teachers, the fourth-most while sitting on the curb gazing at—I admit it, I admit it!—an American coin) was aroused by the name Elsie when I found out that the name Elsie was the name of the woman up the block, which woman—O Elsie, Elsie, Elsie!—was my playmate Harvey Weidenfeld's—oh, wow!—mother.

Okay, so now I find out that Stevens' wife, his daughter Holly's mother, that she also was an Elsie.

Okay, what next do I find?

That where Stevens and his Elsie first lived in New York was where their landlord had Stevens' Elsie model for him so that the landlord—otherwise, in the official manifestation of himself, a sculptor—could enter the result in a U.S. Mint competition for the face that would newly ornament the U.S. Mint's newly-to-be-minted ten-cent piece.

The dime.

Get this.

It wins.

He wins.

The Stevenses' landlord wins.

It's therefore Elsie Stevens' face that's there on the ten-cent piece driving me—when I am eight and nine and ten—crazy with feelings.

Plus which, it's such a swell face, or that version of it is, that the U.S. Mint decides to let it go be the face that goes on the fifty-cent piece, too.

The half dollar.

So that face—you get it, you get it?—the face that a million years ago my insides were getting all swimmy over—turns out to have been the face of—well, of my derived-from's missus.

But here's the capper, topper, pay-off.

Which is that where they made their residence, the Stevenses, when they first got together as marrieds and first set up housekeeping here in New York, and which was where Mr. Weinman, that landlord/sculptor I was telling you about, got Elsie Stevens—O Elsie, Elsie, Elsie!— to sit for him for the coin thing I was just telling you about, that where that was, that where (according to a Holly Stevens footnote in the compilation of letters I was, wasn't I, just telling you about) all those goings-on were going on was three doors from the selfsame address where I, Gordon—O Gordon, Gordon, Gordon, shame!—kept conducting oh-so-many shameless romances from 1969 to 1994, which latter year was the year my wife of thirty-one years died.

So will you look?

Will you just look at how far somebody will go for him to look as if he is not just any old nameless belatedness but—look, look!—an identifiably indictable one?

Nominated by M. D. Elevitch

THE NUDE DETECTIVE, A COMPLAINT

by DOROTHY BARRESI

from BAKUNIN

for God

Your devices are sensitive.

In rain and in snow,
in moonlight that clatters down

its bright plates and crockery
like a voice in the head,

you stay. You lend to our windows
a fishing pole

and a microphone.
But why?

Are you some under-assistant's
last hireling?

Nothing, not even faith or crazy envy can explain
how we provoke you to this patience

hour by hour by hour.
And if our daily static can be removed,

our *yeses*
turned to *no* on tape

the way technology puts
plastic hearts in men, or

cheese in jars,
then surely we don't deserve

such a careful listening.
Such bare attention to what we do

only makes us act worse.
A kiss, a gasp—

how long before you drag
your sunburned knuckles in some fleshly

circles on the ground?
How long before you order Moo Shu Pork then drip

plum sauce on the bedclothes?
Mr. Never-Kissed and Tell, Mr.

Truly Exposed,
we're speaking out at last.

You wearing only a porkpie hat
like Donatello's David,

you with dark circles under wholly
permanent eyes, we wish you'd get a life

and beat it for good this time, you goddamn,
you shivering

angel who loves us more than we love ourselves.

Nominated by Bakunin and David Rivard

GOOSEBERRY MARSH

by GRETCHEN LEGLER

from ORION and ALL THE POWERFUL INVISIBLE THINGS: A
SPORTSWOMAN'S NOTEBOOK (Seal Press)

THIS FALL ON Gooseberry Marsh the weather is warm and the water is high. As Craig and I load the canoe on the grassy shore of the marsh, the sky is turning from rosy-gold to gray-blue. The blackbirds that make their homes in the reeds are singing by the hundreds, a loud, high, rocks-in-a-bucket screeching. Above us, lines of geese cross the lightening sky.

This is the first fall of our not living with each other, of living apart: Craig in the big house, me in a small apartment. But we decided to hunt together anyway, hanging onto this sure thing, hunting at Gooseberry Marsh, this thing we have shared for so many years.

We try in a polite and partly exhausted way to pretend that nothing is different, that we still love each other, but something subtle has shifted beneath us. It is more than the awkward and uneasy rearranging of our lives. In preparing for this trip, I bought *our* supplies with *my* money and brought the food to *Craig's* house. When we get *home* from hunting I will unpack *our* decoys and *our* coolers full of wet birds, do *my* laundry, and then I will leave for *my* apartment. We both feel embarrassed and sad when we catch ourselves saying, "Next time we should wear waders," for we both know there probably will be no next time.

But something more has changed. It is hard for me now even to reach out to hold his hand. The intimacy we had, the warm space between our bodies, has stretched so that it feels like nothing. Between us now is only this coolness, as we stand so close together on the shore of the marsh.

Even with the high water this year, we have to pull our canoe through the faint, watery channel between the forest of reeds that separates the two parts of the marsh. We both lean forward, grasp bunches of reeds in our fists and on three we pull.

"One, two, three, pull," I call. "One, two, three, pull." We inch along. This is maddening. I can't steer the bow. Because Craig is pulling so hard in the stern and not watching, the canoe gets jammed nose first in the reeds. We have to back out and start over. I twist around in my seat in the bow and glare at Craig.

"Don't pull unless I say so," I say.

"Just shut up and do it," he says, wearily, coldly. "This isn't a big deal."

A sourness rises up in me. The nape of my neck bristles. He has never said anything like this to me. Ever. He has hardly raised his voice to me in seven years, not even in the midst of my most dangerous rages. I am so startled I fall silent. As we move out of the reeds into the pond again, I say quietly, "You were a jerk. You should apologize."

"Okay," he says mockingly. "I'm sorry I hurt your feelings."

On the far end of the pond we see frightened mallards and teal rise up, quacking. We know they will come back later. The sky around us now is a faint pink. The day is fast coming on. We open the green canvas packs in the middle of the canoe and one by one unravel the lead weights and string from around the necks of our plastic mallards and our plastic bluebills, placing the decoys carefully in a configuration we think will draw ducks close enough to shoot—one long line to the right of the place where we will hide in the reeds, a bunch to the left, and sets of three and four scattered about. I reach into the pocket of my canvas hunting jacket to feel the hard, cold wood of my duck call. It has always been my job to do the calling.

After our decoys are set and we have driven the canoe into the reeds, pulled reeds down over us, stretched a camouflage tarp over us, we wait. We hear sharp echoes from hunters shooting far off on other ponds. The first ducks to come to us are teal. They are small and tan, only as big as a grown man's fist. They land on the water and we can see by the twinge of powdery blue on their wings that they are blue-winged teal. We have set some ethical guidelines to stick to, as we have every year. We will shoot no hens, and no birds sitting on the water.

We don't shoot the teal on the water, but I rise up to scare them into flight so that we can take a shot. We miss.

The next birds are mallards and we shoot a hen. She falls into the water and flaps around, dipping her head in and out of the water, slapping her wings. Then she sits up, confused and frightened, and paddles toward the reeds. We know that if she gets into the reeds we will never find her again, that she will go in there and die, probably be eaten by a fox or a weasel, or, eventually, by the marsh itself. But I will still see our shooting her as a waste. My heart cramps up as we follow this bird in our canoe, paddling fast, trying to mark where she entered the reeds. We look for her for nearly an hour, straining our eyes for curls of soft breast feathers on the water among the reed stems. I engage in this search with a kind of desperation. But she is gone.

"If it's still alive, it'll come out," Craig says. He is impatient to get back to our blind. While we have been looking, another flock flew over and flared off, seeing us plainly in the water.

I feel defeated and sad. We paddle back to our spot in the reeds, drive our canoe into the grass, pull the long reeds over us to hide again and wait. Half an hour passes. The sun is out now and I am sweating in all the wool and cotton underneath my canvas hunting jacket. I doze off. I am bored. I take my duck call out of my pocket and practice making quacking noises.

Quack Quack Quack

Craig rolls his eyes. "Stop it. You might scare them away."

I throw the call to him at the other end of the canoe. "You do it then," I say, stuffing my hands back in the deep pockets of my coat."

The next birds to come over are bluebills, and I shoot one as it is flying away over my right shoulder. The momentum of its flight carries it into the reeds behind me. Again we spend forty-five minutes looking for the bird. We don't find the bluebill either. I want to keep looking. I insist we try again. Craig says, "We'll never find it. Give it up."

The next birds to come in are wood ducks, mostly males. We shoot at them just as they have set their wings and two fall in a mess of feathers and shot, the pellets dropping like hail on the water. We paddle out to pick them up. One is breast-down in the water and when I reach down with my bare hand and pull it up by the neck, I gasp. Its breast has been shot away. I shot away its breast. The white feathers are laid open, dark red breast meat split open, gaping, the heart smashed, the beak smashed, the head crushed. I swallow down something nasty rising in my throat. We pick up the other wood duck and head back into

563

the reeds. I hold the broken wood duck on my lap. What is left of its blood is soaking through my tan pants onto my long underwear. The warm heavy body lies across my knee. I am stroking this bird's elaborate, feathery purple and orange and white crest, letting tears come up to the surface and roll down my wind-chapped face.

Craig says, "Let's get the camouflage back on the boat, and then you can play."

"Play?" I ask him. At this moment I hate him fiercely. I vow that I will never hunt with him again. I wonder why I ever did. Why I married him, stayed with him. Why I hunt at all. "I'm not playing," I whisper hoarsely. Later, after we have been quiet for a time, I say to him, "Maybe you want to hunt with a man, someone who doesn't cry." He doesn't answer me.

Still later, when we are cleaning the ducks onshore and I reach my hand into the cavity of the ravaged wood duck, scraping my hand on the broken bones such that I bleed, I ask him "What would a man hunter do about this bird? Would he cry?"

Craig says, "No, he would throw it away." And there is a hardness in what he has said, so that I barely recognize his voice.

After the ducks are emptied of their hearts and livers and green, reeking, grass-filled crops, we line them up as before on the banks of the marsh and sprinkle cornmeal on them, in front of them, beside them, behind them. This time I complete the ritual with a sick resignation, as if there is nothing now that I can say or do that will make amends for this—for this hunting gone all wrong, for this hunting when the love between us has gone all wrong.

There is nothing I can do for this now, except take this wood duck home, save its skin, and give the lovely feathers to my father, who will make beautiful dry flies out of them to catch trout with in Montana. I will salvage what breast meat I can from this wreckage and make a soup or a stew; something good to eat, something hot and rich to share with my friends, or to eat alone.

Hunting with Craig has never been like this. My heart aches and I am afraid. I hate what we have done this year. It feels like murder. In the beginning, when Craig and I were first in love, everything was different. I wonder if I will ever hunt again. I wonder if I can make sense of what has happened here. I think now that hunting for us has everything to do with love; with the way we feel about ourselves and each other. The heaviness or lightness of our hearts, our smallness or our generosity, shows in the way we hunt; in the way we treat the bluebills and mallards and teal that we shoot and eat; in the way we treat each other. I want to correct this imbalance between Craig and me and inside myself. I want to go hunting, but not this way.

Part of what hunting meant for us, when we were together, was feasting. It wasn't the shooting that ever mattered, but what we did with this food we gathered: how we prepared the ducks to eat, how we shared them with friends, how we raised our glasses before we ate, at a long table lit by candles, covered with a lacy white cloth, and thanked the ducks for their lives. Several times a year, at Easter, at Thanksgiving and at Christmas, Craig and I prepared banquets for our friends. Nearly everything we cooked for our feasts was from our garden, or collected from the woods, or killed by us. This, I think now, was why I hunted and why I still want to. Because I want this kind of intimate relationship with the food I eat.

There were some things—flour, sugar, oranges, walnuts, chutney—that Craig and I served at our feasts that we could not grow or collect ourselves. For these items I would shop at our local grocery store. To get to the checkout counter in the store, I usually walked down the meat aisle. There was hardly ever a whole animal for sale, only parts. There were double-breasted cut-up fryers with giblets. Three-legged fryers and the budget packs—two split breasts with backs, two wings, two legs, two giblets, and two necks. There were boneless, skinless thighs; packages of only drumsticks; plastic containers of livers. There were breaded, skinless, boneless breasts in a thin box—microwavable, ninety-five percent fat free, shrink wrapped, "all natural" and farm fresh. The meat cases were cool, so cool I could hardly smell the meat, only a sanitary wateryness. The smell was different from the smell of wet ducks and blood in the bottom of our canoe. The smell was different from the smell of the warm gut-filled cavity I reached my hand into when I cleaned a bird. The smell was different from the smell in the kitchen when we pulled out all the ducks' feathers, piling them up in a soft mound on the kitchen table; different from the smell when we dipped the birds in warm wax, wax that we then let harden and pulled off in thick flakes along with the duck's pinfeathers.

The birds in the store were pared down and down and down so that what was left had no relationship to what these animals were alive. They were birds pared down and down and down, cut and sliced until all that was left were grotesque combinations of named parts. It always felt obscene to me. What were these birds like whole? It was hard, standing amid the dry coolness rising up from the meat cases, to imagine any life; hard to construct a picture of these birds flying, walking, making morning noise, pecking for insects in the grass, fighting over corn, laying eggs. Hard to imagine them in any way but stacked in their airless cages.

The Russian philosopher and critic Mikhail Bakhtin tells us that the ritual of feasting serves as a way to bridge humans' most basic fear—fear of what Bakhtin calls "the other," fear of that which is not subject to human control, fear of nature. In his writing about banquets and feasting in the novels of sixteenth-century French author François Rabelais, Bakhtin says that in the act of eating, as in the act of drinking, of making love, of giving birth, the beginning and the end of life are linked and interwoven. In Rabelais's novels, eating celebrates these joyful crossings or joinings, at the same time that it celebrates the destruction of the powerful other. In feasting, the mysterious unknown is taken into the human body, it is consumed.

One year, two weeks before Christmas, Craig and I invited twelve of our friends to our house for a feast. We spent all day preparing for this meal. I sliced through the dense brilliant layers of three red cabbages and set the purple shreds to simmer in a pot with honey. I stuffed our ducks with apples, oranges, onions, and raisins, spread the slippery pale breasts with butter and garlic, sprinkling on thyme and rosemary. We took handfuls of dried morel mushrooms from a coffee can above the refrigerator, plumped them again with white wine, sautéed them in butter.

Craig scooped out the insides of a pumpkin from the garden for a pie. He walked to the freezer on the porch and brought back a jar of frozen blueberries. Another pie. The squash from the garden was piled in a cardboard box in the basement. I walked down the stairs into the dark cool, collected four acorn squash, carried them upstairs into the steamy kitchen, peeled off their tough green and orange skins, chopped them, added butter and onions and carrots, cooked the mixture, and puréed it for soup.

We were drinking wine and dancing as we cooked. We were full of joy. We felt generous. To feed all of these people, our friends, with food that we knew in some intimate way, food we had grown or ani-

566

mals we had killed ourselves, was a kind of miracle. The meal we concocted was nearly perverse in its abundance.

Appetizer: venison liver paté and hot spiced wine.

First course: acorn squash soup sprinkled with fresh ground nutmeg.

Second course: spinach and beet green salad with chutney dressing.

Third course: barbecued venison steaks, wild rice, morel mushrooms, buttered beets, and honeyed carrots.

Fourth course: roast duck with plum gravy, new potatoes in butter and parsley sauce and sweet-and-sour red cabbage with honey, vinegar, and caraway seeds.

Dessert: rhubarb pie, blueberry pie, pumpkin pie. Ice cream.

Then brandy. Coffee. Tea. As we sat and talked, we ate tart, green and red, thinly sliced apples, slivers of pear, and cheese and grapes.

In eating these foods—these ducks that we shot out of the sky, that fell, tumbling wing over head, with loud splashes into the cold pond beside our canoe; pumpkin pie that came from a pumpkin that grew all summer long in our backyard garden, surviving three weeks of me cutting open its stalk, scraping out squash borers with the tip of a paring knife; these mushrooms, collected over April and May in the just-leafing-out Minnesota woods full of cardinals, scarlet tanagers, bloodroot, new violets, nesting grouse, and baby rabbits; this venison, from a big-shouldered, spreading-antlered, randy buck Craig killed in November, which we tracked by following the bloody trail it left on bushes and dried grass and leaves—in eating these foods, in this passing of lives into ours, this passing of other blood and muscle into our own blood and muscle, into our own tongues and hearts; in this bridging we were taking up not only food for our bodies, but something that is wild that we wanted for ourselves. Perhaps it was our own power we were eating. Perhaps it was our own ability to grow, to shoot, to find food for ourselves, that we were eating; our ability to engage creatively with the world. We were eating what we wanted so much. We were eating life.

Audre Lorde has written about the erotic and its potential to help us redefine our relationships with ourselves, with each other, and with the world. Lorde, who died from cancer in 1992, wrote about the erotic as a way of knowing the world, as a source of power that is unlike any other source of power.

We live in a racist, patriarchal, and anti-erotic society, Lorde wrote in "Uses of the Erotic: The Erotic as Power." We live in a pornographic society that insists on the separation of so many inseparable things; that insists on ways of thinking that separate the body from the world, the body from the mind, nature from culture, men from women, black from white; a society that insists on bounded categories of difference.

But we can use erotic power to resist those splitting forces. The erotic is the sensual bridge that connects the spiritual and the political. It has to do with love. The word itself comes from the Greek word *eros,* the personification of love in all its aspects—born of chaos and personifying creative power and harmony. *Eros* is a nonrational power. *Eros* is awareness. *Eros* is not about what we do but about how acutely and fully we can feel in the doing, says Lorde. Its opposite, the pornographic, emphasizes sensation without feeling. Pornographic relationships are those that are born not of human erotic feeling and desire, not of a love of life and love of the body, but those relationships, those ideas, born of a fear of bodily knowledge and a desire to silence the erotic.

Everything we have ever learned in our lives tells us to suspect feeling. To doubt feeling. To doubt the power of the erotic and to confuse it, conflate it with the pornographic. But the two are at opposite ends of the world. One is about parts, not wholes. One numbs us to the irrationality, the comedy, of eating animals that are strangers to us, who come to us as perverse combinations of wings and breasts.

I understand the horror among some people I know over my shooting and eating a duck. But while I have become accustomed to hunting and eating wild duck, they are accustomed to buying and eating chicken from the store. Our actions are somehow similar yet also fundamentally different. Buying and eating a shrink-wrapped fryer feels to me like eating reduced to the necessities of time, convenience, cleanliness.

Lorde asks when we will be able, in our relationships with one another and with the world, to risk sharing the erotic's electric charge without having to look away, and without distorting the enormously powerful and creative nature of that exchange. Embracing the erotic means accepting our own mortality, our own bodiedness. Embracing the erotic means not looking away from our relationship with what we eat. And that can turn hunting into a relationship of love; at least not something brutal.

One spring I was walking around Lake of the Isles in Minneapolis with a friend. We were walking fast, dressed in sweatpants and tennis shoes. She would rather have run, but because I was recovering from knee surgery, I could only walk. We took long strides and when I stretched out my leg I could feel the scars there, the manufacturing of new tissue that gave me a strong knee.

We were talking about nothing in particular. About her job as an editor with an agricultural magazine, about running, about lifting weights, about books we had read. Suddenly I shouted, interrupting her. "Look at that."

She looked to where I was pointing and turned back to me to see what it was I was so excited about.

"Look at the ducks," I said. "All those ducks." As we came upon a gaggle of mallards, we stopped to stare. I was fascinated by the greenheads, how when they moved their heads turned violet and emerald in the light. How there was one duck there with a broken bill and a goose with only one foot. There was one female among the group of males. Two of the males were chasing her. It was mating season.

My friend and I moved on. She talked to me about her lover who teaches writing and literature at a local college. We stopped again because I'd seen a wake in the water, a silvery "V" streaming out behind a fast-moving muskrat. "Where?" She squinted.

"There" I said, pointing.

"What is it?"

"A muskrat," I said, watching it as it moved toward a small island, its whiskered nose in the air.

I hear geese honking outside my window in the middle of the city. I used to track the garter snake in our garden from its sunny place in the bean bed to its home under the house, its entryway a piece of bent-up siding. I watch squirrels in the trash cans at the university. I pay attention to spider webs.

Can I call this love? Can I say that I love the swimming greenheads in Lake of the Isles, when every fall I make an adventure out of killing them? Does killing have anything to do with love? What kind of language allows this paradox? This tragic conflation of violence and love is part of what I try to resist in the world, yet here I am, in the midst of it. How is my love for the greenheads, the swimming muskrat, the Canada goose different from the feelings other hunters have for the animals they kill? Can I have a relationship with these animals alive?

Or is the killing, the eating, that magical bridging, a crucial part of my love, part of my relationship with these animals, with the world? What does it mean, that in my body, helping to keep me alive, to make me joyful, to share joy with people I love, is the breast of a greenhead mallard that I shot down on a cool autumn day and scooped from the cold water with my hand?

Nominated by Seal Press

VOUS ÊTES PLUS BEAUX QUE VOUS NE PENSIEZ

by KENNETH KOCH

from POETRY

I

Botticelli lived
In a little house
In Florence
Italy
He went out
And painted Aphrodite
Standing on some air
Above a shell
On some waves
And he felt happy
He
Went into a café
And cried
I'll buy
Everybody a drink
And for me
A *punt e mes*
Celebrities thronged
To look at his painting
Never had anyone seen
So beautiful a painted girl
The real girl he painted
The model
For Aphrodite sits

571

With her chin in her hand
Her hand on her wrist
Her elbow
On a table
And she cries,
"When I was
Naked I was believed,
Will be, and am."

2

Sappho lived
In a little house
Made out of stone
On the island
In Greece of Lesbos
And she lived
To love other women
She loved girls
She went out
And was tortured by loving someone
And then was
Tortured by
Loving someone else
She wrote great
Poems
About these loves
Poems so great
That they actually seem
Like torture themselves
Torture to know
So much sweetness
Can be given
And can be taken away.

3

George Gordon Lord Byron lived
In a little house
In England
He came out
Full of fire
And wild
Creative spirits
He got himself in trouble all the time
IIe made love to his sister
He was a devil to his wife
And she to him!
Byron was making love
Part of the time
In ottava rima
And part of the time
Really
Teresa Guiccioli lived
In a big palace
In Venice
And Byron made love to her
Time after time after time.

4

Saint Francis of Assisi lived
In a little house
Full of fine
And expensive things
His father
Was a billionaire
(SIR Francis of Assisi)
And his mother was a lady
Most high and rare
Baby Francis stayed there
And then he went out
He found God
He saw God

He gave all
His clothes away
Which made
His father mad
Very mad
Saint Francis gave
To poor
People and to animals
Everything he had
Now he has a big church
Built to him in Assisi
His father has nothing
Not even
A mound of earth
With his name
SIR
FRANCIS OF ASSISI
Above it
Carved on a stone.

5

Borges lived
In a little house
In Buenos Aires
He came out
And wrote
Stories, and
When he was blind
Was director
Of the National Library
La Biblioteca Nacional
No one at the Library
Knew he was a famous man
They were amazed
At the elegant women
Who came to pick him up—
Like a book!—
At the Library's day's end.

6

Vladimir Mayakowsky lived
In a little house
In Russia
He came out
And painted pictures
And wrote poems
"To the Eiffel Tower"
"To My Passport"
"At the Top of My Lungs"
"A Cloud in Trousers."
Before he died—
Was it suicide
Or was he murdered
By the Secret Police?
Crowds of fifty thousand gathered
To hear him read his lines.

7

Maya Plisetskaya lived
In a little house
In Russia
There was snow
All around
And often
For weeks at a time
Maya Plisetskaya's feet
Didn't touch the ground
The way, afterwards
They never seemed to touch
The stage
She said The age
When you begin
To understand dance
Is the same
As that at which
You start to lose
Your "elevation."

8

Ludwig Wittgenstein lived
In a little house
In Austria
He came out
And went to live
In another house
In England
He kept coming out
And going back in
He wrote philosophy
Books that showed
We do not know how we know
What we mean
By words like Out and In
He was revered like a god
For showing this
And he acted like a god
In mid-career
He completely changed his mind.

Frank O'Hara lived
In a little house
In Grafton, Massachusetts
Sister and brother
Beside him.
He took out
Toilet articles from his house
And he took out
Candles and books
And he took out
Music and pictures and stones
And to himself he said
Now you are out
Of the house Do something
Great! He came

To New York
He wrote "Second Avenue," "Biotherm"
And "Hatred"
He played the piano
He woke up
In a construction site
At five a.m., amazed.

10

Jean Dubuffet lived
In a little house
In the south of France
He came out
And made paintings
He went back in
And made some more
Soon Jean Dubuffet had
A hundred and five score
He also did sculptures,
And paintings
That were like sculptures
And even some sculptures
That were like
Paintings Such
Is our modern world
And among the things
He did
Was a series
Of portraits
Of his artist and writer
Friends A large series
Entitled You Look
Better than You Thought You
Did *Vous Êtes*
Plus Beaux que
Vous ne Pensiez.

Nominated by Philip Booth, J. Allyn Rosser, Richard Tayson, Dean Young

JAGET

by ANNE CARSON

from CHICAGO REVIEW

"A jaget is a jaget is a jaget."—Gertrude Stein

Jaget in Gunnar Ekelöff

A world is every human.
A world is every human peopled
by blind others in dark uproar
against the jaget who rules over them as king.
In every soul are thousand souls captured.
In every world are thousand worlds folded
and these blind these underworlds
are real and alive although too soon
they become as the jaget is. And we

kings and counts of the thousand possible ones within us
are ourselves underourselves captured
in some larger one whose jaget
we understand as little as our overself
his overself. From their death and love
our feelings took color

as when a big steamship passes
far out under horizon where it lies
so evening blank and we know nothing of it

578

until a swell comes to us onshore—
first one so another and more, many
they strike and foam until everything is
as it was. Everything is otherwise.

So grips us shadows a strange unease
when something tells us people have travelled on
and some of the possible ones got free.

Jaget in Emily Brontë

There are two trees in a lonely field;
they breathe a spell to me;
A dreary jaget their dark boughs yield,
All waving solemnly.

Jaget in Pindar (Fragment 131)

All bodies follow strong death.
But still left alive after is
a jaget made of the time-substance:

yes it is the only God part.

Sleeps when limbs are active
but to sleepers in dreams,
it shows a crack that runs
between delight and pain.

Wittgenstein on Jaget

The idea that in order to get clear about the meaning of a general term
one had to find the common jaget in all its applications has shackled
philosophical investigation. . . .

Jaget and the Slave Trade

One of the most remarkable artifacts recovered by classical archaeolo-
gists is a private letter written on lead about 530 B.C. Found at Berezan
on the north coast of the Black Sea. The letter refers to itself as

TO MOLIBDION ("a little jaget of lead"). There being no word for "letter" in those days. The author writes in acute distress (he was in danger of enslavement). Did he expect a quick lead answer? Poor man.

Aristotle on Jaget

Wherefore in some men jaget does not occur even under strong stimulus, by reason of suffering or age—as if you pressed a seal on running water—while for others, worn away like old walls of houses or hardened on the surface, no impression penetrates it.

Jaget Research

Monkeys wander in the pure, dry air of the laboratory with—this may interest you, you tell us you used to sculpt—the jaget projection strip removed from their thalamus (other monkeys have everything except the jaget protection strip removed). We saw them on the overhead slide represented by black monkey-shaped outlines with dotted lines for jaget (the others as dotted lines ending in heavy black executioner's gloves). Given discrimination tasks they score badly. In a world without jaget, who cares which metal lever drops the food drawer? (Meanwhile, monkeys for whom the world is now nothing *but* jaget were described as lashing, biting, butting, gripping, or stroking the metal elbows of the food box in a fever.)

Jaget and Its Double

The real drawback of being mad is not that consciousness is crushed and torn but that Artaud cannot say so, fascinating as this would be, while it is happening. But only later when somewhat "recovered" (so much less convincingly). The mad state is, as he emphasizes again and again, empty. Teeming with emptiness. Knotted on emptiness. Immodest in its emptiness. You can pull emptiness out of it by the handful, pull it out endlessly. For jaget he uses the term "cruelty."

Jaget and the Tao

We find references to a certain Jageh-tzu who travelled (downstream) on rivers with folded arms. His historicity is doubtful. His book written on straw does not survive. When the bright moon flooded the plain he thought, *This journey is endless*. When police tigers were released to devour him, they lay down with sulky eyes. No one knows where Jageh-tzu went. Gliding above the forests.

Jaget in Hölderlin

Reach it to me someone.
Filled with dark light.
The fragrant jaget.
So I can rest. For sweet
Would sleep under shadows be.
Not good.
To empty your soul.
With mortal thoughts. But good
Is a conversation and to say.
What the heart means, to hear
About days of love.
And facts, that happened.

Jaget in Celan

Let it go

❀

rolling toward the abyss.

Nominated by Chicago Review

SCAR VEGAS

fiction by TOM PAINE

from THE OXFORD AMERICAN

THE COWBOYS CRACKED MY RIBS but they are taped firm. I am now in Vegas after frying across the Texas panhandle in July top down because the top was broke up good when I was thrown through outside Amarillo, my first real stop after Galveston. I like the convertible top up myself and I like air-conditioning on full cold and the radio low. I do not like the sky night or day and keep my eyes on the yellow lines heading under the car when I am moving on. A pretty girl throws me the finger as I roll down the strip. It's soft asphalt hot in Vegas.

The door to 1137 is cracked and I kick it open slow with my boot toe. The cowboy boots screw up my knees and they click with floating bone. The knees are wanting for oil or I am higher on the odometer than yesterday. Room 1137 is empty. I take off my shades and hang them slow in my shirt. I click my knees in the empty room and breath easy the air-conditioned air. No air-conditioning in the Galveston prison.

My sister in her wedding dress jumps from behind the door. She grabs my jewels. She whispers, "Ain't you surprised, Johnny?"

No. I ain't surprised. I ain't never surprised. This world ain't never sprung nothing on me. Some people get themselves hit by lightning and other strange things but that ain't me at all.

Her hold on my crotch is not too bad. My sister's name is Janey but everybody always calls her Fruit. We are the Loops. Fruit is stunted but busty and hippy and blond as bleach and smells like peppermint. It's not candy but perfume. When Fruit was a girl she wore peppermint perfume and she still wears it to this very day here in this hotel in Vegas the day before her wedding.

Fruit says, "Say Uncle."

She squeezes more and down I go to my knees. We Loops are stubborn people and she ought to of known I wasn't going to say what she said to say. Things generally happen without my two cents. All I got is the right to open and close my mouth when it strikes me and not a minute before.

Fruit tightens up her hand more. She squeezes once hard. I thud over on the carpet. She says, "I'm glad you came, Johnny."

The groom is at the door to room 1137 in a cut-off shirt and shorts. I figure it's the groom. He looks like a bull at a rodeo before the gate swings open. This groom is snorting and comes into the room as if zapped by an electric cattle prod. Fruit freezes. He yanks her up like he's yanking a flower out of the ground, roots and all. He swings her in a circle hooting and hollering. She is smiling in a concerned way as she goes round and clips me with a heel in the eye. Fruit goes round and round in her wedding dress.

The groom is a semipro football player, number 22, Breezy Bonaventure. He flings my sister Fruit. A shotput in a wedding dress. She rolls across the bed and is lost on the floor behind. Breezy looks at the bed. Where'd she go? He looks angry. Soon enough I see him forget her. A dog forgetting a stick. When I asked Fruit when I called from Austin why she was marrying she whispered because she was sick of waiting.

Breezy sticks his head in the little fridge and slaps the wall with his hand. His legs are the color of Ivory soap. He pulls out two beers and sticks them on either side of his hips under the elastic band of his team shorts and a third he unscrews in his teeth and spits the top across the room. Fruit climbs up on the bed and hides her face in a pillow. Breezy doesn't know me from a hole in the wall and comes over scratching his chin looking me over and finally he says pointing his beer, "Who you?"

"He's my brother Johnny," says Fruit from the pillow.

"Hell no," says Breezy. "You never said nothing about a brother."

"I did so say," says Fruit.

Breezy leaves Room 1137. Fruit says, "What'd you say, Johnny?"

"I didn't say nothing," I say.

Nobody called me Johnny in prison. Everybody called me Loop.

My sister Fruit has never played the slots and I buy her a bucket of quarters. In prison I made about a quarter an hour and she has a

583

bucket of long hours in her hand. Fruit skips down between the machines in her wedding dress.

I do not like to gamble and done Vegas too many times. I am not lucky. Some people are lucky. The big finger in the sky is pointed at them. The big finger in the sky never so much as took the time to poke me in the eye.

Fruit puts the bucket of quarters down next to a slot. Fruit's got the slot arm.

"Go on," I say. "Give her a good yank."

I click my knees and Fruit pulls all lemons.

Fruit is looking at me.

"What?" I say.

"You cut your hair."

"Long time ago."

She is real quiet.

"You ain't never—" she says.

"Ain't never what?"

"Called or nothing."

"I called," I say. "I called and I come."

"One call. Four years," she says. "You was calling for cash. You was in prison."

Fruit says nothing more. I am now thinking about prison in Galveston. Two years. In prison there was a cellmate name of Reginald. All the time he says he is looking at the sky at night. There ain't no sky. Nothing but the bottom of my bunk all covered with stains. Reginald says once to me he's long ago given up on people. Says after you are done with people there ain't nothing left to do but wait for a sign.

Fruit takes the quarters to another slot. She goes off down the long line of slots and she puts quarters from her bucket in the buckets of all the old ladies smoking butts at the slot machines. None of them even see. Fruit stops at the end of the row of slots and climbs on a stool.

He is overboned. An old steer. His clothes are beat but ironed and his cowboy hat is low over his eyes and clean to new. His belt hangs low and his thumbs are hooked in his belt. He leans over Fruit like a tree in a hurricane. He is grinning and rubbing his nose with his thumb. He pulls back and stands up and wrestles up his pants some and moves back in again and raises his hand to her hair.

He touches her bleached hair with that horse hand because he ain't got no choice. He strokes her bleached hair and Fruit spins around and tries to slap away his big hand. She says something and the Texan moves in to give her a kiss. Fruit tries to hit him where it counts with her knee. Her knee is driving like a piston but can't do much in all the cloth of her wedding dress. The Texan is holding onto her by the shoulders and shaking her hard.

The Texan never knows what hits him but I know. Breezy Bonaventure's skull spears him in the spine flat out. The Texan slams into two slots and is on the floor, a sorry sack of skin and bones. Fruit is on the floor in a wad of wedding dress. It takes five security guards to pull Breezy off the Texan. Breezy is foaming. The Texan is twitching. I ain't moved a muscle.

I don't want no trouble.

The hotel got it on videotape. Breezy sees these replays all the time as a football player. He asks for a copy. The manager says it isn't allowed, however much he'd like to oblige. The manager has a lot of paint in his hair and his teeth are far too bright and he looks afraid like if things go down he's going down much worse. The office is a jungle with plants.

We three look at him in his office.

"We are a family hotel," the manager says.

"Yeah," says Breezy. "Family."

"Things like this shouldn't happen to a bride," says the manager.

"No sir," I say. "They sure shouldn't."

"Not to as pretty a bride as this young lady," says the manager.

Breezy shows his teeth again. The manager stands up short behind his desk. What the manager does is lead us up to a door on the seventeenth floor and give Fruit a key. We all stick our heads in when the door opens and take a look round. The room is three times bigger than the last room. Big enough to spin donuts in a car. The whole place is bright pink. I put on my shades. Breezy goes into the room and walks in a circle and says, "Got any beer?" The manager shows him this wall that opens and there are all the beers in the world. Fruit sits in a big pink chair. She rolls from side to side to look at the room on account of her neck being sore.

"This is all for us?" she says.

"We service thousands of brides a year," says the manager.

"That right?" I say.

"We're a family hotel," says the manager. "A place you can tell your friends and neighbors about when they're planning a wedding or choosing a family destination."

"Sure," says Breezy. "Family."

We all look at the manager. He crawls out backwards. I shut the door and get a beer and give one to Breezy. He shoots the cap across the room and it plinks off the window. There is another big Vegas hotel right across and I look out and see into a hundred rooms. Fruit slides off the chair and goes to the fridge. She gets a bottle of champagne. Breezy pulls the cork and the foam goes down his arm. Fruit takes the bottle and pulls open the glass door and goes out on the porch.

"You really her brother?" says Breezy.

"Yes I am," I say. "I am."

Breezy chugs his beer and tosses the empty across the floor. He belches and rubs his foot. I slide open the glass door and go out on the porch.

"Fruit," I say, "How come you never tell this guy you got a brother?"

"You was in prison."

"So?" I say. "Lot of people in prison. I'm your only family."

"So?" she says.

The sky is white and sick with heat.

"Nice dress," I say.

"I made it," she says. "I made it."

"How long you say you know this guy?"

"Three weeks."

"You make the dress in three weeks?"

"No," she says. "The dress was a year."

"Pretty."

Fruit spits and we watch it fall. It goes a long way before it hits the building. We don't say nothing but I spit and it goes further down. Fruit spits and it goes further yet. Fruit gets a kick out of this so I do it with her for a long time and we drink the champagne. When I go back inside Fruit stays on the porch.

Breezy has a grapefruit in each hand. Down at the end of the room he has lined up six empty beers. He rolls the grapefruit across the pink carpet. A strike. He sets up the beers again. He goes back down the end and rolls another grapefruit and rolls a split. I sit down on the couch and Breezy bowls. He throws a gutter ball into the bedroom. He takes another grapefruit from the basket on the marble table. He throws a strike.

My sister Fruit comes flying in from the porch. I turn my head to look at her. She says, "Some guy is jerking off over there."

586

Breezy catches his swing and turns to her. His nostrils twitch. Fruit points at the hotel across the way.

"He was standing in the window naked," she says. "He was looking over and waving his thing at me."

Breezy breaks for the porch. I go to the window. Fruit is next to me. Breezy is out on the porch pointing and screaming at the other hotel. I shut the door to the porch. Breezy takes off his shirt and waves it at the pervert. His face is blue.

"Can you see the guy, Fruit?"

"He's gone," says Fruit.

Breezy barrels back in the suite. He takes the basket of fruit and drop kicks it. Breezy picks up a round pink lamp. He shatters it on the marble table and cuts his hand. He stops and looks stupid at the blood. He snorts. He chugs a beer. He lies face down on the couch. His hand hangs off the couch and is dripping blood slowly off his fingers on the pink carpet. Fruit and I sit and say nothing.

Breezy snores.

Breezy says Fruit is in heat. So I go down to the lobby that night when the Sarasota Panthers come to town. I go to greet the team as the brother of the bride. Soon as I am down there by the waterfall I see them. The whole team is standing in their uniforms. All padded up and their cleats *clack, clickety, clack* and they are tossing footballs through the waterfall. People sitting near the waterfall stand up and applaud.

A guy in a crew cut raises his hand and they stop throwing the football. His nose is all broke up and he has two black eyes. His squint says: You is an asshole. He raises his hand and they stop throwing footballs and he shouts up the inside of the hotel, "Breezy, where the hell are you?"

I go to meet and greet but Crewcut stiff-arms me and says, "Out of my way, asshole." The manager brings over a handful of keys and leads them to the elevators. The manager don't know me now. The whole team tries to push into an elevator. There is a happy brawl. The second elevator comes and there is another happy brawl. I turn and there is a player pushing a shopping cart filled with beer across the lobby. He is wearing his uniform but no pads. He has black hair and a chipped tooth and sticks out his hand.

"Lucas Fairweather," he says. "Tight end."

"Johnny Loop," I say. "Dead end."

"Friend of Fruit's?"

"Brother of Fruit."

"Fruit's a nice girl."

His skin is slick and maybe he is Indian.

"Want a beer?" says Lucas. He points down at the shopping cart. I feel a case. It is cool. Way up at the top of the hotel the Sarasota Panthers are screaming. I put my cool hand on my forehead.

"You all right, bud?" Lucas says. "You don't look too hot."

Lucas pushes his shopping cart toward the waterfall and I hold on to the metal wire edge. The Sarasota Panthers are howling from the top of the hotel. I sit down on the edge of the waterfall and Lucas sits down. Lucas opens the beer and hands it to me. Big orange fish swim over to us when Lucas sticks his fingers in the water.

"Where you from?"

"Amarillo," I say. "Least that's the last stop."

Both of us look around the big hotel. People are going every which way. From the casino room I hear bells and whistles and see a red light flashing and people freeze and crane their necks to see who won the jackpot. It must be a big jackpot because people come unfroze and are getting sucked into the casino like there is a big magnet in there. One old lady gets knocked over in the rush and everyone is stepping right over her and she puts her hands over her head. I stick my fingers in the pond and the fish dart away.

"Hell," I say. "Truth is, I ain't never been lucky."

"Everybody got some luck."

"No. I ain't never been lucky. I can see it now clear."

"Another beer?"

"Uh huh."

Lucas sticks his hand in the water and the fish come over.

"See?" I say. "You're lucky. The fish comes right to you."

"You stick your hand in," says Lucas. "They'll come right over to you."

The beer bottle is dropped from twenty stories up the hotel. There is not much of a splash in the pond and no one notices but the two of us sitting there. The water settles back and all the pieces of the beer bottle are winkling around on the blue bottom of the pond. The fish are long gone to the other side. The Sarasota Panthers are all howling up there at the top of the hotel.

"You're lucky that didn't hit you," says Lucas.

"Nope," I say. "That ain't luck."

"It could of hit you."

"Nope."

"Sure it could of," Lucas says. "You were lucky."

"Luck ain't something that don't happen," I says. "Lots of things don't happen. Luck is something that happens. When you been fingered out."

Lucas is taking off his shoes and socks. He pulls up his pants to his knees and steps over into the pond. He walks right out there in the pond. When he gets there he bends down and picks up the glass and piles it like plates in his other hand. He walks right back and steps over and walks right across the floor to the reception desk and he hands that glass to the girl. The marble floor is all wet footsteps. While I look the footsteps dry right up.

Lucas and I sit there and drink beers and talk about nothing. Lucas is getting cut from the team soon because he's lost his killer instinct. Lucas knows when he lost the instinct but doesn't want to talk about it and he doesn't want to talk about being cut from the team. So we look at the fish and drink beers.

The Sarasota Panthers bail out of the elevator. One has a case of beer under each arm. Breezy is in the center of them. Crewcut makes him chug beers. The Panthers behind Breezy keep looking up the inside of the hotel. I look up in time to see the football coming down from up near the glass roof. Breezy looks up and drops his beer and raises his arms as if to catch the ball. At the last second Crewcut gives Breezy a shove and the ball hits Breezy smack in the face. The ball bounces straight up in the air. Crewcut grabs it and hands it to Breezy, who is pissed off then grinning like there is nothing better than to have a football dropped twenty stories onto your face. The laces leave a red scar across his cheek. Crewcut starts whooping over and over, "Pervert Hunt!" The Sarasota Panthers file out of the hotel after Crewcut. Lucas gets up and follows and I follow Lucas.

In the heat outside the hotel I am dizzy. Prison was hot as hell and so is the desert. I splash some water from a fountain on my face and we go into the hotel across the street and back into the air-conditioning where I am better.

The Sarasota Panthers go right to the elevators and fight to fit into one and also the second. We go up in the third with a Panther.

"What floor?" say Lucas.

"Seventeen," says the Panther. "The pervert's on seventeen."

"What pervert?" says Lucas.

589

"Some guy pulling his pud checking out Fruit. Who's this asshole?" The Panther thumbs toward me.

"My friend's the asshole," says Lucas. "You got a problem?"

"I ain't got a problem. That pervert's got a problem. Yanking his chain and the woman's in a wedding dress. That's who's got a problem. I ain't got a problem. That pervert's got a problem. We're his problem now. He's got to deal with us. We're going to clean up his act. We're going to polish the floor with his face."

On the seventeenth the team goes into a huddle. Lucas and I lean against the wall. Lucas rustles up two beers. The team is huddled for a while and they clap and break and half the team goes one way and the other half goes the other way. Lucas and I slump down against the wall of the hotel. Lucas clinks his beer to mine. It is too quiet down both ways of the hall.

Lucas pulls up his sleeve and shows me a tattoo.

"Kind of looks like a tiger," I say.

"A panther," says Lucas. "A Florida panther. Our team logo. Now I'm cut from the team I don't know what to do about it."

"Do about what?"

"The tattoo."

"Why you got to do something? Lots of people got tattoos from things they don't do no more. Says you were once part of something."

Crewcut sticks his head around the corner and pulls it back. They are all sneaking around the floor. One tiptoes by and leaves a case of beer near us at the elevator.

We both drain our beers. Lucas keeps shaking his head. I go and get a couple more beers. We both have our legs straight out in the hall and Lucas is flopped half over. If someone came out of the elevator they might've thought we were gunned down. Nobody came through the hall and there was nothing but the sound of the air conditioner. A low hum.

"You hear the air conditioner, Lucas?"

Lucas listens and shakes his head.

"You ever think you ain't part of it all?"

"Part of what, Johnny?"

"The score," I say. "People is making a killing all around you and you have less than nothing to do with it. They don't even see you. Sometimes it makes me sick."

"I don't know, Johnny."

"I do know," I say. "I do know."

"You know what?"

"I don't know," I say.

"Sure you do, Johnny. You know."

"I don't know if I know," I say. "But I know they don't know me. That's all I know for sure."

Lucas is flat on the floor now. I put a beer in his hand and say, "Thanks for calling me Johnny."

I sit back with my head against the wall and sip the beer. We sit there for some time then I hear a ruckus down the hall. The sound keeps getting bigger and soon enough they come around the corner. The whole team. Under Crewcut's arm is a worm of a man. A skinny bald guy in a dirty muscle undershirt and boxers. He has about three grey hairs left on his head and looks about three feet long. Crewcut drops him on the floor and puts his boot on him. He squirms around like a worm but Crewcut pushes down on his ribs with his foot.

"The pervert?" I say.

"Yeah," says Crewcut. "What's it to you?"

Someone says, "He's a pal of Fairweather's."

Lucas pulls up to a sitting position.

"Are you sure it's him?" I say.

"Tissues spread all over the floor," says Crewcut. "He's been spanking all right."

"At least he's neat," I say. "Using tissues."

All the Sarasota Panthers are looking down at the worm on the ground. I say to the worm, "What's your name?"

The worm on the floor looks at me and says, "Ray Candleman."

"You waving your little thing at a bride?"

"No," Candleman says. "No bride."

"Hell," says Crewcut. "This is the pervert. Got a clear view of Fruit. We could see her from his room."

"How'd you get in his room?"

"We knocked, asshole."

Crewcut scoops up old Ray Candleman and goes into the stairwell. The Sarasota Panthers follow. I get Lucas up and we follow the team up a few levels to the roof. It's just about dark. The roof is all gravel and tar. The strip is lit bright and it looks like a carnival. There are a couple of broken chairs. Ray Candleman is bouncing like a sack of meal on Crewcut's shoulder. He looks happy and I figure he's gone round the bend. Crewcut drops him on the ground near the far edge of the roof. He kicks him and Candleman gets to his feet. He is wearing yellow socks up his skinny shanks.

Crewcut says to him, "Jump, you piece of shit."

The team circles. Candleman looks behind him and down twenty stories. Candleman smiles. A slow, stupid smile. A smile as if these are all his pals. A smile as if he's never had this many buddies. A smile as if he's ready to jump if it will make all these buddies stand around and talk up Ray Candleman some more.

Lucas pulls on my sleeve and says, "Let's go play the slots. I don't want to see this."

We go down to the casino and Lucas goes in to play the slots and I go to the bar. I see her looking over. She is dressed all in shiny spangles like her dress is made of a million little spoons. She keeps looking and I look behind me to see if maybe she is looking at someone else. There is nobody behind me. She is still looking and I point to my chest and she nods and I just about fall off my stool. I figure she must be a whore and try to settle down but she doesn't look like a whore somehow so I can't settle down. Her eyebrows make her look surprised and her lips are open just a crack. She comes over sweet as pie and after a drink I ask her and she isn't a whore, she's a schoolteacher from Iowa just trying to get over a divorce with some of her girlfriends. She tells me she stays away from the slots because she isn't lucky and I say I know just how you feel, no doubt about it. She tells me she grew up on a farm. She is ten times better looking than any woman who ever looked at me twice in my entire life.

Ray Candleman is naked on the floor of the hotel room and curled up on his side with his knees to his scrawny chest. There is no one else in the room but me and Ray Candleman. I kick him soft with the toe of my boot because I am thinking he maybe is dead. I am thinking he is dead but there is no blood or bruises. He is stiff under my toe and heavy. I kick him hard and his back rolls forward some and flops right back again. Now I think he is dead. I kick him hard again in the back. Now I am sure he is dead.

"You bastard, Ray," I say. "Don't you be dead."

I bend over and put my hand on his shoulder. The skin is hot as hell. His right eyebrow pops up and one eye flies open. It opens wide and Ray Candleman lays on me a slow wink like we are the best of buddies.

"Johnny?" someone says. "Johnny?"

"Who's there?" I say.

"Johnny Loop?"

Someone is talking to me and saying my name but I can't see anyone and it is pissing me off.

"Johnny? Johnny?"

Sure enough I wake up from a dream. The whole Ray Candleman dead on the floor thing was a dream. I am on my side and there is Lucas Fairweather, his face stuck in mine.

"Johnny?"

"What?"

"Johnny?"

I hear someone go "He's conscious?"

Lucas blows his bad breath in my face again. I try and sit up but they push me back down. I struggle and swing my arm and hear one holler but there is such pain in my back that it drops me back down.

"Damn," I say. "I been stabbed."

"Johnny," says Lucas. "You're in the hospital."

Lucas moves out of the way and I see a tall doctor. His face is all mouth. His mouth says, "You've had a nephrectomy, Mr. Loop. You're stable now."

"Say again?"

The doctor shakes his head and scratches his nose.

"Your right kidney, Mr. Loop," he says.

"What about it?"

"It's gone," he says. "It's been surgically removed."

"What the hell are you talking about?"

The doctor is shaking his head again.

"It's true, Johnny," says Lucas. "That thing's long gone."

I pull myself up even though it hurts like hell and say to the Doc, "Well how about you put it right back in where you found it? I got to get on to my sister's wedding."

Lucas says, "The wedding was yesterday, Johnny. You never showed up. Fruit thought you skipped town. Everybody's gone."

"Don't screw with me."

"I found you in the bar," says Lucas. "You were having a beer but you were all messed up. You said your back hurt and I took a look and brought you here."

All this time my hand is checking out this bandage on my back from my ass up to my ribs.

593

"He was having a beer?" says the Doc. "That's amazing. That's really amazing. He must have an amazing constitution."

"What's that mean?"

"It means you're tough," say Lucas.

The Doc looks at me for a long while and says nothing. He pulls out his pen as if to poke me but turns and jabs over and over at an X-ray on the wall.

"You can see it here," says the Doc. "See the clips on the aorta at the renal junction? The clips on the minor arteries? This zipper here is where they stapled you up, Mr. Loop. A very neat job. I've seen them botch it. Can you see your other kidney here? You'll be able to live off that kidney, Mr. Loop."

"I was on my back. That's the last thing I remember. She was from Iowa."

The Doc put his pen slowly back in his pocket. "It's not as uncommon as you might suppose, Mr. Loop. I've seen three cases this year. On the black market your kidney might be worth a hundred thousand or more. Some people are desperate."

"No kidding," I say. "A hundred thousand?"

"Consider yourself lucky to be alive, Mr. Loop," says the Doc. "They might have taken both kidneys."

"They," I say quietly.

"Mr. Loop? Did you say something?"

"How many people come to Vegas in a year?" I say. "You know?"

"I don't know," says the Doc. "Millions."

"Millions?"

"Must be," says the Doc. "Why do you ask?"

"And you've only seen two others like me this year."

"Three."

"Three others?"

"No," says the Doc. "A total of three. Maybe two last year. Why?"

"Nothing," I say.

The doctor's beeper goes off and off he goes. Lucas looks at the clock and says, "Hey, Johnny. You're going to be okay."

"Lucas?" I say. "You hear that?"

"Hear what?"

"You hear him say how much that kidney of mine is worth to them?"

"I heard it."

"Would you have ever thought it?"

"Not me, Johnny," says Lucas. "Nothing in my body will ever be worth that much."

"Lucas?"

"Johnny?"

"You want to see the scar?"

"I've already seen it."

"Is it something?"

"It's something all right."

Lucas walks alongside the bed later when I am rolled to a room and then he has to go back to Sarasota. He shakes my hand and is gone like he was never there. Out the window of the hospital I see all the colored lights of Vegas. Every light is someone throwing the dice or pulling the slot or getting hit at the blackjack table. Late that night I ring for the nurse and ask her to bring me a mirror. She gives it to me and turns and is leaving the room before I even have a grip. I get the bandages in hand and with a couple of good yanks pull the whole taped mess down.

In the mirror I see it looks like a long angry yellowish mouth with silver braces. It looks like a greasy mouth that might open and my ugly insides might vomit out all over the floor. I touch the metal zipper holding it all back with the tip of my finger. It will scar bad.

Until I fall asleep I imagine over and over them fingering me, Johnny Loop, out of all the crowds of nobodies and losers.

Nominated by The Oxford American

THE COAT

fiction by FLANNERY O'CONNOR

from DOUBLETAKE

Rosa found him rolled over in the mud down by the gully. She started. The wash basket fell off her head and six white shirts—washed, pressed, and folded—flapped face-down in the mud. One of them was in reach of his hand, a rigid, immobile hand, strangely white against the soft red clay it lay in. She felt like sinking into the clay herself. It had taken her all afternoon to iron them shirts. She picked them up except the one that almost touched him. She fished that up with a stick and dropped it into the basket. Then she looked at him again. He seemed almost to have been pressed down in the clay, his thin body and outstretched arms forming a weird white cross in the relief on the red. Light-colored trousers clung to his wet body and Rosa noticed that a thin coating of ice had begun to form around his arms and back. He had on no coat.

"Whoever killed him ain't lef' nothin' for nobody else," she muttered. "Done took the coat offen his back. These niggers 'round here ain't got no sense." Allus got caught in some devilment an' got theysevs in the 'lectric chair. 'Thout gittin' nothin' out it neither. Niggers was funny that way, she mused. Wonder howcome she was different? Allus had been. Even when she was little, she was brightern Lizzie an' Boon. She was scrawny but she was bright. And scrawny as she was, she had got Abram. Strongest nigger in Bell's Quarters was hers. He was devilish like the rest of 'em, but, Lord, that nigger was strong! He could er strangled that man there wit one er his hans. She looked down at the cross apprehensively. Might er done it too 'cepin' he had gone in town for keresene an' that had carried him t'other way. This would be one time Abram wouldn't be mess up in nothin'. He warn't a bad nigger, couldn't help stealin' now an' then, er gittin' hissef drunk, er fightin'. It was in his blood like sense was in hers. Abram had sense too—almost as much as she had—when he warn't drunk; but git that nigger drunk and he'd forget he a king an' gonna git him a throne someday. Him an' her—they gonna have 'em a throne, Abram say. He gonna git 'em a throne. Would too. Long's he won't drunk an' didn't git hissef in trouble. But he warn't mess up in this killin' here. This was some other nigger's doin', er maybe a white man's. Maybe.

Vaguely she wondered if they might think she had killed the man.

They sho would if they seen her tracks leadin' up to him. Now how they gonna know them her tracks? They warn't God Amighty. Rosa put the basket on her head again and went back home.

She was sorting the Grocery-Store-Wilkinson's wash from the Sheriff-Thomases when Abram came in. She heard three, slow, deliberate footsteps and thought it was someone else. Then the door creaked and he peered in. She knew he was drunk by the way he opened the door. If it had weighed a hundred, he couldn't have done it more slowly. Cheap wine—allus got him. Abram closed the door behind him with infinite care and tiptoed to the bed where she had the wash laid out.

"You ain't gonna lie down on that wash, nigger!" she screamed as he lowered himself to the Sheriff's stiff, green-striped shirt. Abram rolled over on the floor.

"Where the keresene?" she demanded.

Abram yawned. "I ain't been after it yet," he murmured.

"What you waitin' on? We ain't got enough but for tonight, an' to-morrer's Sunday. You ain't got no sense." She slapped another shirt on the pile. "Usin' my keresene money to git yosef drunk wit. I ain't got no money to be payin' for yo' liquor, nigger," she stormed.

Abram fumbled in his pocket. "Here yo' seventy-fi' cents," he said softly.

She took the money suspiciously. "Then what you stole to git yosef drunk wit?

"Ain't stole nothin'. Found it."

"What you found?"

"Lemme go to sleep, Rosa," he whined.

"What you found, I say?"

"Just a ol' coat."

"What it have in it?"

"Ain't had nothin' in it."

"How you git drunk off an ol' coat then?"

"I eschanged it for a lil' wine at Branches sto'. Lemme go to sleep, Rosa," he pleaded.

She folded her arms and stared at him. He could feel her eyes singeing the back of his neck. He rose slowly and sheepishly held a five-dollar bill out to her. "Here de money I found in de pocket, Rosa."

She felt the fear slowly clamp down on her, numbing the thing that beat in her chest. "You ain't got no sense," she moaned. "Why you have to go eschange that coat at Branches? They finds that man an' you done showed yosef eschangin' his coat, they git you sho'."

Abram stared. "Don't you want the money, Rosa?" he mumbled.

She snatched it from him and flung it to the floor. He backed away in amazement. "I ain't found no more, Rosa. Honest I ain't. I didn't git but fo' dollars for dat coat an' I done drunk it all."

"Howcome you got to kill somebody? Ain't you got enough to do 'thout gittin' yosef mess up like that? I don't want to have to tell people you done got yosef in the 'lectric chair when they asks how you is."

"I ain't kill nobody, Rosa. Where you git dat idea?"

"You ain't got sense enough to jest kill him an' git his money an' go—you got to eschange his coat," she said bitterly, "an' there's probly a hunnert people knows that his coat."

"Dat whose coat?" Abram's voice rose to an unnatural tenor.

"You knows there ain't no sense triflin' 'round wit me, Abram, pretendin' you don't know what I talkin' 'bout. When they finds that dead man roll over in that gully an' sees his coat up there at Branches an' you done eschanged it, they gon put you in the 'lectric chair 'fore you gits chance to turn 'round good." It was fine she had some sense to take care of Abram wit. He needed her. "An' who that man?" she demanded.

"I ain't seen no man," Abram whispered. He dropped down on the bed. "What I gonna do, Rosa? Was he a white man?"

"You know he white good's you know you black."

"What I gonna do?" he mumbled.

"This ain't none er my doin'," she sniffed. "I ain't kill nobody."

"I ain't kill nobody neither," he said sullenly.

"I knows when you lyin' good's I know my name, Abram." She stalked over to a pile of clothes bags in the corner and began to draw out the musty-smelling shirts and sheets the Brinsons always sent.

"I goin' an' git dat coat," Abram said suddenly.

598

"You jest drunk," she muttered. "How many seen you eschange that coat? They allus fo' er five white men in there 'sides a passel er niggers. What gonna keep them from 'membering 'bout it when that man's found?" She was bright. Allus.

Abram limped back to the bed. "I reckon I go off an' hide for a spell," he said.

"That's yo' affair." She inspected the front of Joe Brinson's shirt as if its state of grime was all that interested her. They'd git him whether he hid or not. They allus got 'em. "Ain't got sense enough to kill him an' git. Got to go sportin' his coat all 'round," she muttered.

Abram looked up. He could feel advice coming.

"Ain't got sense enough to bury what he done kill befo' they finds it." She opened another wash bag. "I sho' ain't gonna go out in the dark by myself an' git filthy buryin' him."

Abram shook his head. "What I want to bury him for? I goin' over to Rivertred an' lie low."

"An' they be waitin' on yo' do' step when you come back. Or else they be out there to git you. You better listen to somebody wit some sense."

"I got my own sense."

"You ain't usin' it then."

"I reckon I ain't," Abram sighed.

He was still rolled over in the mud—the same way she had seen him before—when they came. Abram set the lamp down.

"It'll be easy to cover him over wit dis slime," he suggested.

"An' have him juttin' out like a rock for the rain to wash off? You ain't got no sense. Start diggin'."

"Where?"

"Right next to him. Then you can roll him over into it."

Of course, she knew she'd have to tell him everything to do. She was smartern him. Knowd it when she married him. But he was smartern them other niggers. He was the onliest one she would er had—him that gonna be the king. She found a stump and sat down.

Abram's shovel slid rhythmically in and out of the mud. The lamp's shining into his face made crystals of the big drops of sweat erupting on his forehead and silvered his cheekbones and the ridge of his nose. He was a king awready. White folks could be kings in the day time when the light was in their favor; but niggers was kings at night. "Quit yo' slackin' up. I don't wan' have to set on this stump all night." Abram would jest fit a throne—slouched down in them purple drapes. She'd have to be supervisin' it for him so's he wouldn't git hissef drunk. That'd make her a queen. "Start makin' that hole longer. He ain't round." There they'd be—her an' Abram—settin' side by side. Wit other folks washin' their clothes. "Thow that rock out er there. You gonna break that shovel befo' we done paid for it." Said she'd never keep Abram. Done shown 'em though. He was drunk but he was hers. Scrawny as she was. She watched the moon rolling unconcernedly among the clouds. That would be the way her an' Abram would do— jest roll on 'bout their business 'thout mindin' nobody; but plenty er folks mindin' them—like those shadows that changed when the moon come through 'em.

"Ain't dat deep enough?" Abram asked after a while.

She got up and peered into the hole. "Naw, that ain't deep enough. Jest keep goin'. You got the energy to kill him, you got the energy to bury him."

"Suppose somebody fin' us here?"

"Who gonna fin' us here this time er night?"

"Maybe they out lookin' for him."

"Well, they ain't gonna know to look here 'til somebody pass an' tell 'em they seen him."

"Howcome you didn't tell nobody, Rosa?"

"Why I wan' git mysef mess up in that? He done ruin six shirts awready. Leastwise, you done ruin 'em—sportin' his coat 'round, leavin' him rolled over in the open like he suppose to be sunnin' hissef. Hurry up. I done tol' you I ain't gonna set on this stump all night."

"Ain't it deep enough yet?"

"I done tol' you it ain't."

Abram pushed the shovel in again. "Half dis slime runnin' back in," he remarked.

"If you throw it far enough, it ain't gonna get back in."

"I'll have to wait 'til de moon git from behind dat cloud so's I kin see." Abram stuck his shovel in the ground and looked around for a place to sit.

"You kin see well enough by that lamp. You jest tryin' to rest."

"Lamp goin' out. You didn't put enough keresene in it. Dere it go now," Abram said happily as the lamp sputtered and the darkness absorbed his shadow.

Rosa got up. "I goin' back up there an' git you another one. You be settin' here all night waitin' for that moon to come out. Don't you see all them clouds?"

600

"Be powerful dark goin' up dere by yosef," he suggested.

"I done it befo'. You set there an' if that moon do come out for a few minutes, you git yosef at it an' make haste. You ain't worth all this wearyment."

She started cautiously up the path, digging her heels into the soft earth and, where it was steep and slippery, feeling for roots to pull up on with her free hand. Hadn't been for her, he'd be gittin' hissef in the 'lectric chair wit all his drunkness. He was drunk but he was strong. Strong like a king—even strongern that man at the fair. Biggern him, too. Howcome this path warn't so slippery in the day time? Must be these shoes wit their wore-down heels. She clutched on a root to steady herself. Now that lamp was draggin'. Suddenly she felt herself falling backwards. She grasped at the ground to steady herself but she felt only mud slipping through her fingers. She heard the lamp crash a second before she stopped rolling and when she felt about her on the ground, broken glass cut her fingers. "An' this the onliest good lamp we got," she muttered. "Reckon I'll wait on the moon to git itsef from behin' that cloud befo' I git up," she groaned. "Ain't gonna do Abram no good wit my neck broke." It just had a minute to go. She could see the end of the cloud becoming fringed with light. In a second, there it'd be, an' it'd take it a couple er minutes to git 'round to that other cloud an' by that time, she would be on the good path.

There it was! Slidin' out like a slow freight from the tunnel. Now where is I? she wondered. She got stiffly up and looked about her. Down the hill between the trees she could see the gully and to its left, stationary as a part of the rock he was enthroned on, Abram, gazing up at the moon, his shovel like a scepter idle by his side. "Howcome he don't git hissef up an' tend to that man now the moon out?" she muttered. That jest like him—settin' there dreamin' like he owned the country. That would be the way he'd set on a throne. Like he was holdin' it up 'stead er it holdin' him. An' her probly havin' to hold 'em both up. "Abram!" she shrilled, "git yosef offen that rock an' start diggin'." To her satisfaction the king scrambled off his throne and the scepter became a shovel again. Havin' to holler at him like he was one er Lizzie's chillun. He was her chile, though, the onliest one she'd got. She chuckled. Warn't nothin' wrong wit his ears neither. Hmp! He better had heard her. She found the path again and clawed her way up, reaching the edge of the hill just as the moon slid under cover. Now the road was straight and she could run.

601

The shack was dark and she had to feel her way to the shelf where they kept the other lamp and the matches. Like as not wouldn't be no keresene in it neither. She shook it. Jest like she thought. Good thing she kept candles. Where'd that Abram be if it warn't for her? He'd probly be sleepin' in that bed there like nothin' had happened an' then gittin' hissef in the 'lectric chair. She put the candle stumps and the matches in her pocket and left the shack.

The steep, winding path that led down into the gully seemed even longer and darker as she stood where the good road ended and lit a candle to light her way down. That Abram better be workin' when she got there. Her trapesyin' 'round all night wit all that washin' she got to do in the mornin'! Going down was harder than going up. The trees were scattered thinly and the small plants were of little use to clutch. Rosa held the candle low by her side and with her knees bent and her free hand grasping for an occasional tree to steady on, groped her way down the path. Farther on she felt broken glass under her feet. This where she seen Abram from, too. Now where was he? She leaned against a tree and tried to find where she had looked before. T'warn't no use lookin' when the moon was in, she thought, but suddenly a lighted area over to the west caught her eye, and there, standing on a rock, was Abram, his head bent, his hands in the air. Now where he git all that light from? Why warn't he diggin'? She crept closer. Was them hounds she heard barkin'? White men! Must be ten of 'em! Wit guns an' dogs. All 'round him. She clung to the tree. They'd got him. Wit all her tryin', they'd got him. 'Possum huntin' more than likely an' found him there. She remembered she had called him. Likely 'tracted 'em. No. They'd er got him anyway. She felt hollow. The devil allus ketched up wit his own; it was in Abram's blood. She snuffed the candle out and looked more closely. There were guns all around him. She edged her way closer. She could hear them talking.

One laughed. "First time I've ever got a coon when I was looking for a 'possum."

"What's yer name, nigger?" another asked.

"I ain't done nothin'," Abram yelled. "I ain't done nothin'."

"Oh, we know you ain't done nothin'. You just nursin' that corpse for its mamma, but what's yer name—just for the record?" The man poked a gun at his side.

Abram stiffened. "I ain't done nothin'," he muttered.

He won't gonna tell 'em. Rosa knew he won't. They didn't know Abram. He was drunk an' when he was drunk, he didn't have no truck wit strangers who was rough wit him. He roused up an' fought.

"Who's he killed?" one man asked.

"Never seen him before."

"Who is he, nigger?"

"I ain't done nothin'," Abram insisted.

"I believe this nigger's a looney," one man growled.

"Oh, he'll talk with some persuasion." A man in a plaid jacket strode toward Abram. "Listen, nigger," he snarled, "open up or get hell beat out you." He prodded the gun into Abram's side. "Get off that rock," he ordered.

"He ain't gonna do it," Rosa whispered. "He gon stan' there like a king. He gonna kill that man. He gon . . ."

Abram wrenched the gun from its owner and like a black streak darted past the startled group and up the open side of the gully. Rosa groaned. Ef only he'd er come this side she might could er helped him.

Several of the men raised their guns.

Rosa clung to the tree. She heard four shots and a scream. Later that night when she crawled home—after they had taken his body, them men what didn't have no business wit it—she wondered if it hadn't been better them gittin' him that way. Them 'lectric chairs—she shuddered—weren't fit for no king; and all that week, though she lay on her bed with what the neighbor women called the "fall fevers," there was a little core of something light buried in the dark weight her head was.

Toward the end of the week she was just well enough to walk (although she couldn't feel that she was walking) out to Mrs. Wilkinson's car that had honked three times loudly in front of her door. She was able to take the wash bundle out of the back of the automobile and to stand almost straight while Mrs. Wilkinson told her that there were two of Roy's shirts in there, three of her own summer dresses—that she wanted done with extra carefulness—and Mr. Wilkinson's light hunting jacket which she would find simply filthy. He had lost it last week in the woods and found that some colored man had taken ten dollars out of the pocket and exchanged the coat at Branches for four pints of cheap wine. Wasn't that ridiculous? She knew Mr. Wilkinson had paid at least twenty dollars for that coat. And oh yes, she told Rosa, there were six of her best luncheon napkins and a table runner in the bundle and for heaven's sake, she told her, she was not to lose any of the napkins. She had the hardest time imaginable keeping up with them; last year she had lost three and the year before, two. And she told Rosa how in the beginning there had been sixteen.

Nominated by Genie Chipps

From the editors of *DoubleTake*: *We decided, with respect to the O'Connor story, to call it an "exploration"—a young Georgia lady of promise and means struggling hard to look at foolishness and fear as they exert their toll on us, no matter our background. Pride is, of course, the sin of sins (George Eliot's "unreflecting egoism"), and in that regard, none of us is spared, as Miss O'Connor, scarcely over twenty, knew when she wrote "The Coat." She would never again try so fully to attend to black people, immerse herself in their thoughts and manner of expression—and, indeed, this story would go unpublished during her lifetime, and until now. . . . O'Connor would go on to achieve far greater control over the fiction, short and long, that she'd give us until her life ended, less than twenty years after this story was fashioned, but she would never want to surrender a fierce determination, already evident in this early writing, to confront smugness in all its variations: among the propertied, their all too apparent displays of vanity; among the persecuted, their natural, telling mimicry of those who lord it over them, a copycat resort to "airs" that is, finally, a measure of their humanity; and not least, among the "interleckchuls," whom she never ceased arraigning, through the implication of her spelling, and in occasionally lengthy epistolary asides—such assaults, though, meant not to spare herself, but as confessional gestures.*

SPECIAL MENTION

(The editors also wish to mention the following important works published recently by small presses. Listing is in no particular order.)

POETRY

Cookie Monster—Abdi Ali (Agni)
Variations of Themes From The Doors—Mark Svenvold (Virginia Quarterly)
The Woodchuck—Jean Nordhaus (Marlboro Review)
Game 5—Nola Garrett (Poet Lore)
Sirens—Sally Ball (Virginia Quarterly)
On the Grand Canyon's North Rim—Alan Michael Parker (College English)
Wu-Wei Deductible—C. L. Rawlins (Caldera)
Monologue of the Signified—Bruce Beasley (Ontario Review)
Vacancies—Gregory Thielen (Poems and Plays)
Blue China—Jane Yeh (TriQuarterly)
My Little Esperanto—Caroline Finkelstein (Ploughshares)
Musee—Scott Cairns (Prairie Schooner)
Sub Rosa—Elton Glaser (Iowa Review)
Poem Ending Everette—Ralph Adamo (Laurel Review)
Wolf—Ron Koertge (14 Hills)
Driving to Work—William Hathaway (Exquisite Corpse)
Grief—Cal Bedient (Agni)
On The Beach—Tom Clark (Exquisite Corpse)
Sex Before Dog—Stephen Dobyns (Marlboro Review)
The Sky Drank In—Gillian Conoley (American Letters and Commentary)
Nonesuch—Mary Jo Bang (Colorado Review)

ESSAYS

A Nasty Man—Kenneth Bernard (Salmagundi)

Mockingbird Years—Emily Fox Gordon (Boulevard)

Homestead—Annick Smith (*Homestead,* Milkweed)

Earth Bone Connected to the Spirit Bone—Adrian C. Louis (Ploughshares)

Royal Crown—Bret Lott (Creative Nonfiction)

Blind Is the Bookless Man—Bill Holm (*The Heart Can Be Filled Anywhere on Earth,* Milkweed)

Bungee—DeWitt Henry (Iowa Review)

Tommy Two—Mark Spragg (Northern Lights)

Klan of the Grandmother—Rebecca McClanahan (Southern Review)

M.—Mark Rudman (Raritan)

Toward A Small Theory of the Visible—John Berger (Threepenny Review)

Ferrule—Chris Arthur (American Scholar)

The Cult of the Adolescent: Commercial Indoctrination and The Collapse of Civic Virtue—David Bosworth (Georgia Review)

Hanging From the Trestle While the Train Goes By—George Garrett (Witness)

Smoke—Jake Grant (North Carolina Literary Review)

Tahiti—Frederick Seidel (Raritan Review)

The Binding of Books and the Matter of Spirit—Jack Matthews (Antioch Review)

Poisoned Fruit: Crossing Cultural Boundaries—Arthur Goldhammer (Salmagundi)

Dancing Among the Ghosts: An Okinawa Journal—James D. Houston (Manoa)

Fear of Happiness—Louise Glück (Michigan Quarterly)

The Gangster We Are All Looking For—Lê Thi Diem Thúy (Massachusetts Review)

How I Came Into My Inheritance—Dorothy Gallagher (Raritan Review)

What's In A Name—Francesca Kazan (Gettysburg Review)

A Punishment Seminar—Gary Fincke (Shenandoah)

Tracking My Father—Mary Gordon (DoubleTake)

Present Among Us—Carolyn Forché (DoubleTake)

Great Teacher—Judith Grossman (Yale Review)

Scavenging—Jonathan Franzen (Antioch Review)

Deleting Childhood: Computers and the Life of Children—Mary Ann Lieser (Plain)

Communion—Bill McKibben (DoubleTake)

A Psychohistory of the Homosexual Body—Danniel Harris (Salmagundi)

How I Remember Him—Rose Ryan (Boston Review)

Night Carrier—Steve Faulkner (DoubleTake)

Mornings In Quarain—Barry Lopez (Gettysburg Review)

Mothers' Regrets—Melody Ermachild Chavis (Shambala Sun)

Present Among Us—Carolyn Forché (DoubleTake)

The Talking Horse—Beth Ferris (Northern Lights)

FICTION

San—Lan Samantha Chang (Story)

Lokey Man—Susan Dodd (Ohio Review)

Boy Looking Into Infinity—Joyce Carol Oates (Agni)

The Talk Talked Between Worms—Lee. K. Abbott (Georgia Review)

"Woman Loses Cookie Bake-Off, Sets Self On Fire"—Robert Olen Butler (Gettysburg Review)

from The Carriage Stone—Sigbjørn Hølmebakk (Dufour Editions)

Their Story—Thomas Glave (Kenyon Review)

City Life—Mary Gordon (Ploughshares)

Two Prose Pieces—Severo Sarduy (Conjunctions)

On Becoming A Snake Woman—Jennifer Rahim (Caribbean Writer)

Day 'n Night—Rachel M. Resnick (Crescent Review)

The Miracle—Stephen Dixon (StoryQuarterly)

Two Stories—Rikki Ducornet (Conjunctions)

Tell Me Something—Tom McNeal (Epoch)

Last Wash—Alice Mattison (Boulevard)

Fourteen—Bo Caldwell (Ploughshares)

The Adornment of Days—Aryeh Lev Stollman (Southwest Review)

Dr. Rapallo—Stephen Menick (Press)

We're So Famous—Jaime Clarke (Mississippi Review)

Fox and Geese—David Reimer (Ontario Review)

The Artist—Bhargavi C. Mandava (*Where The Oceans Meet*, Seal Press)

The Book of the Milky Way—Eugene Mirabelli (Third Coast)

The Bride Wore Red—Robbie Clipper Sethi (*The Bride Wore Red*, Bridge Works)

Every Building Wants to Fall—Rhian Margaret Ellis (Epoch)

A Real Disaster—Rhidin Brook (Paris Review)
Saboteur—Ha Jin (Antioch Review)
Entre Toutes Les Femmes—Elisabeth Panttaja Brink (Buffalo Spree)
The Baker's Wife—Sara Powers (Zoetrope)
The Son and Heir—Alexander Häusser (Grand Street)
The Merman—Cary Holladay (Happy)
The Egg Man—Cary Holladay (American Literary Review)
The Accident—Donald Hall (Ohio Review)
Horse, Horse, Horse—William Powers (Another Chicago Magazine)
The Team—Daśa Śali (Ontario Review)
Redemption—Robin Hemley (Another Chicago Magazine)
A Lit Window Is Someone Awake—Sharon Wahl (Literal Latté)
At The Village Hall—William Monahan (Old Crow)
Something To Be Proud Of—James Meek (The Baffler)
In Hiding—Robert Boyers (Michigan Quarterly Review)
My Black Rachmaninoff—Richard Burgin (Ontario Review)
Bob Darling—Carolyn Cooke (Paris Review)
Bathwater—Carrie Pomeroy (Laurel Review)
Bright Wings—Dabney Stuart (Kenyon Review)
Nones—Solon Timothy Woodward (Ontario Review)
Age of Wonders—Jayne Anne Phillips (DoubleTake)
Voyager—Kit Reed (Yale Review)
Air Mail—Jeffrey Eugenides (Yale Review)
Flying Cranes—Mikhail Iossel (Boulevard)
from Craven Images—Alan Isler (Bridge Works Press)
The Underwater Town—Robin Hemley (Shenandoah)
Catering—S. L. Wisenberg (Willow Review)
The Boys At Night—Robert Cohen (Glimmer Train)
Ice—Alyce Miller (Michigan Quarterly Review)
The Baker—Samuel Roberts (Press)
Circumnavigation—Steve Lattimore (American Short Fiction)
Ash—Jon Billman (ZYZZYVA)
Give the Pig A Chance—David Rice (Give the Pig A Chance, Bilingual Review)
Are We Pleasing You Tonight—Frederick Busch (Five Points)
Her Wild American Self—M. Evelina Galang (Calyx)

CONTRIBUTORS' NOTES

DANNIE ABSE is a native of Cardiff, Wales. His first book of poems appeared in 1948 and he has published nine more, most recently *White Coat, Purple Coat* (Persea Books, 1989) and *Intermittent Journals* (Dufour Editions, 1995).

PAUL ALLMAN's stories have appeared in *Gem, The Iowa Review,* and *Paris Transcontinental.* His first novel, *Otis,* was issued by St. Martin's in 1994.

RITA ARIYOSHI is a photographer, journalist and author of *Majui On My Mind* (Mutual Publishing, 1985). Her brother and three cousins were killed in the war in Vietnam.

RANE ARROYO is a Puerto Rican poet from Chicago. His most recent book is *Pale Ramon* (Zoland Books, 1998). He teaches at the University of Toledo.

ANDREA BARRETT is the author of four novels and the short fiction collection, *Ship Fever and Other Stories* (Norton, 1996) which won the National Book Award. She lives in Rochester, New York.

CHARLES BAXTER is the author of three novels and four volumes of short stories, most recently *Believers* (Pantheon, 1997). He teaches at the University of Michigan.

MOLLY BENDALL last appeared in this series in *Pushcart Prize XX.* Her *After Estrangement* was published by Peregrine Smith in 1992. She lives in Venice, California.

GINA BERRIAULT's latest collection of short stories, *Women in Their Beds* (Counterpoint Press) won the National Book Critics Circle Award, the PEN-Faulkner Award and the Micheal Rea Award for the short story.

LINDA BIERDS is the author most recently of *The Ghost Trio* (Holt). She lives in Washington state.

DAN BROWN's poems have appeared in *Partisan Review* and *Poetry Northwest*, among other journals. His debut collection, *Matter*, is just out from Crosstown Books.

RON CARLSON is the author of four books of fiction, including *Hotel Eden*, just out from Norton. He lives in Scottsdale, Arizona.

ANNE CARSON is a professor of classics at McGill University in Montreal. She is the author of *Plainwater* (Knopf, 1995) and *Glass, Irony and God* (New Directions, 1995).

TURNER CASSITY's first collection, *Watchboy*, was published in 1966 and has been followed by nine additional volumes. From 1962 to 1991 he was a librarian at Emory University in Atlanta. He is now retired in lives in Georgia and California.

MARILYN CHIN teaches at San Diego State. She has published books with Milkweed and Greenfield Review Press.

JEFF CLARK's first book of poems, *The Little Door Slides Back*, is just out from Sun & Moon. He lives in San Francisco.

JOSHUA CLOVER is the author of *Madonna Anno Domini* (LSU Press) which includes this poem. He lives in Berkeley, California.

SUSAN DAITCH is the author of the novels *L. C.* (Harcourt, 1987); *The Colorist* (Vintage, 1990). She teaches at Sarah Lawrence College.

KIANA DAVENPORT is a *hapa-haole*, of Native Hawaiian and Anglo-American descent. She is the author of four novels, most recently *Shark Dialogues* (Plume/Penguin, 1995). Her story here is based on her stay at a river-station on the Sepik River in Papua, New Guinea.

CLAIRE DAVIS teaches at Lewis-Clark State College in Idaho. Her work has been published in *American Literary Review, CutBank, Puerto Del Sol, The Southern Review* and elsewhere.

CHARD DE NIORD's poetry has appeared in *Gettysburg Review, Southern Review,* and *Ploughshares.* He is the author of *Asleep in the Fire.*

JUNOT DIAZ was born and raised in Santo Domingo, Dominican Republic. His story collection, *Drown,* was published by Riverhead. He is currently working on a novel.

JANICE EIDUS has just published a new collection of fiction from City Lights titled *The Celibacy Club.* She has won two O'Henry Awards and published two novels.

THOMAS SAYERS ELLIS is a co-founding member of The Dark Room Collective and he teaches at Case Western Reserve and Bennington College. His *The Good Junk* was published by Graywolf in 1996 and his poetry appeared in *Best American Poetry 1997.*

NATHAN ENGLANDER lives in Jerusalem, where he is at work on his first collection of stories. He was born and raised in New York City and received an M.F.A. from the Iowa Writers' Workshop in 1996. This is his first published story.

PERCIVAL EVERETT is the author of *Big Picture,* a collection of short stories from Graywolf. He teaches in the Creative Writing Department at UCLA, Riverside.

TOMAS FILER's "Civilization" is part of a work-in-progress that ranges over the 500 year history of a canyon suburb in Los Angeles. Other stories in the series have appeared in *Cream City Review* and *Kansas Quarterly.*

REGINALD GIBBONS just retired as editor of *TriQuarterly.* He has published several volumes of poetry and his novel, *Sweetbitter,* was published in 1994.

ELIZABETH GILBERT has published in *Esquire, Story, Mississippi Review,* and *Ploughshares.* Her collection, *Pilgrims,* is just out.

ALBERT GOLDBARTH received the National Book Critics Circle Award for his collection, *Heaven and Earth.* New collections are due soon from Ohio University Press and David Godine.

SAM HAMILL founded Copper Canyon Press in 1972 and has published more than thirty books. He lives near Port Townsend, Washington.

DAVID HAYWARD's poems have appeared in *DoubleTake, Three-penny Review,* and *Fourteen Hills.* He is a copy editor and lives in San Francisco.

MICHAEL HEFFERNAN directs the MFA creative writing program at the University of Arkansas, Fayetteville. His *Love's Answer* won the Iowa Poetry Prize from the University of Iowa Press in 1993.

LEWIS HYDE is Luce Professor of Art and Politics at Kenyon College. "Two Accidents" is part of a book on the creativity of tricksters to be published by Farrar Straus & Giroux.

RICHARD JACKSON's latest book of poems is *Alive All Day* (Cleveland State University Press, 1992). He is a past poetry co-editor of *The Pushcart Prize.*

RACHEL KADISH was a fellow at the Bunting Institute. She is working on a novel, *From A Sealed Room,* forthcoming from Putnam.

BRIGIT KELLY teaches at the University of Illinois, Urbana. Her second book, *Song,* was published by BOA Editions in 1995.

KRISTIN KING earned an MFA from the University of Washington and lives in Seattle. She has won recognition from the Writers at Work program and the Utah Arts Council.

KENNETH KOCH received a Bollingen Prize in 1995. His latest volume is *The Art of Poetry,* a book of writings about poetry from The University of Michigan Press.

GRETCHEN LEGLER lives in Anchorage, Alaska and teaches at The University of Alaska. Seal Press just published her *All the Powerful Invisible Things: A Sportswoman's Notebook.*

DANA LEVIN will be Poet-In-Residence at Pitzer College in 1998. Her work has appeared in *Sojourner, Literal Latté, Countermeasures* and *Boston Review.*

LARRY LEVIS died in May, 1996. He published six collections of poems, the most recent of which, *Elegy,* just appeared from the University of Pittsburgh Press. He was Professor of English at Virginia Commonwealth University, Richmond, and received a Lamont Prize, a Guggenheim Foundation grant and a National Poetry Series selection.

P. H. LIOTTA is the author of the memoir, *Learning to Fly: A Season With the Peregrine Falcon;* and a novel and poetry collection. He received the 1997 Robert H. Winner Memorial Award from the Poetry Society of America.

GORDON LISH is a former editor at *Esquire* and *Knopf*. He now edits *The Quarterly* full time. His books are available from Four Walls Eight Windows.

THOMAS LYNCH is the author of two books of poems from Knopf and Jonathan Cape/Random House. His *The Undertaking: Life and Studies from the Dismal Trade* is just out from Norton.

JAMES ALAN MCPHERSON is the author of two story collections: *Hue and Cry* and *Elbow Room*.

KATHERINE MIN is working on a novel, *The Naked Woman*. She was a MacDowell colonist recently and her fiction has appeared in *Ploughshares, Threepenny Review* and *Prairie Schooner*.

RICK MOODY is the author most recently of *Purple America* (Little, Brown). He is fiction editor of *The Pushcart Prize*, and won Pushcart's Editors' Book Award for his novel, *Garden State*.

MIKE NEWIRTH was born in 1970 on Long Island where he later tended bar on the East End. He now lives in Chicago. His work will appear in the forthcoming *Twenties in the Nineties*.

JOSIP NOVAKOVICH teaches at the University of Cincinnati. He is the author of two story collections from Graywolf. A new collection appears in 1998.

FLANNERY O'CONNOR died in 1964. She was the author of the novels *The Violent Bear It Away* and *Wise Blood* and the story collection *Everything That Rises Must Converge*.

TOM PAINE lives in Vermont. His stories have been picked by *Best New Stories from the South*, the O'Henry collection, and *Pushcart Prize* XXI.

PAMELA PAINTER lives in Boston and Wellfleet, Massachusetts. She is the author of *Getting to Know the Weather*. Her fiction has appeared in *Harpers, Kenyon Review, Atlantic* and elsewhere. She teaches at Emerson College.

ROBERT PINSKY is Poet Laureate of the United States. His most recent book is *The Figured Wheel: New and Collected Poems 1966–1996*.

FRANK POLITE lives in Youngstown, Ohio and is the author of two recent poetry collections: *Flamingo* (Pangborn Books) and *Letters of Transit* (City Minor).

BIN RAMKE is editor of *Denver Quarterly*. His most recent poetry collection is *Massacre of the Innocents* (University of Iowa Press, 1995).

DONALD RAWLEY's latest book is *Slow Dance on The Fault Line* (HarperCollins). He lives in Sherman Oaks, California.

STACEY RICHTER lives in Tucson, Arizona where she works as a film critic. She has won prizes for her fiction, her poetry and her short films.

JESSICA ROEDER's fiction has appeared in *Threepenny Review, Alaska Quarterly Review* and *Primavera* and her poems have been published in *American Poetry Review* and *Denver Quarterly*.

MARY RUEFLE won a Whiting Award in 1994. Her *Cold Pluto* was published by Carnegie-Mellon in 1996. She lives in Bennington, Vermont.

KAY RYAN is the author of *Elephant Rocks*, (Grove/Atlantic). and three other poetry collections. She lives in Fairfax, California.

ALBERT SAIJO was born in 1926 in Los Angeles, studied Zen in the 1950's, traveled with Jack Kerouac and Lew Welch, farmed in Northern California in the 60's to 80's and is described as "a devout practitioner, thinker and poet-philosopher." His most recent book is *Outspeaks a Rhapsody* (Bamboo Ridge).

MAUREEN SEATON is the author of books of poetry from The University of Iowa Press (which includes "L.A. Dream #2"), New Rivers and Eighth Mountain. She lives in Chicago.

GERALD SHAPIRO is the author of a story collection, *From Hunger,* (University of Missouri Press). His stories have appeared in *The Gettysburg Review, The Southern Review* and *The Missouri Review*.

CHARLES SIMIC is author of the poetry collection, *A Wedding in Hell*. He lives in New Hampshire.

JULIA SLAVIN has published stories in *Crescent Review, Cottonwood, Gargoyle* and *WordWrights*. She lives in Washington D.C. with her husband and two children.

LEE SMITH's most recent novel is *Saving Grace* (Putnam). She is also the author of *Oral History* and nine other books. She lives in Chapel Hill, North Carolina.

GARY SNYDER won the Pulitzer Prize and, most recently The Bollingen Prize. His most recent collection is *Mountains and Rivers Without End* (Counterpoint).

A. E. STALLINGS lives in Decatur, Georgia. Her poems have appeared in *The American Voice, The Formalist,* and *Best American Poetry 1994.*

DAVID ST. JOHN's *Study For The World's Body* (HarperCollins, 1995) was nominated for a National Book Award. He lives in Venice, California.

JULIA VINOGRAD lives in Berkeley, California. She won the Before Columbus American Book Award and has published many volumes of her poems.

SYLVIA WATANABE is a Japanese-American born on the island of Mauai. She is the author of the story collection, *Talking to the Dead,* (Doubleday, 1992).

GORDON WEAVER is the author of four novels and seven story collections. His *Four Decades: New and Selected Stories* is just out from the University of Missouri Press and includes "Return of the Boyceville Flash."

STEVE YARBROUGH's two collections of fiction are *Family Men* (1990) and *Mississippi History* (1994) both published by the University of Missouri Press. He lives and teaches in Fresno, California.

PRESSES FEATURED IN THE PUSHCART PRIZE EDITIONS SINCE 1976

Acts
Agni Review
Ahsahta Press
Ailanthus Press
Alaska Quarterly Review
Alcheringa/Ethnopoetics
Alice James Books
Ambergris
Amelia
American Letters and Commentary
American Literature
American PEN
American Poetry Review
American Scholar
American Short Fiction
The American Voice
Amicus Journal
Amnesty International
Anaesthesia Review
Another Chicago Magazine
Antaeus
Antietam Review
Antioch Review
Apalachee Quarterly
Aphra

Aralia Press
The Ark
Ascensius Press
Ascent
Aspen Leaves
Aspen Poetry Anthology
Assembling
Atlanta Review
Autonomedia
The Baffler
Bakunin
Bamboo Ridge
Barlenmır House
Barnwood Press
The Bellingham Review
Bellowing Ark
Beloit Poetry Journal
Bennington Review
Bilingual Review
Black American Literature Forum
Black Rooster
Black Scholar
Black Sparrow
Black Warrior Review
Blackwells Press

Bloomsbury Review
Blue Cloud Quarterly
Blue Unicorn
Blue Wind Press
Bluefish
BOA Editions
Bomb
Bookslinger Editions
Boulevard
Boxspring
Bridges
Brown Journal of Arts
Burning Deck Press
Caliban
California Quarterly
Calyx
Callaloo
Calliope
Calliopea Press
Canto
Capra Press
Caribbean Writer
Carolina Quarterly
Cedar Rock
Center
Chariton Review
Charnel House
Chattahochee Review
Chelsea
Chicago Review
Chouteau Review
Chowder Review
Cimarron Review
Cincinnati Poetry Review
City Lights Books
Clown War
CoEvolution Quarterly
Cold Mountain Press
Colorado Review
Columbia: A Magazine of Poetry
    and Prose
Confluence Press
Confrontation

Conjunctions
Copper Canyon Press
Cosmic Information Agency
Countermeasures
Counterpoint
Crawl Out Your Window
Crazyhorse
Crescent Review
Cross Cultural Communications
Cross Currents
Crosstown Books
Cumberland Poetry Review
Curbstone Press
Cutbank
Dacotah Territory
Daedalus
Dalkey Archive Press
Decatur House
December
Denver Quarterly
Domestic Crude
Doubletake
Dragon Gate Inc.
Dreamworks
Dryad Press
Duck Down Press
Durak
East River Anthology
Ellis Press
Empty Bowl
Epoch
Ergo!
Exquisite Corpse
Faultline
Fiction
Fiction Collective
Fiction International
Field
Fine Madness
Firebrand Books
Firelands Art Review
Five Fingers Review
Five Trees Press

The Formalist
Frontiers: A Journal of Women Studies
Gallimaufry
Genre
The Georgia Review
Gettysburg Review
Ghost Dance
Glimmer Train
Goddard Journal
David Godine, Publisher
Graham House Press
Grand Street
Granta
Graywolf Press
Green Mountains Review
Greenfield Review
Greensboro Review
Guardian Press
Gulf Coast
Hanging Loose
Hard Pressed
Harvard Review
Hayden's Ferry Review
Hermitage Press
Hills
Holmgangers Press
Holy Cow!
Home Planet News
Hudson Review
Hungry Mind Review
Icarus
Icon
Iguana Press
Indiana Review
Indiana Writes
Intermedia
Intro
Invisible City
Inwood Press
Iowa Review
Ironwood
Jam To-day

The Journal
The Kanchenjuga Press
Kansas Quarterly
Kayak
Kelsey Street Press
Kenyon Review
Latitudes Press
Laughing Waters Press
Laurel Review
L'Epervier Press
Liberation
Linquis
Literal Latté
The Literary Review
The Little Magazine
Living Hand Press
Living Poets Press
Logbridge-Rhodes
Louisville Review
Lowlands Review
Lucille
Lynx House Press
Magic Circle Press
Malahat Review
Mānoa
Manroot
Marlboro Review
Massachusetts Review
Mho & Mho Works
Micah Publications
Michigan Quarterly
Mid-American Review
Milkweed Editions
Milkweed Quarterly
The Minnesota Review
Mississippi Review
Mississippi Valley Review
Missouri Review
Montana Gothic
Montana Review
Montemora
Moon Pony Press
Mr. Cogito Press

MSS
Mulch Press
Nada Press
New America
New American Review
The New Criterion
New Delta Review
New Directions
New England Review
New England Review and Bread
    Loaf Quarterly
New Letters
New Virginia Review
New York Quarterly
New York University Press
Nimrod
North American Review
North Atlantic Books
North Dakota Quarterly
North Point Press
Northern Lights
Northwest Review
Notre Dame Review
O. ARS
O·Blēk
Obsidian
Obsidian II
Oconee Review
October
Ohio Review
Old Crow Review
Ontario Review
Open Places
Orca Press
Orchises Press
Orion
Oxford American
Oxford Press
Oyez Press
Painted Bride Quarterly
Painted Hills Review
Paris Press

Paris Review
Parnassus: Poetry in Review
Partisan Review
Passages North
Penca Books
Pentagram
Penumbra Press
Pequod
Persea: An International Review
Pipedream Press
Pitcairn Press
Pitt Magazine
Ploughshares
Poet and Critic
Poetry
Poetry East
Poetry Ireland Review
Poetry Northwest
Poetry Now
Prairie Schooner
Prescott Street Press
Press
Promise of Learnings
Provincetown Arts
Puerto Del Sol
Quarry West
The Quarterly
Quarterly West
Raccoon
Rainbow Press
Raritan: A Quarterly Review
Red Cedar Review
Red Clay Books
Red Dust Press
Red Earth Press
Release Press
Review of Contemporary Fiction
Revista Chicano-Riquena
Rhetoric Review
River Styx
Rowan Tree Press
Russian *Samizdat*

Salmagundi
San Marcos Press
Sea Pen Press and Paper Mill
Seal Press
Seamark Press
Seattle Review
Second Coming Press
Semiotext(e)
Seven Days
The Seventies Press
Sewanee Review
Shankpainter
Shantih
Sheep Meadow Press
Shenandoah
A Shout In the Street
Sibyl-Child Press
Side Show
Small Moon
The Smith
Solo
Some
The Sonora Review
Southern Poetry Review
Southern Review
Southwest Review
Spectrum
The Spirit That Moves Us
St. Andrews Press
Story
Story Quarterly
Streetfare Journal
Stuart Wright, Publisher
Sulfur
The Sun
Sun & Moon Press
Sun Press
Sunstone
Sycamore Review
Tamagwa
Tar River Poetry
Teal Press

Telephone Books
Telescope
Temblor
Tendril
Texas Slough
The MacGuffin
Third Coast
13th Moon
THIS
Thorp Springs Press
Three Rivers Press
Threepenny Review
Thunder City Press
Thunder's Mouth Press
Tikkun
Tombouctou Books
Toothpaste Press
Transatlantic Review
TriQuarterly
Truck Press
Undine
Unicorn Press
University of Illinois Press
University of Iowa Press
University of Massachusetts Press
University of Pittsburgh Press
Unmuzzled Ox
Unspeakable Visions of the Individual
Vagabond
Vignette
Virginia Quarterly
Volt
Wampeter Press
Washington Writers Workshop
Water Table
Western Humanities Review
Westigan Review
White Pine Press
Wickwire Press
Willow Springs
Wilmore City
Witness

Word Beat Press
Word-Smith
Wormwood Review
Writers Forum
Xanadu
Yale Review

Yardbird Reader
Yarrow
Y'Bird
Zeitgeist Press
ZYZZYVA

CONTRIBUTING SMALL PRESSES FOR THIS EDITION

(These presses made or received nominations for this edition of *The Pushcart Prize*. See the *International Directory of Little Magazines and Small Presses,* Dustbooks, P.O. Box 100, Paradise, CA 95967, for subscription rates, manuscript requirements and a complete international listing of small presses.)

A

The Acorn, P.O. Box 39, Somerset, CA 95684
The Advocado Press, P.O. Box 145, Louisville, KY 40201
Agni, Boston Univ., 236 Bay State Rd., Boston, MA 02215
Alamo Square Press, P.O. Box 29478, Los Angeles, CA 90029
Alaska Quarterly Review, Univ. of Alaska, Anchorage, AK 99508
Alligator Juniper, Prescott College, 220 Grove Ave., Prescott, AZ 86301
Alpha Beat Press, 31A Waterloo St., New Hope, PA 18038
Amaranth, P.O. Box 184, Trumbull, CT 06611
American Letters & Commentary, 850 Park Ave., Ste. 5B, New York, NY 10021
American Literary Review, Univ. of North Texas, P.O. Box 13827, Denton, TX 76203
The American Scholar, 1811 Q St., NW, Washington, DC 20009
American Short Fiction, P.O. Box 7819, Austin, TX 78713
The American Voice, 332 W. Broadway, Louisville, KY 40202
Amherst Writers & Artists, P.O. Box 1076, Amherst, MA 01004
The Amicus Journal, 40 W. 20th St., New York, NY 10011
Angelflesh Press, P.O. Box 141123, Grand Rapids, MI 49514
Another Chicago Magazine, 3709 N. Kenmore, Chicago, IL 60613
Antietam Review, 7 W. Franklin St., Hagerstown, MD 21740
Antioch Review, P.O. Box 148, Yellow Springs, OH 45387
Art & Academe, 209 E. 23rd St., New York, NY 10010
Artful Dodge, English Dept., College of Wooster, Wooster, OH 44691
Ascent, English Dept., Concordia College, Moorhead, MN 56562
Asian Pacific American Journal, 10 E. 53rd St., New York, NY 10022
Atlanta Review, P.O. Box 8248, Atlanta, GA 30306
Autonomedia, P.O. Box 568, Brooklyn, NY 11211

Avec Books, P.O. Box 1059, Penngrove, CA 94951
Axe Factory, 2653 Sperry St., Philadelphia, PA 19152

B

Baffler, P.O. Box 378293, Chicago, IL 60637
Bakunin, Box 1853, Simi Valley, CA 93062
Ballast Quarterly Review, 2022 X Ave., Dysart, IA 52224
Bamboo Ridge Press P.O. Box 61781, Honolulu, HI 96839
Barracuda Press, P.O. Box 1730, Escondido, CA 92033
Belletrist Review, P.O. Box 596, Plainville, CT 06062
Bellingham Review, M5-9053, West Washington Univ., Bellingham, WA 98225
Beloit Poetry Journal, RFD 2, Box 154, Ellsworth, ME 04605
Berkeley Fiction Review, 703 Eshleman Hall, Univ. of California, Berkeley, CA 94720
Berkeley Hills Books, P.O. Box 9877, Berkeley, CA 94709
Bilingual Press, Arizona State Univ., P.O. Box 872702, Tempe, AZ 85287
Black Ice, box 494, Univ. of Colorado, Boulder, CO 80309
Black Warrior Review, P.O. Box 2936, Tuscaloosa, AL 35486
Block's Magazine, 1419 Chapin St., Beloit, WI 53511
Blue Heron, 24450 N.W. Hansen Rd., Hillsboro, OR 97124
Blue Sofa Press, 524 Orleans St., St. Paul, MN 55107
BOA Editions, 200 East Ave., Rochester, NY 14604
Boston Review, E53-407, Massachusetts Inst. of Tech., Cambridge, MA 02139
Bottom Dog Press, Firelands College, Huron, OH 44839
Bottomfish, DeAnza College, 21250 Stevens Creek Blvd., Cupertino, CA 95014
Boulevard, 4579 Laclede Ave., #332, St. Louis, MO 63108
Briar Cliff Review, Briar Cliff Colege, 3303 Rebecca St., Sioux City, IA 51204
Bridge Works Publishing Co., Bridge Lane, Box 1798, Bridgehampton, NY 11932
Brilliant Corners, Lycoming College, Williamsport, PA 17701
Burning Car, P.O. Box 26692, San Francisco, CA 94126
Burning Deck, 71 Elmgrove Ave., Providence, RI 02906
Button, Box 26, Lunenburg, MA 01462

C

Callaloo, 2715 N. Charles St., Baltimore, MD 21218
Calyx, P.O. Box B, Corvallis, OR 97339
The Camel Press, c/o Gen'l Delivery, Big Cove Tannery, PA 17212
Canio's Editions, P.O. Box 1962, Sag Harbor, NY 11963
Canterbury Press, 5540 Vista Del Amigo, Anaheim, CA 92807
Cape Perpetua Press, P.O. Box 1005, Yachats, OR 97498
The Caribbean Writer, Univ. of Virgin Islands, RR02, Box 10,000, Kingshill, St. Croix, U.S. Virigin Islands, 00850
Carolina Quarterly, Univ. of North Carolina, Chapel Hill, NC 27499
Chariton Review, Truman State Univ., Kirksville, MO 63501
Chattahoochee Review, DeKalb College, Dunwoody, GA 30338
Chelsea, Box 773, Cooper Sta., New York, NY 10276
Chicago Review, Univ. of Chicago, 5801 S. Kenwood Ave., Chicago, IL 60637
Chiron Review, 522 E. South Ave., St. John, KS 67576
Cities and Roads, P.O. Box 10886, Greensboro, NC 27404
Clearwood Publishers, P.O. Box 52, Bella Vista, CA 96008
Clock Watch Review, Eng. Dept., Illinois Wesleyan Univ., Bloomington, IL 61702

Colorado Review, Colorado State University, Ft. Collins, CO 80523
Common Boundary, 5272 River Rd., Ste. 650, Bethesda, MD 20816
The Compendium, P.O. Box 542327, Houston, TX 77254
Confluence, P.O. Box 336, Belpre, OH 45714
Confrontation, English Dept., C.W. Post of L.I.U., Brookville, NY 11548
Conjunctions, Bard College, Annandale-on-Hudson, NY 12504
Connecticut Review, English Dept., So. Connecticut St. Univ., New Haven, CT 06515
Conservatory of American Letters, P.O. Box 298, Thomaston, ME 04861
Contemporary Arts Publishing, P.O. Box 148486, Chicago, IL 60614
Coracle, 1516 Euclid Ave., Berkeley, CA 94708
Countermeasures, Humanities Dept., College of Santa Fe, Santa Fe, NM 87505
Crab Creek Review, 4462 Whitman Ave., No. Upper Seattle, WA 98103
Crab Orchard Review, English Dept., So. Illinois Univ., Carbondale, IL 62901
The Crescent Review, P.O. Box 15069, Chevy Chase, MD 20825
Cross Connect, Inc., P.O. Box 2317, Philadelphia, PA 19103
Crosstown Books, P.O. Box Cathedral Station, New York, NY 10025
Cups, 10 East 39th St., 7th fl., New York, NY 10016
CutBank, English Dept., Univ. of Montana, Missoula, MT 58912

D

Dalkey Archive Press, Illinois State Univ., Campus Box 4241, Normal, IL 61790
John Daniel & Co., Publishers, P.O. Box 21922, Santa Barbara, CA 93121
Daughters of Nyx, P.O. Box 1100, Stevenson, WA 98648
Defined Providence, 26 E. Fort Lee Rd., #2B, Bogota, NJ 07603
Denver Quarterly, English Dept., Univ. of Denver, Denver, CO 80208
Dirigible, 216 Willow St., New Haven, CT 06511
Dufour Editions, Inc., P.O. Box 7, Chester Springs, PA 19425

E

The Ear, Irvine Valley College, 5500 Irvine Center Dr., Irvine, CA 92620
Edgewise Press, 24 Fifth Ave., Ste. 224, New York, NY 10011
El Locofoco, Rt. 2, Box 4914, Eagle Pass, TX 78852
Emergence, P.O. Box 1615, Bridgeview, IL 60455
Emigre, 4475 "D" St., Sacramento, CA 95819
Epoch, 251 Goldwin Smith Hall, Cornell Univ., Ithaca, NY 14853
Equestrian Press, 1317 N. 78th St., Seattle, WA 98103
Etcetera, 156 Maple St., New Haven, CT 06511
Eureka Literary Magazine, Eureka College, P.O. Box 280, Eureka, IL 61530
Event, Douglas College, P.O. Box 2503, New Westminster, B.C. V3L 5B2 CANADA
Exit 13 Magazine, 22 Oakwood Ct., Fanwood, NJ 07023

F

Farmer's Market, Elgin Community College, 1700 Spartan Dr., Elgin, IL 60123
Fiction International, English Dept., San Diego State Univ., San Diego, CA 92182
Fine Madness, P.O. Box 31138, Seattle, WA 98103
First Intensity, P.O. Box 665, Lawrence, KS 66044

Five Points, English Dept., Georgia State Univ., 33 Gilmer St. SE, Atlanta, GA 30303
Florida Review, English Dept., Univ. of Central Florida, Orlando, FL 32816
Flying Horse, P.O. Box 445, Marblehead, MA 01945
Flyway, English Dept., Iowa State Univ., Ames, IA 50011
Forkroads, Box 150, Spencertown, NY 12165
The Formalist, 320 Hunter Dr., Evansville, IN 47711
Four Way Books, P.O. Box 607, Marshfield, MA 02050
Free Lunch, P.O. Box 7647, Laguna Niguel, CA 92607

G

Gettysburg Review, Gettysburg College, Gettysburg, PA 17325
Glimmer Train, 710 SW Madison, #504, Portland, OR 97205
Graffiti Rag, 5647 Oakman Blvd., Dearborn, MI 48126
Grand Street, 131 Varick St., Rm. 906, New York, NY 10013
Grand Tour, P.O. Box 66, Thorofare, NJ 08086
Graywolf Press, 2402 University Ave., Ste. 203, St. Paul, MN 55114
Green Hills Literary Lantern, P.O. Box 375, Trenton, MO 64683
Green Mountains Review, Johnson State College, Johnson, VT 05656
Greensboro Review, Univ. of North Carolina, Greensboro, NC 27412

H

Haight Ashbury Literary Journal, 558 Joost Ave., San Francisco, CA 94127
Hammers, 1718 Sherman Ave., Ste. 203, Evanston, IL 60201
Harvard Review, Harvard College Library, Cambridge, MA 02138
Hayden's Ferry Review, Box 871502, Arizona State Univ., Tempe, AZ 85287
Helicon Nine, P.O. Box 22412, Kansas City, MO 64113
High Plains Literary Review, 180 Adams St., Ste. 250, Denver, CO 80206
Highpoint Press, P.O. Box 958, Cambridge, MA 02140
Hubbub, 5344 SE 38th Ave., Portland, OR 97202
The Hudson Review, 684 Park Ave., New York, NY 10021
Hungry Mind Press, 57 Macalester St., St. Paul, MN 55105

I

Ibis, P.O. Box 133, Falls Village, CT 06031
Ice Cube Press, 205 N. Front St., North Liberty, IA 52317
Icon, Kent State Univ., 4314 Mahoning Ave., NW, Warren, OH 44483
The Iconoclast, 1675 Amazon Rd., Mohegan Lake, NY 10647
Indiana Review, 465 Ballantine, Indiana Univ., Bloomington, IN 47405
The Iowa Review, 308 EPB, Univ. of Iowa, Iowa City, IA 52242
Italian Americana, Univ. of Rhode Island, 80 Washington St., Providence, RI 02908

J

Janus, P.O. Box 376, Collingswood, NJ 08108
Java Snob Review, P.O. Box 54, Bellevue, MI 49021
The Journal, English Dept., Ohio State Univ., Columbus, OH 43210

The Journal of African Travel-Writing, P.O. Box 346, Chapel Hill, NC 27514
Journal of New Jersey Poets, County College of Morris, Rt. 10 & Center Grove Rd., Randolph, NJ 07869

K

Kalliope, Florida Community College, 3939 Roosevelt Blvd., Jacksonville, FL 32205
Kansas Quarterly/Arkansas Review, English & Philosophy Dept., P.O. Box 1890, State Univ., AR 72467
Kaya, 133 W. 25th St., Ste. 35, New York, NY 10001
Keen Science Fiction, 907 W. 17th Ave., Spokane, WA 99203
Kelsey Review, Mercer County Community College, P.O. Box B, Trenton, NJ 08690
Kelsey Street Press, 2718 Ninth St., Berkeley, CA 94710
The Kenyon Review, Kenyon College, Gambier, OH 43022
Kestrel, Fairmont State College, Fairmont, WV 26554

L

The Laurel Review, English Dept., Northwest Missouri State Univ., Maryville, MO 64468
The Ledge, 78-03 83rd St., Glendale, NY 11385
Leviathan, P.O. Box 4248, Tallahassee, FL 32315
Lips, P.O. Box 1345, Montclair, NJ 07042
Literal Latté, 61 E 8th St., Ste. 240, New York, NY 10003
The Literary Review, Fairleigh Dickinson Univ., 285 Madison Ave., Madison, NJ 07940
Livingston Press, Univ. of West Alabama, Livingston, AL 35470
Lone Stars Magazine, 4219 Flinthill Dr., San Antonio, TX 78230
The Longneck, P.O. Box 659, Vermillion, SD 57069
Lost Prophet Press, 3300 3rd Ave. South, Minneapolis, MN 55408
The Lowell Review, P.O. Box 184, Struthers, OH 44471
Lucidity, Rt. 2, Box 94, Eureka Springs, AR 72631
Lynx Eye, 1880 Hill Dr., Los Angeles, CA 90041

M

The MacGuffin, Schoolcraft College, 18600 Haggerty Rd., Livonia, MI 48152
MagiCircle, P.O. Box 1123, Davis, CA 95617
Mala Revija, 3413 Alta Vista Dr., Chattanooga, TN 37411
Manoa, English Dept., Univ. of Hawaii, Honolulu, HI 96822
Many Beaches Press, 1527 N. 36th., Sheboygan, WI 53081
Many Mountains Moving, 420 22nd St., Boulder, CO 80302
ManyTracks, Rt. 1, Box 52, Cooks, MI 49817
Marlboro Review, P.O. Box 243, Marlboro, VT 05344
The Massachusetts Review, Univ. of Massachusetts, Amherst, MA 01003
Barbara Matteau Editions, P.O. Box 381280, Cambridge, MA 02238
The Maverick Press, Rt. 2, Box 4915, Eagle Pass, TX 78852
Medicinal Purposes Literary Review, 86-37 120th St., #2D, Richmond Hill, NY 11418
Melting Trees Review, 2026 Mt. Meigs Rd., #2, Montgomery, AL 36107
Meridian Writers Collective, P.O. Box 12376, Philadelphia, PA 19119
Michigan Quarterly Review, Univ. of Michigan, 3032 Rackham Bldg., Ann Arbor, MI 48109

Mid-American Review, English Dept., Bowling Green State Univ., Bowling Green, OH 43403
Midstream, 110 E. 59 St., New York, NY 10022
Midwest Villages & Voices, P.O. Box 40214, St. Paul, MN 55104
Milkweed Editions, 430 First Ave. N, Ste. 400, Minneapolis, MN 55401
Mind in Motion, P.O. Box 7070, Big Bear Lake, CA 92315
Mind Purge, NT Box 5471, Denton, TX 76203
Mississippi Review, Box 5144, Univ. of Southern Mississippi, Hattiesburg, MS 39406
The Missouri Review, 1507 Hillcrest Hall, Univ. of Missouri, Columbia, MO 65211
Mockingbird, P.O. Box 761, Davis, CA 95617
Mudfish, 184 Franklin St., New York, NY 10013

N

The Nebraska Review, Creative Writing Program, Univ. of Nebraska, Omaha, NE 68182
Nerve Cowboy, P.O. Box 4973, Austin, TX 78765
New Letters, Univ. of Missouri, 5100 Rockhill Rd., Kansas City, MO 64110
New Millenium Writings, 821 Indian Gap Rd., Sevierville, TN 37876
New Orleans Review, Box 195, Loyola Univ., 6363 St. Charles Ave., New Orleans, LA 70118
New Poets Series, Inc., 541 Piccadilly Rd., Baltimore, MD 21204
New Renaissance, 26 Heath Rd., #11, Arlington, MA 02174
Nightshade Press, P.O. Box 76, Troy, ME 04987
Nine Muses Books, 3541 Kent Creek Rd., Winston, OR 97496
No Exit, P.O. Box 454, South Bend, IN 46624
North Carolina Literary Review, English Dept., ECU, Greenville, NC 27858
Northbrae Books, 2140 Shattuck Ave., Ste. 2122, Berkeley, CA 94704
Northeast Corridor, Beaver College, 450 S. Easton Rd., Glenside, PA 19038
Northern Lights, P.O. Box 8084, Missoula, MT 59807
The Northridge Review, 24043 Bessemer St., Woodland Hills, CA 91367
Notre Dame Review, Notre Dame University, Notre Dame, IN 46556

O

Oasis, P.O. Box 626, Largo, FL 33779
Old Crow Review, P.O. Box 662, Amherst, MA 01004
Ontario Review, 9 Honey Brook Dr., Princeton, NJ 08540
Opojaz, Inc., see Boulevard
Orchises Press, George Mason Univ., Fairfax, VA 22030
Orion, 195 Main St., Great Barrington, MA 01230
Osiris, P.O. Box 297, Deerfield, MA 07342
Other Voices, English Dept., Univ. of Illinois, 601 S. Morgan St., Chicago, IL 60607
The Oxford American, P.O. Drawer 1156, Oxford, MS 38655

P

Palo Alto Review, Palo Alto College, 1400 W. Villaret, San Antonio, TX 78224
Pangolin Papers, Box 241, Nordland, WA 98358
Papier-Mache, 135 Aviation Way, #14, Watsonville, CA 95076
Paris Press, P.O. Box 487, Ashfield, MA 01330
The Paris Review, 541 East 72nd St., New York, NY 10021

Pearl, 3030 E. Second St., Long Beach, CA 90803
Pearl River Press, P.O. Box 8416, Mobile, AL 36689
Pecan Grove Press, Box AL-1, Camino Santa Maria, San Antonio, TX 78228
Piedmont Literary Review, 3750 Woodside Ave., Lynchburg, VA 24503
Pivot, 250 Riverside Dr., #23, New York, NY 10025
Plain, 60805 Pigeon Point, Barnesville, OH 43713
The Plum Review, P.O. Box 1347, Philadelphia, PA 19105
Pod Publishing, Box 1124, Mercer Island, WA 98040
Poems & Plays, P.O. Box 70, Middle Tennessee Univ., Murfreesboro, TN 37132
Poet Lore, 4508 Walsh St., Bethesda, MD 20815
Poetry Calendar, 611 Broadway, Ste. 905, New York, NY 10012
Poetry in Motion, P.O. Box 173, Bayport, MN 55003
Poetry Miscellany, 3413 Alta Vista Dr., Chattanooga, TN 37411
Poetry Motel, 1911 E. First St., Duluth, MN 55812
The Poetry Project, 131 E. 10th St., New York, NY 10003
The Poet's Guild, P.O. Box 161236, Sacramento, CA 95816
Porcupine, P.O. Box 259, Cedarburg, WI 53012
Potomac Review, P.O. Box 354, Port Tobacco, MD 20677
Potpourri, P.O. Box 8278, Prairie Village, KS 66208
Prairie Schooner, P.O. Box 880334, Univ. of Nebraska, Lincoln, NE 68588
Press, 2124 Broadway, Ste. 323, New York, NY 10023
Prologue Press, 375 Riverside Dr., 14-C, New York, NY 10025
Provincetown Arts, 650 Commercial St., Provincetown, MA 02657
Puerto Del Sol, Box 3-E, New Mexico State Univ., Las Cruces, NM 88001

Q

QECE, 406 Main St., #3C, Collegeville, PA 19426
Quarterly West, 312 Olpin Union, Univ. of Utah, Salt Lake City, UT 84112

R

Raritan, Rutgers State Univ. of New Jersey, New Brunswick, NJ 08903
Rencounter, 1717 E. Birch, #G105, Brea, CA 92821
The Rio Grande Review, Univ. of Texas, Hudspeth Hall, El Paso, TX 79968
River Oak Review, P.O. Box 3127, Oak Park, IL 60303
Ronsdale Press, 3350 W. 21st Ave., Vancouver, B.C. V6S 1G7, CANADA
Rosebud, P.O. Box 459, Cambridge, WI, 53523

S

Salmagundi, Skidmore College, Saratoga Springs, NY 12866
Salt Hill Journal, English Dept., Syracuse Univ., Syracuse, NY 13244
Santa Monica Review, Santa Monica College, Santa Monica, CA 90405
Sarabande Books, 2234 Dundee Rd., Ste. 200, Louisville, KY 40205
Satire, P.O. Box 340, Hancock, MD 21750
Satori Press, 904 Silver Spur Rd., #323, Rolling Hills Estates, CA 90274
Savannah Literary Journal, P.O. Box 9561, Savannah, GA 31412
SCOP, Box 376, College Park, MD 20740

Seal Press, 3131 Western Ave. #410, Seattle, WA 98121
Seneca Review, Hobart & William Smith College, Geneva, NY 14456
Shamal Books, GPO Box 16, New York, NY 10116
Shenandoah, Washington & Lee Univ., Lexington, VA 24450
Sistersong, P.O. Box 7405, Pittsburgh, PA 15213
Skylark, Purdue Univ., 2200 169th St., Hammond, IN 46323
Slipstream, Box 2071, New Market Sta., Niagara Falls, NY 14301
Slest Ltd, P.O. Box 1238 Simpsonville, SC 29681
Snowy Egret, P.O. Box 9, Bowling Green, IN 47833
Solo, 5146 Foothill Rd., Carpinteria, CA 93013
Somersault Press, 404 Vista Heights Rd., Richmond, CA 94805
South Carolina Review, English Dept., Clemson Univ., Clemson, SC 29634
Southwest Manuscripters, see Satori Press
Southwest Review, P.O. Box 750374, Southern Methodist Univ., Dallas, TX 75275
Sou'wester, English Dept., Southern Illinois Univ., Edwardsville, IL 62026
Spinsters Ink, 32 E. First St., #330, Duluth, MN 55802
Spout, 28 W. Robie St., St. Paul, MN 55107
Steppingstone, P.O. Box 327, Chatham, MA 02633
Story Quarterly, P.O. Box 1416, Northbrook, IL 60065
Street News, 150-11 78th Rd., Kew Garden Hills, NY 11367
Sulphur River, P.O. Box 19228, Austin, TX 78760
The Sun, 107 N. Roberson St., Chapel Hill, NC 27516
Sweet Annie & Sweet Pea Review, 7750 Highway F-24 West, Baxter, IA 50028
Sycamore Review, English Dept., Purdue Univ., West Lafayette, IN 47907
Sycamore Roots, see Ice Cube Press

T

Talking River Review, Lewis & Clark State College, Lewiston, ID 83501
Tamarack Publishing, P.O. Box 7, Rhinelander, WI 54501
Tamaqua, Humanities Dept., Parkland College, 2400 W. Bradley Ave., Champaign, IL 61821
Tampa Review, 401 W. Kennedy Blvd., Tampa, FL 33606
Tar River Poetry, English Dept., East Carolina Univ., Greenville, NC 27858
Texture Press, P.O. Box 720157, Norman, OK 73072
Theme, Box 74109, Mctairie, LA 70033
Thin Air, P.O. Box 23549, Flagstaff, AZ 86002
Third Coast, English Dept., West Michigan Univ., Kalamazoo, MI 49007
Threepenny Review, P.O. Box 9131, Berkeley, CA 94709
Tia Chucha Press, P.O. Box 476969, Chicago, IL 60647
Tomorrow Magazine, see Contemporary Arts Publishing
Transfer Magazine, Creative Writing Dept., San Francisco State Univ., San Francisco, CA 94132
Trask House Books, 3222 NE Schuyler, Portland, OR 97212
TriQuarterly, Northwestern Univ., 2020 Ridge Ave., Evanston, IL 60208
Turning Wheel, P.O. Box 4650, Berkeley, CA 94704

U

Under the Sun, English Dept., Box 5053, Tennessee Technical Univ., Cookeville, TN 38505
University of Arkansas Press, 201 Ozark Ave., Fayetteville, AR 72701
University of Georgia Press, 330 Research Dr., Athens, GA 30602
University of Massachusetts Press, Box 429, Amherst, MA 01004
University of Wisconsin Press, 114 N. Murray St., Madison, WI 53715

University Press of New England, 23 S. Main St., Hanover, NH 03755
The Urbanite, P.O. Box 4737, Davenport, IA 52808

V

Verse, English dept., College of William & Mary, Williamsburg, VA 23187
Vignette, P.O. Box 109, Hollywood, CA 90078
Voices Israel, Box 5780, 46157 Herzlia, ISRAEL
Voyage Publishing, P.O. Box 1386, Anacortes, WA 98221
Voyager Publishing, P.O. Box 2215, Stillwater, MN 55082

W

Washington Review, Box 50132, Washington, DC 20091
Washington Square, Creative Writing Prog., New York Univ., 19 Univ. Pl., New York, NY 10003
West Wind Review, English Dept., Southern Oregon State College, Ashland, OR 97520
Western Humanities Review, Univ of Utah, Salt Lake City, UT 84112
Whetstone, Box 1255, Barrington, IL 60011
White Pine Press, 10 Village Sq. #28, Fredonia, NY 14063
Wild Duck Review, 419 Spring St., Ste. D, Nevada City, CA 95959
Wild Earth, P.O. Box 455, Richmond, VT 05477
Witness, 27055 Orchard Lake Rd., Farmington Hills, MI 48334
The Worcester Review, 6 Chatham St., Worcester, MA 01608
The Word Works, P.O. Box 42164, Washington, DC 20015
Wordcraft of Oregon, P.O. Box 3235, La Grande, OR 97850

Y

Yale Review, Yale University, New Haven, CT 06520
The Yalobusha Review, P.O. Box 186, University, MS 38677

Z

Zeitgeist Press, 1630 University Ave. #34, Berkeley, CA 94703
Zoetrope, 126 Fifth Ave., Ste. 300, New York, NY 10011
ZYZZYVA, 41 Sutter St., Ste. 1400, San Francisco, CA 94104

INDEX

The following is a listing in alphabetical order by author's last name of works reprinted in the first twenty-two *Pushcart Prize* editions.

634

636

637

638

641

643

644

647

651

654